CW01190251

Jane Austen's

L E T T E R S

to her sister Cassandra
and others

Jane Austen's
LETTERS

to her sister Cassandra
and others

COLLECTED AND EDITED
by
R. W. CHAPMAN

SECOND EDITION

OXFORD UNIVERSITY PRESS
OXFORD NEW YORK TORONTO MELBOURNE

Oxford University Press, Walton Street, Oxford OX2 6DP

OXFORD LONDON GLASGOW

NEW YORK TORONTO MELBOURNE WELLINGTON

KUALA LUMPUR SINGAPORE JAKARTA HONG KONG TOKYO

DELHI BOMBAY CALCUTTA MADRAS KARACHI

NAIROBI DAR ES SALAAM CAPE TOWN

ISBN 0 19 212102 2

First edition 1932
Second edition 1952
Reprinted (with corrections) 1959, 1964, 1969, and 1979

All rights reserved. No part of this publication may be reproduced, stored in a retrieval system, or transmitted, in any form or by any means, electronic, mechanical, photocopying, recording, or otherwise, without the prior permission of Oxford University Press

Printed in Great Britain
at the University Press, Oxford
by Eric Buckley
Printer to the University

PREFACE

THE extant letters of Jane Austen have not hitherto been collected. The majority of them are of two groups: those to which James Edward Austen-Leigh had access in compiling his *Memoir* of his aunt[1]—they had been preserved in his own branch of the family or by the daughters of Charles Austen; and those which were inherited by the first Lord Brabourne from his mother, Jane Austen's niece Fanny Knight (Lady Knatchbull), and published by him.[2] Mr. Austen-Leigh printed a part only of the letters which were at his disposal. Lord Brabourne's edition is substantially complete; but he omitted certain passages and suppressed some names. A third group of letters, those to Francis Austen, were first published by Mr. and Miss Hubback in *Jane Austen's Sailor Brothers*.[3]

The late William Austen-Leigh and Mr. R. A. Austen-Leigh in compiling their *Life and Letters of Jane Austen*[4] had access to the originals of many of these letters, and also to unpublished letters or parts of letters from the same sources. But it was no part of their plan to edit the letters as a whole. Almost every extant letter is quoted by them, but relatively few are given entire.

There is thus still room for an edition of the letters; and the present edition, so far as concerns the letters hitherto recorded, is tolerably well based. I have seen either the originals, or recent and trustworthy copies,

[1] 1870; second edition 1871. [2] 1884. [3] 1906.
[4] 1913; second edition 1913; now out of print.

of all the letters of which the ownership is stated in my list. Unfortunately the letters to Cassandra edited by Lord Brabourne were dispersed many years ago; and some thirty of these I have failed to trace. I have little doubt that they are in the hands of private collectors; and the publication of this edition will probably reveal some of their hiding-places.

There is, however, no reason to suspect that Lord Brabourne's text is seriously corrupt. He sent the originals to the printer, and the printer had little excuse for misreading Jane Austen's hand.

It is not very likely that any considerable hoard of Jane Austen's letters will hereafter come to light. There is no hope of any more to Cassandra; for it is known that she destroyed many, and those which she kept passed to her nieces and have been published. I long cherished hopes of letters to her brother Henry, to whom she is more likely to have revealed literary secrets than to any other correspondent; but I have seen a letter written to J. E. Austen-Leigh by his half-sister, in which it is stated that 'no letters to Uncle Henry have been kept'.

It is improbable that any more letters are preserved in the family.[1] There is more hope of letters addressed to cousins or acquaintances, such as those numbered 8, 145, and 148.

My first duty has been to secure accurate texts of all letters of which I was able to examine the originals.

[1] But the letter (74.1) to Martha Lloyd, sold in 1930 by a descendant of her husband Sir Francis Austen, was unknown to the authors of the *Life*.

To those who are familiar with the letters it will be apparent that I have been able to do a good deal in addition and correction, as well as in the restoration of Jane Austen's spelling and punctuation. I have not thought it necessary to record my improvements; I believe I am justified in saying that all divergences from my predecessors have been verified and may be trusted.

Another duty could not be evaded, though its performance is difficult, and often involves a choice of evils. There is an element of solemn absurdity in any commentary on familiar letters such as these. Yet Lord Brabourne was right in saying that they cannot be understood, or fully enjoyed, without some knowledge of the many hundreds of persons to whom they make familiar allusion. Lord Brabourne's solution was to furnish discursive introductions to the letters as a whole and to their several sections. There is much to be said for this method, but I did not feel that it was open to me. Nor have I felt able to print brief notes on the same pages as the text. This has the advantage of conveying information rapidly and easily to those who want it; but it has the grave disadvantage that it obtrudes such information upon those who resent it.

I hope it will be thought that my solution of these difficulties is not unsatisfactory. In the notes appended to each volume I give summary identifications of any persons who are *ambiguously* mentioned in the text.[1] In my indexes (which no one will or can *read*)

[1] See the note prefixed to the notes on vol. i, which helps the reader to distinguish the commonest Christian names.

I set out the relationships of the various families, and give somewhat full particulars (when I could get them) of all persons, however obscure or unimportant, who are mentioned in the letters. To those who may think these indexes absurdly and pedantically elaborate, probably no excuses are worth offering; to those who welcome them I confess myself aware that with more leisure and industry, or with a better command of the sources of information, they might have been made more accurate and less incomplete.

PREFACE TO THE SECOND EDITION

THE text of this edition is little altered except by the addition of the letters printed at the end and numbered 78.1 (a notable accession of knowledge), 122.1, 141.1, and 149. Since my text was first printed I have had access to the originals of 2, 10, 39, 58, 63, 72, 75–9, 82, 89, 92, 96, 97, 111, 114, 123. These have yielded a few more additions (in 10 and 82) and slight verbal corrections. It did not seem worth while to sacrifice the plates of many pages merely to restore Jane Austen's spelling and punctuation, which are adequately represented by the text as a whole.

I have left my list of acknowledgements as it stood in 1932. I now add my thanks to those friends and correspondents who have furnished additions or corrections in the notes and indexes: especially to Miss A. L. Tallmadge of Evanston and Mrs. Henry G. Burke of Baltimore.

ACKNOWLEDGEMENTS

For the use of original letters and other manuscripts I am indebted to the descendants of Jane Austen's brothers—Miss Isabel Lefroy, Mr. E. C. Austen-Leigh, Mr. R. A. Austen-Leigh, Mr. L. A. Austen-Leigh and his co-heirs, Lord Brabourne, Captain Ernest Austen, R.N., Mrs. Spanton, the late Miss Jane Austen, Miss Florence Austen—and to the following: Dr. J. Pierpont Morgan, Mr. R. B. Adam, the Rev. R. G. Binnall, Mr. Oliver R. Barrett, Lady Charnwood, the late Cleveland H. Dodge, Mrs. M. A. De Wolfe Howe, Sir Alfred Law, the late Miss Amy Lowell, Mr. H. V. Marrot, Mr. Harold Murdock, Sir John Murray, Miss A. L. Sillar, Miss Anne Tucker.

Messrs. Maggs, and Messrs. Sessler of Philadelphia, have helped me to trace letters recorded in auction sale catalogues.

My chief obligation is to Mr. Richard Austen-Leigh, without whose sanction this edition would not have been undertaken, and without whose help it could hardly have been carried through. He placed at my disposal many family manuscripts which throw light on the letters, and many notes of his own, and throughout gave me the full benefit of his unrivalled knowledge of Jane Austen's life and surroundings.

The late J. W. Horrocks had a wide knowledge of family history in Hampshire and especially in Southampton; almost all my information on the Southampton period is due to him.

Mr. R. H. New and Mr. F. Page have been assiduous in the search for minute particulars in the Bodleian and British Museum.

I am further indebted for occasional assistance to a very large number of persons. The list which follows is long, but I am afraid it is not complete: Rev. L. Brooke Barnett, Rector of Ashe; Mr. E. G. Bayford; Mr. C. F. Bell; Mr. W. M. Bevan; the Rev. S. G. Brade-Birks, Vicar of Godmersham; the Rev. Canon E. Brook-Jackson; Dame Georgiana Buller; Prof. Geoffrey Callender; Mr. Herbert

Chitty; Mr. J. H. Coltart; Mr. Davidson Cook; Mr. W. H. Curtis of Alton; members of the de Bary family; Miss M. Hope Dodds; the Hon. Mrs. Dudley-Ryder, formerly of 26 Hans Place; Mr. Ralph Edwards; the late Lord Fitz-walter, of Goodnestone, the Hon Sir John Fortescue; Sir William Foster; Mr. J. C. B. Gamlen; Miss Belle da Costa Greene; Mr. F. H. H. Guillemarde; Mr. D. W. Herdman, Public Librarian at Cheltenham; Mr. E. V. Hewkin of the G.P.O.; Mr. Ellice Hicks Beach; Mr. C. B. Hogan; Mr. Archibald Jacob; the Rev. J. L. Beaumont; Mr. Hilary Jenkinson; Mr. Walter Johnson; the late Lord Kilbracken; the Hon. Michael Knatchbull; the late Colonel Lionel Knight and Mrs. Knight of Chawton; Mrs. Montagu Knight; Mrs. Koch and Miss Tallmadge, of Evanston, Illinois; the Marquis of Lansdowne; Viscountess Lewisham, of Godmer-sham Park; Mr. D. M. Low; Mr. Justice MacKinnon; Mr. Edward Marsh; Mr. H. T. Mead, Librarian at Canterbury; Mr. Philip Morrell, Mr. James Morrell, and Mr. A. H. M. Morrell; Mr. A. H. Hallam Murray; Mrs. Norsworthy; Sir Charles Oman; Dr. C. T. Onions; Mr. R. H. Paranjpye; the late Sir William Portal, Miss Evelyn Portal of Free-mantle, and Mr. E. R. Portal of Hardenhuish; Mr. L. F. Powell; Mr. J. U. Powell and Mr. Austin Poole, of St. John's College, Oxford; Sir D'Arcy Power; Mrs. Horatia Powlett; Mr. P. E. Roberts; Mr. S. C. Roberts; Mr. W. Roberts; Sir Humphry Rolleston; Mr. Michael Sadleir; the Rev. D. M. Salmon, Rector of Streatham; Lord Saye and Sele; Miss Jean Smith; Mr. A. H. Stenning; Mrs. C. G. Stirling; Miss C. Linklater Thomson; Dr. G. M. Trevelyan; the late Dr. Paget Toynbee; Prof. G. S. Veitch; Mr. C. Wanklyn of Lyme Regis; Mr. F. D. Wardle, of Messrs. Stone, King, and Wardle, 13 Queen Square, Bath; Sir Alfred Welby; Mr. Leonard Whibley; Mr. J. S. Williamson, formerly of 64 Sloane Street; Miss E. G. Withycombe; Mr. R. W. M. Wright, Director of the Bath Libraries; officials of the Public Record Office and of Somerset House.

CONTENTS

PREFACE . . . . . . Page v

PREFACE TO THE SECOND EDITION . . ,, viii

ACKNOWLEDGEMENTS . . . . ,, ix

LIST OF LETTERS . . . . . ,, xvii

LIST OF ILLUSTRATIONS . . . . . ,, xxxv

AUTHORITIES . . . . . . ,, xxxvii

INTRODUCTION . . . . . . ,, xxxix

LETTERS . . . . . Pages 1–515

1796

NOS.

January. From Steventon to Cassandra at Kintbury 1–2
August. From Cork Street to Cassandra . . 3
September. From Rowling to Cassandra at Steventon 4–7

1798

April. From Steventon to Philadelphia Walter . 8
October. From Dartford to Cassandra at Godmersham 9
October–December. From Steventon to Cassandra at Godmersham 10–16

1799

January. From Steventon to Cassandra at Godmersham 17–18
May–June. From 13 Queen Square, Bath, to Cassandra at Steventon 19–22

NOS.

1800

October–November. From Steventon to Cassandra at Godmersham 23–25, 27

November. From Steventon to Martha Lloyd at Ibthrop 26

From Ibthrop to Cassandra at Godmersham 28

1801

January. From Steventon to Cassandra at Godmersham 29–33

February. From Manydown to Cassandra in Berkeley Street 34

May. From Paragon, Bath, to Cassandra at Ibthrop and Kintbury 35–38

1804

September. From Lyme to Cassandra at Ibthrop . 39

1805

January. From Green Park Buildings, Bath, to Francis Austen, H.M.S. *Leopard* . . 40–42

April. From 25 Gay Street, Bath, to Cassandra at Ibthrop 43–44

August. From Godmersham to Cassandra at Goodnestone 45

From Goodnestone to Cassandra at Godmersham 46–47

1807

January–February. From Southampton to Cassandra at Godmersham 48–50

1808

June. From Godmersham to Cassandra at Castle Square, Southampton 51–54

October–December. From Castle Square, Southampton, to Cassandra at Godmersham . . 55–62

Contents

NOS.

1809

January. From Castle Square, Southampton, to Cassandra at Godmersham 63–66

April. From Castle Square, Southampton, to Messrs. Crosbie in London 67

July. From Chawton to Francis Austen . . 68

NOS.

1811

April. From Sloane Street to Cassandra at Godmersham 69–71

May–June. From Chawton to Cassandra at Godmersham 72–74

1812

November. From Chawton to Martha Lloyd at Barton[1] 74.1

1813

January–February. From Chawton to Cassandra at Steventon and Manydown . . . 75–78

February. From Chawton to Martha Lloyd[2] . 78.1

May. From Sloane Street to Cassandra at Chawton 79–80

July. From Chawton to Francis Austen in the Baltic 81

September. From 10 Henrietta Street to Cassandra at Chawton 82–83

September. From Godmersham to Francis Austen in the Baltic 85

September–October. From Godmersham to Cassandra at Chawton 84, 86–87

October–November. From Godmersham to Cassandra at 10 Henrietta Street . . . 88–91

[1] See p. 499. [2] See p. 503.

NOS.

1814

March. From 10 Henrietta Street to Cassandra at Chawton 92–94

May or June. From Chawton to Anna Austen at Steventon 95

June. From Chawton to Cassandra at 10 Henrietta Street 96–97

August. From Chawton to Anna Austen at Steventon 98

From 23 Hans Place to Cassandra at Chawton 99

September. From Chawton to Anna Austen at Steventon 100–102

November. From Chawton to Fanny Knight at Goodnestone 103

From Chawton to Anna Lefroy at Hendon 104

November–December. From 23 Hans Place to Anna Lefroy at Hendon 105, 107

November. From 23 Hans Place to Fanny Knight at Godmersham 106

From Chawton to Anna Lefroy at Hendon 108

November or December. From 23 Hans Place to Anna Lefroy at Hendon 109

1815

September. From Chawton to Anna Lefroy at Wyards 110

October–December. From 23 Hans Place to Cassandra at Chawton 111, 116–118

From 23 Hans Place to Caroline Austen at Steventon 112, 119

NOS.

November–December. From 23 Hans Place to J. S. Clarke at Carlton House . . . 113, 120
From 23 Hans Place to John Murray 114, 115, 121, 122

December. To Charles Thomas Haden[1] . 122.1
To Lady Morley 123
To Anna Lefroy 124

1816

March, April, July. From Chawton to Caroline Austen at Steventon . . . 125, 128, 128.1, 131

April. From Chawton to J. S. Clarke . . 126
From Chawton to John Murray . . 127

June and ?. From Chawton to Anna Lefroy 129, 135

July and December. From Chawton to Edward Austen at Steventon 130, 134

September. From Chawton to Cassandra at Cheltenham 132, 133

1817

January. From Chawton to Cassandra, daughter of Charles Austen, at 22 Keppel Street . . . 136

January–March. From Chawton to Caroline Austen at Steventon 137, 138, 143

January. From Chawton to Alethea Bigg at Streatham 139

February–March. From Chawton to Fanny Knight at Godmersham 140–142

March. From Chawton to Caroline Austen[2] . 141.1

April. From Chawton to Charles Austen at 22 Keppel Street 144

May. From Chawton to Anne Sharp at Doncaster. 145
From College Street, Winchester, to Edward Austen at Oxford 146

[1] See p. 510.
[2] See p. 511.

		NOS
	From College Street to an unknown correspondent	147
n.d.	To Catherine Ann Prowting	148
n.d.	To Caroline Austen?[1]	149

ADDENDA . . . . . *Page* 499

APPENDIX

1. Letters from Cassandra Austen to Fanny Knight after Jane Austen's death . . *Page* 513
2. Jane Austen's Will . . . . „ 519

NOTES

INDEXES

I. Jane Austen's Family
II. Other Persons (with Addenda)
III. Places
IV. General Topics
V. Authors, Books, Plays
VI. Jane Austen's Novels
VII. Jane Austen's English
VIII. Names of Ships

[1] See p. 512.

LIST OF LETTERS

THIS list shows the ownership, &c., of the originals, or, if these are untraced, the best authority for the text.

The ownership of some of the letters has been discovered, or has altered, since the text was printed off; this list gives the latest state of my information. In particular, Letters 2 and 82 have been traced and collated; for additions and corrections to these letters, see the notes.

At the eleventh hour, indeed a little later, I am indebted to Mrs. R. M. Mowll, a descendant of Sir Francis Austen, for the privilege of publishing Jane Austen's letter to Martha Lloyd of 2 Sept. 1814. See page 506. It was not practicable to include this interesting document in the indexes.

The publisher is indebted to Mr. David Gilson for providing a corrected version of Letter 127.

1979

List of Letters

NO.	RECIPIENT.	PLACE.	DATE.
1	Cassandra Austen	Steventon	Sat. 9 Jan. ⟨1796⟩
2	Cassandra Austen	Steventon	Thurs. ⟨14⟩ Jan. ⟨1796⟩
3	Cassandra Austen	Cork Street	Tues. ⟨Aug. 1796⟩
4	Cassandra Austen	Rowling	Thurs. 1 Sept. ⟨1796⟩
5	Cassandra Austen	Rowling	Mon. 5 Sept. ⟨1796⟩
6	Cassandra Austen	Rowling	Thurs. 15 Sept. 1796
7	Cassandra Austen	Rowling	Sun. 18 Sept. 1796
8	? Philadelphia Walter	Steventon	Sun. 8 Apr. ⟨1798⟩
9	Cassandra Austen	Bull and George, Dartford	Wed. 24 Oct. ⟨1798⟩
10	Cassandra Austen	Steventon	Sat. 27 Oct. ⟨1798⟩
11	Cassandra Austen	Steventon	Sat. 17 Nov. 1798
12	Cassandra Austen	Steventon	Sun. 25 Nov. ⟨1798⟩
13	Cassandra Austen	Steventon	⟨Sat.⟩ 1 Dec. ⟨1798⟩
14	Cassandra Austen	Steventon	Tues. 18 Dec. 1798
15	Cassandra Austen	Steventon	Mon. 24 Dec. ⟨1798⟩
16	Cassandra Austen	Steventon	Fri. 28 Dec. ⟨1798⟩
17	Cassandra Austen	Steventon	Tues. 8 Jan. ⟨1799⟩
18	Cassandra Austen	Steventon	Mon. 21 Jan. ⟨1799⟩
19	Cassandra Austen	13 Queen Square	Fri. 17 May ⟨1799⟩
20	Cassandra Austen	13 Queen Square	Sun. 2 June ⟨1799⟩
21	Cassandra Austen	13 Queen Square	Tues. 11 June ⟨1799⟩
22	Cassandra Austen	13 Queen Square	Wed. 19 June ⟨1799⟩

ORIGINAL.	PREVIOUS PUBLICATION (WHOLE OR PART).
.. .. ..	*Brabourne* I 125 ; *Life* 87, 98.
Sir Alfred Law	*Brabourne* I 130 ; *Life* 88, 99.
Facsimile in O. F. Adams	*Brabourne* I 133 ; *Life* 99.
.. .. ..	*Brabourne* I 134 ; *Life* 100.
Harold Murdock	*Brabourne* I 138 ; *Life* 101.
Pierpont Morgan Library	*Brabourne* I 141 ; *Life* 102.
Pierpont Morgan Library	*Brabourne* I 146 ; *Life* 103.
Rev. R. G. Binnall	Not published.
.. .. ..	*Brabourne* I 153 ; *Life* 109.
Mrs. Raymond Hartz	*Brabourne* I 156 ; *Life* 111.
.. .. ..	*Brabourne* I 162 ; *Life* 84, 113.
.. .. ..	*Brabourne* I 167 ; *Life* 113.
.. .. ..	*Brabourne* I 171 ; *Life* 115.
Pierpont Morgan Library	*Brabourne* I 176 ; *Life* 116.
.. .. ..	*Brabourne* I 182 ; *Life* 118.
Oliver R. Barrett	*Brabourne* I 190 ; *Life* 121.
.. .. ..	*Brabourne* I 191 ; *Life* 122.
[Sotheby Catalogue May 1891]	*Brabourne* I 198 ; *Life* 124.
Harvard Library	*Brabourne* I 206 ; *Life* 127.
Pierpont Morgan Library	*Brabourne* I 211 ; *Life* 129.
Australian National Library	*Brabourne* I 215 ; *Life* 130.
Pierpont Morgan Library	*Brabourne* I 220 ; *Life* 131.

NO.	RECIPIENT.	PLACE.	DATE.
23	Cassandra Austen	Steventon	Sat. 25 Oct. 1800
24	Cassandra Austen	Steventon	Sat. 1 Nov. 1800
25	Cassandra Austen	Steventon	Sat. 8 Nov. 1800
26	Martha Lloyd	Steventon	Wed. 12 Nov. ⟨1800⟩
27	Cassandra Austen	Steventon	Thurs. 20 Nov. 1800
28	Cassandra Austen	Ibthrop	Sun. 30 Nov. 1800
29	Cassandra Austen	Steventon	Sat. 3 Jan. 1801
30	Cassandra Austen	Steventon	Thurs. 8 Jan. 1801
31	Cassandra Austen	Steventon	Wed. 14 Jan. ⟨1801⟩
32	Cassandra Austen	Steventon	Wed. 21 Jan. 1801
33	Cassandra Austen	Steventon	Sun. 25 Jan. ⟨1801⟩
34	Cassandra Austen	Manydown	Wed. 11 Feb. 1801
35	Cassandra Austen	Paragon	Tues. 5 May ⟨1801⟩
36	Cassandra Austen	Paragon	Tues. 12 May ⟨1801⟩
37	Cassandra Austen	Paragon	Thurs. 21 May ⟨1801⟩
38	Cassandra Austen	Paragon	Tues. 26 May ⟨1801⟩
39	Cassandra Austen	Lyme	Fri. 14 Sept. ⟨1804⟩

ORIGINAL.	PREVIOUS PUBLICATION (WHOLE OR PART).
Pierpont Morgan Library	*Brabourne* I 230 ; *Life* 141.
Pierpont Morgan Library	*Brabourne* I 235 ; *Life* 143.
L. A. Austen-Leigh	*Memoir*[2] 58 ; *Life* 145.
New York Public Library	*Memoir*[2] 61 ; *Life* 148.
Pierpont Morgan Library	*Brabourne* I 241 ; *Life* 150.
L. A. Austen-Leigh	*Life* 153.
Pierpont Morgan Library	*Brabourne* I 248 ; *Life* 156.
Pierpont Morgan Library	*Brabourne* I 255 ; *Life* 158.
Pierpont Morgan Library	*Brabourne* I 261 ; *Life* 159.
Pierpont Morgan Library	*Brabourne* I 266 ; *Life* 161.
.. .. ..	*Brabourne* I 272 ; *Life* 162.
British Museum	*Memoir*[1] 81, *Memoir*[2] 64 ; *Life* 163.
Fitzwilliam Museum, Cambridge	*Brabourne* I 278 ; *Life* 165.
Pierpont Morgan Library	*Brabourne* I 284 ; *Life* 166.
Pierpont Morgan Library	*Brabourne* I 289 ; *Life* 168.
Charles B. Hogan	*Memoir*[1] 83, *Memoir*[2] 65 ; *Life* 169.
Mrs. Henry Burke	*Memoir*[1] 89, *Memoir*[2] 68 ; *Life* 177.

NO.	RECIPIENT.	PLACE.	DATE.
40	Francis Austen	Green Park Buildings	Mon. 21 Jan. 1805
41	Francis Austen	Do.	Tues. 22 Jan. ⟨1805⟩
42	Francis Austen	Do.	Tues. 29 Jan. ⟨1805⟩
43	Cassandra Austen	25 Gay Street	Mon. 8 Apr. ⟨1805⟩
44	Cassandra Austen	Gay Street	Sun. 21 Apr. ⟨1805⟩
45	Cassandra Austen	Godmersham	Sat. 24 Aug. ⟨1805⟩
46	Cassandra Austen	Goodnestone	Tues. 27 Aug. ⟨1805⟩
47	Cassandra Austen	Goodnestone	Fri. 30 Aug. ⟨1805⟩
48	Cassandra Austen	Southampton	Wed. 7 Jan. ⟨1807⟩
49	Cassandra Austen	Southampton	⟨Sun.⟩ 8 Feb. ⟨1807⟩
50	Cassandra Austen	Southampton	Fri. 20 Feb. 1807
51	Cassandra Austen	Godmersham	Wed. 15 June ⟨1808⟩
52	Cassandra Austen	Godmersham	Mon. 20 June 1808
53	Cassandra Austen	Godmersham	Sun. 26 June 1808
54	Cassandra Austen	Godmersham	Thurs. 30 June 1808
55	Cassandra Austen	Castle Square	Sat. 1 Oct. 1808
56	Cassandra Austen	Castle Square	Fri. 7 Oct. 1808
57	Cassandra Austen	Castle Square	⟨Thurs.⟩ 13 Oct. 1808
58	Cassandra Austen	Castle Square	Sat. 15 Oct. ⟨1808⟩
59	Cassandra Austen	Castle Square	Mon. 24 Oct. ⟨1808⟩
60	Cassandra Austen	Castle Square	Sun. 21 Nov. ⟨1808⟩
61	Cassandra Austen	Castle Square	Fri. 9 Dec. 1808
62	Cassandra Austen	Castle Square	Tues. 27 Dec. ⟨1808⟩

ORIGINAL.	PREVIOUS PUBLICATION (WHOLE OR PART).
British Museum	*Sailor Brothers* 115 ; *Life* 181.
British Museum	*Sailor Brothers* 116 ; *Life* 180.
British Museum	*Sailor Brothers* 129.
L. A. Austen-Leigh	*Memoir*[2] 70 ; *Life* 183.
Jerome Kern (1927)	*Memoir*[1] 93, *Memoir*[2] 74 ; *Life* 185.
Harvard College Library	*Brabourne* I 298 ; *Life* 189.
.. .. ..	*Brabourne* I 303 ; *Life* 190.
.. .. ..	*Brabourne* I 307 ; *Life* 191.
.. .. ..	*Brabourne* I 312 ; *Life* 198.
Pierpont Morgan Library	*Brabourne* I 320 ; *Life* 199.
R. B. Adam	*Brabourne* I 329 ; *Life* 201.
.. .. ..	*Brabourne* I 341 ; *Life* 204.
Pierpont Morgan Library	*Brabourne* I 350 ; *Life* 206.
Pierpont Morgan Library	*Brabourne* I 358 ; *Life* 207.
Pierpont Morgan Library	*Brabourne* I 366 ; *Life* 207.
Pierpont Morgan Library	*Brabourne* II 4 ; *Life* 210.
Pierpont Morgan Library	*Brabourne* II 11 ; *Life* 212.
Pierpont Morgan Library	*Brabourne* II 18 ; *Life* 213.
Hist. Soc. of Pennsylvania	*Brabourne* II 21 ; *Life* 214.
.. .. ..	*Brabourne* II 25 ; *Life* 216.
Pierpont Morgan Library	*Brabourne* II 32 ; *Life* 219.
Pierpont Morgan Library	*Brabourne* II 38 ; *Life* 221.
.. .. ..	*Brabourne* II 46 ; *Life* 223.

NO.	RECIPIENT.	PLACE.	DATE.
63	Cassandra Austen	Castle Square	Tues. 10 Jan. ⟨1809⟩
64	Cassandra Austen	Castle Square	Tues. 17 Jan. 1809
65	Cassandra Austen	Castle Square	Tues. 24 Jan. 1809
66	Cassandra Austen	Castle Square	Mon. 30 Jan. 1809
67	Crosbie & Co.	Southampton	⟨Wed.⟩ 5 Apr. 1809
68	Francis Austen	Chawton	⟨Wed.⟩ 26 July 1809
69	Cassandra Austen	Sloane Street	Thurs. 18 Apr. 1811
70	Cassandra Austen	Sloane Street	Thurs. 25 Apr. 1811 ?
71	Cassandra Austen	Sloane Street	Tues. ⟨30 Apr. 1811⟩
72	Cassandra Austen	Chawton	Wed. 29 May ⟨1811⟩
73	Cassandra Austen	Chawton	Fri. 31 May 1811
74	Cassandra Austen	Chawton	Thurs. 6 June 1811
74.1	Martha Lloyd	Chawton	Sun. 29 Nov. ⟨1812⟩
75	Cassandra Austen	Chawton	Sun. 24 Jan. ⟨1813⟩
76	Cassandra Austen	Chawton	Fri. 29 Jan. ⟨1813⟩
77	Cassandra Austen	Chawton	Thurs. 4 Feb. ⟨1813⟩
78	Cassandra Austen	Chawton	Tues. 9 Feb. ⟨1813⟩
78.1	Martha Lloyd	Chawton	Tues. 16 Feb. ⟨1813⟩
79	Cassandra Austen	Sloane Street	Thurs. 20 May ⟨1813⟩
80	Cassandra Austen	Sloane Street	Mon. 24 May ⟨1813⟩

List of Letters

ORIGINAL.	PREVIOUS PUBLICATION (WHOLE OR PART).
Maine Hist. Soc.	*Brabourne* II 53 ; *Life* 224.
Pierpont Morgan Library	*Brabourne* II 59 ; *Life* 226.
Pierpont Morgan Library	*Brabourne* II 66 ; *Life* 227.
Pierpont Morgan Library	*Brabourne* II 72 ; *Life* 228.
(Contemporary copy, not by J. A.—British Museum)	*Life* 230.
British Museum	*Times* 16 Dec. 1930 (part).

Pierpont Morgan Library	*Brabourne* II 82 ; *Life* 244.
British Museum	*Brabourne* II 89 ; *Life* 246.
Pierpont Morgan Library	*Brabourne* II 97 ; *Life* 251.
Hist. Soc. of Pennsylvania	*Brabourne* II 100 ; *Life* 251.
Pierpont Morgan Library	*Brabourne* II 105 ; *Life* 252.
Pierpont Morgan Library	*Brabourne* II 111 ; *Life* 254.

New York Public Library	Not published (see p. 499).

T. Edward Carpenter	*Memoir*^{1} 135, *Memoir*^{2} 99 (where extracts from Nos. 75 and 78 are printed together); *Life* 258.
T. Edward Carpenter	*Memoir*^{1} 131, *Memoir*^{2} 97; *Life* 260.
T. Edward Carpenter	*Memoir*^{1} 133, *Memoir*^{2} 99; *Life* 261.
T. Edward Carpenter	*Memoir*^{1} 133, *Memoir*^{2} 99 (see above on No. 75); *Life* 262.
Mrs. Henry Burke	Not published (see p. 503).
T. Edward Carpenter	*Memoir*^{2} 102; *Life* 265.
Pierpont Morgan Library	*Brabourne* II 139; *Life* 267.

List of Letters

NO.	RECIPIENT.	PLACE.	DATE.
81	Francis Austen	Chawton	⟨Sat.⟩ 3 July 1813
82	Cassandra Austen	Henrietta Street	Wed. 15 Sept. ⟨1813⟩
83	Cassandra Austen	Henrietta Street	Thurs. ⟨16 Sept. 1813⟩
84	Cassandra Austen	Godmersham	Thurs. 23 Sept. ⟨1813⟩
85	Francis Austen	Godmersham	⟨Sat.⟩ 25 Sept. 1813
86	Cassandra Austen	Godmersham	Mon. 11 Oct. 1813
87	Cassandra Austen	Godmersham	Thurs. 14 Oct. 1813
88	Cassandra Austen	Godmersham	Thurs. 21 Oct. ⟨1813⟩
89	Cassandra Austen	Godmersham	Tues. 26 Oct. ⟨1813⟩
90	Cassandra Austen	Godmersham	Wed. 3 Nov. 1813
91	Cassandra Austen	Godmersham	Sat. 6 Nov. ⟨1813⟩
92	Cassandra Austen	Henrietta Street	Wed. 2 Mar. ⟨1814⟩
93	Cassandra Austen	Henrietta Street	Sat. 5 Mar. ⟨1814⟩
94	Cassandra Austen	Henrietta Street	Wed. 9 Mar. ⟨1814⟩
95	Anna Austen	⟨Chawton⟩	⟨May or June 1814⟩
96	Cassandra Austen	Chawton	Tues. 13 (14) June ⟨1814⟩
97	Cassandra Austen	⟨Chawton⟩	Thurs. 23 June ⟨1814⟩
98	Anna Austen	Chawton	Wed. 10 Aug. ⟨1814⟩
99	Cassandra Austen	23 Hans Place	Tues. ⟨Aug. 1814⟩
99.1	Martha Lloyd	23 Hans Place	Fri. 2 Sep. 1814
100	Anna Austen	Chawton	⟨Fri.⟩ 9 Sept. ⟨1814⟩
101	Anna Austen	Chawton	Wed. 28 Sept. ⟨1814⟩

List of Letters

ORIGINAL.	PREVIOUS PUBLICATION (WHOLE OR PART).
British Museum	*Sailor Brothers* 233; *Life* 85, 270.
Sir Alfred Law	*Brabourne* II 145; *Life* 273.
Cleveland H. Dodge	*Brabourne* II 154; *Life* 276.
Pierpont Morgan Library	*Brabourne* II 159; *Life* 276.
British Museum	*Sailor Brothers* 243; *Life* 278.
Pierpont Morgan Library	*Brabourne* II 169; *Life* 282.
Harvard College Library	*Brabourne* II 177; *Life* 283.
.. .. ..	*Brabourne* II 189; *Life* 285.
Mrs. Henry Burke	*Brabourne* II 194; *Life* 285.
Pierpont Morgan Library	*Brabourne* II 200; *Life* 287.
Pierpont Morgan Library	*Brabourne* II 209; *Life* 288.
Sotheby 3 May 1948	*Memoir*[2] 104; *Life* 291.
Pierpont Morgan Library	*Brabourne* II 222; *Life* 294.
Pierpont Morgan Library	*Brabourne* II 231; *Life* 295.
St. John's College, Oxford	*Brabourne* II 304; *Life* 354.
Mrs. Henry Burke	*Brabourne* II 234; *Life* 303.
Haverford College	*Brabourne* II 236; *Life* 304.
St. John's College, Oxford	*Memoir*[1] 119, *Memoir*[2] 91; *Brabourne* II 305; *Life* 354.
Pierpont Morgan Library	*Brabourne* II 240; *Life* 305.
Mrs. R. M. Mowll	
St. John's College, Oxford	*Memoir*[1] 120, *Memoir*[2] 91; *Brabourne* II 310; *Life* 357.
St. John's College, Oxford	*Memoir*[1] 111, 120, *Memoir*[2] 85, 91; *Brabourne* II 315; *Life* 359.

NO.	RECIPIENT.	PLACE.	DATE.
102	Anna Austen	.. ..	.. ..
103	Fanny Knight	Chawton	Fri. 18 Nov. ⟨1814⟩
104	Anna Lefroy	⟨Chawton⟩	Tues. 22 Nov. 1814
105	Anna Lefroy	Hans Place	⟨Tues. 29 Nov. 1814⟩
106	Fanny Knight	Hans Place	Wed. 30 Nov. ⟨1814⟩
107	Anna Lefroy	Hans Place	Wed. ⟨ Dec. 1814⟩
108	⟨Anna Lefroy⟩	⟨Chawton⟩	n.d.
109	Anna Lefroy	⟨Hans Place⟩	⟨Nov. or Dec. 1814 ?⟩
110	Anna Lefroy	Chawton	Fri. 29 Sept. ⟨1815⟩
111	Cassandra Austen	Hans Place	Tues. 17 Oct. ⟨1815⟩
112	Caroline Austen	Hans Place	Mon. 30 Oct. ⟨1815⟩
113	J. S. Clarke	⟨Hans Place⟩	⟨Wed.⟩ 15 Nov. 1815
114	⟨John Murray⟩	⟨Hans Place⟩	⟨? Nov. 1815⟩
115	John Murray	Hans Place	Thurs. 23 Nov. ⟨1815⟩
116	Cassandra Austen	Hans Place	Fri. 24 Nov. ⟨1815⟩
117	Cassandra Austen	Hans Place	Sun. 26 Nov. ⟨1815⟩
118	Cassandra Austen	Hans Place	Sat. 2 Dec. 1815
119	Caroline Austen	.. ..	6 Dec. ⟨? 1815⟩
120	J. S. Clarke	⟨Hans Place⟩	⟨Mon.⟩ 11 Dec. 1815

ORIGINAL.	PREVIOUS PUBLICATION (WHOLE OR PART).
(Copy by F. C. Lefroy—Miss Lefroy)	Not published.
Lord Brabourne	*Brabourne* II 277 ; *Life* 308, 342.
Miss Lefroy	*Brabourne* II 320.
R. A. Austen-Leigh (fragment); Miss Lefroy (fragment, and copy by Mrs. Bellas); Lady Charnwood (fragment)	*Memoir*[1] 116, *Memoir*[2] 88 ; *Brabourne* II 321 ; *Life* 361.
Lord Brabourne	*Brabourne* II 284 ; *Life* 308, 345.
St. John's College, Oxford	*Memoir*[1] 121, *Memoir*[2] 92 ; *Brabourne* II 322 ; *Life* 361.
Miss Lefroy (fragment) [now, 1931, R.W.C.]	*Memoir*[1] 116, 173, *Memoir*[2] 89, 131 ; *Brabourne* II 323 (misplaced) ; *Life* 362.
R. A. Austen-Leigh	*Memoir*[1] 173, *Memoir*[2] 131.
Miss Lefroy	*Brabourne* II 324.
Mrs. Henry Burke	*Life* 309.
L. A. Austen-Leigh	*Life* 365.
Copy by J. A.—Pierpont Morgan Library	*Memoir*[1] 149, *Memoir*[2] 112 ; *Life* 312.
Earl Stanhope	Not published.
.. .. ..	*Memoir*[2] 122 ; *Life* 314.
Pierpont Morgan Library	*Brabourne* II 249 ; *Life* 315.
New York Public Library	*Brabourne* II 253 ; *Life* 316.
Pierpont Morgan Library	*Brabourne* II 258 ; *Life* 317.
L. A. Austen-Leigh	*Life* 363.
Copy by J. A.—T. E. Carpenter	*Memoir*[1] 152 ; *Memoir*[2] 114 ; *Life* 319.

NO.	RECIPIENT.	PLACE.	DATE.
121	John Murray	Hans Place	⟨Mon.⟩ 11 Dec. ⟨1815⟩
122	John Murray	Hans Place	⟨Mon.⟩ 11 Dec. ⟨1815⟩
122.1	Charles Thomas Haden	Hans Place	Thurs. ⟨14 Dec. 1815⟩
123	The Countess of Morley	.. ..	⟨Sun.⟩ 31 Dec. 1815
124	Anna Lefroy	.. .	⟨? Dec. 1815⟩
125	Caroline Austen	Chawton	Wed. 13 Mar. ⟨1816⟩
126	J. S. Clarke	Chawton	⟨Mon.⟩ 1 Apr. 1816
127	John Murray	Chawton	⟨Mon.⟩ 1 Apr. 1816
128	Caroline Austen	Chawton	Sun. 21 Apr. ⟨1816⟩
128·1	Caroline Austen	⟨Chawton⟩	⟨Sun. 21 Apr. 1816⟩
129	Anna Lefroy	Chawton	Sun. 23 June ⟨1816⟩
130	Edward Austen	Chawton	Tues. 9 July 1816
131	Caroline Austen	Chawton	Mon. 15 July ⟨1816⟩
132	Cassandra Austen	⟨Chawton⟩	⟨Wed.⟩ 4 Sept. 1816
133	Cassandra Austen	Chawton	Sun. 8 Sept. ⟨1816⟩
134	Edward Austen	Chawton	Mon. 16 Dec. ⟨1816⟩
135	Anna Lefroy	⟨Chawton⟩	Thurs. ⟨late in 1816⟩

ORIGINAL.	PREVIOUS PUBLICATION (WHOLE OR PART).
Lt.-Col. Sir John Murray	*Memoir*[2] 122; *Life* 318.
.. .. ..	*Memoir*[2] 124; *Life* 319.
Mrs. Henry Burke	Not published.
Mrs. Henry Burke	*Memoir*[1] 140, *Memoir*[2] 126; *Life* 326.
R. A. Austen-Leigh	*Memoir*[1] 203, *Memoir*[2] 148.
L. A. Austen-Leigh	*Life* 365.
Copy by J. A.—T. E. Carpenter	*Memoir*[1] 156, *Memoir*[2] 116; *Life* 323.
Mrs. D. H. Warren	*Memoir*[2] 124; *Life* 327.
(Copies—L. A. Austen-Leigh and Miss Lefroy)	Not published.
L. A. Austen-Leigh	Not published.
(Copy by Mrs. Bellas—Miss Lefroy)	*Brabourne* II 326.
L. A. Austen-Leigh	*Memoir*[1] 208, *Memoir*[2] 151; *Life* 371.
L. A. Austen-Leigh	*Life* 364.
L. A. Austen-Leigh	*Life* 374.
Pierpont Morgan Library	*Brabourne* II 262; *Life* 375.
L. A. Austen-Leigh	*Biographical Notice* (in *Northanger Abbey*, 1818; short extract); *Memoir*[1] 212, *Memoir*[2] 153; *Life* 377.
(Copy by Anna Lefroy—Miss Lefroy)	Not published.

NO.	RECIPIENT.	PLACE.	DATE.
136	Cassandra Austen (daughter of Charles Austen)	Chawton	⟨Wed.⟩ 8 Jan. 1817
137	Caroline Austen	Chawton	Thurs. 23 Jan. 1817
138	Caroline Austen	.. ..	Wed. ⟨1817⟩
139	Alethea Bigg	Chawton	⟨Fri.⟩ 24 Jan. 1817
140	Fanny Knight	Chawton	Thurs. 20 Feb. ⟨1817⟩
141	Fanny Knight	Chawton	Thurs. 13 Mar. ⟨1817⟩
141.1	Caroline Austen	Chawton	⟨Fri.⟩ 14 March ⟨1817⟩
142	Fanny Knight	Chawton	Sun. 23 Mar. ⟨1817⟩
143	Caroline Austen	Chawton	Wed. 26 Mar. ⟨1817⟩
144	Charles Austen	Chawton	Sun. 6 Apr. ⟨1817⟩
145	Anne Sharp	Chawton	⟨Thurs.⟩ 22 May ⟨1817⟩
146	Edward Austen	College Street, Winton	Tues. 27 May 1817
147	.. ..	⟨College Street⟩	⟨end of May 1817⟩
148	C. A. Prowting	⟨Chawton⟩	——

ORIGINAL.	PREVIOUS PUBLICATION (WHOLE OR PART).
Pierpont Morgan Library	*Brabourne* II 327.
L. A. Austen-Leigh	*Memoir*[2] 160 ; *Life* 366.
L. A. Austen-Leigh	*Life* 367.
.. .. ..	*Memoir*[2] 158 ; *Life* 379.
Lord Brabourne	*Brabourne* II 290 ; *Life* 348, 383.
Lord Brabourne	*Brabourne* II 295 ; *Life* 351, 383.
Lady Charnwood	Not published.
Lord Brabourne	*Brabourne* II 299 ; *Life* 352, 383.
L. A. Austen-Leigh	*Life* 367.
British Museum	*Memoir*[1] 207, *Memoir*[2] 150 (short extract) ; *Life* 385.
Mrs. Henry Burke	*Times* 1 Feb. 1926.
L. A. Austen-Leigh	*Memoir*[2] 163 ; *Life* 389.
.. .. ..	*Biographical Notice* (in *Northanger Abbey*, 1818) ; *Memoir*[1] 207, 224, *Memoir*[2] 150, 164 ; *Life* 391.
Miss Tucker	Not published.

LIST OF ILLUSTRATIONS

A Drawing by Cassandra Austen . . *Frontispiece*

A coloured drawing from the Lefroy MS. This, which is signed and dated by Cassandra Austen (CEA 1804), was inserted by Anna Lefroy in her volume of family history. It is the only drawing in the book not of her own composition. Its place in the volume, coming just before a copy of one of J. A.'s letters, and the fact that it has no descriptive legend, suggest that it was a portrait of Jane; for otherwise its presence would have called for explanation. Moreover, there are at least two copies of it (one of which I have seen) in other family collections. There is, I think, a presumption that it is Jane Austen; at least it is a pleasing example of Cassandra's talent. I have preferred it to the two known portraits of Jane which are familiar.[1]

Cottages at Steventon; from a drawing by Anna Lefroy *p.* xlvi

Astley's Amphitheatre; from Ackermann's *Repository* 1808 . . . . . . *Facing page* 6

Steventon Rectory 1814; from a drawing in the possession of R. A. Austen-Leigh 16

Jane Austen's Parents; from *Chawton Manor*, 1911 . 64

Axford and Paragon Buildings. From Nattes's *Bath*, 1806 128

Lyme Regis; from a lithograph made for Daniel Dunster, *c.* 1844, when the *Three Cups* was burned down . 136

Sydney Gardens. From Nattes's *Bath*, 1806 . . 144

Goodnestone Park 160

Godmersham Park; from Hasted's *Kent* . . 168

Southampton in 1819, showing Lord Lansdowne's Castle; from a print lent by Mr. H. B. Lankester . . 192

Edward Austen (Knight); from a miniature by Sir William Ross; *Chawton Manor*, 1911 208

[1] This conjecture has been verified. See my *Jane Austen*, 1948, 213.

List of Illustrations

Elizabeth Austen (née Bridges); from a miniature by Cosway; *Chawton Manor*, 1911 . . *Facing page* 216

Chawton Cottage; from a *Times* photograph, 1 Jan. 1926 266

Chawton House; from a print by G. F. Prosser . . 304

Covent Garden Theatre; from Ackermann's *Repository*, 1808 322

Godmersham Park; from Hasted's *Kent* . . 330

The High Street, Canterbury. From a lithograph by Thomas Sidney Cooper (1803–1902) . . . 362

Miss O'Neill as *Isabella*; from a print by Cheesman after Boaden 418

Carlton House; from Ackermann's *Repository*, 1808 . 450

Banknote of Austen, Maunde, and Tilson (by permission of the Institute of Bankers) 458

Steventon Manor; from a drawing by Anna Lefroy *Page* 520

Plan of the Neighbourhood of Steventon . . . 521

Bookplates of Austen of Broadford and Austen of Sevenoaks 522

Map of Hampshire 523

Plan of Hans Place, showing Henry Austen's houses, 64 Sloane Street and 23 Hans Place . . 524

Chawton Church; from a drawing by Anna Lefroy . 525

Plan of Chawton 526

Emma; the Dedication, from the first edition *Facing Note* 69

AUTHORITIES

MSS. of the Letters

SEE the Preface. For a fuller account of the MSS. see the Introduction to my edition of the *Memoir* (Oxford 1926). The table printed above indicates the ownership of all letters I have traced;[1] I have seen the originals, or photographs, of all these letters.

Other Primary Authorities

Opinions of *Mansfield Park* and *Emma* collected by J. A. from her acquaintance, and preserved in her handwriting. See *Plan of a Novel*, &c., Oxford 1926. Cited as *Opinions.*

Henry Austen: anonymous *Biographical Notice* prefixed to the first edition of *Northanger Abbey and Persuasion* 1818; somewhat expanded as introduction to Bentley's collected edition of the novels, 1833.

Caroline Austen: unpublished Reminiscences by J. A.'s niece, in the possession of Mr. E. C. Austen-Leigh. 'The entries in my Mother's well-kept pocket-books are the authorities on which I write.'

Anna Lefroy: unpublished Reminiscences by J. A.'s niece, in the possession of Miss Isabel Lefroy. Cited as *Lefroy MS.*

James Edward Austen-Leigh: *Memoir* of his Aunt, published 1870; second edition (expanded) 1871. Cited as *Memoir.*

The same: *Recollections of the Early Days of the Vine Hunt. . . . By a Sexagenarian.* Privately printed 1865.

Powlett Correspondence. Unpublished letters from Frank Temple, son of William Johnston Temple (Boswell's correspondent and ancestor of the Archbishop), to his sister Anne, Mrs. Charles Powlett; and between the latter and her husband; in the possession of Mrs. Horatia Powlett.

R. A. Austen-Leigh, *Austen Papers* 1704–1856. Privately printed 1942.

[1] I have indicated (1959) all changes of ownership known to me.

Authorities

Lybbe Powys, Mrs. Philip: *Passages from the Diaries of Mrs. P. L. P. of Hardwick House, Oxon., 1756–1808.* Edited by Emily J. Climenson. 1899.

Secondary Authorities

Letters of Jane Austen, 1884. Edited, from MSS. inherited from his mother (Fanny Knight, Lady Knatchbull, J. A.'s niece), by her son Edward Knatchbull Hugessen, first Lord Brabourne. This edition is still the sole authority for nearly twenty letters, the originals of which have not been traced. Cited as *Brabourne.*

Mrs. Bellas, daughter of Anna Lefroy: (1) unpublished volume of reminiscences, based on her mother's volume but with substantial additions; in the possession of Miss Isabel Lefroy. (2) Unpublished notes in her copy of Lord Brabourne's edition of the Letters, in the possession of Miss C. L. Thomson.

Jane Austen's Sailor Brothers, by J. H. and E. C. Hubback, 1906. Cited as *Sailor Brothers.*

Jane Austen's Life and Letters, by W. and R. A. Austen-Leigh, 1913; second edition, 1913. Now unhappily out of print. The authors of the *Life* had access to almost all the originals known to me of the Letters, and to almost all the unpublished documents described above, as well as to other family papers. The present edition of the Letters makes no attempt to supersede their work, which gives a full account of J. A.'s environment, and is indispensable. Cited as *Life.*

Mary Augusta Austen-Leigh: *Memoir* of her father J. E. A.-L. Privately printed 1911.

William Austen-Leigh and Montagu George Knight: *Chawton Manor and its Owners.* 1911.

Constance Hill: *Jane Austen, Her Homes and her Friends.* 1901, third ed. 1923. Miss Hill had access to Lefroy and other MSS.

Bibliography

Geoffrey Keynes: *Jane Austen: A Bibliography.* 1929. See also R. W. C. in the *Cambridge Bibliography of English Literature.*

INTRODUCTION

JANE AUSTEN'S letters have had some detractors and some apologists. They have received little whole-hearted praise even from the 'idolators' of the novels. It has been assumed that they have little interest except for the few brief rays with which they illumine the history of the novels, and would be hardly readable if their author were not otherwise famous. A familiar complaint is that they have nothing to say about the great events that were shaking Europe—a kind of negative criticism seldom elsewhere applied to family correspondence. A familiar defence is that the letters have been robbed of their general interest by Cassandra Austen's pious destruction of all that she supposed might possibly excite general curiosity. We know from their niece Caroline that 'her letters to Aunt Cassandra were, I daresay, open and confidential. My Aunt looked them over and burnt the greater part as she told me three or four years before her own death. She left or gave some as legacies to the nieces, but of those that I have seen several had portions cut out.' [1]

Doubtless this suppression has cost us much that we should value. But we may suspect that it has not materially affected the impression we should have received from a richer survival. The sisters were, for the greater part of their joint lives, together, and in conditions of the closest intimacy. They were from time to time separated by long visits, and then corresponded regularly. But the purpose of their letters

[1] Quoted in *Personal Aspects of Jane Austen* by M. A. Austen-Leigh, 1920, p. 145.

was to exchange information not only between themselves, but between two branches of a large family. There are indications that these letters and others like them were read by, and to, a number of people. Even if this had not been so, it would not have been consonant with the sisters' temperament, or with their way of life, to exchange letters of sentiment or disquisition. It would not have suited Jane Austen's sense of propriety to charge her sister sixpence (or thereabouts) for opinions on religion or politics, on life or letters, which were known already, or would keep. But news would not wait, and news must always give satisfaction. Only on rare and emergent occasions, I believe, was the ordinary tenor of news interrupted.[1]

I must add, though with reluctance, my impression that Cassandra Austen was not the correspondent who best evoked her sister's powers. The letters to the nieces show more flow of fancy, less attention to the business of news. And the two letters,[2] recovered in recent years, to friends outside the family are notably above the average in variety and vigour.

But I would not seem to be apologetic where I see no need for apology. Are these letters in fact uninteresting? I have not found them so. Even if Jane Austen had no other claim to be remembered, her letters would be memorable. Read with attention, they yield a picture of the life of the upper middle class of that time which is surely without a rival. And they depict not only manners, but also persons. Jane Austen's own family, with its ramifications by marriage, is itself a larger—I had almost said, a more

[1] 'I am quite dependent on the communications of our friends, or my own wits,' p. 245. [2] Numbers 74·1 and 145.

ambitious—subject than any she attempted in her novels. And though the characterization is incidental, and hardly ever deliberate, it is by the same hand as Lady Bertram and Mrs. Norris. Round the family is grouped a gallery of lesser persons, all of whom—if they are not merely named—acquire some individuality. It is difficult not to remember even Mr. Robert Mascall, though we hardly know more of him than that he 'eats a great deal of butter'. There are in these five hundred pages characters chiefly conspicuous for their amiability: Cassandra herself, and Edward, and the two sailors, and Martha Lloyd, and old Mrs. Knight. There are public characters—not many of these—like Mr. Crabbe, seen or not seen at a distance, or Mr. Lushington, M.P., M.F., who could talk well about Milton; 'I daresay he is ambitious and insincere'. There are brilliant and versatile characters, notably Henry Austen, who reminds us of Henry Tilney and even of Henry Crawford, but had more of 'genius' than any man in the novels; attractive young people, like Fanny Knight and her 'agreeable, idle brothers', Anna Austen, and Mr. Haden; mixed characters, like Mrs. James Austen, and Miss Sharp, and 'that puss Cassy', and Mr. Moore, Rector of Wrotham; and farcical characters, like Mrs. Henry Digweed, and Mrs. Stent, and Miss Milles of Canterbury, whom the late A. B. Walkley guessed to be the prototype of Miss Bates. Many of these persons have, no doubt, assumed some artificial importance to an editor who has made it his business to hunt for facts about them. I can urge, on the other side, that ten years' intimacy has raised, not lessened, my regard. I cannot be mistaken in the belief that, in their several degrees, they are alive. How they are brought to life, without quotation and almost without description, may be perceived but can hardly be explained.

The letters are, like most letters, occasional, unstudied, and inconsequent. Their themes are accidental; their bulk, that of a quarto sheet. As a series, though they have connexion, they have no coherence; they straggle over twenty years, and lack a plot. Their details, therefore, unlike the details of *Emma*, are not the ingredients or the embellishments of a rounded composition. If they can be called works of art, they are so only because, as their writer reminds us,[1] 'an artist cannot do anything slovenly'. But as fragments—fragments of observation, of characterization, of criticism—they are in the same class as the material of the novels; and in some respects they have a wider range.

But with all their vividness, are these letters trifling? Can they be plausibly called 'a desert of trivialities punctuated by occasional oases of clever malice'?[2] Life, wrote Johnson, 'is made up of little things'. Trifles are dear to all our hearts, if they are attached to the objects of our affection—whether persons or things. 'The tables are come. . . . They are both covered with green baize and send their best Love.'[3] The writer of these letters was never ashamed to be minute. 'You know how interesting the purchase of a spongecake is to me.'[4] The question, for that posterity whom she did not here address, is not whether she

[1] *Act.* 23; p. 30.

[2] H. W. Garrod in ***Essays by Divers Hands*** (R. Society of Literature), viii, 1928.

[3] p. 82, cf. pp. 162, 381.

[4] p. 191.

wrote of trifles, but whether she makes the small change of her life important, amusing, and endearing to us her unlicensed readers; or, on the contrary, reveals a cold heart, a meagre intelligence, and a petty spirit. We know that Jane Austen the novelist had a genius for the particular; a zest for the small concerns or belongings of her creatures, which her genius made communicable. The readers of *Mansfield Park* were not told how much Mrs. Norris gave William Price at parting. But her family knew that Miss Austen could tell them, if she chose, what the 'something considerable' was. So the secret got out, and still delights each new participant. The eager, affectionate interest which the letters show in matters of domestic concern ('Pray, where did the boys sleep?'[1]) is scarcely less infectious.

But the enchantment which enthusiasts have sometimes found in these letters will not be universally admitted. It will be admitted by those only in whose own experience little things—like nicknames, or family jokes, or the arrangement of the furniture—are inseparable from the deeper joys, and even from the deeper sorrows of life; and by those only who find wisdom and humanity in this correspondence, as well as—or in despite of—its devotion to minutiae. To those who do not find these qualities in them, the letters may appear not merely trivial, but hard and cold. Even their professed admirers have deplored their occasional cynicism. The charge should be met, though I ought to confess that I do not well comprehend it. The letters abound in gentle or playful malice; and sharper strokes are frequent. Mr. Robert Mascall

[1] Page 369.

is not the only person whose character is blasted in a phrase. Some mercy is shown to foolishness:

'Dear Mrs. Digweed! I cannot bear that she should not be foolishly happy after a Ball.'[1]

But not very much:

'If the Brother should luckily be a little sillier than the Colonel, what a treasure for Eliza.'[2]
'She was highly rouged, and looked rather quietly and contentedly silly than anything else.'[3]

There is none at all for meanness or pretence.

'They live in a handsome style and are rich, and she seemed to like to be rich, and we gave her to understand that we were far from being so; she will soon feel therefore that we are not worth her acquaintance.'[4]
'I would not give much for Mr. Rice's chance of living at Deane; he builds his hope, I find, not upon anything that his mother has written, but upon the effect of what he has written himself. He must write a great deal better than those eyes indicate if he can persuade a perverse and narrow-minded woman to oblige those whom she does not love.'[5]

This may be thought censorious by those who have no taste for satire. But the unpublished portrait of Mrs. Rice deserves the charge of cruelty no more and no less than the published portrait of Mrs. Norris; and it has been remarked that Jane Austen does justice to the virtues which Mrs. Norris had. Whatever be thought of these asperities, they are not spiteful.

The author of *Pride and Prejudice* was not insensible of the beauty of candour; of the virtue which Elizabeth Bennet, praising her sister, calls 'candour without

[1] Page 345. [2] Page 210. [3] Page 128.
[4] Page 175. [5] Page 117.

ostentation or design—to take the good of every body's character, and make it still better, and say nothing of the bad'. She, like her Elizabeth, knew that her own distinctive talent lay in an opposite direction. Neither of them scrupled to use it. But it is unfair to conclude, because Miss Austen can be exquisitely wicked, that she was deficient in the softer emotions; just as it is unfair to deny her all romantic sentiment because there, too, she knew her limitations, and declared she 'could no more write a romance than an epic poem'.[1]

As I lay aside the desultory employment of many years, during which I have indulged a harmless curiosity about the births, marriages, and deaths of unimportant people, the details of travel, and the economy of country houses, I cannot forbear to remind myself of the closing sentences of *The Last Chronicle of Barset.*

'To me Barset has been a real country, and its city a real city, and the spires and towers have been before my eyes, and the voices of the people are known to my ears, and the pavements of the city ways are familiar to my footsteps.'

That Godmersham and Chawton were and are real places, as Barset and Mansfield were not, makes I think no important difference. The miracle of communication is the same.

[1] Page 452.

COTTAGES AT STEVENTON
from a drawing by Anna Lefroy

1. *To Cassandra Austen. Saturday* 9 *Jan.* ⟨1796⟩

Address (Brabourne): To Miss Austen | Rev. Mr. Fowle's, Kintbury, Newbury

Original not traced.

Brabourne i. 125; *Life* 87, 98 (extracts).

Steventon: Saturday January 9

In the first place I hope you will live twenty-three years longer. Mr. Tom Lefroy's birthday was yesterday, so that you are very near of an age.

After this necessary preamble I shall proceed to inform you that we had an exceeding good ball last night, and that I was very much disappointed at not seeing Charles Fowle of the party, as I had previously heard of his being invited. In addition to our set at the Harwoods' ball, we had the Grants, St. Johns, Lady Rivers, her three daughters and a son, Mr. and Miss Heathcote, Mrs. Lefevre, two Mr. Watkins, Mr. J. Portal, Miss Deanes, two Miss Ledgers, and a tall clergyman who came with them, whose name Mary would never have guessed.

We were so terrible good as to take James in our carriage, though there were three of us before; but indeed he deserves encouragement for the very great improvement which has lately taken place in his dancing. Miss Heathcote is pretty, but not near so handsome as I expected. Mr. H. began with Elizabeth, and afterwards danced with her again; but *they* do not know how *to be particular*. I flatter myself, however, that they will profit by the three successive lessons which I have given them.

You scold me so much in the nice long letter which I have this moment received from you, that I am almost afraid to tell you how my Irish friend and I behaved. Imagine to yourself everything most profligate and shocking in the way of dancing and sitting down together. I *can* expose myself, however, only *once more,* because he leaves the country soon after next Friday, on which day we *are* to have a dance at Ashe after all. He is a very gentlemanlike, good-looking, pleasant young man, I assure you. But as to our having ever met, except at the three last balls, I cannot say much; for he is so excessively laughed at about me at Ashe, that he is ashamed of coming to Steventon, and ran away when we called on Mrs. Lefroy a few days ago.

We left Warren at Dean Gate, in our way home last night, and he is now on his road to town. He left his love, &c., to you, and I will deliver it when we meet. Henry goes to Harden to-day in his way to his Master's degree. We shall feel the loss of these two most agreeable young men exceedingly, and shall have nothing to console us till the arrival of the Coopers on Tuesday. As they will stay here till the Monday following, perhaps Caroline will go to the Ashe ball with me, though I dare say she will not.

I danced twice with Warren last night, and once with Mr. Charles Watkins, and, to my inexpressible astonishment, I entirely escaped John Lyford. I was forced to fight hard for it, however. We had a very good supper, and the greenhouse was illuminated in a very elegant manner.

We had a visit yesterday morning from Mr. Benjamin Portal, whose eyes are as handsome as ever. Everybody is extremely anxious for your return, but as you cannot come home by the Ashe ball, I am glad that

I have not fed them with false hopes. James danced with Alithea, and cut up the turkey last night with great perseverance. You say nothing of the silk stockings; I flatter myself, therefore, that Charles has not purchased any, as I cannot very well afford to pay for them; all my money is spent in buying white gloves and pink persian. I wish Charles had been at Manydown, because he would have given you some description of my friend, and I think you must be impatient to hear something about him.

Henry is still hankering after the Regulars, and as his project of purchasing the adjutancy of the Oxfordshire is now over, he has got a scheme in his head about getting a lieutenancy and adjutancy in the 86th, a new-raised regiment, which he fancies will be ordered to the Cape of Good Hope. I heartily hope that he will, as usual, be disappointed in this scheme. We have trimmed up and given away all the old paper hats of Mamma's manufacture; I hope you will not regret the loss of yours.

After I had written the above, we received a visit from Mr. Tom Lefroy and his cousin George. The latter is really very well-behaved now; and as for the other, he has but *one* fault, which time will, I trust, entirely remove—it is that his morning coat is a great deal too light. He is a very great admirer of Tom Jones, and therefore wears the same coloured clothes, I imagine, which *he* did when he was wounded.

Sunday.—By not returning till the 19th, you will exactly contrive to miss seeing the Coopers, which I suppose it is your wish to do. We have heard nothing from Charles for some time. One would suppose they must have sailed by this time, as the wind is so favourable. What a funny name Tom has got for his vessel! But he has no taste in names, as we well know, and I dare say he christened it himself. I am sorry for the Beaches' loss of their little girl, especially as it is the one so much like me.

I condole with Miss M. on her losses and with Eliza on her gains, and am ever yours,

J. A.

2. *To Cassandra Austen. Thursday* ⟨14⟩ *Jan.* ⟨1796⟩

Address: Miss Austen | The Rev. Mr. Fowle's, Kintbury, Newbury
Postmark: 16 IA 1796.
Sir Alfred Law.
Brabourne i. 130 (misdated 16 Jan.); *Life* 88, 99 (extracts).

Steventon: Thursday January 16

I have just received yours and Mary's letter, and I thank you both, though their contents might have been more agreeable. I do not at all expect to see you on Tuesday, since matters have fallen out so unpleasantly; and if you are not able to return till after that day, it will hardly be possible for us to send for you before Saturday, though for my own part I care so little about the ball that it would be no sacrifice to me to give it up for the sake of seeing you two days earlier. We are extremely sorry for poor Eliza's illness. I trust, however, that she has continued to recover since you wrote, and that you will none of you be the worse for your attendance on her. What a good-for-nothing fellow Charles is to bespeak the stockings! I hope he will be too hot all the rest of his life for it!

I sent you a letter yesterday to Ibthorp, which I suppose you will not receive at Kintbury. It was not very long or very witty, and therefore if you never receive it, it does not much signify. I wrote principally to tell you that the Coopers were arrived and in good health. The little boy is very like Dr. Cooper, and the little girl is to resemble Jane, they say.

Our party to Ashe to-morrow night will consist of Edward Cooper, James (for a ball is nothing without *him*), Buller, who is now staying with us, and I. I look forward with great impatience to it, as I rather expect to receive an offer from my friend in the course of the evening. I shall refuse him, however, unless he promises to give away his white coat.

I am very much flattered by your commendation of my last letter, for I write only for fame, and without any view to pecuniary emolument.

Edward is gone to spend the day with his friend, John Lyford, and does not return till to-morrow. Anna is now here ; she came up in her chaise to spend the day with her young cousins, but she does not much take to them or to anything about them, except Caroline's spinning-wheel. I am very glad to find from Mary that Mr. and Mrs. Fowle are pleased with you. I hope you will continue to give satisfaction.

How impertinent you are to write to me about Tom, as if I had not opportunities of hearing from him myself ! The *last* letter that I received from him was dated on Friday, 8th, and he told me that if the wind should be favourable on Sunday, which it proved to be, they were to sail from Falmouth on that day. By this time, therefore, they are at Barbadoes, I suppose. The Rivers are still at Manydown, and are to be at Ashe to-morrow. I intended to call on the Miss Biggs yesterday had the weather been tolerable. Caroline,

Anna, and I have just been devouring some cold souse, and it would be difficult to say which enjoyed it most.

Tell Mary that I make over Mr. Heartley and all his estate to her for her sole use and benefit in future, and not only him, but all my other admirers into the bargain wherever she can find them, even the kiss which C. Powlett wanted to give me, as I mean to confine myself in future to Mr. Tom Lefroy, for whom I do not care sixpence. Assure her also, as a last and indubitable proof of Warren's indifference to me, that he actually drew that gentleman's picture for me, and delivered it to me without a sigh.

Friday.—At length the day is come on which I am to flirt my last with Tom Lefroy, and when you receive this it will be over. My tears flow as I write at the melancholy idea. Wm. Chute called here yesterday. I wonder what he means by being so civil. There is a report that Tom is going to be married to a Lichfield lass. John Lyford and his sister bring Edward home to-day, dine with us, and we shall all go together to Ashe. I understand that we are to draw for partners. I shall be extremely impatient to hear from you again, that I may know how Eliza is, and when you are to return.

With best love, &c., I am affectionately yours,

J. Austen

ASTLEY'S AMPHITHEATRE

3. *To Cassandra Austen. Tuesday* ⟨*Aug.* 1796⟩

No address.
Original not traced.
***Brabourne* i. 133 ; *Life* 99.**

Cork Street: Tuesday morn ⟨August 1796⟩

My dear Cassandra

Here I am once more in this scene of dissipation and vice, and I begin already to find my morals corrupted. We reached Staines yesterday, I do not (know) when, without suffering so much from the heat as I had hoped to do. We set off again this morning at seven o'clock, and had a very pleasant drive, as the morning was cloudy and perfectly cool. I came all the way in the chaise from Hertford Bridge.

Edward and Frank are both gone out to seek their fortunes ; the latter is to return soon and help us seek ours. The former we shall never see again. We are to be at Astley's to-night, which I am glad of. Edward has heard from Henry this morning. He has not been at the races at all, unless his driving Miss Pearson over to Rowling one day can be so called. We shall find him there on Thursday.

I hope you are all alive after our melancholy parting yesterday, and that you pursued your intended avocation with success. God bless you ! I must leave off, for we are going out.

Yours very affectionately,

J. Austen

Everybody's love.

4. *To Cassandra Austen.* *Thursday* 1 *Sept.* ⟨1796⟩

Address (Brabourne): Miss Austen, Steventon, Overton, Hants
Original not traced.
Brabourne i. 134; *Life* 101 (extracts).

Rowling: Thursday September 1

My dearest Cassandra

The letter which I have this moment received from you has diverted me beyond moderation. I could die of laughter at it, as they used to say at school. You are indeed the finest comic writer of the present age.

Since I wrote last, we have been very near returning to Steventon so early as next week. Such, for a day or two, was our dear brother Henry's scheme, but at present matters are restored, not to what they were, for my absence seems likely to be lengthened still farther. I am sorry for it, but what can I do?

Henry leaves us to-morrow for Yarmouth, as he wishes very much to consult his physician there, on whom he has great reliance. He is better than he was when he first came, though still by no means well. According to his present plan, he will not return here till about the 23rd, and bring with him, if he can, leave of absence for three weeks, as he wants very much to have some shooting at Godmersham, whither Edward and Elizabeth are to remove very early in October. If this scheme holds, I shall hardly be at Steventon before the middle of that month; but if you cannot do without me, I could return, I suppose, with Frank if he ever goes back. He enjoys himself here very much, for he has just learnt to turn, and is so delighted with the employment, that he is at it all day long.

I am sorry that you found such a conciseness in the

strains of my first letter. I must endeavour to make you amends for it, when we meet, by some elaborate details, which I shall shortly begin composing.

I have had my new gown made up, and it really makes a very superb surplice. I am sorry to say that my new coloured gown is very much washed out, though I charged everybody to take great care of it. I hope yours is so too. Our men had but indifferent weather for their visit to Godmersham, for it rained great part of the way there and all the way back. They found Mrs. Knight remarkably well and in very good spirits. It is imagined that she will shortly be married again. I have taken little George once in my arms since I have been here, which I thought very kind. I have told Fanny about the bead of her necklace, and she wants very much to know where you found it.

To-morrow I shall be just like Camilla in Mr. Dubster's summer-house; for my Lionel will have taken away the ladder by which I came here, or at least by which I intended to get away, and here I must stay till his return. My situation, however, is somewhat preferable to hers, for I am very happy here, though I should be glad to get home by the end of the month. I have no idea that Miss Pearson will return with me.

What a fine fellow Charles is, to deceive us into writing two letters to him at Cork! I admire his ingenuity extremely, especially as he is so great a gainer by it.

Mr. and Mrs. Cage and Mr. and Mrs. Bridges dined with us yesterday. Fanny seemed as glad to see me as anybody, and enquired very much after you, whom she supposed to be making your wedding-clothes. She is as handsome as ever, and somewhat fatter. We had a very pleasant day, and some *liqueurs* in the evening. Louisa's figure is very much improved ; she is as stout again as she was. Her face, from what I could see of it one evening, appeared not at all altered. She and the gentlemen walked up here on Monday night—she came in the morning with the Cages from Hythe.

Lady Hales, with her two youngest daughters, have been to see us. Caroline is not grown at all coarser than she was, nor Harriet at all more delicate. I am glad to hear so good an account of Mr. Charde, and only fear that my long absence may occasion his relapse. I practise every day as much as I can—I wish it were more for his sake. I have heard nothing of Mary Robinson since I have been (here). I expect to be well scolded for daring to doubt, whenever the subject is mentioned.

Frank has turned a very nice little butter-churn for Fanny. I do not believe that any of the party were aware of the valuables they had left behind ; nor can I hear anything of Anna's gloves. Indeed I have not enquired at all about them hitherto.

We are very busy making Edward's shirts, and I am proud to say that I am the neatest worker of the party. They say that there are a prodigious number of birds hereabouts this year, so that perhaps *I* may kill a few. I am glad to hear so good an account of Mr. Limprey and J. Lovett. I know nothing of my mother's handkerchief, but I dare say I shall find it soon.

I am very affectionately yours,

Jane

5. *To Cassandra Austen. Monday 5 Sept.* ⟨1796⟩

Address : lost.
Harold Murdock (one leaf). Facsimile in W. H. Helm, *Jane Austen and her Country-House Comedy*, 1909. Pages 3–4 were already missing when Lord Brabourne published the letter. He indicates a hiatus after *five volumes*, but this is not exact; the sentence last printed was a postscript, added to page 1.
Brabourne i. 138 ; *Life* 101.

Rowling Monday 5th Sept[1]

My dear Cassandra

I shall be extremely anxious to hear the Event of your Ball, & shall hope to receive so long & minute an account of every particular that I shall be tired of reading it. Let me know how many besides their fourteen Selves & Mr & Mrs Wright, Michael will contrive to place about their Coach, and how many of the Gentlemen, Musicians & Waiters, he will have persuaded to come in their Shooting Jackets. I hope John Lovett's accident will not prevent his attending the Ball, as you will otherwise be obliged to dance with Mr. Tincton the whole Evening. Let me know how J. Harwood deports himself without the Miss Biggs;—and which of the Marys will carry the day with my Brother James. *We* were at a Ball on Saturday I assure you. We dined at Goodnestone & in the Evening danced two Country Dances and the Boulangeries.—I opened the Ball with Edwd Bridges; the other couples, were Lewis Cage & Harriot, Frank and Louisa, Fanny & George. Elizth played one Country dance, Lady Bridges the other, which she made Henry dance with her; and Miss Finch played the Boulangeries—On reading over the last three or four Lines, I am aware of my having expressed myself in so doubtful a manner that if I did not tell you to the contrary, You might imagine it was Lady Bridges who made Henry dance with her, at the same time that she was playing—which if not impossible must appear a very improbable Event to you.—But it was Eliz: who danced—.

We supped there, & walked home at night under the shade of two Umbrellas.—Today the Goodnestone Party begins to disperse & spread itself abroad. Mr. & Mrs. Cage & George repair to Hythe. Lady Waltham, Miss Bridges & Miss Mary Finch to Dover, for the health of the two former.—I have never seen Marianne at all.—

On Thursday Mr. & Mrs. Bridges return to Danbury; Miss Harriot Hales accompanies them to London in her way to Dorsetshire. Farmer Clarinbould died this morning, & I fancy Edward means to get some of his Farm if he can cheat Sir Brook enough in the agrement.—We have just got some venison from Godmersham, which the two Mr. Harveys are to devour tomorrow; and on friday or Saturday the Goodnestone people are to finish their Scraps. Henry went away on friday as he purposed *without fayl*;—You will hear from him soon I imagine, as he talked of writing to Steventon shortly. Mr. Richard Harvey is going to be married; but as it is a great secret, & only known to half the Neighbourhood, you must not mention it. The Lady's name is Musgrove.—I am in great Distress.—I cannot determine whether I shall give Richis half a guinea or only five Shillings when I go away. Counsel me, amiable Miss Austen, and tell me which will be the most.—We walked Frank last night to Crixhall ruff, and he appeared much edified. Little

Edward was breeched yesterday for good & all, and was whipped, into the Bargain. Pray remember me to Everybody who does not enquire after me. Those who do, remember me without bidding. . . .

Give my Love to Mary Harrison, & tell her I wish whenever she is attached to a young Man, some *respectable* Dr. Marchmont may keep them apart for five Volumes.

6. *To Cassandra Austen.* *Thursday* 15 *Sept.* 1796

Address: Miss Austen | Steventon | Overton | Hants
Postmark: 17 SE 96
Pierpont Morgan Library. 2 leaves 4°
Brabourne i. 141; *Life* 102 (extracts). One sentence unpublished.

Rowling: Thursday 15th Septr

My dear Cassandra

We have been very gay since I wrote last; dining at Nackington, returning by Moonlight, and everything quite in Stile, not to mention Mr. Claringbould's Funeral which we saw go by on Sunday. I beleive I told you in a former Letter that Edward had some idea of taking the name of Claringbould; but that scheme is over, tho' it would be a very eligible as well as a very pleasant plan, would any one advance him Money enough to begin on. We rather expected Mr. Milles to have done so on Tuesday; but to our great Surprise, nothing was said on the subject, and unless it is in your power to assist your Brother with five or six Hundred pounds, he must entirely give up the idea. At Nackington we met Lady Sondes' picture over the Mantlepeice in the Dining room, and the pictures of her three Children in an Antiroom, besides

Mr. Scott, Miss Fletcher, Mr. Toke, Mr. J. Toke, and the Archdeacon Lynch. Miss Fletcher and I were very thick, but I am the thinnest of the two—She wore her purple Muslin, which is pretty enough, tho' it does not become her complexion. There are two Traits in her character which are pleasing ; namely, she admires Camilla, & drinks no cream in her Tea. If you should ever see Lucy, You may tell her, that I scolded Miss Fletcher for her negligence in writing, as she desired me to do, but without being able to bring her to any proper sense of Shame—That Miss Fletcher says in her defence that as every Body whom Lucy knew when she was in Canterbury, has now left it, she has nothing at all to write to her about. By *Everybody*, I suppose Miss Fletcher means that a new set of Officers have arrived there—. But this is a note of my own.—Mrs. Milles, Mr. John Toke, & in short everybody of any Sensibility enquired in tender Strains after You ; and I took an opportunity of assuring Mr. J. T. that neither he nor his Father need longer keep themselves single for You—. We went in our two Carriages to Nackington ; but how we divided, I shall leave you to surmise, merely observing that as Eliz: and I were without Hat or Bonnet, it would not have been very convenient for us to go in the Chair.—We went by Bifrons, & I contemplated with a melancholy pleasure, the abode of Him, on whom I once fondly doated.—We dine to-day at Goodnestone, to meet my Aunt Fielding from Margate, and a Mr. Clayton, her professed Admirer ; at least so I imagine. Lady Bridges has received very good accounts of Marianne, who is already certainly the better for her Bathing.—So—his royal Highness Sir Thomas Williams has at length sailed— ; the

Papers say 'on a Cruize.' But I hope they are gone to Cork, or I shall have written in vain. Give my Love to Jane, as she arrived at Steventon Yesterday, I dare say. I sent a message to Mr. Digweed from Edward, in a letter to Mary Lloyd, which she ought to receive today; but as I know that the Harwoods are not very exact as to their Letters, I may as well repeat it to You—. Mr. Digweed is to be informed that Illness has prevented Seward's coming over to look at the intended Repairs at the Farm, but that he will come, as soon as he can. Mr. Digweed may also be informed if you think proper, that Mr. & Mrs. Milles are to dine here tomorrow, and that Mrs. Joan Knatchbull is to be asked to meet them.—Mr. Richard Harvey's match is put off till he has got a Better Christian name, of which he has great Hopes. Mr. Children's two Sons are both going to be married, John & George—. They are to have one wife between them; a Miss Holwell, who belongs to the Black Hole at Calcutta.—I depend on hearing from James very soon; he promised me an account of the Ball, and by this time he must have collected his Ideas enough, after the fatigue of dancing, to give me one. Edward & Fly went out yesterday very early in a couple of Shooting Jackets, and came home like a couple of Bad Shots, for they killed nothing at all. They are out again today, & are not yet returned. Delightful Sport!—They are just come home; Edward with his two Brace, Frank with his Two and a half. What amiable Young Men!

Friday—Your Letter & one from Henry are just come, and the contents of both accord with my Scheme more than I had dared expect—In one particular I could wish it otherwise, for Henry is very indifferent indeed—. You must not expect us quite so early however as wednesday the 20th—on that day se'night according to our present plan we may be with You. Frank had never any idea of going away before Monday the 26th. I shall write to Miss Pearson immediately & press her returning with us, which Henry thinks very likely, & particularly eligible.

Buy Mary Harrison's Gown by all means. You shall have mine for ever so much money, tho' if I am tolerably rich when I get home, I shall like it very much myself.

Till we know whether she accompanies us or not, we can say nothing in reply to my Father's kind offer—.

As to the mode of our travelling to Town, *I* want to go in a Stage Coach, but Frank will not let me. As you are likely to have the Williams' & Lloyds with you next week, you would hardly find room for us then.

If anybody wants anything in Town, they must send their Commissions to Frank, as *I* shall merely pass thro' it.—The Tallow Chandler is Penlington, at the Crown & Beehive Charles Street, Covent Garden.

7. *To Cassandra Austen.* *Sunday* 18 *Sept.* 1796

Address: Miss Austen | Steventon | Overton | Hants
Postmark: 19 SE 96
Pierpont Morgan Library. 2 leaves 4o
Brabourne i. 146; *Life* 103 (extracts).

Rowling: Sunday 18th Septr

My dear Cassandra

This morning has been spent in Doubt & Deliberation; in forming plans, and removing Difficulties, for

Back front of Steventon Rectory. 1814

it ushered in the Day with an Event which I had not intended should take place so soon by a week. Frank has rec[d] his appointment on Board the Captain John Gore, commanded by the Triton, and will therefore be obliged to be in Town on wednesday—and tho' I have every Disposition in the world to accompany him on that day, I cannot go on the Uncertainty of the Pearsons being at Home; as I should not have a place to go to, in case they were from Home. I wrote to Miss P. on friday, and hoped to receive an answer from her this morning, which would have rendered everything smooth and Easy, and would have enabled us to leave this place to-morrow, as Frank on first receiving his Appointment, intended to do. He remains till Wednesday merely to accomodate me. I have written to her again to-day and desired her to answer it by return of post—On Tuesday therefore I shall positively know whether they can receive me on Wednesday—If they cannot, Edward has been so good as to promise to take me to Greenwich on the Monday following which was the day before fixed on, if that suits them better—. If I have no answer at all on Tuesday, I must suppose Mary is not at Home, and must wait till I do hear; as after having invited her to go to Steventon with me, it will not quite do, to go home and say no more about it.—

My Father will be so good as to fetch home his prodigal Daughter from Town, I hope, unless he wishes me to walk the Hospitals, Enter at the Temple, or mount Guard at St. James. It will hardly be in Frank's power to take me home; nay, it certainly will not. I shall write again as soon as I get to Greenwich.—

What dreadful Hot weather we have !—It keeps one in a continual state of Inelegance.—If Miss Pearson should return with me, pray be careful not to expect too much Beauty. I will not pretend to say that on a *first veiw*, she quite answered the opinion I had formed of her.—My Mother I am sure will be disappointed, if she does not take great care. From what I remember of her picture, it is no great resemblance. I am very glad that the idea of returning with Frank occurred to me, for as to Henry's coming into Kent again, the time of its taking place is so very uncertain, that I should be waiting for *Dead-men's Shoes.*

I had once determined to go with Frank to-morrow and take my chance &c. ; but they dissuaded me from so rash a step—as I really think on consideration it would have been; for if the Pearsons were not at home, I should inevitably fall a Sacrifice to the arts of some fat Woman who would make me drunk with Small Beer.—

Mary is brought to bed of a Boy ; both doing very well. I shall leave you to guess what Mary, I mean.—Adieu, with best Love to all your agreable Inmates. Do not let the Lloyds go on any account before I return, unless Miss P. is of the party.

How ill I have written. I begin to hate myself.

Yrs ever,

J: Austen

The Triton is a new 32 Frigate, just launched at Deptford.—Frank is much pleased with the prospect of having Capt: Gore under his command.

8. ⟨*To Philadelphia Walter*⟩. *Sunday* 8 *April* ⟨1798⟩

No address or postmark.
Rev. R. G. Binnall. One leaf 4°, the other leaf lost.
Not published.

Steventon Sunday April 8th
⟨1798 in another hand⟩

My dear Cousin

As Cassandra is at present from home, you must accept from my pen, our sincere Condolance on the melancholy Event which Mrs Humphries Letter announced to my Father this morning.—The loss of so kind & affectionate a Parent, must be a very severe affliction to all his Children, to yourself more especially, as your constant residence with him has given you so much the more constant & intimate Knowledge of his Virtues.—But the very circumstance which at present enhances your loss, must gradually reconcile you to it the better;—the Goodness which made him valuable on Earth, will make him Blessed in Heaven.—This consideration must bring comfort to yourself, to my Aunt, & to all his family & friends; & this comfort must be heightened by the consideration of the little Enjoyment he was able to receive from this World for some time past, & of the small degree of pain attending his last hours. I will not press you to write before you would otherwise feel equal to it, but when you can do it without pain, I hope we shall receive from you as good an account of my Aunt & yourself, as can be expected in these early days of Sorrow.—My Father & Mother join me in every kind wish, & I am my dear Cousin,

Yours affec:^{tely}
Jane Austen

9. *To Cassandra Austen.* *Wednesday* 24 *Oct.* ⟨1798⟩

Address (Brabourne) : Miss Austen, Godmersham Park, Faversham
Original not traced.
Brabourne i. 153 ; *Life* 109 (extracts).

'Bull and George,' Dartford :
Wednesday October 24

My dear Cassandra

You have already heard from Daniel, I conclude, in what excellent time we reached and quitted Sittingbourne, and how very well my mother bore her journey thither. I am now able to send you a continuation of the same good account of her. She was very little fatigued on her arrival at this place, has been refreshed by a comfortable dinner, and now seems quite stout. It wanted five minutes of twelve when we left Sittingbourne, from whence we had a famous pair of horses, which took us to Rochester in an hour and a quarter ; the postboy seemed determined to show my mother that Kentish drivers were not always tedious, and really drove as fast as *Cax*.

Our next stage was not quite so expeditiously performed ; the road was heavy and our horses very indifferent. However, we were in such good time, and my mother bore her journey so well, that expedition was of little importance to us ; and as it was, we were very little more than two hours and a half coming hither, and it was scarcely past four when we stopped at the inn. My mother took some of her bitters at Ospringe, and some more at Rochester, and she ate some bread several times.

We have got apartments up two pair of stairs, as we could not be otherwise accommodated with a sitting-room and bed-chambers on the same floor, which we wished to be. We have one double-bedded and one single-bedded room ; in the former my mother and I are to sleep. I shall leave you to guess who is to occupy the other. We sate down to dinner a little after five, and had some beef-steaks and a boiled fowl, but no oyster sauce.

I should have begun my letter soon after our arrival but for a little adventure which prevented me. After we had been here a quarter of an hour it was discovered that my writing and dressing boxes had been by accident put into a chaise which was just packing off as we came in, and were driven away towards Gravesend in their way to the West Indies. No part of my property could have been such a prize before, for in my writing-box was all my worldly wealth, *7l.*, and my dear Harry's deputation. Mr. Nottley immediately despatched a man and horse after the chaise, and in half an hour's time I had the pleasure of being as rich as ever; they were got about two or three miles off.

My day's journey has been pleasanter in every respect than I expected. I have been very little crowded and by no means unhappy. Your watchfulness with regard to the weather on our accounts was very kind and very effectual. We had one heavy shower on leaving Sittingbourne, but afterwards the clouds cleared away, and we had a very bright *chrystal* afternoon.

My father is now reading the 'Midnight Bell,' which he has got from the library, and mother sitting by the fire. Our route to-morrow is not determined. We have none of us much inclination for London, and if

Mr. Nottley will give us leave, I think we shall go to Staines through Croydon and Kingston, which will be much pleasanter than any other way; but he is decidedly for Clapham and Battersea. God bless you all!

Yours affectionately,

J. A.

I flatter myself that *itty Dordy* will not forget me at least under a week. Kiss him for me.

10. *To Cassandra Austen. Saturday* 27 *Oct.* ⟨1798⟩

***Address*: Miss Austen, Godmersham Park, Faversham, Kent**
Mrs. R. E. Hartz. For passages omitted here see p. 512.
***Brabourne* i. 156; *Life* 111 (extracts).**

Steventon: Saturday October 27

My dear Cassandra

Your letter was a most agreeable surprise to me to-day, and I have taken a long sheet of paper to show my gratitude.

We arrived here yesterday between four and five, but I cannot send you quite so triumphant an account of our last day's journey as of the first and second. Soon after I had finished my letter from Staines, my mother began to suffer from the exercise & fatigue of travelling so far, and she was a good deal indisposed. She had not a very good night at Staines, but bore her journey better than I had expected, and at Basingstoke, where we stopped more than half an hour, received much comfort from a mess of broth and the sight of Mr. Lyford, who recommended her to take twelve drops of laudanum when she went to bed as a composer, which she accordingly did.

James called on us just as we were going to tea, and my mother was well enough to talk very cheerfully to him before she went to bed. James seems to have taken to his old trick of coming to Steventon in spite of Mary's reproaches, for he was here before breakfast and is now paying us a second visit. They were to have dined here to-day, but the weather is too bad. I have had the pleasure of hearing that Martha is with them. James fetched her from Ibthorp on Thursday, and she will stay with them till she removes to Kintbury.

We met with no adventures at all in our journey yesterday, except that our trunk had once nearly slipped off, and we were obliged to stop at Hartley to have our wheels greased.

Whilst my mother and Mr. Lyford were together I went to Mrs. Ryder's and bought what I intended to buy, but not in much perfection. There were no narrow braces for children and scarcely any notting silk; but Miss Wood, as usual, is going to town very soon, and will lay in a fresh stock. I gave 2*s.* 3*d.* a yard for my flannel, and I fancy it is not very good, but it is so disgraceful and contemptible an article in itself that its being comparatively good or bad is of little importance. I bought some Japan ink likewise, and next week shall begin my operations on my hat, on which you know my principal hopes of happiness depend.

I am very grand indeed; I had the dignity of dropping out my mother's laudanum last night. I carry about the keys of the wine and closet, and twice since I began this letter have had orders to give in the kitchen. Our dinner was very good yesterday, and the chicken boiled perfectly tender; therefore I shall not be obliged to dismiss Nanny on that account.

Almost everything was unpacked and put away last night. Nanny chose to do it, and I was not sorry to be busy. I have unpacked the gloves and placed yours in your drawer. Their colour is light and pretty, and I believe exactly what we fixed on.

Your letter was chaperoned here by one from Mrs. Cooke, in which she says that 'Battleridge' is not to come out before January, and she is so little satisfied with Cawthorn's dilatoriness that she never means to employ him again.

Mrs. Hall, of Sherborne, was brought to bed yesterday of a dead child, some weeks before she expected, owing to a fright. I suppose she happened unawares to look at her husband.

There has been a great deal of rain here for this last fortnight, much more than in Kent, and indeed we found the roads all the way from Staines most disgracefully dirty. Steventon lane has its full share of it, and I don't know when I shall be able to get to Deane.

I hear that Martha is in better looks and spirits than she has enjoyed for a long time, and I flatter myself she will now be able to jest openly about Mr. W.

The spectacles which Molly found are my mother's, the scissors my father's. We are very glad to hear such a good account of your patients, little and great. My dear itty Dordy's remembrance of me is very pleasing to me—foolishly pleasing, because I know it will be over so soon. My attachment to him will be more durable. I shall think with tenderness and delight on his beautiful and smiling countenance and interesting manners till a few years have turned him into an ungovernable, ungracious fellow.

The books from Winton are all unpacked and put away; the binding has compressed them most conveniently, and there is now very good room in the bookcase for all that we wish to have there. I believe the servants were very glad to see us. Nanny was, I am sure. She confesses that it was very dull, and yet she had her child with her till last Sunday. I understand that there are some grapes left, but I believe not many; they must be gathered as soon as possible, or this rain will entirely rot them.

I am quite angry with myself for not writing closer; why is my alphabet so much more sprawly than yours? Dame Tilbury's daughter has lain in. Shall I give her any of your baby clothes? The laceman was here only a few days ago. How unfortunate for both of us that he came so soon! Dame Bushell washes for us only one week more, as Sukey has got a place. John Steevens' wife undertakes our purification. She does not look as if anything she touched would ever be clean, but who knows? We do not seem likely to have any other maidservant at present, but Dame Staples will supply the place of one. Mary has hired a young girl from Ashe who has never been out to service to be her scrub, but James fears her not being strong enough for the place.

Earle Harwood has been to Deane lately, as I think Mary wrote us word, and his family then told him that they would receive his wife, if she continued to behave well for another year. He was very grateful, as well he might; their behaviour throughout the whole affair has been particularly kind. Earle and his wife live in the most private manner imaginable at

Portsmouth, without keeping a servant of any kind. What a prodigious innate love of virtue she must have, to marry under such circumstances!

It is now Saturday evening, but I wrote the chief of this in the morning. My mother has not been down at all to-day; the laudanum made her sleep a good deal, and upon the whole I think she is better. My father and I dined by ourselves. How strange! He and John Bond are now very happy together, for I have just heard the heavy step of the latter along the passage.

James Digweed called to-day, and I gave him his brother's deputation. Charles Harwood, too, has just called to ask how we are, in his way from Dummer, whither he has been conveying Miss Garrett, who is going to return to her former residence in Kent. I *will* leave off, or I shall not have room to add a word to-morrow.

Sunday.—My mother has had a very good night, and feels much better to-day.

I have received my Aunt's letter, and thank you for your scrap. I will write to Charles soon. Pray give Fanny and Edward a kiss from me, and ask George if he has got a new song for me. 'Tis really very kind of my Aunt to ask us to Bath again; a kindness that deserves a better return than to profit by it.

Yours ever,

J. A.

11. *To Cassandra Austen. Saturday* 17 *Nov.* 1798

Address (Brabourne): Miss Austen, Godmersham
Original not traced.
Brabourne i. 162; *Life* 84, 113 (extracts).

Saturday, November 17, 1798.

My dear Cassandra

If you paid any attention to the conclusion of my last letter, you will be satisfied, before you receive this, that my mother has had no relapse, and that Miss Debary comes. The former continues to recover, and though she does not gain strength very rapidly, my expectations are humble enough not to outstride her improvements. She was able to sit up nearly eight hours yesterday, and to-day I hope we shall do as much. . . . So much for my patient—now for myself.

Mrs. Lefroy did come last Wednesday, and the Harwoods came likewise, but very considerately paid their visit before Mrs. Lefroy's arrival, with whom, in spite of interruptions both from my father and James, I was enough alone to hear all that was interesting, which you will easily credit when I tell you that of her nephew she said nothing at all, and of her friend very little. She did not once mention the name of the former to *me*, and I was too proud to make any enquiries; but on my father's afterwards asking where he was, I learnt that he was gone back to London in his way to Ireland, where he is called to the Bar and means to practise.

She showed me a letter which she had received from her friend a few weeks ago (in answer to one written by her to recommend a nephew of Mrs. Russell to his notice at Cambridge), towards the end of which was a sentence to this effect: 'I am very sorry to hear of Mrs. Austen's illness. It would give me particular pleasure to have an opportunity of improving my acquaintance with that family—with a hope of creating to myself a nearer interest. But at present I cannot indulge any expectation of it.' This is rational enough; there is less love and more sense in it than sometimes appeared before, and I am very well satisfied. It will all go on exceedingly well, and decline away in a very reasonable manner. There seems no likelihood of his coming into Hampshire this Christmas, and it is therefore most probable that our indifference will soon be mutual, unless his regard, which appeared to spring from knowing nothing of me at first, is best supported by never seeing me.

Mrs. Lefroy made no remarks on the letter, nor did she indeed say anything about him as relative to me. Perhaps she thinks she has said too much already. She saw a great deal of the Mapletons while she was in Bath. Christian is still in a very bad state of health, consumptive, and not likely to recover.

Mrs. Portman is not much admired in Dorsetshire; the good-natured world, as usual, extolled her beauty so highly, that all the neighbourhood have had the pleasure of being disappointed.

My mother desires me to tell you that I am a very good housekeeper, which I have no reluctance in doing, because I really think it my peculiar excellence, and for this reason—I always take care to provide such things as please my own appetite, which I consider as the chief merit in housekeeping. I have had some ragout veal, and I mean to have some haricot mutton to-morrow. We are to kill a pig soon.

There is to be a ball at Basingstoke next Thursday. Our assemblies have very kindly declined ever since we laid down the carriage, so that dis-convenience and dis-inclination to go have kept pace together.

My father's affection for Miss Cuthbert is as lively as ever, and he begs that you will not neglect to send him intelligence of her or her brother, whenever you have any to send. I am likewise to tell you that one of his Leicestershire sheep, sold to the butcher last week, weighed 27 lb. and $\frac{1}{4}$ per quarter.

I went to Deane with my father two days ago to see Mary, who is still plagued with the rheumatism, which she would be very glad to get rid of, and still more glad to get rid of her child, of whom she is heartily tired. Her nurse is come, and has no particular charm either of person or manner; but as all the Hurstbourne world pronounce her to be the best nurse that ever was, Mary expects her attachment to increase.

What fine weather this is! Not very becoming perhaps early in the morning, but very pleasant out of doors at noon, and very wholesome—at least everybody fancies so, and imagination is everything. To Edward, however, I really think dry weather of importance. I have not taken to fires yet.

I believe I never told you that Mrs. Coulthard and Anne, late of Manydown, are both dead, and both died in childbed. We have not regaled Mary with this news. Harry St. John is in Orders, has done duty at Ashe, and performs very well.

I am very fond of experimental housekeeping, such as having an ox-cheek now and then; I shall have one next week, and I mean to have some little dumplings put into it, that I may fancy myself at Godmersham.

I hope George was pleased with my designs. Perhaps they would have suited him as well had they been less elaborately finished; but an artist cannot do anything slovenly. I suppose baby grows and improves.

Sunday.—I have just received a note from James to say that Mary was brought to bed last night, at eleven o'clock, of a fine little boy, and that everything is going on very well. My mother had desired to know nothing of it before it should be all over, and we were clever enough to prevent her having any suspicion of it, though Jenny, who had been left here by her mistress, was sent for home. . . .

I called yesterday on Betty Londe, who enquired particularly after you, and said she seemed to miss you very much, because you used to call in upon her very often. This was an oblique reproach at me. which I am sorry to have merited, and from which I will profit. I shall send George another picture when I write next, which I suppose will be soon, on Mary's account. My mother continues well.

Yours,

J. A.

12. *To Cassandra Austen. Sunday* 25 *Nov.* ⟨1798⟩

Address (Brabourne): Miss Austen, Godmersham Park
Original not traced.
Brabourne i. 167; *Life* 113 (extracts).

Steventon: Sunday November 25

My dear Sister

I expected to have heard from you this morning, but no letter is come. I shall not take the trouble of announcing to you any more of Mary's children, if, instead of thanking me for the intelligence, you always sit down and write to James. I am sure nobody can desire your letters so much as I do, and I don't think anybody deserves them so well.

Having now relieved my heart of a great deal of malevolence, I will proceed to tell you that Mary continues quite well, and my mother tolerably so. I saw the former on Friday, and though I had seen her comparatively hearty the Tuesday before, I was really amazed at the improvement which three days had made in her. She looked well, her spirits were perfectly good, and she spoke much more vigorously than Elizabeth did when we left Godmersham. I had only a glimpse at the child, who was asleep ; but Miss Debary told me that his eyes were large, dark, and handsome. *She* looks much as she used to do, is netting herself a gown in worsteds, and wears what Mrs. Birch would call a *pot hat*. A short and compendious history of Miss Debary !

I suppose you have heard from Henry himself that his affairs are happily settled. We do not know who furnishes the qualification. Mr. Mowell would have readily given it, had not all his Oxfordshire property been engaged for a similar purpose to the Colonel. Amusing enough !

Our family affairs are rather deranged at present, for Nanny has kept her bed these three or four days, with a pain in her side and fever, and we are forced to have two charwomen, which is not very comfortable. She is considerably better now, but it must still be some time, I suppose, before she is able to do anything. You and Edward will be amused, I think, when you know that Nanny Littlewart dresses my hair.

The ball on Thursday was a very small one indeed, hardly so large as an Oxford smack. There were but seven couples, and only twenty-seven people in the room.

The Overton Scotchman has been kind enough to rid me of some of my money, in exchange for six shifts and four pair of stockings. The Irish is not so fine as I should like it; but as I gave as much money for it as I intended, I have no reason to complain. It cost me 3*s*. 6*d*. per yard. It is rather finer, however, than our last, and not so harsh a cloth.

We have got 'Fitz-Albini;' my father has bought it against my private wishes, for it does not quite satisfy my feelings that we should purchase the only one of Egerton's works of which his family are ashamed. That these scruples, however, do not at all interfere with my reading it, you will easily believe. We have neither of us yet finished the first volume. My father is disappointed—*I* am not, for I expected nothing better. Never did any book carry more internal evidence of its author. Every sentiment is completely Egerton's. There is very little story, and what there is told in a strange, unconnected way. There are many characters introduced, apparently merely to be delineated. We have not been able to recognise any of them hitherto, except Dr. and Mrs. Hey and Mr. Oxenden, who is not very tenderly treated.

You must tell Edward that my father gives 25*s*. a piece to Seward for his last lot of sheep, and, in return for this news, my father wishes to receive some of Edward's pigs.

We have got Boswell's 'Tour to the Hebrides,' and

are to have his 'Life of Johnson;' and, as some money will yet remain in Burdon's hands, it is to be laid out in the purchase of Cowper's works. This would please Mr. Clarke, could he know it.

By the bye, I have written to Mrs. Birch among my other writings, and so I hope to have some account of all the people in that part of the world before long. I have written to Mrs. E. Leigh too, and Mrs. Heathcote has been ill-natured enough to send me a letter of enquiry; so that altogether I am tolerably tired of letter-writing, and, unless I have anything new to tell you of my mother or Mary, I shall not write again for many days; perhaps a little repose may restore my regard for a pen. Ask little Edward whether Bob Brown wears a great coat this cold weather.

13. *To Cassandra Austen.* ⟨*Saturday*⟩ 1 *Dec.* ⟨1798⟩

Address (Brabourne): Miss Austen, Godmersham Park, Faversham
Original not traced.
Brabourne i. 171; *Life* 115 (extracts).

Steventon: December 1.

My dear Cassandra

I am so good as to write to you again thus speedily, to let you know that I have just heard from Frank. He was at Cadiz, alive and well, on October 19, and had then very lately received a letter from you, written as long ago as when the 'London' was at St. Helen's. But his *raly* latest intelligence of us was in one from me of September 1, which I sent soon after we got to Godmersham. He had written a packet full for his dearest friends in England, early in October, to go by the 'Excellent;' but the 'Excellent' was not sailed, nor likely to sail, when he despatched this to me. It comprehended letters for both of us, for Lord Spencer, Mr. Daysh, and the East India Directors. Lord St. Vincent had left the fleet when he wrote, and was gone to Gibraltar, it was said to superintend the fitting out of a private expedition from thence against some of the enemies' ports; Minorca or Malta were conjectured to be the objects.

Frank writes in good spirits, but says that our correspondence cannot be so easily carried on in future as it has been, as the communication between Cadiz and Lisbon is less frequent than formerly. You and my mother, therefore, must not alarm yourselves at the long intervals that may divide his letters. I address this advice to you two as being the most tender-hearted of the family.

My mother made her *entrée* into the dressing-room through crowds of admiring spectators yesterday afternoon, and we all drank tea together for the first time these five weeks. She has had a tolerable night, and bids fair for a continuance in the same brilliant course of action to-day. . . .

Mr. Lyford was here yesterday; he came while we were at dinner, and partook of our elegant entertainment. I was not ashamed at asking him to sit down to table, for we had some pease-soup, a sparerib, and a pudding. He wants my mother to look yellow and to throw out a rash, but she will do neither.

I was at Deane yesterday morning. Mary was very well, but does not gain bodily strength very fast. When I saw her so stout on the third and sixth days, I expected to have seen her as well as ever by the end of a fortnight.

James went to Ibthorp yesterday to see his mother and child. Letty is with Mary at present, of course exceedingly happy, and in raptures with the child. Mary does not manage matters in such a way as to make me want to lay in myself. She is not tidy enough in her appearance; she has no dressing-gown to sit up in; her curtains are all too thin, and things are not in that comfort and style about her which are necessary to make such a situation an enviable one. Elizabeth was really a pretty object with her nice clean cap put on so tidily and her dress so uniformly white and orderly. We live entirely in the dressing-room now, which I like very much; I always feel so much more elegant in it than in the parlour.

No news from Kintbury yet. Eliza sports with our impatience. She was very well last Thursday. Who is Miss Maria Montresor going to marry, and what is to become of Miss Mulcaster?

I find great comfort in my stuff gown, but I hope you do not wear yours too often. I have made myself two or three caps to wear of evenings since I came home, and they save me a world of torment as to hair-dressing, which at present gives me no trouble beyond washing and brushing, for my long hair is always plaited up out of sight, and my short hair curls well enough to want no papering. I have had it cut lately by Mr. Butler.

There is no reason to suppose that Miss Morgan is dead after all. Mr. Lyford gratified us very much yesterday by his praises of my father's mutton, which they all think the finest that was ever ate. John Bond begins to find himself grow old, which John Bonds ought not to do, and unequal to much hard work; a man is therefore hired to supply his place as to labour, and John himself is to have the care of the sheep. There are not more people engaged than before, I believe; only men instead of boys. I fancy so at least, but you know my stupidity as to such matters. Lizzie Bond is just apprenticed to Miss Small, so we may hope to see her able to spoil gowns in a few years.

My father has applied to Mr. May for an alehouse for Robert, at his request, and to Mr. Deane, of Winchester, likewise. This was my mother's idea, who thought he would be proud to oblige a relation of Edward in return for Edward's accepting his money. He sent a very civil answer indeed, but has no house vacant at present. May expects to have an empty one soon at Farnham, so perhaps Nanny may have the honour of drawing ale for the Bishop. I shall write to Frank to-morrow.

Charles Powlett gave a dance on Thursday, to the great disturbance of all his neighbours, of course, who, you know, take a most lively interest in the state of his finances, and live in hopes of his being soon ruined.

We are very much disposed to like our new maid; she knows nothing of a dairy, to be sure, which, in our family, is rather against her, but she is to be taught it all. In short, we have felt the inconvenience of being without a maid so long, that we are determined to like her, and she will find it a hard matter to displease us. As yet, she seems to cook very well, is uncommonly stout, and says she can work well at her needle.

Sunday.—My father is glad to hear so good an account of Edward's pigs, and desires he may be told, as encouragement to his taste for them, that Lord Bolton is particularly curious in *his* pigs, has had pigstyes of a most elegant construction built for them, and visits them every morning as soon as he rises.

Affectionately yours,

J. A.

14. *To Cassandra Austen.* *Tuesday* 18 *Dec.* 1798

Address: Miss Austen | Godmersham Park | Faversham | Kent
Postmark: 20 DE 98
Pierpont Morgan Library. 2 leaves 4°
Brabourne i. 176; *Life* 116 (extracts). A few words unpublished.

Steventon Tuesday Decr 18th

My dear Cassandra

Your letter came quite as soon as I expected, and so your letters will always do, because I have made it a rule not to expect them till they come, in which I think I consult the ease of us both.—It is a great satisfaction to us to hear that your Business is in a way to be settled, & so settled as to give you as little inconvenience as possible.—You are very welcome to my father's name, & to his Services if they are ever required in it.—I shall keep *my* ten pounds too to wrap myself up in next winter.—I took the liberty a few days ago of asking your Black velvet Bonnet to lend me its cawl, which it very readily did, & by which I have been enabled to give a considerable improvement of dignity to my Cap, which was before too *nidgetty* to please me.—I shall wear it on Thursday, but I hope you will not be offended with me for following your advice as to its ornaments only in part.—I still venture to retain the narrow silver round it, put twice round without any bow, & instead of the black military feather shall put in the Coquelicot one, as being smarter;—& besides Coquelicot is to be all the fashion this winter.—After the Ball, I shall probably make it entirely black.—I am sorry that our dear Charles begins to feel the Dignity of Ill-usage.—My father will write to Admiral Gambier.—He must already have received so much satisfaction from his acquaintance & Patronage of Frank, that he will be delighted I dare say to have another of the family introduced to him.—I think it would be very right in Charles to address Sir Thos on the occasion ; tho' I cannot approve of *your* scheme of writing to him (which you communicated to me a few nights ago) to request him to come home & convey you to Steventon. —To do you justice however, you had some doubts of the propriety of such a measure yourself.—I am very much obliged to my dear little George for his message, for his *Love* at least ;—his *Duty* I suppose was only in consequence of some hint of my favourable intentions towards him from his father or Mother.—I am sincerely rejoiced however that I ever was born, since it has been the means of procuring him a dish of Tea.—Give my best Love to him. This morning has been made very gay to us, by visits from our two lively Neighbours Mr. Holder & Mr. John Harwood. I have received a very civil note from Mrs. Martin requesting my name as a Subscriber to her Library which opens the 14th of January, & my name, or rather Yours is accordingly given. My Mother finds the Money.—Mary subscribes too, which I am glad of, but hardly expected.—As an inducement to subscribe Mrs. Martin tells us that her Collection is not to consist only of Novels, but of every kind of Literature, &c. &c—She might have spared this pretension to *our* family, who are great Novel-readers & not ashamed of being so ;—

but it was necessary I suppose to the self-consequence of half her Subscribers.—I hope & imagine that Edward Taylor is to inherit all Sir Edw: Dering's fortune as well as all his own father's.—I took care to tell Mrs. Lefroy of your calling on her Mother, & she seemed pleased with it.—I enjoyed the hard black Frosts of last week very much, & one day while they lasted walked to Deane by myself.—I do not know that I ever did such a thing in my life before.—Charles Powlett has been very ill, but is getting well again ;—his wife is discovered to be everything that the Neighbourhood could wish her, silly & cross as well as extravagant. Earle Harwood & his friend Mr. Bailey came to Deane yesterday, but are not to stay above a day or two.—Earle has got the appointment to a Prison ship at Portsmouth, which he has been for some time desirous of having ; & he & his wife are to live on board for the future.—We dine now at half after Three, & have done dinner I suppose before you begin—We drink tea at half after six.—I am afraid you will despise us.—My father reads Cowper to us in the evening, to which I listen when I can. How do you spend your Evenings ?—I guess that Elizth works, that you read to her, & that Edward goes to sleep.—My mother continues hearty, her appetite & nights are very good, but her Bowels are still not entirely settled, & she sometimes complains of an Asthma, a Dropsy, Water in her Chest & a Liver Disorder. The third Miss Irish Lefroy is going to be married to a Mr. Courteney, but whether James or Charles I do not know.—Miss Lyford is gone into Suffolk with her Brother & Miss Lodge—. Everybody is now very busy in making up an income for the two latter. Miss

Lodge has only 800£ of her own, & it is not supposed that her Father can give her much, therefore the good offices of the Neighbourhood will be highly acceptable. —John Lyford means to take pupils.—James Digweed has had a very ugly cut—how could it happen? It happened by a young horse which he had lately purchased, & which he was trying to back into its stable; —the animal kicked him down with his forefeet, & kicked a great hole in his head;—he scrambled away as soon as he could, but was stunned for a time, & suffered a good deal of pain afterwards. Yesterday he got up the Horse again, & for fear of something worse, was forced to throw himself off.—*Wednesday*.— I have changed my mind, & changed the trimmings of my Cap this morning; they are now such as you suggested;—I felt as if I should not prosper if I strayed from your directions, & I think it makes me look more like Lady Conyngham now than it did before, which is all that one lives for now.—I beleive I *shall* make my new gown like my robe, but the back of the latter is all in a peice with the tail, & will 7 yards enable me to copy it in that respect? Mary went to Church on Sunday, & had the weather been smiling, we should have seen her here before this time.— Perhaps I may stay at Manydown as long as Monday, but not longer—Martha sends me word that she is too busy to write to me now, and but for your letter I should have supposed her deep in the study of Medecine preparatory to their removal from Ibthrop. —The letter to Gambier goes today.—I expect a very stupid Ball, there will be nobody worth dancing with, & nobody worth talking to but Catherine; for I believe Mrs. Lefroy will not be there; Lucy is to go with Mrs. Russell.—People get so horridly poor & economical in this part of the World, that I have no patience with them.—Kent is the only place for happiness, Everybody is rich there;—I must do similar justice however to the Windsor neighbourhood.—I have been forced to let James & Miss Debary have two sheets of your Drawing paper, but they sha'nt have any more. There are not above 3 or 4 left, besides one of a smaller & richer sort.—Perhaps you may want some more if you come thro' Town in your return, or rather buy some more, for your wanting it will not depend on your coming thro' Town I imagine.—I have just heard from Martha & Frank—his letter was written on the 12th Nov^{r}—all well, & nothing particular.

J. A.

15. *To Cassandra Austen.* *Monday* 24 *Dec.* ⟨1798⟩

Address (Brabourne): Miss Austen, Godmersham Park, Faversham, Kent
Original not traced.
Brabourne i. 182; *Life* 118 (extracts).

Steventon: Monday night December 24.

My dear Cassandra

I have got some pleasant news for you which I am eager to communicate, and therefore begin my letter sooner, though I shall not *send* it sooner than usual.

Admiral Gambier, in reply to my father's application, writes as follows:—'As it is usual to keep young officers in small vessels, it being most proper on account of their inexperience, and it being also a situation where they are more in the way of learning their duty, your son has been continued in the "Scorpion;" but I have mentioned to the Board of Admiralty his wish to be in a frigate, and when a proper opportunity offers and it is judged that he has taken his turn in a small ship, I hope he will be removed. With regard to your son now in the "London" I am glad I can give you the assurance that his promotion is likely to take place very soon, as Lord Spencer has been so good as to say he would include him in an arrangement that he proposes making in a short time relative to some promotions in that quarter.'

There! I may now finish my letter and go and hang myself, for I am sure I can neither write nor do anything which will not appear insipid to you after this. *Now* I really think he will soon be made, and only wish we could communicate our foreknowledge of the event to him whom it principally concerns. My father has written to Daysh to desire that he will inform us, if he can, when the commission is sent. Your chief wish is now ready to be accomplished; and could Lord Spencer give happiness to Martha at the same time, what a joyful heart he would make of yours!

I have sent the same extract of the sweets of Gambier to Charles, who, poor fellow, though he sinks into nothing but an humble attendant on the hero of the piece, will, I hope, be contented with the prospect held out to him. By what the Admiral says, it appears as if he had been designedly kept in the 'Scorpion.' But I will not torment myself with conjectures and suppositions; facts shall satisfy me.

Frank had not heard from any of us for ten weeks when he wrote to me on November 12 in consequence of Lord St. Vincent being removed to Gibraltar. When his commission is sent, however, it will not be so long on its road as our letters, because all the Government despatches are forwarded by land to his lordship from Lisbon with great regularity.

I returned from Manydown this morning, and found my mother certainly in no respect worse than when I left her. She does not like the cold weather, but that we cannot help. I spent my time very quietly and very pleasantly with Catherine. Miss Blachford is agreeable enough. I do not want people to be very agreeable, as it saves me the trouble of liking them a great deal. I found only Catherine and her when I got to Manydown on Thursday. We dined together and went together to Worting to seek the protection of Mrs. Clarke, with whom were Lady Mildmay, her eldest son, and a Mr. and Mrs. Hoare.

Our ball was very thin, but by no means unpleasant. There were thirty-one people, and only eleven ladies out of the number, and but five single women in the room. Of the gentlemen present you may have some idea from the list of my partners—Mr. Wood, G. Lefroy, Rice, a Mr. Butcher (belonging to the Temples, a sailor and not of the 11th Light Dragoons), Mr. Temple (not the horrid one of all), Mr. Wm. Orde (cousin to the Kingsclere man), Mr. John Harwood, and Mr. Calland, who appeared as usual with his hat in his hand, and stood every now and then behind Catherine and me to be talked to and abused for not dancing. We teased him, however, into it at last. I was very glad to see him again after so long a separation, and he was altogether rather the genius and flirt of the evening. He enquired after you.

There were twenty dances, and I danced them all, and without any fatigue. I was glad to find myself capable of dancing so much, and with so much satisfaction as I did; from my slender enjoyment of the Ashford balls (as assemblies for dancing) I had not thought myself equal to it, but in cold weather and with few couples I fancy I could just as well dance for a week together as for half an hour. My black cap was openly admired by Mrs. Lefroy, and secretly I imagine by everybody else in the room.

Tuesday.—I thank you for your long letter, which I will endeavour to deserve by writing the rest of this as closely as possible. I am full of joy at much of your information; that you should have been to a ball, and have danced at it, and supped with the Prince, and that you should meditate the purchase of a new muslin gown, are delightful circumstances. *I* am determined to buy a handsome one whenever I can, and I am so tired and ashamed of half my present stock, that I even blush at the sight of the wardrobe which contains them. But I will not be much longer libelled by the possession of my coarse spot; I shall turn it into a petticoat very soon. I wish you a merry Christmas, but *no* compliments of the season.

Poor Edward! It is very hard that he, who has everything else in the world that he can wish for, should not have good health too. But I hope with the assistance of stomach complaints, faintnesses, and sicknesses, he will soon be restored to that blessing likewise. If his nervous complaint proceeded from a suppression of something that ought to be thrown out, which does not seem unlikely, the first of these disorders may really be a remedy, and I sincerely wish it may, for I know no one more deserving of happiness without alloy than Edward is.

I cannot determine what to do about my new gown ; I wish such things were to be bought ready-made. I have some hopes of meeting Martha at the christening at Deane next Tuesday, and shall see what she can do for me. I want to have something suggested which will give me no trouble of thought or direction.

Again I return to my joy that you danced at Ashford, and that you supped with the Prince. I can perfectly comprehend Mrs. Cage's distress and perplexity. She has all those kind of foolish and incomprehensible feelings which would make her fancy herself uncomfortable in such a party. I love her, however, in spite of all her nonsense. Pray give 't'other Miss Austen's' compliments to Edward Bridges when you see him again.

I insist upon your persevering in your intention of buying a new gown ; I am sure you must want one, and as you will have *5l.* due in a week's time, I am certain you may afford it very well, and if you think you cannot, I will give you the body-lining.

Of my charities to the poor since I came home you shall have a faithful account. I have given a pair of worsted stockings to Mary Hutchins, Dame Kew, Mary Steevens, and Dame Staples ; a shift to Hannah Staples, and a shawl to Betty Dawkins ; amounting in all to about half a guinea. But I have no reason to suppose that the *Battys* would accept of anything, because I have not made them the offer.

I am glad to hear such a good account of Harriet Bridges ; she goes on now as young ladies of seventeen ought to do, admired and admiring, in a much more rational way than her three elder sisters, who had so little of that kind of youth. I dare say she fancies Major Elkington as agreeable as Warren, and if she can think so, it is very well.

I was to have dined at Deane to-day, but the weather is so cold that I am not sorry to be kept at home by the appearance of snow. We are to have company to dinner on Friday: the three Digweeds and James. We shall be a nice silent party, I suppose. Seize upon the scissors as soon as you possibly can on the receipt of this. I only fear your being too late to secure the prize.

The Lords of the Admiralty will have enough of our applications at present, for I hear from Charles that he has written to Lord Spencer himself to be removed. I am afraid his Serene Highness will be in a passion, and order some of our heads to be cut off.

My mother wants to know whether Edward has ever made the hen-house which they planned together. I am rejoiced to hear from Martha that they certainly continue at Ibthorp, and I have just heard that I am sure of meeting Martha at the christening.

You deserve a longer letter than this; but it is my unhappy fate seldom to treat people so well as they deserve. . . . God bless you!

Yours affectionately,

Jane Austen

Wednesday.—The snow came to nothing yesterday, so I *did* go to Deane, and returned home at nine o'clock at night in the little carriage, and without being very cold.

16. *To Cassandra Austen.* *Friday* 28 *Dec.* 1798

Address: Miss Austen Godmersham Park Faversham Kent
Postmark: illegible.
Oliver R. Barrett. Two leaves 4°
Brabourne i. 190; *Life* 121.

My dear Cassandra

Frank is made.—He was yesterday raised to the Rank of Commander & appointed to the Petterel Sloop, now at Gibraltar.—A Letter from Daysh has just announced this, & as it is confirmed by a very friendly one from Mr Mathew to the same effect transcribing one from Admiral Gambier to the General, We have no reason to suspect the truth of it.—As soon as you have cried a little for Joy, you may go on, & learn farther that the India House have taken *Captn Austen's* Petition into consideration—this comes from Daysh—& likewise that Lieut: Charles John Austen is removed to the *Tamer* Frigate—this comes from the Admiral.—We cannot find out where the Tamer is, but I hope we shall now see Charles here at all Events.

This letter is to be dedicated entirely to good News.—If you will send my father an account of your Washing & Letter expences &c, he will send you a draft for the amount of it, as well as for your next quarter, & for Edward's Rent.—If you don't buy a muslin Gown now on the strength of this Money, & Frank's promotion, I shall never forgive you.—

Mrs Lefroy has just sent me word that Lady Dortchester means to invite me to her Ball on the 8th of January, which tho' an humble Blessing compared with what the last page records, I do not consider as any Calamity. I cannot write any more now, but I have written enough to make you very happy, & therefore may safely conclude.——

Yours affec[ly]

Jane

Steventon Friday Dec[r] 28th

17. *To Cassandra Austen. Tuesday* 8 *Jan.* ⟨1799⟩

Address (Brabourne) : Miss Austen, Godmersham Park, Faversham
Original not traced.
Brabourne i. 191 ; _Life_ 122 (extracts).

Steventon : Tuesday January 8

My dear Cassandra

You must read your letters over *five* times in future before you send them, and then, perhaps, you may find them as entertaining as I do. I laughed at several parts of the one which I am now answering.

Charles is not come yet, but he must come this morning, or he shall never know what I will do to him. The ball at Kempshott is this evening, and I have got him an invitation, though I have not been so considerate as to get him a partner. But the cases are different between him and Eliza Bailey, for he is not in a dying way, and may therefore be equal to getting a partner for himself. I believe I told you that Monday was to be the ball night, for which, and for all other errors into which I may ever have led you, I humbly ask your pardon.

Elizabeth is very cruel about my writing music, and, as a punishment for her, I should insist upon always writing out all hers for her in future, if I were not punishing myself at the same time.

I am tolerably glad to hear that Edward's income is so good a one—as glad as I can be at anybody's being rich except you and me—and I am thoroughly rejoiced to hear of his present to you.

I am not to wear my white satin cap to-night, after all; I am to wear a mamalone cap instead, which Charles Fowle sent to Mary, and which she lends me. It is all the fashion now; worn at the opera, and by Lady Mildmays at Hackwood balls. I hate describing such things, and I dare say you will be able to guess what it is like. I have got over the dreadful epocha of mantua-making much better than I expected. My gown is made very much like my blue one, which you always told me sat very well, with only these variations: the sleeves are short, the wrap fuller, the apron comes over it, and a band of the same completes the whole.

I assure you that I dread the idea of going to Brighton as much as you do, but I am not without hopes that something may happen to prevent it.

F—— has lost his election at B——, and perhaps they may not be able to see company for some time. They talk of going to Bath, too, in the spring, and perhaps they may be overturned in their way down, and all laid up for the summer.

Wednesday.—I have had a cold and weakness in one of my eyes for some days, which makes writing neither very pleasant nor very profitable, and which will probably prevent my finishing this letter myself. My mother has undertaken to do it for me, and I shall leave the Kempshott ball for her.

You express so little anxiety about my being murdered under Ash Park Copse by Mrs. Hulbert's servant, that I have a great mind not to tell you whether I was or not, and shall only say that I did not return home that night or the next, as Martha kindly made room for me in her bed, which was the shut-up one in the new nursery. Nurse and the child slept upon the floor, and there we all were in some confusion and great comfort. The bed did exceedingly well for us, both to lie awake in and talk till two o'clock, and to sleep in the rest of the night. I love Martha better than ever, and I mean to go and see her, if I can, when she gets home. We all dined at the Harwoods' on Thursday, and the party broke up the next morning.

This complaint in my eye has been a sad bore to me, for I have not been able to read or work in any comfort since Friday, but one advantage will be derived from it, for I shall be such a proficient in music by the time I have got rid of my cold, that I shall be perfectly qualified in *that* science at least to take Mr. Roope's office at Eastwell next summer; and I am sure of Elizabeth's recommendation, be it only on Harriet's account. Of my talent in drawing I have given specimens in my letters to you, and I have nothing to do but to invent a few hard names for the stars.

Mary grows rather more reasonable about her child's beauty, and says that she does not think him really handsome; but I suspect her moderation to be something like that of W—— W——'s mama. Perhaps Mary has told you that they are going to enter more into dinner parties; the Biggs and Mr. Holder dine there to-morrow, and I am to meet them. I shall sleep there. Catherine has the honour of giving her name to a set, which will be composed of two

Withers, two Heathcotes, a Blachford, and no Bigg except herself. She congratulated me last night on Frank's promotion, as if she really felt the joy she talked of.

My sweet little George! I am delighted to hear that he has such an inventive genius as to face-making. I admired his yellow wafer very much, and hope he will choose the wafer for your next letter. I wore my green shoes last night, and took my *white fan* with me; I am very glad he never threw it into the river.

Mrs. Knight giving up the Godmersham estate to Edward was no such prodigious act of generosity after all, it seems, for she has reserved herself an income out of it still; this ought to be known, that her conduct may not be overrated. I rather think Edward shows the most magnanimity of the two, in accepting her resignation with such incumbrances.

The more I write, the better my eye gets, so I shall at least keep on till it is quite well, before I give up my pen to my mother.

Mrs. Bramston's little moveable apartment was tolerably filled last night by herself, Mrs. H. Blackstone, her two daughters, and me. I do not like the Miss Blackstones; indeed, I was always determined not to like them, so there is the less merit in it. Mrs. Bramston was very civil, kind, and noisy. I spent a very pleasant evening, chiefly among the Manydown party. There was the same kind of supper as last year, and the same want of chairs. There were more dancers than the room could conveniently hold, which is enough to constitute a good ball at any time.

I do not think I was very much in request. People were rather apt not to ask me till they could not help it ; one's consequence, you know, varies so much at times without any particular reason. There was one gentleman, an officer of the Cheshire, a very good-looking young man, who, I was told, wanted very much to be introduced to me ; but as he did not want it quite enough to take much trouble in effecting it, we never could bring it about.

I danced with Mr. John Wood again, twice with a Mr. South, a lad from Winchester, who, I suppose, is as far from being related to the bishop of that diocese as it is possible to be, with G. Lefroy, and J. Harwood, who, I think, takes to me rather more than he used to do. One of my gayest actions was sitting down two dances in preference to having Lord Bolton's eldest son for my partner, who danced too ill to be endured. The Miss Charterises were there, and played the parts of the Miss Edens with great spirit. Charles never came. Naughty Charles ! I suppose he could not get superseded in time.

Miss Debary has replaced your two sheets of drawing-paper with two of superior size and quality ; so I do not grudge her having taken them at all now. Mr. Ludlow and Miss Pugh of Andover are lately married, and so is Mrs. Skeete of Basingstoke, and Mr. French, chemist, of Reading.

I do not wonder at your wanting to read 'First Impressions' again, so seldom as you have gone through it, and that so long ago. I am much obliged to you for meaning to leave my old petticoat behind you. I have long secretly wished it might be done, but had not courage to make the request.

Pray mention the name of Maria Montresor's lover when you write next. My mother wants to know it, and I have not courage to look back into your letters to find it out.

I shall not be able to send this till to-morrow, and you will be disappointed on Friday ; I am very sorry for it, but I cannot help it.

The partnership between Jeffereys, Toomer, and Legge is dissolved ; the two latter are melted away into nothing, and it is to be hoped that Jeffereys will soon break, for the sake of a few heroines whose money he may have. I wish you joy of your birthday twenty times over.

I *shall* be able to send this to the post to-day, which exalts me to the utmost pinnacle of human felicity, and makes me bask in the sunshine of prosperity, or gives me any other sensation of pleasure in studied language which you may prefer. Do not be angry with me for not filling my sheet, and believe me yours affectionately,

J. A.

18. *To Cassandra Austen. Monday* 21 *Jan.* ⟨1799⟩

Address (Brabourne) : Miss Austen, Godmersham Park, Faversham, Kent
Original not traced.
Brabourne i. 198 ; *Life* 124 (extracts).

Steventon : Monday January 21

My dear Cassandra

I will endeavour to make this letter more worthy your acceptance than my last, which was so shabby a one that I think Mr. Marshall could never charge you with the postage. My eyes have been very indifferent since it was written, but are now getting better once more; keeping them so many hours open on Thursday night, as well as the dust of the ball-room, injured them a good deal. I use them as little as I can, but *you* know, and *Elizabeth* knows, and everybody who ever had weak eyes knows, how delightful it is to hurt them by employment, against the advice and entreaty of all one's friends.

Charles leaves us to-night. The 'Tamar' is in the Downs, and Mr. Daysh advises him to join her there directly, as there is no chance of her going to the westward. Charles does not approve of this at all, and will not be much grieved if he should be too late for her before she sails, as he may then hope to get into a better station. He attempted to go to town last night, and got as far on his road thither as Dean Gate; but both the coaches were full, and we had the pleasure of seeing him back again. He will call on Daysh to-morrow to know whether the 'Tamar' has sailed or not, and if she is still at the Downs he will proceed in one of the night coaches to Deal. I want to go with him, that I may explain the country to him properly between Canterbury and Rowling, but the unpleasantness of returning by myself deters me. I should like to go as far as Ospringe with him very much indeed, that I might surprise you at Godmersham.

Martha writes me word that Charles was very much admired at Kintbury, and Mrs. Lefroy never saw anyone so much improved in her life, and thinks him handsomer than Henry. He appears to far more advantage here than he did at Godmersham, not surrounded by strangers and neither oppressed by a pain in his face or powder in his hair.

James christened Elizabeth Caroline on Saturday morning, and then came home. Mary, Anna, and Edward have left us of course; before the second went I took down her answer to her cousin Fanny.

Yesterday came a letter to my mother from Edward Cooper to announce, not the birth of a child, but of a living; for Mrs. Leigh has begged his acceptance of the Rectory of Hamstall-Ridware in Staffordshire, vacant by Mr. Johnson's death. We collect from his letter that he means to reside there, in which he shows his wisdom. Staffordshire is a good way off; so we shall see nothing more of them till, some fifteen years hence, the Miss Coopers are presented to us, fine, jolly, handsome, ignorant girls. The living is valued at 140*l.* a year, but perhaps it may be improvable. How will they be able to convey the furniture of the dressing-room so far in safety?

Our first cousins seem all dropping off very fast. One is incorporated into the family, another dies, and a third goes into Staffordshire. We can learn nothing of the disposal of the other living. I have not the smallest notion of Fulwar's having it. Lord Craven has probably other connections and more intimate ones, in that line, than he now has with the Kintbury family.

Our ball on Thursday was a very poor one, only eight couple and but twenty-three people in the room; but it was not the ball's fault, for we were deprived of two or three families by the sudden illness of Mr. Wither, who was seized that morning at Winchester with a return of his former alarming complaint. An express was sent off from thence to the family; Catherine and Miss Blachford were dining with Mrs. Russell. Poor Catherine's distress must have been very great. She was prevailed on to wait till the Heathcotes could come from Wintney, and then with those two and Harris proceeded directly to Winchester. In such a disorder his danger, I suppose, must always be great ; but from this attack he is now rapidly recovering, and will be well enough to return to Manydown, I fancy, in a few days.

It was a fine thing for conversation at the ball. But it deprived us not only of the Biggs, but of Mrs. Russell too, and of the Boltons and John Harwood, who were dining there likewise, and of Mr. Lane, who kept away as related to the family. Poor man !—I mean Mr. Wither—his life is so useful, his character so respectable and worthy, that I really believe there was a good deal of sincerity in the general concern expressed on his account.

Our ball was chiefly made up of Jervoises and Terrys, the former of whom were apt to be vulgar, the latter to be noisy. I had an odd set of partners : Mr. Jenkins, Mr. Street, Col. Jervoise, James Digweed, J. Lyford, and Mr. Briggs, a friend of the latter. I had a very pleasant evening, however, though you will probably find out that there was no particular reason for it ; but I do not think it worth while to wait for enjoyment until there is some real opportunity for it. Mary behaved very well, and was not at all fidgetty. For the history of her adventures at the ball I refer you to Anna's letter.

When you come home you will have some shirts to make up for Charles. Mrs. Davies frightened him into buying a piece of Irish when we were in Basingstoke. Mr. Daysh supposes that Captain Austen's commission has reached him by this time.

Tuesday.—Your letter has pleased and amused me very much. Your essay on happy fortnights is highly ingenious, and the talobert skin made me laugh a good deal. Whenever I fall into misfortune, how many jokes it ought to furnish to my acquaintance in general, or I shall die dreadfully in their debt for entertainment.

It began to occur to me before you mentioned it that I had been somewhat silent as to my mother's health for some time, but I thought you could have no difficulty in divining its exact state—you, who have guessed so much stranger things. She is tolerably well—better upon the whole than she was some weeks ago. She would tell you herself that she has a very dreadful cold in her head at present; but I have not much compassion for colds in the head without fever or sore throat.

Our own particular little brother got a place in the coach last night, and is now, I suppose, in town. I have no objection at all to your buying our gowns there, as your imagination has pictured to you exactly such a one as is necessary to make me happy. You quite abash me by your progress in notting, for I am still without silk. You must get me some in town or in Canterbury; it should be finer than yours.

I thought Edward would not approve of Charles being a crop, and rather wished you to conceal it from him at present, lest it might fall on his spirits and retard his recovery. My father furnishes him with a pig from Cheesedown; it is already killed and cut up, but it is not to weigh more than nine stone; the season is too far advanced to get him a larger one. My mother means to pay herself for the salt and the trouble of ordering it to be cured by the sparibs, the souse, and the lard. We have had one dead lamb.

I congratulate you on Mr. E. Hatton's good fortune. I suppose the marriage will now follow out of hand. Give my compliments to Miss Finch.

What time in March may we expect your return in? I begin to be very tired of answering people's questions on that subject, and, independent of *that*, I shall be very glad to see you at home again, and then if we can get Martha and shirk . . . who will be so happy as we?

I think of going to Ibthorp in about a fortnight. My eyes are pretty well, I thank you, if you please.

Wednesday, 23rd.—I wish my dear Fanny many returns of this day, and that she may on every return enjoy as much pleasure as she is now receiving from her doll's-beds.

I have just heard from Charles, who is by this time at Deal. He is to be Second Lieutenant, which pleases him very well. The 'Endymion' is come into the Downs, which pleases him likewise. He expects to be ordered to Sheerness shortly, as the 'Tamar' has never been refitted.

My father and mother made the same match for you last night, and are very much pleased with it. *He* is a beauty of my mother's.

Yours affectionately,
Jane

19. *To Cassandra Austen.* *Friday* 17 *May* ⟨1799⟩

Address (Brabourne): Miss Austen, Steventon, Overton, Hants
Harvard Library.
Brabourne i. 206; *Life* 127 (extracts).

13, Queen's Square, Friday May 17

My dearest Cassandra

Our journey yesterday went off exceedingly well; nothing occurred to alarm or delay us. We found the roads in excellent order, had very good horses all the way, and reached Devizes with ease by four o'clock. I suppose John has told you in what manner we were divided when we left Andover, and no alteration was afterwards made. At Devizes we had comfortable rooms and a good dinner, to which we sat down about five; amongst other things we had asparagus and a lobster, which made me wish for you, and some cheesecakes, on which the children made so delightful a supper as to endear the town of Devizes to them for a long time.

Well, here we are at Bath; we got here about one o'clock, and have been arrived just long enough to go over the house, fix on our rooms, and be very well pleased with the whole of it. Poor Elizabeth has had a dismal ride of it from Devizes, for it has rained almost all the way, and our first view of Bath has been just as gloomy as it was last November twelvemonth.

I have got so many things to say, so many things equally unimportant, that I know not on which to decide at present, and shall therefore go and eat with the children.

We stopped in Paragon as we came along, but as it

was too wet and dirty for us to get out, we could only see Frank, who told us that his master was very indifferent, but had had a better night last night than usual. In Paragon we met Mrs. Foley and Mrs. Dowdeswell with her yellow shawl airing out, and at the bottom of Kingsdown Hill we met a gentleman in a buggy, who, on minute examination, turned out to be Dr. Hall—and Dr. Hall in such very deep mourning that either his mother, his wife, or himself must be dead. These are all of our acquaintance who have yet met our eyes.

I have some hopes of being plagued about my trunk; I *had* more a few hours ago, for it was too heavy to go by the coach which brought Thomas and Rebecca from Devizes; there was reason to suppose that it might be too heavy likewise for any other coach, and for a long time we could hear of no waggon to convey it. At last, however, we unluckily discovered that one was just on the point of setting out for this place, but at any rate the trunk cannot be here till to-morrow; so far we are safe, and who knows what may not happen to procure a farther delay?

I put Mary's letter into the post-office at Andover with my own hand.

We are exceedingly pleased with the house; the rooms are quite as large as we expected. Mrs. Bromley is a fat woman in mourning, and a little black kitten runs about the staircase. Elizabeth has the apartment within the drawing-room; she wanted my mother to have it, but as there was no bed in the inner one, and the stairs are so much easier of ascent, or my mother so much stronger than in Paragon as not to regard the double flight, it is settled for us to be above, where we have two very nice-sized rooms, with dirty quilts and everything comfortable. I have the outward and larger apartment, as I ought to have; which is quite as large as our bedroom at home, and my mother's is not materially less. The beds are both as large as any at Steventon, and I have a very nice chest of drawers and a closet full of shelves—so full indeed that there is nothing else in it, and it should therefore be called a cupboard rather than a closet, I suppose.

Tell Mary that there were some carpenters at work in the inn at Devizes this morning, but as I could not be sure of their being Mrs. W. Fowle's relations, I did not make myself known to them.

I hope it will be a tolerable afternoon. When first we came, all the umbrellas were up, but now the pavements are getting very white again.

My mother does not seem at all the worse for her journey, nor are any of us, I hope, though Edward seemed rather fagged last night, and not very brisk this morning; but I trust the bustle of sending for tea, coffee, and sugar, &c., and going out to taste a cheese himself, will do him good.

There was a very long list of arrivals here in the newspaper yesterday, so that we need not immediately dread absolute solitude; and there is a public breakfast in Sydney Gardens every morning, so that we shall not be wholly starved.

Elizabeth has just had a very good account of the three little boys. I hope you are very busy and very comfortable. I find no difficulty in doing my eyes. I like our situation very much; it is far more cheerful than Paragon, and the prospect from the drawing-room window, at which I now write, is rather picturesque, as it commands a perspective view of the left side of Brock Street, broken by three Lombardy poplars in the garden of the last house in Queen's Parade.

I am rather impatient to know the fate of my best gown, but I suppose it will be some days before Frances can get through the trunk. In the meantime I am, with many thanks for your trouble in making it, as well as marking my silk stockings,

Yours very affectionately,

Jane

A great deal of love from everybody.

20. *To Cassandra Austen.* *Sunday* 2 *June* ⟨1799⟩

Address: Miss Austen | Steventon | Overton | Hants
Postmark: BATH. The dated postmark cut away.
Pierpont Morgan Library. 2 leaves 4°. A piece cut away, 14 lines lost.
Brabourne i. 211; *Life* 129 (extracts). One sentence unpublished.

13. Queen Square—Sunday June 2d.

My dear Cassandra

I am obliged to you for two letters, one from Yourself & the other from Mary, for of the latter I knew nothing till on the receipt of yours yesterday, when the Pigeon Basket was examined & I received my due.—As I have written to her since the time which ought to have brought me her's, I suppose she will consider herself as I chuse to consider her, still in my debt.—I will lay out all the little Judgement I have in endeavouring to get such stockings for Anna as she will approve;—but I do not know that I shall execute Martha's commission at all, for I am not fond of ordering shoes, & at any rate they shall all have flat heels.—What must I tell you of Edward ?—Truth or Falsehood ?—I will try the former, & you may chuse for yourself another time.—He was better yesterday than he had been for two or three days before, about as well as while he was at Steventon—. He drinks at the Hetling Pump, is to bathe tomorrow, & try Electricity on Tuesday ;—he proposed the latter himself to Dr. Fellowes, who made no objection to it, but I fancy we are all unanimous in expecting no advantage from it. At present I have no great notion of our staying here beyond the Month.—I heard from Charles last week—they were to sail on Wednesday.—My Mother seems remarkably well.—My Uncle overwalked himself at first, and can now only travel in a Chair, but is otherwise very well.—My Cloak is come home and here follows the pattern of it's lace.—If you

do not think it wide enough, I can give $\frac{\text{d}}{3}$ a yard more for yours, & not go beyond the two guineas, for my Cloak altogether does not cost quite two pounds.—I like it very much, & can now exclaim with delight, like J. Bond at Hay-Harvest, 'This is what I have been looking for these three years.'—I saw some gauzes in a shop in Bath Street yesterday at only $\frac{3}{4}$ a yard, but they were not so good or so pretty as mine.—Flowers are very much worn, & Fruit is still more the thing. Eliz: has a bunch of Strawberries, & I have seen Grapes, Cherries, Plumbs & Apricots—There are likewise Almonds & raisins, french plumbs & Tamarinds at the Grocers, but I have never seen any of them in hats.—A plumb or greengage would cost three shillings ;—Cherries & grapes about 5 I beleive—but this is at some of the dearest shops ;—My aunt has told me of a very cheap one near Walcot Church, to which I shall go in quest of something for you.—I have never seen an old Woman at the Pump room.—Eliz: has given me a hat, and it is not only a pretty hat, but a pretty *stile* of hat too—It is something like Eliza's only instead of being all straw, half of it is narrow purple ribbon.—I flatter myself however that you can understand very little of it, from this description—. Heaven forbid that I should ever offer such encouragement to Explanations, as to give a clear one on any occasion myself.—But I must write no more of ⟨*seven lines cut out*⟩ it so.—I spent friday evening with the Mapletons, & was obliged to submit to being pleased in spite of my inclination. We took a very charming walk from 6 to 8 up Beacon Hill, & across some fields to the Village of Charlcombe, which is sweetly situated in a little green Valley, as a Village with such a name ought to be.—Marianne is sensible & intelligent, and even Jane considering how fair she is, is not unpleasant. We had a Miss North & a Mr. Gould of our party ;—the latter walked home with me after Tea ;—he is a very young Man, just entered of Oxford, wears Spectacles, & has heard that Evelina was written by Dr. Johnson.—I am afraid I cannot

JANE AUSTEN'S PARENTS

undertake to carry Martha's shoes home, for, tho' we had plenty of room in our Trunks when we came, We shall have many more things to take back, & I must allow besides for *my* packing.—There is to be a grand gala on tuesday evening in Sydney Gardens ;—a Concert, with Illuminations & fireworks ;—to the latter Eliz: & I look forward with pleasure, & even the Concert will have more than it's usual charm with me, as the gardens are large enough for me to get pretty well beyond the reach of its sound.—In the morning Lady Willoughby is to present the Colours to some Corps of Yeomanry or other, in the Crescent—& that such festivities may have a proper commencement, we think of going to ⟨*seven lines cut out*⟩

I am quite pleased with Martha & Mrs. Lefroy for wanting the pattern of our Caps, but I am not so well pleased with your giving it to them—. Some wish, some prevailing wish is necessary to the animation of everybody's Mind, & in gratifying this, you leave them to form some other which will not probably be half so innocent.—I shall not forget to write to Frank.—Duty & Love &c.

Yours affec[ly]

Jane

My uncle is quite surprised at my hearing from you so often ; but as long as we can keep the frequency of our correspondence from Martha's uncle, we will not fear our own.

21. *To Cassandra Austen.* *Tuesday* 11 *June* ⟨1799⟩

Address: Miss Austen, Steventon, Overton, Hants
Australian National Library.
Brabourne i. 215; *Life* 130 (extracts).

13, Queen Square, Tuesday June 11.

My dear Cassandra

Your letter yesterday made me very happy. I am heartily glad that you have escaped any share in the impurities of Deane, and not sorry, as it turns out, that our stay here has been lengthened. I feel tolerably secure of our getting away next week, though it is certainly possible that we may remain till Thursday the 27th. I wonder what we shall do with all our intended visits this summer! I should like to make a compromise with Adlestrop, Harden, and Bookham, that Martha's spending the summer at Steventon should be considered as our respective visits to them all.

Edward has been pretty well for this last week, and as the waters have never *dis*agreed with him in any respect, we are inclined to hope that he will derive advantage from them in the end. Everybody encourages us in this expectation, for they all say that the effect of the waters cannot be negative, and many are the instances in which their benefit is felt afterwards more than on the spot. He is more comfortable here than I thought he would be, and so is Elizabeth, though they will both, I believe, be very glad to get away—the latter especially, which one can't wonder at *somehow*. So much for Mrs. Piozzi. I had some thoughts of writing the whole of my letter in her style, but I believe I shall not.

Though you have given me unlimited powers concerning your sprig, I cannot determine what to do about it, and shall therefore in this and in every other future letter continue to ask you for directions. We have been to the cheap shop, and very cheap we found it, but there are only flowers made there, no fruit; and as I could get four or five very pretty sprigs of the former for the same money which would procure only one Orleans plumb—in short, could get more for three or four shillings than I could have means of bringing home—I cannot decide on the fruit till I hear from you again. Besides, I cannot help thinking that it is more natural to have flowers grow out of the head than fruit. What do you think on that subject?

I would not let Martha read 'First Impressions' again upon any account, and am very glad that I did not leave it in your power. She is very cunning, but I saw through her design; she means to publish it from memory, and one more perusal must enable her to do it. As for 'Fitzalbini,' when I get home she shall have it, as soon as ever she will own that Mr. Elliott is handsomer than Mr. Lance, that fair men are preferable to black; for I mean to take every opportunity of rooting out her prejudices.

Benjamin Portal is here. How charming that is! I do not exactly know why, but the phrase followed so naturally that I could not help putting it down. My mother saw him the other day, but without making herself known to him.

I am very glad you liked my lace, and so are you, and so is Martha, and we are all glad together. I have got your cloak home, which is quite delightful—as delightful at least as half the circumstances which are called so.

I do not know what is the matter with me to-day, but I cannot write quietly; I am always wandering away into some exclamation or other. Fortunately I have nothing very particular to say.

We walked to Weston one evening last week, and liked it very much. Liked *what* very much? Weston? No, *walking* to Weston. I have not expressed myself properly, but I hope you will understand me.

We have not been to any public place lately, nor performed anything out of the common daily routine of No. 13, Queen Square, Bath. But to-day we were to have dashed away at a very extraordinary rate, by dining out, had it not so happened that we do not go.

Edward renewed his acquaintance lately with Mr. Evelyn, who lives in the Queen's Parade, and was invited to a family dinner, which I believe at first Elizabeth was rather sorry at his accepting; but yesterday Mrs. Evelyn called on us, and her manners were so pleasing that we liked the idea of going very much. The Biggs would call her a nice woman. But Mr. Evelyn, who was indisposed yesterday, is worse to-day, and we are put off.

It is rather impertinent to suggest any household care to a housekeeper, but I just venture to say that the coffee-mill will be wanted every day while Edward is at Steventon, as he always drinks coffee for breakfast.

Fanny desires her love to you, her love to grand-papa, her love to Anna, and her love to Hannah; the latter is particularly to be remembered. Edward desires his love to you, to grandpapa, to Anna, to little Edward, to Aunt James and Uncle James, and he hopes all your turkeys and ducks, and chicken and guinea fowls are very well; and he wishes you very much to send him a printed letter, and so does Fanny—and they both rather think they shall answer it. EA.

'On more accounts than one you wished our stay here to be lengthened beyond last Thursday.' There is some mystery in this. What have you going on in Hampshire besides the *itch* from which you want to keep us?

Dr. Gardiner was married yesterday to Mrs. Percy and her three daughters.

Now I will give you the history of Mary's veil, in the purchase of which I have so considerably involved you that it is my duty to economise for you in the flowers. I had no difficulty in getting a muslin veil for half a guinea, and not much more in discovering afterwards that the muslin was thick, dirty, and ragged, and therefore would by no means do for a united gift. I changed it consequently as soon as I could, and, considering what a state my imprudence had reduced me to, I thought myself lucky in getting a black lace one for sixteen shillings. I hope the half of that sum will not greatly exceed what you had intended to offer upon the altar of sister-in-law affection.

Yours affectionately, Jane

They do not seem to trouble you much from Manydown. I have long wanted to quarrel with them, and I believe I shall take this opportunity. There is no denying that they are very capricious—for they like to enjoy their elder sister's company when they can.

22. *To Cassandra Austen.* *Wednesday* 19 *June* ⟨1799⟩

Address : Miss Austen | Steventon | Overton | Hants
Postmark : BATH. The dated postmark illegible.
Pierpont Morgan Library. 2 leaves 4°.
Brabourne i. 220 ; *Life* 131 (extracts). The additions dictated by the children are unpublished.

13. Queen Square—Wednesday June 19th.

My dear Cassandra

The Children were delighted with your letters, as I fancy they will tell you themselves before this is concluded.—Fanny expressed some surprise at the wetness of the Wafers, but it did not lead to any suspicion of the Truth.—Martha & You were just in time with your commissions, for two o'clock on monday was the last hour of my receiving them ;—the office is now closed.—John Lyford's history is a melancholy one.—I feel for his family, & when I know that his Wife was really fond of him, I will feel for her too, but at present I cannot help thinking their loss the greatest.—Edward has not been well these last two days ; his appetite has failed him, & he has complained of sick & uncomfortable feelings, which with other Symptoms make us think of the Gout—perhaps a fit of it might cure him, but I cannot wish it to begin at Bath.—He made an important purchase Yesterday ; no less so than a pair of Coach Horses ; his friend Mr. Evelyn found them out & recommended them, & if the judgement of a Yahoo can ever be depended on, I suppose it may now, for I beleive Mr. Evelyn has all his life thought more of Horses than of anything else.—Their Colour is black & their size not large—their price sixty Guineas, of which the Chair Mare was taken as fifteen—but this is of course to be a secret.—Mrs. Williams need not pride herself on her knowledge of Dr. Mapleton's success here;—she knows no more than everybody else knows in Bath.—There is not a Physician in the place who writes so many Prescriptions as he does—I cannot help wishing that Edward had not been tied down to Dr. Fellowes, for had he come disengaged, we should all have recommended Dr. Mapleton; my Uncle & Aunt as earnestly as ourselves.—I do not see the Miss Mapletons very often, but just as often as I like; we are always very glad to meet, & I do not wish to wear out our satisfaction.—Last Sunday We all drank tea in Paragon; my Uncle is still in his flannels, but is getting better again.—On Monday, Mr. Evelyn was well enough for us to fulfil our engagement with him;—the visit was very quiet & uneventful; pleasant enough.—We met only another Mr. Evelyn, his cousin, whose wife came to Tea.—Last night we were in Sidney Gardens again, as there was a repetition of the Gala which went off so ill on the 4th.—We did not go till nine, & then were in very good time for the Fire-works, which were really beautiful, & surpassing my expectation;—the illuminations too were very pretty.—The weather was as favourable, as it was otherwise a fortnight ago.—The Play on Saturday is *I hope* to conclude our Gaieties here, for nothing but a lengthened stay will make it otherwise. We go with Mrs. Fellowes.—Edward will not remain at Steventon longer than from Thursday to the following Monday I beleive, as the Rent-day is to be fixed for the *consecutive* friday.—I can recollect nothing more to say at present;—perhaps Breakfast may assist my ideas. I was deceived—my breakfast supplied only two ideas, that the rolls were good, & the butter bad ;—But the Post has been more friendly to me, it has brought me a letter from Miss Pearson. You may remember that I wrote to her above two months ago about the parcel under my care, & as I had heard nothing from her since, I thought myself obliged to write again two or three days ago, for after all that had passed I was determined that the Correspondence should never cease thro' my means—. This second letter has produced an apology for her silence, founded on the Illness of several of the family.—The exchange of packets is to take place through the medium of Mr. Nutt, probably one of the Sons belonging to Woolwich Academy, who comes to Overton in the beginning of July.—I am tempted to suspect from some parts of her Letter, that she has a matrimonial project in veiw—I shall question her about it when I answer her Letter ; but all this you know is *en Mystere* between ourselves.—Edward has seen the Apothecary to whom Dr. Millman recommended him, a sensible, intelligent Man, since I began this—& he attributes his present little feverish indisposition to his having ate something unsuited to his Stomach.—I do not understand that Mr. Anderton suspects the Gout at all ;—The occasional particular glow in the hands & feet, which we considered as a symptom of that Disorder, he only calls the effect of the Water in promoting a better circulation of the blood. I cannot help thinking from your account of Mrs. E. H. that Earle's vanity has tempted him to invent the account of her former way of Life, that his triumph in securing her might be greater ;—I dare say she was nothing but an innocent Country Girl in fact.—Adeiu—. I shall not write again before Sunday, unless anything particular happens.

Yours ever
Jane

We shall be with you on Thursday to a very late Dinner—later I suppose than my father will like for himself—but I give him leave to eat one before. You must give us something very nice, for we are used to live well.

My dear Cassandra

I thank you for your pretty letter ;—My little Brothers were very well when Mama heard from Sackree. I have given all your messages except to my Uncle & Aunt Perrot, & I have not seen them since I had your letter. I am very happy at Bath, but I am afraid Papa is not much better for drinking the Waters.—Mama's best Love.—Is the other chaffinche's nest in the Garden hatched ?—Your affec: Neice F A G—P.S.—Yes, I shall be very glad to home & see brothers.

My dear Aunt Cassandra—I hope you are very well. Grandmama hopes the white Turkey lays, & that you have eat up the black one.—We like Gooseberry Pye & Gooseberry pudding very much.—Is that the same Chaffinches Nest that we saw before we went away ? & pray will you send me another printed Letter when you write to Aunt Jane again—If you like it.—

E A

23. *To Cassandra Austen.* *Saturday* 25 *Oct.* 1800

Address : Miss Austen | Godmersham Park | Faversham | Kent
Postmarks : OVERTON and OCT 2 (8 ?) 1800
Pierpont Morgan Library. 2 leaves 4°.
Brabourne i. 230 ; *Life* 141 (extracts).

Steventon : Saturday evening Oct 25.

My dear Cassandra

I am not yet able to acknowledge the receipt of any parcel from London, which I suppose will not occasion you much surprise.—I was a little disappointed today, but not more than is perfectly agreable ; & I hope to be disappointed again tomorrow, as only one coach comes down on sundays.—You have had a very pleasant Journey of course, & have found Elizabeth & all the Children very well on your arrival at Godmersham, & I congratulate you on it. Edward is rejoicing this evening I dare say to find himself once more at home, from which he fancies he has been absent a great while.—His son left behind him the very fine chestnuts which had been selected for planting at Godmersham, & the drawing of his own which he had intended to carry to George ;—the former will therefore be deposited in the soil of Hampshire instead of Kent ; the latter, I have already consigned to another Element. We have been exceedingly busy ever since you went away. In the first place we have had to rejoice two or three times every day at your having such very delightful weather for the whole of your Journey—& in the second place we have been obliged to take advantage of the delightful weather ourselves by going to see almost all our Neighbours.—On Thursday we walked to Deane, yesterday to Oakley Hall &

Oakley, & today to Deane again.—At Oakley Hall we did a great deal—eat some sandwiches all over mustard, admired Mr. Bramston's Porter & Mrs. Bramston's Transparencies, & gained a promise from the latter of two roots of hearts-ease, one all yellow & the other all purple, for you. At Oakley we bought ten pair of worsted stockings, & a shift.—The shift is for Betty Dawkins, as we find she wants it more than a rug.—She is one of the most grateful of all whom Edward's charity has reached, or at least she expresses herself more warmly than the rest, for she sends him a 'sight of thanks.' This morning we called at the Harwoods, & in their dining-room found Heathcote & Chute for ever—Mrs. Wm Heathcote & Mrs. Chute—the first of whom took a long ride yesterday morning with Mrs. Harwood into Lord Carnarvon's Park & fainted away in the evening, & the second walked down from Oakley Hall attended by Mrs. Augusta Bramston. They had meant to come on to Steventon afterwards, but we knew a trick worth two of that.—If I had thought of it in time, I would have said something civil to her about Edward's never having had any serious idea of calling on Mr. Chute while he was in Hampshire; but unluckily it did not occur to me.—Mrs. Heathcote is gone home today; Catherine had paid her an early visit at Deane in the morning, & brought a good account of Harris.—James went to Winchester fair yesterday, & bought a new horse; & Mary has got a new maid—two great acquisitions, one comes from Folly Farm, is about five years old, used to draw, & thought very pretty; & the other is neice to Dinah at Kintbury.—James called by my father's desire on Mr. Bayle to inquire into the cause of his being so horrid.—Mr. Bayle did not attempt to deny his being horrid, & made many apologies for it ;—he did not plead his having a drunken self, he talked only of a drunken foreman &c &c, & gave hopes of the Table's being at Steventon on Monday se'night next.—We have had no letter since you left us, except one from Mr. Serle of Bishop's Stoke to enquire the character of James Elton.—Our whole Neighbourhood is at present very busy greiving over poor Mrs. Martin, who has totally failed in her business, & had very lately an execution in her house.—Her own Brother & Mr. Rider are the principal creditors, & they have seized her effects in order to prevent other people's doing it.—There has been the same affair going on, we are told, at Wilson's, & my hearing nothing of you makes me apprehensive that You, your fellow travellers & all your effects, might be seized by the Bailiffs when you stopt at the Crown & sold altogether for the benefit of the creditors. In talking of Mr. Deedes's new house, Mrs. Bramston told us one circumstance, which, that we should be ignorant of it before must make Edward's conscience fly into his face ; she told us that one of the sitting rooms at Sandling, an oval room with a Bow at one end, has the very remarkable & singular feature of a fireplace with a window, the centre window of the Bow, exactly over the mantlepeice.—*Sunday.*—This morning's unpromising aspect makes it absolutely necessary for me to observe once more how peculiarly fortunate you have been in your weather, and then I will drop the subject for ever.—Our Improvements have advanced very well ;—the Bank along the *Elm Walk* is sloped down for the reception of Thorns & Lilacs ; & it is settled that the other side of the path is to continue turf'd & be planted with Beech, Ash, & Larch.—*Monday.* I am glad I had no means of sending this yesterday, as I am now able to thank you for executing my Commissions so well.—I like the Gown very much & my mother thinks it very ugly.—I like the Stockings also very much & greatly prefer having only two pair of that quality to three of an inferior sort.—The Combs are very pretty, & I am much obliged to you for your present; but am sorry you should make me so many.—The Pink Shoes are not particularly beautiful, but they fit me very well—the others are faultless.—I am glad that I have still my Cloak to expect. Among my other obligations, I must not omit to number your writing me so long a letter in a time of such hurry. I am amused by your going to Milgate at last,—& glad that you have so charming a day for your Journey home.—

My father approves his Stockings very highly—& finds no fault with any part of Mrs. Hancock's bill except the charge of 3*s* 6*d* for the Packing box.

The weather does not know how to be otherwise than fine.—I am surprised that Mrs. Marriot should not be taller—Surely You have made a mistake.—Did Mr. Roland make you look well ?—

Yours affec^{ly}

J. A.

24. *To Cassandra Austen. Saturday* 1 *Nov.* 1800

Address: Miss Austen | Godmersham Park | Faversham | Kent
Postmark: NOV 3 1800
Pierpont Morgan Library. 2 leaves 4°.
Brabourne i. 235 ; *Life* 143 (extracts).

Steventon : Saturday Nov 1st.

My dear Cassandra

You have written I am sure, tho' I have received no letter from you since your leaving London ;—the Post, & not yourself must have been unpunctual.—We have at last heard from Frank ; a letter from him to you came yesterday, & I mean to send it on as soon as I can get a ditto, (*that* means a frank,) which I hope to do in a day or two.—En attendant, You must rest satisfied with knowing that on the 8th of July the Petterell with the rest of the Egyptian Squadron was off the Isle of Cyprus, whither they went from Jaffa for Provisions &c., & whence they were to sail in a day or two for Alexandria, there to wait the result of the English proposals for the Evacuation of Egypt. The rest of the letter, according to the present fashionable stile of Composition, is cheifly Descriptive ; of his Promotion he knows nothing, & of Prizes he is guiltless.—Your letter is come ; it came indeed twelve lines ago, but I could not stop to acknowledge it before, & I am glad it did not arrive till I had completed my first sentence, because the sentence had been made ever since yesterday, & I think forms a very good beginning.—Your abuse of our Gowns amuses, but does not discourage me ; I shall take mine to be made up next week, & the more I look at it, the better it pleases me.—My Cloak came on tuesday, & tho' I expected a good deal, the beauty of the lace astonished me.—It is too handsome to be worn, almost too handsome to be looked at.—The Glass is all safely arrived also, & gives great satisfaction. The wine glasses are much smaller than I expected, but I suppose it is the proper size.—*We* find no fault with your manner of performing any of our commissions, but if you like to think yourself remiss in any of them, pray do.—My Mother was rather vexed that you could not go to Penlington's, but she has since written to him, which does just as well.—Mary is disappointed of course about her Locket, & of course delighted about the Mangle which is safe at Basingstoke.—You will thank Edward for it on their behalf &c. &c., & as you know how much it was wished for, will not feel that you are inventing Gratitude.—Did you think of our Ball on thursday evening, & did you suppose me at it ?—You might very safely, for there I was.—On wednesday morning it was settled that Mrs. Harwood, Mary & I should go together, and shortly afterwards a very civil note of invitation for me came from Mrs. Bramston, who wrote I beleive as soon as she knew of the Ball. I might likewise have gone with Mrs. Lefroy, & therefore with three methods of going, I must have been more at the Ball than anybody else.—I dined & slept at Deane.—Charlotte & I did my hair, which I fancy looked very indifferent ; nobody abused it however, & I retired delighted with my success.—It was a pleasant Ball, & still more good than pleasant, for there were nearly 60 people, & sometimes we had 17 couple.—The Portsmouths, Dorchesters, Boltons, Portals & Clerks were there, & all the meaner & more usual &c. &c.'s.—There was a scarcity of Men in general, & a still greater scarcity of any that were good for much.—I danced nine dances out of ten, five with Stephen Terry, T. Chute & James Digweed & four with Catherine.—There was commonly a couple of Ladies standing up together, but not often any so amiable as ourselves.—I heard no news, except that Mr. Peters who was not there, is supposed to be particularly attentive to Miss Lyford.—You were enquired after very prettily, & I hope the whole assembly now understands that you are gone into Kent, which the families in general seemed to meet in ignorance of.—Lord Portsmouth surpassed the rest in his attentive recollection of you, enquired more into the length of your absence, & concluded by desiring to be 'remembered to you when I wrote next.'—Lady Portsmouth had got a different dress on, & Lady Bolton is much improved by a wig.—The three Miss Terries were there, but no Anne;—which was a great disappointment to me; I hope the poor girl had not set her heart on her appearance that Even[g] so much as I had.—Mr. Terry is ill, in a very low way. I said civil things for Edward to Mr. Chute, who amply returned them by declaring that had he known of my brother's being at Steventon he should have made a point of calling on him to thank him for his civility about the Hunt.—I have heard from Charles, & am to send his shirts by half dozens as they are finished;—one sett will go next week.—The Endymion is now waiting only for orders, but may wait for them perhaps a month.—Mr. Coulthard was unlucky in very narrowly missing another unexpected Guest at Chawton, for Charles had actually set out & got half the way thither in order to spend one day with Edward, but turned back on discovering the distance to be considerably more than he had fancied, & finding himself & his horse to be very much tired.—I should regret it the more if his friend Shipley had been of the party, for Mr. Coulthard might not have been so well pleased to see only one come at a time.

Miss Harwood is still at Bath, & writes word that she never was in better health & never more happy. Jos: Wakeford died last Saturday, & my father buried him on Thursday. A deaf Miss Fonnereau is at Ashe, which has prevented Mrs. Lefroy's going to Worting or Basingstoke, during the absence of Mr. Lefroy.— My Mother is very happy in the prospect of dressing a new Doll which Molly has given Anna. My father's feelings are not so enviable, as it appears that the farm cleared 300£ last year.—James & Mary went to Ibthrop for one night last monday, & found Mrs. Lloyd not in very good looks.—Martha has been lately at Kintbury, but is probably at home by this time.— Mary's promised maid has jilted her, & hired herself elsewhere.—The Debaries persist in being afflicted at the death of their Uncle, of whom they now say they saw a great deal in London.—Love to all.—I am glad George remembers me.

Yours very affec:tely

J. A.

I am very unhappy.—In re-reading your letter I find I might have spared myself my Intelligence of Charles.—To have written only what you knew before !—You may guess how much I feel.

I wore at the Ball your favourite gown, a bit of muslin of the same round my head, border'd with Mrs. Cooper's band—& one little Comb.—

25. *To Cassandra Austen.* *Saturday* 8 *Nov.* 1800

Address: Miss Austen | Godmersham Park | Faversham | Kent
Postmarks: OVERTON and NOV 11 1800
L. A. Austen-Leigh. 2 leaves 4°.
*Memoir*² 58; *Life* 145. A large part unpublished.

Steventon Saturday Even^g—Novr 8

My dear Cassandra,

Having just finished the first volume of Les Veillees du Chateau, I think it a good opportunity for beginning a letter to you while my mind is stored with Ideas worth transmitting.—I thank you for so speedy a return to my two last, & particularly thank you for your anecdote of Charlotte Graham & her cousin Harriet Bailey, which has very much amused both my Mother & myself. If you can learn anything farther of that interesting affair I hope you will mention it.—I have two messages; let me get rid of them, & then my paper will be my own.—Mary fully intended writing to you by Mr Chute's frank, & only happened intirely to forget it—but will write soon— & my father wishes Edward to send him a memorandum in your next letter, of the price of the hops.— The Tables are come, & give general contentment. I had not expected that they would so perfectly suit the fancy of us all three, or that we should so well agree in the disposition of them; but nothing except their own surface can have been smoother;—The two ends put together form our constant Table for everything, & the centre peice stands exceedingly well under the glass; holds a great deal most commodiously, without looking awkwardly.—They are both covered with green baize & send their best Love.—The Pembroke has got its destination by the sideboard, & my mother has great delight in keeping her money & papers locked up.—The little Table which used to stand there, has most conveniently taken itself off into the best bed-room, & we are now in want only of the chiffoniere, which is neither finished nor come.—So much for that subject; I now come to another, of a very different nature, as other subjects are very apt to be.—Earle Harwood has been again giving uneasiness to his family, & Talk to the Neighbourhood;—in the present instance however he is only unfortunate & not in fault.—About ten days ago, in cocking a pistol in the guard-room at Marcou, he accidentally shot himself through the Thigh. Two young Scotch Surgeons in the Island were polite enough to propose taking off the Thigh at once, but to that he would not consent; & accordingly in his wounded state was put on board a Cutter & conveyed to Haslar Hospital at Gosport; where the bullet was extracted, & where he now is I hope in a fair way of doing well.—The surgeon of the Hospital wrote to the family on the occasion, & John Harwood went down to him immediately, attended by James, whose object in going was to be the means of bringing back the earliest Intelligence to M^r^ and Mrs Harwood, whose anxious sufferings particularly those of the latter, have of course been dreadful. They went down on tuesday, & James came back the next day, bringing such favourable accounts as greatly to lessen the distress of the family at Deane, tho' it will probably be a long while before Mrs Harwood can be quite at ease.—*One* most material comfort however they have; the assurance of it's being really an accidental wound, which is not only positively declared by Earle himself, but is likewise testified by the particular direction of the bullet. Such a wound could not have been received in a duel. —At present he is going on very well, but the Surgeon will not declare him to be in no danger.—John Harwood came back last night, & will probably go to him again soon. James had not time at Gosport to take any other steps towards seeing Charles, than the very few which conducted him to the door of the assembly room in the Inn, where there happened to be a Ball on the night of their arrival. A likely spot enough for the discovery of a Charles: but I am glad to say that he was not of the party, for it was in general a very ungenteel one, & there was hardly a pretty girl in the room.—I cannot possibly oblige you by not wearing my gown, because I have it made up on purpose to wear it a great deal, & as the discredit will be my own, I feel the less regret.—You must learn to like it yourself & make it up at Godmersham; it may easily be done; it is only protesting it to be very beautiful, & you will soon think it so.—Yesterday was a day of great business with me; Mary drove me all in the rain to Basingstoke, & still more all in the rain back again, because it rained harder; and soon after our return to Dean a sudden invitation & an own postchaise took us to Ash Park, to dine tete a tete with Mr Holder, Mr Gauntlett & James Digweed; but our tete a tete was cruelly reduced by the non-attendance of the two latter.—We had a very quiet evening, I beleive Mary found it dull, but I thought it very pleasant. To sit in idleness over a good fire in a well-proportioned room is a luxurious sensation.—Sometimes we talked & sometimes we were quite silent; I said two or three amusing things, & Mr Holder made a few infamous puns.—I have had a most affectionate letter from Buller; I was afraid he would oppress me by his felicity & his love for his wife, but this is not the case; he calls her simply Anna without any angelic embellishments, for which I respect & wish him happy—and throughout the whole of his letter indeed he seems more engrossed by his feelings towards our family, than towards her, which you know cannot give any one disgust.—He is very pressing in his invitation to us all to come & see him at Colyton, & my father is very much inclined to go there next Summer.—It is a circumstance that may considerably assist the Dawlish scheme.—Buller has desired me to write again, to give him more particulars of us all.—Mr Heathcote met with a genteel little accident the other day in hunting; he got off to lead his horse over a hedge or a house or a something, & his horse in his haste trod upon his leg, or rather ancle I beleive, & it is not certain whether the small bone is not broke.—Harris seems still in a poor way, from his bad habit of body; his hand bled again a little the other day, & Dr Littlehales has been with him lately. Martha has accepted Mary's invitation for Ld Portsmouth's Ball.—He has not yet sent out his *own* invitations, but *that* does not signify; Martha comes, & a Ball there must be.—I think it will be too early in her Mother's absence for me to return with her.—Mr Holder told Wm Portal a few days ago that Edward objected to the narrowness of the path which his plantation has left in one part of the Rookery.—Wm Portal has since examined it himself, acknowledges it to be much too narrow, & promises to have it altered.

He wishes to avoid the necessity of removing the end of his plantation with it's newly-planted quick &c, but if a proper footpath cannot be made by poking away the bank on the other side, he will not spare the former.—I have finished this on sunday morning

am y^{rs} ever J A.

Sunday Evening.—We have had a dreadful storm of wind in the forepart of this day, which has done a great deal of mischeif among our trees.—I was sitting alone in the dining room, when an odd kind of crash startled me—in a moment afterwards it was repeated ; I then went to the window, which I reached just in time to see the last of our two highly valued Elms descend into the Sweep ! ! ! ! ! The other, which had fallen I suppose in the first crash, & which was the nearest to the pond, taking a more easterly direction sunk amongst our screen of chesnuts and firs, knocking down one spruce fir, beating off the head of another, & stripping the two corner chesnuts of several branches, in its fall.—This is not all.—One large Elm out of two on the left hand side, as you enter what I call the Elm walk, was likewise blown down, the Maypole bearing the weathercock was broke in two, and what I regret more than all the rest, is that all the three Elms which grew in Hall's meadow & gave such ornament to it, are gone.—Two were blown down, & the other so much injured that it cannot stand.—I am happy to add however that no greater Evil than the loss of Trees has been the consequence of the Storm in this place, or in our immediate neighbourhood.—We greive therefore in some comfort.

You spend your time just as quietly & comfortably

as I supposed you would.—We have all seen & admired Fanny's letter to her Aunt.—The Endymion sailed on a cruize last friday.

I hope it is true that Edward Taylor is to marry his cousin Charlotte. Those beautiful dark Eyes will then adorn another Generation at least in all their purity.—

Mr Holder's paper tells us that sometime in last August, Capt: Austen & the Petterell were very active in securing a Turkish Ship (driven into a Port in Cyprus by bad weather) from the French.—He was forced to burn her however.—You will see the account in the Sun I dare say.—

26. *To Martha Lloyd, Wednesday* 12 Nov. ⟨1800⟩

Address: Miss Lloyd | Up-Hurstbourne | Andover
Postmark: OVERTON
New York Public Library. 2 leaves 4°.
*Memoir*² 61; *Life* 148. A few sentences unpublished.

Steventon Wednesday Even^g^. Nov:^r^ 12th

My dear Martha

I did not receive your note yesterday till after Charlotte had left Deane, or I would have sent my answer by her, instead of being the means, as I now must be, of lessening the Elegance of your new Dress for the Hurstbourn Ball by the value of $\frac{d}{3}$.—You are very good in wishing to see me at Ibthrop so soon, & I am equally good in wishing to come to you; I beleive our Merit in that respect is much upon a par, our Self-denial mutually strong.—Having paid this tribute of praise to the Virtue of both, I shall have done with Panegyric & proceed to plain matter of fact.

—In about a fortnight's time I hope to be with you; I have two reasons for not being able to come before; I wish so to arrange my visit as to spend some days with you after your Mother's return, in the 1st place that I may have the pleasure of seeing her, & in the 2d, that I may have a better chance of bringing you back with me.—Your promise in my favour was not quite absolute, but if your Will is not perverse, you & I will do all in our power to overcome your scruples of conscience.—I hope we shall meet next week to talk all this over, till we have tired ourselves with the very idea of my visit, before my visit begins.—Our invitations for the 19th are arrived, & very curiously are they worded.—Mary mentioned to you yesterday poor Earle's unfortunate accident I dare say; he does not seem to be going on very well; the two or three last posts have brought rather less & less favourable accounts of him. This morning's letter states the apprehensions of the Surgeon that the violent catchings of his Patient have done material injury to the bone, which from the first has appeared so nearly broken that any particular irritation or sudden movement might make the fracture certain.—John Harwood is gone to Gosport again to day.—We have two families of friends that are now in a most anxious state; for tho' by a note from Catherine this morning there seems now to be a revival of hope at Manydown, it's continuance may be too reasonably doubted.—Mr. Heathcote however who has broken the small bone of his leg, is so good as to be doing very well. It would be really too much to have three people to care for!—

Mary has heard from Cassandra to day; she is now gone with Edward & Elizabeth to the Cages for two or three Nights.—You distress me cruelly by your request about Books ; I cannot think of any to bring with me, nor have I any idea of our wanting them. I come to you to be talked to, not to read or hear reading. I can do *that* at home ; & indeed I am now laying in a stock of intelligence to pour out on you as *my* share of Conversation.—I am reading Henry's History of England, which I will repeat to you in any manner you may prefer, either in a loose, disultary, unconnected strain, or dividing my recital as the Historian divides it himself, into seven parts, The Civil & Military—Religion—Constitution—Learning & Learned Men—Arts & Sciences—Commerce Coins & Shipping—& Manners ;—so that for every evening of the week there will be a different subject ; The friday's lot, Commerce, Coin & Shipping, You will find the least entertaining ; but the next Eveng:'s portion will make amends.—With such a provision on my part, if you will do your's by repeating the French Grammar, & Mrs Stent will now & then ejaculate some wonder about the Cocks & Hens, what can we want ?—Farewell for a short time—You are to dine here on tuesday to meet James Digweed, whom you must wish to see before he goes into Kent.—We all unite in best Love, & I am

Yr very affecte JA.—

It is reported at Portsmouth that Sir T. Williams is going to be married—It has been reported indeed twenty times before, but Charles is inclined to give some credit to it now, as they hardly ever see him on board, & he looks very much like a Lover.—

Thursday.—The Harwoods have received a much

better account of Earle this morning ; & Charles, from whom I have just had a letter, has been assured by the Hospital-Surgeon that the wound is in as favourable a state as can be.

27. *To Cassandra Austen.* *Thursday* 20 *Nov.* 1800

Address : Miss Austen | Godmersham Park | Faversham | Kent
Postmarks : OVERTON and NOV 22 00
Pierpont Morgan Library. 2 leaves 4°.
Brabourne i. 241 ; *Life* 150 (extracts). A few words unpublished.

Steventon Thursday Novr 20th

My dear Cassandra

Your letter took me quite by surprise this morning ; you are very welcome however, & I am very much obliged to you.—I beleive I drank too much wine last night at Hurstbourne ; I know not how else to account for the shaking of my hand today ;—You will kindly make allowance therefore for any indistinctness of writing by attributing it to this venial Error.—Naughty Charles did not come on tuesday ; but good Charles came yesterday morning. About two o'clock he walked in on a Gosport Hack.—His feeling equal to such a fatigue is a good sign, & his finding no fatigue in it a still better.—We walked down to Deane to dinner, he danced the whole Evening, & today is no more tired than a gentleman ought to be.—Your desiring to hear from me on Sunday will perhaps bring in you a more particular account of the Ball than you may care for, because one is prone to think much more of such things the morning after they happen, than when time has entirely driven them out of one's recollection.—It was a pleasant Evening, Charles found it remarkably so, but I cannot tell why, unless the absence of Miss Terry—towards whom his conscience reproaches him with now being perfect indifferent—was a releif to him.—There were only twelve dances, of which I danced nine, & was merely prevented from dancing the rest by the want of a partner. —We began at 10, supped at 1, & were at Deane before 5.—There were but 50 people in the room; very few families indeed from our side of the Country, & not many more from the other.—My partners were the two St. Johns, Hooper Holder—and very prodigious—Mr. Mathew, with whom I called the last, & whom I liked the best of my little stock.—There were very few Beauties, & such as there were, were not very handsome. Miss Iremonger did not look well, & Mrs. Blount was the only one much admired. She appeared exactly as she did in September, with the same broad face, diamond bandeau, white shoes, pink husband, & fat neck.—The two Miss Coxes were there; I traced in one the remains of the vulgar, broad featured girl who danced at Enham eight years ago;—the other is refined into a nice, composed looking girl like Catherine Bigg.—I looked at Sir Thomas Champneys & thought of poor Rosalie; I looked at his daughter & thought her a queer animal with a white neck.—Mrs. Warren, I was constrained to think a very fine young woman, which I much regret. She has got rid of some part of her child, & danced away with great activity, looking by no means very large.—Her husband is ugly enough; uglier even than his cousin John; but he does not look so *very* old.—The Miss Maitlands are both prettyish; very like Anne; with brown skins, large dark eyes, & a good deal of nose.—The General has got the Gout, and Mrs. Maitland the Jaundice.—Miss Debary, Susan & Sally all in black, but without any Statues, made their appearance, & I was as civil to them as their bad breath would allow me. They told me nothing new of Martha.—I mean to go to her on Thursday, unless Charles should determine on coming over again with his friend Shipley for the Basingstoke ball, in which case I shall not go till friday.—I shall write to you again however before I set off, & I shall hope to hear from you in the mean time. If I do not stay for the Ball, I would not on any account do so uncivil a thing by the Neighbourhood as to set off at that very time for another place, & shall therefore make a point of not being later than Thursday *morning*.—Mary said that I looked very well last night; I wore my aunt's gown & handkercheif, & my hair was at least tidy, which was all my ambition.—I will now have done with the Ball; & I will moreover go and dress for dinner.—*Thursday Even^{g}*. Charles leaves us on saturday, unless Henry should take us in his way to the Island, of which we have some hopes, & then they will probably go together on sunday.—The young lady whom it is suspected that Sir Thomas is to marry, is Miss Emma Wabshaw;—she lives somewhere between Southampton and Winchester, is handsome, accomplished, amiable, & everything but rich.—He is certainly finishing his house in a great hurry.—Perhaps the report of his being to marry a Miss Fanshawe might originate in his attentions to this very lady; the names are not unlike.—Miss Summers has made my gown very well indeed, & I grow more and more pleased with it.—Charles does not like it, but my father and Mary do; my Mother is very much rec⟨oncile⟩d to it, & as for James, he gives it the preference over everything of the kind he ever saw; in proof of which I am desired to say that if you like to sell yours, Mary will buy it.—We had a very pleasant day on monday at Ashe; we sat down 14 to dinner in the study, the dining room being not habitable from the Storm's having blown down it's chimney.—Mrs. Bramston talked a good deal of nonsense, which Mr. Bramston & Mr. Clerk seemed almost equally to enjoy.—There was a whist & a casino table, & six outsiders.—Rice & Lucy made love, Mat: Robinson fell asleep, James & Mrs. Augusta alternately read Dr. Jenner's pamphlet on the cow pox, & I bestowed my company by turns on all. On enquiring of Mrs. Clerk, I find that Mrs. Heathcote made a great blunder in her news of the Crooks & Morleys; it is young Mr. Crooke who is to marry the second Miss Morley—& it is the Miss Morleys instead of the second Miss Crooke, who were the beauties at the Music meeting.—This seems a more likely tale, a better devised Impostor.—The three Digweeds all came on tuesday, & we played a pool at Commerce.—James Digweed left Hampshire today. I think he must be in love with you, from his anxiety to have you go to the Faversham Balls, & likewise from his supposing, that the two Elms fell from their greif at your absence. Was not it a galant idea?—It never occurred to me before, but I dare say it was so.—Hacker has been here today, putting in the fruit trees.—A new plan has been suggested concerning the plantation of the new inclosure on the right hand side of the Elm Walk—the doubt is whether it would be better to make a little orchard of it, by planting apples, pears & cherries, or whether it should be larch, Mountain-ash & acacia.—What is your opinion?—I say nothing, & am ready to agree with anybody.—You & George walking to Eggerton!—What a droll party!—Do the Ashford people still come to Godmersham Church every Sunday in a cart?—It is *you* that always disliked Mr. N. Toke so much, not *I*.—I do not like his wife, & I do not like Mr. Brett, but as for Mr. Toke, there are few people whom I like better.—Miss Harwood & her friend have taken a house 15 miles from Bath; she writes very kind letters, but sends no other particulars of the situation.—Perhaps it is one of the first houses in Bristol.—Farewell. Charles sends you his best love & Edward his worst.—If you think the distinction improper, you may take the worst yourself.—He will write to you when he gets back to his Ship—& in the meantime desires that you will consider me as

Your affec: sister

J. A.

Charles likes my gown now.

Friday.—I have determined to go on Thursday, but of course not before the post comes in.—Charles is in very good looks indeed. I had the comfort of finding out the other evening who all the fat girls with short noses were that disturbed me at the 1st H. ball. They all prove to be Miss Atkinsons of En⟨. . . .⟩.

I rejoice to say that we have just had another letter from our dear Frank.—It is to you, very short, written from Larnica in Cyprus & so lately as the 2^d^ of October.—He came from Alexandria & was to return there in 3 or 4 days, knew nothing of his promotion, & does not write above twenty lines, from a doubt of the letter's ever reaching you & an idea of all letters being open'd at Vienna.—He wrote a few days before to you from Alexandria by the Mercury, sent with dispatches to Lord Keith.—Another letter must be oweing to us besides this,—*one* if not *two*—because none of these are to me.—Henry comes tomorrow, for one night only.—

My mother has heard from Mrs. E. Leigh. Lady S & S—— and her daughter are going to remove to Bath. —Mrs. Estwick is married again to a Mr. Sloane, a young Man under age—without the knowledge of either family.—He bears a good character however.—

28. *To Cassandra Austen.* *Sunday* 30 *Nov.* 1800

Address: Miss Austen | Godmersham Park | Faversham | Kent
Postmarks: ANDOVER and DEC 2 1800
L. A. Austen-Leigh. 2 leaves 4°.
Life 153. A large part unpublished.

Ibthrop Sunday Novr 30th

My dear Cassandra

Shall you expect to hear from me on Wednesday or not?—I think you will, or I should not write, as the three days & half which have passed since my last letter was sent, have not produced many materials towards filling another sheet of paper.—But like Mrs Hastings, 'I do not despair'—& you perhaps like the faithful Maria may feel still more certain of the happy Event.—I have been here ever since a quarter after three on thursday last, by the Shrewsbury Clock, which I am fortunately enabled absolutely to ascertain, because Mrs. Stent once lived at Shrewsbury, or at least at Tewksbury.—I have the pleasure of thinking myself a very welcome Guest, & the pleasure of spending my time very pleasantly.—Martha looks very well, & wants me to find out that she grows fat; but I cannot carry my complaisance farther than to beleive whatever she asserts on the subject.—Mrs. Stent gives us quite as much of her company as we wish for, & rather more than she used to do; but perhaps not more than is to our advantage in the end, because it is too dirty even for such desperate walkers as Martha and I to get out of doors, & we are therefore confined to each other's society from morning till night, with very little variety of Books or Gowns. Three of the Miss Debaries called here the morning after my arrival, but I have not yet been able to return their civility;—You know it is not an uncommon circumstance in this parish to have the road from Ibthrop to the Parsonage much dirtier and more impracticable for walking than the road from the Parsonage to Ibthrop.—I left my Mother very well when I came away, & left her with strict orders to continue so.—My Journey was safe & not unpleasant; —I spent an hour in Andover, of which Messrs Painter & Pridding had the larger part;—twenty minutes however fell to the lot of Mrs Poore & her mother, whom I was glad to see in good looks & spirits.—The latter asked me more questions than I had very well time to answer; the former I beleive is very big; but I am by no means certain;—she is either very big, or not at all big, I forgot to be accurate in my observation at the time, & tho' my thoughts are now more about me on the subject, the power of exercising them to any effect is much diminished.—The two youngest boys only were at home; I mounted the highly-extolled staircase & went into the elegant Drawing room, which I fancy is now Mrs Harrison's apartment;—and in short did everything that extraordinary Abilities can be supposed to compass in so short a space of time.—The endless Debaries are of course very well acquainted with the lady who is to marry Sir Thomas, & all her family. I pardon them however, as their description of her is favourable.—Mrs Wapshire is a widow, with several sons & daughters, a good fortune, & a house in Salisbury; where Miss Wapshire has been for many years a distinguished beauty.—She is now seven or eight & twenty, and tho' still handsome less handsome than she has been.—This promises better, than the bloom of seventeen; & in addition to this, they say that she has always been remarkable for the propriety of her behaviour, distinguishing her far above the general class of Town Misses, & rendering her of course very unpopular among them.—I hope I have now gained the real truth, & that my letters may in future go on without conveying any farther contradictions of what was last asserted about Sir Thomas Williams and Miss Wapshire.—I wish I could be certain that her name were Emma; but her being the Eldest daughter leaves that circumstance doubtful. At Salisbury the match is considered as certain & as near at hand.—Martha desires her best love, & will be happy to welcome any letter from you to this house, whether it be addressed to herself or to me—and in fact, the difference of direction will not be material.—*She* is pleased with my Gown, & particularly bids me say that if you could see me in it for five minutes, she is sure you would be eager to make up your own.—I have been obliged to mention this, but have not failed to blush the whole time of my writing it.—Part of the money & time which I spent at Andover were devoted to the purchase of some figured cambric muslin for a frock for Edward—a circumstance from which I derive two pleasing reflections; it has in the first place opened to me a fresh source of self-congratulation on being able to make so munificent a present, & secondly it has been the means of informing me that the very pretty manufacture in question may be bought for $\frac{s \quad d}{4 \;,, \; 6}$ p^{r} y^{d}—yard & half wide.—Martha has promised to return with me, & our plan is to have a nice black frost for walking to Whitechurch, & there throw ourselves into a postchaise, one upon the other, our heads hanging out at one door, & our feet at the opposite.—If you have never heard that Miss Dawes has been married these two months, I will mention it in my next.—Pray do not forget to go to the Canterbury Ball. I shall despise you all most insufferably if you do.—By the bye, there will not be any Ball, because Delmar lost so much by the Assemblies last winter that he has protested against opening his rooms this year.—I have charged my Myrmidons to send me an account of the Basingstoke Ball; I have placed my spies at different places that they may collect the more; & by so doing, by sending Miss Bigg to the Townhall itself, & posting my Mother at Steventon I hope to derive from their various observations a good general idea of the whole.—

Monday.—Martha has this moment received your letter—I hope there is nothing in it requiring an immediate answer as we are at dinner, & she has neither time to read nor I to write.—Y^rs ever

J A.

29. *To Cassandra Austen. Saturday* 3 *Jan.* 1801

Address: Miss Austen | Godmersham Park | Faversham | Kent
Postmarks: OVERTON and JAN 6 1801
Pierpont Morgan Library. 2 leaves 4°.
Brabourne i. 248 ; *Life* 156 (extracts).

Steventon: Saturday Jan^ry 3^d.

My dear Cassandra

As you have by this time received my last letter, it is fit that I should begin another ; & I begin with the hope, which is at present uppermost in my mind, that you often wore a white gown in the morning, at the time of all the gay party's being with you. Our visit at Ash Park last Wednesday, went off in a come-cá way ; we met Mr. Lefroy & Tom Chute, played at cards & came home again.—James & Mary dined here on the following day, & at night Henry set off in the Mail for London.—He was as agreable as ever during his visit, & has not lost anything in Miss Lloyd's estimation.—Yesterday, we were quite alone, only our four selves ;—but today the scene is agreeably varied by Mary's driving Martha to Basingstoke, & Martha's afterwards dining at Deane.—My Mother looks forward with as much certainty as you can do, to our keeping two Maids—my father is the only one not in the secret.—We plan having a steady Cook, & a young giddy Housemaid, with a sedate, middle aged Man, who is to undertake the double office of Husband to the former & sweetheart to the latter.—No Children of course to be allowed on either side.—You feel more for John Bond, than John Bond deserves ;—I am sorry to lower his Character, but he is not ashamed to own himself, that he has no doubt at all of getting a good place, & that he had even an offer many years ago from a Farmer Paine of taking him into his service whenever he might quit my father's.—There are three parts of Bath which we have thought of as likely to have Houses in them.—Westgate Buildings, Charles Street, & some of the short streets leading from Laura Place or Pulteney St: Westgate Buildings, tho' quite in the lower part of the Town are not badly situated themselves ; the street is broad, & has rather a good appearance. Charles Street however I think is preferable ; the buildings are new, & it's nearness to Kingsmead fields would be a pleasant circumstance.—Perhaps you may remember, or perhaps you may forget that Charles Street leads from the Queen Square Chapel to the two Green park-Streets.—The Houses in the streets near Laura Place I should expect to be above our price.—Gay Street would be too high, except only the lower house on the left hand side as you ascend ; towards *that* my Mother has no disinclination ;—it used to be lower rented than any other house in the row, from some inferiority in the apartments. But above all other's, her wishes are at present fixed on the corner house in Chapel row, which opens into Prince's Street. Her knowledge of it however is confined only to the outside, & therefore she is equally uncertain of it's being really desirable as of its being to be had.—In the meantime she assures you that she will do everything in her power to avoid Trim St altho' you have not expressed the fearful presentiment of it, which was rather expected.—We know that Mrs. Perrot will want to get us into Axford Buildings, but we all unite in particular dislike of that part of the Town, & therefore hope to escape. Upon all these different situations, You and Edward may confer together, & your opinion of each will be expected with eagerness.—As to our Pictures, the Battle peice, Mr. Nibbs, Sir Wm East, & all the old heterogenous, miscellany, manuscript, Scriptoral peices dispersed over the House are to be given to James.—Your own Drawings will not cease to be your own—& the two paintings on Tin will be at your disposal.—My Mother says that the French agricultural Prints in the best bed-room were given by Edward to his two Sisters. Do you or he know anything about it ?—She has written to my Aunt, & We are all impatient for the answer.—I do not know how to give up the idea of our both going to Paragon in May ;—*Your* going I consider as indispensably necessary, & I shall not like being left behind ; there is no place here or hereabouts that I shall want to be staying at—& tho' to be sure the keep of two will be more than of one, I will endeavour to make the difference less by disordering my Stomach with Bath bunns ; & as to the *trouble* of accomodating us, whether there are one or two, it is much the same.—According to the first plan, my mother & our two selves are to travel down together ; & my father follow us afterwards—in about a fortnight or three weeks.—We have promised to spend a couple of days at Ibthrop in our way.—We must all meet at Bath you know before we set out for the Sea, & everything considered I think the first plan as good as any. My father & mother wisely aware of the difficulty of finding in all Bath such a bed as their own, have resolved on taking it with them ;—All the beds indeed that we shall want are to be removed, viz:—besides theirs, our own two, the best for a spare one, & two for servants—and these necessary articles will probably be the only material ones that it ⟨wou⟩ld answer to send down.—I do not think it will be worth while to remove any of our chests of Drawers—We shall be able to get some of a much more commo⟨dious⟩ form, made of deal, & painted to look very neat ; & I flatter myself that for little comforts of all kinds, our apartment will be one of the most complete things of the sort all over Bath—Bristol included.—We have thought at times of removing the side-board, or a pembroke table, or some other peice of furniture—but upon the whole it has ended in thinking that the trouble & risk of the removal would be more than the advantage of having them at a place, where everything may be purchased. Pray send your opinion.—Martha has as good as promised to come to us again in March.—Her spirits are better than they were.—I have now attained the true art of letter-writing, which we are always told, is to express on paper exactly what one would say to the same person by word of mouth ; I have been talking to you almost as fast as I could the whole of this letter.—Your Christmas Gaieties are really quite surprising ; I think they would satisfy even Miss Walter herself.—I hope the ten shillings won by Miss Foote may make everything easy between her & her cousin Frederick.—So, Lady Bridges—in the delicate language of Coulson Wallop, is *in for it* !—I am very glad to hear of the Pearsons' good fortune.—It is a peice of promotion which I know they looked forward to as very desirable some years ago, on Capt: Lockyer's illness.—It brings them a considerable increase of Income, & a better house.—My Mother bargains for having no trouble at all in furnishing our house in Bath—& I have engaged for your willingly undertaking to do it all.—I get more & more reconciled to the idea of our removal. We have lived long enough in this Neighbourhood, the Basingstoke Balls are certainly on the decline, there is something interesting in the bustle of going away, & the prospect of spending future summers by the Sea or in Wales is very delightful.—For a time we shall now possess many of the advantages which I have often thought of with Envy in the wives of Sailors or Soldiers.—It must not be generally known however that I am not sacrificing a great deal in quitting the Country—or I can expect to inspire no tenderness, no interest in those we leave behind.—The threatened Act of Parliament does not seem to give any alarm.

My father is doing all in his power to encrease his Income by raising his Tythes &c., & I do not despair of getting very nearly six hundred a year.—In what part of Bath do you mean to place your *Bees* ?—We are afraid of the South Parade's being too hot.

Monday.—Martha desires her best Love, & says a great many kind things about spending some time with you in March—& depending on a large return from us both in the Autumn.—Perhaps I may not write again before Sunday.—

Yours affec[ly]

J. A.

30. *To Cassandra Austen.* *Thursday* 8 *Jan.* 1801

Address: Miss Austen | Godmersham Park | Faversham | Kent
Postmarks: OVERTON and JAN 10 1801
Pierpont Morgan Library. 2 leaves 4°.
Brabourne i. 255; *Life* 158 (extracts).

Steventon Thursday Jan[ry] 8th

My dear Cassandra

The 'Perhaps' which concluded my last letter being only a 'perhaps,' will not occasion your being overpowered with Surprise, I dare say, if you *should* receive this before tuesday, which unless circumstances are very perverse will be the case.—I received yours with much general Philanthropy & still more peculiar good will two days ago; & I suppose I need not tell you that it was very long, being written on a foolscap sheet, & very entertaining, being written by you.—Mr. Payne has been dead long enough for Henry to be out of mourning for him before his last visit, tho' we knew nothing of it till about that time. Why he died, or of what complaint, or to what Noblemen he bequeathed his four daughters in marriage we have not heard.—I am glad that the Wildmans' are going to give a Ball, & hope you will not fail to benefit both yourself & me, by laying out a few kisses in the purchase of a frank.—I beleive you are right in proposing to delay the Cambric muslin, & I submit with a kind of voluntary reluctance.—Mr. Peter Debary has declined Dean curacy; he wishes to be settled nearer London. A foolish reason!, as if Deane were not near London in comparison of Exeter or York.—Take the whole world through, & he will find many more places at a greater distance from London than Deane, than he will at a less.—What does he think of Glencoe or Lake Katherine ?—I feel rather indignant that any possible objection should be raised against so valuable a peice of preferment, so delightful a situation !—that Deane should not be universally allowed to be as near the Metropolis as any other country villages.—As this is the case however, as Mr. Peter Debary has shewn himself a Peter in the blackest sense of the Word, We are obliged to look elsewhere for an heir ; & my father has thought it a necessary compliment to James Digweed to offer the Curacy to him, tho' without considering it as either a desirable or an eligible situation for him.—Unless he is in love with Miss Lyford, I think he had better not be settled exactly in this neighbourhood, & unless he is very much in love with her indeed, he is not likely to think a salary of 50£ equal in value or efficacy to one of 75£.—Were *you* indeed to be considered as one of the fixtures of the house !—but you were never actually erected in it either by Mr. Egerton Brydges or Mrs. Lloyd.—Martha & I dined yesterday at Deane to meet the Powletts & Tom Chute, which we did not fail to do.—Mrs. Powlett was at once expensively & nakedly dress'd ; we have had the satisfaction of estimating her Lace & her Muslin ; & she said too little to afford us much other amusement.—Mrs. John Lyford is so much pleased with the state of widowhood as to be going to put in for being a widow again ;—she is to marry a Mr. Fendall, a banker in Gloucester, a man of very good fortune, but considerably older than herself & with three little children.—Miss Lyford has never been here yet ; she can come only for a day, & is not able to fix the day.—I fancy Mr. Holder will have the Farm, & without being obliged to depend on the accomodating spirit of Mr. William Portal; he will probably have it for the remainder of my father's lease.—This pleases us all much better than it's falling into the hands of Mr. Harwood or Farmer Twitchen.—Mr. Holder is to come in a day or two to talk to my father on the subject, & then John Bond's interest will not be forgotten.—I have had a letter today from Mrs. Cooke. Mrs. Laurel is going to be married to a Mr. Hinchman, a rich East Indian. I hope Mary will be satisfied with this proof of her cousin's existence & welfare, & cease to torment herself with the idea of his bones being bleaching in the Sun on Wantage Downs.—Martha's visit is drawing towards it's close, which we all four sincerely regret.—The wedding-day is to be celebrated on the 16th because the 17th falls on Saturday—& a day or two before the 16th Mary will drive her sister to Ibthrop to find all the festivity she can in contriving for everybody's comfort, & being thwarted or teized by almost everybody's temper.—Fulwar, Eliza, & Tom Chute are to be of the party;—I know of nobody else.—I was asked, but declined it.—Eliza has seen Lord Craven at Barton, & probably by this time at Kintbury, where he was expected for one day this week.—She found his manners very pleasing indeed.—The little flaw of having a Mistress now living with him at Ashdown Park, seems to be the only unpleasing circumstance about him.—From Ibthrop, Fulwar & Eliza are to return with James and Mary to Deane.—The Rices are *not* to have an house on Weyhill;—for the present he has Lodgings in Andover, & they are in veiw of a dwelling hereafter in Appleshaw, that village of wonderful Elasticity, which stretches itself out for the reception of everybody who does not wish for a house on Speen Hill.—Pray give my love to George, tell him that I am very glad to hear he can skip so well already, & that I hope he will continue to send me word of his improvement in the art.—I think you judge very wisely in putting off your London visit—& I am mistaken if it be not put off for some time.—You speak with such noble resignation of Mrs. Jordan & the Opera House that it would be an insult to suppose consolation required—but to prevent your thinking with regret of this rupture of your engagement with Mr. Smithson, I must assure you that Henry suspects him to be a great miser.—

Friday. No answer from my Aunt.—She has no time for writing I suppose in the hurry of selling furniture, packing cloathes & preparing for their removal to Scarletts.—You are very kind in planning presents for me to make, & my Mother has shewn me exactly the same attention—but as I do not chuse to have Generosity dictated to me, I shall not resolve on giving my cabinet to Anna till the first thought of it has been my own. Sidmouth is now talked of as our summer abode; get all the information therefore about it that you can from Mrs. C. Cage.

My father's old Ministers are already deserting him to pay their court to his Son; the brown Mare, which as well as the black was to devolve on James at our removal, has not had patience to wait for that, & has settled herself even now at Deane.—The death of Hugh Capet, which like that of Mr. Skipsey—tho' undesired was not wholly unexpected, being purposely effected, has made the immediate possession of the

Mare very convenient; & everything else I suppose will be seized by degrees in the same manner.—Martha & I work at the books every day.—

Yours affec^ly J. A.

31. *To Cassandra Austen. Wednesday* 14 *Jan.* ⟨1801⟩

Address: Miss Austen | Godmersham Park | Faversham | Kent
Postmarks: OVERTON and JAN (figures illegible)
Pierpont Morgan Library. 2 leaves 4º.
Brabourne i. 261; *Life* 159 (extracts).

Steventon: Wednesday Jan^ry 14th.

Poor Miss Austen!—It appears to me that I have rather oppressed you of late by the frequency of my letters. You had hoped not to hear from me again before tuesday but Sunday shewed you with what a merciless Sister you had to deal.—I cannot recall the past, but you shall not hear from me quite so often in future.—Your letter to Mary was duly received before she left Dean with Martha yesterday morning, & it gives us great pleasure to know that the Chilham Ball was so agreable & that you danced four dances with Mr. Kemble.—Desirable however as the latter circumstance was I cannot help wondering at it's taking place;—Why did you dance four dances with so stupid a Man?—why not rather dance two of them with some elegant brother-officer who was struck with your appearance as soon as you entered the room?—Martha left you her best Love; she will write to you herself in a short time; but trusting to my memory rather than her own, she has nevertheless desired me to ask you to purchase for her two bottles of Steele's Lavender Water when you are in Town, provided you should go to the Shop on your own account;—otherwise you may be sure that she would not have you recollect the request.—James dined with us yesterday, wrote to Edward in the Evening, filled three sides of paper, every line inclining too much towards the North-East, & the very first line of all scratched out, and this morning he joins His lady in the fields of Elysium & Ibthrop.—Last friday was a very busy day with us. We were visited by Miss Lyford and Mr. Bayle.—The latter began his operations in the house, but had only time to finish the four sitting-rooms; the rest is deferred till the spring is more advanced & the days longer.—He took his paper of appraisement away with him, & therefore we only know the Estimate he has made of one or two articles of furniture, which my father particularly enquired into. I understand however that he was of opinion that the whole would amount to more than two hundred pounds, & it is not imagined that this will comprehend the Brewhouse, & many other &c. &c.—Miss Lyford was very pleasant, & gave my mother such an account of the houses in Westgate Buildings, where Mrs. Lyford lodged four years ago, as made her think of a situation there with great pleasure; but your opposition will be without difficulty, decisive, & my father in particular who was very well inclined towards the Row before, has now ceased to think of it entirely.—At present the Environs of Laura-place seem to be his choice. His veiws on the subject are much advanced since I came home; he grows quite ambitious, & actually requires now a comfortable & a creditable looking house.—On Saturday Miss Lyford went to her long home—that is to say, it was a long way off; & soon afterwards a party of fine Ladies issuing from a well-known, commodious green Vehicle, their heads full of Bantam-cocks and Galinies, entered the house.—Mrs. Heathcote, Mrs. Harwood, Mrs. James Austen, Miss Bigg, Miss Jane Blachford. Hardly a day passes in which we do not have some visitor or other; yesterday came Mrs. Bramstone, who is very sorry that she is to lose us, & afterwards Mr. Holder, who was shut up for an hour with my father & James in a most aweful manner. —John Bond est a lui.—Mr. Holder was perfectly willing to take him on exactly the same terms with my father, & John seems exceedingly well satisfied.— The comfort of not changing his home is a very material one to him, and since such are his unnatural feelings his belonging to Mr. Holder is the every thing needful; but otherwise there would have been a situation offering to him which I had thought of with particular satisfaction, viz= under Harry Digweed, who if John had quitted Cheesedown would have been eager to engage him as superintendant at Steventon, would have kept an horse for him to ride about on, would probably have supplied him with a more permanent home, & I think would certainly have been a more desirable Master altogether.—John & Corbett are not to have any concern with each other;—there are to be two Farms and two Bailiffs.—We are of opinion that it would be better in only one.—This morning brought my Aunt's reply, & most thoroughly affectionate is it's tenor. She thinks with the greatest pleasure of our being settled in Bath; it is an event which will attach her to the place more than anything else could do, &c., &c.—She is moreover very urgent with my mother not to delay her visit in Paragon if she should continue unwell, & even recommends her spending the whole winter with them.—At present, & for many days past my mother has been quite stout, & she wishes not to be obliged by any relapse to alter her arrangements.—Mr. and Mrs. Chamberlayne are in Bath, lodging at the Charitable Repository;—I wish the scene may suggest to Mrs. C. the notion of selling her black beaver bonnet for the releif of the poor.—Mrs. Welby has been singing Duetts with the Prince of Wales.—My father has got above 500 Volumes to dispose of;—I want James to take them at a venture at half a guinea a volume.—The whole repairs of the parsonage at Deane, Inside & out, Coachbox, Basket & Dickey will not much exceed 100£.—Have you seen that Major Byng, a nephew of Lord Torrington is dead?—That must be Edmund.—

Friday. I thank you for yours, tho' I should have been more grateful for it, if it had not been charged 8*d.* instead of 6*d.*, which has given me the torment of writing to Mr. Lambould on the occasion.—I am rather surprised at the Revival of the London visit—but Mr. Doricourt has travelled; he knows best. That James Digweed has refused Dean Curacy I suppose he has told you himself—tho' probably the subject has never been mentioned between you.—Mrs. Milles flatters herself falsely; it has never been Mrs. Rice's wish to have her son settled near herself—& there is now a hope entertained of her relenting in favour of Deane.—Mrs. Lefroy & her son in law were here yesterday; *she* tries not to be sanguine, but *he* was in excellent spirits.—I rather wish they may have the Curacy. It will be an amusement to Mary to superintend their Household management, & abuse them for expense, especially as Mrs. L. means to advise them to put their washing out.—

Yours affec^ly^ J. A.

32. *To Cassandra Austen. Wednesday* 21 *Jan.* 1801

Address: Miss Austen | Godmersham Park | Faversham | Kent
Postmarks: OVERTON and JAN 23 1801
Pierpont Morgan Library. 2 leaves 4°.
Brabourne i. 266; *Life* 161 (extracts). Two sentences unpublished.

Steventon Wednesday Jan^ry^ 21st

Expect a most agreable Letter; for not being overburdened with subject—(having nothing at all to say)—I shall have no check to my Genius from beginning to end.—Well—& so, Frank's letter has made you very happy, but you are afraid he would not have patience to stay for the Haarlem, which you wish him to have done as being safer than the Merchantman.—Poor fellow! to wait from the middle of November to the end of December, & perhaps even longer! it must be sad work!—especially in a place where the ink is so abominably pale.—What a surprise to him it must have been on the 20th of Octr to be visited, collar'd & thrust out of the Petterell by Captn Inglis!—He kindly passes over the poignancy of his feelings in quitting his Ship, his Officers & his Men.—What a pity it is that he should not be in England at the time of this promotion, because he certainly would have had an appointment!—so everybody says, & therefore it must be right for me to say it too.—Had he been really here, the certainty of the appointment I dare say would not have been half so great—but as it could not be brought to the proof, his absence will be always a lucky source of regret.—Eliza talks of having read in a Newspaper that all the 1st Lieut^{s} of the Frigates whose Captains were to be sent into Line-of-Battle ships, were to be promoted to the rank of Commanders—. If it be true, Mr. Valentine may afford himself a fine Valentine's knot, & Charles may perhaps become 1st of the Endymion—tho' I suppose Capt: Durham is too likely to bring a villain with him under that denomination. I dined at Deane yesterday, as I told you I should;—& met the two Mr. Holders.—We played at Vingt-un, which as Fulwar was unsuccessful, gave him an opportunity of exposing himself as usual.—Eliza says she is quite well, but she is thinner than when we saw her last, & not in very good looks. I suppose she has not recovered from the effects of her illness in December.—She cuts her hair too short over her forehead, & does not wear her cap far enough upon her head—in spite of these many disadvantages however, I can still admire her beauty.—They all dine here today. Much good may it do us all. William & Tom are much as usual; Caroline is improved in her person; I think her now really a pretty Child. She is still very shy, & does not talk much. Fulwar goes next month into Gloucestershire, Leicestershire & Warwickshire, & Eliza spends the time of his absence at Ibthrop & Deane; she hopes therefore to see you before it is long. Lord Craven was prevented by Company at home, from paying his visit at Kintbury, but as I told you before, Eliza is greatly pleased with him, & they seem likely to be on the most friendly terms.—Martha returns into this country next tuesday, & then begins her two visits at

Deane.—I expect to see Miss Bigg every day, to fix the time for my going to Manydown ; I think it will be next week, & I shall give you notice of it if I can, that you may direct to me there.—The Neighbourhood have quite recovered the death of Mrs. Rider—so much so, that I think they are rather rejoiced at it now ; her things were so very dear !—& Mrs. Rogers is to be all that is desirable. Not even Death itself can fix the friendship of the World.—

You are not to give yourself the trouble of going to Penlingtons when you are in Town ; my father is to settle the matter when he goes there himself ; You are only to take special care of the Bills of his in your hands, & I dare say will not be sorry to be excused the rest of the business.—*Thursday.* Our party yesterday was very quietly pleasant. Today we all attack Ash Park, & tomorrow I dine again at Deane. What an eventful week !—Eliza left me a message for you which I have great pleasure in delivering; she will write to you & send you your Money next Sunday.—Mary has likewise a message—. She will be much obliged to you if you can bring her the pattern of the Jacket & Trowsers, or whatever it is, that Elizth's boys wear when they are first put into breeches— ; or if you could bring her an old suit itself she would be very glad, but that I suppose is hardly do-able. I am happy to hear of Mrs. Knight's amendment, whatever might be her complaint. I cannot think so ill of her however in spite of your insinuations, as to suspect her of having lain-in.—I do not think she would be betrayed beyond an *Accident* at the utmost.—The Wylmots being robbed must be an amusing thing to their acquaintance, & I hope it is as much their pleasure as it seems their avocation to be subjects of general Entertainment.—I have a great mind not to acknowledge the receipt of your letter, which I have just had the pleasure of reading, because I am so ashamed to compare the sprawling lines of this with it !—But if I say all that I have to say, I hope I have no reason to hang myself.—Caroline was only brought to bed on the 7th of this month, so that her recovery does seem pretty rapid.—I have heard twice from Edward on the occasion, & his letters have each been exactly what they ought to be—chearful & amusing.—He dares not write otherwise to *me*—but perhaps he might be obliged to purge himself from the guilt of writing Nonsense by filling his shoes with whole pease for a week afterwards.—Mrs. G. has left him 100£.—his wife & son 500£. each. I join with you in wishing for the Environs of Laura place, but do not venture to expect it.—My Mother hankers after the Square dreadfully, & it is but natural to suppose that my Uncle will take *her* part.—It would be very pleasant to be near Sidney Gardens !—we might go into the Labyrinth every day.—You need not endeavour to match my mother's mourning Calico—, she does not mean to make it up any more.—Why did not J. D. make his proposals to you ? I suppose he went to see the Cathedral, that he might know how he should like to be married in it.—Fanny shall have the Boarding-school as soon as her Papa gives me an opportunity of sending it—& I do not know whether I may not by that time have worked myself up into so generous a fit as to give it to her for ever.—

We have a Ball on Thursday too—. I expect to go to it from Manydown.—Do not be surprised, or imagine that Frank is come if I write again soon. It will only be to say that I am going to M—& to answer your ⟨ques⟩tion about my Gown.

33. *To Cassandra Austen. Sunday* 25 *Jan.* ⟨1801⟩

Address (Brabourne): Miss Austen, Godmersham Park, Faversham, Kent
Original not traced.
***Brabourne* i. 272; *Life* 162 (extracts).**

Steventon: Sunday January 25.

I have nothing to say about Manydown, but I write because you will expect to hear from me, and because if I waited another day or two, I hope your visit to Goodnestone would make my letter too late in its arrival. I dare say I shall be at M. in the course of this week, but as it is not certain you will direct to me at home.

I shall want two new coloured gowns for the summer, for my pink one will not do more than clear me from Steventon. I shall not trouble you, however, to get more than one of them, and that is to be a plain brown cambric muslin, for morning wear; the other, which is to be a very pretty yellow and white cloud, I mean to buy in Bath. Buy two brown ones, if you please, and both of a length, but one longer than the other—it is for a tall woman. Seven yards for my mother, seven yards and a half for me; a dark brown, but the kind of brown is left to your own choice, and I had rather they were different, as it will be always something to say, to dispute about which is the prettiest. They must be cambric muslin.

How do you like this cold weather? I hope you have all been earnestly praying for it as a salutary relief from the dreadfully mild and unhealthy season preceding it, fancying yourself half putrified from the want of it, and that now you all draw into the fire, complain that you never felt such bitterness of cold before, that you are half starved, quite frozen, and wish the mild weather back again with all your hearts.

Your unfortunate sister was betrayed last Thursday into a situation of the utmost cruelty. I arrived at Ashe Park before the Party from Deane, and was shut up in the drawing-room with Mr. Holder alone for ten minutes. I had some thoughts of insisting on the housekeeper or Mary Corbett being sent for, and nothing could prevail on me to move two steps from the door, on the lock of which I kept one hand constantly fixed. We met nobody but ourselves, played at *vingt-un* again, and were very cross.

On Friday I wound up my four days of dissipation by meeting William Digweed at Deane, and am pretty well, I thank you, after it. While I was there a sudden fall of snow rendered the roads impassable, and made my journey home in the little carriage much more easy and agreeable than my journey down.

Fulwar and Eliza left Deane yesterday. You will be glad to hear that Mary is going to keep another maid. I fancy Sally is too much of a servant to find time for everything, and Mary thinks Edward is not so much out of doors as he ought to be; there is therefore to be a girl in the nursery.

I would not give much for Mr. Rice's chance of living at Deane; he builds his hope, I find, not upon anything that his mother has written, but upon the effect of what he has written himself. He must write a great deal better than those eyes indicate if he can persuade a perverse and narrow-minded woman to oblige those whom she does not love.

Your brother Edward makes very honourable mention of you, I assure you, in his letter to James, and seems quite sorry to part with you. It is a great comfort to me to think that my cares have not been thrown away, and that you are respected in the world. Perhaps you may be prevailed on to return with him and Elizabeth into Kent, when they leave us in April, and I rather suspect that your great wish of keeping yourself disengaged has been with that view. Do as you like; I have overcome my desire of your going to Bath with my mother and me. There is nothing which energy will not bring one to.

Edward Cooper is so kind as to want us all to come to Hamstall this summer, instead of going to the sea, but we are not so kind as to mean to do it. The summer after, if you please, Mr. Cooper, but for the present we greatly prefer the sea to all our relations.

I dare say you will spend a very pleasant three weeks in town. I hope you will see everything worthy notice, from the Opera House to Henry's office in Cleveland Court; and I shall expect you to lay in a stock of intelligence that may procure me amusement for a twelvemonth to come. You will have a turkey from Steventon while you are there, and pray note down how many full courses of exquisite dishes M. Halavant converts it into.

I cannot write any closer. Neither my affection for you nor for letter-writing can stand out against a Kentish visit. For a three months' absence I can be a very loving relation and a very excellent correspondent, but beyond that I degenerate into negligence and indifference.

I wish you a very pleasant ball on Thursday, and myself another, and Mary and Martha a third, but they will not have theirs till Friday, as they have a scheme for the Newbury Assembly.

Nanny's husband is decidedly against her quitting service in such times as these, and I believe would be very glad to have her continue with us. In some respects she would be a great comfort, and in some we should wish for a different sort of servant. The washing would be the greatest evil. Nothing is settled, however, at present with her, but I should think it would be as well for all parties if she could suit herself in the meanwhile somewhere nearer her husband and child than Bath. Mrs. H. Rice's place would be very likely to do for her. It is not many, as she is herself aware, that she is qualified for.

My mother has not been so well for many months as she is now.

Adieu. Yours sincerely, J. A.

34. *To Cassandra Austen.* *Wednesday* 11 *Feb.* 1801

Address: Miss Austen | 24. Upper Berkeley Street | Portman Square | London
Postmarks: BASINGSTOKE and FEB 13 1801
British Museum (1925). Formerly in the collection described in *Times Literary Supplement* 14 Jan. 1926. 2 leaves 4°.
Memoir[1] 81, *Memoir*[2] 64 (extract); *Life* 163 (extract). A large part unpublished.

Manydown Wednesday Feb 11th

My dear Cassandra

As I have no Mr Smithson to write of *I* can date my letters.—Yours to my Mother has been forwarded to me this morning, with a request that I would take on me the office of acknowledging it. I should not however have thought it necessary to write so soon, but for the arrival of a letter from Charles to myself.—It was written last Saturday from off the Start, & conveyed to Popham Lane by Cap^{tn} Boyle in his way to Midgham. He came from Lisbon in the Endymion, & I will copy Charles' account of his conjectures about Frank.—' He has not seen my brother lately, nor does he expect to find him arrived, as he met Capt: Inglis at Rhodes going up to take command of the Petterel as he was coming down, but supposes he will arrive in less than a fortnight from this time, in some ship which is expected to reach England about that time with dispatches from Sir Ralph Abercrombie.'—The event must shew what sort of a Conjuror Capt: Boyle is.—The Endymion has not been plagued with any more prizes.—Charles spent three pleasant days in Lisbon.—They were very well satisfied with their Royal Passenger, whom they found fat, jolly & affable, who talks of Ly Augusta as his wife & seems much attached to her.—When this letter was written, the Endymion was becalmed, but Charles hoped to reach Portsmouth by monday or tuesday; and as he particularly enquires for Henry's direction, you will e'er long I suppose receive further intelligence of him; He received my letter, communicating our plans, before he left England, was much surprised of course, but is quite reconciled to them, & means to come to Steventon once more while Steventon is ours.—Such I beleive are all the particulars of his Letter, that are worthy of travelling into the Regions of Wit, Elegance, fashion, Elephants & Kangaroons. My visit to Miss Lyford begins tomorrow, & ends on Saturday, when I shall have an opportunity of returning here at no expence as the Carriage must take Cath: to Basingstoke.—She meditates your returning into Hampshire together, & if the Time should accord, it would not be undesirable. She talks of staying only a fortnight, & as that will bring your stay in Berkeley Street to three weeks, I suppose you would not wish to make it longer.—Do not let this however retard your coming down, if you had intended a much earlier return.—I suppose whenever you come, Henry would send you in his carriage a stage or two, where you might be met by John, whose protection you would we imagine think sufficient for the rest of your Journey. He might ride on the Bar, or might even sometimes meet with the accomodation of a sunday-chaise.—James has offered to meet you anywhere, but as that would be to give him trouble without any counterpoise of convenience, as he has no intention of going to London at present on his own account, we suppose that you would rather accept the attentions of John.—We spend our time here as quietly as usual. One long morning visit is what generally occurs, & such a one took place yesterday. We went to Baugherst. The place is not so pretty as I expected, but perhaps the Season may be against the beauty of Country. The house seemed to have all the comforts of little Children, dirt & litter. Mr Dyson as usual looked wild, & Mrs Dyson as usual looked big.—Mr Bramston called here the morning before,—et voila tout.—I hope you are as well satisfied with having my coloured Muslin Gown as a white one. Everybody sends their Love—& I am sincerely yours

J A.

35. *To Cassandra Austen. Tuesday* 5 *May* ⟨1801⟩

Address (Brabourne): Miss Austen, Mrs. Lloyd's, Up Hurstbourne, Andover
Fitzwilliam Museum, Cambridge.
Brabourne i. 278; *Life* 165 (extracts).

Paragon: Tuesday May 5

My dear Cassandra

I have the pleasure of writing from my *own* room up two pair of stairs, with everything very comfortable about me.

Our journey here was perfectly free from accident or event; we changed horses at the end of every stage, and paid at almost every turnpike. We had charming weather, hardly any dust, and were exceedingly agreeable, as we did not speak above once in three miles.

Between Luggershall and Everley we made our grand meal, and then with admiring astonishment perceived in what a magnificent manner our support had been provided for. We could not with the utmost exertion consume above the twentieth part of the beef. The cucumber will, I believe, be a very acceptable present, as my uncle talks of having inquired the price of one lately, when he was told a shilling.

We had a very neat chaise from Devizes; it looked almost as well as a gentleman's, at least as a very shabby gentleman's; in spite of this advantage, however, we were above three hours coming from thence to Paragon, and it was half after seven by your clocks before we entered the house.

Frank, whose black head was in waiting in the Hall window, received us very kindly; and his master and mistress did not show less cordiality. They both look very well, though my aunt has a violent cough. We drank tea as soon as we arrived, and so ends the account of our journey, which my mother bore without any fatigue.

How do you do to-day? I hope you improve in sleeping—I think you must, because *I* fall off; I have been awake ever since five and sooner; I fancy I had too much clothes over me; I thought I *should* by the feel of them before I went to bed, but I had not courage to alter them. I am warmer here without any fire than I have been lately with an excellent one.

Well, and so the good news is confirmed, and Martha triumphs. My uncle and aunt seemed quite surprised that you and my father were not coming sooner.

I have given the soap and the basket, and each have been kindly received. *One* thing only among all our concerns has not arrived in safety: when I got into the chaise at Devizes I discovered that your drawing ruler was broke in two; it is just at the top where the cross-piece is fastened on. I beg pardon.

There is to be only one more ball—next Monday is the day. The Chamberlaynes are still here. I begin to think better of Mrs. C——, and upon recollection believe she has rather a long chin than otherwise, as she remembers us in Gloucestershire when we were very charming young women.

The first view of Bath in fine weather does not answer my expectations; I think I see more distinctly through rain. The sun was got behind everything, and the appearance of the place from the top of Kingsdown was all vapour, shadow, smoke, and confusion.

I fancy we are to have a house in Seymour Street, or thereabouts. My uncle and aunt both like the situation. I was glad to hear the former talk of all the houses in New King Street as too small; it was my own idea of them. I had not been two minutes in the dining-room before he questioned me with all his accustomary eager interest about Frank and Charles, their views and intentions. I did my best to give information.

I am not without hopes of tempting Mrs. Lloyd to settle in Bath; meat is only 8*d.* per pound, butter12*d.*, and cheese 9½*d.* You must carefully conceal from her, however, the exorbitant price of fish: a salmon has been sold at 2*s.* 9*d.* per pound the whole fish. The Duchess of York's removal is expected to make that article more reasonable—and till it really appears so, say nothing about salmon.

Tuesday night.—When my uncle went to take his second glass of water I walked with him, and in our morning's circuit we looked at two houses in Green Park Buildings, one of which pleased me very well. We walked all over it except into the garret; the dining-room is of a comfortable size, just as large as you like to fancy it; the second room about 14 ft. square. The apartment over the drawing-room pleased me particularly, because it is divided into two, the smaller one a very nice-sized dressing-room, which upon occasion might admit a bed. The aspect is south-east. The only doubt is about the dampness of the offices, of which there were symptoms.

Wednesday.—Mrs. Mussell has got my gown, and I will endeavour to explain what her intentions are. It is to be a round gown, with a jacket and a frock front, like Cath. Bigg's, to open at the side. The jacket is all in one with the body, and comes as far as the pocket-holes—about half a quarter of a yard deep, I suppose, all the way round, cut off straight at the corners with a broad hem. No fulness appears either in the body or the flap ; the back is quite plain in this form , and the sides equally so. The front is sloped round to the bosom and drawn in, and there is to be a frill of the same to put on occasionally when all one's handkerchiefs are dirty—which frill *must* fall back. She is to put two breadths and a-half in the tail, and no gores—gores not being so much worn as they were. There is nothing new in the sleeves : they are to be plain, with a fulness of the same falling down and gathered up underneath, just like some of Martha's, or perhaps a little longer. Low in the back behind, and a belt of the same. I can think of nothing more, though I am afraid of not being particular enough.

My mother has ordered a new bonnet, and so have I ; both white strip, trimmed with white ribbon. I find my straw bonnet looking very much like other people's, and quite as smart. Bonnets of cambric muslin on the plan of Lady Bridges' are a good deal worn, and some of them are very pretty ; but I shall defer one of that sort till your arrival. Bath is getting so very empty that I am not afraid of doing too little. Black gauze cloaks are worn as much as anything. I shall write again in a day or two. Best love.

Yours ever, J. A.

We have had Mrs. Lillingstone and the Chamberlaynes to call on us. My mother was very much struck with the odd looks of the two latter ; *I* have only seen *her*. Mrs. Busby drinks tea and plays at cribbage here to-morrow; and on Friday, I believe, we go to the Chamberlaynes'. Last night we walked by the Canal.

36. *To Cassandra Austen.* *Tuesday* 12 *May* ⟨1801⟩

Address: Miss Austen | Mrs Lloyd's | Hurstbourn Tarrant | Andover
Postmark: BATH
Pierpont Morgan Library. 2 leaves 4o.
Brabourne i. 284; *Life* 166 (extracts). A few words unpublished.

Paragon Tuesday May 12th.

My dear Cassandra

My mother has heard from Mary & I have heard from Frank; we therefore know something now of our concerns in distant quarters, & you I hope by some means or other are equally instructed, for I do not feel inclined to transcribe the letter of either.—You know from Elizabeth I dare say that my father & Frank, deferring their visit to Kippington on account of Mr. M. Austen's absence are to be at Godmersham today; & James I dare say has been over to Ibthrop by this time to enquire particularly after Mrs. Lloyd's health, & forestall whatever intelligence of the sale I might attempt to give.—Sixty-one guineas & a half for the three cows gives one some support under the blow of only Eleven Guineas for the Tables. Eight for my Pianoforte, is about what I really expected to get; I am more anxious to know the amount of my books, especially as they are said to have sold well.—

My Adventures since I wrote last, have not been very numerous; but such as they are, they are much at your service.—We met not a creature at Mrs. Lillingstone's, & yet were not so very stupid as I expected, which I attribute to my wearing my new bonnet & being in good looks.—On Sunday we went to Church twice, & after evening service walked a little in the Crescent fields, but found it too cold to stay long. Yesterday morning we looked into a house in Seymour St: which there is reason to suppose will soon be empty, and as we are assured from many quarters that no inconvenience from the river is felt in those Buildings, we are at liberty to fix in them if we can;—but this house was not inviting;—the largest room downstairs, was not much more than fourteen feet square, with a western aspect.—In the evening I hope you honoured my Toilette & Ball with a thought; I dressed myself as well as I could, & had all my finery much admired at home. By nine o'clock my Uncle, Aunt & I entered the rooms & linked Miss Winstone on to us.—Before tea, it was rather a dull affair; but then the before tea did not last long, for there was only one dance, danced by four couple.—Think of four couple, surrounded by about an hundred people, dancing in the upper Rooms at Bath!—After tea we *cheered up*; the breaking up of private parties sent some scores more to the Ball, & tho' it was shockingly & inhumanly thin for this place, there were people enough I suppose to have made five or six very pretty Basingstoke assemblies.—I then got Mr. Evelyn to talk to, & Miss Twisleton to look at; and I am proud to say that I have a very good eye at an Adultress, for tho' repeatedly assured that another in the same party was the *She*, I fixed upon the right one from the first.—A resemblance to Mrs. Leigh was my guide. She is not so pretty as I expected; her face has the same defect of baldness as her sister's, & her features not so handsome ;—she was highly rouged, & looked rather quietly & contentedly silly than anything else. —Mrs. Badcock & two young Women were of the same party, except when Mrs. Badcock thought herself obliged to leave them to run round the room after her drunken Husband.—His avoidance, & her pursuit, with the probable intoxication of both, was an amusing scene.—The Evelyns returned our visit on saturday ;—we were very happy to meet, & all that ;—they are going tomorrow into Gloucestershire, to the Dolphins for ten days.—Our acquaintance Mr. Woodward is just married to a Miss Rowe, a young lady rich in money & music.—I thank you for your Sunday's letter, it is very long & very agreable—. I fancy you know many more particulars of our sale than we do— ; we have heard the price of nothing but the Cows, Bacon, Hay, Hops, Tables, & my father's Chest of Drawers & Study Table.—Mary is more minute in her account of their own Gains than in ours—probably being better informed in them.—I will attend to Mrs. Lloyd's commission—& to her abhorrence of Musk when I write again.—I have bestowed three calls of enquiry on the Mapletons, & I fancy very beneficial ones to Marianne, as I am always told that she is better. I have not seen any of them.—Her complaint is a billious fever.—I like my dark gown very much indeed, colour, make, & everything.—I mean to have my new white one made up now, in case we should go to the rooms again next monday, which is to be really the last time.

Wednesday. Another stupid party last night ; perhaps if larger they might be less intolerable, but here there were only just enough to make one card table,

AXFORD AND PARAGON BUILDINGS, BATH

with six people to look on, & talk nonsense to each other. Ly Fust, Mrs. Busby & a Mrs. Owen sat down with my Uncle to Whist within five minutes after the three old *Toughs* came in, & there they sat with only the exchange of Adm: Stanhope for my Uncle till their chairs were announced.—I cannot anyhow continue to find people agreable ;—I respect Mrs. Chamberlayne for doing her hair well, but cannot feel a more tender sentiment.—Miss Langley is like any other short girl with a broad nose & wide mouth, fashionable dress, & exposed bosom.—Adm: Stanhope is a gentlemanlike Man, but then his legs are too short, & his tail too long.—Mrs. Stanhope could not come ; I fancy she had a private appointment with Mr. Chamberlayne, whom I wished to see more than all the rest.—My uncle has quite got the better of his lameness, or at least his walking with a stick is the only remains of it. —He & I are soon to take the long-plann'd walk to the Cassoon—& on friday we are all to accompany Mrs. Chamberlayne & Miss Langley to Weston. My Mother had a letter yesterday from my father ; it seems as if the W. Kent scheme were entirely given up.—He talks of spending a fortnight at Godmersham & then returning to Town.—

Y[rs] ever J. A.

Excepting a slight cold, my mother is very well ; she has been quite free from feverish or billious complaints since her arrival here.

37. *To Cassandra Austen.* *Thursday* 21 *May* ⟨1801⟩

Address : Miss Austen | The Revd F. C. Fowle's | Kintbury | Newbury
Postmark : BATH
Pierpont Morgan Library. 2 leaves 4°.
Brabourne i. 289 ; *Life* 168 (extracts).

Paragon Thursday May 21st.

My dear Cassandra

To make long sentences upon unpleasant subjects is very odious, & I shall therefore get rid of the one now uppermost in my thoughts as soon as possible.—Our views on G. P. Buildings seem all at an end ; the observation of the damps still remaining in the offices of an house which has been only vacated a week, with reports of discontented families & putrid fevers, has given the coup de grace.—We have now nothing in veiw.—When you arrive, we will at least have the pleasure of examining some of these putrifying Houses again ;—they are so very desirable in size & situation, that there is some satisfaction in spending ten minutes within them.—I will now answer the enquiries in your last letter. I cannot learn any other explanation of the coolness between my Aunt & Miss Bond than that the latter felt herself slighted by the former's leaving Bath last summer without calling to see her before she went.—It seems the oddest kind of quarrel in the world ; they never visit, but I beleive they speak very civilly if they meet ; My Uncle & Miss Bond certainly do. The 4 Boxes of Lozenges at $\overset{s}{1}-\overset{d}{1}-\frac{1}{2}$ per box, amount as I was told to $\overset{s}{4}-\overset{d}{6}$ and as the sum was so trifling, I thought it better to pay at once than contest the matter. I have just heard from Frank ;

my father's plans are now fixed; you will see him at Kintbury on friday, and unless inconvenient to you we are to see you both here on Monday the 1st of June.—Frank has an invitation to Milgate, which I beleive he means to accept.—Our party at Ly Fust's was made up of the same set of people that you have already heard of; the Winstones, Mrs. Chamberlayne, Mrs. Busby, Mrs. Franklyn & Mrs. Maria Somerville; yet I think it was not quite so stupid as the two preceding parties here.—The friendship between Mrs. Chamberlayne & me which you predicted has already taken place, for we shake hands whenever we meet. Our grand walk to Weston was again fixed for Yesterday, & was accomplished in a very striking manner; Every one of the party declined it under some pretence or other except our two selves, & we had therefore a tete a tete; but *that* we should equally have had after the first two yards, had half the Inhabitants of Bath set off with us.—It would have amused you to see our progress;—we went up by Sion Hill, & returned across the fields;—in climbing a hill Mrs. Chamberlayne is very capital; I could with difficulty keep pace with her—yet would not flinch for the world.—On plain ground I was quite her equal—and so we posted away under a fine hot sun, *She* without any parasol or any shade to her hat, stopping for nothing, & crossing the Church Yard at Weston with as much expedition as if we were afraid of being buried alive.—After seeing what she is equal to, I cannot help feeling a regard for her.—As to Agreableness, she is much like other people.—Yesterday Evening we had a short call from two of the Miss Arnolds, who came from Chippenham on Business; they are very civil, and not too genteel, and upon hearing that we wanted a House recommended one at Chippenham. This morning we have been visitted again by Mrs. & Miss Holder; they wanted us to fix an evening for drinking tea with them, but my Mother's still remaining cold allows her to decline everything of the kind.—As *I* had a separate invitation however, I beleive I shall go some afternoon. It is the fashion to think them both very detestable, but they are so civil, & their gowns look so white and so nice (which by the bye my Aunt thinks an absurd pretension in this place) that I cannot utterly abhor them, especially as Miss Holder owns that she has no taste for Music.—After they left us, I went with my Mother to help look at some houses in New King Street, towards which she felt some kind of inclination—but their size has now satisfied her;—they were smaller than I expected to find them. One in particular out of the two, was quite monstrously little;—the best of the sittingrooms not so large as the little parlour at Steventon, and the second room in every floor about capacious enough to admit a very small single bed.—We are to have a tiny party here tonight; I hate tiny parties—they force one into constant exertion.—Miss Edwards & her father, Mrs. Busby & her nephew Mr. Maitland, & Mrs. Lillingstone are to be the whole;—and I am prevented from setting my black cap at Mr. Maitland by his having a wife & ten children.—My Aunt has a very bad cough; do not forget to have heard about *that* when you come, & I think she is deafer than ever. My Mother's cold disordered her for some days, but she seems now very well;—her resolution as to remaining here, begins to give way a little; she will not like being left behind.

& will be glad to compound Matters with her enraged family.—You will be sorry to hear that Marianne Mapleton's disorder has ended fatally; she was beleived out of danger on Sunday, but a sudden relapse carried her off the next day.—So affectionate a family must suffer severely; & many a girl on early death has been praised into an Angel I beleive, on slighter pretensions to Beauty, Sense & Merit than Marianne.—Mr. Bent seems *bent* upon being very detestable, for he values the books at only 70£. The whole World is in a conspiracy to enrich one part of our family at the expence of another.—Ten shillings for Dodsley's Poems however please me to the quick, & I do not care how often I sell them for as much. When Mrs. Bramston has read them through I will sell them again.—I suppose you can hear nothing of your Magnesia.—

Friday. You have a nice day for your Journey in whatever way it is to be performed—whether in the Debary's Coach or on your own twenty toes.—When you have made Martha's bonnet you must make her a cloak of the same sort of materials; they are very much worn here, in different forms—many of them just like her black silk spencer, with a trimming round the armholes instead of sleeves;—some are long before, & some long all round like C. Bigg's.—Our party last night supplied me with no new idea for my Letter—.

Yrs Ever J. A.

The Pickfords are in Bath & have called here.—*She* is the most elegant looking Woman I have seen since I left Martha—*He* is as raffish in his appearance as I would wish every Disciple of Godwin to be.—We drink tea tonight with Mrs. Busby.—I scandalized her nephew cruelly ; he has but three children instead of Ten.—

Best Love to everybody.

38. *To Cassandra Austen.* *Tuesday* 26 *May* ⟨1801⟩

Address : Miss Austen | The Revd F. C. Fowle's | Kintbury | Newbury
Postmark : BATH
C. B. Hogan. Formerly in the collection described in *Times Literary Supplement* 14 Jan. 1926. 2 leaves 4°. Endorsed 'May 26th 1801'. This letter was sold with the 'topaze crosses' which it authenticates, and with which it should always be preserved.
Memoir[1] 83, *Memoir*[2] 65 (extract) ; *Life* 169 (extracts). A large part unpublished.

Paragon—Tuesday May 26th

My dear Cassandra

For your letter from Kintbury & for all the compliments on my writing which it contained, I now return you my best thanks.—I am very glad that Martha goes to Chilton ; a very essential temporary comfort her presence must afford to Mrs Craven, and I hope she will endeavour to make it a lasting one by exerting those kind offices in favour of the young Man, from which you were both with-held in the case of the Harrison family by the mistaken tenderness of one part of ours.—The Endymion came into Portsmouth on Sunday, & I have sent Charles a short letter by this day's post.—My adventures since I wrote to you three days ago have been such as the time would easily contain ; I walked yesterday morning with Mrs Chamberlayne to Lyncombe & Widcombe, and in the evening I drank tea with the Holders.—Mrs Chamberlayne's pace was not quite so magnificent on this second trial as in the first; it was nothing more than I could keep up with, without effort; and for many, many yards together on a raised narrow footpath I led the way.—The walk was very beautiful as my companion agreed, whenever I made the observation—And so ends our friendship, for the Chamberlaynes leave Bath in a day or two.—Prepare likewise for the loss of Lady Fust, as you will lose before you find her.—My evening visit was by no means disagreable. Mrs Lillingston came to engage Mrs Holder's conversation, & Miss Holder & I adjourned after tea into the inner Drawingroom to look over Prints & talk pathetically. She is very unreserved & very fond of talking of her deceased brother & sister, whose memories she cherishes with an enthusiasm which tho' perhaps a little affected, is not unpleasing. She has an idea of your being remarkably lively; therefore get ready the proper selection of adverbs, & due scraps of Italian & French.—I must now pause to make some observation on Mrs Heathcote's having got a little Boy; I wish her well to wear it out—& shall proceed. —Frank writes me word that he is to be in London tomorrow; some money Negociation from which he hopes to derive advantage, hastens him from Kent, & will detain him a few days behind my father in Town. —I have seen the Miss Mapletons this morning; Marianne was buried yesterday, and I called without expecting to be let in, to inquire after them all.—On the servant's invitation however I sent in my name, & Jane & Christiana who were walking in the Garden came to me immediately, and I sat with them about ten minutes.—They looked pale & dejected, but were more composed than I had thought probable.—When

I mentioned your coming here on Monday, they said that they should be very glad to see you.—We drink tea tonight with Mrs Lysons;—Now this, says My Master will be mighty dull.—On friday we are to have another party, & a sett of new people to you.—The Bradshaws & Greaves's, all belonging to one another; & I hope the Pickfords.—Mrs Evelyn called very civilly on sunday, to tell us that Mr Evelyn had seen Mr Philips the proprietor of No. 12 G. P. B. and that Mr Philips was very willing to raise the kitchen floor;—but all this I fear is fruitless—tho' the water may be kept out of sight, it cannot be sent away, nor the ill effects of its nearness be excluded.—I have nothing more to say on the subject of Houses;—except that we were mistaken as to the aspect of the one in Seymour Street, which instead of being due west is North-west.—I assure you in spite of what I might chuse to insinuate in a former letter, that I have seen very little of Mr Evelyn since my coming here; I met him this morning for only the 4th time, & as to my anecdote about Sidney Gardens, I made the most of the story because it came in to advantage, but in fact he only asked me whether I were to be at Sidney Gardens in the evening or not.—There is now something like an engagement between us & the Phaeton, which to confess my frailty I have a great desire to go out in;—whether it will come to anything must remain with him.—I really beleive he is very harmless; people do not seem afraid of him here, and he gets Groundsel for his birds & all that.—My Aunt will never be easy till she visits them;—she has been repeatedly trying to fancy a necessity for it now on our accounts, but she meets with no encouragement.—

LYME REGIS
from a Lithograph (*c.* 1844)

She ought to be particularly scrupulous in such matters & she says so herself—but nevertheless. . . . Well—I am come home from M[rs] Lysons as yellow as I went;—you cannot like your yellow gown half so well as I do, nor a quarter neither. M[r] Rice & Lucy are to be married, one on the 9th & the other on the 10th of July. Yrs affe[ly] JA.

Wednesday.—I am just returned from my airing in the very bewitching Phaeton & four, for which I was prepared by a note from M[r] E. soon after breakfast: We went to the top of Kingsdown & had a very pleasant drive: One pleasure succeeds another rapidly—On my return I found your letter & a letter from Charles on the table. The contents of yours I suppose I need not repeat to you; to thank you for it will be enough.—I give Charles great credit for remembering my Uncle's direction, & he seems rather surprised at it himself.—He has received 30£ for his share of the privateer & expects 10£ more—but of what avail is it to take prizes if he lays out the produce in presents to his sisters. He has been buying gold chains & Topaze crosses for us;—he must be well scolded. The Endymion has already received orders for taking Troops to Egypt—which I should not like at all if I did not trust to Charles' being removed from her somehow or other before she sails. He knows nothing of his own destination he says,—but desires me to write directly as the Endymion will probably sail in 3 or 4 days.—He will receive my yesterday's letter today, and I shall write again by this post to thank & reproach him.—We shall be unbearably fine.—I have made an engagement for you for Thursday the 4th of

June; if my mother & aunt should not go to the fireworks, w[h] I dare say they will not, I have promised to join M[r] Evelyn & Miss Wood. Miss Wood has lived with them you know ever 'since my son died'.

I will engage M[rs] Mussell as you desire. She made my dark gown very well & may therefore be trusted I hope with yours—but she does not always succeed with lighter colours.—My white one I was obliged to alter a good deal. Unless anything particular occurs I shall not write again.

39. *To Cassandra Austen.* *Friday* 14 *Sept.* ⟨1804⟩

Address: Miss Austen | M[rs] Lloyd's | Up. Hurstbourne | Andover
Postmark: none.
Mrs. Henry Burke; formerly in the collection described in *Times Literary Supplement* 14 Jan. 1926.
Memoir[1] 89, *Memoir*[2] 68 (extracts); *Life* 177 (extracts). Part unpublished.

Lyme Friday Sept 14.

My dear Cassandra

I take the first sheet of this fine striped paper to thank you for your letter from Weymouth, and express my hopes of your being at Ibthrop before this time. I expect to hear that you reached it yesterday evening, being able to get as far as Blandford on Wednesday. Your account of Weymouth contains nothing which strikes me so forcibly as there being no ice in the town. For every other vexation I was in some measure prepared, and particularly for your disappointment in not seeing the Royal Family go on board on Tuesday, having already heard from Mr. Crawford that he had seen you in the very act of being too late, but for there being no ice what could prepare me? Weymouth is altogether a shocking place, I perceive, without recommendation of any kind, & worthy only of being frequented by the inhabitants of Gloucester. I am really very glad that we did not go there, & that Henry & Eliza saw nothing in it to make them feel differently. You found my letter at Andover, I hope, yesterday, and have now for many hours been satisfied that your kind anxiety on my behalf was as much thrown away as kind anxiety usually is. I continue quite well; in proof of which I have bathed again this morning. It was absolutely necessary that I should have the little fever and indisposition which I had: it has been all the fashion this week in Lyme. Miss Anna Cove was confined for a day or two & her Mother thinks she was saved only by a timely Emetic (prescribed by Dr Robinson) from a serious illness & Miss Bonham has been under Mr Carpenter's care for several days with a sort of nervous fever, & tho' she is now well enough to walk abroad she is still very tall & does not come to the Rooms. We all of us attended them both on Wednesday evening & last evening I suppose I must say or Martha will think Mr Peter Debary slighted. My mother had her pool of commerce each night & divided the first with Le Chevalier, who was lucky enough to divide the other with somebody else. I hope he will always win enough to empower him to treat himself with so great an indulgence as cards must be to him. He enquired particularly after you, not being aware of your departure. We are quite settled in our Lodgings by this time as you may suppose, & everything goes on in the usual order. The servants behave very well, & make no difficulties, tho' nothing certainly can exceed the inconvenience of the offices, except the general dirtiness of the house & furniture & all its inhabitants. Hitherto the weather has been just what we could wish—the continuance of the dry season is very necessary to our comfort. I endeavour as far as I can to supply your place & be useful, & keep things in order. I detect dirt in the water-decanter as fast as I can & give the Cook physic which she throws off her stomach. I forget whether she used to do this, under your administration. James is the delight of our lives, he is quite an uncle Toby's annuity to us. My mother's shoes were never so well blacked before, & our plate never looked so clean. He waits extremely well, is attentive, handy, quick and quiet, & in short has a great many more than all the cardinal virtues (for the cardinal virtues in themselves have been so often possessed that they are no longer worth having) & amongst the rest, that of wishing to go to Bath, as I understand from Jenny. He has the laudable thirst I fancy for travelling, which in poor James Selby was so much reprobated; & part of his disappointment in not going with his master, arose from his wish of seeing London. My mother is at this moment reading a letter from my aunt. Yours to Miss Irvine of which she had had the perusal (which by the bye in your place I should not like) has thrown them into a quandary about Charles & his prospects. The case is that my mother had previously told my aunt, without restriction, that a sloop (which my aunt calls a Frigate) was reserved in the East for Charles; whereas you had replied to Miss Irvine's enquiries on the subject with less explicitness & more caution. Never mind, let them puzzle on together.

As Charles will equally go to the E. Indies, my uncle cannot be really uneasy, & my aunt may do what she likes with her frigates. She talks a great deal of the violent heat of the weather—we know nothing of it here. My uncle has been suffering a good deal lately; they mean however to go to Scarlets about this time unless prevented by bad accounts of Cook. The Coles have got their infamous plate upon our door. I dare say *that* makes a great part of the massy plate so much talked of. The Irvines' house is nearly completed. I believe they are to get into it on Tuesday: my aunt owns it to have a comfortable appearance, & only 'hopes the kitchen may not be damp'. I have not heard from Charles yet, which rather surprises me—some ingenious addition of his own to the proper direction perhaps prevents my receiving his letter. I have written to Buller & I have written to Mr Pyne, on the subject of the broken lid; it was valued by Anning here we were told at five shillings, & as that appeared to us beyond the value of all the furniture in the room together, we have referred ourselves to the owner. The Ball last night was pleasant, but not full for Thursday. My father staid very contentedly till half-past nine (we went a little after eight), and then walked home with James and a lanthorn, though I believe the lanthorn was not lit, as the moon was up; but this lanthorn may sometimes be a great convenience to him. My mother and I staid about an hour later. Nobody asked me the two first dances; the two next I danced with Mr. Crawford, and had I chosen to stay longer might have danced with Mr. Granville, Mrs. Granville's son, whom my dear friend Miss Armstrong offered to introduce to me, or with a new odd-looking man who had been eyeing me for some time, and at last, without any introduction, asked me if I meant to dance again. I think he must be Irish by his ease, and because I imagine him to belong to the hon^bl Barnwalls, who are the son, and son's wife of an Irish viscount, bold queer-looking people, just fit to be quality at Lyme. Mrs. Fraser (?) & the Schuylers went away—I do not know where—last Tuesday for some days & when they return the Schuylers I understand are to remain here a very little while longer. I called yesterday morning (ought it not in strict propriety to be termed yester-morning ?) on Miss Armstrong and was introduced to her father and mother. Like other young ladies she is considerably genteeler than her parents. Mrs. Armstrong sat darning a pair of stockings the whole of my visit. But I do not mention this at home, lest a warning should act as an example. We afterwards walked together for an hour on the Cobb ; she is very converseable in a common way ; I do not perceive wit or genius, but she has sense and some degree of taste, and her manners are very engaging. She seems to like people rather too easily. She thought the Downes pleasant etc etc. I have seen nothing of M^r & Mrs Manhood. My aunt mentions Mrs. Holder's being returned from Cheltenham so her summer ends before theirs begins. Hooper was heard of well at the Madeiras. Eliza would envy him. I hope Martha thinks you looking better than when she saw you in Bath. Jenny has fastened up my hair to-day in the same manner that she used to do up Miss Lloyd's—which makes us both very happy. I need not say that we are particularly anxious for your next letter to know how you find M[rs] Lloyd & Martha. Say everything kind for us to the latter. The former I fear must be beyond any remembrance of or from the absent.

Y[rs] affect[ly]

J. A.

Friday Even[g]. The bathing was so delightful this morning & Molly so pressing with me to enjoy myself that I believe I staid in rather too long, as since the middle of the day I have felt unreasonably tired. I shall be more careful another time, & shall not bathe to-morrow as I had before intended. Jenny & James are walked to Charmouth this afternoon. I am glad to have such an amusement for him, as I am very anxious for his being at once quiet & happy. He can read, & I must get him some books. Unfortunately he has read the 1st vol. of Robinson Crusoe. We have the Pinckards newspaper however which I shall take care to lend him.

40. *To Francis Austen. Monday* 21 *Jan.* 1805

Address: Capt. Austen | HMS Leopard | Dungeness | New Romney (Downs and Portsmouth added later)
Postmarks: BATH DEAL N⟨EW RO⟩MNEY and JA 25 1805
Captain Ernest Austen R.N. 2 leaves 4o.
J. H. and E. C. Hubback, *Jane Austen's Sailor Brothers*, 1906, 125; *Life* 181 (extracts).

Green Park B[gs] Monday Jan[ry] 21st

My dearest Frank

I have melancholy news to relate, & sincerely feel for your feelings under the shock of it.—I wish I could better prepare you for it. But having said so much, your mind will already forestall the sort of event which I have to communicate.—Our dear Father has closed his virtuous & happy life, in a death almost as free from suffering as his Children could have wished. —He was taken ill on Saturday morning, exactly in the same way as heretofore, an oppression in the head, with fever, violent tremulousness, & the greatest degree of Feebleness. The same remedy of Cupping, which had before been so successful, was immediately applied to—but without such happy effects. The attack was more violent, & at first he seemed scarcely at all releived by the operation.—Towards the Evening however he got better, had a tolerable night, & yesterday morning was so greatly amended as to get up & join us at breakfast as usual, & walk about with only the help of a stick, & every symptom was then so favourable that when Bowen saw him at one, he felt sure of his doing perfectly well.—But as the day advanced, all these comfortable appearances gradually changed ; the fever grew stronger than ever, & when Bowen saw him at ten at night, he pronounc'd his situation to be most alarming.—At nine this morning he came again—& by his desire a Physician was called in ;—Dr. Gibbs—But it was then absolutely a lost case—. Dr. Gibbs said that nothing but a Miracle could save him, and about twenty minutes after Ten he drew his last gasp.—Heavy as is the blow, we can already feel that a thousand comforts remain to us to soften it. Next to that of the consciousness of his worth & constant preparation for another World, is the remembrance of his having suffered, comparatively speaking, nothing. Being quite insensible of his own state, he was spared all the pain of separation,

SYDNEY GARDENS, BATH

& he went off almost in his Sleep.—My Mother bears the Shock as well as possible; she was quite prepared for it, & feels all the blessing of his being spared a long Illness. My Uncle & Aunt have been with us, & shew us every imaginable kindness. And to-morrow we shall I dare say have the comfort of James's presence, as an express has been sent to him.—We write also of course to Godmersham & Brompton. Adieu my dearest Frank. The loss of such a Parent must be felt, or we should be Brutes—. I wish I could have given you better preparation—but it has been impossible.—Yours Ever affec[ly]

J A.

41. *To Francis Austen. Tuesday* 22 *Jan.* ⟨1805⟩

Address: Capt. Austen | HMS Leopard | Portsmouth
Postmark: none.
Capt. Ernest Austen R.N. 2 leaves 4°. Endorsed 'January 23rd 1805'.
Hubback, *Sailor Brothers*, 127; *Life* 180 (with omissions).

Green Park B[gs] Tuesday Even[g], Jan[ry] 22[d]

My dearest Frank

I wrote to you yesterday; but your letter to Cassandra this morning, by which we learn the probability of your being by this time at Portsmouth, obliges me to write to you again, having unfortunately a communication as necessary as painful to make to you.—Your affectionate heart will be greatly wounded, & I wish the shock could have been lessen'd by a better preparation;—but the Event has been sudden, & so must be the information of it. We have lost an Excellent Father.—An illness of only eight & forty hours carried him off yesterday morning between ten

& eleven. He was seized on saturday with a return of the feverish complaint, which he had been subject to for the three last years; evidently a more violent attack from the first, as the applications which had before produced almost immediate releif, seemed for some time to afford him scarcely any.—On Sunday however he was much better, so much so as to make Bowen quite easy, & give us every hope of his being well again in a few days.—But these hopes gradually gave way as the day advanced, & when Bowen saw him at ten that night he was greatly alarmed.—A Physician was called in yesterday morning, but he was at that time past all possibility of cure—& Dr. Gibbs and Mr. Bowen had scarcely left his room before he sunk into a Sleep from which he never woke.—Everything I trust & beleive was done for him that was possible!—It has been very sudden!—within twenty four hours of his death he was walking with only the help of a stick, was even reading!—We had however some hours of preparation, & when we understood his recovery to be hopeless, most fervently did we pray for the speedy release which ensued. To have seen him languishing long, struggling for Hours, would have been dreadful! & thank God! we were all spared from it. Except the restlessness & confusion of high Fever, he did not suffer—& he was mercifully spared from knowing that he was about to quit the Objects so beloved, so fondly cherished as his wife & Children ever were.—His tenderness as a Father, who can do justice to?—My Mother is tolerably well; she bears up with great fortitude, but I fear her health must suffer under such a shock.—An express was sent for James, & he arrived here this morning before eight o'clock.—The funeral is to be on Saturday, at Walcot Church.—The Serenity of the Corpse is most delightful!—It preserves the sweet, benevolent smile which always distinguished him.—They kindly press my Mother to remove to Steventon as soon as it is all over, but I do not beleive she will leave Bath at present. We must have this house for three months longer, & here we shall probably stay till the end of that time.—

We all unite in Love, & I am affec[ly] Yours

J A.

42. *To Francis Austen. Tuesday* 29 *Jan.* ⟨1805⟩

Address: Capt. Austen | HMS Leopard | Portsmouth
Postmark: BATH
Capt. Ernest Austen R.N. 2 leaves 4°. Endorsed 'January 29th 1805'.
Hubback, *Sailor Brothers*, 129.

Green Park B[gs] Tuesday Jan[ry] 29.

My dearest Frank

My Mother has found among our dear Father's little personal property, a small astronomical Instrument which she hopes you will accept for his sake. It is, I beleive a Compass & Sun-Dial, & is in a Black chagreen Case. Would you have it sent to you now, & with what direction?—There is also a pair of Scissars for you.—We hope these are articles that may be useful to you, but we are sure they will be valuable.—I have not time for more.

Yours very affec[ly]

J A.

43. *To Cassandra Austen.* *Monday* 8 *April* ⟨1805⟩

Address: Miss Austen | Up. Hurstbourn | Andover | April 11th (i.e. Thursday, when the letter was finished).
Postmark: BATH
L. A. Austen-Leigh. 2 leaves 4°.
Memoir[2] 70; *Life* 183. A large part unpublished.

25 Gay St Monday

My dear Cassandra

Here is a day for you! Did Bath or Ibthrop ever see a finer 8th of April?—It is March & April together, the glare of one & the warmth of the other. We do nothing but walk about; as far as your means will admit I hope you profit by such weather too. I dare say you are already the better for change of place. We were out again last night; Miss Irvine invited us, when I met her in the Crescent, to drink tea with them, but I rather declined it, having no idea that my Mother would be disposed for another Evening visit there so soon; but when I gave her the message I found her very well inclined to go;—and accordingly on leaving Chapel we walked to Lansdown.—Richard Chamberlayne & a young Ripley from Mr Morgan's school, were there; & our visit did very well.—This morning we have been to see Miss Chamberlayne look hot on horseback.—Seven years & four months ago we went to the same Ridinghouse to see Miss Lefroy's performance!—What a different set are we now moving in! But seven years I suppose are enough to change every pore of one's skin, & every feeling of one's mind.—We did not walk long in the Crescent yesterday, it was hot & not crouded enough; so we went into the field, & passed close by Stephen Terry and Miss Seymour again.—I have not yet seen her face, but neither her dress nor air have anything of the Dash or Stilishness which the Browns talked of; quite the contrary indeed, her dress is not even smart, & her appearance very quiet. Miss Irvine says she is never speaking a word. Poor Wretch, I am afraid she is *en Penitence*.—Here has been that excellent Mrs. Coulthard calling, while my Mother was out & I was beleived to be so; I always respected her as a good-hearted, friendly woman;—And the Brownes have been here; I find their affidavits on the Table. —The Ambuscade reached Gibraltar on the 9th of March and found all well; so say the papers.—We have had no letters from anybody, but I expect to hear from Edward tomorrow, & from you soon afterwards.—How happy they are at Godmersham now!—I shall be very glad of a letter from Ibthrop, that I may know how you all are there, & particularly yourself. This is nice weather for M[rs] J. Austen's going to Speen, & I hope she will have a pleasant visit there. I expect a prodigious account of the Christening dinner; perhaps it brought you at last into the company of Miss Dundas again.—

Tuesday. I received your letter last night, & wish it may be soon followed by another to say that all is over; but I cannot help thinking that Nature will struggle again & produce a revival. Poor woman! May her end be peaceful & easy, as the Exit we have witnessed! And I dare say it will. If there is no revival, suffering must be all over; even the consciousness of Existence I suppose was gone when you wrote. The Nonsense I have been writing in this and in my last letter, seems out of place at such a time;

but I will not mind it, it will do you no harm, & nobody else will be attacked by it.—I am heartily glad that you can speak so comfortably of your own health & looks, tho' I can scarcely comprehend the latter being really approved. Could travelling fifty miles produce such an immediate change ?—You were looking so very poorly here ; everybody seem'd sensible of it.—Is there a charm in an hack postchaise ?—But if there were, Mrs. Craven's carriage might have undone it all.—I am much obliged to you for the time & trouble you have bestowed on Mary's cap, & am glad it pleases her ; but it will prove a useless gift at present I suppose.—Will not she leave Ibthrop on her Mother's death ?—As a companion You will be all that Martha can be supposed to want ; & in that light, under those circumstances your visit will indeed have been well-timed, & your presence & support have the utmost value.—Miss Irvine spent yesterday Evening with us, & we had a very pleasant walk to Twerton. On our return we heard with much surprise that Mr Buller had called while we were out. He left his address, & I am just returned from seeing him & his wife in their Lodgings, 7 Bath S^{t}. His Errand as you may suppose, is health. It had been often recommended to him to try Bath, but his coming now seems to have been chiefly in consequence of his sister Susan's wish that he would put himself under the care of Mr Bowen.—Having so very lately heard from Colyton & that account so tolerable, I was very much astonished—but Buller has been worse again since he wrote to me.—His Habit has always been billious, but I am afraid it must be too late for these waters to do him any good ; for tho' he is altogether in a more comfortable state as to Spirits & appetite than when I saw him last, & seems equal to a good deal of quiet walking, his appearance has exactly that of a confirmed Decline.—The Children are not come, so that poor Mrs Buller is away from all that can constitute enjoyment with her.—I shall be glad to be of any use to her, but she has that sort of quiet composedness of mind which always seems sufficient to itself.—What honour I come to!—I was interrupted by the arrival of a Lady to enquire the character of Anne, who is returned from Wales & ready for service.—And I hope I have acquitted myself pretty well; but having a very reasonable Lady to deal with, one who only required a *tolerable* temper, my office was not difficult. —Were I going to send a girl to school I would send her to this person; to be rational in anything is great praise, especially in the ignorant class of school mistresses—& she keeps the School in the upper Crescent.—Since I wrote so far, I have walked with my Mother to St James' Square & Paragon; neither family at home. I have also been with the Cookes trying to fix Mary for a walk this afternoon, but as she was on the point of taking a *long* walk with some other Lady, there is little chance of her joining us. I should like to know how far they are going; she invited me to go with them ⟨&⟩ when I excused myself as rather tired & mentioned my coming from S^t^ J⟨ames'⟩ Square, she said 'that *is* a long walk indeed'. They want us to drink te⟨a⟩ with them tonight, but I do not know whether my mother will have nerves for it.—We are engaged tomorrow Evening. What request we are in!—Mrs Chamberlayne expressed to her neice her wish of being intimate enough with us to ask us to drink tea with her in a quiet way—we have therefore offered her ourselves & our quietness thro' the same medium.—Our Tea and sugar will last a great while.—I think we are just the kind of people & party to be treated about among our relations ;—we cannot be supposed to be very rich.—The Mr Duncans called yesterday with their Sisters, but were not admitted, which rather hurt me. In the Evening we met Mr John, & I am sorry to say that he has got a very bad cold—they have all had bad colds—& he has but just caught his.—Jenny is very glad to hear of your being better, & so is Robert, with whom I left a message to that effect—as my Uncle has been very much in earnest about your recovery.—I assure you, you were looking very ill indeed, & I do not beleive much of your being looking well already. People think you in a very bad way I suppose, & pay you Compliments to keep up your Spirits.

Thursday. I was not able to go on yesterday, all my Wit & leisure were bestowed on letters to Charles & Henry. To the former I wrote in consequence of my Mother's having seen in the papers that the Urania was waiting at Portsmouth for the convoy for Halifax ;—this is nice, as it is only three weeks ago that you wrote by the Camilla.—The Wallop race seem very fond of Nova Scotia. I wrote to Henry because I had a letter from him, in which he desired to hear from me very soon. His to me was most affectionate & kind, as well as entertaining ;—there is no merit to him in *that*, he cannot help being amusing. —He expresses himself as greatly pleased with the Screen, & says that he does not know whether he is 'most delighted with the idea or the Execution '.—

Eliza of course goes halves in all this, and there is also just such a message of warm acknowledgement from her respecting the Broche as you would expect.—He mentions having sent one of Miss Gibson's Letters to Frank, by favour of Gen: Tilson, now waiting at Spithead. Would it be possible for us to do something like it, through Mr Turner's means ? I did not know before, that the Expedition were going to Frank.—One thing more Henry mentions which deserves your hearing ; he offers to meet us on the Sea-coast if the plan, of which Edward gave him some hint, takes place. Will not this be making the Execution of such a plan, more desirable & delightful than Ever.—He talks of the rambles we took together last Summer with pleasing affection.—Mrs Buller goes with us to our Chapel tomorrow ;—which I shall put down as 'Attention ye First '. I hope she will keep an account too.—My Mother's cold is not so bad today as I expected. ⟨It is che⟩ifly in her head, & she has not fever enough to affec⟨t⟩ her appetite.—C. Fowle has this moment left us. He has taken N° 20, from Michaelmas.—Y^rs^ Ever, J A.

Mary Cooke did walk with us on tuesday, & we drank tea in Alfred S^t^. But we could not keep our Engagement with Mrs Chamberlayne last night, my Mother having unluckily caught a cold which seems likely to be rather heavy.—Buller has begun the Waters, so that it will soon appear whether they can do anything for him.—

44. *To Cassandra Austen.* *Sunday* 21 *April* ⟨1805⟩

Address: Miss Austen | Ibthrop | Up. Hurstbourn | Andover
Postmark: none.
Jerome Kern (1927). Formerly in the collection described in *Times Literary Supplement* 14 Jan. 1926. 2 leaves 4°. Endorsed 'From Bath—April 1805'.
Memoir[1] 93, *Memoir*[2] 74 (extracts); *Life* 185 (extracts). A large part unpublished.

Gay St Sunday Evening, April 21st

My dear Cassandra

I am much obliged to you for writing to me again so soon; your letter yesterday was quite an unexpected pleasure. Poor Mrs Stent! it has been her lot to be always in the way; but we must be merciful, for perhaps in time we may come to be Mrs Stents ourselves, unequal to anything & unwelcome to everybody.—We shall be very glad to see you whenever you can get away, but I have no expectation of your coming before the 10th or 11th of May.—Your account of Martha is very comfortable indeed, & now we shall be in no fear of receiving a worse. This day, if she has gone to Church, must have been a trial of her feelings, but I hope it will be the last of any acuteness.—James may not be a Man of Business, but as a 'Man of Letters' he is certainly very useful; he affords you a most convenient communication with the Newbury Post.—You were very right in supposing I wore my crape sleeves to the Concert, I had them put in on the occasion; on my head I wore my crape & flowers, but I do not think it looked particularly well.—My Aunt is in a great hurry to pay me for my Cap, but cannot find in her heart to give me good money. 'If I have any intention of going to the Grand Sydney-Garden Breakfast, if there is any party I wish to join, Perrot will take out a ticket for me.' Such an offer I shall of course decline; & all the service she will render me therefore, is to put it out of my power to go at all, whatever may occur to make it desirable.—Yesterday was a busy day with me, or at least with my feet & my stockings; I was walking almost all day long; I went to Sydney Gardens soon after one, & did not return till four, & after dinner I walked to Weston.—My morning engagement was with the Cookes, & our party consisted of George & Mary, a Mr & Miss Bendish who had been with us at the Concert, & the youngest Miss Whitby;—not Julia, we have done with her, she is very ill, but Mary; Mary Whitby's turn is actually come to be grown up & have a fine complexion & wear great square muslin shawls. I have not expressly enumerated myself among the party, but there I was, & my cousin George was very kind & talked sense to me every now & then in the intervals of his more animated fooleries with Miss Bendish, who is very young & rather handsome, & whose gracious manners, ready wit, & solid remarks put me somewhat in mind of my old acquaintance Lucy Lefroy.—There was a monstrous deal of stupid quizzing, & common-place nonsense talked, but scarcely any wit;—all that border'd on it, or on sense came from my Cousin George, whom altogether I like very well.—Mr Bendish seems nothing more than a tall young man.—I met Mr F. Bonham the other day, & almost his first salutation was 'So Miss Austen your cousin is come'.—My Evening Engagement & walk was with Miss Armstrong, who had called on me the day before, & gently upbraided me in her turn with change of manners to her since she had been in Bath, or at least of late. Unlucky me! that my notice should be of such consequence & my Manners so bad! —She was so well-disposed, & so reasonable that I soon forgave her, & made this engagement with her in proof of it.—She is really an agreable girl, so I think I may like her, & her great want of a companion at home, which may well make any tolerable acquaintance important to her, gives her another claim on my attention. I shall endeavour as much as possible to keep my Intimacies in their proper place, & prevent their clashing.—I have been this morning with Miss Irvine; it is not in my power to return her evening-visits at present. I must pay her as I can.—On tuesday we are to have a party. It came into my wise head that tho' my Mother did not go out of an evening, there was no reason against her seeing her friends at home, & that it would be as well to get over the Chamberlaynes visit now, as to delay it. I accordingly invited them this morning, Mrs C. fixed on tuesday, & I rather think they will all come; the possibility of it will deter us from asking M^{r} & Mrs L. P. to meet them.—I asked Miss Irvine, but she declined it, as not feeling quite stout, & wishing to keep quiet;—but her Mother is to enliven our circle.—Bickerton has been at home for the Easter Holidays, & returns tomorrow; he is a very sweet boy, both in manner & countenance. He seems to have the attentive, affectionate feelings of Fulwar-William—who by the bye is actually fourteen—what are we to do?—I have never seen Bickerton without his immediately enquiring whether I had heard from you—from 'Miss

Cassandra ', was his expression at first.—As far as I can learn, the Family are very much pleased with Bath, & excessively overcome by the heat, or the cold, or whatever happens to be the weather.—They go on with their Masters & Mistresses, & are to have a Miss ; Amelia is to take lessons of Miss Sharpe.—Among so many friends it will be well if I do not get into a scrape ; & now here is Miss Blachford come. I should have gone distracted if the Bullers had staid. —The Cookes leave Bath next week I believe, & my Cousin goes earlier.—The papers announce the Marriage of the Rev. Edward Bather, Rector of some place in Shropshire to a Miss Emma Halifax—a wretch !—he does not deserve an Emma Halifax's maid Betty.—Mr Hampson is here ; this must interest Martha ; I met him the other morning in his way (as he said) to Green Park B^{gs} ; I trusted to his forgetting our number in Gay S^{t} when I gave it him, & so I conclude he has, as he ⟨has⟩ not yet called.—Mrs Stanhope has let her house from Midsummer, so we shall get rid of them. She is lucky in disposing of it so soon, as there is an astonishing number of Houses at this time vacant in that end of the Town.—Mrs Elliot is to quit hers at Michaelmas.—I wonder whether Mr Hampson's friend Mr Saunders is any relation to the famous Saunders whose letters have been lately published !—I am quite of your opinion as to the folly of concealing any longer our intended Partnership with Martha, & whenever there has of late been an enquiry on the subject I have always been sincere ; & I have sent word of it to the Mediterranean in a letter to Frank.—None of *our* nearest connections I think will be unprepared for it ; & I do not know how to suppose that Martha's have not foreseen it.—When I tell you that we have been visiting a Countess this morning, you will immediately with great justice, but no truth, guess it to be Lady Roden. No, it is Lady Leven, the mother of L[d] Balgonie. On receiving a message from Lord & Lady Leven thro' the Mackays declaring their intention of waiting on us, we thought it right to go to them. I hope we have not done too much, but the friends & admirers of Charles must be attended to.—They seem very reasonable, good sort of people, very civil, & full of his praise.—We were shewn at first into an empty Drawing-room, & presently in came his Lordship, not knowing who we were, to apologise for the servant's mistake, & tell a lie himself, that Lady Leven was not within.—He is a tall, gentlemanlike man, with spectacles, & rather deaf:—after sitting with him ten minutes we walked away; but Lady L. coming out of the Dining parlour as we passed the door, we were obliged to attend her back to it, & pay our visit over again.—She is a stout woman, with a very handsome face.—By this means we had the pleasure of hearing Charles's praises twice over;—they think themselves excessively obliged to him, & estimate him so highly as to wish L[d] Balgonie when he is quite recovered, to go out to him.—The young man is much better, & is gone for the confirmation of his health, to Penzance.—There is a pretty little Lady Marianne of the party, to be shaken hands with & asked if she remembers M[r] Austen.—

Monday. The Cookes' place seems of a sort to suit Isaac, if he means to go to service again, & does not object to change of Country. He will have a good soil, & a good Mistress, & I suppose will not mind taking physic now & then. The only doubt which occurs to me is whether Mr Cooke may not be a disagreable, fidgetty Master, especially in matters concerning the Garden.—Mr Mant has not yet paid my Mother the remainder of her money, but she has very lately received his apology for it, with his hope of being able to close the account shortly.—You told me some time ago that Tom Chute had had a fall from his horse, but I am waiting to know how it happened before I begin pitying him, as I cannot help suspecting it was in consequence of his taking orders; very likely as he was going to do Duty or returning from it.—

Tuesday. I have not much more to add. My Uncle & Aunt drank tea with us last night, & in spite of my resolution to the contrary, I could not help putting forward to invite them again this Evening. I thought it was of the first consequence to avoid anything that might seem a slight to them. I shall be glad when it is over, & hope to have no necessity for having so many dear friends at once again.—I shall write to Charles by the next Packet, unless you tell me in the meantime of your intending to do it. Beleive me if you chuse

Yr affecte Sister.

45. *To Cassandra Austen. Saturday* 24 *Aug.* ⟨1805⟩

Address: Miss Austen | Goodnestone Farm | Wingham | Bye Bag
Postmark: FEVERSHAM
Harvard College Library. 2 leaves 4°.
Brabourne i. 298 ; *Life* 189 (extracts).

Godmersham Park, Saturday Augst 24

My dear Cassandra

How do you do ? & how is Harriot's cold ?—I hope you are at this time sitting down to answer these questions.—Our visit to Eastwell was very agreable, I found Ly Gordon's manners as pleasing as they had been described, & saw nothing to dislike in Sir Janison, excepting once or twice a sort of sneer at Mrs Anne Finch. He was just getting into Talk with Elizth as the carriage was ordered, but during the first part of the visit he said very little.—Your going with Harriot was highly approved of by everyone ; & only too much applauded as an act of virtue on your part. I said all I could to lessen your merit.—The Mrs Finches were afraid you would find Goodnestone very dull ; I wished when I heard them say so, that they could have heard Mr E. Bridges's solicitude on the subject & have known all the amusements that were planned to prevent it.—They were very civil to me, as they always are ;—Fortune was also very civil to me in placing Mr E. Hatton by me at dinner.—I have discovered that Ly Elizth for a woman of her age & situation, has astonishingly little to say for herself, & that Miss Hatton has not much more.—Her eloquence lies in her fingers ; they were most fluently harmonious.—George is a fine boy, & well behaved, but Daniel cheifly delighted me ; the good humour

GOODNESTONE.

KENT.

of his countenance is quite bewitching. After Tea we had a cribbage Table, & he & I won two rubbers of his brother & M[rs] Mary.—M[r] Brett was the only person there besides our two families. It was considerably past eleven before we were at home, & I was so tired as to feel no envy of those who were at Ly Yates' Ball.—My good wishes for it's being a pleasant one, were I hope successful. Yesterday was a very quiet day with us; my noisiest efforts were writing to Frank, & playing at Battledore & Shuttlecock with William; he & I have practiced together two mornings, & improve a little; we have frequently kept it up *three* times, & once or twice *six*. The two Edwards went to Canterbury in the chair, & found M[rs] Knight as you found her I suppose the day before, chearful but weak.—Fanny was met walking with Miss Sharp & Miss Milles, the happiest Being in the world; she sent a private message to her Mama implying as much—'Tell Mama that I am quite Palmerstone!'—If little Lizzy used the same Language, she would I dare say send the same message from Goodnestone.—In the evening we took a quiet walk round the Farm, with George & Henry to animate us by their races & merriment.—Little Edw[d] is by no means better, & his papa & mama have determined to consult D[r] Wilmot. Unless he recovers his strength beyond what is now probable, his brothers will return to School without him, & he will be of the party to Worthing.—If Sea-Bathing should be recommended he will be left there with us, but this is not thought likely to happen.—I have been used very ill this morning, I have received a letter from Frank which I ought to have had when Eliz[th] & Henry had theirs, & which in it's way from

Albany to Godmersham has been to Dover & Steventon. It was finished on ye 16th, & tells what theirs told before as to his present situation; he is in a great hurry to be married, & I have encouraged him in it, in the letter which ought to have been an answer to his.—He must think it very strange that I do not acknowledge the receipt of his, when I speak of those of the same dates to Eliz: & Henry; & to add to my injuries I forgot to number mine on the outside.—I have found your white mittens, they were folded up within my clean nightcap, & send their duty to you.—Eliz: has this moment proposed a scheme, which will be very much for my pleasure, if equally convenient to the other party; it is that when you return on Monday, I should take your place at Goodnestone for a few days.—Harriot cannot be insincere, let her try for it ever so much, & therefore I defy her to accept this self-invitation of mine, unless it be really what perfectly suits her.—As there is no time for an answer, I shall go in the Carriage on Monday, & can return with you, if my going on to Goodnestone is at all inconvenient.—The Knatchbulls come on Wednesday to dinner, & stay only till Friday morng. at the latest.—Frank's letter to me is the only one that you or I have received since Thursday.—Mr Hall walked off this morng. to Ospringe, with no inconsiderable Booty. He charged Elizth ${}^{s}_{5}$ for every time of dressing her hair, & ${}^{s}_{5}$ for every lesson to Sace, allowing nothing for the pleasures of his visit here, for meat drink & Lodging, the benefit of Country air, & the charms of Mrs Salkeld's & Mrs Sace's society.—Towards me he was as considerate, as I had hoped for, from my relationship to you, charging me only ${}^{s}_{2}.{}^{d}_{6}$

for cutting my hair, tho' it was as thoroughly dress'd after being cut for Eastwell, as it had been for the Ashford Assembly.—He certainly respects either our Youth or our poverty.—My writing to you to day prevents Eliz^th's^ writing to Harriot, for which Evil I implore the latter's pardon.—Give my best Love to her—& kind remembrances to her Brothers.—Yours very affec^ly^

J A.

You are desired to bring back with you Henry's picture of Rowling for the Mrs Finches.

Eliz^th^ hopes you will not be later here on Monday than 5 o'clock, on Lizzy's account.—

As I find on looking into my affairs, that instead of being very rich I am likely to be very poor, I cannot afford more than ten shillings for Sackree; but as we are to meet in Canterbury I need not have mentioned this. It is as well however, to prepare you for the sight of a Sister sunk in poverty, that it may not overcome your Spirits.

We have heard nothing from Henry since he went.—Daniel told us that he went from Ospringe in one of the Coaches.

46. *To Cassandra Austen. Tuesday* 27 *Aug.* ⟨1805⟩

Address (Brabourne): Miss Austen, Edward Austen's Esq. | Godmersham Park, Faversham
Original not traced.
Brabourne i. 303; *Life* 190 (extract).

Goodnestone Farm: Tuesday August 27

My dear Cassandra

We had a very pleasant drive from Canterbury, and reached this place about half-past four, which seemed to bid fair for a punctual dinner at five ; but scenes of great agitation awaited us, and there was much to be endured and done before we could sit down to table.

Harriot found a letter from Louisa Hatton, desiring to know if she and her brothers were to be at the ball at Deal on Friday, and saying that the Eastwell family had some idea of going to it, and were to make use of Rowling if they did ; and while I was dressing she came to me with another letter in her hand, in great perplexity. It was from Captain Woodford, containing a message from Lady Forbes, which he had intended to deliver in person, but had been prevented from doing.

The offer of a ticket for this grand ball, with an invitation to come to her house at Dover before and after it, was Lady Forbes's message. Harriot was at first very little inclined, or rather totally disinclined, to profit by her ladyship's attention ; but at length, after many debates, she was persuaded by me and herself together to accept the ticket. The offer of dressing and sleeping at Dover she determined on Marianne's account to decline, and her plan is to be conveyed by Lady Elizabeth Hatton.

I hope their going is by this time certain, and will be soon known to be so. I think Miss H. would not have written such a letter if she had not been all but sure of it, and a little more. I am anxious on the subject, from the fear of being in the way if they do not come to give Harriot a conveyance. I proposed and pressed being sent home on Thursday, to prevent the possibility of being in the wrong place, but Harriot would not hear of it.

There is no chance of tickets for the Mr. Bridgeses, as no gentlemen but of the garrison are invited.

With a civil note to be fabricated to Lady F., and an answer written to Miss H., you will easily believe that we could not begin dinner till six. We were agreeably surprised by Edward Bridges's company to it. He had been, strange to tell, too late for the cricket match, too late at least to play himself, and, not being asked to dine with the players, came home. It is impossible to do justice to the hospitality of his attentions towards me; he made a point of ordering toasted cheese for supper entirely on my account.

We had a very agreeable evening, and here I am before breakfast writing to you, having got up between six and seven; Lady Brydges's room must be good for early rising.

Mr. Sankey was here last night, and found his patient better, but I have heard from a maidservant that she has had but an indifferent night.

Tell Elizabeth that I did not give her letter to Harriot till we were in the carriage, when she received it with great delight, and could read it in comfort.

As you have been here so lately, I need not particularly describe the house or style of living, in which all seems for use and comfort; nor need I be diffuse on the state of Lady Brydges's bookcase and corner-shelves upstairs. What a treat to my mother to arrange them!

Harriot is constrained to give up all hope of seeing Edward here to fetch me, as I soon recollected that Mr. and Mrs. Charles Knatchbull's being at Godmersham on Thursday must put it out of the question.

Had I waited till after breakfast, the chief of all

this might have been spared. The Duke of Gloucester's death sets my heart at ease, though it will cause some dozens to ache. Harriot's is not among the number of the last ; she is very well pleased to be spared the trouble of preparation. She joins me in best love to you all, and will write to Elizabeth soon. I shall be very glad to hear from you, that we may know how you all are, especially the two Edwards.

I have asked Sophie if she has anything to say to Lizzy in acknowledgment of the little bird, and her message is that, with her love, she is very glad Lizzy sent it. She volunteers, moreover, her love to little Marianne, with the promise of bringing her a doll the next time she goes to Godmersham.

John is just come from Ramsgate, and brings a good account of the people there. He and his brother, you know, dine at Nackington ; we are to dine at four, that we may walk afterwards. As it is now two, and Harriot has letters to write, we shall probably not get out before.

Yours affectionately,

J. A.

Three o'clock.—Harriot is just come from Marianne, and thinks her upon the whole better. The sickness has not returned, and a headache is at present her chief complaint, which Henry attributes to the sickness.

47. *To Cassandra Austen.* *Friday* 30 *Aug.* ⟨1805⟩

Address (Brabourne): Miss Austen, Edward Austen's Esq. | Godmersham Park, Faversham
Original not traced.
Brabourne i. 307 ; *Life* 191 (extract).

Goodnestone Farm : Friday August 30

My dear Cassandra

I have determined on staying here till Monday. Not that there is any occasion for it on Marianne's account, as she is now almost as well as usual, but Harriot is so kind in her wishes for my company that I could not resolve on leaving her to-morrow, especially as I had no reason to give for its necessity. It would be inconvenient to me to stay with her longer than the beginning of next week, on account of my clothes, and therefore I trust it will suit Edward to fetch or send for me on Monday, or Tuesday if Monday should be wet. Harriot has this moment desired me to propose his coming hither on Monday, and taking me back the next day.

The purport of Elizabeth's letter makes me anxious to hear more of what we are to do and not to do, and I hope you will be able to write me your own plans and opinions to-morrow. The journey to London is a point of the first expediency, and I am glad it is resolved on, though it seems likely to injure our Worthing scheme. I expect that *we* are to be at Sandling, while *they* are in town.

It gives us great pleasure to hear of little Edward's being better, and we imagine, from his mama's expressions, that he is expected to be well enough to return to school with his brothers.

Marianne was equal to seeing me two days ago; we sat with her for a couple of hours before dinner, and the same yesterday, when she was evidently better, more equal to conversation, and more cheerful than during our first visit. She received me very kindly, and expressed her regret in not having been able to see you.

She is, of course, altered since we saw her in October, 1794. Eleven years could not pass away even in health without making some change, but in her case it is wonderful that the change should be so little. I have not seen her to advantage, as I understand she has frequently a nice colour, and her complexion has not yet recovered from the effects of her late illness. Her face is grown longer and thinner, and her features more marked, and the likeness which I remember to have always seen between her and Catherine Bigg is stronger than ever, and so striking is the voice and manner of speaking that I seem to be really hearing Catherine, and once or twice have been on the point of calling Harriot 'Alethea.' She is very pleasant, cheerful, and interested in everything about her, and at the same time shows a thoughtful, considerate, and decided turn of mind.

Edward Bridges dined at home yesterday; the day before he was at St. Albans; to-day he goes to Broome, and to-morrow to Mr. Hallett's, which latter engagement has had some weight in my resolution of not leaving Harriot till Monday.

We have walked to Rowling on each of the two last days after dinner, and very great was my pleasure in going over the house and grounds. We have also found time to visit all the principal walks of this place,

W. Watts del. et Sculp.

GODMERSHAM PARK in Kent, the Seat of THOMAS KNIGHT ESQ.[r]

except the walk round the top of the park, which we shall accomplish probably to-day.

Next week seems likely to be an unpleasant one to this family on the matter of game. The evil intentions of the Guards are certain, and the gentlemen of the neighbourhood seem unwilling to come forward in any decided or early support of their rights. Edward Bridges has been trying to arouse their spirits, but without success. Mr. Hammond, under the influence of daughters and an expected ball, declares he will do nothing.

Harriot hopes my brother will not mortify her by resisting all her plans and refusing all her invitations ; she has never yet been successful with him in any, but she trusts he will now make her all the amends in his power by coming on Monday. She thanks Elizabeth for her letter, and you may be sure is not less solicitous than myself for her going to town.

Pray say everything kind for us to Miss Sharpe, who could not regret the shortness of our meeting in Canterbury more than we did. I hope she returned to Godmersham as much pleased with Mrs. Knight's beauty and Miss Milles's judicious remarks as those ladies respectively were with hers. You must send me word that you have heard from Miss Irvine.

I had almost forgot to thank you for your letter. I am glad you recommended 'Gisborne,' for having begun, I am pleased with it, and I had quite determined not to read it.

I suppose everybody will be black for the D. of G. Must we buy lace, or will ribbon do ?

We shall not be at Worthing so soon as we have been used to talk of, shall we ? This will be no evil to us, and we are sure of my mother and Martha being happy together. Do not forget to write to Charles. As I am to return so soon, we shall not send the pincushions.

Yours affectionately, J. A.

You continue, I suppose, taking hartshorn, and I hope with good effect.

48. *To Cassandra Austen. Wednesday* 7 *Jan.* ⟨1807⟩

Address (Brabourne): Miss Austen, Godmersham Park, | Faversham, Kent
Original not traced.
Brabourne i. 312 ; *Life* 198 (extracts).

Southampton : Wednesday January 7

My dear Cassandra

You were mistaken in supposing I should expect your letter on Sunday ; I had no idea of hearing from you before Tuesday, and my pleasure yesterday was therefore unhurt by any previous disappointment. I thank you for writing so much ; you must really have sent me the value of two letters in one. We are extremely glad to hear that Elizabeth is so much better, and hope you will be sensible of still further amendment in her when you return from Canterbury.

Of your visit there I must now speak 'incessantly ;' it surprises, but pleases me more, and I consider it as a very just and honourable distinction of you, and not less to the credit of Mrs. Knight. I have no doubt of your spending your time with her most pleasantly in quiet and rational conversation, and am so far from thinking her expectations of you will be deceived, that my only fear is of your being so agreeable, so much to her taste, as to make her wish to keep you with her for ever. If that should be the case, we must remove to Canterbury, which I should not like so well as Southampton.

When you receive this, our guests will be all gone or going; and I shall be left to the comfortable disposal of my time, to ease of mind from the torments of rice puddings and apple dumplings, and probably to regret that I did not take more pains to please them all.

Mrs. J. Austen has asked me to return with her to Steventon; I need not give my answer; and she has invited my mother to spend there the time of Mrs. F. A.'s confinement, which she seems half inclined to do.

A few days ago I had a letter from Miss Irvine, and as I was in her debt, you will guess it to be a remonstrance, not a very severe one, however; the first page is in her usual retrospective, jealous, inconsistent style, but the remainder is chatty and harmless. She supposes my silence may have proceeded from resentment of her not having written to inquire particularly after my hooping cough, &c. She is a funny one.

I have answered her letter, and have endeavoured to give something like the truth with as little incivility as I could, by placing my silence to the want of subject in the very quiet way in which we live. Phebe has repented, and stays. I have also written to Charles, and I answered Miss Buller's letter by return of post, as I intended to tell you in my last.

Two or three things I recollected when it was too late, that I might have told you; one is, that the Welbys have lost their eldest son by a putrid fever at Eton, and another that Tom Chute is going to settle in Norfolk.

You have scarcely ever mentioned Lizzy since your being at Godmersham. I hope it is not because she is altered for the worse.

I cannot yet satisfy Fanny as to Mrs. Foote's baby's name, and I must not encourage her to expect a good one, as Captain Foote is a professed adversary to all but the plainest; he likes only Mary, Elizabeth, Anne, &c. Our best chance is of 'Caroline,' which in compliment to a sister seems the only exception.

He dined with us on Friday, and I fear will not soon venture again, for the strength of our dinner was a boiled leg of mutton, underdone even for James; and Captain Foote has a particular dislike to underdone mutton; but he was so good-humoured and pleasant that I did not much mind his being starved. He gives us all the most cordial invitation to his house in the country, saying just what the Williams ought to say to make us welcome. Of them we have seen nothing since you left us, and we hear that they are just gone to Bath again, to be out of the way of further alterations at Brooklands.

Mrs. F. A. has had a very agreeable letter from Mrs. Dickson, who was delighted with the purse, and desires her not to provide herself with a christening dress, which is exactly what her young correspondent wanted; and she means to defer making any of the caps as long as she can, in hope of having Mrs. D.'s present in time to be serviceable as a pattern. She desires me to tell you that the gowns were cut out before your letter arrived, but that they are long enough for Caroline. The *Beds*, as I believe they are called, have fallen to Frank's share to continue, and of course are cut out to admiration.

'Alphonsine' did not do. We were disgusted in twenty pages, as, independent of a bad translation, it has indelicacies which disgrace a pen hitherto so pure; and we changed it for the 'Female Quixotte,' which now makes our evening amusement; to me a very high one, as I find the work quite equal to what I remembered it. Mrs. F. A., to whom it is new, enjoys it as one could wish; the other Mary, I believe, has little pleasure from that or any other book.

My mother does not seem at all more disappointed than ourselves at the termination of the family treaty; she thinks less of *that* just now than of the comfortable state of her own finances, which she finds on closing her year's accounts beyond her expectation, as she begins the new year with a balance of 30*l.* in her favour; and when she has written her answer to my aunt, which you know always hangs a little upon her mind, she will be above the world entirely. You will have a great deal of unreserved discourse with Mrs. K., I dare say, upon this subject, as well as upon many other of our family matters. Abuse everybody but me.

Thursday.—We expected James yesterday, but he did not come; if he comes at all now, his visit will be a very short one, as he must return to-morrow, that Ajax and the chair may be sent to Winchester on Saturday. Caroline's new pelisse depended upon her mother's being able or not to come so far in the chair; how the guinea that will be saved by the same means of return is to be spent I know not. Mrs. J. A. does not talk much of poverty now, though she has no hope of my brother's being able to buy another horse *next* summer.

Their scheme against Warwickshire continues, but

I doubt the family's being at Stoneleigh so early as James says he must go, which is May.

My mother is afraid I have not been explicit enough on the subject of her wealth; she began 1806 with 68*l.*, she begins 1807 with 99*l.*, and this after 32*l.* purchase of stock. Frank too has been settling his accounts and making calculations, and each party feels quite equal to our present expenses; but much increase of house-rent would not do for either. Frank limits himself, I believe, to four hundred a year.

You will be surprised to hear that Jenny is not yet come back; we have heard nothing of her since her reaching Itchingswell, and can only suppose that she must be detained by illness in somebody or other, and that she has been each day expecting to be able to come on the morrow. I am glad I did not know beforehand that she was to be absent during the whole or almost the whole of our friends being with us, for though the inconvenience has not been nothing, I should have feared still more. Our dinners have certainly suffered not a little by having only Molly's head and Molly's hands to conduct them; she fries better than she did, but not like Jenny.

We did *not* take our walk on Friday, it was too dirty, nor have we yet done it; we may perhaps do something like it to-day, as after seeing Frank skate, which he hopes to do in the meadows by the beech, we are to treat ourselves with a passage over the ferry. It is one of the pleasantest frosts I ever knew, so very quiet. I hope it will last some time longer for Frank's sake, who is quite anxious to get some skating; he tried yesterday, but it would not do.

Our acquaintance increase too fast. He was recognised lately by Admiral Bertie, and a few days since arrived the Admiral and his daughter Catherine to wait upon us. There was nothing to like or dislike in either. To the Berties are to be added the Lances, with whose cards we have been endowed, and whose visit Frank and I returned yesterday. They live about a mile and three-quarters from S. to the right of the new road to Portsmouth, and I believe their house is one of those which are to be seen almost anywhere among the woods on the other side of the Itchen. It is a handsome building, stands high, and in a very beautiful situation.

We found only Mrs. Lance at home, and whether she boasts any offspring besides a grand pianoforte did not appear. She was civil and chatty enough, and offered to introduce us to some acquaintance in Southampton, which we gratefully declined.

I suppose they must be acting by the orders of Mr. Lance of Netherton in this civility, as there seems no other reason for their coming near us. They will not come often, I dare say. They live in a handsome style and are rich, and she seemed to like to be rich, and we gave her to understand that we were far from being so; she will soon feel therefore that we are not worth her acquaintance.

You must have heard from Martha by this time. We have had no accounts of Kintbury since her letter to me.

Mrs. F. A. has had one fainting fit lately; it came on as usual after eating a hearty dinner, but did not last long.

I can recollect nothing more to say. When my letter is gone, I suppose I shall.

Yours affectionately, J. A.

I have just asked Caroline if I should send her love to her godmama, to which she answered 'Yes.'

49. *To Cassandra Austen.* ⟨*Sunday*⟩ 8 *Feb.* 1807

Address: Miss Austen | Godmersham Park | Faversham | Kent
Postmarks: SOUTHAMPTON and FEB 10 1807
Pierpont Morgan Library. 2 leaves 4°.
Brabourne i. 320; *Life* 199 (extracts). A few lines unpublished.

Southampton Feb. 8th

My dearest Cassandra

My expectation of having nothing to say to you after the conclusion of my last, seems nearer Truth than I thought it would be, for I feel to have but little. I need not therefore be above acknowledging the receipt of yours this morng; or of replying to every part of it which is capable of an answer; & you may accordingly prepare for my ringing the Changes of the Glads & Sorrys for the rest of the page.—Unluckily however I see nothing to be glad of, unless I make it a matter of Joy that Mrs. Wylmot has another son, & that Ld Lucan has taken a Mistress, both of which Events are of course joyful to the Actors;—but to be sorry I find many occasions, the first is that your return is to be delayed, & whether I ever get beyond the first is doubtful. It is no use to lament.—I never heard that even Queen Mary's Lamentation did her any good, & I could not therefore expect benefit from mine.—We are all sorry, & now that subject is exhausted. I heard from Martha yesterday: she spends this week with the Harwoods, goes afterwards with James & Mary for a few days to see Peter Debary & two of his sisters at Eversley—the Living of which he has gained on the death of Sir R. Cope—& means to be here on ye 24th, which will be Tuesday fortnight. I shall be truely glad if she can keep to her day, but dare not depend on it;—& am so apprehensive of farther detention that, if nothing else occurs to create it, I cannot help thinking she will marry Peter Debary.—It vexed me that I could not get any fish for Kintbury while their family was large; but so it was, & till last Tuesday I could procure none. I then sent them four pair of small soals, & should be glad to be certain of their arriving in good time, but I have heard nothing about them since, & had rather hear nothing than Evil.—They cost six shillings, & as they travelled in a Basket which came from Kintbury a few days before with Poultry &c, I insist upon treating you with the Booking *whatever it may be*, You are only Eighteen pence in my debt.—Mrs. E. Leigh did not make the slightest allusion to my Uncle's Business, as I remember telling you at the time, but you shall have it as often as you like. My Mother wrote to her a week ago.—Martha's rug is just finished, & looks well, tho' not quite so well as I had hoped. I see no fault in the Border, but the Middle is dingy.— My Mother desires me to say that she will knit one for you, as soon as you return to chuse the colours & pattern. I am sorry I have affronted you on the subject of Mr. Moore, but I do not mean ever to like him; & as to pitying a young woman merely because she cannot live in two places at the same time, & at once enjoy the comforts of being married & single, I shall not attempt it, even for Harriet.—You see I have a spirit, as well as yourself. Frank & Mary cannot at all approve of your not being at home in time to help them in their finishing purchases, & desire me to say that, if you are not, they shall be as spiteful as possible & chuse everything in the stile most likely to vex you, knives that will not cut, glasses that will not hold, a sofa without a seat, & a Bookcase without shelves.—Our Garden is putting in order, by a Man who bears a remarkably good character, has a very fine complexion & asks something less than the first. The shrubs which border the gravel walk he says are only sweetbriar & roses, & the latter of an indifferent sort;—we mean to get a few of a better kind therefore, & at my own particular desire he procures us some Syringas. I could not do without a Syringa, for the sake of Cowper's Line.—We talk also of a Laburnam.—The Border under the Terrace Wall, is clearing away to receive Currants & Gooseberry Bushes, & a spot is found very proper for raspberries.—The alterations & improvements within doors too advance very properly, & the offices will be made very convenient indeed.—Our Dressing-Table is constructing on the spot, out of a large Kitchen Table belonging to the House, for doing which we have the permission of Mr. Husket Lord Lansdown's Painter,—domestic Painter I sh^d^ call him, for he lives in the Castle.—Domestic Chaplains have given way to this more necessary office, & I suppose whenever the Walls want no touching up, he is employed about my Lady's face.—The morning was so wet that I was afraid we should not be able to see our little visitor, but Frank who alone could go to Church called for her after service, & she is now talking away at my side & examining the Treasures of my Writing-desk drawer;—very happy I beleive;—not at all shy of course.—Her name is Catherine & her Sister's Caroline.—She is something like her Brother, & as short for her age, but not so well-looking.—What is become of all the Shyness in the World ?—Moral as well as Natural Diseases disappear in the progress of time, & new ones take their place.—Shyness & the Sweating Sickness have given way to Confidence & Paralytic complaints.—I am sorry to hear of Mrs. Whitfield's encreasing Illness, & of poor Marianne Bridges's having suffered so much; —these are some of my sorrows,—& that Mrs. Deedes is to have another Child I suppose I may lament.—The death of Mrs. W. K. we had seen;—I had no idea that anybody liked her, & therefore felt nothing for any Survivor, but I am now feeling away on her Husband's account, and think he had better marry Miss Sharpe.—I have this instant made my present, & have the pleasure of seeing it smiled over with genuine satisfaction. I am sure I may on this occasion call Kitty Foote, as Hastings did H. Egerton, my 'very valuable Friend.'—*Even*^g^.—Our little visitor has just left us, & left us highly pleased with her;—she is a nice, natural, openhearted, affectionate girl, with all the ready civility which one sees in the best Children in the present day;—so unlike anything that I was myself at her age, that I am often all astonishment & shame.—Half her time here was spent at Spillikins, which I consider as a very valuable part of our Household furniture, & as not the least important Benefaction from the family of Knight to that of Austen.—But I must tell you a story. Mary has for some time had notice from Mrs. Dickson of the intended arrival of a certain Miss Fowler in this place; —Miss F. is an intimate friend of Mrs. D. & a good deal known as such to Mary.—On Thursday last she called here while we were out;—Mary found on our return her card with only her name on it, & she had left word that she w[d] call again.—The particularity of this made us talk, & among other conjectures Frank said in joke 'I dare say she is staying with the Pearsons.'—The connection of the names struck Mary, & she immediately recollected Miss Fowler's having been very intimate with persons so called ;—and upon putting everything together we have scarcely a doubt of her being actually staying with the only Family in the place whom we cannot visit.—What a Contretems !—in the Language of France ; What an unluckiness ! in that of M[de] Duval :—The Black Gentleman has certainly employed one of his menial imps to bring about this complete tho' trifling mischeif.—Miss F. has never called again, but we are in daily expectation of it.—Miss P. has of course given her a proper understanding of the Business ;—it is evident that Miss F. did not expect or wish to have the visit returned, & Frank is quite as much on his guard for his wife as we c[d] desire for her sake or our own.—We shall rejoice in being so near Winchester when Edward belongs to it, & can never have our spare bed filled more to our satisfaction than by him. Does he leave Eltham at Easter ?—We are reading Clarentine, & are surprised to find how foolish it is. I remember liking it much less on a 2[d] reading than at the 1st & it does not bear a 3[d] at all. It is full of unnatural conduct & forced difficulties, without striking merit of any kind.—

Miss Harrison is going into Devonshire to attend Mrs. Dusautoy as usual.—Miss Jackson is married to young Mr. Gunthorpe, & is to be very unhappy. He swears, drinks, is cross, jealous, selfish & Brutal ;—the match makes *her* family miserable, & has occasioned *his* being disinherited.—The Browns are added to our list of acquaintance ; He commands the Sea Fencibles here under Sir Tho. & was introduced at his own desire by the latter when we saw him last week.—As yet the Gentlemen only have visited, as Mrs. B. is ill, but she is a nice looking woman & wears one of the prettiest straw Bonnets in the place.—*Monday.* The Garret-beds are made, & ours will be finished today. I had hoped it w^d be finished on Saturday, but neither Mrs. Hall nor Jenny were able to give help enough for that ; & I have as yet done very little & Mary nothing at all. This week we shall do more, & I sh^d like to have all the 5 Beds completed by the end of it.—There will then be the Window-Curtains, sofa-cover, & a carpet to be altered. I should not be surprised if we were to be visited by James again this week ; he gave us reason to expect him soon ; & if they go to Eversley he cannot come next week.—

I am sorry & angry that his Visits should not give one more pleasure ; the company of so good & so clever a Man ought to be gratifying in itself ;—but his Chat seems all forced, his Opinions on many points too much copied from his Wife's, & his time here is spent I think in walking about the House & banging the doors, or ringing the bell for a glass of water.—

There, I flatter myself I have constructed you a smartish Letter, considering my want of Materials. But like my dear Dr. Johnson I beleive I have dealt more in Notions than Facts.—

I hope your Cough is gone & that you are otherwise well.—And remain with Love,

Y^{rs} $affec^{tely}$ J. A.

50. *To Cassandra Austen.* *Friday* 20 *Feb.* 1807

Address : Miss Austen | Godmersham Park | Faversham | Kent
Postmarks : SOUTHAMPTON and FEB 23 1807
R. B. Adam. 2 leaves 4°.
Brabourne i. 329 ; *Life* 201 (extracts).

Southampton Friday Feby 20th

My dear Cassandra

We have at last heard something of Mr Austen's Will. It is beleived at Tunbridge that he has left everything after the death of his widow to Mr. M^y^ Austen's 3^d^ son John ; & as the said John was the only one of the Family who attended the Funeral, it seems likely to be true.—Such ill-gotten wealth can never prosper !—I really have very little to say *this* week, & do not feel as if I should spread that little into the shew of much. I am inclined for short sentences.—Mary will be obliged to you to take notice how often Eliz^th^ nurses her Baby in the course of the 24 hours, how often it is fed & with what ;—you need not trouble yourself to *write* the result of your observations, your return will be early enough for the communication of them.—You are recommended to bring away some flower-seeds from Godmersham, particularly Mignionette seed.—My Mother has heard this morn^g^ from Paragon. My Aunt talks much of the violent colds prevailing in Bath, from which my Uncle has suffered ever since their return, & she has herself a cough much worse than any she ever had before, subject as she has always been to bad ones.—She writes in good humour & chearful spirits however. The negociation between them & Adlestrop so happily over indeed, what can have power to vex her materially ?

—Elliston, she tells us has just succeeded to a considerable fortune on the death of an Uncle. I would not have it enough to take *him* from the Stage; *she* should quit her business, & live with him in London.—We could not pay our visit on Monday, the weather altered just too soon; & we have since had a touch of almost everything in the weather way;—two of the severest frosts since the winter began, preceded by rain, hail & snow.—Now we are smiling again.

Saturday.—I have received your letter, but I suppose you do not expect me to be gratified by it's contents. I confess myself much disappointed by this repeated delay of your return, for tho' I had pretty well given up all idea of your being with us before our removal, I felt sure that March would not pass quite away without bringing you. Before April comes, of course something else will occur to detain you. But as *you* are happy, all this is selfishness, of which here is enough for one page.—Pray tell Lizzy that if I had imagined her Teeth to be really out, I should have said before what I say now, that it was a very unlucky fall indeed, that I am afraid it must have given her a great deal of pain, & that I dare say her Mouth looks very comical.—I am obliged to Fanny for the list of Mrs. Coleman's Children, whose names I had not however quite forgot; the new one I am sure will be Caroline.—I have got Mr. Bowen's Recipe for you, it came in my aunt's letter.—You must have had more snow at G^{m}, than we had here;—on Wednesday morn^{g} there was a thin covering of it over the fields & roofs of the Houses, but I do not think there was any left the next day. Everybody used to Southampton says that Snow never lies more than 24 hours near it, & from what we have observed ourselves, it is very true.—Frank's going into Kent depends of course upon his being unemployed, but as the 1st Lord after promising L[d] Moira that Capt. A. should have the first good Frigate that was vacant, has since given away two or three fine ones, he has no particular reason to expect an appointment now.—*He* however has scarcely spoken about the Kentish Journey; I have my information cheifly from her, & she considers her own going thither as more certain if he sh[d] be at sea, than if not.—Frank has got a very bad cough, for an Austen;—but it does not disable him from making very nice fringe for the Drawingroom-Curtains.—Mrs. Day has now got the Carpet in hand, & Monday I hope will be the last day of her employment here. A fortnight afterwards she is to be called again from the shades of her red-check'd bed in an alley near the end of the High Street to clean the new House & air the Bedding.—We hear that we are envied our House by many people, & that the Garden is the best in the Town.—There will be green baize enough for Martha's room & ours;—not to cover them, but to lie over the part where it is most wanted, under the Dressing Table. Mary is to have a peice of carpetting for the same purpose; my Mother says *she* does not want any;—& it may certainly be better done without in her room than in Martha's & ours, from the difference of their aspect.—I recommend M[rs] Grant's Letters, as a present to the latter;—what they are about, nor how many volumes they form I do not know, having never heard of them but from Miss Irvine, who speaks of them as a new & much admired work, & as one which has pleased her highly.—I have enquired for the book here, but find it quite unknown. I beleive *I* put five breadths of Linon also into my flounce ; I know I found it wanted more than I had expected, & that I sh[d] have been distressed if I had not bought more than I beleived myself to need, for the sake of the even Measure, on which we think so differently.—A light morn[g] gown will be a very necessary purchase for you, & I wish you a pretty one. I shall buy such things whenever I am tempted, but as yet there is nothing of the sort to be seen.—We are reading Barretti's other book, & find him dreadfully abusive of poor M[r] Sharpe. I can no longer take his part against you, as I did nine years ago.—*Sunday*.—This post has brought me Martha's own assurance of her coming on tuesday even[g] which nothing is now to prevent except William should send her word that there is no *remedy* on that day.—Her letter was put into the post at Basingstoke on their return from Eversley, where she says they have spent their time very pleasantly ; she does not own herself in any danger of being tempted back again however, & as she signs by her maiden name we are at least to suppose her not married yet.—They must have had a cold visit, but as she found it agreable I suppose there was no want of Blankets, and we may trust to her Sister's taking care that her love of many should be known.—She sends me no particulars, having time only to write the needful.—

I wish You a pleasant party tomorrow, & not more than you like of Miss Hatton's neck.—Lady B. must have been a shameless woman if she named H. Hales as within her Husband's reach. It is a peice of impertinence indeed in a Woman to pretend to fix on any one, as if she supposed it c[d] be only ask & have. A Widower with 3 children has no right to look higher than his daughter's Governess.—I am forced to be abusive for want of subject, having really nothing to say.—When Martha comes, she will supply me with matter; I shall have to tell you how she likes the House & what she thinks of Mary.—You must be very cold today at G[m].—We are cold here. I expect a severe March, a wet April, & a sharp May.—And with this prophecy I must conclude.—My love to everybody,—Y[rs] affec[tely] J Austen

51. *To Cassandra Austen.* *Wednesday* 15 *June* ⟨1808⟩

Address *(Brabourne)*: **Miss Austen, Castle Square, Southampton**
Original not traced.
***Brabourne* i. 341; *Life* 204 (extracts).**

Godmersham: Wednesday June 15

My dear Cassandra

Where shall I begin? Which of all my important nothings shall I tell you first? At half after seven yesterday morning Henry saw us into our own carriage, and we drove away from the Bath Hotel; which, by-the-bye, had been found most uncomfortable quarters—very dirty, very noisy, and very ill-provided. James began his journey by the coach at five. Our first eight miles were hot; Deptford Hill brought to my mind our hot journey into Kent fourteen years ago; but after Blackheath we suffered nothing, and as the day advanced it grew quite cool. At Dartford, which we reached within the two hours and three-quarters, we went to the Bull, the same inn at which we breakfasted in that said journey, and on the present occasion had about the same bad butter.

At half-past ten we were again off, and, travelling on without any adventure reached Sittingbourne by three. Daniel was watching for us at the door of the George, and I was acknowledged very kindly by Mr. and Mrs. Marshall, to the latter of whom I devoted my conversation, while Mary went out to buy some gloves. A few minutes, of course, did for Sittingbourne; and so off we drove, drove, drove, and by six o'clock were at Godmersham.

Our two brothers were walking before the house as we approached, as natural as life. Fanny and Lizzy met us in the Hall with a great deal of pleasant joy; we went for a few minutes into the breakfast parlour, and then proceeded to our rooms. Mary has the Hall chamber. I am in the Yellow room—very literally—for I am writing in it at this moment. It seems odd to me to have such a great place all to myself, and to be at Godmersham without you is also odd.

You are wished for, I assure you: Fanny, who came to me as soon as she had seen her Aunt James to her room, and stayed while I dressed, was as energetic as usual in her longings for you. She is grown both in height and size since last year, but not immoderately, looks very well, and seems as to conduct and manner just what she was and what one could wish her to continue.

Elizabeth, who was dressing when we arrived, came to me for a minute attended by Marianne, Charles, and Louisa, and, you will not doubt, gave me a very affectionate welcome. That I had received such from Edward also I need not mention; but I do, you see, because it is a pleasure. I never saw him look in better health, and Fanny says he is perfectly well.

I cannot praise Elizabeth's looks, but they are probably affected by a cold. Her little namesake has gained in beauty in the last three years, though not all that Marianne has lost. Charles is not quite so lovely as he was. Louisa is much as I expected, and Cassandra I find handsomer than I expected, though at present disguised by such a violent breaking-out that she does not come down after dinner. She has charming eyes and a nice open countenance, and seems likely to be very lovable. Her size is magnificent.

I was agreeably surprised to find Louisa Bridges still here. She looks remarkably well (legacies are very wholesome diet), and is just what she always was. John is at Sandling. You may fancy our dinner party therefore; Fanny, of course, belonging to it, and little Edward, for that day. He was almost too happy, his happiness at least made him too talkative.

It has struck ten; I must go to breakfast.

Since breakfast I have had a *tête-à-tête* with Edward in his room; he wanted to know James's plans and mine, and from what his own now are I think it already nearly certain that I shall return when they do, though not with them. Edward will be going about the same time to Alton, where he has business with Mr. Trimmer, and where he means his son should join him; and I shall probably be his companion to that place, and get on afterwards somehow or other.

I should have preferred a rather longer stay here certainly, but there is no prospect of any later conveyance for me, as he does not mean to accompany Edward on his return to Winchester, from a very natural unwillingness to leave Elizabeth at that time. I shall at any rate be glad not to be obliged to be an incumbrance on those who have brought me here, for, as James has no horse, I must feel in their carriage that I am taking his place. We were rather crowded yesterday, though it does not become me to say so, as I and my boa were of the party, and it is not to be supposed but that a child of three years of age was fidgety.

I need scarcely beg you to keep all this to yourself, lest it should get round by Anna's means. She is very kindly inquired after by her friends here, who all regret her not coming with her father and mother.

I left Henry, I hope, free from his tiresome complaint, in other respects well, and thinking with great pleasure of Cheltenham and Stoneleigh.

The brewery scheme is quite at an end : at a meeting of the subscribers last week it was by general, and I believe very hearty, consent dissolved.

The country is very beautiful. I saw as much as ever to admire in my yesterday's journey.

Thursday.—I am glad to find that Anna was pleased with going to Southampton, and hope with all my heart that the visit may be satisfactory to everybody. Tell her that she will hear in a few days from her mamma, who would have written to her now but for this letter.

Yesterday passed quite *à la* Godmersham : the gentlemen rode about Edward's farm, and returned in time to saunter along Bentigh with us ; and after dinner we visited the Temple Plantations, which, to be sure, is a Chevalier Bayard of a plantation. James and Mary are much struck with the beauty of the place. To-day the spirit of the thing is kept up by the two brothers being gone to Canterbury in the chair.

I cannot discover, even through Fanny, that her mother is fatigued by her attendance on the children. I have, of course, tendered my services, and when Louisa is gone, who sometimes hears the little girls read, will try to be accepted in her stead. She will not be here many days longer. The Moores are partly expected to dine here to-morrow or Saturday.

I feel rather languid and solitary—perhaps because I have a cold; but three years ago we were more animated with you and Harriot and Miss Sharpe. We shall improve, I dare say, as we go on.

I have not yet told you how the new carriage is liked—very well, very much indeed, except the lining, which does look rather shabby.

I hear a very bad account of Mrs. Whitefield; a very good one of Mrs. Knight, who goes to Broadstairs next month. Miss Sharpe is going with Miss Bailey to Tenby. The Widow Kennet succeeds to the post of laundress.

Would you believe it my trunk is come already; and, what completes the wondrous happiness, nothing is damaged. I unpacked it all before I went to bed last night, and when I went down to breakfast this morning presented the rug, which was received most gratefully, and met with universal admiration. My frock is also given, and kindly accepted.

Friday.—I have received your letter, and I think it gives me nothing to be sorry for but Mary's cold, which I hope is by this time better. Her approbation of her child's hat makes me very happy. Mrs. J. A. bought one at Gayleard's for Caroline, of the same shape, but brown and with a feather.

I hope Huxham is a comfort to you; I am glad you

are taking it. I shall probably have an opportunity of giving Harriot your message to-morrow ; she does not come here, they have not a day to spare, but Louisa and I are to go to her in the morning. I send your thanks to Eliza by this post in a letter to Henry.

Lady Catherine is Lord Portmore's daughter. I have read Mr. Jefferson's case to Edward, and he desires to have his name set down for a guinea and his wife's for another ; but does not wish for more than one copy of the work. Your account of Anna gives me pleasure. Tell her, with my love, that I like her for liking the quay. Mrs. J. A. seems rather surprised at the Maitlands drinking tea with you, but that does not prevent my approving it. I hope you had not a disagreeable evening with Miss Austen and her niece. You know how interesting the purchase of a sponge-cake is to me.

I am now just returned from Eggerton ; Louisa and I walked together and found Miss Maria at home. Her sister we met on our way back. *She* had been to pay her compliments to Mrs. Inman, whose chaise was seen to cross the park while we were at dinner yesterday.

I told Sackree that you desired to be remembered to her, which pleased her ; and she sends her duty, and wishes you to know that she has been into the great world. She went on to town after taking William to Eltham, and, as well as myself, saw the ladies go to Court on the 4th. She had the advantage indeed of me in being in the Palace.

Louisa is not so handsome as I expected, but she is not quite well. Edward and Caroline seem very happy here ; he has nice playfellows in Lizzy and

Charles. They and their attendant have the boys' attic. Anna will not be surprised that the cutting off her hair is very much regretted by several of the party in this house ; I am tolerably reconciled to it by considering that two or three years may restore it again.

You are very important with your Captain Bulmore and Hotel Master, and I trust, if your trouble overbalances your dignity on the occasion, it will be amply repaid by Mrs. Craven's approbation, and a pleasant scheme to see her.

Mrs. Cooke has written to my brother James to invite him and his wife to Bookham in their way back, which, as I learn through Edward's means, they are not disinclined to accept, but that my being with them would render it impracticable, the nature of the road affording no conveyance to James. I shall therefore make them easy on that head as soon as I can.

I have a great deal of love to give from everybody.

Yours most affectionately, Jane

My mother will be glad to be assured that the size of the rug does perfectly well. It is not to be used till winter.

52. *To Cassandra Austen. Monday* 20 *June* 1808

Address : Miss Austen | Castle Square | Southampton
Postmarks : FEVERSHAM and JUN 23 1808
Pierpont Morgan Library. 2 leaves 4°.
Brabourne i. 350 ; *Life* 206 (extracts).

Godmersham Monday June 20th.

My dear Cassandra

I will first talk of my visit to Canterbury, as Mrs. J. A.'s letter to Anna cannot have given you every

A NEAR VIEW of SOUTHAMPTON, IN 1819.

particular of it, which you are likely to wish for.—I had a most affectionate welcome from Harriot & was happy to see her looking almost as well as ever. She walked with me to call on Mrs. Brydges, when Eliz[th] & Louisa went to Mrs. Milles' ;—Mrs. B. was dressing & c[d] not see us, & we proceeded to the White Friars, where Mrs. K. was alone in her Drawing room, as gentle & kind & friendly as usual.—She enquired after every body, especially my Mother & yourself.—We were with her a quarter of an hour before Eliz. & Louisa, hot from Mrs. Baskerville's Shop, walked in ;—they were soon followed by the Carriage, & another five minutes brought Mr. Moore himself, just returned from his morn[g] ride. Well !—& what do I think of Mr. Moore ?—I will not pretend in one meeting to *dislike* him, whatever Mary may say, but I can honestly assure her that I saw nothing in him to admire.—His manners, as you have always said, are gentlemanlike—but by no means winning. He made one formal enquiry after you.—I saw their little girl, & very small & very pretty she is ; her features are as delicate as Mary Jane's, with nice dark eyes, & if she had Mary Jane's fine colour, she w[d] be quite complete.—Harriot's fondness for her seems just what is amiable & natural, & not foolish.—I saw Caroline also, & thought her very plain.—Edward's plan for Hampshire does not vary, he only improves it with the kind intention of taking me on to Southampton, & spending one whole day with you ; & if it is found practicable, Edward Jun[r] will be added to our party for that one day also, which is to be Sunday y[e] 10th of July.—I hope you may have beds for them. We are to begin our Journey on y[e] 8th & reach you late on y[e] 9th.—This morning brought me a letter from Mrs. Knight, containing the usual Fee, & all the usual Kindness. She asks me to spend a day or two with her this week, to meet Mrs. C. Knatchbull, who with her Husband comes to the W. Friars today—& I beleive I shall go.—I have consulted Edw[d]—& think it will be arranged for Mrs. J. A.'s going with me one morn[g], my staying the night, & Edward's driving me home the next Even[g].—Her very agreable present will make my circumstances quite easy. I shall reserve half for my Pelisse.—I hope, by this early return I am sure of seeing Catherine & Alethea ;—& I propose that either with or without them you & I & Martha shall have a snug fortnight while my Mother is at Steventon.—We go on very well here, Mary finds the Children less troublesome than she expected, & independant of *them*, there is certainly not much to try the patience or hurt the spirits at Godmersham.—I initiated her yesterday into the mysteries of Inman-ism.—The poor old Lady is as thin & chearful as ever, & very thankful for a new acquaintance.—I had called on her before with Eliz. & Louisa.—I find John Bridges grown very old & black, but his manners are not altered ; he is very pleasing, & talks of Hampshire with great admiration.—Pray let Anna have the pleasure of knowing that she is remembered with kindness both by Mrs. Cooke & Miss Sharpe. Her manners must be very much worsted by your description of them, but I hope they will improve by this visit.—Mrs. Knight finishes her letter with 'Give my best Love to Cassandra when you write to her.'—I shall like spending a day at the White Friars very much.—We breakfasted in the Library this morn[g] for the first time, & most of the party have been complaining all day of the heat ; but Louisa & I feel alike as to weather, & are cool and comfortable.—Wednesday.—The Moores came yesterday in their Curricle between one & two o'clock, & immediately after the noonshine which succeeded their arrival, a party set off for Buckwell to see the Pond dragged ;—Mr. Moore, James, Edward & James-Edward on horseback, John Bridges driving Mary in his gig.—The rest of us remained quietly & comfortably at home.—We had a very pleasant Dinner, at the lower end of The table at least ; the merriment was cheifly between Edw[d] Louisa, Harriot & myself.—Mr. Moore did not talk so much as I expected, & I understand from Fanny, that I did not see him at all as he is in general ;—our being strangers made him so much more silent & quiet. Had I had no reason for observing what he said & did, I sh[d] scarcely have thought about him.—His manners to her want Tenderness—& he was a little violent at last about the impossibility of her going to Eastwell.—I cannot see any unhappiness in her however ; & as to kind-heartedness &c. she is quite unaltered.—Mary was disappointed in *her* beauty, & thought *him* very disagreable ; James admires *her*, & finds *him* conversible & pleasant. I sent my answer by them to Mrs. Knight, my double acceptance of her note & her invitation, which I wrote without much effort ; for I was rich—& the rich are always respectable, whatever be their stile of writing.—I am to meet Harriot at dinner to-morrow ;—it is one of the Audit days, and Mr. M. dines with the Dean, who is just come to Canterbury.—On Tuesday there is to be a family meeting at Mrs. C. Milles's.—Lady Bridges & Louisa from Goodnestone, the Moores, & a party from this House, Elizth John Bridges & myself. It will give me pleasure to see Lady B.—she is now quite well.—Louisa goes home on friday, & John with her ; but he returns the next day. These are our engagements ; make the most of them.—Mr. Waller is dead I see ;—I cannot greive about it, nor perhaps can his Widow very much.—Edward began cutting S^{t}foin on saturday & I hope is likely to have favourable weather ;—the crop is good.—There has been a cold & sorethroat prevailing very much in this House lately, the Children have almost all been ill with it, & we were afraid Lizzy was going to be very ill one day ; she had specks & a great deal of fever.—It went off however, & they are all pretty well now.—I want to hear of your gathering Strawberries, we have had them three times here.—I suppose you have been obliged to have in some white wine, & must visit the Store Closet a little oftener than when you were quite by yourselves.—One begins really to expect the St. Albans now, & I wish she may come before Henry goes to Cheltenham, it will be so much more convenient to him. He will be very glad if Frank can come to him in London, as his own Time is likely to be very precious, but does not depend on it.—I shall not forget Charles next week.—So much did I write before breakfast—& now to my agreable surprise I have to acknowledge another Letter from you.—I had not the least notion of hearing before tomorrow, & heard of Russell's being about to pass the Windows without any anxiety. You are very amiable & very clever to write such long Letters ; every page of yours has more lines than this, & every line more words than the average of mine. I am quite ashamed

—but you have certainly more little events than we have. Mr. Lyford supplies you with a great deal of interesting Matter (Matter Intellectual, not physical) —but I have nothing to say of Mr. Scudamore. And now, that is such a sad stupid attempt at Wit, about Matter, that nobody can smile at it, & I am quite out of heart. I am sick of myself, & my bad pens.—I have no other complaint however, my languor is entirely removed.—Ought I to be very much pleased with Marmion ?—as yet I am not.—James reads it aloud in the Even[g]—the short Even[g]—beginning at about 10, & broken by supper.—Happy Mrs. Harrison & Miss Austen !—You seem to be always calling on them.—I am glad your various civilities have turned out so well ; & most heartily wish you success & pleasure in your present engagement.—I shall think of you tonight as at Netley, & tomorrow too, that I may be quite sure of being right—& therefore I guess you will not go to Netley at all.—This is a sad story about Mrs. Powlett. I should not have suspected her of such a thing.—She staid the Sacrament I remember, the last time that you & I did.—A hint of it, with Initials, was in yesterday's Courier ; and Mr. Moore guessed it to be L[d] Sackville, beleiving there was no other Viscount S. in the peerage, & so it proved—L[d] Viscount Seymour not being there.—Yes, I enjoy my apartment very much, & always spend two or three hours in it after breakfast.—The change from Brompton Quarters to these is material as to Space.—I catch myself going on to the Hall Chamber now & then.—Little Caroline looks very plain among her Cousins, and tho' she is not so headstrong or humoursome as they are, I do not think her at all more engaging.—Her brother is to go with us to Canterbury tomorrow, & Fanny completes the party. I fancy Mrs. K. feels less interest in that branch of the family than any other. I dare say she will do her *duty* however, by the Boy.—His Uncle Edward talks nonsense to him delightfully—more than he can always understand. The two Morrises are come to dine & spend the day with him. Mary wishes my Mother to buy whatever she thinks necessary for Anna's shifts ;—& hopes to see her at Steventon soon after y[e] 9th of July, if that time is as convenient to my Mother as any other.—I have hardly done justice to what she means on the subject, as her intention is that my Mother sh[d] come at whatever time she likes best.—They will be at home on y[e] 9th.—I always come in for a morning visit from Crondale, & Mr. & Mrs. Filmer have just given me my due. He & I talked away gaily of Southampton, the Harrisons Wallers &c.—Fanny sends her best Love to you all, & will write to Anna very soon.—Yours very affec[ly] Jane

I want some news from Paragon.—I am almost sorry that Rose Hill Cottage sh[d] be so near suiting us, as it does not quite.

53. *To Cassandra Austen.* *Sunday* 26 *June* 1808

Address : Miss Austen | Castle Square | Southampton
Postmarks : FEVERSHAM and JUN 27 1808
Pierpont Morgan Library. 2 leaves 4º.
Brabourne i. 358 ; *Life* 207 (extracts).

Godmersham, Sunday June 26th.

My dear Cassandra

I am very much obliged to you for writing to me on Thursday, & very glad that I owe the pleasure of hearing from you again so soon, to such an agreable cause ; but you will not be surprised, nor perhaps so angry as I sh[d] be, to find that Frank's History had reached me before, in a letter from Henry.—We are all very happy to hear of his health & safety ;—he wants nothing but a good Prize to be a perfect Character.—This scheme to the Island is an admirable thing for his wife ; she will not feel the delay of his return, in such variety.—How very kind of Mrs. Craven to ask her !—I think I quite understand the whole Island arrangements, & shall be very ready to perform my part in them. I hope my Mother will go—& I trust it is certain that there will be Martha's bed for Edward when he brings me home. What can you do with Anna ?—for her bed will probably be wanted for young Edward.—His Father writes to Dr. Goddard today to ask leave, & we have the Pupil's authority for thinking it will be granted.—I have been so kindly pressed to stay longer here, in consequence of an offer of Henry's to take me back some time in September, that not being able to detail all my objections to such a plan, I have felt myself obliged to give Edw[d] and Eliz[th] one private reason for my wishing to be at home in July.—They feel the strength of it, & say no more ;—& one can rely on their secrecy.—After this, I hope we shall not be disappointed of our Friends' visit ;—my honour, as well as my affection will be concerned in it.—Eliza[th] has a very sweet scheme of our accompanying Edward into Kent next Christmas. A Legacy might make it very feasible ;—a Legacy is our sovereign good.—In the mean while, let me remember that I have now some money to spare, & that I wish to have my name put down as a subscriber to Mr. Jefferson's works. My last Letter was closed before it occurred to me how possible, how right, & how gratifying such a measure w^{d} be.—Your account of your Visitors' good Journey, voyage, & satisfaction in everything gave me the greatest pleasure. They have nice weather for their introduction to the Island, & I hope with such a disposition to be pleased, their general Enjoyment is as certain as it will be just.—Anna's being interested in the Embarkation shows a Taste that one values.—Mary Jane's delight in the water is quite ridiculous. Elizabeth supposes Mrs. Hall will account for it, by the Child's knowledge of her Father's being at sea.—Mrs. J. A. hopes as I said in my last, to see my Mother soon after her return home, & will meet her at Winchester on any day, she will appoint.—And now I beleive I have made all the needful replys & communications; & may disport myself as I can on my Canterbury visit.—It was a very agreable visit. There was everything to make it so; Kindness, conversation, & variety, without care or cost.—Mr. Knatchbull from Provendar was at the W. Friars when we arrived, & staid dinner, which with Harriot—who came as you may suppose in a great hurry, ten minutes after the time—made our number 6.—Mr. K. went away early;—Mr. Moore succeeded him, & we sat quietly working & talking till 10, when he ordered his wife away, & we adjourned to the Dressing room to eat our Tart & Jelly.—Mr. M. was not unagreable, tho' nothing seemed to go right with him. He is a sensible Man, & tells a story well.—Mrs. C. Knatchbull & I breakfasted tete a tete the next day, for her Husband was gone to Mr. Toke's, & Mrs. Knight had a sad headache which kept her in bed.

She had had too much company the day before ;—after my coming, which was not till past two, she had Mrs. M of Nackington, a Mrs. & Miss Gregory, & Charles Graham ; & she told me it had been so all the morning.—Very soon after breakfast on friday Mrs. C. K.—who is just what we have always seen her—went with me to Mrs. Brydges' & Mrs. Moore's, paid some other visits while I remained with the latter, & we finished with Mrs. C. Milles, who luckily was not at home, & whose new House is a very convenient short cut from the Oaks to the W. Friars.—We found Mrs. Knight up and better—but early as it was—only 12 o'clock—we had scarcely taken off our Bonnets before company came, Ly. Knatchbull & her Mother ; & after them succeeded Mrs. White, Mrs. Hughes & her two Children, Mr. Moore, Harriot & Louisa, & John Bridges, with such short intervals between any, as to make it a matter of wonder to me, that Mrs. K. & I should ever have been ten minutes alone, or have had any leisure for comfortable Talk.—Yet we had time to say a little of Everything.—Edward came to dinner, & at 8 o'clock he and I got into the Chair, & the pleasures of my visit concluded with a delightful drive home.—Mrs. & Miss Brydges seemed very glad to see me.—The poor old Lady looks much as she did three years ago, & was very particular in her enquiries after my Mother ;—and from her, & from the Knatchbulls, I have all manner of kind Compliments to give you both. As Fanny writes to Anna by this post, I had intended to keep my Letter for another day, but recollecting that I must keep it two, I have resolved rather to finish & send it now. The two letters will not interfere I dare say ; on the contrary, they may throw light on each other.—Mary begins to fancy, because she has received no message on the subject, that Anna does not mean to answer her Letter; but it must be for the pleasure of fancying it. I think Eliz[th] better & looking better than when we came.—Yesterday I introduced James to Mrs. Inman;—in the evening John Bridges returned from Goodnestone—& this morn[g] before we had left the Breakfast Table we had a visit from Mr. Whitfield, whose object I imagine was principally to thank my Eldest Brother for his assistance. Poor Man!—he has now a little intermission of his excessive solicitude on his wife's account, as she is rather better.—James does Duty at Godmersham today.—The Knatchbulls had intended coming here next week, but the Rentday makes it impossible for them to be received, & I do not think there will be any spare time afterwards. They return into Somersetshire by way of Sussex & Hants, & are to be at Fareham—& perhaps may be in Southampton, on which possibility I said all that I thought right—& if they are in the place, Mrs. K. has promised to call in Castle Square;—it will ⟨be⟩ about the end of July.—She seems to have a prospect however of being in that Country again in the Spring for a longer period, & will spend a day with us if she is.—You & I need not tell eachother how glad we shall be to receive attention from, or pay it to anyone connected with Mrs. Knight.—I cannot help regretting that now, when I feel enough her equal to relish her society, I see so little of the latter.—The Milles' of Nackington dine here on friday & perhaps the Hattons.—It is a compliment as much due to me, as a call from the Filmers.—When you write to the Island, Mary will be glad to have Mrs. Craven informed with her Love that she is now sure it will not be in her power to visit Mrs. Craven during her stay there, but that if Mrs. Craven can take Steventon in her way back, it will be giving my brother & herself great pleasure.—She also congratulates her namesake on hearing from her Husband.—That said namesake is rising in the World ;—she was thought excessively improved in her late visit.—Mrs. Knight thought her so, last year.—Henry sends us the welcome information of his having had no face-ache since I left them.—You are very kind in mentioning old Mrs. Williams so often. Poor Creature! —I cannot help hoping that each Letter may tell of her sufferings being over.—If she wants sugar, I sh[d] like to supply her with it.—The Moores went yesterday to Goodnestone, but return tomorrow. After Tuesday we shall see them no more—tho' Harriot is very earnest with Edw[d] to make Wrotham in his Journey, but we shall be in too great a hurry to get nearer to it than Wrotham Gate.—He wishes to reach Guilford on friday night—that we may have a couple of hours to spare for Alton.—I shall be sorry to pass the door at Seale without calling, but it must be so—& I shall be nearer to Bookham than I c[d] wish, in going from Dorking to Guilford—but till I have a travelling purse of my own, I must submit to such things.—The Moores leave Canterbury on friday—& go for a day or two to Sandling.—I really hope Harriot is altogether very happy—but she cannot feel quite so much at her ease with her Husband, as the wives she has been used to.—

Good-bye. I hope you have been long recovered from your worry on Thursday morn[g],—& that you do not much mind not going to the Newbury Races.—I am withstanding those of Canterbury. Let that strengthen you.—

Y^rs very sincerely

Jane

54. *To Cassandra Austen.* *Thursday* 30 *June* 1808

Address: Miss Austen | Castle Square | Southampton
Postmarks: FEVERSHAM and JUL 2 1808
Pierpont Morgan Library. 2 leaves 4°.
Brabourne i. 366 ; *Life* 207 (extracts).

Godmersham, Thursday June 30th.

My dear Cassandra

I give you all joy of Frank's return, which happens in the true sailor way, just after our being told not to expect him for some weeks.—The Wind has been very much against him, but I suppose he must be in our Neighbourhood by this time. Fanny is in hourly expectation of him here.—Mary's visit in the Island is probably shortened by this Event. Make our kind Love & Congratulations to her.—What cold, disagreeable weather, ever since Sunday!—I dare say you have Fires every day. My kerseymere Spencer is quite the comfort of our Even^g walks.—Mary thanks Anna for her Letter, & wishes her to buy enough of her new coloured frock to make a shirt handkf.—I am glad to hear of her Aunt Maitland's kind present.—We want you to send us Anna's height, that we may know whether she is as tall as Fanny;—and pray can you tell me of any little thing that w^d be probably acceptable to Mrs. F. A.—I wish to bring her something;—has she a silver knife—or w^d you recommend a Broche?

I shall not spend more than half a guinea about it.—Our Tuesday's Engagement went off very pleasantly ; we called first on Mrs. Knight, & found her very well ; & at dinner had only the Milles' of Nackington in addition to Goodnestone & Godmersham & Mrs. Moore.—Lady Bridges looked very well, & w^{d} have been very agreable I am sure, had there been time enough for her to talk to me, but as it was, she c^{d} only be kind & amiable, give me good-humoured smiles & make friendly enquiries.—Her son Edward was also looking very well, & with manners as un-altered as hers. In the $Even^{g}$ came Mr. Moore, Mr. Toke, Dr. & Mrs. Walsby & others ;—one Card Table was formed, the rest of us sat & talked, & at half after nine we came away.—Yesterday my two Brothers went to Canterbury, and J. Bridges left us for London in his way to Cambridge, where he is to take his Master's Degree.—Edward & Caroline & their Mama have all had the Godmersham Cold ; the former with sore-throat & fever which his Looks are still suffering from. —*He* is very happy here however, but I beleive the little girl will be glad to go home ;—her Cousins are too much for her.—We are to have Edward, I find, at Southampton while his Mother is in Berkshire for the Races & are very likely to have his Father too. If circumstances are favourable, that will be a good time for our scheme to Beaulieu. Lady E. Hatton called here a few mornings ago, her Daughter $Eliz^{th}$ with her, who says as little as ever, but holds up her head & smiles & is to be at the Races.—Annamaria was there with Mrs. Hope, but we are to see her here tomorrow.—So much was written before breakfast ; it is now half past twelve, & having heard Lizzy read,

I am moved down into the Library for the sake of a fire which agreably surprised us when we assembled at Ten, & here in warm & happy solitude proceed to acknowledge this day's Letter. We give you credit for your spirited voyage, & are very glad it was accomplished so pleasantly, & that Anna enjoyed it so much. —I hope you are not the worse for the fatigue—but to embark at 4 you must have got up at 3, & most likely had no sleep at all.—Mary's not chusing to be at home, occasions a general small surprise.—As to Martha, she has not the least chance in the world of hearing from me again, & I wonder at her impudence in proposing it.—I assure you I am as tired of writing long letters as you can be. What a pity that one should still be so fond of receiving them !—Fanny Austen's Match is quite news, & I am sorry she has behaved so ill. There is some comfort to *us* in her misconduct, that we have not a congratulatory Letter to write. James & Edward are gone to Sandling today ;—a nice scheme for James, as it will shew him a new & fine Country. Edward certainly excels in doing the Honours to his visitors, & providing for their amusement.—They come back this Even[g].—Elizabeth talks of going with her three girls to Wrotham while her husband is in Hampshire ;—she is improved in looks since we first came, & excepting a cold, does not seem at all unwell. She is considered indeed as more than usually active for her situation & size.—I have tried to give James pleasure by telling him of his Daughter's Taste, but if he felt, he did not express it.—*I* rejoice in it very sincerely.—Henry talks, or rather writes of going to the Downes, if the St. Albans continues there—but I hope it will be settled otherwise.—I had everybody's congratulations on her arrival, at Canterbury ; it is pleasant to be among people who know one's connections & care about them ; & it amuses me to hear John Bridges talk of ' Frank.'—I have thought a little of writing to the Downs, but I shall not ; it is so very certain that he w^d^ be somewhere else when my Letter got there.—Mr. Tho. Leigh is again in Town—or was very lately. Henry met with him last sunday in St. James's Church.—He owned being come up unexpectedly on Business—which we of course think can be only *one* business—& he came post from Adlestrop in one day, which—if it c^d^ be doubted before—convinces Henry that he will live for ever.—Mrs. Knight is kindly anxious for our Good, & thinks Mr. L. P. *must* be desirous for his *Family's* sake to have everything settled.—Indeed, I do not know where we are to get our Legacy—but we will keep a sharp look-out.—Lady B. was all in prosperous Black the other day.—A Letter from Jenny Smalbone to her Daughter brings intelligence which is to be forwarded to my Mother, the calving of a Cow at Steventon.—I am also to give her Mama's Love to Anna, & say that as her Papa talks of writing her a Letter of comfort she will *not* write, because she knows it w^d^ certainly prevent his doing so.—When are calculations ever right ?—I could have sworn that Mary must have heard of the St. Albans return, & w^d^ have been wild to come home, or to be doing something.—Nobody ever feels or acts, suffers or enjoys, as one expects.—I do not at all regard Martha's disappointment in the Island ; she will like it the better in the end.—I cannot help thinking & re-thinking of your going to the Island so heroically. It puts me in mind of Mrs. Hastings' voyage down the

Ganges, & if we had but a room to retire into to eat our fruit, we w^d^ have a picture of it hung there.—Friday July 1st—The weather is mended, which I attribute to my writing about it—& I am in hopes, as you make no complaint, tho' on the Water & at 4 in the morn^g^—that it has not been so cold with you.—It will be two years tomorrow since we left Bath for Clifton, with what happy feelings of Escape!—This post has brought me a few lines from the amiable Frank, but he gives us no hope of seeing him here.—We are not unlikely to have a peep at Henry who, unless the St. Albans moves quickly, will be going to the Downs, & who will not be able to be in Kent without giving a day or two to Godmersham.—James has heard this morn^g^ from Mrs. Cooke, in reply to his offer of taking Bookham in his way home, which is kindly accepted; & Edwd has had a less agreeable answer from Dr. Goddard, who actually refuses the petition. Being once fool enough to make a rule of never letting a Boy go away an hour before the Breaking up Hour, he is now fool enough to keep it.—We are all disappointed.—His Letter brings a double disappointment, for he has no room for George this summer.—My Brothers returned last night at 10, having spent a very agreable day in the usual routine. They found Mrs. D. at home, & Mr. D. returned from Business abroad, to dinner. James admires the place very much, & thinks the two Eldest girls handsome—but Mary's beauty has the preference.—The number of Children struck him a good deal, for not only are their own Eleven all at home, but the three little Bridgeses are also with them.—James means to go once more to Cant^y^ to see his friend Dr. Marlowe, who

EDWARD AUSTEN (KNIGHT)
from a miniature by Sir William Ross

is coming about this time;—*I* shall hardly have another opportunity of going there. In another week I shall be at home—& then, my having been at Godmersham will seem like a Dream, as my visit at Brompton seems already. The Orange Wine will want our Care soon.—But in the meantime for Elegance & Ease & Luxury—; the Hattons & Milles' dine here today—& I shall eat Ice & drink French wine, & be above vulgar Economy. Luckily the pleasures of Friendship, of unreserved Conversation, of similarity of Taste & Opinions, will make good amends for Orange Wine.—

Little Edw[d] is quite well again.—

Y[rs] affec: with Love from all, J. A.

55. *To Cassandra Austen. Saturday* 1 *Oct.* 1808

Address: Miss Austen | Edward Austen's Esq[r] | Godmersham Park | Faversham | Kent
Postmarks: SOUTHAMPTON and OCT 3 1808
Pierpont Morgan Library. 2 leaves 4[o].
Brabourne ii. 4; *Life* 210 (extracts). A few lines unpublished.

Castle Square, Saturday Oct[r] 1.

My dear Cassandra

Your letter this morning was quite unexpected, & it is well that it brings such good news to counterbalance the disappointment to me of losing my first sentence, which I had arranged full of proper hopes about your Journey, intending to commit them to paper today, & not looking for certainty till tomorrow. —We are extremely glad to hear of the birth of the Child, & trust everything will proceed as well as it begins;—his Mama has our best wishes, & he our second best for health & comfort—tho' I suppose unless he has our best too, we do nothing for *her.*—We are glad it was all over before your arrival;—& I am most happy to find who the Godmother is to be.—My Mother was some time guessing the names.—Henry's present to you gives me great pleasure, & I shall watch the weather for him at this time with redoubled interest.—We have had 4 brace of Birds lately, in equal Lots from Shalden & Neatham.—Our party at Mrs. Duer's produced the novelties of two old Mrs. Pollens & Mrs. Heywood, with whom My mother made a Quadrille Table; & of Mrs. Maitland & Caroline, & Mr. Booth without his sisters at Commerce.—I have got a Husband for each of the Miss Maitlands;—Col[n] Powlett & his Brother have taken Argyle's inner House, & the consequence is so natural that I have no ingenuity in planning it. If the Brother sh[d] luckily be a little sillier than the Colonel, what a treasure for Eliza.—Mr. Lyford called on tuesday to say that he was disappointed of his son & daughter's coming, & must go home himself the following morn[g];—& as I was determined that he sh[d] not lose every pleasure I consulted him on my complaint. He recommended cotton moistened with oil of sweet almonds, & it has done me good.—I hope therefore to have nothing more to do with Eliza's receipt than to feel obliged to her for giving it as I very sincerely do.—Mrs. Tilson's remembrance gratifies me, & I will use her patterns if I can; but poor Woman! how can she be honestly breeding again?—I have just finished a Handkf. for Mrs. James Austen, which I expect her Husband to give me an opportunity of sending to her ere long. Some fine day in

October will certainly bring him to us in the Garden, between three & four o'clock.—*She* hears that Miss Bigg is to be married in a fortnight. I wish it may be so.—About an hour & half after your toils on Wednesday ended, ours began;—at seven o'clock, Mrs. Harrison, her two daughters & two Visitors, with Mr. Debary & his eldest sister walked in; & our Labour was not a great deal shorter than poor Elizabeth's, for it was past eleven before we were delivered. —A second pool of Commerce, & all the longer by the addition of the two girls, who during the first had one corner of the Table & Spillikens to themselves, was the ruin of us;—it completed the prosperity of Mr. Debary however, for he won them both.—Mr. Harrison came in late, & sat by the fire—for which I envied him, as we had our usual luck of having a very cold Even[g]. It rained when our company came, but was dry again before they left us.—The Miss Ballards are said to be remarkably well-informed; their manners are unaffected and pleasing, but they do not talk quite freely enough to be agreable—nor can I discover any right they had by Taste or Feeling to go their late Tour.—Miss Austen & her nephew are returned—but Mr. Choles is still absent;—'still absent' say you, 'I did not know that he was gone anywhere'—Neither did I know that Lady Bridges was at Godmersham at all, till I was told of her being *still* there, which I take therefore to be the most approved method of announcing arrivals & departures.—Mr. Choles is gone to drive a Cow to Brentford, & his place is supplied to us by a Man who lives in the same sort of way by odd jobs, & among other capabilities has that of working in a garden, which my Mother will not forget, if we ever have another garden here.—In general however she thinks much more of Alton, & really expects to move there.—Mrs. Lyell's 130 Guineas rent have made a great impression. To the purchase of furniture, whether here or there, she is quite reconciled, & talks of the *Trouble* as the only evil.—I depended upon Henry's liking the Alton plan, & expect to hear of something perfectly unexceptionable there, through him.—Our Yarmouth Division seem to have got nice Lodgings ;—& with fish almost for nothing, & plenty of Engagements & plenty of each other, must be very happy.—My mother has undertaken to cure six Hams for Frank ;—at first it was a distress, but now it is a pleasure.—She desires me to say that she does not doubt your making out the Star pattern very well, as you have the Breakfast-room-rug to look at.—We have got the 2[d] vol. of Espriella's Letters, & I read it aloud by candlelight. The Man describes well, but is horribly anti-english. He deserves to be the foreigner he assumes. Mr. Debary went away yesterday, & I being gone with some partridges to St. Maries lost his parting visit.—I have heard today from Miss Sharpe, & find that she returns with Miss B. to Hinckley, & will continue there at least till about Christmas, when she thinks they may both travel southward.—Miss B. however is probably to make only a temporary absence from Mr. Chessyre, & I sh[d] not wonder if Miss Sharpe were to continue with her ;—unless anything more eligible offer, she certainly *will*. She describes Miss B. as very anxious that she should do so.—Sunday.—I had not expected to hear from you again so soon, & am much obliged to you for writing as you did ; but now as you must have a great deal of the business upon your hands, do not trouble yourself with me for the present;—I shall consider silence as good news, & not expect another Letter from you till friday or Saturday.—You must have had a great deal more rain than has fallen here ;—cold enough it has been but not wet, except for a few hours on Wednesday Even[g], & I could have found nothing more plastic than dust to stick in ;—now indeed we are likely to have a wet day—-& tho' Sunday, my Mother begins it without any ailment.—Your plants were taken in one very cold blustering day & placed in the Dining room, & there was a frost the very same night.—If we have warm weather again they are to be put out of doors, if not my Mother will have them conveyed to their Winter quarters.—I gather some Currants every now & then, when I want either fruit or employment.—Pray tell my little Goddaughter that I am delighted to hear of her saying her lesson so well.—You have used me ill, you have been writing to Martha without telling me of it, & a letter which I sent her on wednesday to give her information of you, must have been good for nothing. I do not know how to think that something will not still happen to prevent her returning by ye 10th—And if it does, I shall not much regard it on my own account, for I am now got into such a way of being alone that I do not wish even for her.—The Marquis has put off being cured for another year ;—after waiting some weeks in vain for the return of the Vessel he had agreed for, he is gone into Cornwall to order a Vessel built for himself by a famous Man in that Country, in which he means to go abroad a twelvemonth hence.—

Everybody who comes to Southampton finds it either their duty or pleasure to call upon us ; Yesterday we were visited by the eldest Miss Cotterel, just arrived from Waltham. Adeiu—With Love to all,

Y[rs] affec:[ly] J A.

We had two Pheasants last night from Neatham. Tomorrow Even[g] is to be given to the Maitlands ;— we are just asked, to meet Mrs. Heywood & Mrs. Duer.

56. *To Cassandra Austen.* *Friday* 7 *Oct.* 1808

Address: Miss Austen | Edward Austen's Esq[r] | Godmersham Park | Faversham | Kent
Postmarks: SOUTHAMPTON and OCT 10 1808
Pierpont Morgan Library. 2 leaves 4°.
Brabourne ii. 11 ; *Life* 212 (extracts).

Castle Square, Friday Oct. 7.—

My dear Cassandra

Your letter on Tuesday gave us great pleasure, & we congratulate you all upon Elizabeth's hitherto happy recovery ;—tomorrow or Sunday I hope to hear of it's advancing in the same stile.—We are also very glad to know that you are so well yourself, & pray you to continue so.—I was rather surprised on Monday by the arrival of a letter for you from your Winchester Correspondent, who seemed perfectly unsuspicious of your being likely to be at Godmersham ;—I took complete possession of the Letter by reading, paying for, & answering it ;—and he will have the Biscuits today, —a very proper day for the purpose, tho' I did not think of it at the time.—I wish my Brother joy of completing his 30th year—& hope the day will be remembered better than it was six years ago.—The

Masons are now repairing the Chimney, which they found in such a state as to make it wonderful that it sh[d] have stood so long, & next to impossible that another violent wind should not blow it down. We may therefore thank *you* perhaps for saving us from being thumped with old bricks.—You are also to be thank'd by Eliza's desire for your present to her of dyed sattin, which is made into a bonnet, & I fancy surprises her by it's good appearance.—My Mother is preparing mourning for Mrs. E. K.—she has picked her old silk pelisse to peices, & means to have it dyed black for a gown—a very interesting scheme, tho' just now a little injured by finding that it must be placed in Mr. Wren's hands, for Mr. Chambers is gone.—As for Mr. Floor, he is at present rather low in our estimation ; how is your blue gown ?—Mine is all to peices.—I think there must have been something wrong in the dye, for in places it divided with a Touch.—There was four shillings thrown away ;—to be added to my subjects of never failing regret.—We found ourselves tricked into a thorough party at Mrs. Maitland's, a quadrille & a Commerce Table, & Music in the other room. There were two pools at Commerce, but I would not play more than one, for the Stake was three shillings, & I cannot afford to lose that, twice in an even[g].—The Miss Ms. were as civil & as silly as usual. —You know of course that Martha comes today ; yesterday brought us notice of it, & the Spruce Beer is brewed in consequence.—On wednesday I had a letter from Yarmouth to desire me to send Mary's flannels & furs, &c—& as there was a packing case at hand, I could do it without any trouble.—On Tuesday Even[g] Southampton was in a good deal of alarm for about an hour; a fire broke out soon after nine at Webbes, the Pastrycook, & burnt for some time with great fury. I cannot learn exactly how it originated, at the time it was said to be their Bakehouse, but now I hear it was in the back of their Dwelling house, & that one room was consumed.—The Flames were considerable, they seemed about as near to us as those at Lyme, & to reach higher. One could not but feel uncomfortable, & I began to think of what I should do, if it came to the worst;—happily however the night was perfectly still, the Engines were immediately in use, & before ten the fire was nearly extinguished—tho' it was twelve before everything was considered safe, & a Guard was kept the whole night. Our friends the Duers were alarmed, but not out of their good Sense or Benevolence.—I am afraid the Webbes have lost a great deal—more perhaps from ignorance or plunder than the Fire;—they had a large stock of valuable China, & in order to save it, it was taken from the House, & thrown down anywhere.—The adjoining House, a Toyshop, was almost equally injured—& Hibbs, whose House comes next, was so scared from his senses that he was giving away all his goods, valuable Laces &c, to anybody who w^d^ take them.—The Croud in the High S^t^ I understand was immense; Mrs. Harrison, who was drinking tea with a Lady at Millar's, could not leave it twelve o'clock.—Such are the prominent features of our fire. Thank God! they were not worse.—

Saturday.—Thank you for your Letter, which found me at the Breakfast-Table, with my *two* companions. —I am greatly pleased with your account of Fanny; I found her in the summer just what you describe,

ELIZABETH AUSTEN (*née* BRIDGES)
from a miniature by Richard Cosway

almost another Sister,—& could not have supposed that a neice would ever have been so much to me. She is quite after one's own heart; give her my best Love, & tell her that I always think of her with pleasure.—I am much obliged to you for enquiring about my ear, & am happy to say that Mr. Lyford's prescription has entirely cured me. I feel it a great blessing to hear again.—Your gown shall be unpicked, but I do not remember it's being settled so before.—Martha was here by half past six, attended by Lyddy; —they had some rain at last, but a very good Journey on the whole; & if Looks & Words may be trusted Martha is very happy to be returned. We receive her with Castle Square-weather, it has blown a gale from the N.W. ever since she came—& we feel ourselves in luck that the Chimney was mended yesterday.—She brings several good things for the Larder, which is now very rich; we had a pheasant & hare the other day from the Mr. Grays of Alton. Is this to entice us to Alton, or to keep us away?—Henry had probably some share in the two last baskets from that Neighbourhood, but we have not seen so much of his handwriting even as a direction to either. Martha was an hour & half in Winchester, walking about with the three boys & at the Pastrycook's.—She thought Edward grown, & speaks with the same admiration as before of his Manners;—she saw in George a little likeness to his uncle Henry.—I am glad you are to see Harriot, give my Love to her.—I wish you may be able to accept Lady Bridges's invitation, tho' *I* could not her son Edward's;—she is a nice Woman, & honours me by her remembrance.—Do you recollect whether the Manydown family send about their Wedding Cake ?—Mrs. Dundas has set her heart upon having a peice from her friend Catherine, & Martha who knows what importance she attaches to the sort of thing, is anxious for the sake of both that there sh^d^ not be a disappointment.—Our weather I fancy has been just like yours, we have had *some* very delightful days, our 5th & 6th were what the 5th & 6th of October should always be, but we have always wanted a fire *within* doors, at least except for just the middle of the day.—Martha does not find the key, which you left in my charge for her, suit the keyhole—& wants to know whether you think you can have mistaken it.—It should open the interior of her High Drawers—but she is in no hurry about it.

Sunday.—It is cold enough now for us to prefer dining upstairs to dining below without a fire, & being only three we manage it very well, & today with two more we shall do just *as* well, I dare say ; Miss Foote & Miss Wethered are coming. My mother is much pleased with Elizabeth's admiration of the rug—& pray tell Elizabeth that the new mourning gown is to be made double *only* in the body & sleeves.—Martha thanks you for your message, & desires you may be told with her best Love that your wishes are answered & that she is full of peace & comfort here.—I do not think however that *here* she will remain a great while, she does not herself expect that Mrs. Dundas will be able to do with her long. She *wishes* to stay with us till Christmas if possible.—Lyddy goes home to-morrow ; she seems well, but does not mean to go to service at present.—The Wallops are returned. Mr. John Harrison has paid his visit of duty & is gone.—We have got a new Physician, a Dr. Percival, the son of a famous Dr. Percival of Manchester, who wrote moral tales for Edward to give to me.—When you write again to Catherine, thank her on my part for her very kind & welcome mark of friendship. I shall value such a Broche very much.—Good bye my dearest Cassandra.

Yrs very affec:ly J A.

Have you written to Mrs. E. Leigh ?—Martha will be glad to find Anne in work at present, & I am as glad to have her so found.—We must turn our black pelisses into new, for velvet is to be very much worn this winter.—

57. *To Cassandra Austen.* ⟨*Thursday*⟩ 13 *Oct.* 1808

Address **: Miss Austen | Edward Austen's Esqr | Godmersham Park | Faversham | Kent**
Postmarks **: SOUTHAMPTON and OCT 14 1808**
Pierpont Morgan Library. 2 leaves 4o.
Brabourne **ii. 18 ;** ***Life*** **213 (extracts).**

Castle Square, Octr 13.

My dearest Cassandra

I have received your Letter, & with most melancholy anxiety was it expected, for the sad news reached us last night, but without any particulars ; it came in a short letter to Martha from her sister, begun at Steventon, & finished in Winchester.—We have felt, we do feel, for you all—as you will not need to be told—for you, for Fanny, for Henry, for Lady Bridges, & for dearest Edward, whose loss and whose sufferings seem to make those of every other person nothing.—God be praised ! that you can say what you do of him—that he has a religious Mind to bear him up, & a Disposition that will gradually lead him to comfort.—My dear, dear Fanny!—I am so thankful that she has you with her!—You will be everything to her, you will give her all the Consolation that human aid can give.—May the Almighty sustain you all—& keep you my dearest Cassandra well—but for the present I dare say you are equal to everything.—You will know that the poor Boys are at Steventon, perhaps it is best for them, as they will have more means of exercise & amusement there than they c[d] have with us, but I own myself disappointed by the arrangement;—I should have loved to have them with me at such a time. I shall write to Edward by this post.—We shall of course hear from you again very soon, & as often as you can write.—We will write as you desire, & I shall add Bookham. Hamstall I suppose you write to yourselves, as you do not mention it.—What a comfort that Mrs. Deedes is saved from present misery & alarm—but it will fall heavy upon poor Harriot—& as for Lady B.—but that her fortitude does seem truely great, I should fear the effect of such a Blow & so unlooked for. I long to hear more of you all.—Of Henry's anguish, I think with greif and solicitude; but he will exert himself to be of use & comfort. With what true sympathy our feelings are shared by Martha, you need not be told;—she is the friend & sister under every circumstance. We need not enter into a Panegyric on the Departed—but it is sweet to think of her great worth—of her solid principles, her true devotion, her excellence in every relation of Life. It is also consolatory to reflect on the shortness of the sufferings which led her from this World to a better.—Farewell for the present, my dearest Sister. Tell Edward that we feel for him & pray for him.—

Y^rs affec^tely J Austen

I will write to Catherine.

Perhaps you can give me some directions about Mourning.

58. *To Cassandra Austen.*

Address: Miss Austen Edward Austen's Esq. Godmersham Park Faversham Kent. *Postmark*: OCT 17 1808.
Historical Soc. of Pennsylvania.
Brabourne ii. 21; *Life* 214 (extracts).

Castle Square: Saturday night October 15.

My dear Cassandra,

Your accounts make us as comfortable as we can expect to be at such a time. Edward's loss is terrible, and must be felt as such, and these are too early days indeed to think of moderation in grief, either in him or his afflicted daughter, but soon we may hope that our dear Fanny's sense of duty to that beloved father will rouse her to exertion. For his sake, and as the most acceptable proof of love to the spirit of her departed mother, she will try to be tranquil and resigned. Does she feel you to be a comfort to her, or is she too much overpowered for anything but solitude?

Your account of Lizzy is very interesting. Poor child! One must hope the impression *will* be strong, and yet one's heart aches for a dejected mind of eight years old.

I suppose you see the corpse? How does it appear? We are anxious to be assured that Edward will not attend the funeral, but when it comes to the point I think he must feel it impossible.

Your parcel shall set off on Monday, and I hope the shoes will fit; Martha and I both tried them on. I shall send you such of your mourning as I think most likely to be useful, reserving for myself your stockings and half the velvet, in which selfish arrangement I know I am doing what you wish.

I am to be in bombazeen and crape, according to what we are told is universal *here*, and which agrees with Martha's previous observation. My mourning, however, will not impoverish me, for by having my velvet pelisse fresh lined and made up, I am sure I shall have no occasion *this winter* for anything new of that sort. I take my cloak for the lining, and shall send yours on the chance of its doing something of the same for you, though I believe your pelisse is in better repair than mine. *One* Miss Baker makes my gown and the other my bonnet, which is to be silk covered with crape.

I have written to Edward Cooper, and hope he will not send one of his letters of cruel comfort to my poor brother; and yesterday I wrote to Alethea Bigg, in reply to a letter from her. She tells us in confidence that Catherine is to be married on Tuesday se'nnight. Mr. Hill is expected at Manydown in the course of the ensuing week.

We are desired by Mrs. Harrison and Miss Austen to say everything proper for them to yourself and Edward on this sad occasion, especially that nothing but a wish of not giving additional trouble where so much is inevitable prevents their writing themselves to express their concern. They seem truly to feel concern.

I am glad you can say what you do of Mrs. Knight and of Goodnestone in general; it is a great relief to me to know that the shock did not make any of them ill. But what a task was yours to announce it! *Now* I hope you are not overpowered with letter-writing, as Henry and John can ease you of many of your correspondents.

Was Mr. Scudamore in the house at the time, was any application attempted, and is the seizure at all accounted for?

Sunday.—As Edward's letter to his son is not come here, we know that you must have been informed as early as Friday of the boys being at Steventon, which I am glad of.

Upon your letter to Dr. Goddard's being forwarded to them, Mary wrote to ask whether my mother wished to have her grandsons sent to her. We decided on their remaining where they were, which I hope my brother will approve of. I am sure he will do us the justice of believing that in such a decision we sacrificed inclination to what we thought best.

I shall write by the coach to-morrow to Mrs. J. A., and to Edward, about their mourning, though this day's post will probably bring directions to them on that subject from yourselves. I shall certainly make use of the opportunity of addressing our nephew on the most serious of all concerns, as I naturally did in my letter to him before. The poor boys are, perhaps, more comfortable at Steventon than they could be here, but you will understand *my feelings* with respect to it.

To-morrow will be a dreadful day for you all. Mr. Whitfield's will be a severe duty. Glad shall I be to hear that it is over.

That you are for ever in our thoughts you will not doubt. I see your mournful party in my mind's eye under every varying circumstance of the day; and in the evening especially figure to myself its sad gloom: the efforts to talk, the frequent summons to melancholy orders and cares, and poor Edward, restless in misery, going from one room to the other, and perhaps not seldom upstairs, to see all that remains of his Elizabeth. Dearest Fanny must now look upon herself as his prime source of comfort, his dearest friend; as the being who is gradually to supply to him, to the extent that is possible, what he has lost. This consideration will elevate and cheer her.

Adieu. You cannot write too often, as I said before. We are heartily rejoiced that the poor baby gives you no particular anxiety. Kiss dear Lizzy for us. Tell Fanny that I shall write in a day or two to Miss Sharpe.

My mother is not ill.

Yours most truly, J. Austen

Tell Henry that a hamper of apples is gone to him from Kintbury, and that Mr. Fowle intended writing on Friday (supposing him in London) to beg that the charts, &c., may be consigned to the care of the Palmers. Mrs. Fowle has also written to Miss Palmer to beg she will send for them.

59. *To Cassandra Austen. Monday* 24 *Oct.* ⟨1808⟩

Address **(Brabourne): Miss Austen, Edward Austen Esq. | Godmersham Park, Faversham, Kent**
Original not traced.
Brabourne **ii. 25 ;** ***Life*** **216 (extracts);**

Castle Square : Monday October 24

My dear Cassandra,

Edward and George came to us soon after seven on Saturday, very well, but very cold, having by choice travelled on the outside, and with no great coat but what Mr. Wise, the coachman, good-naturedly spared them of his, as they sat by his side. They were so much chilled when they arrived, that I was afraid they must have taken cold ; but it does not seem at all the case ; I never saw them looking better.

They behave extremely well in every respect, showing quite as much feeling as one wishes to see, and on every occasion speaking of their father with the liveliest affection. His letter was read over by each of them yesterday, and with many tears ; George sobbed aloud, Edward's tears do not flow so easily ; but as far as I can judge they are both very properly impressed by what has happened. Miss Lloyd, who is a more impartial judge than I can be, is exceedingly pleased with them.

George is almost a new acquaintance to me, and I find him in a different way as *engaging as Edward.*

We do not want amusement : bilbocatch, at which George is indefatigable, spillikins, paper ships, riddles, conundrums, and cards, with watching the flow and ebb of the river, and now and then a stroll out, keep us well employed ; and we mean to avail ourselves of our kind papa's consideration, by not returning to Winchester till quite the evening of Wednesday.

Mrs. J. A. had not time to get them more than one suit of clothes; their others are making here, and though I do not believe Southampton is famous for tailoring, I hope it will prove itself better than Basingstoke. Edward has an old black coat, which will save *his* having a second new one; but I find that black pantaloons are considered by them as necessary, and of course one would not have them made uncomfortable by the want of what is usual on such occasions.

Fanny's letter was received with great pleasure yesterday, and her brother sends his thanks and will answer it soon. We all saw what she wrote, and were very much pleased with it.

To-morrow I hope to hear from you, and to-morrow we must think of poor Catherine. To-day Lady Bridges is the heroine of our thoughts, and glad shall we be when we can fancy the meeting over. There will then be nothing so very bad for Edward to undergo.

The 'St. Albans,' I find, sailed on the very day of my letters reaching Yarmouth, so that we must not expect an answer at present; we scarcely feel, however, to be in suspense, or only enough to keep our plans to ourselves. We have been obliged to explain them to our young visitors, in consequence of Fanny's letter, but we have not yet mentioned them to Steventon. We are all quite familiarised to the idea ourselves; my mother only wants Mrs. Seward to go out at Midsummer.

What sort of a kitchen garden is there? Mrs. J. A. expresses her fear of our settling in Kent, and, till this proposal was made, we began to look forward to it here; my mother was actually talking of a house at Wye. It will be best, however, as it is.

Anne has just given her mistress warning; she is going to be married; I wish she would stay her year.

On the subject of matrimony, I must notice a wedding in the Salisbury paper, which has amused me very much, Dr. Phillot to Lady Frances St. Lawrence. *She* wanted to have a husband I suppose, once in her life, and *he* a Lady Frances.

I hope your sorrowing party were at church yesterday, and have no longer *that* to dread. Martha was kept at home by a *cold, but I went with my two nephews, and I saw Edward was much affected by the sermon, which, indeed, I could have supposed purposely addressed* to the afflicted, if the text had not naturally come in the course of Dr. Mant's observations on the Litany: 'All that are in danger, necessity, or tribulation,' was the subject of it. The weather did not allow us afterwards to get farther than the quay, where George was very happy as long as we could stay, flying about from one side to the other, and skipping on board a collier immediately.

In the evening we had the Psalms and Lessons, and a sermon at home, to which they were very attentive; but you will not expect to hear that they did not return to conundrums the moment it *was over*. Their aunt has written pleasantly of them, which was more than I hoped.

While I write now, George is most industriously making and naming paper ships, at which he afterwards shoots with horse-chestnuts, brought from Steventon on purpose; and Edward equally intent over the 'Lake of Killarney,' twisting himself about in one of our great chairs.

Tuesday.—Your close-written letter makes me quite ashamed of my wide lines; you have sent me a great deal of matter, most of it very welcome. As to your lengthened stay, it is no more than I expected, and what must be, but you cannot suppose I like it.

All that you say of Edward is truly comfortable; I began to fear that when the bustle of the first week was over, his spirits might for a time be more depressed; and perhaps one must still expect something of the kind. If *you* escape a bilious attack, I shall wonder almost as much as rejoice. I am glad you mentioned where Catherine goes to-day; it is a good plan, but sensible people may generally be trusted to form such.

The day began cheerfully, but it is not likely to continue what it should, for them or for us. *We had a little water party* yesterday; I and my two nephews went from the Itchen Ferry up to Northam, where we landed, looked into the 74, and walked home, and it was so much enjoyed that I had intended to take them to Netley to-day; the tide is just right for our going immediately after noonshine, but I am afraid there will be rain; if we cannot get so far, however, we may perhaps go round from the ferry to the quay.

I had not proposed doing more than cross the Itchen yesterday, but it proved so pleasant, and so much to the satisfaction of all, that when we reached the middle of the stream we agreed to be rowed up the river; both the boys rowed great part of the way, and their questions and remarks, as well as their enjoyment, were very amusing; George's enquiries were endless, and his eagerness in everything reminds me often *of his Uncle Henry*.

Our evening was equally agreeable in its way: I introduced *speculation*, and it was so much approved that we hardly knew how to leave off.

Your idea of an early dinner to-morrow is exactly what we propose, for, after writing the first part of this letter, it came into my head that at this time of year we have not summer evenings. We shall watch the light to-day, that we may not give them a dark drive to-morrow.

They send their best love to papa and everybody, with George's thanks for the letter brought by this post. Martha begs my brother may be assured of her interest in everything relating to him and his family, and of her sincerely partaking our pleasure in the receipt of every good account from Godmersham.

Of Chawton I think I can have nothing more to say, but that everything you say about it in the letter now before me will, I am sure, as soon as I am able to read it to her, make my mother consider the plan with more and more pleasure. We had formed the same views on H. Digweed's farm.

A very kind and feeling letter is arrived to-day from Kintbury. Mrs. Fowle's sympathy and solicitude on such an occasion you will be able to do justice to, and to express it as she wishes to my brother. Concerning *you*, she says: 'Cassandra will, I know, excuse my writing to her; it is not to save myself but *her* that I omit so doing. Give my best, my kindest love to her, and tell her I feel for her as I know she would for me on the same occasion, and that I most sincerely hope her health will not suffer.'

We have just had two hampers of apples from Kintbury, and the floor of our little garret is almost covered. Love to all.

Yours very affectionately, J. A.

60. *To Cassandra Austen.* *Sunday* 20 *Nov.* ⟨1808⟩

Address: Miss Austen | Edw: Austen's Esqr | Godmersham Park | Faversham | Kent
Postmarks: SOUTHAMPTON and NOV 21 (year illegible)
Pierpont Morgan Library. 2 leaves 4°.
Brabourne ii. 32; *Life* 219 (extracts).

Castle Square, Sunday Novr 21 (*sic*).—

Your letter my dear Cassandra, obliges me to write immediately, that you may have the earliest notice of Frank's intending if possible to go to Godmersham exactly at the time now fixed for your visit to Goodnestone. He resolved almost directly on the receipt of your former Letter, to try for an extension of his Leave of absence that he might be able to go down to you for two days, but charged me not to give you any notice of it, on account of the uncertainty of success;—Now however, I must give it, & now perhaps he may be giving it himself—for I am just in the hateful predicament of being obliged to write what I know will somehow or other be of no use.—He meant to ask for five days more, & if they were granted, to go down by Thursday-night's Mail & spend friday & saturday with you;—& he considered his chance of succeeding by no means bad.—I hope it will take place as he planned, & that your arrangements with Goodnestone may admit of suitable alteration.—Your news of Edw: Bridges was *quite* news, for

I have had no letter from Wrotham.—I wish him happy with all my heart, & hope his choice may turn out according to his own expectations, & beyond those of his Family—and I dare say it will. Marriage is a great Improver—& in a similar situation Harriet may be as amiable as Eleanor.—As to Money, that will come you may be sure, because they cannot do without it.—When you see him again, pray give him our Congratulations & best wishes.—This Match will certainly set John & Lucy going.—There are six Bed-chambers at Chawton; Henry wrote to my Mother the other day, & luckily mentioned the number—which is just what we wanted to be assured of. He speaks also of Garrets for store-places, one of which she immediately planned fitting up for Edward's Man-servant—& now perhaps it must be for our own—for she is already quite reconciled to our keeping one. The difficulty of doing without one, had been thought of before.—His name shall be Robert, if you please.—Before I can tell you of it, you will have heard that Miss Sawbridge is married. It took place I beleive on Thursday, Mrs. Fowle has for some time been in the secret, but the Neighbourhood in general were quite unsuspicious. Mr. Maxwell *was* tutor to the young Gregorys—consequently they must be one of the happiest Couple in the World, & either of them worthy of Envy—for *she* must be excessively in love, and he mounts from nothing, to a comfortable Home.—Martha has heard him very highly spoken of.—They continue for the present at Speen Hill.—I have a Southampton Match to return for your Kentish one, Capt. G. Heathcote & Miss A. Lyell; I have it from Alethea—& like it, because I had made it before.

Yes, the Stoneleigh business is concluded, but it was not till yesterday that my Mother was regularly informed of it, tho' the news had reached us on Monday Even[g] by way of Steventon. My Aunt says as little as may be on the subject by way of information, & nothing at all by way of satisfaction. She reflects on Mr. T. Leigh's dilatoriness, & looks about with great diligence & success for Inconvenience & Evil—among which she ingeniously places the danger of her new Housemaids catching cold on the outside of the Coach, when she goes down to Bath—for a carriage makes her sick.—John Binns has been offered their place, but declines it—as she supposes, because he will not wear a Livery.—Whatever be the cause, I like the effect.—In spite of all my Mother's long and intimate knowledge of the Writer, she was not up to the expectation of such a Letter as this; the discontentedness of it shocked & surprised her—but *I* see nothing in it out of Nature—tho' a sad nature.

She does not forget to wish for Chambers, you may be sure.—No particulars are given, not a word of arrears mentioned—tho' in her letter to James they were in a *general way* spoken of. The amount of them is a matter of conjecture, & to my Mother a most interesting one; she cannot fix any time for their beginning, with any satisfaction to herself, but Mrs. Leigh's death—& Henry's two Thousand pounds neither agrees with that period nor any other.—I did not like to own, our previous information of what was intended last July—& have therefore only said that if we could see Henry we might hear many particulars, as I had understood that some confidential conversation had passed between him & Mr. T. L. at Stoneleigh. We have been as quiet as usual since Frank & Mary left us ;—Mr. Criswick called on Martha that very morn[g] in his way home again from Portsmouth, & we have had no visitor since.—We called on the Miss Lyells one day, & heard a good account of Mr. Heathcote's canvass, the success of which of course exceeds his expectation.—Alethea in her Letter hopes for *my interest,* which I conclude means Edward's—& I take this opportunity therefore of requesting that he will bring in Mr. Heathcote.—Mr. Lance told us yesterday that Mr. H. had behaved very handsomely & waited on Mr. Thistlethwaite to say that if *he* (Mr. T.) would stand, *he* (Mr. H.) would not oppose him ; but Mr. T. declined it, acknowledging himself still smarting under the payment of late Electioneering costs.—The Mrs. Hulberts, we learn from Kintbury, come to Steventon this week, & bring Mary Jane Fowle with them, in her way to Mrs. Nunes ;—she returns at Christmas with her Brother.—*Our* Brother we may perhaps see in the course of a few days—& we mean to take the opportunity of his help, to go one night to the play. Martha ought to see the inside of the Theatre once while she lives in Southampton, & I think she will hardly wish to take a second veiw.—The Furniture of Bellevue is to be sold tomorrow, & we shall take it in our usual walk if the Weather be favourable. How could you have a wet day on Thursday ?—with us it was a Prince of days, the most delightful we have had for weeks, soft, bright, with a brisk wind from the south west ;—everybody was out & talking of spring—& Martha and I did not know how to turn back.—on Friday Even[g] we had some very blowing weather—from 6 to 9, I think we never heard it worse, even here.—And one night we had so much rain that it forced it's way again into the store closet—& tho' the Evil was comparatively slight, & the Mischief nothing, I had some employment the next day in drying parcels &c. I have now moved still more out of the way.—

Martha sends her best Love, & thanks you for admitting her to the knowledge of the pros & cons about Harriet Foote—she has an interest in all such matters.—I am also to say that she wants to see you. —Mary Jane missed her papa & mama a good deal at first, but now does very well without them.—I am glad to hear of little John's being better;—& hope your accounts of Mrs. Knight will also improve. Adeiu. Remember me affec^{tely} to everybody, & beleive me

Ever yours,   J A.

61. *To Cassandra Austen.* *Friday* 9 *Dec.* 1808

Address: Miss Austen | Edw: Austen's Esqr | Godmersham Park | Faversham | Kent
Postmark: DEC 10 1808
Pierpont Morgan Library. 2 leaves 4°. A piece cut away, 4 lines lost.
Brabourne ii. 38; *Life* 221 (extracts).

Castle Square, Friday Decr 9.

Many thanks my dear Cassandra, to you & Mr. Deedes for your joint & agreable composition, which took me by surprise this morning. He has certainly great merit as a Writer, he does ample justice to his subject, & without being diffuse, is clear & correct; & tho' I do not mean to compare his Epistolary powers with yours, or to give him the same portion of my Gratitude, he certainly has a very pleasing way of winding up a whole, & speeding Truth into the world.—' But all this, as my dear Mrs. Piozzi says, is flight & fancy & nonsense—for my Master has his great casks to mind, & I have my little Children'— It is *you* however in this instance, that have the little Children—& *I* that have the great cask—, for we are brewing Spruce Beer again;—but my meaning really is, that I am extremely foolish in writing all this unnecessary stuff, when I have so many matters to write about, that my paper will hardly hold it all. Little Matters they are to be sure, but highly important.—In the first place, Miss Curling is actually at Portsmouth—which I was always in hopes would not happen.—I wish her no worse however than a long & happy abode there. *Here*, she w[d] probably be dull, & I am sure she w[d] be troublesome.—The Bracelets are in my possession, & everything I could wish them to be. They came with Martha's pelisse, which likewise gives great satisfaction.—Soon after I had closed my last letter to you, we were visited by Mrs. Dickens & her Sisterinlaw Mrs. Bertie, the wife of a lately made Admiral;—Mrs. F. A. I beleive was their first object— but they put up with us very kindly, & Mrs. D. finding in Miss Lloyd a friend of Mrs. Dundas had another motive for the acquaintance. She seems a really agreable Woman—that is, her manners are gentle & she knows a great many of our Connections in West Kent.—Mrs. Bertie lives in the Polygon, & was out when we returned her visit—which are *her* two virtues.—

A larger circle of acquaintance & an increase of amusement is quite in character with our approaching removal.—Yes—I mean to go to as many Balls as possible, that I may have a good bargain. Everybody is very much concerned at our going away, & everybody is acquainted with Chawton & speaks of it as a remarkably pretty village ; & everybody knows the House we describe—but nobody fixes on the right.—I am very much obliged to Mrs. Knight for such a proof of the interest she takes in me—& she may depend upon it, that I *will* marry Mr. Papillon, whatever may be his reluctance or my own.—I owe her much more than such a trifling sacrifice.—Our Ball was rather more amusing than I expected, Martha liked it very much, & I did not gape till the last quarter of an hour.—It was past nine before we were sent for, & not twelve when we returned.—The room was tolerably full, & there were perhaps thirty couple of Dancers ;—the melancholy part was, to see so many dozen young Women standing by without partners, & each of them with two ugly naked shoulders !—It was the same room in which we danced 15 years ago !—I thought it all over—& in spite of the shame of being so much older, felt with thankfulness that I was quite as happy now as then.—We paid an additional shilling for our Tea, which we took as we chose in an adjoining, & very comfortable room.—There were only 4 dances, & it went to my heart that the Miss Lances (one of them too named Emma !) should have partners only for two.—You will not expect to hear that *I* was asked to dance—but I was—by the Gentleman whom we met *that Sunday* with Cap^{n} D'Auvergne. We have always kept up a bowing acquaintance since, & being pleased with his black eyes, I spoke to him at the Ball, which brought on me this civility ; but I do not know his name—& he seems so little at home in the English Language that I beleive his black eyes may be the best of him.—Capt. D'Auvergne has got a ship.—Martha & I made use of the very favourable state of yesterday for walking, to pay our duty at Chiswell—we found Mrs. Lance at home & alone, & sat out three other Ladies who soon came in.—We went by the Ferry, & returned by the Bridge, & were scarcely at all fatigued.—Edward must have enjoyed the last two days ;—You, I presume had a *cool* drive to Canterbury. Kitty Foote came on Wednesday, & her Even^{g} visit began early enough for the last part, the apple pye of our dinner, for we never dine now till five.—Yesterday I, or rather you had a letter from Nanny Hilliard, the object of which is that she w^{d} be very much obliged to us if we w^{d} get Hannah a place.—I am sorry that I cannot assist her ;—if you can, let me know, as I shall not answer the letter immediately. Mr. Sloper is married again, not much to Nanny's, or anybody's satisfaction ;—the Lady was Governess to Sir Robert's natural Children, & seems to have nothing to recommend her.—I do not find however that Nanny is likely to lose her place in consequence.—She says not a word of what service she wishes for Hannah, or what Hannah can do—but a Nursery I suppose, or something of that kind, must be the Thing.—Having now cleared away my smaller articles of news, I come to a communication of some weight—no less than that my Uncle & Aunt are going to allow James £100. a year. We hear of it through Steventon ;—Mary sent us the other day an extract from my Aunt's letter on the subject—in which the Donation is made with the greatest kindness, & intended as a Compensation for his loss in the Conscientious refusal of Hampstead Living—£100. a year being all that he had at the time called its worth—as I find it was always intended at Steventon to divide the real Income with Kintbury.—Nothing can be more affectionate than my Aunt's Language in making the present, & likewise in expressing her hope of their being much more together in future, than to her great regret, they have of late years been.—My Expectations for my Mother do not rise with this Event. We will allow a little more time however, before we fly out.—If not prevented by Parish Business, James comes to us on Monday. The Mrs. Hulberts & Miss Murden are their Guests at present, & likely to continue such till Christmas.—Anna comes home on ye 19th. The Hundred a year begins next Ladyday.—I am glad you are to have Henry with you again; with him & the Boys, you cannot but have a chearful, & at times even a merry Christmas.—Martha is so ⟨*Two lines cut out*⟩

We want to be settled at Chawton in time for Henry to come to us for some shooting, in October at least;—but a little earlier, & Edward may visit us after taking his boys back to Winchester;—suppose we name the 4th of Sept^r^—will not that do?—I have but one thing more to tell you. Mrs. Hill called on my Mother yesterday while we were gone to Chiswell—& in the course of the visit asked her whether she knew anything of a Clergyman's family of the name of *Alford* who had resided in our part of Hampshire.—Mrs. Hill had been applied to, as likely to give some information of them on account of their probable vicinity to Dr. Hill's Living—by a Lady, or for a Lady, who had known Mrs. & the two Miss Alfords in Bath, whither they had removed it seems from Hampshire—& who now wishes to convey to the Miss Alfords some work, or trimming, which she has been doing for them—but the Mother & Daughters have left Bath, & the Lady cannot learn where they are gone to.—While my Mother gave us the account, the probability of its being ourselves, occurred to us, and it had previously struck herself ⟨*Two lines cut out*⟩

likely—& even indispensably to be *us*, is that she mentioned Mr. Hammond as now having the Living or Curacy, which the Father had had.—I cannot think who our kind Lady can be—but I dare say we shall not like the work.—

Distribute the affec^{te} Love of a Heart not so tired as the right hand belonging to it.—

Yours Ever Sincerely J A.

62. *To Cassandra Austen.* *Tuesday* 27 *Dec.* ⟨1808⟩

Address (Brabourne): Miss Austen, Edward Austen's, Esq. | Godmersham Park, Faversham, Kent
Original not traced.
Brabourne ii. 46 ; *Life* 223 (extracts).

Castle Square: Tuesday December 27

My dear Cassandra,

I can now write at leisure and make the most of my subjects, which is lucky, as they are not numerous this week.

Our house was cleared by half-past eleven on Saturday, and we had the satisfaction of hearing yesterday that the party reached home in safety soon after five.

I was very glad of your letter this morning, for, my mother taking medicine, Eliza keeping her bed with a cold, and Choles not coming, made us rather dull and dependent on the post. You tell me much that gives me pleasure, but I think not much to answer. I wish I *could* help you in your needlework. I have two hands and a new thimble that lead a very easy life.

Lady Sondes' match surprises, but does not offend me; had her first marriage been of affection, or had there been a grown-up single daughter, I should not have forgiven her; but I consider everybody as having a right to marry *once* in their lives for love, if they can, and provided she will now leave off having bad headaches and being pathetic, I can allow her, I can *wish* her, to be happy.

Do not imagine that your picture of your *tête-à-tête* with Sir B. makes any change in our expectations here; he could not be really reading, though he held the newspaper in his hand; he was making up his mind to the deed, and the manner of it. I think you will have a letter from him soon.

I heard from Portsmouth yesterday, and as I am to send them more clothes, they cannot be expecting a very early return to us. Mary's face is pretty well, but she must have suffered a great deal with it; an abscess was formed and opened.

Our evening party on Thursday produced nothing more remarkable than Miss Murden's coming too, though she had declined it absolutely in the morning, and sitting very ungracious and very silent with us from seven o'clock till half after eleven, for so late was it, owing to the chairmen, before we got rid of them.

The last hour, spent in yawning and shivering in a wide circle round the fire, was dull enough, but the tray had admirable success. The widgeon and the preserved ginger were as delicious as one could wish. But as to our black butter, do not decoy anybody to Southampton by such a lure, for it is all gone. The first pot was opened when Frank and Mary were here, and proved not at all what it ought to be ; it was neither solid nor entirely sweet, and on seeing it Eliza remembered that Miss Austen had said she did not think it had been boiled enough. It was made, you know, when we were absent. Such being the event of the first pot, I would not save the second, and we therefore ate it in unpretending privacy ; and though not what it ought to be, part of it was very good.

James means to keep three horses on this increase of income ; at present he has but one. Mary wishes the other two to be fit to carry women, and in the purchase of one Edward will probably be called upon to fulfil his promise to his godson. We have now pretty well ascertained James's income to be eleven hundred pounds, curate paid, which makes us very happy—the ascertainment as well as the income.

Mary does not talk of the garden ; it may well be a disagreeable subject to her, but her husband is persuaded that nothing is wanting to make the first new one good but trenching, which is to be done by his own servants and John Bond, by degrees, not at the expense which trenching the other amounted to.

I was happy to hear, chiefly for Anna's sake, that a ball at Manydown was once more in agitation ; it is called a child's ball, and given by Mrs. Heathcote to Wm. Such was its beginning at least, but it will probably swell into something more. Edward was invited during his stay at Manydown, and it is to take place between this and Twelfth-day. Mrs. Hulbert has taken Anna a pair of white shoes on the occasion.

I forgot in my last to tell you that we hear, by way of Kintbury and the Palmers, that they were all well at Bermuda in the beginning of Nov.

Wednesday.—Yesterday must have been a day of sad remembrance at Gm. I am glad it is over. We spent Friday evening with our friends at the boarding-house, and our curiosity was gratified by the sight of their fellow-inmates, Mrs. Drew and Miss Hook, Mr. Wynne and Mr. Fitzhugh; the latter is brother to Mrs. Lance, and very much the gentleman. He has lived in that house more than twenty years, and, poor man! is so totally deaf that they say he could not hear a cannon, were it fired close to him; having no cannon at hand to make the experiment, I took it for granted, and talked to him a little with my fingers, which was funny enough. I recommended him to read Corinna.

Miss Hook is a well-behaved, genteelish woman; Mrs. Drew well behaved, without being at all genteel. Mr. Wynne seems a chatty and rather familiar young man. Miss Murden was quite a different creature this last evening from what she had been before, owing to her having with Martha's help found a situation in the morning, which bids very fair for comfort. When she leaves Steventon, she comes to board and lodge with Mrs. Hookey, the chemist—for there is no Mr. Hookey. I cannot say that I am in any hurry for the conclusion of her present visit, but I was truly glad to see her comfortable in mind and spirits ; at her age, perhaps, one may be as friendless oneself, and in similar circumstances quite as captious.

My mother has been lately adding to her possessions in plate—a whole tablespoon and a whole dessert-spoon, and six whole teaspoons—which makes our sideboard border on the magnificent. They were mostly the produce of old or useless silver. I have turned the **11***s*. in the list into **12***s*., and the card looks all the better ; a silver tea-ladle is also added, which will at least answer the purpose of making us sometimes think of John Warren.

I have laid Lady Sondes' case before Martha, who does not make the least objection to it, and is particularly pleased with the name of Montresor. I do not agree with her there, but I like his rank very much, and always affix the ideas of strong sense and highly elegant manners to a general.

I must write to Charles next week. You may guess in what extravagant terms of praise Earle Harwood speaks of him. He is looked up to by everybody in all America.

I shall not tell you anything more of Wm. Digweed's china, as your silence on the subject makes you unworthy of it. Mrs. H. Digweed looks forward with great satisfaction to our being her neighbours. I would have her enjoy the idea to the utmost, as I suspect there will not be much in the reality. With equal pleasure *we* anticipate an intimacy with her husband's bailiff and his wife, who live close by us, and are said to be remarkably good sort of people.

Yes, yes, we *will* have a pianoforte, as good a one as can be got for thirty guineas, and I will practise country dances, that we may have some amusement for our nephews and nieces, when we have the pleasure of their company.

Martha sends her love to Henry, and tells him that he will soon have a bill of Miss Chaplin's, about 14*l*., to pay on her account ; but the bill shall not be sent in till his return to town. I hope he comes to you in good health, and in spirits as good as a first return to Godmersham can allow. With his nephews he will force himself to be cheerful, till he really is so. Send me some intelligence of Eliza ; it is a long while since I have heard of her.

We have had snow on the ground here almost a week ; it is now going, but Southampton must boast no longer. We all send our love to Edward junior and his brothers, and I hope Speculation is generally liked.

Fare you well.

Yours affectionately,   J. Austen

My mother has not been out of doors this week, but she keeps pretty well. We have received through Bookham an indifferent account of your godmother.

63. *To Cassandra Austen. Tuesday* 10 *Jan.* ⟨1809⟩

Address (Brabourne) : Miss Austen, Edward Austen's, Esq. | Godmersham Park, Faversham, Kent
Maine Historical Society.
Brabourne ii. 53 ; *Life* 224 (extracts).

Castle Square : Tuesday January 10

I am not surprised, my dear Cassandra, that you did not find my last letter very full of matter, and I wish this may not have the same deficiency ; but we are doing nothing ourselves to write about, and I am therefore quite dependent upon the communications of our friends, or my own wits.

This post brought me two interesting letters, yours and one from Bookham, in answer to an enquiry of mine about your good godmother, of whom we had lately received a very alarming account from Paragon. Miss Arnold was the informant there, and she spoke of Mrs. E. L. having been very dangerously ill, and attended by a physician from Oxford.

Your letter to Adlestrop may perhaps bring you information from the spot, but in case it should not, I must tell you that she is better ; though Dr. Bourne cannot yet call her out of danger ; such was the case last Wednesday, and Mrs. Cooke's having had no later account is a favourable sign. I am to hear again from the latter *next* week, but not *this*, if everything goes on well.

Her disorder is an inflammation on the lungs, arising from a severe chill, taken in church last Sunday three weeks ; her mind all pious composure, as may be supposed. George Cooke was there when her illness began ; his brother has now taken his place. Her age and feebleness considered, one's fears cannot but preponderate, though her amendment has already surpassed the expectation of the physician at the beginning. I am sorry to add that *Becky* is laid up with a complaint of the same kind.

I am very glad to have the time of your return at all fixed ; we all rejoice in it, and it will not be later than I had expected. I dare not hope that Mary and Miss Curling may be detained at Portsmouth so long or half so long ; but it would be worth twopence to have it so.

The 'St. Albans' perhaps may soon be off to help bring home what may remain by this time of our poor army, whose state seems dreadfully critical. The 'Regency' seems to have been heard of only here; my most political correspondents make no mention of it. Unlucky that I should have wasted so much reflection on the subject.

I can now answer your question to my mother more at large, and likewise more at small—with equal perspicuity and minuteness; for the very day of our leaving Southampton is fixed; and if the knowledge is of no *use* to Edward, I am sure it will give him pleasure. Easter Monday, April 3, is the day; we are to sleep that night at Alton, and be with our friends at Bookham the next, if they are then at home; there we remain till the following Monday, and on Tuesday, April 11, hope to be at Godmersham. If the Cookes are absent, we shall finish our journey on the 5th. These plans depend of course upon the weather, but I hope there will be no settled cold to delay us materially.

To make you amends for being at Bookham, it is in contemplation to spend a few days at Barton Lodge in our way *out* of Kent. The hint of such a visit is most affectionately welcomed by Mrs. Birch, in one of her odd pleasant letters lately, in which she speaks of *us* with the usual distinguished kindness, declaring that she shall not be at all satisfied unless a very *handsome* present is made us immediately from one quarter.

Fanny's not coming with you is no more than we expected, and as we have not the hope of a bed for her, and shall see her so soon afterwards at Godmersham, we cannot wish it otherwise.

William will be quite recovered, I trust, by the time you receive this. What a comfort his cross-stitch must have been! Pray tell him that I should like to see his work very much. I hope our answers this morning have given satisfaction; we had great pleasure in Uncle Deedes' packet; and pray let Marianne know, in private, that I think she is quite right to work a rug for Uncle John's coffee urn, and that I am sure it must give great pleasure to herself now, and to him when he receives it.

The preference of Brag over Speculation does not greatly surprise me, I believe, because I feel the same myself; but it mortifies me deeply, because Speculation was under my patronage; and, after all, what is there so delightful in a pair royal of Braggers? It is but three nines or three knaves, or a mixture of them. When one comes to reason upon it, it cannot stand its ground against Speculation—of which I hope Edward is now convinced. Give my love to him if he is.

The letter from Paragon before mentioned was much like those which had preceded it, as to the felicity of its writer. They found their house so dirty and so damp that they were obliged to be a week at an inn. John Binns had behaved most unhandsomely and engaged himself elsewhere. They *have* a man, however, on the same footing, which my aunt does not like, and she finds both him and the new maid-servant very, very inferior to Robert and Martha. Whether they mean to have any other domestics does not appear, nor whether they are to have a carriage while they are in Bath.

The Holders are as usual, though I believe it is not

very usual for them to be happy, which they now are at a great rate, in Hooper's marriage. The Irvines are not mentioned. The American lady improved as we went on; but still the same faults in part recurred.

We are now in Margiana, and like it very well indeed. We are just going to set off for Northumberland to be shut up in Widdrington Tower, where there must be two or three sets of victims already immured under a very fine villain.

Wednesday.—Your report of Eliza's health gives me great pleasure, and the progress of the bank is a constant source of satisfaction. With such increasing profits, tell Henry that I hope he will not work poor High-diddle so hard as he used to do.

Has your newspaper given a sad story of a Mrs. Middleton, wife of a farmer in Yorkshire, her sister, and servant, being almost frozen to death in the late weather, her little child quite so? I hope this sister is not our friend Miss Woodd, and I rather think her brother-in-law had moved into Lincolnshire, but their name and station accord too well. Mrs. M. and the maid are said to be tolerably recovered, but the sister is likely to lose the use of her limbs.

Charles's rug will be finished to-day, and sent to-morrow to Frank, to be consigned by him to Mr. Turner's care; and I am going to send Marmion out with it—very generous in me, I think.

As we have no letter from Adlestrop, we may suppose the good woman was alive on Monday, but I cannot help expecting bad news from thence or Bookham in a few days. Do you continue quite well?

Have you nothing to say of your little namesake? We join in love and many happy returns.

Yours affectionately, J. Austen

The Manydown ball was a smaller thing than I expected, but it seems to have made Anna very happy. At *her* age it would not have done for *me.*

64. *To Cassandra Austen.* *Tuesday* 17 *Jan.* 1809

***Address*: Miss Austen | Edwd Austen's Esqr | Godmersham Park Faversham | Kent**
***Postmarks*: SOUTHAMPTON and JAN 19 1809**
Pierpont Morgan Library. 2 leaves 4°.
***Brabourne* ii. 59; *Life* 226 (extracts). Two sentences unpublished.**

Castle Square, Tuesday Jany 17.

My dear Cassandra

I am happy to say that we had no second Letter from Bookham last week. Yours has brought its usual measure of satisfaction and amusement, and I beg your acceptance of all the Thanks due on the occasion.—Your offer of Cravats is very kind, and happens to be particularly adapted to my wants—but it was an odd thing to occur to you. Yes—we have got another fall of snow, and are very dreadful; everything seems to turn to snow this winter.—I hope you have had no more illness among you, and that William will be soon as well as ever. His working a footstool for Chawton is a most agreable surprise to me, and I am sure his Grandmama will value it very much as a proof of his affection and Industry—but we shall never have the heart to put our feet upon it.—I beleive I must work a muslin cover in sattin stitch, to keep it from the dirt.—I long to know what his colours are—I guess greens and purples.—Edw[d] and Henry have started a difficulty respecting our Journey, which I must own with some confusion, had never been thought of by us ; but if the former expected by it, to prevent our travelling into Kent entirely he will be disappointed, for we have already determined to go the Croydon road, on leaving Bookham, and sleep at Dartford.—Will not that do ?—There certainly does seem no convenient restingplace on the other road.—Anna went to Clanville last friday, and I have hopes of her new Aunt's being really worth her knowing.—Perhaps you may never have heard that James and Mary paid a morn[g] visit there in form some weeks ago, and Mary tho' by no means disposed to like her, was very much pleased with her indeed. *Her* praise to be sure, proves nothing more than Mrs. M.'s being civil and attentive to them, but her being so is in favour of her having good sense.—Mary writes of Anna as improved in person, but gives her no other commendation.—I am afraid her absence now may deprive her of one pleasure, for that silly Mr. Hammond is actually to give his Ball on friday.—We had some reason to expect a visit from Earle Harwood and James this week, but they do not come.—Miss Murden arrived last night at Mrs. Hookey's, as a message and a basket announced to us—You will therefore return to an enlarged and of course improved society here, especially as the Miss Williamses are come back.—We were agreably surprised the other day by a visit from your Beauty and mine, each in a new Cloth Mantle and Bonnet, and I daresay you will value yourself much on the modest propriety of Miss W.'s taste, hers being purple, and Miss Grace's scarlet. I can easily suppose that your six weeks here will be fully occupied, were it only in lengthening the waist of your gowns. I have pretty well arranged my spring and summer plans of that kind, and mean to wear out my spotted Muslin before I go.—You will exclaim at this—but mine really has signs of feebleness, which with a little care may come to something.—Martha and Dr. Mant are as bad as ever; he runs after her in the street to apologise for having spoken to a Gentleman while *she* was near him the day before.—Poor Mrs. Mant can stand it no longer; she is retired to one of her married Daughters.—We hear through Kintbury that Mrs Esten was unluckily to lie in at the same time with Mrs C. A.—

When William returns to Winchester Mary Jane is to go to Mrs. Nunes for a month, and then to Steventon for a fortnight, and it seems likely that she and her Aunt Martha may travel into Berkshire together.—We shall not have a Month of Martha after your return—and that Month will be a very interrupted and broken one;—but we shall enjoy ourselves the more, when we *can* get a quiet half hour together. —To set against your new Novel of which nobody ever heard before and perhaps never may again, We have got *Ida of Athens* by Miss Owenson; which must be very clever, because it was written as the Authoress says, in three months.—We have only read the Preface yet; but her Irish Girl does not make me expect much.—If the warmth of her Language could affect the Body it might be worth reading in this weather.—

Adeiu—I must leave off to stir the fire and call on Miss Murden.

Even^g^. I have done them both, the first very often.

—We found our friend as comfortable, as she can ever allow herself to be in cold weather;—there is a very neat parlour behind the shop for her to sit in, not very light indeed, being a la Southampton, the middle of Three deep—but very lively, from the frequent sound of the pestle and mortar.—We afterwards called on the Miss Williamses, who lodge at Dusautoys; Miss Mary only was at home, and she is in very indifferent health.—Dr. Hacket came in while we were there, and said that he never remembered such a severe winter as this, in Southampton before. It is bad, but *we* do not suffer as we did last year, because the wind has been more N.E.—than N.W.— For a day or two last week, my Mother was very poorly, with a return of *one* of her old complaints— but it did not last long, and seems to have left nothing bad behind it.—She began to talk of a serious Illness, her two last having been preceded by the same symptoms; but—thank Heaven! she is now quite as well as one can expect her to be in Weather, which deprives her of Exercise.—

Miss M. conveys to us a third volume of sermons from Hamstall, just published; and which we are to like better than the two others;—they are professedly *practical*, and for the use of country Congregations.— I have just recieved some verses in an unknown hand, and am desired to forward them to my nephew Edw[d] at Godmersham.

"Alas! poor Brag, thou boastful Game!—
What now avails thine empty name?—
Where now thy more distinguish'd fame?—
My day is o'er, and Thine the same.—
For thou like me art thrown aside,
At Godmersham, this Christmas Tide;

And now across the Table wide,
Each Game save Brag or Spec: is tried."—
"Such is the mild Ejaculation,
Of tender hearted Speculation."—

Wednesday.—I expected to have a Letter from somebody to-day, but I have not. Twice every day, I think of a Letter from Portsmouth.—Miss Murden has been sitting with us this morn[g]—as yet she seems very well pleased with her situation. The worst part of her being in Southampton will be the necessity of our walking with her now and then, for she talks so loud that one is quite ashamed, but our Dining hours are luckily very different, which we shall take all reasonable advantage of.—M[rs] H[y] D. has been brought to bed some time. I suppose *we* must stand to the next.

The Queen's Birthday moves the Assembly to this night, instead of last—and as it is always fully attended, Martha and I expect an amusing shew.—We were in hopes of being independant of other companions by having the attendance of Mr. Austen and Capt. Harwood, but, as they fail us, we are obliged to look out for other help, and have fixed on the Wallops as least likely to be troublesome.—I have called on them this morn[g] and found them very willing ;—and I am sorry that you must wait a whole week for the particulars of the Even[g].—I propose being asked to dance by our acquaintance Mr. Smith, now *Capt*[n] Smith, who has lately re-appeared in Southampton—but I shall decline it.—He saw Charles last August.—What an alarming Bride Mrs. Col[n] Tilson must have been. Such a parade is one of the most immodest peices of Modesty that one can imagine. To *attract* notice could have been her only wish.--It augurs ill for his family—it announces not *great* sense, and therefore ensures boundless Influence. —I hope Fanny's visit is now taking place.—You have said scarcely anything of her lately, but I trust you are as good friends as ever.—Martha sends her Love, and hopes to have the pleasure of seeing you when you return to Southampton. You are to understand this message, as being merely for the sake of a Message, to oblige me.—

Y[rs] affec[tely]— J. Austen

Henry never sent his Love to me in your last—but I send him Mine.—

65. *To Cassandra Austen. Tuesday* 24 *Jan.* 1809

Address: Miss Austen | Edw[d] Austen Esq[r] | Godmersham Park | Faversham | Kent
Postmarks: SOUTHAMPTON and ⟨JA⟩N 25 ⟨18⟩09
Pierpont Morgan Library. 2 leaves 4°.
Brabourne ii. 66; *Life* 227 (extracts).

Castle Square, Tuesday Jan[y] 24.

My dear Cassandra

I will give you the indulgence of a letter on Thursday this week, instead of Friday, but I do not require you to write again before Sunday, provided I may beleive you and your finger going on quite well.—Take care of your precious self, do not work too hard, remember that Aunt Cassandras are quite as scarce as Miss Beverleys.—I had the happiness yesterday of a letter from Charles, but I shall say as little about it as possible, because I know *that* excruciating Henry will have had a Letter likewise; to make all my intelligence valueless.—It was written at Bermuda on ye 7, & 10 of Dec^r;—all well, and Fanny still only in expectation of being otherwise. He had taken a small prize in his late cruize; a French schooner laden with Sugar, but Bad weather parted them, and she had not yet been heard of;—his cruize ended Decr 1st—My September Letter was the latest he had recieved.—This day three weeks you are to be in London, and I wish you better weather—not but that you may have worse, for we have now nothing but ceaseless snow or rain and insufferable dirt to complain of—no tempestuous winds, nor severity of cold. Since I wrote last, we have had something of each, but it is not genteel to rip up old greivances.—You used me scandalously by not mentioning Ed. Cooper's sermons;—I tell you everything, and it is unknown the Mysteries you conceal from me.—And to add to the rest you persevere in giving a final e to Invalid thereby putting it out of one's power to suppose Mrs. E. Leigh even for a moment, a veteran Soldier.—She, good Woman, is I hope destined for some further placid enjoyment of her own Excellence in this World, for her recovery advances exceedingly well.—I had this pleasant news in a letter from Bookham last Thursday, but as the letter was from Mary instead of her Mother, you will guess her account was not equally good from home.—Mrs. Cooke had been confined to her bed some days by Illness, but was then better, and Mary wrote in confidence of her continuing to mend. I have desired to hear again soon. You rejoice me by what you say of Fanny—I hope she will not turn good-for-nothing this ever so long;—we thought of and talked of her yesterday with sincere affection, and wished her a long enjoyment of all the happiness to which she seems born.—While she gives happiness to those about her, she is pretty sure of her own share.—I am gratified by her having pleasure in what I write—but I wish the knowledge of my being exposed to her discerning Criticism, may not hurt my stile, by inducing too great a solicitude. I begin already to weigh my words and sentences more than I did, and am looking about for a sentiment, an illustration or a metaphor in every corner of the room. Could my Ideas flow as fast as the rain in the Store closet it would be charming.—We have been in two or three dreadful states within the last week, from the melting of the snow &c.—and the contest between us and the Closet has now ended in our defeat; I have been obliged to move almost everything out of it, and leave it to splash itself as it likes.—You have by no means raised my curiosity after Caleb;—My disinclination for it before was affected, but now it is real; I do not like the Evangelicals.—Of course I shall be delighted, when I read it, like other people, but till I do I dislike it.—I am sorry my verses did not bring any return from Edward, I was in hopes they might—but I suppose he does not rate them high enough.—It might be partiality, but they seemed to me purely classical—just like Homer and Virgil, Ovid and Propria que Maribus.—I had a nice, brotherly letter from Frank the other day, which after an interval of nearly three weeks, was very welcome.—No orders were come on friday, and none were come yesterday, or we sh^{d} have heard to-day.—I had supposed Miss C. would share her Cousin's room here, but a message in this Letter proves the Contrary;—I will make the Garret as comfortable as I can, but the possibilities of that apartment are not great.—My Mother has been talking to Eliza about our future home—and *she*, making no difficulty at all of the sweetheart, is perfectly disposed to continue with us, but till she has written home for *Mother's* approbation, cannot quite decide.—*Mother* does not like to have her so far off;—at Chawton she will be nine or ten miles nearer, which I hope will have its due influence—As for Sally, she means to play John Binns with us, in her anxiety to belong to our Household again. Hitherto, she appears a very good Servant.—You depend upon finding all your plants dead, I hope.—They look very ill I understand.—Your silence on the subject of our Ball, makes me suppose your Curiosity too great for words. We were very well entertained, and could have staid longer but for the arrival of my List shoes to convey me home, and I did not like to keep them waiting in the cold. The room was tolerably full, and the Ball opened by Miss Glyn;—the Miss Lances had partners, Capt. D'auvergne's friend appeared in regimentals, Caroline Maitland had an officer to flirt with, and Mr. John Harrison was deputed by Capt. Smith, being himself absent, to ask me to dance.—Everything went well you see, especially after we had tucked Mrs. Lance's neckhandkerf in behind, and fastened it with a pin.—We had a very full and agreable account of Mr. Hammond's Ball, from Anna last night; the same fluent pen has sent similar information I know into Kent.—She seems to have been as happy as one could wish her—and the complacency of her Mama in doing the Honours of the Even^{g} must have made her pleasure almost as great.—The Grandeur of the Meeting was beyond my hopes.—I should like to have seen Anna's looks and performance—but that sad cropt head must have injured the former.—

Martha pleases herself with beleiving that if *I* had kept her counsel, you w[d] never have heard of D[r] M.'s late behaviour, as if the very slight manner in which I mentioned it could have been all on which you found your Judgement.—I do not endeavour to undeceive her, because I wish her happy at all events, and know how highly she prizes happiness of any kind. She is moreover so full of kindness for us both, and sends you in particular so many good wishes about your finger, that I am willing to overlook a venial fault; and as Dr. M. is a Clergyman their attachment, however immoral, has a decorous air.—Adeiu, sweet You.—This is greivous news from Spain.—It is well that Dr. Moore was spared the knowledge of such a son's death.—

Y[rs] affec:[ly] J. Austen

Anna's hand gets better and better, it begins to be too good for any consequence.

We send best Love to dear little Lizzy and Marianne in particular.

The Portsmouth paper gave a melancholy history of a poor Mad Woman, escaped from Confinement, who said her Husband and Daughter of the name of Payne lived at Ashford in Kent. Do you own them?

66. *To Cassandra Austen.* *Monday* 30 *Jan.* 1809

Address: Miss Austen | Edwd Austen's Esqr | Godmersham Park | Faversham | Kent
Postmark: JAN 31 1809
Pierpont Morgan Library. 2 leaves 4°.
Brabourne ii. 72; *Life* 228 (extracts).

Castle Square: Monday Jany 30.

My dear Cassandra

I was not much surprised yesterday by the agreable surprise of your letter, & extremely glad to receive the assurance of your finger being well again. Here is such a wet Day as never was seen!—I wish the poor little girls had better weather for their Journey; they must amuse themselves with watching the raindrops down the Windows. Sackree I suppose feels quite brokenhearted.—I cannot have done with the weather without observing how delightfully mild it is; I am sure Fanny must enjoy it with us.—Yesterday was a very blowing day; we got to Church however, which we had not been able to do for two Sundays before.—I am not at all ashamed about the name of the Novel, having been guilty of no insult towards your handwriting; the Dipthong I always saw, but knowing how fond you were of adding a vowel wherever you could, I attributed it to that alone—& the knowledge of the truth does the book no service; the only merit it could have, was in the name of Caleb, which has an honest, unpretending sound; but in Cœlebs, there is pedantry & affectation.—Is it written only to Classical Scholars? —I shall now try to say only what is necessary, I am weary of meandering—so expect a vast deal of small matter concisely told, in the next two pages.—Mrs.

Cooke has been very dangerously ill, but is now I hope safe.—I had a letter last week from George, Mary being too busy to write, & at that time the Disorder was called of the Typhus kind, & their alarm considerable —but yesterday brought me a much better account from Mary; the origin of the complaint being now ascertained to be Billious, & the strong medicines requisite, promising to be effectual.—Mrs. E. L. is so much recovered as to get into the Dressing-room every day. —A letter from Hamstall gives us the history of Sir Tho. Williams' return;—the Admiral, whoever he might be, took a fancy to the Neptune, & having only a worn out 74 to offer in lieu of it, Sir Tho. declined such a command, & is come home Passenger. Lucky Man! to have so fair an opportunity of escape.— I hope His wife allows herself to be happy on the occasion, & does not give all her thoughts to being nervous.—A great event happens this week at Hamstall, in young Edward's removal to school; he is going to Rugby & is very happy in the idea of it;—I wish his happiness may last, but it will be a great change, to become a raw school boy from being a pompous Sermon-Writer, & a domineering Brother.—It will do him good I dare say.—Caroline has had a great escape from being burnt to death lately;—as her husband gives the account, we must beleive it true.—Miss Murden is gone—called away by the critical state of Mrs. Pottinger, who has had another severe stroke, & is without Sense or Speech. Miss Murden wishes to return to Southampton if circumstances suit, but it must be very doubtful.—We have been obliged to turn away Cholles, he grew so very drunken & negligent, & we have a man in his place called Thomas.—

Martha desires me to communicate something concerning herself which she knows will give you pleasure, as affording her very particular satisfaction; it is, that she is to be in Town this spring with Mrs. Dundas.—I need not dilate on the subject—you understand enough of the whys & wherefores to enter into her feelings, & to be conscious that of all possible arrangements, it is the one most acceptable to her.—She goes to Barton on leaving us—& the Family remove to Town in April.—What you tell me of Miss Sharpe is quite new, & surprises me a little;—I feel however as you do. She is born, poor thing! to struggle with Evil—& her continuing with Miss B. is I hope a proof that Matters are not always so very bad between them as her Letters sometimes represent.—Jenny's marriage I had heard of, & supposed you would do so too from Steventon, as I knew you were corresponding with Mary at the time. I hope she will not sully the respectable name she now bears.—Your plan for Miss Curling is uncommonly considerate & friendly, & such as she must surely jump at. Edward's going round by Steventon, as I understand he promises to do, can be no reasonable objection, Mrs. J. Austen's hospitality is just of the kind to enjoy such a visitor.—We were very glad to know Aunt Fanny was in the Country when we read of the Fire.—Pray give my best Comp[ts] to the Mrs. Finches, if they are at G[m].—I am sorry to find that Sir J. Moore has a mother living, but tho' a very Heroick son, he might not be a very necessary one to her happiness.—Deacon Morrell may be more to Mrs. Morrell.—I wish Sir John had united something of the Christian with the Hero in his death.—Thank Heaven! we have had no one to care for particularly among the Troops—no one in fact nearer to us than Sir John himself. Col. Maitland is safe & well; his Mother & sisters were of course anxious about him, but there is no entering much into the solicitudes of that family.—My Mother is well, & gets out when she can with the same enjoyment, & apparently the same strength as hitherto.—She hopes you will not omit begging Mrs. Seward to get the Garden cropped for us—supposing she leaves the House too early, to make the Garden any object to herself.—We are very desirous of receiving *your* account of the House—for your observations will have a motive which can leave nothing to conjecture & suffer nothing from want of Memory.—For one's own dear self, one ascertains & remembers everything.—Lady Sondes is an impudent Woman to come back into her old Neighbourhood again; I suppose she pretends never to have married before—& wonders how her Father & Mother came to have her christen'd Lady Sondes.—

The store closet I hope will never do so again—for much of the Evil is proved to have proceeded from the Gutter being choked up, & we have had it cleared. —We had reason to rejoice in the Child's absence at the time of the Thaw, for the Nursery was not habitable.—We hear of similar disasters from almost everybody.—No news from Portsmouth. We are very patient.—Mrs. Charles Fowle desires to be kindly remembered to you. She is warmly interested in my Brother and his Family.—

Yrs very affec:ly J. Austen

67. *To Crosbie & Co.* ⟨*Wednesday*⟩ 5 *April* 1809

No address or postmark.
British Museum (1925). Formerly in the collection described in *Times Literary Supplement* 14 Jan. 1926. One leaf 4°. Endorsed 'Copy of a Letter to Mess[rs] Crosbie & Co. & M[r] Crosbie's reply'. Not autograph. Preserved with N° 67a.
***Life* 230.**

Gentlemen

In the spring of the year 1803 a MS. Novel in 2 vol. entitled Susan was sold to you by a Gentleman of the name of Seymour, & the purchase money £10. rec[d] at the same time. Six years have since passed, & this work of which I am myself the Authoress, has never to the best of my knowledge, appeared in print, tho' an early publication was stipulated for at the time of sale. I can only account for such an extraordinary circumstance by supposing the MS. by some carelessness to have been lost; & if that was the case, am willing to supply you with another copy if you are disposed to avail yourselves of it, & will engage for no farther delay when it comes into your hands. It will not be in my power from particular circumstances to command this copy before the Month of August, but then, if you accept my proposal, you may depend on receiving it. Be so good as to send me a Line in answer as soon as possible, as my stay in this place will not exceed a few days. Should no notice be taken of this address, I shall feel myself at liberty to secure the publication of my work, by applying elsewhere. I am Gentlemen &c. &c.

M. A. D.

April 5. 1809.

Direct to M[rs] Ashton Dennis
Post Office, Southampton

67a. *From Richard Crosby.* ⟨*Saturday*⟩ 8 *April* 1809

Address: Mrs Ashton Dennis | Post Office | Southampton
Postmark: AP 10 1809
British Museum (1925). See N° 67. One leaf.
Life 231.

Madam

We have to acknowledge the receipt of your letter of the 5th inst. It is true that at the time mentioned we purchased of Mr Seymour a MS. novel entitled *Susan* and paid him for it the sum of 10£ for which we have his stamped receipt as a full consideration, but there was not any time stipulated for its publication, neither are we bound to publish it, Should you or anyone else (*sic*) we shall take proceedings to stop the sale. The MS. shall be yours for the same as we paid for it

For R. Crosby & Co.

I am yours etc.

Richard Crosby

London

Ap 8 1809.

68. *To Francis Austen.* ⟨*Wednesday*⟩ 26 *July* 1809

Address: Captn Austen RN.
Postmark: none.
Captain Ernest Austen R.N. 2 leaves 4°.
Unpublished.

Chawton, July 26.—1809.—

My dearest Frank, I wish you joy
Of Mary's safety with a Boy,
Whose birth has given little pain
Compared with that of Mary Jane.—

May he a growing Blessing prove,
And well deserve his Parents' Love !—
Endow'd with Art's & Nature's Good,
Thy name possessing with thy Blood,
In him, in all his ways, may we
Another Francis William see !—
Thy infant days may he inherit,
Thy warmth, nay insolence of spirit ;—
We would not with one fault dispense
To weaken the resemblance.

May he revive thy Nursery sin,
Peeping as daringly within,
His curley Locks but just descried,
With, ' Bet, my be not come to bide.'—

Fearless of danger, braving pain,
And threaten'd very oft in vain,
Still may one Terror daunt his soul,
One needful engine of Controul
Be found in this sublime array,
A neighbouring Donkey's aweful Bray.
So may his equal faults as Child,
Produce Maturity as mild !
His saucy words & fiery ways
In early Childhood's pettish days,
In Manhood, shew his Father's mind
Like him, considerate & kind ;
All Gentleness to those around,
And eager only not to wound.

Then like his Father too, he must,
To his own former struggles just,
Feel his Deserts with honest Glow,
And all his self-improvement know.—

A native fault may thus give birth
To the best blessing, conscious Worth.—

As for ourselves, we're very well;
As unaffected prose will tell.—
Cassandra's pen will paint our state,
The many comforts that await
Our Chawton home, how much we find
Already in it, to our mind;
And how convinced, that when complete
It will all other Houses beat
That ever have been made or mended,
With rooms concise, or rooms distended.
You'll find us very snug next year,
Perhaps with Charles & Fanny near,
For now it often does delight us
To fancy them just over-right us.—

J. A.---

CHAWTON COTTAGE
(The Times, 1 *Jan.* 1926; *reproduced by permission*)

69. *To Cassandra Austen. Thursday* 18 *April* 1811

Address: Miss Austen | Edw[d] Austen's Esq[re] | Godmersham Park | Faversham | Kent
Postmark: AP 20 1811
Pierpont Morgan Library. 2 leaves 4°. A piece cut away, 1 line lost.
Brabourne ii. 82; *Life* 244 (extracts).

Sloane St. Thursday April 18.

My dear Cassandra

I have so many little matters to tell you of, that I cannot wait any longer before I begin to put them down.—I spent tuesday in Bentinck S[t]; the Cookes called here & took me back; & it was quite a Cooke day, for the Miss Rolles paid a visit while I was there, & Sam Arnold dropt in to tea. The badness of the weather disconcerted an excellent plan of mine, that of calling on Miss Beckford again, but from the middle of the day it rained incessantly. Mary & I, after disposing of her Father & Mother, went to the Liverpool Museum, & the British Gallery, & I had some amusement at each, tho' my preference for Men & Women, always inclines me to attend more to the company than the sight.—Mrs. Cooke regrets very much that she did not see you when you called, it was owing ⟨to some⟩ blunder among the servants, for she did not know of our visit till we were gone.—She seems tolerably well; but the nervous part of her Complaint I fear increases, & makes her more and more unwilling to part with Mary.—I have proposed to the latter that she should go to Chawton with me, on the supposition of my travelling the Guildford road—& *she*, I do beleive, would be glad to do it, but perhaps it may be impossible; unless a Brother can be at home at that time, it certainly must.—George comes to them to day. I did not see Theo' till late on Tuesday ; he was gone to Ilford, but he came back in time to shew his usual, nothing-meaning, harmless, heartless Civility.—Henry, who had been confined the whole day to the Bank, took me in his way home ; & after putting Life & Wit into the party for a quarter of an hour, put himself & his Sister into a Hackney coach.—I bless my stars that I have done with tuesday !—But alas !—Wednesday was likewise a day of great doings, for Manon & I took our walk to Grafton House, & I have a good deal to say on that subject.—I am sorry to tell you that I am getting very extravagant & spending all my Money ; & what is worse for *you*, I have been spending yours too ; for in a Linendraper's shop to which I went for check'd muslin, & for which I was obliged to give seven shillings a yard, I was tempted by a pretty coloured muslin, and bought 10 y^{ds} of it, on the chance of your liking it ;—but at the same time if it sh^{d} not suit you, you must not think yourself at all obliged to take it ; it is only 3/6 p^{r} y^{d}, & I sh^{d} not in the least mind keeping the whole.—In texture, it is just what we prefer, but it's resemblance to green cruels I must own is not great, for the pattern is a small red spot.—⟨*One line cut out*⟩ & now I beleive I have done all my commissions, except Wedgwood. I liked my walk very much ; it was shorter than I had expected, & the weather was delightful. We set off immediately after breakfast & must have reached Grafton House by ½ past 11—, but when we entered the Shop, the whole Counter was thronged, & we waited *full* half an hour before we c^{d} be attended to. When we were served however, I was very well satisfied with my purchases, my Bugle Trimming at 2/4^{d} & 3 p^{r} silk stock^{gs} for a little less than 12./s a p^{r}—In my way back, who sh^{d} I meet but Mr. Moore, just come from Beckenham. I beleive he would have passed me, if I had not made him stop—but we were delighted to meet. I soon found however that he had nothing new to tell me, & then I let him go.—Miss Burton has made me a very pretty little Bonnet—& now nothing can satisfy me but I must have a straw hat, of the riding hat shape, like Mrs. Tilson's; & a young woman in this Neighbourhood is actually making me one. I am really very shocking; but it will not be dear at a Guinea.—Our Pelisses are 17/s. each—she charges only 8/ for the making, but the Buttons seem expensive;—*are* expensive, I might have said—for the fact is plain enough.—We drank tea again yesterday with the Tilsons, & met the Smiths.—I find all these little parties very pleasant. I like Mr. S. Miss Beaty is good-humour itself, & does not seem much besides. We spend tomorrow even^{g} with them, & are to meet the Col^{n} & Mrs. *Cantelo* Smith, you have been used to hear of; & if she is in good humour, are likely to have excellent singing.—To night I might have been at the Play, Henry had kindly planned our going together to the Lyceum, but I have a cold which I sh^{d} not like to make worse before Saturday;—so I stay within, all this day.—Eliza is walking out by herself. She has plenty of business on her hands just now—for the day of the party is settled, & drawing near:—above 80 people are invited for next tuesday Even^{g} & there is to be some very good Music, 5 professionals, 3 of them Glee singers, besides Amateurs.—Fanny will listen to this. One of the Hirelings, is a Capital on the Harp, from which I expect great pleasure.—The foundation of the party was a dinner to Henry Egerton & Henry Walter—but the latter leaves Town the day before. I am sorry—as I wished *her* prejudice to be done away—but sh[d] have been more sorry if there had been no invitation.—I am a wretch, to be so occupied with all these Things, as to seem to have no Thoughts to give to people & circumstances which really supply a far more lasting interest—the Society in which You are—but I do think of you all I assure you, & want to know all about everybody, & especially about your visit to the W. Friars; 'mais le moyen' not to be occupied by one's own concerns?—

Saturday.—Frank is superseded in the Caledonia. Henry brought us this news yesterday from Mr. Daysh &—he heard at the same time that Charles may be in England in the course of a month.—Sir Edw[d] Pellew succeeds Lord Gambier in his command, & some captain of his, succeeds Frank; & I beleive the order is already gone out. Henry means to enquire farther to day;—he wrote to Mary on the occasion.—This is something to think of.—Henry is convinced that he will have the offer of something else, but does not think it will be at all incumbent on him to accept it; & then follows, what will he do? & where will he live?—I hope to hear from you today. How are you, as to Health, strength, Looks, stomach &c.?—I had a very comfortable account from Chawton yesterday.—If the weather permits, Eliza & I walk into London this morn[g]. *She* is in want of chimney lights for Tuesday;—& *I*, of an ounce of darning cotton.—She has resolved not to venture to the Play tonight. The D'Entraigues & Comte Julien cannot come to the Party—which was at first a greif, but she has since supplied herself so well with Performers that it is of no consequence;—their not coming has produced our going to them tomorrow Even[g]—which I like the idea of. It will be amusing to see the ways of a French circle. I wrote to Mrs. Hill a few days ago, & have received a most kind & satisfactory answer; my time, the first week in May, exactly suits her; & therefore I consider my Goings as tolerably fixed. I shall leave Sloane St. on the 1st or 2[d] & be ready for James on ye 9th;—& if his plan alters, I can take care of myself.—I have explained my veiws here, & everything is smooth & pleasant; & Eliza talks kindly of conveying me to Streatham.—We met the Tilsons yesterday Even[g]—but the singing Smiths sent an excuse—which put our Mrs. Smith out of humour.—

We are come back, after a good dose of Walking & Coaching, & I have the pleasure of your letter.—I wish I had James's verses, but they were left at Chawton. When I return thither, if Mrs. K. will give me leave, I will send them to her.—Our first object to day was Henrietta St. to consult with Henry, in consequence of a very unlucky change of The play for this very night—Hamlet instead of King John—& we are to go on Monday to Macbeth, instead, but it is a disappointment to us both.

Love to all.

Yours affec:[ly] Jane

70. *To Cassandra Austen.* *Thursday* 25 *April* ⟨1811⟩

Address: Miss Austen | Edw[d] Austen's Esq[re] | Godmersham Park | Faversham
Postmark: AP 2⟨ ⟩ ⟨18⟩11
British Museum.
Brabourne ii. 89 ; *Life* 246 (extracts).

Sloane S[t] Thursday April 25

My dearest Cassandra

I can return the compliment by thanking you for the unexpected pleasure of *your* Letter yesterday, & as I like unexpected pleasure, it made me very happy; And indeed, you need not apologise for your Letter in any respect, for it is all very fine, but not *too* fine I hope to be written again, or something like it. I think Edward will not suffer much longer from heat; by the look of Things this morn[g] I suspect the weather is rising into the balsamic Northeast. It has been hot here, as you may suppose, since it was so hot with you, but I have not suffered from it at all, nor felt it in such a degree as to make me imagine it would be anything in the country. Everybody has talked of the heat, but I set it all down to London.—I give you joy of our new nephew, & hope if he ever comes to be hanged, it will not be till we are too old to care about it.—It is a great comfort to have it so safely & speedily over. The Miss Curlings must be hard worked in writing so many Letters, but the novelty of it may recommend it to *them*;—mine was from Miss Eliza, & she says that my Brother may arrive today.—No indeed, I am never too busy to think of S & S. I can no more forget it, than a mother can forget her sucking child; & I am much obliged to you for your enquiries. I have had two sheets to correct, but the last only brings us to W.s first appearance. Mrs K. regrets in the most flattering manner that she must wait *till* May, but I have scarcely a hope of its being out in June.—Henry does not neglect it; he *has* hurried the Printer, & says he will see him again today.—It will not stand still during his absence, it will be sent to Eliza.—The *Incomes* remain as they were, but I will get them altered if I can.—I am very much gratified by Mrs K.s interest in it; & whatever may be the event of it as to my credit with her, sincerely wish her curiosity could be satisfied sooner than is now probable. I think she will like my Elinor, but cannot build on any thing else. Our party went off extremely well. There were many solicitudes; alarms & vexations beforehand of course, but at last everything was quite right. The rooms were dressed up with flowers &c, & looked very pretty.—A glass for the Mantlepiece was lent, by the Man who is making their own.—Mr Egerton & Mr Walter came at 1/2 past 5, & the festivities began with a pr of very fine Soals. Yes, Mr Walter—for he postponed his leaving London on purpose—which did not give much pleasure at the time, any more than the circumstance from which it rose, his calling on Sunday & being asked by Henry to take the family dinner on that day, which he did—but it is all smooth'd over now;—& she likes him very well.—At 1/2 past 7 arrived the Musicians in two Hackney coaches, & by 8 the lordly company began to appear. Among the earliest were George & Mary Cooke, & I spent the greatest part of the eveng very pleasantly with them.—The Drawg room being soon hotter than we liked, we placed ourselves in the connecting Passage, which was comparatively cool, & gave us all the advantage of the Music at a pleasant distance, as well as that of the first veiw of every new comer.—I was quite surrounded by acquaintance, especially Gentlemen; & what with Mr Hampson, Mr Seymour, Mr W. Knatchbull, Mr Guillemarde, Mr Cure, a Capt Simpson, brother to *the* Capt Simpson, besides Mr Walter & Mr Egerton, in addition to the Cookes & Miss Beckford & Miss Middleton, I had quite as much upon my hands as I could do.—Poor Miss B. has been suffering again from her old complaint, & looks thinner than ever. She certainly goes to Cheltenham the beginning of June. We were all delight & cordiality of course. Miss M. seems very happy, but has not beauty enough to figure in London. —Including everybody we were 66—which was considerably more than Eliza had expected, & quite enough to fill the Back Draw^g^ room, & leave a few to be scattered about in the other, & in the passage. The Music was extremely good. It opened (tell Fanny, with ' Poike pe Parp pin praise pof Prapela '— & of the other Glees I remember, ' In Peace Love tunes,' ' Rosabelle,' ' The red cross Knight,' & ' Poor Insect.' Between the Songs were Lessons on the Harp, or Harp & Piano Forte together—& the Harp Player was Wiepart, whose name seems famous, tho' new to me.—There was one female singer, a short Miss Davis all in blue, bringing up for the Public Line, whose voice was said to be very fine indeed; & all the Performers gave great satisfaction by doing what they were paid for, & giving themselves no airs.—No amateur could be persuaded to do anything.—The House was not clear till after 12.—If you wish to hear more of it, you must put your questions, but I seem rather to have exhausted than spared the subject.—This said Capt. Simpson told us, on the authority of some other Capt[n] just arrived from Halifax, that Charles was bringing the Cleopatra home, & that she was probably by this time in the Channel—but as Capt. S. was certainly in liquor, we must not quite depend on it.—It must give one a sort of expectation however, & will prevent my writing to him any more. —I would rather he sh[d] not reach England till I am at home, & the Steventon party gone. My Mother & Martha both write with great satisfaction of Anna's behaviour. She is quite an Anna with variations—but she cannot have reached her last, for that is always the most flourishing & shewey—she is at about her 3[d] or 4th which are generally simple & pretty.—Your Lilacs are in leaf, *ours* are in bloom.—The Horse chesnuts are quite out, & the Elms almost.—I had a pleasant walk in Kensington G[s] on Sunday with Henry, M[r] Smith & M[r] Tilson—everything was fresh & beautiful.—We *did* go to the play after all on Saturday, we went to the Lyceum, & saw the Hypocrite, an old play taken from Moliere's *Tartuffe*, & were well entertained. Dowton & Mathews were the good actors. Mrs Edwin was the Heroine—& her performance is just what it used to be.—I have no chance of seeing M[rs] Siddons.—She *did* act on Monday, but as Henry was told by the Boxkeeper that he did not think she would, the places, & all thought of it, were given up. I should particularly have liked seeing her in Constance, & could swear at her with little effort for disappointing me.—Henry has been to the Watercolour Exhibition, which open'd on Monday,

& is to meet us there again some morn[g].—If Eliza cannot go—(& she has a cold at present) Miss Beaty will be invited to be my companion.—Henry leaves Town on Sunday afternoon—but he means to write soon himself to Edward—& will tell his own plans.—The Tea is this moment setting out.—Do not have your col[d] muslin unless you really want it, because I am afraid I c[d] not send it to the Coach without giving trouble here.—Eliza caught her cold on Sunday in our way to the D'Entraigues ;—the Horses actually gibbed on this side of Hyde Park Gate—a load of fresh gravel made it a formidable Hill to them, and they refused the collar ;—I believe there was a sore shoulder to irritate.—Eliza was frightened, & we got out—& were detained in the Even[g] air several minutes. —The cold is in her chest—but she takes care of herself, & I hope it may not last long.—This engagement prevented M[r] Walter's staying late—he had his coffee & went away.—Eliza enjoyed her even[g] very much & means to cultivate the acquaintance—& I see nothing to dislike in them, but their taking quantities of snuff.—Monsieur the old Count, is a very fine looking man, with quiet manners, good enough for an Englishman—& I believe is a Man of great Information & Taste. He has some fine Paintings, which delighted Henry as much as the Son's music gratified Eliza—& among them, a Miniature of Philip 5. of Spain, Louis 14.s Grandson, which exactly suited *my* capacity.—Count Julien's performance is very wonderful. We met only M[rs] Latouche & Miss East—& we are just now engaged to spend next Sunday Even[g] at M[rs] L.s—& to meet the D'Entraigues ;—but M. le Comte must do without Henry. If he w[d] but speak english, *I* would take to him.—Have you ever mentioned the leaving off Tea to Mrs K. ?—Eliza has just spoken of it again.—The Benefit *she* has found from it in sleeping, has been very great.—I shall write soon to Catherine to fix my day, which will be Thursday.—We have no engagements but for Sunday. Eliza's cold makes quiet adviseable.—Her party is mentioned in this morning's paper. I am sorry to hear of poor Fanny's state.—From *that* quarter I suppose is to be the alloy of her happiness.—I *will* have no more to say.—

Y^rs^ affec^ly^

J. A.

Give my Love particularly to my God-daughter.

71. *To Cassandra Austen. Tuesday* ⟨30 *April* 1811⟩

Address **: none. The letter was no doubt enclosed in another, see the first paragraph.**
Postmark **: none. The date is fixed by the allusion to No. 70.**
Pierpont Morgan Library. 2 leaves 4°.
Brabourne **ii. 97 ;** ***Life*** **251 (extracts).**

Sloane St Tuesday.

My dear Cassandra

I had sent off my Letter yesterday before yours came, which I was sorry for ; but as Eliza has been so good as to get me a frank, your questions shall be answered without much further expense to you.—The best direction to Henry at Oxford will be *The Blue Boar, Cornmarket.*—I do *not* mean to provide another trimming for my Pelisse, for I am determined to spend no more money, so I shall wear it as it is, longer than I ought, & then—I do not know.—My head dress was a Bugle band like the border to my gown, & a flower of Mrs. Tilson's.—I depended upon hearing something of the Even[g] from Mr. W. K.—& am very well satisfied with his notice of me. 'A pleasing looking young woman,'—that must do;—one cannot pretend to anything better now—thankful to have it continued a few years longer!—It gives me sincere pleasure to hear of Mrs. Knight's having had a tolerable night at last—but upon this occasion I wish she had another name, for the two *Nights* jingle very much.—We have tried to get Self-controul, but in vain.—I *should* like to know what her Estimate is—but am always half afraid of finding a clever novel *too clever*—& of finding my own story and my own people all forestalled. Eliza has just rec[d] a few lines from Henry to assure her of the good conduct of his Mare. He slept at Uxbridge on Sunday, & wrote from Wheatfield.—We were not claimed by Hans place yesterday, but are to dine there today.—Mr. Tilson called in the even[g].—but otherwise we were quite alone all day, & after having been out a good deal, the change was very pleasant.—I like your opinion of Miss Allen much better than I expected, & have now hopes of her staying a whole twelvemonth.—By this time I suppose she is hard at it, governing away—poor creature! I pity her, tho' they *are* my neices. Oh! yes, I remember Miss Emma Plumbtree's *Local* consequence perfectly.—

'I am in a Dilemma, for want of an Emma,'
'Escaped from the Lips, of Henry Gipps.'—

But really, I was never much more put to it, than in contriving an answer to Fanny's former message. What is there to be said on the subject?—Pery pell—or pare pey? or po.—or at the most, Pi pope pey pike pit.—I congratulate Edward on the Weald of Kent Canal-Bill being put off till another Session, as I have just had the pleasure of reading. There is always something to be hoped from Delay.—

'Between Session and Session	'And the villainous Bill'
'The first Prepossession'	'May be forced to lie still'
'May rouse up the Nation,	'Against Wicked Men's will.'

There is poetry for Edward and his Daughter. I am afraid I shall not have any for you.—I forgot to tell you in my last, that our cousin Miss Payne called in on Saturday & was persuaded to stay dinner.—She told us a great deal about her friend Lady Cath. Brecknell, who is most happily married—& Mr. Brecknell is very religious, & has got black Whiskers. —I am glad to think that Edw[d] has a tolerable day for his drive to Goodnestone, & *very* glad to hear of his kind promise of bringing you to Town. I hope everything will arrange itself favourably. The 16th is now to be Mrs. Dundas's day.—I mean, if I can, to wait for your return, before I have my new gown made up—from a notion of their making up to more advantage together—& as I find the Muslin is not so wide as it *used to be*, some contrivance may be necessary.—I expect the Skirt to require one half breadth cut in gores, besides two Whole breadths.—

Eliza has not yet quite resolved on inviting Anna—but I think she will.—

Yours very affec[ly] Jane

72. *To Cassandra Austen. Wednesday* 29 *May* 1811

Address: Miss Austen, Godmersham Park | Faversham Kent. *Postmark*: 30 (?) MA 1811.
Historical Soc. of Pennsylvania.
Brabourne ii. 100 ; *Life* 251 (extracts).

Chawton : Wednesday May 29

It was a mistake of mine, my dear Cassandra, to talk of a tenth child at Hamstall. I had forgot there were but eight already.

Your enquiry after my uncle and aunt were most happily timed, for the very same post brought an account of them. They are again at Gloucester House enjoying fresh air, which they seem to have felt the want of in Bath, and are tolerably well, but not more than tolerable. My aunt does not enter into particulars, but she does not write in spirits, and we imagine that she has never entirely got the better of her disorder in the winter. Mrs. Welby takes her out airing in her barouche, which gives her a headache—a comfortable proof, I suppose, of the uselessness of the new carriage when they have got it.

You certainly must have heard before I can tell you that Col. Orde has married our cousin, Margt. Beckford, the Marchess. of Douglas's sister. The papers say that her father disinherits her, but I think too well of an Orde to suppose that she has not a handsome independence of her own.

The chicken are all alive and fit for the table, but we save them for something grand. Some of the flower seeds are coming up very well, but your mignonette makes a wretched appearance. Miss Benn has been equally unlucky as to hers. She had seed from four different people, and none of it comes up. Our young piony at the foot of the fir-tree has just blown and looks very handsome, and the whole of the shrubbery border will soon be very gay with pinks and sweet-williams, in addition to the columbines already in bloom. The syringas, too, are coming out. We are likely to have a great crop of Orleans plumbs, but not many greengages—on the standard scarcely any, three or four dozen, perhaps, against the wall. I believe I told you differently when I first came home, but I can now judge better than I could then.

I have had a medley and satisfactory letter this morning from the husband and wife at Cowes; and, in consequence of what is related of their plans, we have been talking over the possibility of inviting them here in their way from Steventon, which is what one should wish to do, and is, I daresay, what they expect; but, supposing Martha to be at home, it does not seem a very easy thing to accommodate so large a party. My mother offers to give up her room to Frank and Mary, but there will then be only the best for two maids and three children.

They go to Steventon about the 22nd, and I *guess*—for it is quite a guess—will stay there from a fortnight to three weeks.

I must not venture to press Miss Sharpe's coming at present; we may hardly be at liberty before August.

Poor John Bridges! we are very sorry for his situation and for the distress of the family. Lady B. is in *one way* severely tried. And our own dear brother suffers a great deal, I dare say, on the occasion.

I have not much to say of ourselves. Anna is nursing a cold caught in the arbour at Faringdon, that she may be able to keep her engagement to Maria M. this evening, when I suppose she will make it worse.

She did not return from Faringdon till Sunday, when H. B. walked home with her, and drank tea here. She was with the Prowtings almost all Monday. She went to learn to make feather trimmings of Miss Anna, and they kept her to dinner, which was rather lucky, as we were called upon to meet Mrs. and Miss Terry the same evening at the Digweeds; and, though Anna was of course invited too, I think it always safest to keep her away from the family lest she should be doing too little or too much.

Mrs. Terry, Mary, and Robert, with my aunt Harding and her daughter, came from Dummer for a day and a night—all very agreeable and very much delighted with the new house and with Chawton in general.

We sat upstairs and had thunder and lightning as usual. I never knew such a spring for thunder-storms as it has been. Thank God! we have had no bad ones here. I thought myself in luck to have my uncomfortable feelings shared by the mistress of the house, as that procured blinds and candles. It had been excessively hot the whole day. Mrs. Harding is a good-looking woman, but not much like Mrs. Toke, inasmuch as she is very brown and has scarcely any teeth; she seems to have some of Mrs. Toke's civility but does not profess being so silly. Miss H. is an elegant, pleasing, pretty-looking girl, about nineteen, I suppose, or nineteen and a half, or nineteen and a quarter, with flowers in her head and music at her finger ends. She plays very well indeed. I have seldom heard anybody with more pleasure. They were at Godington four or five years ago. My cousin, Flora Long, was there last year.

My name is Diana. How does Fanny like it? What a change in the weather! We have a fire again now.

Harriet Benn sleeps at the Great House to-night and spends to-morrow with us; and the plan is that we should all walk with her to drink tea at Faringdon, for her mother is now recovered, but the state of the weather is not very promising at present.

Miss Benn has been returned to her cottage since the beginning of last week, and has now just got another girl; she comes from Alton. For many days Miss B. had nobody with her but her niece Elizabeth, who was delighted to be her visitor and her maid. They both dined here on Saturday while Anna was at Faringdon; and last night an accidental meeting and a sudden impulse produced Miss Benn and Maria Middleton at our tea-table.

If you have not heard it is very fit you should, that Mr. Harrison has had the living of Fareham given him by the Bishop, and is going to reside there; and now it is said that Mr. Peach (beautiful wiseacre) wants to have the curacy of Overton, and, if he *does* leave Wootton, James Digweed wishes to go there. Fare you well.

Yours affectionately, Jane Austen

The chimneys at the Great House are done. Mr. Prowting has opened a gravel pit, very conveniently for my mother, just at the mouth of the approach to his house; but it looks a little as if he meant to catch all his company. Tolerable gravel.

73. *To Cassandra Austen.* *Friday* 31 *May* 1811

Address: Miss Austen | Edwd. Austen's esqre. | Godmersham Park | Faversham.
Postmark: 1 JY 1811.
Pierpont Morgan Library. 2 leaves 4°.
Brabourne ii. 105; *Life* 252 (extracts).

Chawton Friday May 31st.—

My dear Cassandra

I have a magnificent project.—The Cookes have put off their visit to us; they are not well enough to leave home at present, & we have no chance of seeing them till I do not know when—probably never, in this house. This circumstance has made me think the present time would be favourable for Miss Sharp's coming to us; it seems a more disengaged period with us, than we are likely to have later in the summer; if Frank & Mary do come, it can hardly be before the middle of July, which will be allowing a reasonable length of visit for Miss Sharpe supposing she begins it when you return; & if you & Martha do not dislike the plan, & she can avail herself of it, the opportunity of her being conveyed hither will be excellent.—I shall write to Martha by this post, & if neither You nor she make any objection to my proposal, I shall make the invitation directly—& as there is no time to lose, you must write by return of post if you have any reason for not wishing it done.—It was her intention I beleive to go first to Mrs. Lloyd—but such a means of getting here may influence her otherwise.—We have had a Thunder storm again this morng. Your letter came to comfort me for it.—I have taken your hint, slight as it was, & have written to Mrs. Knight, & most sincerely do I hope it will not be in vain. I cannot endure the idea of her giving away her own wheel, & have told her no more than the truth, in saying that I could never use it with comfort;—I had a great mind to add that if she persisted in giving it, I would spin nothing with it but a rope to hang myself—but I was afraid of making it appear a less serious matter of feeling than it really is.—I am glad you are so well yourself, & wish everybody else were equally so.—I will not say that your Mulberry trees are dead, but I am afraid they are not alive. We shall have pease soon—I mean to have them with a couple of Ducks from Wood Barn & Maria Middleton towards the end of next week.—From Monday to Wednesday Anna is to be engaged at Faringdon, in order that she may come in for the Gaieties of Tuesday (ye 4th), on Selbourne Common, where there are to be Volunteers & Felicities of all kinds. Harriot B. is invited to spend the day with the John Whites, & her Father & Mother have very kindly undertaken to get Anna invited also.—Harriot and Eliz. dined here yesterday, & we walked back with them to Tea;—not my Mother—she has a cold which affects her in the usual way, & was not equal to the walk.—She is better this morn^g^ & I hope will soon physick away the worst part of it.—It has not confined her; she has got out every day that the weather has allowed her.—Poor Anna is also suffering from *her* cold which is worse today, but as she has no sore throat I hope it may spend itself by Tuesday. She had a delightful Even^g^ with the Miss Middletons—Syllabub, Tea, Coffee, Singing, Dancing, a Hot Supper, eleven o'clock, everything that can be imagined agreable.—She desires her best Love to

Fanny, & will answer her letter before she leaves Chawton, & engages to send her a particular account of the Selbourne day. We cannot agree as to which is the eldest of the two Miss Plumbtrees;—send us word. Have you remembered to collect peices for the Patchwork?—We are now at a stand still. I got up here to look for the old Map & can now tell you that it shall be sent tomorrow;—it was among the great parcel in the Dining room.—As to my debt of 3^s. 6 to Edward, I must trouble you to pay it, when you settle with him for your Boots.—We began our China Tea three days ago, & *I* find it very good—my companions know nothing of the matter.—As to Fanny, & her 12 lb. in a twelvemonth, she may talk till she is as black in the face as her own Tea, but I cannot beleive her;—more likely 12 lb. to a quarter.—I have a message to you from Mrs. Cooke;—the substance of it is that she hopes you will take Bookham in your way home, & stay there as long as you can, & that when you must leave them, they will convey you to Guildford.—You may be sure that it is very kindly worded—& that there is no want of attendant $Comp^{ts}$ to my Brother and his family.—I am very sorry for Mary;—but I have some comfort in there being two Curates now lodging in Bookham, besides their own Mr. Warneford from Dorking, so that I think she must fall in love with one or the other.—How horrible it is to have so many people killed!—And what a blessing that one cares for none of them!—I return to my Letter writing from calling on Miss Harriot Webb, who is short & not quite straight, & cannot pronounce an R any better than her Sisters—but she has dark hair, a complexion to suit, & I think has the pleasantest countenance & manner of the three—the most natural.—She appears very well pleased with her new Home—& they are all reading with delight Mrs. H. More's recent publication.—

You cannot imagine—it is not in Human Nature to imagine what a nice walk we have round the Orchard. The row of Beech look very well indeed, & so does the young Quickset hedge in the Garden.—I hear today that an Apricot has been detected on one of the Trees.—My Mother is perfectly convinced *now* that she shall not be overpower'd by her Cleft Wood—& I beleive would rather have more than less.—

Strange to tell, Mr. Prowting was *not* at Miss Lee's wedding—but his Daughters had some cake, & Anna had her share of it.—I continue to like our old Cook quite as well as ever—& but that I am afraid to write in her praise, I could say that she seems just the Servant for us.—Her Cookery is at least tolerable;—her pastry is the only deficiency.—God bless you.—& I hope June will find you well & bring us together.—

Y[rs] Ever Jane

I hope you understand that I do not expect you to write on Sunday, if you like my plan.—I shall consider silence as consent.

74. *To Cassandra Austen.* *Thursday* 6 *June* 1811

Address : Miss Austen | Edwd Austen's Esqre | Godmersham Park | Faversham | Kent
Postmark : 7 JU 1811
Pierpont Morgan Library. 2 leaves 4°.
Brabourne ii. 111 ; *Life* 254 (extracts).

Chawton Thursday June 6.

By this time my dearest Cassandra, you know Martha's plans. I was rather disappointed I confess to find that she could not leave Town till after ye 24th, as I had hoped to see you here the week before. The delay however is not great, & everything seems generally arranging itself for your return very comfortably. I found Henry perfectly pre-disposed to bring you to London if agreable to yourself ; he has not fixed his day for *going* into Kent, but he must be back again before ye 20th.—You may therefore think with something like certainty of the close of your Godmersham visit, & will have I suppose about a week for Sloane St. He travels in his Gig—& should the weather be tolerable, I think you must have a delightful Journey.—I have given up all idea of Miss Sharpe's travelling with you & Martha, for tho' you are both all compliance with my scheme, yet as *you* knock off a week from the end of her visit, & *Martha* rather more from the beginning, the thing is out of the question.—I have written to her to say that after the middle of July we shall be happy to receive her—& I have added a welcome if she could make her way hither *directly* ; but I do not expect that she will.—I have also sent our invitation to Cowes.—We are very sorry for the disappointment you have all had in

Lady B.'s illness ;—but a division of the proposed party is with you by this time, & I hope may have brought you a better account of the rest.—Give my Love & Thanks to Harriot ;—who has written me charming things of your looks, & diverted me very much by poor Mrs. C. Milles's continued perplexity.—I had a few lines from Henry on Tuesday to prepare us for himself and his friend, & by the time that I had made the sumptuous provision of a neck of Mutton on the occasion, they drove into the Court—but lest you should not immediately recollect in how many hours a neck of Mutton may be certainly procured, I add that they came a little after twelve—both tall, & well, & in their different degrees, agreable.—It was a visit of only 24 hours—but very pleasant while it lasted.—Mr. Tilson took a sketch of the Great House before dinner ;—& after dinner we all three walked to Chawton Park, meaning to go into it, but it was too dirty, & we were obliged to keep on the outside. Mr. Tilson admired the trees very much, but greived that they should not be turned into money.—My Mother's cold is better, & I beleive she only wants dry weather to be very well. It was a great distress to her that Anna sh^{d} be absent, during her Uncle's visit—a distress which I could not share.—She does not return from Faringdon till this even^{g},—& I doubt not, has had plenty of the miscellaneous, unsettled sort of happiness which seems to suit her best.—We hear from Miss Benn, who was on the Common with the Prowtings, that she was very much admired by the Gentlemen in general.—

I like your new Bonnets exceedingly, yours is a shape which always looks well, & I think Fanny's particularly becoming to her.—On Monday I had the pleasure of receiving, unpacking & approving our Wedgwood ware. It all came very safely, & upon the whole is a good match, tho' I think they might have allowed us rather larger leaves, especially in such a Year of fine foliage as this. One is apt to suppose that the Woods about Birmingham must be blighted.—There was no Bill with the Goods—but that shall not screen them from being paid. I mean to ask Martha to settle the account. It will be quite in her way, for she is just now sending my Mother a Breakfast set, from the same place. I hope it will come by the Waggon tomorrow; it is certainly what we want, & I long to know what it is like; & as I am sure Martha has great pleasure in making the present, I will not have any regret. We have considerable dealings with the Waggons at present; a Hamper of Port & Brandy from Southampton, is now in the Kitchen.—Your answer about the Miss Plumtrees, proves you as fine a Daniel as ever Portia was;—for *I* maintained Emma to be the eldest.—We began Pease on Sunday, but our gatherings are very small—not at all like the Gathering in the Lady of the Lake.—Yesterday I had the agreable surprise of finding several scarlet strawberries quite ripe;—had *you* been at home, this would have been a pleasure lost. There are more gooseberries & fewer currants than I thought at first.—We must buy currants for our Wine.—The Digweeds are gone down to see the Stephen Terrys at Southampton, & catch the Kings birthday at Portsmouth. Miss Papillon called on us yesterday, looking handsomer than ever.—Maria Middleton & Miss Benn dine here tomorrow.—We are not to enclose any more Letters to Abingdon St. as perhaps Martha has told you.—

I had just left off writing & put on my Things for walking to Alton, when Anna & her friend Harriot called in their way thither, so we went together. Their business was to provide mourning, against the King's death; & my Mother has had a Bombasin bought for her.—I am not sorry to be back again, for the young Ladies had a great deal to do—& without much method in doing it.—Anna does not come home till tomorrow morn[g].—She has written I find to Fanny—but there does not seem to be a great deal to relate of Tuesday. I had hoped there might be Dancing.—Mrs. Budd died on Sunday Even[g]. I saw her two days before her death, & thought it must happen soon. She suffered much from weakness & restlessness almost to the last. Poor little Harriot seems truely greived. You have never mentioned Harry;—how is he?—

With Love to You all, Y[rs] affec[ly] J. A.

74.1. *To Martha Lloyd. Sunday* 29 *Nov.* 1812. *See p.* 499.

75. *To Cassandra Austen. Sunday* 24 *Jan.* 1813

Address: lost. *Postmark*: none.

T. Edward Carpenter (1948); formerly in the collection described in *Times Literary Supplement* 14 Jan 1926. The second sheet (see p. 295), containing the conclusion (and doubtless the address) was already missing when Mr. Austen-Leigh copied the letter in 1909.

Memoir[1] 133–9, *Memoir*[2] 99–101, where extracts from this letter and N[o] 78 are printed as from one letter (of February); *Life* 258 (extracts). A large part unpublished.

Chawton Sunday even[g] Jan 24

My dear Cassandra

This is exactly the weather we could wish for, if you are but well enough to enjoy it. I shall be glad to hear that you are not confined to the house by an increase of cold. Mr Digweed has used us basely. Handsome is as handsome does, he is therefore a very ill-looking man. I hope you have sent off a letter to me by this day's post, unless you are tempted to wait till to-morrow by one of Mr Chute's franks. We have had no letter since you went away, & no visitor except Miss Benn, who dined with us on Friday; but we have received the half of an excellent Stilton cheese—we presume from Henry. My mother is very well & finds great amusement in the glove-knitting, when this pair is finished she means to knit another, & at present wants no other work. We quite run over with books. *She* has got Sir John Carr's Travels in Spain from Miss B. & *I* am reading a Society octavo, an Essay on the Military Police & Institutions of the British Empire by Capt Pasley of the Engineers, a book which I protested against at first, but which upon trial I find delightfully written & highly entertaining. I am as much in love with the author as ever I was with Clarkson or Buchanan, or even the two Mr Smiths of the city—the first soldier I ever sighed for—but he does write with extraordinary force & spirit. Yesterday moreover brought us Mrs Grant's letters with Mr White's comp^ts^. But I have disposed of them, comp^ts^ & all, for the first fortnight to Miss Papillon—& among so many readers or retainers of books as we have in Chawton I daresay there will be no difficulty in getting rid of them for another fortnight if necessary. I learn from Sir J. Carr that there is no Government House at Gibraltar. I must alter it to the Commissioner's. Our party on Wednesday was not unagreeable, tho' as usual we wanted a better

Master of the House, one less anxious & fidgetty & more conversible. In consequence of a civil note that morning from M[rs] Clement, I went with her & her husband in their Tax-cart—civility on both sides; *I* would rather have walked, & no doubt *they* must have wished I had. I ran home with my own dear Thomas at night in great luxury. Thomas was very useful. We were eleven altogether, as you will find on computation adding Miss Benn & two strange gentlemen, a M[r] Twyford curate of G[t] Worldham, who is living in Alton, & his friend M[r] Wilkes. I don't know that M[r] T. is anything except very dark-complexioned, but M[r] W. was a useful addition, being an easy, talking, pleasantish young man—a *very* young man, hardly 20 perhaps. He is of S[t] John's Cambridge & spoke very highly of H. Walter as a schollar. he said he was considered as the best classick in the University. How such a report would have interested my father! I could see nothing very promising between M[r] P. & Miss P. T. She placed herself on one side of him at first, but Miss Benn obliged her to move up higher; & she had an empty plate, & even asked him to give her some mutton twice without being attended to for some time. There might be design in this, to be sure, on his side; he might think an empty stomach the most favourable for love. Upon M[rs] Digweed's mentioning that she had sent the Rejected Addresses to M[r] Hinton, I began talking to her a little about them, & expressed my hope of their having amused her. Her answer was 'Oh dear yes, very much, very droll indeed—the opening of the House, & the striking up of the Fiddles!' What she meant poor woman, who shall say? I sought no farther. The Papillons have now got the book, & like it very much; their neice Eleanor has recommended it most warmly to them. *She* looks like a rejected addresser. As soon as a whist party was formed, & a round table threatened, I made my mother an excuse & came away, leaving just as many for *their* round table as there were at Mrs Grants. I wish they might be as agreeable a set. It was past 10 when I got home, so I was not ashamed of my dutiful delicacy. The Coulthards were talked of you may be sure, no end of *them*. Miss Terry had heard they were going to rent Mr Bramston's house at Oakley, & Mrs Clement that they were going to live at Streatham. Mrs Digweed & I agreed that the house at Oakley could not possibly be large enough for them, & now we find they have really taken it. Mr Gauntlett is thought very agreeable—& there are *no* children at all. The Miss Sibleys want to establish a Book Society in their side of the country, like ours. What can be a stronger proof of that superiority in ours over the Steventon & Manydown society, which I have always foreseen & felt? No emulation of the kind was ever inspired by *their* proceedings. No such wish of the Miss Sibleys was ever heard in the course of the many years of that Society's existence. And what are their Biglands & their Barrows, their Macartneys & Mackenzies to Capt Pasley's Essay on the Military police of the British Empire, & the rejected addresses? I have walked once to Alton, & yesterday Miss Papillon & I walked together to call on the Garnets. She invited herself very pleasantly to be my companion, when I went to propose to her the indulgence of accommodating us about the Letters from the

Mountains. *I* had a very agreeable walk, & if *she* had not, more shame for her, for I was quite as entertaining as she was. Dame G. is pretty well, & we found her surrounded by her well-behaved, healthy, large-eyed children. I took her an old shift, & promised her a set of our Linen, & my companion left some of her Bank Stock with her. Tuesday has done its duty & I have had the pleasure of reading a very comfortable letter. It contains so much that I feel obliged to write down the whole of this page, & perhaps something in a cover. When my parcel is finished I shall walk with it to Alton. I believe Miss Benn will go with me. She spent yesterday evening with us. As I know Mary is interested in her not being neglected by her neighbours, pray tell her that Miss B dined last Wednesday at Mr Papillon's—on Thursday with Capt & Mrs Clement—friday here, Saturday with Mrs Digweed, & Sunday with the Papillons again. I had fancied that Martha w^d^ be at Barton from last Saturday, but am best pleased to be mistaken. I hope she is now quite well. Tell her that I hunt away the rogues every night from under her bed, they feel the difference of her being gone. Miss Benn wore her new shawl last night, sat in it the whole evening, & seemed to enjoy it very much.

'A very sloppy lane' last Friday. What an odd sort of country you must be in! I cannot at all understand it! It was just greasy here on Friday in consequence of the little snow that had fallen in the night. Perhaps it *was* cold on Wednesday, yes I believe it certainly was, but nothing terrible. Upon the whole the weather for winter weather is delightful, the walking excellent. I cannot imagine what sort of a place

Steventon can be! My mother sends her love to Mary, with thanks for her kind intentions & enquiries as to the Pork & will prefer receiving her share from the two *last* Pigs: she has great pleasure in sending her a pair of garters, & is very glad that she had them ready knit. Her letter to Anna is to be forwarded if any opportunity offers, otherwise it may wait for her return. Mrs Leigh's letter came this morning, we are glad to hear anything so tolerable of Scarlets. Poor Charles & his frigate—But there could be no chance of his having one, while it was thought such a certainty. I can hardly believe Brother Michael's news. We have no such idea in Chawton at least. Mrs Bramston is the sort of woman I detest. Mr Cottrell is worth ten of her. It is better to be given the lie direct than to excite no interest. . . .

76. *To Cassandra Austen.* *Friday* 29 *Jan.* ⟨1813⟩

No address or postmark.

T. Edward Carpenter (1948); formerly in the collection described in *Times Literary Supplement* 14 Jan. 1926.

***Memoir*[1] 131, *Memoir*[2] 97 (extracts); *Life* 260 (extracts). Part unpublished.**

Chawton Friday Jany 29

I hope you received my little parcel by J. Bond on Wednesday evening my dear Cassandra, & that you will be ready to hear from me again on Sunday, for I feel that I must write to you to-day. Your parcel is safely arrived & everything shall be delivered as it ought. Thank you for your note. As you had not heard from me at that time it was very good in you to write, but I shall not be so much your debtor soon.

I want to tell you that I have got my own darling child from London; on Wednesday I received one copy sent down by Falknor with three lines from Henry to say that he had given another to Charles, & sent a 3d by the coach to Godmersham—just the two sets which I was least eager for the disposal of. I wrote to him immediately to beg for my two other sets, unless he would take the trouble of forwarding them at once to Steventon & Portsmouth—not having an idea of his leaving Town before to-day; by your account however he was gone before my letter was written. The only evil is the delay: nothing more can be done till his return—Tell James & Mary so with my love. For *your* sake I am as well pleased that it should be so, as it might be unpleasant to you to be in the neighbourhood at the first burst of the business. The Advertisement is in our paper to-day for the first time 18s. He shall ask £1. 1. for my two next & £1. 8 for my stupidest of all. I shall write to Frank that he may not think himself neglected. Miss Benn dined with us on the very day of the books coming & in the evening we set fairly at it, and read half the first vol. to her, prefacing that, having intelligence from Henry that such a work would soon appear, we had desired him to send it whenever it came out, and I believe it passed with her unsuspected. She was amused, poor soul! *That* she could not help, you know, with two such people to lead the way, but she really does seem to admire Elizabeth. I must confess that I think her as delightful a creature as ever appeared in print, and how I shall be able to tolerate those who do not like *her* at least I do not know. There are a few typical errors; and a 'said he,' or a

' said she,' would sometimes make the dialogue more immediately clear ; but

I do not write for such dull elves
As have not a great deal of ingenuity themselves.

The second volume is shorter than I could wish, but the difference is not so much in reality as in look, there being a larger proportion of narrative in that part. I have lop't and crop't so successfully, however, that I imagine it must be rather shorter than S. & S. altogether. Now I will try to write of something else, & it shall be a complete change of subject—ordination—I am glad to find your enquiries have ended so well. If you could discover whether Northamptonshire is a country of Hedgerows I should be glad again. We admire your Charades excessively—but as yet have guessed only the 1st. The others seem very difficult. There is so much beauty in the versification however, that the finding them out is but a secondary pleasure. I grant you that *this is* a cold day, & am sorry to think how cold you will be through the process of your visit at Manydown. I hope you will wear your China crape. Poor wretch! I can see you shivering away with your miserable feeling feet. What a vile character Mr Digweed turns out, quite beyond anything & everything—instead of going to Steventon, they are to have a dinner-party next Tuesday! I am sorry to say that I cd not eat a mince-pie at Mr Papillon's; I was rather headachey that day & could not venture on anything sweet except jelly, but *that* was excellent. There were no stewed pears—but Miss Benn had some almonds & raisins. By the bye she desired to be kindly remembered to you when I wrote last & I forgot it. Betsy sends her duty to you & hopes you are well—& her love to Miss Caroline & hopes she has got rid of her cough. It was such a pleasure to her to think her oranges were so well timed that I daresay she was rather glad to hear of the cough. Since I wrote this letter we have been visited by M[rs] Digweed, her sister & Miss Benn. I gave M[rs] D. her little parcel which she opened here, & seemed much pleased with—and she desired me to make her best thanks etc. to Miss Lloyd for it. Martha may guess how full of wonder & gratitude she was.

77. *To Cassandra Austen.* *Thursday* 4 *Feb.* ⟨1813⟩

No address or postmark.

T. Edward Carpenter (1948); formerly in the collection described in *Times Literary Supplement* 14 Jan. 1926.

Memoir[1] 133, *Memoir*[2] 99 (extract); *Life* 261 (extracts). A large part unpublished.

Chawton, Thursday Feb[y] 4

My dear Cassandra

Your letter was truly welcome, and I am much obliged to you all for your praise; it came at a right time, for I had had some fits of disgust. Our second evening's reading to Miss Benn had not pleased me so well, but I believe something must be attributed to my mother's too rapid way of getting on: and though she perfectly understands the characters herself, she cannot speak as they ought. Upon the whole, however, I am quite vain enough and well satisfied enough. The work is rather too light, and bright, and sparkling; it wants shade; it wants to be stretched out here and there with a long chapter of sense, if it could be had; if not, of solemn specious nonsense, about something unconnected with the story; an essay on writing, a critique on Walter Scott, or the history of Buonaparté, or anything that would form a contrast, and bring the reader with increased delight to the playfulness and epigrammatism of the general style. I doubt your quite agreeing with me here. I know your starched notions. The caution observed at Steventon with regard to the possession of the book is an agreeable surprise to me, & I heartily wish it may be the means of saving you from everything unpleasant—but you must be prepared for the neighbourhood being perhaps already informed of there being such a Work in the World & in the Chawton World! Dummer will do that you know. It was spoken of here one morning when Mrs D. called with Miss Benn. The greatest blunder in the printing that I have met with is in page 220, v. 3, where two speeches are made into one. There might as well have been no suppers at Longbourn; but I suppose it was the remains of Mrs. Bennett's old Meryton habits. I am sorry for your disappointment about Manydown & fear this week must be a heavy one. As far as one may venture to judge at a distance of 20 miles, you must miss Martha. For *her* sake I was glad to hear of her going as I suppose she must have been growing anxious & wanting to be again in scenes of agitation & exertion. She had a lovely day for her journey. I walked to Alton, & dirt excepted found it delightful, it seemed like an old Feby come back again. Before I set out we were visited by Mrs Edwards, & while I was gone Miss Beckford & Maria, & Miss Woolls & Harriet B. called, all of whom my Mother was glad to see, & I very glad to escape. John M. is sailed & now Miss B thinks his father will really try for a house, & has hopes herself of avoiding Southampton, this is as it was repeated to me—& I can tell the Miss Williamses that Miss Beckford has no intention of inviting them to Chawton. Well done you—I thought of you at Manydown in the Drawing-room, & in your China crape, therefore you were in the Breakfast parlour in your brown Bombasin; if I thought of you *so*, you would have been in the Kitchen in your morning stuff. I feel that I have never mentioned the Harwoods in my letters to you, which is shocking enough, but we are sincerely glad to hear all the good of them you send us. There is no chance I suppose, no danger of poor Mrs H.'s being persuaded to come to Chawton at present. I hope John H will not have more debts brought in than he likes. I am pleased with M. T.'s being to dine at Steventon, it may enable you to be yet more decided with Fanny, & help to settle her faith. Thomas was married on Saturday, the wedding was kept at Neatham, & that is all I know about it. Browning is quite a new broom, & at present has no fault. He had lost some of his knowledge of waiting, & is I think rather slow, but he is not noisy, & not at all above being taught. The Back-gate is regularly locked. I did not forget Henry's fee to Thomas. I had a letter from Henry yesterday, written on Sunday from Oxford, mine had been forwarded to him. Edward's information therefore was correct. He says that copies were sent to S. & P. at the same time with the others. He has some thoughts of going to Addlestrop.

78. *To Cassandra Austen.* *Tuesday* 9 *Feb.* ⟨1813⟩

Address: Miss Austen | Manydown | By favour of Mr Gray
Postmark: none.
T. Edward Carpenter (1948); formerly in the collection described in *Times Literary Supplement* 14 Jan. 1926.

Memoir[1] 133–9, *Memoir*[2] 99–101, where extracts from this letter and No 75 are printed as from one letter; *Life* 262 (extracts). A large part unpublished.

Chawton Tuesday Feb. 9

This will be a quick return for yours, my dear Cassandra; I doubt its having much else to recommend it, but there is no saying; it may turn out to be a very long & delightful letter. What a day was yesterday! How many impatient grumbling spirits must have been confined! We felt for you, I could think of nothing to amuse you but packing up your cloathes. My Mother was quite in distress about Edward & Anna, & will not be quite comfortable till she knows how their journeys were settled. In a few hours you will be transported to Manydown & then for Candour & Comfort & Coffee & Cribbage. Perhaps it will be your last visit there. While I think of it, give my love to Alethea (Alethea first mind, she is Mistress) & Mrs Heathcote & kind remembrances to Miss Charlotte Williams. Only think of your having at last the honour of seeing that wonder of wonders, her elder sister! We are very sorry for what you tell us of Deane. If Mrs Heathcote does not marry & comfort him now I shall think she is a Maria & has no heart. Really, either she or Alethea *must* marry him, or where he is to look for happiness? I am exceedingly pleased that you can say what you do, after having gone thro' the whole work—& Fanny's praise is very gratifying. My hopes were tolerably strong of *her*, but nothing like a certainty. Her liking Darcy & Elizabeth is enough, she might hate all the others if she would. I have her opinion under her own hand this morning, but your transcript of it which I read first was not & is not the less acceptable. To *me* it is of course all praise, but the more exact truth which she sends *you* is good enough. We are to see the Boys for a few hours this day se'night & I am to order a chaise for them which I propose 5'o'clock for, & having a 3 o'clock dinner. I am sorry to find that Sackree was worse again when Fanny wrote, she had been seized the night before with a violent shivering & fever & was still so ill as to alarm Fanny, who was writing from her room. Miss Clewes seems the very governess they have been looking for these ten years—longer coming than J. Bond's last shock of corn. If she will but only keep good & amiable & perfect! Clewes is better than Clowes. And is it not a name for Edward to pun on? Is not a clew a nail? Yes, I believe I *shall* tell Anna, & if you see her & do not dislike the commission, you may tell her for me. You know that I meant to do it as handsomely as I could. But she will probably not return in time. Browning goes on extremely well; as far as he has been able to do anything out of doors, my Mother is exceedingly pleased. The dogs seem just as happy with him as with Thomas,—Cook & Betsy I imagine a great deal happier. Poor Cook is likely to be tried by a wet season now, but she has not begun lamenting much yet. Old Philmore I believe is well again. My cold has been an off and on cold almost ever since you went away, but never very bad. I increase it by walking out, & cure it by staying within. On Saturday I went to Alton, & the high wind made it worse—but by keeping house ever since, it is almost gone. I have had letters from my Aunt & from Charles within these few days. My Uncle is quite confined to his chair by a broken chilblain on one foot, & a violent swelling on the other, which my Aunt does not know what to call; there does not seem pain enough for gout. But you had all this history at Steventon perhaps. She talks of being another fortnight at Scarlets; she is really anxious I can believe to get to Bath, as they have an apprehension of their house in Pulteney S^t^ having been broken into. Charles, his wife, & eldest & youngest reached the Namur in health & safety last Sunday se'night. Middle is left in Keppel S^t^. Lady W. has taken to her old tricks of ill-health again, & is sent for a couple of months among her friends. Perhaps she may make *them* sick. I have been applied to for information as to the oath taken in former times of Bell, Book, & Candle but have none to give. Perhaps you may be able to learn something of its origin & meaning at Manydown. Ladies who read those enormous great stupid thick quarto volumes which one always sees in the Breakfast parlour there, must be acquainted with everything in the world. I detest a quarto. Capt Pasley's book is too good for their Society. They will not understand a man who condenses his thoughts into an octavo. I do not mean however to put Mrs H. out of conceit with her Society; if she is satisfied, well; if she thinks others satisfied, still better—I say nothing of the complaints which reach me from all quarters. Kill poor Mrs Sclater if

CHAWTON HOUSE.

you like it while you are at Manydown. Miss Benn dined here on Friday. I have not seen her since—there is still work for one evening more. I know nothing of the Prowtings. The Clements are at home, & are reduced to read. They have got Miss Edgeworth. I have disposed of Mrs Grant for the 2nd fortnight to Mrs Digweed—it can make no difference to *her*, which of the 26 fortnights in the year the 3 vols lay in her house. It is raining furiously, & tho' only a storm I shall probably send my letter to Alton instead of going myself. I had no thought of your writing by Mr Gray. On Sunday or Tuesday I suppose I shall hear. Cook does not think the Mead in a state to be stopped down. If Mrs Freeman is anywhere above ground, give my best comp^ts^ to her.

Yours very affec^tly^

J. Austen

78.1. *To Martha Lloyd. Tues.* 16 *Feb.* 1813. See p. 503

79. *To Cassandra Austen. Thursday* 20 *May* 1813

Address: Miss Austen | Chawton | Alton | Hants
Postmark: 20 MA 1813
T. Edward Carpenter (1948); formerly in the collection described in *Times Literary Supplement* 14 Jan. 1926.
*Memoir*² 102 (extracts); *Life* 265 (extracts). A large part unpublished.

Sloane St Thursday May 20

My dear Cassandra

Before I say anything else, I claim a paper full of halfpence on the drawing-room mantlepiece; I put them there myself, and forgot to bring them with me. I cannot say that I have yet been in any distress for money, but I chuse to have my due, as well as the Devil. How lucky we were in our weather yesterday!

M

This wet morning makes one more sensible of it. We had no rain of any consequence. The head of the curricle was put half up three or four times, but our share of the showers was very trifling, though they seemed to be heavy all round us, when we were on the Hog's-back, and I fancied it might then be raining so hard at Chawton as to make you feel for us much more than we deserved. Three hours and a quarter took us to Guildford, where we staid barely two hours, and had only just time enough for all we had to do there; that is, eating a long comfortable breakfast, watching the carriages, paying Mr Herington, and taking a little stroll afterwards. From some views which that stroll gave us, I think most highly of the situation of Guildford. We wanted all our brothers and sisters to be standing with us in the bowling-green, and looking towards Horsham. I told Mr Herington of the currants, he seemed equally surprised & shocked—& means to talk to the man who put them up—I wish you may find the currants any better for it. He does not expect Sugars to fall. I was very lucky in my gloves—got them at the first shop I went to, though I went into it rather because it was near than because it looked at all like a glove shop, and gave only four shillings for them; upon hearing which everybody at Chawton will be hoping and predicting that they cannot be good for anything, and their worth certainly remains to be proved; but I think they look very well. We left Guildford at twenty minutes before twelve (I hope somebody cares for these minutiæ), and were at Esher in about two hours more. I was very much pleased with the country in general. Between Guildford and Ripley I thought it particularly pretty, also about Painshill & everywhere else; and from a Mr Spicer's grounds at Esher, which we walked into before our dinner, the views were beautiful. I cannot say what we did *not* see, but I should think that there could not be a wood, or a meadow, or palace, or a remarkable spot in England that was not spread out before us on one side or the other. Claremont is going to be sold: a Mr Ellis has it now. It is a house that seems never to have prospered. At 3 we were dining upon veal cutlets & cold ham, all very good, & after dinner we walked forward to be overtaken at the coachman's time, and before he *did* overtake us we were very near Kingston. I fancy it was about half-past six when we reached this house—a twelve hours' business, and the horses did not appear more than reasonably tired. I was very tired too, and very glad to get to bed early, but am quite well to-day. Upon the whole it was an excellent journey & very thoroughly enjoyed by me; the weather was delightful the greatest part of the day. Henry found it too warm, & talked of its being close sometimes, but to my capacity it was perfection. I never saw the country from the Hogsback so advantageously. We ate 3 of the buns in the course of that stage, the remaining 3 made an elegant entertainment for Mr & Mrs Tilson who drank tea with us. Now little Cass & her attendant are travelling down to Chawton. I wish the day were brighter for them. If Cassy should have intended to take any sketches while the others dine she will hardly be able. How will you distinguish the two Betsies? Mrs Perigord arrived at ½ past 3 & is pretty well, & her mother for *her* seems quite well. She sat with me while I breakfasted this morning, talking of Henrietta S^t^, servants & linen, & is too busy in preparing for the future to be out of spirits. If I can, I shall call by & bye on Mrs Hoblyn & Charlotte Craven. Mrs Tilson is going out which prevents my calling on *her*, but I believe we are to drink tea with her. Henry talks of our going to the watercoloured Exhibition to-morrow, & of my calling for him in Henrietta S^t^—if I do, I shall take the opportunity of getting my Mother's gown, so by 3 o'clock in the afternoon she may consider herself the owner of 7 yds of black sarsenet as completely as I hope Martha finds herself of a 16th of the £20,000. I am very snug with the front drawing-room all to myself, & would not say 'Thank you' for any companion but you. The quietness of it does me good. Henry & I are disposed to wonder that the Guildford road should not be oftener preferred to the Bagshot. It is not longer, has much more beauty, & not more hills. If I were Charles I should chuse it, & having him in our thoughts we made enquiries at Esher as to their posting distances. From Guildford to Esher 14 miles, from Esher to Hyde Park Corner 15—which makes it exactly the same as from Bagshot to H. P. Corner, changing at Bedfont, 49 miles altogether each way. I have contrived to pay my two visits, though the weather made me a great while about it, & left me only a few minutes to sit with C. C. She looks very well, and her hair is done up with an elegance to do credit to any education. Her manners are as unaffected and pleasing as ever. She had heard from her mother to-day. Mrs. Craven spends another fortnight at Chilton. I saw nobody but Charlotte, which pleased me best. I was shewn upstairs into a drawing-room, where she came to me, and the appearance of the room, so totally unschool-like, amused me very much; it was full of all the modern elegancies—& if it had not been for some naked Cupids over the Mantlepiece, which must be a fine study for Girls, one should never have smelt instruction. M[rs] Perigord desires her duty to all the ladies.

Yours very affec[tly] J. A.

80. *To Cassandra Austen. Monday* 24 *May* ⟨1813⟩

Address: Miss Austen | Chawton | By favour of Mess[rs] Gray & Vincent
Postmark: none.
Pierpont Morgan Library. 2 leaves 4°. A few words cut away.
Brabourne ii. 139; *Life* 267 (extracts).

Sloane S[t] Monday May 24.

My dearest Cassandra

I am very much obliged to you for writing to me. You must have hated it after a worrying morning.—Your Letter came just in time to save my going to Remnants, & fit me for Christian's, where I bought Fanny's dimity. I went the day before (Friday) to Laytons as I proposed, & got my Mother's gown 7 y[ds] at 6/6. I then walked into No. 10, which is all dirt & confusion, but in a very promising way, & after being present at the opening of a new account to my great amusement, Henry & I went to the Exhibition in Spring Gardens. It is not thought a good collection, but I was very well pleased—particularly (pray tell Fanny) with a small portrait of Mrs. Bingley, excessively like her. I went in hopes of seeing one of her Sister, but there was no Mrs. Darcy;—perhaps however, I may find her in the Great Exhibition which we shall go to, if we have time ;—I have no chance of her in the collection of Sir Joshua Reynolds's Paintings which is now shewing in Pall Mall, & which we are also to visit.—Mrs. Bingley's is exactly herself, size, shaped face, features & sweetness ; there never was a greater likeness. She is dressed in a white gown, with green ornaments, which convinces me of what I had always supposed, that green was a favourite colour with her. I dare say Mrs. D. will be in Yellow. —Friday was our worst day as to weather, we were out in a very long & very heavy storm of hail, & there had been others before, but I heard no Thunder.—Saturday was a good deal better, dry & cold.—I gave 2/6 for the Dimity ; I do not boast of any Bargains, but think both the Sarsenet & Dimity good of their sort.—I have bought your Locket, but was obliged to give 18^{s} for it—which must be rather more than you intended ; it is neat & plain, set in gold. ⟨*Four or five words cut out*⟩—We were to have gone to the Somerset House Exhibition on Saturday, but when I reached Henrietta Street Mr. Hampson was wanted there, & Mr. Tilson & I were obliged to drive about Town after him, & by the time we had done, it was too late for anything but Home.—We never found him after all.—I have been interrupted by Mrs. Tilson.—Poor Woman ! She is in danger of not being able to attend Lady Drummond Smith's Party tonight. Miss Burdett was to have taken her, & now Miss Burdett has a cough & will not go. My cousin Caro*line* is her sole dependance.—The events of Yesterday were, our going to Belgrave Chapel in the morn^{g}, our being prevented by the rain from going to even^{g} service at

S[t] James, Mr. Hampson's calling, Mess[rs] Barlow & Phillips dining here, & Mr. & Mrs. Tilson's coming in the even[g] a l'ordinaire.—*She* drank tea with us both Thursday & Saturday, *he* dined out each day, & on friday we were with them, & they wish us to go to them tomorrow even[g] to meet Miss Burdett, but I do not know how it will end. Henry talks of a drive to Hampstead, which may interfere with it.—I should like to see Miss Burdett very well, but that I am rather frightened by hearing that she wishes to be introduced to *me*.—If I *am* a wild Beast, I cannot help it. It is not my own fault.—There is no change in our plan of leaving London, but we shall not be with you before Tuesday. Henry thinks Monday would appear too early a day. There is no danger of our being induced to stay longer.

I have not quite determined how I shall manage about my Cloathes, perhaps there may be only my Trunk to send by the Coach, or there may be a Band-box with it.—I have taken your gentle hint & written to Mrs. Hill.—The Hoblyns want us to dine with them, but we have refused. When Henry returns he will be dining out a great deal I dare say; as he will then be alone, it will be more desirable;—he will be more welcome at every Table, & every Invitation more welcome to him. He will not want either of us again till he is settled in Henrietta St. This is my present persuasion.—And he will not be settled there, really settled, till late in the Autumn; 'he will not be come to bide,' till after September.—There is a Gentleman in treaty for this house. Gentleman himself is in the Country, but Gentleman's friend came to see it the other day & seemed pleased on the whole.—

Gentleman would rather prefer an increased rent to parting with five hundred G^{s} at once ; & if that is the only difficulty, it will not be minded. Henry is indifferent as to the which.—Get us the best weather you can for Wednesday, Thursday, & Friday. We are to go to Windsor in our way to Henley, which will be a great delight. We shall be leaving Sloane St. about 12—, two or three hours after Charles's party have begun their Journey.—You will miss them, but the comfort of getting back into your own room will be great !—& then the Tea & Sugar !—

I fear Miss Clewes is not better, or you w^{d} have mentioned it.—I shall not write again unless I have any unexpected communication or opportunity to tempt me.—I enclose Mr. Herington's Bill & receipt.

I am very much obliged to Fanny for her Letter ;—it made me laugh heartily ; but I cannot pretend to answer it. Even had I more time, I should not feel at all sure of the sort of Letter that Miss D. would write. I hope Miss Benn is got quite well again & will have a comfortable Dinner with you today.—*Monday even^{g}.*—We have been both to the Exhibition & Sir J. Reynolds',—and I am disappointed, for there was nothing like Mrs. D. at either. I can only imagine that Mr. D. prizes any Picture of her too much to like it should be exposed to the public eye.—I can imagine he w^{d} have that sort of feeling—that mixture of Love, Pride & Delicacy.—Setting aside this disappointment, I had great amusement among the Pictures ; & the Driving about, the Carriage being open, was very pleasant.—I liked my solitary elegance very much, & was ready to laugh all the time, at my being where I was.—I could not but feel that I had naturally small right to be parading about London in a Barouche.—Henry desires Edward may know that he has just bought 3 dozen of Claret for him (Cheap) & ordered it to be sent down to Chawton.—I should not wonder if we got no farther than Reading on Thursday even[g]—& so, reach Steventon only to a reasonable Dinner hour the next day;—but whatever I may write or you may imagine we know it will be something different.—I shall be quiet tomorrow morn[g]; all my business is done, & I shall only call again upon Mrs. Hoblyn, &c.—Love to your much ⟨? redu⟩ced Party.—Y[rs] affec[ly]

J. Austen

81. *To Francis Austen.* ⟨*Saturday*⟩ 3 *July* 1813

Address: Capt[n] Austen | HMS Elephant | Baltic
Postmark: none.
Captain Ernest Austen R.N. 2 leaves 4[o].
Hubback, *Sailor Brothers*, 233; *Life* 85, 270.

Chawton July 3, 1813

My dearest Frank

Behold me going to write you as handsome a Letter as I can. Wish me good luck.—We have had the pleasure of hearing of you lately through Mary, who sent us some of the particulars of Yours of June 18th (I think) written off Rugen, & we enter into the delight of your having so good a Pilot.—Why are you like Queen Eliz[th]?—Because you know how to chuse wise Ministers.—Does not this prove you as great a Captain as she was a Queen?—This may serve as a riddle for you to put forth among your Officers, by way of increasing your proper consequence.—It must be real enjoyment to you, since you are obliged to leave

England, to be where you are, seeing something of a new Country, & one that has been so distinguished as Sweden.—You must have great pleasure in it.—I hope you may have gone to Carlscroon.—Your Profession has it's douceurs to recompense for some of it's Privations ;—to an enquiring & observing Mind like yours, such douceurs must be considerable.—Gustavus-Vasa, & Charles 12th, & Christina, & Linneus—do their Ghosts rise up before you ?—I have a great respect for former Sweden. So zealous as it was for Protestan⟨t⟩ism !—And I have always fancied it more like England than many Countries ;—& according to the Map, many of the names have a strong resemblance to the English. July begins unpleasantly with us, cold & showery, but it is often a baddish month. We had some fine dry weather preceding it, which was very acceptable to the Holders of Hay & the Masters of Meadows.—In general it must have been a good haymaking Season. Edward has got in all his, in excellent order ; I speak only of Chawton ; but here he has had better luck than Mr. Middleton ever had in the 5 years that he was Tenant. Good encouragement for him to come again ; & I really hope he will do so another Year.—The pleasure to us of having them here is so great, that if we were not the best creatures in the World we should not deserve it.—We go on in the most comfortable way, very frequently dining together, & always meeting in some part of every day.—Edward is very well & enjoys himself as thoroughly as any Hampshire born Austen can desire. Chawton is not thrown away upon him.—He talks of making a new Garden ; the present is a bad one & ill situated, near Mr. Papillon's ;—he means to have the new, at the top of the Lawn behind his own house.—We like to have him proving & strengthening his attachment to the place by making it better.—He will soon have all his Children about him, Edward, George & Charles are collected already, and another week brings Henry & William.—It is the custom at Winchester for Georges to come away a fortnight before the Holidays, when they are not to return any more; for fear they should overstudy themselves just at last, I suppose.—Really it is a piece of dishonourable accomodation to the Master.—We are in hopes of another visit from our own true, lawful Henry very soon, he is to be *our* Guest this time.—He is quite well I am happy to say, & does not leave it to *my* pen I am sure to communicate to you the joyful news of his being Deputy Receiver no longer.—It is a promotion which he thoroughly enjoys;—as well he may;—the work of his own mind.—He sends you all his own plans of course.—The scheme for Scotland we think an excellent one both for himself & his nephew.—Upon the whole his Spirits are very much recovered.—If I may so express myself, his Mind is not a Mind for affliction. He is too Busy, too active, too sanguine.—Sincerely as he was attached to poor Eliza moreover, & excellently as he behaved to her, he was always so used to be away from her at times, that her Loss is not felt as that of many a beloved wife might be, especially when all the circumstances of her long and dreadful Illness are taken into the account.—He very long knew that she must die, & it was indeed a release at last.—Our mourning for her is not over, or we should now be putting it on again for Mr. Thos Leigh—the respectable, worthy, clever, agreable Mr Tho. Leigh, who has just closed a good life at the age of 79, & must have died the possessor of one of the finest Estates in England & of more worthless Nephews and Neices than any other private Man in the United Kingdoms.—We are very anxious to know who will have the Living of Adlestrop, & where his excellent sister will find a home for the remainder of her days. As yet she bears his Loss with fortitude, but she has always seemed so wrapt up in him, that I fear she must feel it very dreadfully when the fever of Business is over.—There is another female sufferer on the occasion to be pitied. Poor Mrs. L. P.—who would now have been Mistress of Stonleigh had there been none of that vile compromise, which in good truth has never been allowed to be of much use to them.—It will be a hard trial.—Charles's little girls were with us about a month, & had so endeared themselves that we were quite sorry to have them go. We have the pleasure however of hearing that they are thought very much improved at home—Harriet in health, Cassy in manners.—The latter *ought* to be a very nice Child—Nature has done enough for her—but Method has been wanting:—we thought her very much improved ourselves, but to have Papa & Mama think her so too, was very essential to our contentment.—She will really be a very pleasing Child, if they will only exert themselves a little.—Harriet is a truely sweet-tempered little Darling.—They are now all at Southend together.—Why do I mention *that*?—As if Charles did not write himself.—I hate to be spending my time so needlessly, encroaching too upon the rights of others.—I wonder whether you happened to see Mr. Blackall's marriage in the

Papers last Jany. *We* did. He was married at Clifton to a Miss Lewis, whose Father had been late of Antigua. I should very much like to know what sort of a Woman she is. He was a piece of Perfection, noisy Perfection himself which I always recollect with regard.—We had noticed a few months before his succeeding to a College Living, the very Living which we remembered his talking of & wishing for; an exceeding good one, Great Cadbury in Somersetshire. —I would wish Miss Lewis to be of a silent turn & rather ignorant, but naturally intelligent & wishing to learn;—fond of cold veal pies, green tea in the afternoon, & a green window blind at night.

You will be glad to hear that every Copy of S. & S. is sold & that it has brought me £140 besides the Copyright, if that sh^d^ ever be of any value.—I have now therefore written myself into £250—which only makes me long for more.—I have something in hand—which I hope on the credit of P. & P. will sell well, tho' not half so entertaining. And by the bye—shall you object to my mentioning the Elephant in it, & two or three other of your old Ships? I *have* done it, but it shall not stay, to make you angry.—They are only just mentioned.

July 6.—

Now my dearest Frank I will finish my Letter. I have kept it open on the chance of what a Tuesday's post might furnish in addition, & it furnishes the likelihood of our keeping our neighbours at the G^t^ House some weeks longer than we had expected.—Mr. Scudamore, to whom my Brother referred, is very decided as to G^m^ not being fit to be inhabited at present ;—he talks even of two months more being necessary to sweeten it, but if we have warm weather I dare-say less will do.—My Brother will probably go down & sniff at it himself & receive his rents.—The rent-day has been postponed already.—*We* shall be gainers by their stay, but the young people in general are disappointed, and therefore we c[d] wish it otherwise.—Our Cousins Colonel Tho[s] Austen & Margaretta are going Aid-de-camps to Ireland & Lord Whitworth goes in their Train as Lord Lieutenant ;—good appointments for each.—God bless you.—I hope you continue beautiful & brush your hair, but not all off.—We join in an infinity of Love.

Y[rs] very affec[ly]
Jane Austen

82. *To Cassandra Austen. Wednesday* 15 *Sept.* ⟨1813⟩

Address (Brabourne): Miss Austen, Chawton | By favour of Mr. Gray
Original: see note.
Brabourne ii. 145 ; *Life* 273 (extracts).

Henrietta St. : Wednesday Sept. 15, ½ past 8

Here I am, my dearest Cassandra, seated in the breakfast, dining, sitting-room, beginning with all my might. Fanny will join me as soon as she is dressed and begin her letter.

We had a very good journey, weather and roads excellent ; the three first stages for 1*s*. 6*d*., and our only misadventure the being delayed about a quarter of an hour at Kingston for horses, and being obliged to put up with a pair belonging to a hackney coach and their coachman, which left no room on the barouche box for Lizzy, who was to have gone her last stage there as she did the first ; consequently we were all four within, which was a little crowd.

We arrived at a quarter-past four, and were kindly welcomed by the coachman, and then by his master, and then by William, and then by Mrs. Perigord, who all met us before we reached the foot of the stairs. Mde. Bigeon was below dressing us a most comfortable dinner of soup, fish, bouillée, partridges, and an apple tart, which we sat down to soon after five, after cleaning and dressing ourselves and feeling that we were most commodiously disposed of. The little adjoining dressing-room to our apartment makes Fanny and myself very well off indeed, and as we have poor Eliza's bed our space is ample every way.

Sace arrived safely about half-past six. At seven we set off in a coach for the Lyceum ; were at home again in about four hours and a half ; had soup and wine and water, and then went to our holes.

Edward finds his quarters very snug and quiet. I must get a softer pen. This is harder. I am in agonies. I have not yet seen Mr. Crabbe. Martha's letter is gone to the post.

I am going to write nothing but short sentences. There shall be two full stops in every line. Layton and Shear's *is* Bedford House. We mean to get there before breakfast if it's possible ; for we feel more and more how much we have to do and how little time. This house looks very nice. It seems like Sloane Street moved here. I believe Henry is just rid of Sloane Street. Fanny does not come, but I have Edward seated by me beginning a letter, which looks natural.

Henry has been suffering from the pain in the face

which he has been subject to before. He caught cold at Matlock, and since his return has been paying a little for past pleasure. It is nearly removed now, but he looks thin in the face, either from the pain or the fatigues of his tour, which must have been great.

Lady Robert is delighted with P. and P., and really *was* so, as I understand, before she knew who wrote it, for, of course, she knows now. He told her with as much satisfaction as if it were my wish. He did not tell *me* this, but he told Fanny. And Mr. Hastings! I am quite delighted with what such a man writes about it. Henry sent him the books after his return from Daylesford, but you will hear the letter too.

Let me be rational, and return to my two full stops.

I talked to Henry at the play last night. We were in a private box—Mr. Spencer's—which made it much more pleasant. The box is directly on the stage. One is infinitely less fatigued than in the common way. But Henry's plans are not what one could wish. He does not mean to be at Chawton till the 29th. He must be in town again by Oct. 5. His plan is to get a couple of days of pheasant shooting and then return directly. His wish was to bring you back with him. I have told him your scruples. He wishes you to suit yourself as to time, and if you cannot come till later, will send for you at any time as far as Bagshot. He presumed you would not find difficulty in getting so far. I could not say you would. He proposed your going with him into Oxfordshire. It was his own thought at first. I could not but catch at it for you.

We have talked of it again this morning (for now we have breakfasted), and I am convinced that if you can make it suit in other respects you need not scruple on his account. If you cannot come back with him on the 3rd or 4th, therefore, I do hope you will contrive to go to Adlestrop. By not beginning your absence till about the middle of this month I think you may manage it very well. But you will think all this over. One could wish he had intended to come to you earlier, but it cannot be helped.

I said nothing to him of Mrs. H. and Miss B., that he might not suppose difficulties. Shall not you put *them* into our own room ? This seems to me the best plan, and the maid will be most conveniently near.

Oh, dear me ! when I shall ever have done. We *did* go to Layton and Shear's before breakfast. Very pretty English poplins at 4*s*. 3*d*. ; Irish, ditto at 6*s*. ; *more* pretty, certainly—beautiful.

Fanny and the two little girls are gone to take places for to-night at Covent Garden ; 'Clandestine Marriage' and 'Midas.' The latter will be a fine show for L. and M. They revelled last night in 'Don Juan,' whom we left in hell at half-past eleven. We had scaramouch and a ghost, and were delighted. I speak of *them ; my* delight was very tranquil, and the rest of us were sober-minded. 'Don Juan' was the last of three musical things. 'Five hours at Brighton,' in three acts—of which one was over before we arrived, none the worse—and the 'Beehive,' rather less flat and trumpery.

I have this moment received 5*l*. from kind, beautiful Edward. Fanny has a similar gift. I shall save what I can of it for your better leisure in this place. *My* letter was from Miss Sharpe—nothing particular. A letter from Fanny Cage this morning.

Four o'clock.—We are just come back from doing

Mrs. Tickars, Miss Hare, and Mr. Spence. Mr. Hall is here, and, while Fanny is under his hands, I will try to write a little more.

Miss Hare had some pretty caps, and is to make me one like one of them, only *white* satin instead of blue. It will be white satin and lace, and a little white flower perking out of the left ear, like Harriot Byron's feather. I have allowed her to go as far as 1*l.* 16*s.* My gown is to be trimmed everywhere with white ribbon plaited on somehow or other. She says it will look well. I am not sanguine. They trim with white very much.

I learnt from Mrs. Tickars's young lady, to my high amusement, that the stays now are not made to force the bosom up at all; *that* was a very unbecoming, unnatural fashion. I was really glad to hear that they are not to be so much off the shoulders as they were.

Going to Mr. Spence's was a sad business and cost us many tears; unluckily we were obliged to go a second time before he could do more than just look. We went first at half-past twelve and afterwards at three; papa with us each time; and, alas! we are to go again to-morrow. Lizzy is not finished yet. There have been no teeth taken out, however, nor will be, I believe, but he finds *hers* in a very bad state, and seems to think particularly ill of their durableness. They have been all cleaned, *hers* filed, and are to be filed again. There is a very sad hole between two of her front teeth. [See note for a suppressed passage.]

Thursday Morning, half-past Seven.—Up and dressed and downstairs in order to finish my letter in time for the parcel. At eight I have an appointment with

COVENT GARDEN THEATRE

Madame B., who wants to show me something downstairs. At nine we are to set off for Grafton House, and get that over before breakfast. Edward is so kind as to walk there with us. We are to be at Mr. Spence's again at 11·5; from that time shall be driving about I suppose till four o'clock at least. We are, if possible, to call on Mrs. Tilson.

Mr. Hall was very punctual yesterday, and curled me out at a great rate. I thought it looked hideous, and longed for a snug cap instead, but my companions silenced me by their admiration. I had only a bit of velvet round my head. I did not catch cold however. The weather is all in my favour. I have had no pain in my face since I left you.

We had very good places in the box next the stage-box, front and second row; the three old ones behind of course. I was particularly disappointed at seeing nothing of Mr. Crabbe. I felt sure of him when I saw that the boxes were fitted up with crimson velvet. The new Mr. Terry was Lord Ogleby, and Henry thinks he may do; but there was no acting more than moderate, and I was as much amused by the remembrances connected with 'Midas' as with any part of it. The girls were very much delighted, but still prefer 'Don Juan;' and I must say that I have seen nobody on the stage who has been a more interesting character than that compound of cruelty and lust.

It was not possible for me to get the worsteds yesterday. I heard Edward last night pressing Henry to come to G^{m}, and I think Henry engaged to go there after his November collection. Nothing has been done as to S. and S. The books came to hand too late for him to have time for it before he went.

Mr. Hastings never *hinted* at Eliza in the smallest degree. Henry knew nothing of Mr. Trimmer's death. I tell you these things that you may not have to ask them over again.

There is a new clerk sent down to Alton, a Mr. Edmund Williams, a young man whom Henry thinks most highly of, and he turns out to be a son of the luckless Williamses of Grosvenor Place.

I long to have you hear Mr. H.'s opinion of P. and P. His admiring my Elizabeth so much is particularly welcome to me.

Instead of saving my superfluous wealth for you to spend, I am going to treat myself with spending it myself. I hope, at least, that I shall find some poplin at Layton and Shear's that will tempt me to buy it. If I do, it shall be sent to Chawton, as half will be for you; for I depend upon your being so kind as to accept it, being the main point. It will be a great pleasure to me. Don't say a word. I only wish you could choose too. I shall send twenty yards.

Now for Bath. Poor F. Cage has suffered a good deal from her accident. The noise of the White Hart was terrible to her. They will keep her quiet, I dare say. *She* is not so much delighted with the place as the rest of the party; probably, as she says herself, from having been less well, but she thinks she should like it better in the season. The streets are very empty now, and the shops not so gay as she expected. They are at No. 1 Henrietta Street, the corner of Laura Place, and have no acquaintance at present but the Bramstons.

Lady Bridges drinks at the Cross Bath, her son at the Hot, and Louisa is going to bathe. Dr. Parry seems to be half starving Mr. Bridges, for he is restricted to much such a diet as James's bread, water and meat, and is never to eat so much of that as he wishes, and he is to walk a great deal—walk till he drops, I believe—gout or no gout. It really is to that purpose. I have not exaggerated.

Charming weather for you and us, and the travellers, and everybody. You will take your walk this afternoon, and . . .

83. *To Cassandra Austen.* *Thursday* ⟨16 *Sept.* 1813⟩

Address: Miss Austen | Chawton | By favour of (blank)
Postmark: none.
The late Cleveland H. Dodge. 2 leaves 4°. Endorsed 'Henrietta St. Autumn of 1813'.
Brabourne ii. 154 ; *Life* 276 (extracts). A few lines unpublished.

Henrietta Street—Thursday—after dinner

Thank you my dearest Cassandra for the nice long Letter I sent off this morning.—I hope you have had it by this time & that it has found you all well, & my Mother no more in need of Leeches.—Whether this will be delivered to you by Henry on Saturday even^g^ or by the Postman on Sunday morn^g^ I know not, as he has lately recollected something of an engagement for Saturday which perhaps may delay his visit.—He seems determined to come to you soon however.—I hope you will receive the Gown tomorrow & may be able with tolerable honesty to say that you like the colour ;—it was bought at Grafton House, where, by going very early, we got immediate attendance & went on very comfortably.—I only forgot the one particular thing which I had always resolved to buy there—

a white silk Handkf—& was therefore obliged to give six shillings for one at Crook & Besford's—which reminds me to say that the Worsteds ought also to be at Chawton tomorrow & that I shall be very happy to hear they are approved. I had not much time for deliberation. We are now all four of us young Ladies sitting round the Circular Table in the inner room writing our Letters, while the two Brothers are having a comfortable coze in the room adjoining.—It is to be a quiet evening, much to the satisfaction of 4 of the 6.—My Eyes are quite tired of Dust and Lamps.—The Letter you forwarded from Edwd Junr has been duly received. He has been shooting most prosperously at home, & dining at Chilham Castle & with Mr. Scudamore. My Cap is come home & I like it very much, Fanny has one also; hers is white sarsenet and Lace, of a different shape from mine, more fit for morning, Carriage wear—which is what it is intended for—& is in shape exceedingly like our own Sattin & Lace of last winter—shaped round the face exactly like it, with pipes & more fullness, & a round crown inserted behind. *My* Cap has a peak in front. Large, full Bows of very narrow ribbon (old twopenny) are the thing. One over the right temple perhaps, & another at the left ear.—Henry is not quite well.—His stomach is rather deranged. You must keep him in Rhubarb & give him plenty of Port & Water.—He caught his cold farther back than I told you—before he got to Matlock—somewhere in his Journey from the North—but the ill effects of *that* I hope are nearly gone.—We returned from Grafton House only just in time for breakfast & had scarcely finished breakfast when the carriage came to the door. From 11 to

½ past 3 we were hard at it ;—we *did* contrive to get to Hans Place for 10 minutes. Mrs. T. was as affectionate & pleasing as ever ; & from her appearance I suspect her to be in the family way. Poor Woman ! —Fanny prophecies the Child's coming within 3 or 4 days.

After our return, Mr. Tilson walked up from the Compting House & called upon us ; & these have been all our Visitings.—I have rejoiced more than once that I bought my Writing paper in the Country ; we have not had a q[r] of an hour to spare.—I enclose the Eighteen pence due to my Mother.—The Rose colour was 6/*s*, & the other 4/*s* per y[d]. There was but 2 y[d] and a q[r] of the dark slate in the Shop, but the Man promised to match it and send it off correctly.

Fanny bought her Irish at Newton's in Leicester Sq[re] & I took the opportunity of thinking about your Irish & seeing one piece of the Yard wide at 4/*s*.—and it seemed to me very good—good enough for your purpose.—It might at least be worth your while to go there, if you have no other engagements.—Fanny is very much pleased with the stockings she has bought of Remmington—Silk at 12/*s*.—Cotton at 4..3.—She thinks them great bargains, but I have not seen them yet—as my hair was dressing when the Man & the Stockgs came.—The poor Girls & their Teeth !—I have not mentioned them yet, but we were a whole hour at Spence's, & Lizzy's were filed & lamented over again & poor Marianne had two taken out after all, the two just beyond the Eye teeth, to make room for those in front.—When her doom was fixed, Fanny Lizzy & I walked into the next room, where we heard each of the two sharp hasty Screams.—Fanny's teeth were cleaned too—& pretty as they are, Spence found something to do to them, putting in gold and talking gravely—& making a considerable point of seeing her again before winter;—he had before urged the expediency of L. & M.s being brought to Town in the course of a couple of Months to be further examined, & continued to the last to press for their all coming to him.—My B^r^ would not absolutely promise.—The little girls teeth I can suppose in a critical state, but I think he must be a Lover of Teeth & Money & Mischeif to parade about Fannys.—I would not have had him look at mine for a shilling a tooth & double it.—It was a disagreable hour. We then went to Wedgwoods where my B^r^ & Fanny chose a Dinner Set.—I beleive the pattern is a small-Lozenge in purple, between Lines of narrow Gold;—& it is to have the Crest.

We must have been 3 q^rs^ of an hour at Grafton House, Edward sitting by all the time with wonderful patience. There Fanny bought the Net for Anna's gown, & a beautiful Square veil for herself.—The Edging there is very cheap, I was tempted by some, & I bought some very nice plaiting Lace at 3–4.—

Fanny desires me to tell Martha with her kind Love that Birchall assured her there was no 2^d^ set of Hook's Lessons for Beginners—& that by my advice, she has therefore chosen her a set by another Composer. I thought she w^d^ rather have something than not.—It costs six shillings.—With Love to You all, including Triggs, I remain

Yours very affec^ly^ J. Austen

84. *To Cassandra Austen. Thursday* 23 *Sept.* ⟨1813⟩

Address: Miss Austen | Chawton | Alton | Hants
Postmark: FEVER⟨SHAM⟩. The dated postmark illegible.
Pierpont Morgan Library. 2 leaves 4°.
Brabourne ii. 159; *Life* 276 (extracts). A few lines unpublished.

Godmersham Park—Thursday Sept: 23d.—

My dearest Cassandra

Thank you five hundred & forty times for the exquisite piece of Workmanship which was brought into the room this morng while we were at breakfast—with some very inferior works of art in the same way, & which I read with high glee—much delighted with everything it told whether good or bad.—It is so rich in striking intelligence that I hardly know what to reply to first. I beleive Finery must have it. I am extremely glad that you like the Poplin, I thought it would have my *Mother's* approbation, but was not so confident of *yours*. Remember that it is a present. Do not refuse me. I am very rich.—Mrs. Clement is very welcome to her little Boy & to my Congratulations into the bargain, if ever you think of giving them. I hope she will do well.—Her sister in Lucina, Mrs. H. Gipps does too well we think;—Mary P. wrote on Sunday that she had been three days on the Sofa. Sackree does not approve it. How can Mrs J. Austen be so provokingly ill-judging?—I should have expected better from her professed if not her real regard for my Mother. Now my Mother will be unwell again. Every fault in Ben's blood does harm to hers, & every dinner-invitation he refuses will give her an indigestion.—Well, there is some comfort in the Mrs. Hulbert's not coming to you—& I am happy to hear of the Honey.—I was thinking of it the other day.—Let me know when you begin the new Tea—& the new white wine.—My present Elegancies have not yet made me indifferent to such Matters. I am still a Cat if I see a Mouse.—I am glad you like our caps—but Fanny is out of conceit with hers already; she finds that she has been buying a new cap without having a new pattern, which is true enough.—She is rather out of luck, to like neither her gown nor her cap—but I do not mind it, because besides that I like them both myself, I consider it as a thing of course at her time of Life—one of the sweet taxes of Youth to chuse in a hurry & make bad bargains.—I wrote to Charles yesterday, & Fanny has had a letter from him to day, principally to make enquiries about the time of their visit here, to which mine was an answer beforehand; so he will probably write again soon to fix his week.—I am best pleased that Cassy does not go to you.—Now, what have we been doing since I wrote last? The Mr. Ks came a little before dinner on Monday, & Edwd went to the church with the two Seniors—but there is no Inscription yet drawn up. They are very goodnatured you know & civil & all that—but are not particularly superfine; however, they ate their dinner & drank their Tea & went away, leaving their lovely Wadham in our arms—& I wish you had seen Fanny & me running backwards & forwards with his Breeches from the little chintz to the White room before we went to bed, in the greatest of frights lest he should come upon us before we had done it all.—There had been a mistake in the Housemaids' Preparations & *they* were gone to bed.—He seems a very harmless sort of young Man—nothing to like or dislike in him;—

Godmersham Park in Kent the Seat of Thomas Knight Esq.[r]

Published as the Act directs Nov. 1st 1784 by W. Watts Chelsea

goes out shooting or hunting with the two others all the morn[g]—& plays at whist & makes queer faces in the even[g].—On Tuesday the Carriage was taken to the Painters ;—at one time Fanny & I were to have gone in it, cheifly to call on Mrs. C—Milles and *Moy*—but we found that they were going for a few days to Sandling & w[d] not be at home ;—therefore my Brother & Fanny went to Eastwell in the chair instead. While they were gone the Nackington Milles' called & left their cards.—Nobody at home at Eastwell.—We hear a great deal of Geo. H.'s wretchedness. I suppose he has quick feelings—but I dare say thcy will not kill him.—He is so much out of spirits however that his friend John Plumptre is gone over to comfort him, at Mr. Hatton's desire ; he called here this morn[g] in his way. A handsome young Man certainly, with quiet, gentlemanlike manners.—I set him down as sensible rather than Brilliant.—There is nobody Brilliant nowadays.—He talks of staying a week at Eastwell & then comes to Chilham Cas: for a day or two, & my B[r] invited him to come here afterwards, which he seemed very agreable to.—' 'Tis Night & the Landscape is lovely no more,' but to make amends for that, our visit to the Tyldens is over. My Brother, Fanny, Edw[d] & I went ; Geo. staid at home with W. K.—There was nothing entertaining, or out of the common way. We met only Tyldens & double Tyldens. A Whist Table for the Gentlemen, a grown-up musical young Lady to play Backgammon with Fanny, & engravings of the Colleges at Cambridge for me. In the morn[g] we returned Mrs. Sherer's visit.—I like *Mr.* S. very much.—Well, I have not half done yet ; I am not come up with myself.—My B[r] drove Fanny to Nackington & Cant[y] yesterday, & while they were gone the Faggs paid their duty.—Mary Oxenden is staying at Cant[y] with the Blairs, & Fanny's object was to see her.—The Deedes' want us to come to Sandling for a few days, or at least a day & night ;—at present Edw[d] does not seem well affected—he w[d] rather not be asked to go anywhere—but I rather expect he will be persuaded to go for the one day & night. I read him the cheif of your Letter, he was interested & pleased as he ought, & will be happy to hear from you himself. —Your finding so much comfort from his Cows gave him evident pleasure.—I wonder Henry did not go down on Saturday ;—he does not in general fall *within* a doubtful Intention.—My face is very much as it was before I came away—for the first two or three days it was rather worse—I caught a small cold in my way down & had some pain every even[g]—not to last long, but rather severer than it had been lately. This has worn off however & I have scarcely felt anything for the last two days.—Sackree is pretty well again, only weak ;—much obliged to you for your message &c ;—it was very true that she bless'd herself the whole time that the pain was not in her stomach. I read all the scraps I could of Your letter to her. She seemed to like it—& says she shall always like to hear anything of Chawton now—& I am to make you Miss Clewes's assurance to the same effect, with Thanks and best respects &c.—The girls are much disturbed at Mary Stacey's not admitting Dame L.—Miss C. & I are sorry but not angry ;—we acknowledge Mary Stacey's right & can suppose her to have reason.—Oh ! the Church must have looked very forlorn. We all thought of the empty Pew.—How Bentigh is grown !—and the

Canty.Hill-Plantation!—And the Improvements *within* are very great.—I admire the Chintz room very much.—We live in the Library except at Meals & have a fire every Even^{g}.—The weather is set about changing;—we shall have a settled wet season soon. I must go to bed.

Friday. I am sorry to find that one of the nightcaps here belongs to you—sorry, because it must be in constant wear.—Great Doings again today—Fanny, Lizzy & Mar: are going to Goodnestone for the Fair, which is tomorrow, & stay till Monday, & the Gentlemen are all to dine at Evington. Edwd has been repenting ever since he promised to go & was hoping last night for a wet day—but the morn^{g} is fair.—I shall dine with Miss Clewes & I dare say find her very agreable.—The invitation to the Fair was general; Edwd positively declined his share of that, & I was very glad to do the same.—It is likely to be a baddish Fair—not much upon the Stall, & neither Mary O. nor Mary P.—It is hoped that the Portfolio may be in Cant^{y} this morn^{g}. Sackree's sister found it at Croydon and took it to Town with her, but unluckily did not send it down till she had directions. Fanny C's. screens can be done nothing with, but there are parts of workbags in the parcel, very important in their way.—Three of the Deedes girls are to be at Goodnestone.—We shall not be much settled till this visit is over—settled as to employment I mean;—Fanny and I are to go on with Modern Europe together, but hitherto have advanced only 25 Pages, something or other has always happened to delay or curtail the reading hour.—I ought to have told you before of a purchase of Edward's in Town, he desired you might hear of it, a *Thing* for measuring Timber with, so that you need not have the trouble of finding him in Tapes any longer.—He treated himself with this seven shilling purchase, & bought a new Watch and new Gun for George.—The new gun shoots very well.

Apples are scarce in this Country ; £1—5—a sack.—Miss Hinton should take Hannah Knight.—Mrs. Driver has not yet appeared.—J. Littleworth & the Grey Poney reached Bath safely.—

A letter from Mrs. Cooke, they have been at Brighton a fortnight, stay at least another & Mary is already much better.—Poor Dr. Isham is obliged to admire P. & P—& to send me word that he is sure he shall not like M[de] Darblay's new Novel half so well.—Mrs. C. invented it all of course. He desires his comp[ts] to you & my Mother.—Of the Adlestrop-Living business Mrs. C. says ' It can be now no secret, as the Papers for the necessary Dispensations are going up to the Archbishop's Secretary.—However be it known that we all wish to have it understood that George takes this Trust *entirely* to oblige Mr. Leigh & never will be a shilling benefited by it. Had my consent been necessary, beleive me I sh[d] have withheld it, for I do think it on the part of the Patron a very shabby peice of business.—All these and other *Scrapings* from dear Mrs. E. L. are to accumulate no doubt to help Mr. Twisleton to a secure admission again into England.'—I would wish you therefore to make it known to my Mother as if *this* were the first time of Mrs. Cooke's mentioning it to me.—

I told Mrs. C. of my mother's late oppression in *her head*.—She says on that subject—' Dear Mrs. Austen's is I beleive an attack frequent at her age & mine. Last year I had for some time the Sensation of a Peck Loaf resting on my head, & they talked of cupping me, but I came off with a dose or two of calomel & have never heard of it since.'—

The three Miss Knights & Mrs. Sayce are just off;—the weather has got worse since the early morn[g];—& whether Mrs. Clewes & I are to be Tete a Tete, or to have 4 gentlemen to admire us is uncertain.

I am now alone in the Library, Mistress of all I survey—at least I may say so & repeat the whole poem if I like it, without offence to anybody.—

Martha will have wet Races & catch a bad cold;—in other respects I hope she will have much pleasure at them—& that she is free from Ear ache now. I am glad she likes my cap so well.—I assure you my old one looked so smart yesterday that I was asked two or three times before I set off, whether it was not my new one.—I have this moment seen Mrs. Driver driven up to the Kitchen Door. I cannot close with a grander circumstance or greater wit.—

Yours affec:[ly] J. A.

I am going to write to Steventon so you need not send any news of me there.

Louisa's best Love & a Hundred Thousand Million Kisses.

85. *To Francis Austen.* ⟨*Saturday*⟩ 25 *Sept.* 1813

Address : Captain Austen | HMS. Elephant | Baltic
Postmark : none.
Captain Ernest Austen R.N. 2 leaves 4°.
Hubback, *Sailor Brothers,* 243 ; *Life* 278.

Godmersham Park—Sept: 25. 1813

My dearest Frank

The 11th of this month brought me your letter & I assure you I thought it very well worth its $2^s/3^d$.—I am very much obliged to you for filling me so long a sheet of paper, you are a good one to traffic with in that way, you pay most liberally ;—my Letter was a scratch of a note compared with yours—& then you write so even, so clear both in style & Penmanship, so much to the point & give so much real intelligence that it is enough to kill one.—I am sorry Sweden is so poor & my riddle so bad.—The idea of a fashionable Bathing place in Mecklenburg !—How can people pretend to be fashionable or to bathe out of England ! —Rostock Market makes one's mouth water, our cheapest Butcher's meat is double the price of theirs ;—nothing under 9^d all this summer, & I beleive upon recollection nothing under 10^d.—Bread has sunk & is likely to sink more, which we hope may make Meat sink too. But I have no occasion to think of the price of Bread or of Meat where I am now ;—let me shake off vulgar cares & conform to the happy Indifference of East Kent wealth.—I wonder whether You & the King of Sweden knew that I *was* to come to G^m with my B^r. Yes, I suppose you have rec^d due notice of it by some means or other. I have not been here these 4 years, so I am sure the event deserves to be talked of before & behind as well as in the middle.—We left Chawton on ye 14th,—spent two entire days in Town & arrived here on ye 17th.—My Br, Fanny, Lizzy, Marianne & I composed this division of the Family, & filled his Carriage, inside & out.—Two post-chaises under the escort of George conveyed eight more across the Country, the Chair brought two, two others came on horseback & the rest by the Coach—& so by one means or another we all are removed.—It puts me in mind of the account of St Paul's shipwreck, when all are said by different means to reach the shore in safety. I left my Mother, Cassandra & Martha well, & have had good accounts of them since. At present they are quite alone, but they are going to be visited by Mrs. Heathcote & Miss Bigg—& to have a few days of Henry's company likewise.—I expect to be here about two months. Edward is to be in Hampshire again in November & will take me back.—I shall be sorry to be in Kent so long without seeing Mary, but am afraid it must be so. She has very kindly invited me to Deal, but is aware of the great improbability of my being able to get there.—It would be a great pleasure to me to see Mary Jane again too, as well as her Brothers, new and old.—Charles & his family I do hope to see; they are coming here for a week in October.—We were accomodated in Henrietta St.—Henry was so good as to find room for his 3 neices and myself in his house. Edward slept at an Hotel in the next street.—No. 10 is made very comfortable with cleaning, and Painting & the Sloane St furniture. The front room upstairs is an excellent Dining & common sitting parlour—& the smaller one behind will sufficiently answer his purpose as a Drawg room.—

N

He has no intention of giving large parties of any kind.—His plans are all for the comfort of his Friends & himself.—M[de] Bigeon & her Daughter have a Lodging in his neighbourhood & come to him as often as he likes or as they like. M[de] B. always markets for him as she used to do; & upon our being in the House, was constantly there to do the work.—She is wonderfully recovered from the severity of her Asthmatic complaint.—Of our three even[gs] in Town one was spent at the Lyceum & another at Covent Garden;—the Clandestine Marriage was the most respectable of the performances, the rest were sing-song & trumpery, but did very well for Lizzy & Marianne, who were indeed delighted;—but *I* wanted better acting.—There was no Actor worthy naming.—I beleive the Theatres are thought at a low ebb at present.—Henry has probably sent you his own account of his visit in Scotland. I wish he had had more time & could have gone farther north, & deviated to the Lakes in his way back, but what he was able to do seems to have afforded him great enjoyment & he met with scenes of higher Beauty in Roxburghshire than I had supposed the South of Scotland possessed.—Our nephew's gratification was less keen than our Brother's.—Edward is no Enthusiast in the beauties of Nature. His Enthusiasm is for the sports of the field only.—He is a very promising & pleasing young Man however upon the whole, behaves with great propriety to his Father & great kindness to his Brothers & Sisters—& we must forgive his thinking more of Growse & Partridges than Lakes & Mountains. He & George are out every morn[g] either shooting or with the Harriers. They are both good shots.—Just at present I am Mistress & Miss & altogether here, Fanny being gone to Goodnestone for a day or two, to attend the famous Fair, which makes its yearly distribution of gold paper & coloured persian through all the Family connections.—In this House there is a constant succession of small events, somebody is always going or coming; this morn[g] we had Edw[d] Bridges unexpectedly to breakfast with us, in his way from Ramsgate where is his wife, to Lenham where is his church—& tomorrow he dines and sleeps here on his return.—They have been all the summer at Ramsgate, for *her* health, she is a poor Honey—the sort of woman who gives me the idea of being determined never to be well—& who likes her spasms & nervousness & the consequence they give her, better than anything else.—This is an ill-natured sentiment to send all over the Baltic!—The Mr. Knatchbulls, dear Mrs. Knights Brothers dined here the other day. They came from the Friars, which is still on their hands.—The Elder made many enquiries after you.—Mr. Sherer is quite a new Mr. Sherer to me; I heard him for the first time last Sunday, & he gave us an excellent Sermon—a little too eager sometimes in his delivery, but that is to *me* a better extreme than the want of animation, especially when it evidently comes from the heart as in him. The Clerk is as much like you as ever, I am always glad to see him on that account.—But the Sherers are going away. He has a bad Curate at Westwell, whom he can eject only by residing there himself. He goes nominally for three years, & a Mr. Paget is to have the curacy of G[m]—a married Man, with a very musical wife, which I hope may make her a desirable acquaintance to Fanny.—

I thank you very warmly for your kind consent to my application & the kind hint which followed it.—I was previously aware of what I sh[d] be laying myself open to—but the truth is that the Secret has spread so far as to be scarcely the Shadow of a secret now—& that I beleive whenever the 3[d] appears, I shall not even attempt to tell Lies about it.—I shall rather try to make all the Money than all the Mystery I can of it.—People shall pay for their knowledge if I can make them.—Henry heard P. & P. warmly praised in Scotland, by Lady Rob[t] Kerr & another Lady ;—& what does he do in the warmth of his Brotherly vanity & Love, but immediately tell them who wrote it ! A Thing once set going in that way—one knows how it spreads !—and he, dear Creature, has set it going so much more than once. I know it is all done from affection & partiality—but at the same time, let me here again express to you & Mary my sense of the *superior* kindness which you have shewn on the occasion, in doing what I wished.—I am trying to harden myself. After all, what a trifle it is in all its Bearings, to the really important points of one's existence even in this World !

I take it for granted that Mary has told you of Anna's engagement to Ben Lefroy. It came upon us without much preparation ;—at the same time, there was *that* about her which kept us in a constant preparation for something.—We are anxious to have it go on well, there being quite as much in his favour as the Chances are likely to give her in any Matrimonial connection. I beleive he is sensible, certainly very religious, well connected & with some Independance.—There is an unfortunate dissimularity of Taste between them in one respect which gives us some apprehensions, he hates company & she is very fond of it;—this, with some queerness of Temper on his side & much unsteadiness on hers, is untoward.

I hope Edward's family-visit to Chawton will be yearly, he certainly means it now, but we must not expect it to exceed *two* months in future.—I do not think however, that *he* found *five* too long this summer.—He was very happy there. The new Paint improves this House much, and we find no evil from the smell.

Poor Mr. Trimmer is lately dead, a sad loss to his Family, & occasioning some anxiety to our Brother;—for the present he continues his Affairs in the Son's hands; a matter of great consequence to *them*—I hope he will have no reason to remove his Business.—I remain

Your very affec[te] Sister,

J. Austen

There is to be a 2[d] Edition of S. & S. Egerton advises it.

86. *To Cassandra Austen.* *Monday* 11 *Oct.* 1813

Address: Miss Austen | Chawton | Alton | Hants
Postmarks: FEVERSHAM and 13 OC 1813
Pierpont Morgan Library. 2 leaves 4°.
Brabourne ii. 169; *Life* 282 (extracts).

Godmersham Park Monday Oct[r] 11th

My dearest At: Cass:

I have just asked At. Jane to let me write a little in her letter, but she does not like it so I wont.—Good bye.

You will have Edward's Letter tomorrow. He tells me that he did not send you any news to interfere with mine, but I do not think there is much for anybody to send at present. We had our dinner party on Wed^y with the addition of Mrs. & Miss Milles who were under a promise of dining here in their return from Eastwell whenever they paid their visit of duty there, & it happened to be paid on that day.—Both Mother & Daughter are much as I have always found them.—I like the Mother, 1st because she reminds me of Mrs. Birch & 2dly because she is chearful & grateful for what she is at the age of 90 & upwards.—The day was pleasant enough. I sat by Mr. Chisholme & we talked away at a great rate about nothing worth hearing.—It was a mistake as to the day of the Sherers going being fixed; *they* are ready but are waiting for Mr. Paget's answer.—I enquired of Mrs. Milles after Jemima Brydges & was quite greived to hear that she was obliged to leave Cant^y some months ago on account of her debts & is nobody knows where.—What an unprosperous Family!—On saturday, soon after breakfast Mr. J. P. left us for Norton Court.—I like him very much.—He gives me the idea of a very amiable young Man, only too diffident to be so agreable as he might be.—He was out the cheif of each morning with the other two—shooting & getting wet through.—Tomorrow we are to know whether he & a hundred young Ladies will come here for the Ball.—I do not much expect any.—The Deedes' cannot meet us, they have Engagements at home. I will finish the Deedes' by saying that they are not likely to come here till quite late in my stay—the very last week perhaps—& I do not expect to see the Moores at all.—They are not solicited till after Edward's return from Hampshire. Monday, Nov:^r 15th is the day now fixed for our setting out.—Poor Basingstoke Races !—there seem to have been two particularly wretched days on purpose for them ;—& Weyhill week does not begin much happier.—We were quite surprised by a Letter from Anna at Tollard Royal last Saturday—but perfectly approve her going & only regret they should all go so far, to stay so few days. We had Thunder & Lighten[g] here on Thursday morn[g] between 5 & 7—no very bad Thunder, but a great deal of Light[g].—It has given the commencement of a season of wind & rain ; & perhaps for the next 6 weeks we shall not have two dry days together.—Lizzy is very much obliged to you for your Letter & will answer it soon, but has so many things to do that it may be four or five days before she can. This is quite her own message, spoken in rather a desponding tone.—Your Letter gave pleasure to all of us, we had all the reading of it of course, I *three times*—as I undertook to the great releif of Lizzy, to read it to Sackree, & afterwards to Louisa.—Sackree does not at all approve of Mary Doe & her nuts—on the score of propriety rather than health.—She saw some signs of going after her in George & Henry, & thinks if you could give the girl a check, by rather reproving her for taking anything seriously about nuts which they said to her, it might be of use.—This, of course, is between our three discreet selves—a scene of triennial bliss.—Mrs. Britton called here on Saturday. I never saw her before. She is a large, ungenteel Woman, with self-satisfied & would-be elegant manners.—We are certain of some visitors tomorrow ; Edward Bridges comes for two nights in his way from Lenham to Ramsgate & brings a friend—name unknown—but supposed to be a Mr. Harpur, a neighbouring Clergyman; & Mr. R. Mascall is to shoot with the young Men, which it is to be supposed will end in his staying dinner.—On Thursday, Mr. Lushington M.P. for Canterbury & Manager of the Lodge Hounds, dines here & stays the night.—He is cheifly Young Edward's acquaintance.—If I can, I will get a frank from him & write to you all the sooner. I suppose the Ashford Ball will furnish something.—As I wrote of my nephews with a little bitterness in my last, I think it particularly incumbent on me to do them justice now, & I have great pleasure in saying that they were both at the Sacrament yesterday. After having much praised or much blamed anybody, one is generally sensible of something just the reverse soon afterwards. Now, these two Boys who are out with the Foxhounds will come home & disgust me again by some habit of Luxury or some proof of sporting Mania—unless I keep it off by this prediction. —They amuse themselves very comfortably in the even[g]—by netting; they are each about a rabbit net, & sit as deedily to it, side by side, as any two Uncle Franks could do.—I am looking over Self Control again, & my opinion is confirmed of its being an excellently-meant, elegantly-written Work, without anything of Nature or Probability in it. I declare I do not know whether Laura's passage down the American River, is not the most natural, possible, everyday thing she ever does.—

Tuesday—Dear me! what is to become of me! Such a long Letter! Two & forty lines in the 2[d] Page. —Like Harriot Byron I ask, what am I to do with my Gratitude?—I can do nothing but thank you & go on.—A few of your enquiries I think, are replied to en avance. The name of F. Cage's Draw[g] Master is O'Neil.—We are exceedingly amused with your Shalden news & your self reproach on the subject of Mrs. Stockwell, made me laugh heartily. I rather wondered that Johncock, the only person in the room, could help laughing too.—I had not heard before of her having the Measles. Mrs. H & Alethea's staying till friday was quite new to me ; a good plan however.—I c[d] not have settled it better myself, & am glad they found so much in the house to approve—and I hope they will ask Martha to visit them.—I admire the Sagacity & Taste of Charlotte Williams. Those large dark eyes always judge well.—I will compliment her, by naming a Heroine after her.—Edward has had all the particulars of the Building &c read to him twice over & seems very well satisfied ;—a narrow door to the Pantry is the only subject of solicitude—it is certainly just the door which should not be narrow, on account of the Trays—but if a case of necessity, it must be borne.—I *knew* there was Sugar in the Tin, but had no idea of there being enough to last through your Company. All the better.—You ought not to think this new Loaf better than the other, because *that* was the first of 5 which all came together. Something of fancy perhaps, & something of Imagination.—Dear Mrs. Digweed !—I cannot bear that she sh[d] not be foolishly happy after a Ball.—I hope Miss Yates & her companions were all well the day after their arrival.—I am thoroughly rejoiced that Miss Benn has placed herself in Lodgings—tho' I hope they may not be long necessary.—No Letter from Charles yet.—Southey's Life of Nelson ;—I am tired of Lives of Nelson, being that I never read any. I will read this however, if Frank is mentioned in it.—Here am I in Kent, with one Brother in the same County & another Brother's Wife, & see nothing of them—which seems unnatural—It will not last so for ever I trust.—I sh[d] like to have Mrs. F. A. & her Children here for a week—but not a syllable of that nature is ever breathed.—I wish her last visit had not been so long a one.—I wonder whether Mrs. Tilson has ever lain-in. Mention it, if it ever comes to your knowledge, & we shall hear of it by the same post from Henry. Mr. Rob. Mascall breakfasted here; he eats a great deal of Butter.—I dined upon Goose yesterday, which I hope will secure a good Sale of my 2[d] Edition.—Have you any Tomatas?—Fanny & I regale on them every day.—Disastrous Letters from the Plumptres & Oxendens.—Refusals everywhere—a Blank partout—& it is not quite certain whether we go or not; something may depend upon the disposition of Uncle Edward when he comes—& upon what we hear at Chilham Castle this morn[g]—for we are going to pay visits. We are going to each house at Chilham & to Mystole. I shall like seeing the Faggs.—I shall like it all, except that we are to set out so early that I have not time to write as I would wish.—Edw[d] Bridges's friend is a Mr. Hawker, I find, not Harpur. I would not have you sleep in such an Error for the World.

My brother desires his best Love & Thanks for all your Information. He hopes the roots of the old Beach have been dug away enough to allow a proper covering of Mould & Turf.—He is sorry for the necessity of build[g] the new Coin—but hopes they will contrive that the Doorway should be of the usual width;—if it must be contracted on one side, by widening it on the other.—The appearance need not signify.—And he desires me to say that Your being at Chawton when he is, will be quite necessary. You cannot think it more indispensable than he does. He is very much obliged to you for your attention to everything.—Have you any idea of returning with him to Henrietta S[t] & finishing your visit then ?—Tell me your sweet little innocent Ideas.

Everything of Love & Kindness—proper and improper, must now suffice.—

Y[rs] very affec[ly] J. Austen

87. *To Cassandra Austen.* *Thursday* 14 *Oct.* 1813

Address: Miss Austen | Chawton | Alton | Hants | Free R. Lushington
Postmarks: FEVERSHAM and ⟨OCT⟩ 16 1813
Harvard College Library. 3 leaves 4°.
Brabourne ii. 177 ; *Life* 283 (extracts).

Godmersham Park. Thursday Oct. 14

My dearest Cassandra

Now I will prepare for Mr. Lushington, & as it will be wisest also to prepare for his not coming or my not getting a frank I shall write very close from the first & even leave room for the seal in the proper place.—When I have followed up my last with this, I shall feel somewhat less unworthy of you than the state of our Correspondence now requires. I left off in a great hurry to prepare for our morn[g] visits—of course was ready a good deal the first, & need not have hurried so much—Fanny wore her new gown & cap.—I was surprised to find Mystole so pretty. The Ladies were at home ; I was in luck, & saw Lady Fagg & all her five

Daughters, with an old Mrs. Hamilton from Cant[y] & Mrs. and Miss Chapman from Margate into the Bargain.—I never saw so plain a family, five sisters so very plain !—They are as plain as the Foresters or the Franfraddops or the Sea-graves or the Rivers' excluding Sophy.—Miss Sally Fagg has a pretty figure, & that comprises all the good Looks of the family.—It was stupidish ; Fanny did her part very well, but there was a lack of Talk altogether, & the three friends in the House only sat by & looked at us.—However Miss Chapman's name is Laura & she had a double flounce to her gown.—You really must get some flounces. Are not some of your large stock of white morn[g] gowns just in a happy state for a flounce, too short ?—Nobody at home at either House in Chilham.—Edward Bridges & his friend did not forget to arrive. The friend is a Mr. Wigram, one of the three & twenty Children of a great rich mercantile Sir Robert Wigram, an old acquaintance of the Footes, but very recently known to Edw[d] B.—The history of his coming here, is that intending to go from Ramsgate to Brighton, Edw: B. persuaded him to take Lenham in his way, which gave him the convenience of Mr. W.'s gig & the comfort of not being alone there ; but probably thinking a few days of G[m] would be the cheapest & pleasantest way of entertaining his friend & himself, offered a visit here, & here they stay till tomorrow. Mr. W. is about 5 or 6 & 20, not ill-looking & not agreable.—He is certainly no addition.—A sort of cool, gentlemanlike manner, but very silent.—They say his name is Henry. A proof how unequally the gifts of Fortune are bestowed.—I have seen many a John & Thomas much more agreable. We have got rid of Mr. R. Mascall however ;—I did not like *him* either. He talks too much & is conceited—besides having a vulgarly shaped mouth. He slept here on Tuesday ; so that yesterday Fanny & I sat down to breakfast with six gentlemen to admire us.—We did not go to the Ball.—It was left to her to decide, & at last she determined against it. She knew that it would be a sacrifice on the part of her Father & Brothers if they went—& I hope it will prove that *she* has not sacrificed much.—It is not likely that there sh[d] have been anybody there, whom she wd care for.—*I* was very glad to be spared the trouble of dressing & going & being weary before it was half over, so my gown & my cap are still unworn.—It will appear at last perhaps that I might have done without either.—I produced my Brown Bombasin yesterday & it was very much admired indeed—& I like it better than ever :—You have given many particulars of the state of Chawton House, but still we want more.—Edward wants to be expressly told that all the Round Tower &c. is entirely down, & the door from the Best room stopt up ;—he does not know enough of the appearance of things in that quarter.—He heard from Bath yesterday. Lady B. continues very well & D[r] Parry's opinion is that while the Water agrees with her she ought to remain there, which throws their coming away at a greater Uncertainty than we had supposed.—It will end perhaps in a fit of the Gout which may prevent her coming away. —Louisa thinks her Mother's being so well may be quite as much oweing to her being so much out of doors, as to the Water.—Lady B. is going to try the Hot pump ; the Cross Bath being about to be painted. —Louisa is particularly well herself, & thinks the

Water has been of use to her.—She mentioned our enquiries &c. to Mr. and Mrs. Alex: Evelyn, & had their best Comp[ts] & Thanks to give in return.—Dr. Parry does not expect Mr. E. to last much longer.—Only think of Mrs. Holder's being dead !—Poor woman, she has done the only thing in the World she could possibly do, to make one cease to abuse her.—Now, if you please, Hooper must have it in his power to do more by his Uncle.—Lucky for the little girl !—An Anne Ekins can hardly be so unfit for the care of a Child as a Mrs. Holder. A letter from Wrotham yesterday, offering an early visit here ;—& Mr. & Mrs. Moore & one Child are to come on Monday for 10 days.—I hope Charles & Fanny may not fix the same time—but if they come at all in October they *must*. What is the use of hoping ?—The two parties of Children is the chief Evil. To be sure, here we are, the very thing has happened, or rather worse, a Letter from Charles this very morn[g] which gives us reason to suppose they may come here to day. It depends upon the weather, & the weather now is very fine.—No difficulties are made however & indeed there will be no want of room, but I wish there were no Wigrams & Lushingtons in the way to fill up the Table & make us such a motley set.—I cannot spare Mr. Lushington either because of his frank, but Mr. Wigram does no good to anybody.—I cannot imagine how a Man can have the impudence to come into a Family party for three Days, where he is quite a stranger, unless he knows himself to be agreable on undoubted authority.—He & Mr. Edw. B. are going to ride to Eastwell—& as the Boys are hunting & my B[r] is gone to Cant[y] Fanny & I have a quiet morn[g] before us.—Edward has driven off poor Mrs.

Salkeld.—It was thought a good opportunity of doing something towards clearing the House.—By her own desire *Mrs.* Fanny is to be put in the room next the Nursery, her Baby in a little bed by her ;—& as Cassy is to have the Closet within & Betsey William's little Hole they will be all very snug together.—I shall be most happy to see dear Charles, & he will be as happy as he can with a cross Child or some such care pressing on him at the time.—I should be very happy in the idea of seeing little Cassy again too, did not I fear she wd. disappoint me by some immediate disagreableness.—We had the good old original Brett & Toke calling here yesterday, separately.—Mr. Toke I am always very fond of. He enquired after you & my Mother, which adds Esteem to Passion.—The Charles Cages are staying at Godington.—I *knew* they must be staying somewhere soon.—Ed: Hussey is warned out of Pett, & talks of fixing at Ramsgate.—Bad taste !—He is very fond of the Sea however ;—some Taste in that—& some Judgement too in fixing on Ramsgate, as being by the Sea.—The Comfort of the Billiard Table here is very great.—It draws all the Gentlemen to it whenever they are within, especially after Dinner, so that my B^r^ Fanny & I have the Library to ourselves in delightful quiet.—There is no truth in the report of G. Hatton being to marry Miss Wemyss. He desires it may be contradicted.—Have you done anything about our Present to Miss Benn ?—I suppose she must have a bed at my Mothers whenever she dines there.—How will they manage as to inviting her when you are gone ?—& if they invite how they will contrive to entertain her ?—Let me know as many of your parting arrangements as you can, as to Wine &c.—I wonder whether the Ink bottle has been filled.—Does Butcher's meat keep up at the same price ? and is not Bread lower than 2/6.—Mary's blue gown !—My Mother must be in agonies.—I have a great mind to have *my* blue gown dyed some time or other—I proposed it once to you & you made some objection, I forget what.—It is the fashion of flounces that gives it particular Expediency.—Mrs. & Miss Wildman have just been here. Miss is very plain. I wish Lady B. may be returned before we leave G^{m} that Fanny may spend the time of her Father's absence, at Goodnestone, which is what she would prefer.—*Friday.*—They came. last night at about 7. We had given them up, but I still expected them to come. Dessert was nearly over ;—a better time for arriving than an hour & 1/2 earlier. They were late because they did not set out earlier & did not allow time enough.—Charles did not *aim* at more than reaching Sittingbourn by 3, which cd. not have brought them here by dinner time.—They had a very rough passage, he wd. not have ventured if he had known how bad it wd be. However here they are safe & well, just like their own nice selves, Fanny looking as neat & white this morn^{g} as possible, & dear Charles all affectionate, placid, quiet, chearful good humour. They are both looking very well, but poor little Cassy is grown extremely thin & looks poorly.—I hope a week's Country air & exercise may do her good. I am sorry to say it can be but a week.—The Baby does not appear so large in proportion as she was, nor quite so pretty, but I have seen very little of her.—Cassy was too tired & bewildered just at first to seem to know anybody—We met them in the Hall, the Women & Girl part of us—but before we reached the Library she kissed me very affectionately—& has since seemed to recollect me in the same way. It was quite an even^g of confusion as you may suppose—at first we were all walking about from one part of the House to the other—then came a fresh dinner in the Breakfast room for Charles & his wife, which Fanny & I attended—then we moved into the Library, were joined by the Dining room people, were introduced & so forth.—& then we had Tea & Coffee which was not over till past 10.—Billiards again drew all the odd ones away, & Edwd Charles, the two Fannys & I sat snugly talking. I shall be glad to have our numbers a little reduced, & by the time you receive this we shall be only a family, tho' a large family party. Mr. Lushington goes tomorrow.—Now I must speak of *him*—& I like him very much. I am sure he is clever & a Man of Taste. He got a vol. of Milton last night & spoke of it with Warmth.—He is quite an M.P.—very smiling, with an exceeding good address, & readiness of Language.—I am rather in love with him.—I dare say he is ambitious & Insincere.—He puts me in Mind of Mr. Dundas—. He has a wide smiling mouth & very good teeth, & something the same complexion & nose.—He is a much shorter Man, with Martha's Leave. Does Martha never hear from Mrs. Craven ?—Is Mrs. Craven never at home ?—We breakfasted in the Dining room today & are now all pretty well dispersed & quiet.—Charles & George are gone out shooting together, to Winnigates & Seaton Wood—I asked on purpose to tell Henry. Mr. Lushington & Edwd are gone some other way.—I wish Charles may kill something—but this high wind is against their Sport.—Lady Williams is living at the Rose at Sittingbourn, they called upon her Yesterday; she cannot live at Sheerness & as soon as she gets to Sittingbourn is quite well.—In return for all your Matches, I announce that her Brother William is going to marry a Miss Austen of a Wiltshire Family, who say they are related to us. I talk to Cassy about Chawton; she remembers much but does not volunteer on the subject.—Poor little Love—I wish she were not so very Palmery—but it seems stronger than ever.—I never knew a wife's family-features have such undue influence.—Papa & Mama have not yet made up their mind as to parting with her or not—The cheif, indeed the only difficulty with Mama is a very reasonable one, the Child's being very unwilling to leave them. When it was mentioned to her, she did not like the idea of it at all. At the same time, she has been suffering so much lately from Sea sickness, that her Mama cannot bear to have her much on board this winter.—Charles is less inclined to part with her.—I do not know how it will end, or what is to determine it. He desires his best Love to you & has not written because he has not been able to decide.—They are both very sensible of your Kindness on the occasion.—I have made Charles furnish me with something to say about Young Kendall.—He is going on very well. When he first joined the Namur, my B^r did not find him forward enough to be what they call put in the Office, & therefore placed him under the Schoolmaster, but he is very much improved, & goes into the Office now every afternoon—still attending School in the morn^g. This Cold weather comes very fortunately for Edward's nerves with such a House full, it suits him exactly, he is all alive & chearful. Poor James, on the contrary, must be running his Toes into the fire. I find that Mary Jane Fowle was very near returning with her B^{r} & paying them a visit on board—I forget exactly what hindered her—I beleive their Cheltenham scheme—I am glad something did.—They are to go to Cheltenham on Monday se'night. I don't vouch for their going you know, it only comes from one of the Family. —Now I think I have written you a good sized Letter & may deserve whatever I can get in reply.—Infinities of Love. I must distinguish that of Fanny Senr:—who particularly desires to be remembered to you all. —Yours very affec^{ly}

J. Austen

88. *To Cassandra Austen. Thursday* 21 *Oct.* ⟨1813⟩

Address (Brabourne): Miss Austen, 10 Henrietta St., | Covent Garden, London
Original not traced.
Brabourne ii. 189; *Life* 285 (extract).

Godmersham Park Oct. 18

My dear Aunt Cassandra

I am very much obliged to you for your long letter and for the nice account of Chawton. We are all very glad to hear that the Adams are gone, and hope Dame Libscombe will be more happy now with her deaffy child, as she calls it, but I am afraid there is not much chance of her remaining long sole mistress of her house.

I am sorry you had not any better news to send us of our hare, poor little thing! I thought it would not live long in that *Pondy House*; I don't wonder that Mary Doe is very sorry it is dead, because we promised her that if it was alive when we came back to Chawton, we would reward her for her trouble.

Papa is much obliged to you for ordering the scrubby firs to be cut down; I think he was rather frightened at first about the great oak. Fanny quite believed it, for she exclaimed 'Dear me, what a pity, how could they be so stupid!' I hope by this time they have put up some hurdles for the sheep, or turned out the cart-horses from the lawn.

Pray tell grandmamma that we have begun getting seeds for her; I hope we shall be able to get her a nice collection, but I am afraid this wet weather is very much against them. How glad I am to hear she has had such good success with her chickens, but I wish there had been more bantams amongst them. I am very sorry to hear of poor Lizzie's fate.

I must now tell you something about our poor people. I believe you know old Mary Croucher, she gets *maderer* and *maderer* every day. Aunt Jane has been to see her, but it was on one of her rational days. Poor Will Amos hopes your skewers are doing well; he has left his house in the poor Row, and lives in a barn at Builting. We asked him why he went away, and he said the fleas were so starved when he came back from Chawton that they all flew upon him and *eenermost* eat him up.

How unlucky it is that the weather is so wet! Poor uncle Charles has come home half drowned every day.

I don't think little Fanny is quite so pretty as she was; one reason is because she wears short petticoats, I believe. I hope Cook is better; she was very unwell the day we went away. Papa has given me half-a-dozen new pencils, which are very good ones indeed; I draw every other day. I hope you go and whip Lucy Chalcraft every night.

Miss Clewes begs me to give her very best respects to you; she is very much obliged to you for your kind enquiries after her. Pray give my duty to grandmamma and love to Miss Floyd. I remain, my dear Aunt Cassandra, your very affectionate niece,

Elizth. Knight

Thursday.—I think Lizzy's letter will entertain you. Thank you for yours just received. To-morrow shall be fine if possible. You will be at Guildford before our party set off. They only go to Key Street, as Mr. Street the Purser lives there, and they have promised to dine and sleep with him.

Cassy's looks are much mended. She agrees pretty well with her cousins, but is not quite happy among them; they are too many and too boisterous for her. I have given her your message, but she said nothing, and did not look as if the idea of going to Chawton again was a pleasant one. They have Edward's carriage to Ospringe.

I think I have just done a good deed—extracted Charles from his wife and children upstairs, and made him get ready to go out shooting, and not keep Mr. Moore waiting any longer.

Mr. and Mrs. Sherer and Joseph dined here yesterday very prettily. Edw. and Geo. were absent—gone for a night to Eastling. The two Fannies went to Canty. in the morning, and took Lou. and Cass. to try on new stays. Harriot and I had a comfortable walk together. She desires her best love to you and kind remembrance to Henry. Fanny's best love also. I fancy there is to be another party to Canty. to-morrow —Mr. and Mrs. Moore and me.

Edward thanks Henry for his letter. We are most happy to hear he is so much better. I depend upon you for letting me know what he wishes as to my staying with him or not ; you will be able to find out, I dare say. I had intended to beg you would bring one of my nightcaps with you, in case of my staying, but forgot it when I wrote on Tuesday. Edward is much concerned about his pond : he cannot now doubt the fact of its running out, which he was resolved to do as long as possible.

I suppose my mother will like to have me write to her. I shall try at least.

No ; I have never seen the death of Mrs. Crabbe. I have only just been making out from one of his prefaces that he probably was married. It is almost ridiculous. Poor woman ! I will comfort *him* as well as I can, but I do not undertake to be good to her children. She had better not leave any.

Edw. and Geo. set off this day week for Oxford. Our party will then be very small, as the Moores will be going about the same time. To enliven us, Fanny proposes spending a few days soon afterwards at Fredville. It will really be a good opportunity, as her father will have a companion. We shall all three go to Wrotham, but Edwd. and I stay only a night perhaps. Love to Mr. Tilson.

Yours very affectionately, J. A.

89. *To Cassandra Austen. Tuesday* 26 *Oct.* 1813

***Address*: Miss Austen 10 Henrietta Street | Covent Garden London.**
***Postmark*: 27 oc 1813**
Mrs. Henry Burke.
***Brabourne* ii. 194; *Life* 285 (extracts).**

Godmersham Park Tuesday. Oct: 26.

My dearest Cassandra

You will have had such late accounts from this place as (I hope) to prevent your expecting a Letter from me immediately, as I really do not think I have wherewithal to fabricate one today. I suspect this will be brought to you by our nephews, tell me if it is. —It is a great pleasure to me to think of you with Henry, I am sure your time must pass most comfortably & I trust you are seeing improvement in him every day.—I shall be most happy to hear from you again. Your Saturday's Letter however was quite as long & as particular as I could expect.—I am not at all in a humour for writing; I must write on till I am.—I congratulate Mr. Tilson & hope everything is going on well. Fanny & I depend upon knowing what the Child's name is to be, as soon as you can tell us. I guess Caroline.—Our Gentlemen are all gone to their Sittingbourne Meeting, East & West Kent in one Barouche together—rather—West Kent driving East Kent.—I believe that is not the usual way of the County. We breakfasted before 9 & do not dine till ½ past 6 on the occasion, so I hope we three shall have a long Morning enough.—Mr Deedes & Sir Brook—I do not care for Sir Brook's being a Baronet I will put Mr Deedes first because I like him a great deal the best—they arrived together yesterday—for the Bridges' are staying at Sandling—just before dinner ;—both Gentlemen much as they used to be, only growing a little older. They leave us tomorrow.—You were clear of Guildford by half an hour & were winding along the pleasant road to Ripley when the Charleses set off on friday.—I hope we shall have a visit from them at Chawton in the spring or early part of the summer. They seem well inclined. Cassy had recovered her looks almost entirely, and I find they do not consider the 'Namur' as disagreeing with her in general, only when the weather is so rough as to make her sick.

Our Canterbury scheme took place as proposed, and very pleasant it was—Harriot and I and little George within, my brother on the box with the master coachman. I was most happy to find my brother included in the party. It was a great improvement, and he and Harriot and I walked about together very happily, while Mr. Moore took his little boy with him to tailor's and hair-cutter's.

Our chief business was to call on Mrs. Milles, and we had, indeed, so little else to do that we were obliged to saunter about anywhere and go backwards and forwards as much as possible to make out the time and keep ourselves from having two hours to sit with the good lady—a most extraordinary circumstance in a Canterbury morning.

Old Toke came in while we were paying our visit. I thought of Louisa. Miss Milles was queer as usual, and provided us with plenty to laugh at. She undertook in *three words* to give us the history of Mrs. Scudamore's reconciliation, and then talked on about it for half-an-hour, using such odd expressions, and so foolishly minute, that I could hardly keep my countenance. The death of Wyndham Knatchbull's son will rather supersede the Scudamores. I told her that he was to be buried at Hatch. She had heard, with military honours, at Portsmouth. We may guess how that point will be discussed evening after evening.

Owing to a difference of clocks the coachman did not bring the carriage so soon as he ought by half-an-hour; anything like a breach of punctuality was a great offence, and Mr. Moore was very angry, which I was rather glad of. I wanted to see him angry; and, though he spoke to his servant in a very loud voice and with a good deal of heat, I was happy to perceive that he did not scold Harriot at all. Indeed, there is nothing to object to in his manners to her, and I do believe that he makes her—or she makes herself—very happy. They do not spoil their boy.

It seems now quite settled that we go to Wrotham on Saturday, the 13th, spend Sunday there, and proceed to London on Monday, as before intended. I like the plan. I shall be glad to see Wrotham. Harriot is quite as pleasant as ever. We are very comfortable together, and talk over our nephews and nieces occasionally, as may be supposed, and with much unanimity; and I really like Mr. M. better than I expected—see less in him to dislike.

I begin to perceive that you will have this letter to-morrow. It is throwing a letter away to send it by a visitor; there is never convenient time for reading it, and visitor can tell most things as well. I *had* thought with delight of saving you the postage, but money is dirt. If *you* do not regret the loss of Oxfordshire and Gloucestershire *I* will not, though I certainly had wished for your going very much. 'Whatever is, is best.' There has been one infallible Pope in the world.

George Hatton called yesterday, and I saw him, saw him for ten minutes; sat in the same room with him, heard him talk, saw him bow, and was not in raptures. I discerned nothing extraordinary. I should speak of him as a gentlemanlike young man—*eh! bien tout est dit.* We are expecting the ladies of the family this morning.

How do you like your flounce? We have seen only *plain* flounces. I hope you have not cut off the train of your bombazin. I cannot reconcile myself to giving them up as morning gowns; they are so very sweet by candlelight. I would rather sacrifice my blue one for that purpose; in short, I do not know and I do not care.

Thursday or Friday are now mentioned from Bath as the day of setting off. The Oxford scheme is given up. They will go directly to Harefield. Fanny does not go to Fredville, not yet at least.

She has had a letter of excuse from Mary Plumptre to-day. The death of Mr. Ripley, their uncle by marriage, and Mr. P.'s very old friend, prevents their receiving her. Poor blind Mrs. Ripley must be felt for, if there is any feeling to be had for love or money.

We have had another of Edward Bridges' Sunday visits. I think the pleasantest part of his married life must be the dinners, and breakfasts, and luncheons, and billiards that he gets in this way at Gm. Poor wretch! he is quite the dregs of the family as to luck.

I long to know whether you are buying stockings

HIGH STREET, CANTERBURY

or what you are doing. Remember me most kindly to Mde. B. and Mrs. Perigord. You will get acquainted with my friend, Mr. Philips, and hear him talk from books, and be sure to have something odd happen to you, see somebody that you do not expect, meet with some surprise or other, find some old friend sitting with Henry when you come into the room. Do something clever in that way. Edward and I settled that you went to St. Paul's, Covent Garden, on Sunday. Mrs. Hill will come and see you, or else she won't come and see you and will write instead.

I have had a late account from Steventon, and a baddish one, as far as Ben is concerned. He has declined a curacy (apparently highly eligible), which he might have secured against his taking orders ; and, upon its being made rather a serious question, says he has not made up his mind as to taking orders so early, and that, if her father makes a point of it, he must give Anna up rather than do what he does not approve. He must be maddish. They are going on again at present as before—but it cannot last.—Mary says that Anna is very unwilling to go to Chawton & will get home again as soon as she can.—Good-bye. Accept this indifferent Letter & think it Long & Good.—Miss Clewes is better for some prescription of Mr. Scudamores & indeed seems tolerably stout now.—I find time in the midst of Port & Madeira to think of the 14 Bottles of Mead very often.—Yours very affec^ly^ J. A.

Lady Elizabeth her second Daughter & the two Mrs Finches have just left us.—The two Latter friendly & talking & pleasant as usual.

Harriot and Fanny's best love.

90. *To Cassandra Austen.* *Wednesday* 3 *Nov.* 1813

Address : Miss Austen | 10. Henrietta Street | Covent Garden | London
Postmarks : FEVERSHAM and 4 NO 1813
Pierpont Morgan Library. 2 leaves 4°.
Brabourne ii. 200 ; *Life* 287 (extracts).

Godmersham Park Wednesday Novr 3^{d}.

My dearest Cassandra

I will keep this celebrated Birthday by writing to you, & as my pen seems inclined to write large I will put my lines very close together.—I had but just time to enjoy your Letter yesterday before Edward & I set off in the Chair for Cant^{y}—& I allowed him to hear the cheif of it as we went along. We rejoice sincerely in Henry's gaining ground as he does, & hope there will be weather for him to get out every day this week, as the likeliest way of making him equal to what he plans for the next.—If he is tolerably well, the going into Oxfordshire will make him better, by making him happier.—Can it be, that I have not given you the minutiae of Edward's plans ?—See here they are—To go to Wrotham on Saturday ye 13th, spend Sunday there, & be in Town on Monday to dinner, & if agreable to Henry, spend one whole day with him—which day is likely to be Tuesday, & so go down to Chawton on Wednesday.—But now, I cannot be quite easy without staying a little while with Henry, unless he wishes it otherwise ;—his illness & the dull time of year together make me feel that it would be horrible of me not to offer to remain with him—& therefore, unless you know of any objection, I wish you would tell him with my best Love that I shall be most happy to spend

10 days or a fortnight in Henrietta St—if he will accept me. I do not offer more than a fortnight because I shall then have been some time from home, but it will be a great pleasure to be with him, as it always is. —I have the less regret & scruple on your account, because I shall see you for a day and a half, & because you will have Edward for at least a week.—My scheme is to take Bookham in my way home for a few days & my hope that Henry will be so good as to send me some part of the way thither. I have a most kind repetition of Mrs. Cooke's two or three dozen Invitations, with the offer of meeting me anywhere in one of her airings.—Fanny's cold is much better. By dosing & keeping her room on Sunday, she got rid of the worst of it, but I am rather afraid of what this day may do for her ; she is gone to Canty with Miss Clewes, Liz. & Ma. and it is but roughish weather for any one in a tender state.—Miss Clewes has been going to Canty ever since her return, & it is now just accomplishing. Edward & I had a delightful morng for our Drive *there*, I enjoyed it thoroughly, but the Day turned off before we were ready, & we came home in some rain & the apprehension of a great deal. It has not done us any harm however.—He went to inspect the Gaol, as a visiting Magistrate, & took me with him.—I was gratified—& went through all the feelings which People must go through—I think in visiting such a Building.—We paid no other visits—only walked about snugly together & shopp'd.—I bought a Concert Ticket & a sprig of flowers for my old age.— To vary the subject from Gay to Grave with inimitable address I shall now tell you something of the Bath party—& still a Bath party they are, for a fit of the

Gout came on last week.—The accounts of Lady B. are as good as can be under such a circumstance, Dr. P.—says it appears a good sort of Gout, & her spirits are better than usual, but as to her coming away, it is of course all uncertainty.—I have very little doubt of Edward's going down to Bath, if they have not left it when he is in Hampshire; if he does, he will go on from Steventon, & then return direct to London, without coming back to Chawton.—This detention does not suit his feelings.—It may be rather a good thing however that Dr. P. should see Lady B. with the Gout on her. Harriot was quite wishing for it.—The day seems to improve. I wish my pen would too.—Sweet Mr. Ogle. I dare say he sees all the Panoramas for nothing, has free-admittance everywhere; he is so delightful!—Now, you need not see anybody else.—I am glad to hear of our being likely to have a peep at Charles & Fanny at Christmas, but do not force poor Cass. to stay if she hates it.—You have done very right as to Mrs. F. A.—Your tidings of S & S. give me pleasure. I have never seen it advertised.—Harriot, in a Letter to Fanny today, enquires whether they sell Cloths for Pelisses at Bedford House—& if they do, will be very much obliged to you to desire them to send her down Patterns, with the Width & Prices—they may go from Charing Cross almost any day in the week—but if it is a *ready money* house it will not do, for the Bru of feu the Archbishop says she cannot pay for it immediately.—Fanny & I suspect they do not deal in the Article.—The Sherers I beleive are now really going to go, Joseph has had a Bed here the two last nights, & I do not know whether this is not the day of moving. Mrs. Sherer called yesterday to take leave. The weather looks worse again.—We dine at Chilham Castle tomorrow, & I expect to find some amusement; but more from the Concert the next day, as I am sure of seeing several that I want to see. We are to meet a party from Goodnestone, Lady B. Miss Hawley & Lucy Foote—& I am to meet Mrs. Harrison, & we are to talk about Ben & Anna. 'My dear Mrs. Harrison, I shall say, I am afraid the young Man has some of your Family Madness—& though there often appears to be something of Madness in Anna too, I think she inherits more of it from her Mother's family than from ours.'—That is what I shall say—& I think she will find it difficult to answer me.—I took up your letter again to Refresh me, being somewhat tired; & was struck with the prettiness of the hand; it is really a very pretty hand now & then—so small & so neat!—I wish I could get as much into a sheet of paper.—Another time I will take two days to make a Letter in; it is fatiguing to write a whole long one at once. I hope to hear from you again on Sunday & again on friday, the day before we move.—On Monday I suppose you will be going to Streatham, to see quiet Mr. Hill & eat very bad Baker's bread.—A fall in Bread by the bye. I hope my Mother's Bill next week will shew it. I have had a very comfortable Letter from her, one of her foolscap sheets quite full of little home news.—Anna was there the first of the two Days—. An Anna sent away & an Anna fetched are different things.—This will be an excellent time for Ben to pay his visit—now that we, the formidables, are absent. I did not mean to eat, but Mr. Johncock has brought in the Tray, so I must.—I am all alone, Edward is gone into his Woods.—At this present time

I have five Tables, Eight & twenty Chairs & two fires all to myself.—Miss Clewes is to be invited to go to the Concert with us, there will be my Brother's place & ticket for her, as he cannot go. He & the other connections of the Cages are to meet at Milgate that very day, to consult about a proposed alteration of the Maidstone road, in which the Cages are very much interested. Sir Brook comes here in the morn[g], & they are to be joined by Mr. Deedes at Ashford.—The loss of the Concert will be no great evil to the Squire.—We shall be a party of three Ladies therefore—& to meet three Ladies.—What a convenient Carriage Henry's is, to his friends in general!—Who has it next?—I am glad William's going is voluntary, & on no worse grounds. An inclination for the Country is a venial fault.—He has more of Cowper than of Johnson in him, fonder of Tame Hares & Blank verse than of the full tide of human Existence at Charing Cross.—Oh! I have more of such sweet flattery from Miss Sharp!—She is an excellent kind friend. I am read & admired in Ireland too.—There is a Mrs. Fletcher, the wife of a Judge, an old Lady & very good & very clever, who is all curiosity to know about me—what I am like & so forth—. I am not known to her by *name* however. This comes through Mrs. Carrick, not through Mrs. Gore—You are quite out there.—I do not despair of having my picture in the Exhibition at last—all white & red, with my Head on one Side;—or perhaps I may marry young Mr. D'arblay.—I suppose in the meantime I shall owe dear Henry a great deal of Money for Printing &c.—I hope Mrs. Fletcher will indulge herself with S & S.—If I *am* to stay in H. S[t] & if you should be writing home soon

I wish you w[d] be so good as to give a hint of it—for I am not likely to write there again these 10 days, having written yesterday.

Fanny has set her heart upon it's being a Mr. Brett who is going to marry a Miss Dora Best of this Country. I dare say Henry has no objection. Pray, where did the Boys sleep ?—

The Deedes' come here on Monday to stay till friday—so that we shall end with a flourish the last Canto.—They bring Isabella & one of the Grown ups—& will come in for a Cant[y] Ball on Thursday.—I shall be glad to see them.—Mrs. Deedes & I must talk rationally together I suppose.

Edward does not write to Henry, because of my writing so often. God bless you. I shall be so glad to see you again, & I wish you many happy returns of this Day.—Poor Lord Howard ! How he does cry about it !—

Y[rs] very truly

J. A.

91. *To Cassandra Austen. Saturday* 6 *Nov.* ⟨1813⟩

Address : Miss Austen | 10. Henrietta Street | Covent Garden | London

Postmark : FEVERSHAM. The dated postmark illegible.

Pierpont Morgan Library. 2 leaves 4°.

Brabourne ii. 209 ; *Life* 288 (extracts).

Saturday Nov[r] 6—Godmersham Park

My dearest Cassandra

Having half an hour before breakfast—(very snug, in my own room, lovely morn[g], excellent fire, fancy me) I will give you some account of the last two days. And yet, what is there to be told ? I shall get foolishly minute unless I cut the matter short.—We met only

o

the Brittons at Chilham Castle, besides a Mr. & Mrs. Osborne & a Miss Lee staying in the House, & were only 14 altogether. My B^r^ & Fanny thought it the pleasantest party they had ever known there & I was very well entertained by bits & scraps.—I had long wanted to see Dr. Britton, & his wife amuses me very much with her affected refinement & elegance.—Miss Lee I found very conversible; she admires Crabbe as she ought.—She is at an age of reason, ten years older than myself at least. She was at the famous Ball at Chilham Castle, so of course you remember her.—By the bye, as I must leave off being young, I find many Douceurs in being a sort of Chaperon for I am put on the Sofa near the Fire & can drink as much wine as I like. We had Music in the Even^g^, Fanny & Miss Wildman played, & Mr. James Wildman sat close by & listened, or pretended to listen.—Yesterday was a day of dissipation all through, first came Sir Brook to dissipate us before breakfast—then there was a call from Mr. Sherer, then a regular morn^g^ visit from Lady Honeywood in her way home from Eastwell—then Sir Brook & Edward set off—then we dined (5 in number) at ½ past 4—then we had coffee, & at 6 Miss Clewes, Fanny & I draved away. We had a beautiful night for our frisks.—We were earlier than we need have been, but after a time Lady B. & her two companions appeared, we had kept places for them & there we sat, all six in a row, under a side wall, I between Lucy Foote & Miss Clewes.—Lady B. was much what I expected, I could not determine whether she was rather handsome or very plain.—I liked her, for being in a hurry to have the Concert over & get away, & for getting away at last with a great deal of decision &

promtness, not waiting to compliment & dawdle & fuss about seeing *dear Fanny*, who was half the even^g in another part of the room with her friends the Plumptres. I am growing too minute, so I will go to Breakfast.

When the Concert was over, Mrs. Harrison & I found each other out & had a very comfortable little complimentary friendly chat. She is a sweet Woman, still quite a sweet Woman in herself, & so like her Sister !—I could almost have thought I was speaking to Mrs. Lefroy.—She introduced me to her Daughter, whom I think pretty, but most dutifully inferior to la Mere Beauté. The Faggs & the Hammonds were there, Wm Hammond the only young Man of renown. *Miss* looked very handsome, but I prefer her little, smiling, flirting Sister Julia.—I was just introduced at last to Mary Plumptre, but should hardly know her again. She was delighted with *me* however, good enthusiastic Soul !—And Lady B. found me handsomer than she expected, so you see I am not so very bad as you might think for.—It was 12 before we reached home. We were all dog-tired, but pretty well to-day, Miss Clewes says she has not caught cold, & Fanny's does not seem worse. I was so tired that I began to wonder how I should get through the Ball next Thursday, but there will be so much more variety then in walking about, & probably so much less heat that perhaps I may not feel it more. My China Crape is still kept for the Ball. Enough of the Concert.—I had a Letter from Mary Yesterday. They travelled down to Cheltenham last Monday very safely & are certainly to be there a month.—Bath is still Bath. The H. Bridges' must quit them early next week, &

Louisa seems not quite to despair of their all moving together, but to those who see at a distance there appears no chance of it.—Dr. Parry does not want to keep Lady B. at Bath when she can once move. That is lucky.—You will see poor Mr. Evelyn's death. Since I wrote last, my 2[d] Edit. has stared me in the face.—Mary tells me that Eliza means to buy it. I wish she may. It can hardly depend upon any more Fyfield Estates.—I cannot help hoping that *many* will feel themselves obliged to buy it. I shall not mind imagining it a disagreable Duty to them, so as they do it. Mary heard before she left home, that it was very much admired at Cheltenham, & that it was given to Miss Hamilton. It is pleasant to have such a respectable Writer named. I cannot tire *you* I am sure on this subject, or I would apologise.—What weather ! & what news !—We have enough to do to admire them both.—I hope you derive your full share of enjoyment from each.

I have extended my Lights and increased my acquaintance a good deal within these two days. Lady Honeywood, you know ;—I did not sit near enough to be a perfect Judge, but I thought her extremely pretty & her manners have all the recommendations of ease & goodhumour & unaffectedness ;—& going about with 4 Horses, & nicely dressed herself—she is altogether a perfect sort of Woman.—Oh ! & I saw Mr. Gipps last night—the useful Mr. Gipps, whose attentions came in as acceptably to us in handing us to the Carriage, for want of a better Man, as they did to Emma Plumptre.—I thought him rather a good-looking little Man.—I long for your Letter tomorrow, particularly that I may know my fate as to London.

My first wish is that Henry sh[d] really chuse what he likes best ; I shall certainly not be sorry if he does not want me.—Morning church tomorrow.—I shall come back with impatient feelings. The Sherers are gone, but the Pagets are not come, we shall therefore have Mr. S. again. Mr. Paget acts like an unsteady Man. Dr. Mant however gives him a very good Character ; what is wrong is to be imputed to the Lady.—I dare say the House likes Female Government.—I have a nice long Black & red Letter from Charles, but not communicating much that I did not know. There is some chance of a good Ball next week, as far as Females go. Lady Bridges may perhaps be there with some Knatchbulls.—Mrs. Harrison perhaps with Miss Oxenden & the Miss Papillons—& if Mrs. Harrison, then Lady Fagg will come. The shades of Evening are descending & I resume my interesting Narrative. Sir Brook & my Brother came back about 4, & Sir Brook almost immediately set forward again for Goodnestone.—We are to have Edw[d] B. tomorrow, to pay us another Sunday's visit—the last, for more reasons than one ; they all come home on the same day that we go.—The Deedes' do not come till Tuesday. Sophia is to be the Comer. She is a disputable Beauty that I want much to see. Lady Eliz. Hatton & Annamaria called here this morn[g] ;—Yes, they called,—but I do not think I can say anything more about them. They came & they sat & they went.—*Sunday.*—Dearest Henry ! What a turn he has for being ill ! & what a thing Bile is !—This attack has probably been brought on in part by his previous confinement & anxiety ;—but however it came, I hope it is going fast, & that you will be able to send a very good account of him on Tuesday.—As I hear on Wednesday, of course I shall not expect to hear again on friday. Perhaps a Letter to Wrotham would not have an ill effect. We are to be off on Saturday before the Post comes in, as Edward takes his own Horses all the way. He talks of 9 o'clock. We shall bait at Lenham. Excellent sweetness of you to send me such a nice long Letter;—it made its appearance, with one from my Mother, soon after I & my impatient feelings walked in.—How glad I am that I did what I did!—I was only afraid that *you* might think the offer superfluous, but you have set my heart at ease.—Tell Henry that I *will* stay with him, let it be ever so disagreable to him. Oh! dear me!—I have not time or paper for half that I want to say.—There have been two Letters from Oxford, one from George yesterday. They got there very safely, Edwd two hours behind the Coach, having lost his way in leaving London. George writes cheerfully & quietly—hopes to have Utterson's rooms soon, went to Lecture on wednesday, states some of his expences, and concludes with saying, 'I am afraid I shall be poor.'—I am glad he thinks about it so soon.—I beleive there is no private Tutor yet chosen, but my Brother is to hear from Edwd on the subject shortly.—You, & Mrs. H. & Catherine & Alethea going about together in Henry's carriage seeing sights!—I am not used to the idea of it yet. All that you are to see of Streatham, seen already!—Your Streatham & my Bookham may go hang.—The prospect of being taken down to Chawton by Henry, perfects the plan to me.—I was in hopes of your seeing some illuminations, & you *have* seen them. 'I thought you would came, and you *did* came.' I am sorry *he* is not to *came* from the

Baltic sooner.—Poor Mary !—My Brother has a Letter from Louisa today, of an unwelcome nature;—they are to spend the winter at Bath.—It was just decided on. —Dr. Parry wished it,—not from thinking the Water necessary to Lady B.—but that he might be better able to judge how far his Treatment of her, which is totally different from anything she had been used to—is right; & I suppose he will not mind having a few more of her Ladyship's guineas.—His system is a Lowering one. He took twelve ounces of Blood from her when the Gout appeared, & forbids wine &c.—Hitherto, the plan agrees with her.—*She* is very well satisfied to stay, but it is a sore disappointment to Louisa & Fanny.—

The H. Bridges leave them on Tuesday, & they mean to move into a smaller House. You may guess how Edward feels.—There can be no doubt of his going to Bath now;—I should not wonder if he brought Fanny Cage back with him.—You shall hear from me once more, some day or other.

Yours very affec:ly J. A.

We do not like Mr. Hampson's scheme.

92. *To Cassandra Austen. Wednesday* 2 *March* ⟨1814⟩

Address: To Miss Austen | Chawton | By favour of E. H. Gray Esq
Postmark: none.
E. G. Millar; formerly in the collection described in *Times Literary Supplement* 14 Jan. 1926.
*Memoir*² 104 (extracts); *Life* 291 (extracts). Part unpublished.

Henrietta St Wednesday March 2d

My dear Cassandra

You were wrong in thinking of us at Guildford last night: we were at Cobham. On reaching G. we found that John and the horses were gone on. We therefore did no more there than we had done at Farnham—sit in the carriage while fresh horses were put in, and proceeded directly to Cobham, which we reached by seven, and about eight were sitting down to a very nice roast fowl, &c. We had altogether a very good journey, and everything at Cobham was comfortable. I could not pay Mr. Herington! That was the only alas! of the business. I shall therefore return his bill, and my mother's 2*l*., that you may try your luck. We did not begin reading till Bentley Green. Henry's approbation hitherto is even equal to my wishes. He says it is very different from the other two, but does not appear to think it at all inferior. He has only married Mrs. R. I am afraid he has gone through the most entertaining part. He took to Lady B. and Mrs. N. most kindly, and gives great praise to the drawing of the characters. He understands them all, likes Fanny, and, I think, foresees how it will all be. I finished the 'Heroine' last night, and was very much amused by it. I wonder James did not like it better. It diverted me exceedingly. We went to bed at ten. I was very tired, but slept to a miracle, and am lovely to-day, and at present Henry seems to have no complaint. We left Cobham at half-past eight, stopped to bait and breakfast at Kingston, and were in this house considerably before two quite in the style of Mr. Knight. Nice smiling Mr. Barlowe met us at the door and, in reply to enquiries after news, said that peace was generally expected. I have taken possession of my bedroom, unpacked my bandbox, sent Miss P.'s two letters to the twopenny post, been visited by M[d] B., and am now writing by myself at the new table in the front room. It is snowing. We had some snow-storms yesterday, and a smart frost at night, which gave us a hard road from Cobham to Kingston; but as it was then getting dirty and heavy, Henry had a pair of leaders put on from the latter place to the bottom of Sloane St. His own horses, therefore, cannot have had hard work. I watched for *veils* as we drove through the streets, and had the pleasure of seeing several upon vulgar heads. And now, how do you all do?—you in particular, after the worry of yesterday and the day before. I hope Martha had a pleasant visit again, and that you and my mother could eat your beef-pudding. Depend upon my thinking of the chimney-sweeper as soon as I wake to-morrow. Places are secured at Drury Lane for Saturday, but so great is the rage for seeing Kean that only a third and fourth row could be got; as it is in a front box, however, I hope we shall do pretty well—Shylock, a good play for Fanny—she cannot be much affected, I think. Mrs. Perigord has just been here & I have paid her a shilling for the willow. She tells me that we owe her master for the silk-dyeing. My poor old muslin has never been dyed yet. It has been promised to be done several times. What wicked people dyers are. They begin with dipping their own souls in scarlet sin. Tell my mother that my £6. 15. was duly received, but placed to my account instead of hers, & I have just signed a something which makes it over to her. It is evening; we have drank tea, and I have torn through the third vol. of the 'Heroine.' I do not think it falls off. It is a delightful burlesque, particularly on the Radcliffe style. Henry is going on with 'Mansfield Park.' He admires

H. Crawford: I mean properly, as a clever, pleasant man. I tell you all the good I can, as I know how much you will enjoy it. John Warren and his wife are invited to dine here, and to name their own day in the next fortnight. I do not expect them to come. Wyndham Knatchbull is to be asked for Sunday and if he is cruel enough to consent, somebody must be contrived to meet him. We hear that Mr. Keen is more admired than ever. The two vacant places of our two rows are likely to be filled by Mr. Tilson and his brother General Chownes. I shall be ready to laugh at the sight of Frederick again. It seems settled that I have the carriage on Friday to pay visits, I have therefore little doubt of being able to get to Miss Hares. I am to call upon Miss Spencer: Funny me! There are no good places to be got in Drury Lane for the next fortnight; but Henry means to secure some for Saturday fortnight when you are reckoned upon. I wonder what worse thing than Sarah Mitchell you are forced upon by this time! Give my love to little Cassandra! I hope she found my Bed comfortable last night and has not filled it with fleas. I have seen nobody in London yet with such a long chin as Dr. Syntax, nor anybody quite so large as Gogmagoglicus.

Yours affec^{tely}

J. Austen

Thursday. My Trunk did not come last night—I suppose it will this morning—if not I must borrow stockings & buy shoes & gloves for my visit. I was foolish not to provide better against such a possibility. I have great hope however that writing about it in this way will bring the trunk presently.

93. *To Cassandra Austen. Saturday 5 March* ⟨1814⟩

Address: Miss Austen | Chawton | By favour of Mr Gray
Postmark: none.
Pierpont Morgan Library. 2 leaves 4^{0}. A few words cut away.
Brabourne ii. 222; *Life* 294 (extracts).

Henrietta St Saturday March 5.

My dear Cassandra

Do not be angry with me for beginning another Letter to you. I have read the Corsair, mended my petticoat, & have nothing else to do.—Getting out is impossible. It is a nasty day for everybody. Edward's spirits will be wanting Sunshine, & here is nothing but Thickness & Sleet; and tho' these two rooms are delightfully warm I fancy it is very cold abroad.—Young Wyndham accepts the Invitation. He is such a nice, gentlemanlike, unaffected sort of young Man, that I think he may do for Fanny;—has a sensible, quiet look which one likes.—Our fate with Mrs. L. and Miss E. is fixed for this day senight.—A civil note is come from Miss H. Moore, to apologise for not returning my visit today & ask us to join a small party this Even^{g}.—Thank ye, but we shall be better engaged.—I was speaking to M^{de} B. this morn^{g} about a boil'd Loaf, when it appeared that her Master has no raspberry Jam; *She* has some, which of course she is determined he shall have; but cannot you bring him a pot when you come?—

Sunday.—I find a little time before breakfast for writing.—It was considerably past 4 when they arrived yesterday; the roads were so very bad!—as it was, they had 4 Horses from Cranford Bridge. Fanny was miserably cold at first, but they both seem well.—No possibility of Edwd.'s writing. His opinion however inclines *against* a second prosecution; he thinks it would be a vindictive measure. He might think differently perhaps on the spot.—But things must take their chance.—

We were quite satisfied with Kean. I cannot imagine better acting; but the part was too short, & excepting him and Miss Smith, & *she* did not quite answer my expectation, the parts were ill filled & the Play heavy. We were too much tired to stay for the whole of Illusion (Nour-jahad) which has 3 acts;—there is a great deal of finery & dancing in it, but I think little merit. Elliston was Nour-jahad, but it is a solemn sort of part, not at all calculated for his powers. There was nothing of the *best Elliston* about him. I might not have known him, but for his voice.—A grand thought has struck me as to our Gowns. This 6 weeks mourning makes so great a difference that I shall not go to Miss Hare, till you can come & help chuse yourself; unless you particularly wish the contrary.—It may be hardly worth while perhaps to have the Gowns so expensively made up; we may buy a cap or a *veil* instead;—but we can talk more of this together.—Henry is just come down, he seems well, his cold does not increase. I expected to have found Edward seated at a table writing to Louisa, but I was first.—Fanny I left fast asleep.—She was doing about last night, when *I* went to sleep, a little after one.—I am most happy to find there were but *five* shirts.—She thanks you for your note, & reproaches herself for not having written to you, but I assure her there was no occasion.—The accounts are not capital of Lady B.—Upon the whole I beleive Fanny liked

Bath very well. They were only out three Evengs, to one Play & each of the Rooms ;—Walked about a good deal, & saw a good deal of the Harrisons & Wildmans. —All the Bridgeses are likely to come away together, & Louisa will probably turn off at Dartford to go to Harriot.—Edward is quite ⟨*about five words cut out*⟩.— Now we are come from Church, & all going to write.— Almost everybody was in mourning last night, but my brown gown did very well. Genl: Chowne was introduced to me ; he has not much remains of Frederick.— This young Wyndham does not come after all ; a very long & very civil note of excuse is arrived. It makes one moralize upon the ups & downs of this Life. I have determined to trim my lilac sarsenet with black sattin ribbon just as my China Crape is, 6d width at the bottom, 3d or 4d at top.—Ribbon trimmings are all the fashion at Bath, & I dare say the fashions of the two places are alike enough in that point, to content *me*.—With this addition it will be a very useful gown, happy to go anywhere.—Henry has this moment said that he likes my M. P. better & better ; he is in the 3d volume. I beleive *now* he has changed his mind as to foreseeing the end ; he said yesterday at least, that he defied anybody to say whether H. C. would be reformed, or would forget Fanny in a fortnight.—I shall like to see Kean again excessively, & to see him with you too ;—it appeared to me as if there were no fault in him anywhere ; & in his scene with Tubal there was exquisite acting. Edward has had a correspondence with Mr. Wickham on the Baigent business, & has been shewing me some Letters enclosed by Mr. W. from a friend of his, a Lawyer, whom he had consulted about it, & whose opinion is *for* the prosecution for assault, supposing the Boy is acquitted on the first, which he rather expects.—Excellent Letters; & I am sure he must be an excellent Man. They are such thinking, clear, considerate Letters as Frank might have written. I long to know who he is, but the name is always torn off. He was consulted only as a friend. When Edw[d] gave me *his* opinion against the 2[d] prosecution, he had not read this Letter, which was waiting for him here.—Mr. W. is to be on the Grand Jury. This business must hasten an Intimacy between his family & my Brother's.—Fanny cannot answer your question about button holes till she gets home.—I have never told you, but soon after Henry & I began our Journey, he said, talking of Yours, that he sh[d] desire you to come post at his expence, & added something of the Carriage meeting you at Kingston. He has said nothing about it since.—Now I have just read Mr. Wickham's Letter, by which it appears that the Letters of his friend were sent to my Brother quite confidentially—therefore do'nt tell. By his expression, this friend must be one of the Judges.

A cold day, but bright and clean.—I am afraid your planting can hardly have begun.—I am sorry to hear that there has been a rise in tea. I do not mean to pay Twining till later in the day, when we may order a fresh supply.—I long to know something of the Mead—& how you are off for a Cook. *Monday.* Here's a day!—The Ground covered with snow! What is to become of us?—We were to have walked out early to near shops, & had the Carriage for the more distant.—Mr. Richard Snow is dreadfully fond of us. I dare say he has stretched himself out at Chawton too.—Fanny & I went into the Park yesterday & drove about & were very much entertained ;—and our Dinner & Even^{g} went off very well. Messrs. J. Plumptre and J. Wildman called while we were out ; & we had a glimpse of them both & of G. Hatton too in the Park. *I* could not produce a single acquaintance.—By a little convenient Listening, I now know that Henry wishes to go to G^{m} for a few days before Easter, & has indeed promised to do it.—This being the case, there can be no time for your remaining in London after your return from Adlestrop.—You must not put off your coming therefore ;—and it occurs to me that instead of my coming here again from Streatham, it will be better for you to join me there.—It is a great comfort to have got at the truth. Henry finds he cannot set off for Oxfordshire before the Wednes^{y} which will be ye 23^{d} ; but we shall not have too many days together here previously.—I shall write to Catherine very soon. Well, we have been out, as far as Coventry S^{t}— ; Edwd escorted us there & back to Newtons, where he left us, & I brought Fanny safe home. It was snowing the whole time. We have given up all idea of the Carriage. Edward & Fanny stay another day ; & both seem very well pleased to do so. Our visit to the Spencers is of course put off.—Edwd heard from Louisa this morn^{g}. Her Mother does not get better, & Dr. Parry talks of her beginning the Waters again ; this will be keeping them longer in Bath, and of course is not palateable. You cannot think how much my Ermine Tippet is admired both by Father & Daughter. It was a noble Gift.—Perhaps you have not heard that Edward has a good chance of escaping his Lawsuit. His opponent knocks under. The terms of agreement are not quite settled.—We are to see 'the Devil to pay' to night. I expect to be very much amused.—Excepting Miss Stephens, I daresay Artaxerxes will be very tiresome.—A great many pretty Caps in the Windows of Cranbourn Alley! I hope when you come, we shall both be tempted.—I have been ruining myself in black sattin ribbon with a proper perl edge; & now I am trying to draw it up into kind of roses, instead of putting it in plain double plaits.—Tuesday. My dearest Cassandra in ever so many hurries I acknowledge the receipt of your Letter last night, just before we set off for Covent Garden.—I have no Mourning come, but it does not signify. This very moment has Rich[d] put it on the Table.—I have torn it open & read your note. Thank you, thank you, thank you.—

Edw[d] is amazed at the 64 Trees. He desires his Love & gives you notice of the arrival of a Study Table for himself. It ought to be at Chawton this week. He begs you to be so good as to have it enquired for, & fetched by the Cart; but wishes it not to be unpacked till he is on the spot himself. It may be put in the Hall.—Well, Mr. Hampson dined here & all that. I was very tired of Artaxerxes, highly amused with the Farce, & in an inferior way with the Pantomime that followed. Mr. J. Plumptre joined in the latter part of the Even[g]—walked home with us, ate some soup, & is very earnest for our going to Cov: Gar: again to night to see Miss Stephens in the Farmers Wife. He is to try for a Box. I do not particularly wish him to succeed. I have had enough for the present.—Henry dines to day with Mr. Spencer.—

Yours very affec[ly] J. Austen

94. *To Cassandra Austen. Wednesday* 9 *March* ⟨1814⟩

Address : Miss Austen | Chawton | By favour of Mr Gray
Postmark : none.
Pierpont Morgan Library. 2 leaves 4°.
Brabourne ii. 231 ; *Life* 295 (extracts). One sentence unpublished.

Henrietta St Wednesday March 9.

Well, we went to the Play again last night, & as we were out great part of the morning too, shopping & seeing the Indian Jugglers, I am very glad to be quiet now till dressing time. We are to dine at the Tilsons & tomorrow at Mr. Spencers.—We had not done breakfast yesterday when Mr. J. Plumptre appeared to say that he had secured a Box. Henry asked him to dine here, which I fancy he was very happy to do ; & so, at 5 o'clock we four sat down to table together, while the Master of the House was preparing for going out himself.—The Farmer's Wife is a Musical thing in 3 Acts, & as Edward was steady in not staying for anything more, we were at home before 10—Fanny and Mr. J. P. are delighted with Miss S, & her merit in singing is I dare say very great ; that she gave *me* no pleasure is no reflection upon her, nor I hope upon myself, being what Nature made me on that article. All that I am sensible of in Miss S. is, a pleasing person & no skill in acting. We had Mathews, Liston & Emery ; of course some amusement.—Our friends were off before ½ past 8 this morn^g, & had the prospect of a heavy cold Journey before them. I think they both liked their visit very much, I am sure Fanny did. —Henry sees decided attachment between her & his new acquaintance.—I have a cold too as well as my Mother & Martha. Let it be a generous emulation between us which can get rid of it first.—I wear my gauze gown today, long sleeves & all ; I shall see how they succeed, but as yet I have no reason to suppose long sleeves are allowable. I have lowered the bosom especially at the corners, & plaited black sattin ribbon round the top. Such will be my Costume of Vine leaves & paste. Prepare for a Play the very first evening, I rather think Covent Garden, to see Young in Richard.—I have answered for your little companion's being conveyed to Keppel St immediately.—I have never yet been able to get there myself, but hope I shall soon. What cruel weather this is ! and here is Lord Portsmouth married too to Miss Hanson.—Henry has finished Mansfield Park, & his approbation has not lessened. He found the last half of the last volume *extremely interesting*. I suppose my Mother recollects that she gave me no Money for paying Brecknell & Twining ; and *my* funds will not supply enough.—

We are home in such good time that I can finish my Letter tonight, which will be better than getting up to do it tomorrow, especially as on account of my Cold, which has been very heavy in my head this Eveng—I rather think of lying in bed later than usual. I would not but be well enough to go to Hertford St on any account.—We met only Genl Chowne today, who has not much to say for himself.—I was ready to laugh at the remembrance of Frederick, & such a different Frederick as we chose to fancy him to the real Christopher !—Mrs. Tilson had long sleeves too, & she assured me that they are worn in the evening by many. I was glad to hear this.—She dines here I beleive next Tuesday.

On friday we are to be snug, with only Mr. Barlowe & an evening of Business.—I am so pleased that the Mead is brewed.—Love to all. If Cassandra has filled my Bed with fleas, I am sure they must bite herself.—I have written to Mrs. Hill & care for nobody.

Yours affec^{ly} J. Austen

95. *To Anna Austen.* ⟨*May or June* 1814⟩

Address : Miss Austen | Steventon
Postmark : none.
Miss Isabel Lefroy. One leaf 4^{0}, the first leaf lost. The recto (i. e. page 3) contains the conclusion of a letter signed ' Yr. affect G: M: | C: Austen '. J. A.'s letter is on p. 4. Lord Brabourne writes that the date of this letter is determined by the context. He is referring to _Mrs._ Austen's letter, in which mention is made of a fine crop of gooseberries, not yet ripe.
Brabourne ii. 304 ; _Life_ 354.

My dear Anna—I am very much obliged to you for sending your MS. It has entertained me extremely, all of us indeed; I read it aloud to your G. M.—& A^{t} C.—and we were all very much pleased.—The Spirit does not droop at all. Sir Tho:—Lady Helena, & St. Julian are very well done—& Cecilia continues to be interesting in spite of her being so amiable.—It was very fit that you should advance her age. I like the beginning of D. Forester very much—a great deal better than if he had been very Good or very Bad.—A few verbal corrections were all that I felt tempted to make—the principal of them is a speech of St. Julians to Lady Helena—which you see I have presumed to alter.—As Lady H. is Cecilia's superior, it w^{d} not be correct to talk of *her* being introduced; Cecilia must be the person introduced—and I do not like a Lover's speaking in the 3^{d} person;—it is too much like the formal part of Lord Orville, & I think is not natural. If *you* think differently however, you need not mind me.—I am impatient for more—& only wait for a safe conveyance to return this Book.—

Yours affec[ly]   J. A.

96. *To Cassandra Austen. Tuesday* 14 (misdated 13) *June* ⟨1814⟩

***Address*: Miss Austen, | Henrietta St. | By favour of Mr. Gray**
Mrs. Henry Burke.
***Brabourne* ii. 234 ; *Life* 303 (extracts).**

Chawton : Tuesday June 13

My dearest Cassandra

Fanny takes my mother to Alton this morning, which gives me an opportunity of sending you a few lines without any other trouble than that of writing them.

This is a delightful day in the country, and I hope not much too hot for town. Well, you had a good journey, I trust, and all that, and not rain enough to spoil your bonnet. It appeared so likely to be a wet evening that I went up to the Gt. House between three and four, and dawdled away an hour very comfortably, though Edwd. was not very brisk. The air was clearer in the evening and he was better. We all five walked together into the kitchen garden and along the Gosport road, and they drank tea with us.

You will be glad to hear that G. Turner has another *situation*, something in the cow line, near Rumsey, and he wishes to move immediately, which is not likely to be inconvenient to anybody.

The new nurseryman at Alton comes this morning to value the crops in the garden.

The only letter to-day is from Mrs. Cooke to me. They do not leave home till July, and want me to come to them, according to my promise. And, after considering everything, I have resolved on going. My companions promote it. I will not go, however, till after Edward is gone, that he may feel he has a somebody to give memorandums to, to the last. I must give up all help from his carriage, of course. And, at any rate, it must be such an excess of expense that I have quite made up my mind to it and do not mean to care.

I have been thinking of Triggs and the chair, you may be sure, but I know it will end in posting. They will meet me at Guildford.

In addition to their standing claims on me they admire 'Mansfield Park' exceedingly. Mr. Cooke says 'it is the most sensible novel he ever read,' and the manner in which I treat the clergy delights them very much. Altogether, I must go, and I want you to join me there when your visit in Henrietta St. is over. Put this into your capacious head.

Take care of yourself, and do not be trampled to death in running after the Emperor. The report in Alton yesterday was that they would certainly travel this road either to or from Portsmouth. I long to know what this bow of the Prince's will produce.

I saw Mrs. Andrews yesterday. Mrs. Browning had seen her before. She is very glad to send an Elizabeth.

Miss Benn continues the same. Mr. Curtis, however, saw her yesterday and said her hand was going on as well as possible. Accept our best love.

Yours very affectionately, J. Austen

97. *To Cassandra Austen. Thursday* 23 *June* ⟨1814⟩

Address: Miss Austen | Henrietta St. | By favour of Mr. Gray
Haverford College.
Brabourne ii. 236; *Life* 304 (extracts).

Thursday June 23

Dearest Cassandra

I received your pretty letter while the children were drinking tea with us, as Mr. Louch was so obliging as to walk over with it. Your good account of everybody made us very happy.

I heard yesterday from Frank. When he began his letter he hoped to be here on Monday, but before it was ended he had been told that the naval review would not take place till Friday, which would probably occasion him some delay, as he cannot get some necessary business of his own attended to while Portsmouth is in such a bustle. I hope Fanny has seen the Emperor, and then I may fairly wish them all away. I go to-morrow, and hope for some delays and adventures.

My mother's wood is brought in, but, by some mistake, no bavins. She must therefore buy some.

Henry at White's! Oh, what a Henry! I do not know what to wish as to Miss B., so I will hold my tongue and my wishes.

Sackree and the children set off yesterday, and have not been returned back upon us. They were all very well the evening before. We had handsome presents from the Gt. House yesterday—a ham and the four leeches. Sackree has left some shirts of her master's at the school, which, finished or unfinished, she begs to have sent by Henry and Wm. Mr. Hinton is expected home soon, which is a good thing for the shirts.

We have called upon Miss Dusautoy and Miss Papillon, and been very pretty. Miss D. has a great idea of being Fanny Price—she and her youngest sister together, who is named Fanny.

Miss Benn has drunk tea with the Prowtings, and, I believe, comes to us this evening. She has still a swelling about the fore-finger and a little discharge, and does not seem to be on the point of a perfect cure, but her spirits are good, and she will be most happy, I believe, to accept any invitation. The Clements are gone to Petersfield to look.

Only think of the Marquis of Granby being dead. I hope, if it please Heaven there should be another son, they will have better sponsors and less parade.

I certainly do not *wish* that Henry should think again of getting me to town. I would rather return straight from Bookham; but, if he really does propose it, I cannot say No to what will be so kindly intended. It could be but for a few days, however, as my mother would be quite disappointed by my exceeding the fortnight which I now talk of as the outside—at least, we could not both remain longer away comfortably.

The middle of July is Martha's time, as far as she has any time. She has left it to Mrs. Craven to fix the day. I wish she could get her money paid, for I fear her going at all depends upon that.

Instead of Bath the Deans Dundases have taken a house at Clifton—Richmond Terrace—and she is as glad of the change as even you and I should be, or almost. She will now be able to go on from Berks and visit them without any fears from heat.

This post has brought me a letter from Miss Sharpe. Poor thing! she has been suffering indeed, but is now in a comparative state of comfort. She is at Sir W. P.'s, in Yorkshire, with the children, and there is no appearance of her quitting them. Of course we lose the pleasure of seeing her here. She writes highly of Sir Wm. I do so want him to marry her. There is a Dow. Lady P. presiding there to make it all right. The *Man* is the same; but she does not mention what he is by profession or trade. She does not think Lady P. was privy to his scheme on her, but, on being in his power, yielded. Oh, Sir Wm.! Sir Wm.! how I will love you if you will love Miss Sharp!

Mrs. Driver, &c., are off by Collier, but so near being too late that she had not time to call and leave the keys herself. I have them, however. I suppose one is the key of the linen-press, but I do not ⟨know⟩ what to guess the other.

The coach was stopped at the blacksmith's, and they came running down with Triggs and Browning, and trunks, and birdcages. Quite amusing.

My mother desires her love, and hopes to hear from you.

Yours very affectionately,		J. Austen

Frank and Mary are to have Mary Goodchild to help as *Under* till they can get a cook. *She* is delighted to go.

Best love at Streatham.

98. *To Anna Austen. Wednesday* 10 *Aug.* ⟨1814⟩

Address: Miss Austen
Postmark: none.
Miss Isabel Lefroy. 2 leaves 4°.
Memoir[1] 119, *Memoir*[2] 91; *Brabourne* ii. 305; *Life* 354. A few lines unpublished.

Chawton Wednesday Aug: 10

My dear Anna

I am quite ashamed to find that I have never answered some questions of yours in a former note.—I kept the note on purpose to refer to it at a proper time, & then forgot it.—I like the name 'Which is the Heroine?' very well, & I dare say shall grow to like it very much in time—but 'Enthusiasm' was something so very superior that every common Title must appear to disadvantage.—I am not sensible of any Blunders about Dawlish. The Library was particularly pitiful & wretched 12 years ago, & not likely to have anybody's publication.—There is no such Title as Desborough—either among the Dukes, Marquisses, Earls, Viscounts or Barons.—These were your enquiries.—I will now thank you for your Envelope, received this morning.—I hope Mr W. D. will come.—I can readily imagine Mrs H. D. may be very like a profligate young Lord—I dare say the likeness will be 'beyond every thing.'—Your Aunt Cass:— is as well pleased with St. Julian as ever. I am delighted with the idea of seeing Progillian again.

Wednesday 17.—We have just finished the 1st of the 3 Books I had the pleasure of receiving yesterday; *I* read it aloud—& we are all very much amused, & like the work quite as well as ever.—I depend upon getting through another book before dinner, but there is really a great deal of respectable reading in your 48 Pages. I was an hour about it.—I have no doubt that *6* will make a very good sized volume.—You must be quite pleased to have accomplished so much.—I like Lord P. & his Brother very much;—I am only afraid that Lord P.—'s good nature will make most people like him better than he deserves.—The whole Portman Family are very good—& Lady Anne, who was your great dread, you have succeeded particularly well with.—Bell Griffin is just what she should be.—My Corrections have not been more important than before;—here & there, we have thought the sense might be expressed in fewer words—and I have scratched out Sir Tho: from walking with the other Men to the Stables &c the very day after his breaking his arm—for though I find your Papa *did* walk out immediately after *his* arm was set, I think it can be so little usual as to *appear* unnatural in a book—& it does not seem to be material that Sir Tho: should go with them.—Lyme will not do. Lyme is towards 40 miles distance from Dawlish & would not be talked of there.—I have put Starcross ⟨? instead⟩. If you prefer *Exeter*, that must be always safe.—I have also scratched out the Introduction between Lord P. & his Brother, & Mr. Griffin. A Country Surgeon (dont tell Mr. C. Lyford) would not be introduced to Men of their rank.—And when Mr. Portman is first brought in, he w^{d} not be introduced as *the Honble*.—*That* distinction is never mentioned at such times;—at least I beleive not.—Now, we have finished the 2^{d} book—or rather the 5th—I *do* think you had better omit Lady Helena's postscript;—to those who are acquainted with P. & P. it will seem an Imitation.—And your Aunt C. & I both recommend your making a little alteration in the last scene between Devereux F. and Lady Clanmurray & her Daughter. We think they press him too much—more than sensible Women or well-bred Women would do. *Lady C.* at least, should have discretion enough to be sooner satisfied with his determination of not going with them.—I am very much pleased with Egerton as yet.—I did not expect to like him, but I do; & Susan is a very nice little animated Creature—but St. Julian is the delight of one's Life. He is quite interesting.—The whole of his Break-off with Lady H. is very well done.—

Yes—Russel Square is a very proper distance from Berkeley St.—We are reading the last book.—They must be *two* days going from Dawlish to Bath; They are nearly 100 miles apart.

Thursday. We finished it last night, after our return from drinking tea at the Gt House.—The last chapter does not please us quite so well, we do not thoroughly like the *Play*; perhaps from having had too much of Plays in that way lately. And we think you had better not leave England. Let the Portmans go to Ireland, but as you know nothing of the Manners there, you had better not go with them. You will be in danger of giving false representations. Stick to Bath & the Foresters. There you will be quite at home.—Your Aunt C. does not like desultory novels, & is rather fearful yours will be too much so, that there will be too frequent a change from one set of people to another, & that circumstances will be sometimes introduced of apparent consequence, which will lead to nothing.—It will not be so great an objection to *me*, if it does. I allow much more Latitude than she does—& think Nature and Spirit cover many sins of a wandering story—and People in general do not care so much about it—for your comfort.

I should like to have had more of Devereux. I do not feel enough acquainted with him.—You were afraid of meddling with him I dare say.—I like your sketch of Lord Clanmurray, and your picture of the two poor young girls enjoyments is very good.—I have not yet noticed St. Julian's serious conversation with Cecilia, but I liked it exceedingly ;—what he says about the madness of otherwise sensible Women, on the subject of their Daughters coming out, is worth it's weight in gold.—I do not see that the language sinks. Pray go on.

Yours very affec:ly J. Austen

Twice you have put Dorsetshire for Devonshire. I have altered it.—Mr Griffin must have lived in Devonshire ; Dawlish is half way down the County.—

99. *To Cassandra Austen. Tuesday — Aug.* 1814

Address : Miss Austen | Chawton
Postmark : none.
Pierpont Morgan Library. 2 leaves 4^{0}.
Brabourne ii. 240 ; *Life* 305 (extracts).

23 Hans Place, Tuesday Morng.

My dear Cassandra

I had a very good Journey, not crouded, two of the three taken up at Bentley being Children, the others of a reasonable size ; & they were all very quiet & civil.—We were late in London, from being a great Load & from changing Coaches at Farnham, it was nearly 4 I beleive when we reached Sloane St ; Henry himself met me, & as soon as my Trunk & Basket could be routed out from all the other Trunks & Baskets in the World, we were on our way to Hans Place in the Luxury of a nice large cool dirty Hackney Coach. There were 4 in the Kitchen part of Yalden—& I was told 15 at top, among them Percy Benn; we met in the same room at Egham, but poor Percy was not in his usual Spirits. He would be more chatty I dare say in his way *from* Woolwich. We took up a young Gibson at Holybourn; & in short everybody either *did* come up by Yalden yesterday, or wanted to come up. It put me in mind of my own Coach between Edinburgh & Sterling.—Henry is very well, & has given me an account of the Canterbury Races, which seem to have been as pleasant as one could wish. Everything went well. Fanny had good Partners, Mr. J. P. was her 2^d^ on Thursday, but he did not dance with her any more.—This will content you for the present. I must just add however that there were no Lady Charlottes, they were gone off to Kirby—& that Mary Oxenden, instead of dieing, is going to marry Wm Hammond.—

No James & Edward yet.—Our evening yesterday was perfectly quiet; we only talked a little to Mr. Tilson across the intermediate Gardens; *she* was gone out airing with Miss Burdett.—It is a delightful Place—more than answers my expectation. Having got rid of my unreasonable ideas, I find more space & comfort in the rooms than I had supposed, & the Garden is quite a Love. I am in the front Attic, which is the Bedchamber to be preferred. Henry wants you to see it all, & asked whether you w^d^ return with him from Hampshire; I encouraged him to think you would. He breakfasts here, early, & then rides to Henrietta S^t^.—If it continues fine, John is to drive me there by & bye, & we shall take an airing together; & I do not mean to take any other exercise, for I feel a little tired after my long Jumble.—I live in his room downstairs, it is particularly pleasant from opening upon the garden. I go & refresh myself every now & then, and then come back to Solitary Coolness.—There is *one* maidservant only, a very creditable, cleanlooking young Woman. Richard remains for the present.—

Wednesday Morn^g^.—My Brother and Edwd arrived last night.—They c^d^ not get Places the day before. Their business is about Teeth & Wigs, & they are going after breakfast to Scarman's & Tavistock S^t^—and they are to return to go with me afterwards in the Barouche. I hope to do some of my errands today. I got the Willow yesterday, as Henry was not quite ready when I reached Hen^a^ S^t^.—I saw Mr. Hampson there for a moment. He dines here tomorrow & proposed bringing his son;—so I must submit to seeing George Hampson, though I had hoped to go through Life without it.—It was one of my vanities, like your not reading *Patronage*.—After leaving H. S^t^—we drove to Mrs. Latouches, *they* are always at home—& they are to dine here on friday.—We could do no more, as it began to rain.—We dine at ½ past 4 today, that our Visitors may go to the Play, and Henry & I are to spend the even^g^ with the Tilsons, to meet Miss Burdett, who leaves Town tomorrow.—Mrs. T. called on me yesterday.—Is not this all that can have happened, or been arranged?—Not quite.—Henry wants me to see more of his Hanwell favourite, & has written to invite her to spend a day or two here with me. His scheme is to fetch her on Saturday. I am more & more convinced that he will marry again soon, & like the idea of *her* better than of anybody else at hand.

Now, I have breakfasted & have the room to myself again.—It is likely to be a fine day.—How do you all do?—Henry talks of being at Chawton *about* the 1st of Septr.—He has once mentioned a scheme, which I should rather like—calling on the Birches & the Crutchleys in our way. It may never come to anything, but I must provide for the possibility, by troubling you to send up my Silk Pelisse by Collier on Saturday. I feel it would be necessary on such an occasion;—and be so good as to put up a clean Dressing gown which will come from the Wash on friday. You need not direct it to be left anywhere. It may take it's chance.—We are to call for Henry between 3 & 4—& I must finish this & carry it with me, as he is not always there in the morng before the Parcel is made up.—And before I set off, I must return Mrs. Tilson's visit.—I hear nothing of the Hoblyns & abstain from all enquiry.—

I hope Mary Jane & Frank's Gardens go on well.—Give my love to them all—Nunna Hat's Love to George.—A great many People wanted to mo up in the Poach as well as me.—The wheat looked very well all the way, & James says the same of *his* road.—The same good account of Mrs. C.'s health continues, & her circumstances mend. She gets farther & farther from Poverty. What a comfort! Good bye to You.—

Yours very truly & affecly Jane

All well at Steventon. I hear nothing particular of Ben, except that Edward is to get him some pencils.

99.1. *To Martha Lloyd.* See p. 506.

100. *To Anna Austen.* ⟨*Friday*⟩ 9 *Sept.* ⟨1814⟩

Address : Miss Austen
Postmark : none.
Miss Isabel Lefroy. 2 leaves 4°.
Memoir[1] 120, *Memoir*[2] 91 (extract); *Brabourne* ii. 310; *Life* 357 (extracts).

Chawton Sept: 9.

My dear Anna

We have been very much amused by your 3 books, but I have a good many criticisms to make—more than you will like.—We are not satisfied with Mrs. F.'s settling herself as Tenant & near Neighbour to such a Man as Sir T. H. without having some other inducement to go there; she ought to have some friend living thereabouts to tempt her. A woman, going with two girls just growing up, into a Neighbourhood where she knows nobody but one Man, of not very good character, is an awkwardness which so prudent a woman as Mrs. F. would not be likely to fall into. Remember, she is very prudent;—you must not let her act inconsistently.—Give her a friend, & let that friend be invited to meet her at the Priory, & we shall have no objection to her dining there as she does; but otherwise, a woman in her situation would hardly go there, before she had been visited by other Families.—I like the scene itself, the Miss Lesleys, Lady Anne, & the Music, very much.—Lesley *is* a noble name.—Sir T. H. you always do very well; I have only taken the liberty of expunging one phrase of his, which would not be allowable. 'Bless my Heart'—It is too familiar & inelegant. Your G. M. is more disturbed at Mrs. F.'s not returning the Egertons visit sooner, than anything else. They ought to have called at the

Parsonage before Sunday.—You describe a sweet place, but your descriptions are often more minute than will be liked. You give too many particulars of right hand & left.—Mrs. F. is not careful enough of Susan's health ;—Susan ought not to be walking out so soon after Heavy rains, taking long walks in the dirt. An anxious Mother would not suffer it.—I like your Susan very much indeed, she is a sweet creature, her playfulness of fancy is very delightful. I like her as she is *now* exceedingly, but I am not so well satisfied with her behaviour to George R. At first she seemed all over attachment & feeling, & afterwards to have none at all ; she is so extremely composed at the Ball, & so well-satisfied apparently with Mr. Morgan. She seems to have changed her Character.—You are now collecting your People delightfully, getting them exactly into such a spot as is the delight of my life ;—3 or 4 Families in a Country Village is the very thing to work on—& I hope you will write a great deal more, & make full use of them while they are so very favourably arranged. You are but *now* coming to the heart & beauty of your book ; till the heroine grows up, the fun must be imperfect—but I expect a great deal of entertainment from the next 3 or 4 books, & I hope you will not resent these remarks by sending me no more.—We like the Egertons very well, we see no Blue Pantaloons, or Cocks & Hens ;—there is nothing to *enchant* one certainly in Mr. L. L—but we make no objection to him, & his inclination to like Susan is pleasing.—The Sister is a good contrast—but the name of Rachael is as much as I can bear.—They are not so much like the Papillons as I expected. Your last chapter is very entertaining—the conversation on Genius &c. Mr. St. J.— & Susan both talk in character & very well.—In some former parts, Cecilia is perhaps a little too solemn & good, but upon the whole, her disposition is very well opposed to Susan's —her want of Imagination is very natural.—I wish you could make Mrs. F. talk more, but she must be difficult to manage & make entertaining, because there is so much good common sence & propriety about her that nothing can be very *broad*. Her Economy and her Ambition must not be staring.—The Papers left by Mrs. Fisher is very good.—Of course, one guesses something.—I hope when you have written a great deal more you will be equal to scratching out some of the past. The scene with Mrs. Mellish, I should condemn; it is prosy & nothing to the purpose—& indeed, the more you can find in your heart to curtail between Dawlish & Newton Priors, the better I think it will be. One does not care for girls till they are grown up.—Your Aunt C. quite enters into the exquisiteness of that name. Newton Priors is really a Nonpareil.—Milton w^{d} have given his eyes to have thought of it. Is not the Cottage taken from Tollard Royal ?—

Sunday 18th—I am very glad dear Anna, that I wrote as I did before this sad Event occurred. I have now only to add that your G.Mama does not seem the worse now for the shock.—I shall be very happy to receive more of your work, if more is ready; & you write so fast, that I have great hopes Mr. D. will come freighted back with such a Cargo as not all his Hops or his Sheep could equal the value of.

Your Grandmama desires me to say that she will have finished your Shoes tomorrow & thinks they will look very well;—and that she depends upon seeing you, as you promise, before you quit the Country, & hopes you will give her more than a day.—Yrs affec[ly]

J. Austen

101. *To Anna Austen.* *Wednesday* 28 *Sept.* ⟨1814⟩

Address: Miss Austen | Steventon
Postmark: none.
Miss Isabel Lefroy. 2 leaves 4°.
Memoir[1] 111, 120, *Memoir*[2] 85, 91 (extracts); *Brabourne* ii. 315; *Life* 359.

Chawton Wednesday Sept: 28.

My dear Anna

I hope you do not depend on having your book back again immediately. I keep it that your G:Mama may hear it—for it has not been possible yet to have any public reading. I have read it to your Aunt Cassandra however—in our own room at night, while we undressed—and with a great deal of pleasure. We like the first chapter extremely—with only a little doubt whether Ly Helena is not almost *too* foolish. The matrimonial Dialogue is very good certainly.—I like Susan as well as ever—& begin now not to care at all about Cecilia—she may stay at Easton Court as long as she likes.—Henry Mellish I am afraid will be too much in the common Novel style—a handsome, amiable, unexceptionable Young Man (such as do not much abound in real Life) desperately in Love, & all in vain. But I have no business to judge him so early.—Jane Egerton is a very natural, comprehendable Girl—& the whole of her acquaintance with Susan, & Susan's Letter to Cecilia, very pleasing & quite in character.—But *Miss* Egerton does not entirely satisfy us. She is too formal & solemn, we think, in her advice to her Brother not to fall in love; & it is hardly like a sensible Woman; it is putting it into his head.—We should like a few hints from her better.—We feel really obliged to you for introducing a Lady Kenrick, it will remove the greatest fault in the work, & I give you credit for considerable forbearance as an Author in adopting so much of our opinion.—I expect high fun about Mrs. Fisher and Sir Thomas.—You have been perfectly right in telling Ben of your work, & I am very glad to hear how much he likes it. *His* encouragement & approbation must be quite 'beyond everything.'—I do not at all wonder at his not expecting to like anybody so well as Cecilia *at first*, but shall be surprised if he does not become a Susan-ite in time. Devereux Forester's being ruined by his Vanity is extremely good; but I wish you would not let him plunge into a 'vortex of Dissipation.' I do not object to the Thing, but I cannot bear the expression;—it is such thorough novel slang—and so old, that I dare say Adam met with it in the first novel he opened.—Indeed I did very much like to know Ben's opinion.—I hope he will continue to be pleased with it, I think he must—but I cannot flatter him with their being much Incident. We have no great right to wonder at his not valueing the name of Progillian. *That* is a source of delight which he hardly ever can be quite competent to.—Walter Scott has no business to write novels, especially good ones.—It is not fair.—He has Fame and Profit enough as a Poet, and should not be taking the bread out of other people's mouths.—I do not like him, & do not mean to like Waverley if I can help it—but fear I must.—I am quite determined however not to be pleased with Mrs. West's Alicia de Lacy, should I ever meet with it, which I hope I may not.—I think I *can* be stout against any thing written by Mrs. West.—I have made up my mind to like no Novels really, but Miss Edgeworth's, Yours & my own.—

What can you do with Egerton to increase the interest for him? I wish you c^d contrive something, some family occurrence to draw out his good qualities more—some distress among Brothers or Sisters to releive by the sale of his Curacy—something to ⟨tak⟩e him mysteriously away, & then heard of at York or Edinburgh—in an old great coat.—I would not seriously recommend anything Improbable, but if you c^d invent something spirited for him, it w^d have a good effect.—He might lend all his Money to Captn Morris—but then he w^d be a great fool if he did. Cannot the Morrises quarrel, & he reconcile them?—Excuse the liberty I take in these suggestions.—

Your Aunt Frank's Housemaid has just given her warning, but whether she is worth your having, or w^d take your place I know not.—She was Mrs. Webb's maid before she went to the G^t House. She leaves your Aunt, because she cannot agree with her fellow servants. She is in love with the Man and her head seems rather turned; he returns her affection, but she fancies every body else is wanting to get him too, & envying her. Her previous service must have fitted her for such a place as yours, & she is very active and cleanly.—She is own Sister to the favourite Beatrice.—The Webbs are really gone. When I saw the Waggons at the door, & thought of all the trouble they must have in moving, I began to reproach myself for not having liked them better—but since the Waggons have disappeared, my Conscience has been closed again—& I am excessively glad they are gone.—

I am very fond of Sherlock's Sermons, prefer them to almost any.—

Your affec^{te} Aunt

J. Austen

If you wish me to speak to the Maid, let me know.—

102. *To Anna Austen*

Address: Miss Austen | Steventon

R. A. Austen-Leigh. Copy by F. C. Lefroy, endorsed 'Copy of Note written by Jane Austen to her niece Anne Austen (Mrs B. Lefroy) and given by me (F. C. Lefroy) to Cholmeley Austen Leigh for his collection of Autographs'.

Unpublished.

Miss Jane Austen begs her best Thanks may be conveyed to Mrs Hunter of Norwich for the thread paper which she has been so kind as to send her by Mr Austen, and which will always be very valuable on account of the spirited sketches (made it is supposed by Nicholson or Glover) of those most interesting spots Tarefield Hall, the Mill & above all else Tomb of Howards wife of the faithful representation of which Miss Jane Austen is undoubtedly a good judge having spent so many summers at Tarefield Abbey the delighted guest of the worthy Mrs Wilson.—It is impossible for any likeness to be more complete. Miss J. A.'s tears have flowed over each sweet sketch in such a way as would do Mrs Hs heart good to see, & if Mrs H. could understand all Miss Austen's interest in the subject she would certainly have the kindness to publish at least four volumes more about the Flint family, & especially would give many further particulars on that part of it which M^{rs} H has hitherto handled too briefly viz the history of Mary Flints marriage with Howard.

Miss J. A. cannot close this small Epitome of the miniature of an abridgement of her Thanks & admiration without expressing her sincere hopes that M^{rs} H is provided with a more safe conveyance to London than Alton can now boast—as the Car of Falkenstein which was the pride of that Town was overturned within the last ten days.

103. *To Fanny Knight. Friday* 18 *Nov.* ⟨1814⟩

Address: Miss Knight | Goodnestone Farm | Wingham | Kent
Postmarks: ALTON and 21 NO (year illegible)
Lord Brabourne. 2 leaves 4^{0}. Endorsed 'No 6. Novr 1814'. Facsimile in *Five Letters from Jane Austen to Fanny Knight*, Oxford 1924.
Brabourne ii. 277; *Life* 308, 342 (extracts). The postscript is unpublished, and some phrases and names were suppressed or disguised by Lord Brabourne.

Chawton Nov: 18.—Friday

I feel quite as doubtful as you could be my dearest Fanny as to *when* my Letter may be finished, for I can command very little quiet time at present, but yet I must begin, for I know you will be glad to hear as soon as possible, & I really am impatient myself to be writing something on so very interesting a subject, though I have no hope of writing anything to the purpose. I shall do very little more I dare say than say over again, what you have said before.—I was certainly a good deal surprised *at first*—as I had no suspicion of any change in your feelings, and I have no scruple in saying that you cannot be in Love. My dear Fanny, I am ready to laugh at the idea—and yet it is no laughing matter to have had you so mistaken as to your own feelings—And with all my heart I wish I had cautioned you on that point when first you spoke to me ;—but tho' I did not think you then so *much* in love as you thought yourself, I did consider you as being attached in a degree—quite sufficiently for happiness, as I had no doubt it would increase with opportunity.—And from the time of our being in London together, I thought you really very much in love—But you certainly are not at all—there is no concealing it.—What strange creatures we are !—It seems as if your being secure of him (as you say yourself) had made you Indifferent.—There was a little disgust I suspect, at the Races—& I do not wonder at it. His expressions there would not do for one who had rather more Acuteness, Penetration & Taste, than Love, which was your case. And yet, after all, I *am* surprised that the change in your feelings should be so great.—He is, just what he ever was, only more evidently & uniformly devoted to *you*. This is all the difference.—How shall we account for it ?—My dearest Fanny, I am writing what will not be of the smallest use to you. I am feeling differently every moment, & shall not be able to suggest a single thing that can assist your Mind.—I could lament in one sentence & laugh in the next, but as to Opinion or Counsel I am sure none will ⟨be⟩ extracted worth having from this Letter.—I read yours through the very even^{g} I received it—getting away by myself—I could not bear to leave off, when I had once begun.—I was full of curiosity & concern. Luckily your Aunt C.

dined at the other house, therefore I had not to manœuvre away from *her* ;—& as to anybody else, I do not care.—Poor dear Mr. J. P.!—Oh! dear Fanny, your mistake has been one that thousands of women fall into. He was the *first* young Man who attached himself to you. That was the charm, & most powerful it is.—Among the multitudes however that make the same mistake with yourself, there can be few indeed who have so little reason to regret it ;—*his* Character and *his* attachment leave you nothing to be ashamed of.—Upon the whole, what is to be done? You certainly *have* encouraged him to such a point as to make him feel almost secure of you—you have no inclination for any other person—His situation in life, family, friends, & above all his character—his uncommonly amiable mind, strict principles, just notions, good habits—*all* that *you* know so well how to value, *All* that really is of the first importance—everything of this nature pleads his cause most strongly.—You have no doubt of his having superior Abilities—he has proved it at the University—he is I dare say such a scholar as your agreable, idle Brothers would ill bear a comparison with.—Oh! my dear Fanny, the more I write about him, the warmer my feelings become, the more strongly I feel the sterling worth of such a young Man & the desirableness of your growing in love with him again. I recommend this most thoroughly.—There *are* such beings in the World perhaps, one in a Thousand, as the Creature You and I should think perfection, Where Grace & Spirit are united to Worth, where the Manners are equal to the Heart & Understanding, but such a person may not come in your way, or if he does, he may not be the eldest son of a Man of Fortune, the Brother of your particular friend, & belonging to your own County.—Think of all this Fanny. Mr. J. P.— has advantages which do not often meet in one person. His only fault indeed seems Modesty. If he were less modest. he would be more agreable, speak louder & look Impudenter;—and is not it a fine Character of which Modesty is the only defect?—I have no doubt that he will get more lively & more like yourselves as he is more with you;—he will catch your ways if he belongs to you. And as to there being any objection from his *Goodness*, from the danger of his becoming even Evangelical, I cannot admit *that.* I am by no means convinced that we ought not all to be Evangelicals, & am at least persuaded that they who are so from Reason and Feeling, must be happiest & safest.— Do not be frightened from the connection by your Brothers having most wit. Wisdom is better than Wit, & in the long run will certainly have the laugh on her side; & don't be frightened by the idea of his acting more strictly up to the precepts of the New Testament than others.—And now, my dear Fanny, having written so much on one side of the question, I shall turn round & entreat you not to commit yourself farther, & not to think of accepting him unless you really do like him. Anything is to be preferred or endured rather than marrying without Affection; and if his deficiencies of Manner &c &c strike you more than all his good qualities, if you continue to think strongly of them, give him up at once.—Things are now in such a state, that you must resolve upon one or the other, either to allow him to go on as he has done, or whenever you are together behave with a coldness which may convince him that he has been deceiving himself.—I have no doubt of his suffering a good deal for a time, a great deal, when he feels that he must give you up;—but it is no creed of mine, as you must be well aware, that such sort of Disappointments kill anybody.—Your sending the Music was an admirable Device, it made everything easy, & I do not know how I could have accounted for the parcel otherwise; for tho' your dear Papa most conscientiously hunted about till he found me alone in the Din^g-parlour, your Aunt C. had seen that he *had* a parcel to deliver.—As it was however, I do not think anything was suspected.—We have heard nothing fresh from Anna. I trust she is very comfortable in her new home. Her Letters have been very sensible & satisfactory, with no *parade* of happiness, which I liked them the better for.—I have often known young married Women write in a way I did not like, in that respect.

You will be glad to hear that the first Edit: of M. P. is all sold.—Your Uncle Henry is rather wanting me to come to Town, to settle about a 2^d Edit:—but as I could not very conveniently leave home now, I have written him my Will and pleasure, & unless he still urges it, shall not go.—I am very greedy & want to make the most of it;—but as you are much above caring about money, I shall not plague you with any particulars.—The pleasures of Vanity are more within your comprehension, & you will enter into mine, at receiving the *praise* which every now & then comes to me, through some channel or other.—

Saturday.—Mr. Palmer spent yesterday with us, & is gone off with Cassy this morn^g. We have been expecting Miss Lloyd the last two days, & feel sure of her today.—Mr. Knight and Mr. Edw: Knight are to dine with us.—And on Monday they are to dine with us again, accompanied by their respectable Host & Hostess.—*Sunday.* Your Papa had given me messages to you, but they are unnecessary, as he writes by this post to Aunt Louisa. We had a pleasant party yesterday, at least *we* found it so.—It is delightful to see him so chearful & confident.—Aunt Cass: & I dine at the G^t House today. We shall be a snug half dozen.—Miss Lloyd came, as we expected, yesterday, & desires her Love.—She is very happy to hear of your learning the Harp.—I do not mean to send you what I owe Miss Hare, because I think you would rather not be paid beforehand.—

Yours very affec^ly

J. Austen

Your trying to excite your own feelings by a visit to his room amused me excessively.—The dirty Shaving Rag was exquisite !—Such a circumstance ought to be in print. Much too good to be lost.—Remember me particularly to Fanny C.—I thought you w^d like to hear from me, while you were with her.

104. *To Anna Lefroy. Tuesday* 22 *Nov.* 1814

Address: To | Mrs B. Lefroy | Hendon
Postmark: 24 NO 1814 M 9 (i.e. 9 A.M.)
Miss Isabel Lefroy. One leaf 4°.
Brabourne ii. 320. A few lines unpublished.

My dear Anna

I met Harriet Benn yesterday, she gave her congratulations & desired they might be forwarded to you, and there they are.—Your Father returned to dinner,

Mr Wm Digweed who had business with your Uncle, rode with him.—The cheif news from their country is the death of old Mrs. Dormer.—Your Cousin Edward goes to Winchester today to see his Brother & Cousins, & returns tomorrow. Mrs. Clement walks about in a new Black velvet Pelisse lined with Yellow, & a white Bobbin-net-veil, & looks remarkably well in them.—I think I understand the Country about Hendon from your description. It must be very pretty in Summer.—Should you ⟨? guess⟩ that you were within a dozen miles of the We⟨n from⟩ the atmosphere ?—I shall break my he⟨art⟩ if yo⟨u do⟩ not go to Hadley.—

Make everybody at Hendon admire Mansfield Park.

Your affec: Aunt

Tuesday Nov. 22 J. A.

105. *To Anna Lefroy.* ⟨*Tuesday* 29 *Nov.* 1814⟩

Address : Mrs B. Lefroy | Hendon
Postmark : illegible

This letter as printed by Lord Brabourne begins *I assure you we all came away very much pleased with our visit* and ends *and remain Your affectionate Aunt, J. Austen.* The original of this text consists of three distinct fragments :

(1) R. A. Austen-Leigh. One leaf 8^0, $7\frac{1}{4} \times 4\frac{1}{2}$—pages 1–2 of a letter. Endorsed in pencil ' From Hans Place | Nov 29. 1814 '. Attached is the record that this is part of a letter to Mrs. Lefroy, who in 1869 gave it to her niece Mary A. Austen-Leigh. Page 1 begins *I am very much obliged to you, my dear Anna* and ends *but one remove from Br & Sr.* This was not printed by Lord Brabourne. Page 2 begins *We all came away very much pleased with our visit I assure you* and ends *hugs Mr Younge delightfully.* A pencil mark indicating a fresh paragraph at *We were all at the Play* suggests that the original was sent to the printer ; it seems probable that the printer omitted p. 1 by inadvertence. The transposition of *I assure you* is in Lord Brabourne's manner (and may have been done in proof).

(2) Miss Isabel Lefroy. A scrap, $4\frac{1}{2}$ inches wide, mutilated at the

top; begins *Cassy was excessively*, ends *Benjamin was born in?* The appearance of the paper, and the place of the folds, suggest that this is the upper third (about) of the second leaf, pages 3–4. The piece removed from the top would in that case be just large enough to contain the missing sentence *I am going this morning to see the little girls in Keppel Street.* On the verso is written *Miss J. Austen* three times, and *Hans Place Sloane Street.* This cannot be the direction of *this* letter; J. A. may have used an old 'envelope'.

(3) Lady Charnwood. A scrap, 4½ inches wide, forming the central part of the second leaf; begins *If your Uncle*, ends *J. Austen.* The lower part of the *j* of *Benjamin*, missing in (2), is plain in (3). The direction is on the verso.—The date (Tuesday, Nov: 29) has been cut out (from the foot of p. 3, no doubt) and mounted with the rest of the fragment.

A copy of the letter by Mrs. Bellas, Anna Lefroy's daughter, is in Miss Lefroy's possession. This was made before the mutilation, for it includes the sentence about the little girls (substituting, however, '—— Street' for 'Keppel Street').

Lord Brabourne dates the letter 28 Nov., but the performance of *Isabella* at Covent Garden, referred to as 'last night', was on Monday 28 Nov. A former owner of fragment (1) and Mrs. Bellas concur in the date 29 Nov.

Memoir[1] 116, *Memoir*[2] 88 (extract); *Brabourne* ii. 321; *Life* 361. Part unpublished.

I am very much obliged to you, my dear Anna, & should be very happy to come & see you again if I could, but I have not a day disengaged. We are expecting your Uncle Charles tomorrow; and I am to go the next day to Hanwell to fetch some Miss Moores who are to stay here till Saturday; then comes Sunday & Eliz^th^ Gibson, and on Monday Your Uncle Henry takes us both to Chawton. It is therefore really impossible, but I am very much obliged to You & to Mr B. Lefroy for wishing it.

We should find plenty to say, no doubt, & I should like to hear Charlotte Dewar's Letter; however, though I do not hear it, I am glad she has written to you. I like first Cousins to be first Cousins, & interested about each other. They are but one remove from B^{r} & S^{r}—

We all came away very much pleased with our visit I assure You. We talked of you for about a mile & a half with great satisfaction, & I have been just sending a very good account of you to Miss Beckford, with a description of your dress for Susan & Maria.— Your Uncle & Edwd left us this morning. The hopes of the Former in his Cause, do not lessen.—We were all at the Play last night, to see Miss O'neal in Isabella. I do not think she was quite equal to my expectation. I fancy I want something more than can be. Acting seldom satisfies me. I took two Pocket handkerchiefs, but had very little occasion for either. She is an elegant creature however & hugs Mr Younge delightfully.—

I am going this morning to see the little girls in Keppel Street. Cassy was excessively interested about your marrying, when she heard of it, which was not till she was to drink your health on the wedding day. She asked a thousand questions, in her usual way— What he said to you? & what you said to him?— And we were very much amused one day by Mary Jane's asking 'what Month her *Cousin* Benjamin was born in?'—

If your Uncle were at home he would send his best Love, but I will not impose any base, fictitious remembrance on You.—Mine I can honestly give, & remain Y^{r} affec: Aunt

J. Austen

23 Hans Place

106. *To Fanny Knight. Wednesday* 30 *Nov.* ⟨1814⟩

Address: Miss Knight | Godmersham Park | Faversham
Postmark: 2 ⟨DE ?⟩ 1814
Lord Brabourne. 2 leaves 4⁰. Endorsed 'No. 7 Nov[r] 1814'
Facsimile in *Five Letters from Jane Austen to Fanny Knight*, Oxford 1924.
Brabourne ii. 284; *Life* 308, 345 (extracts). A few words unpublished.

23 Hans Place, Wednesday Nov: 30.

I am very much obliged to you my dear Fanny for your letter, & I hope you will write again soon that I may know you to be all safe & happy at home.—Our visit to Hendon will interest you I am sure, but I need not enter into the particulars of it, as your Papa will be able to answer *almost* every question. I certainly could describe her bed-room, & her Drawers & her Closet better than he can, but I do not feel that I can stop to do it.—I was rather sorry to hear that she *is* to have an Instrument; it seems throwing money away. They will wish the 24 Gs. in the shape of Sheets & Towels six months hence;—and as to her playing, it never can be anything.—Her purple Pelisse rather surprised me.—I thought we had known all Paraphernalia of that sort. I do not mean to blame her, it looked very well & I dare say she wanted it. I suspect nothing worse than it's being got in secret, & not owned to anybody.—She is capable of that you know.—I received a very kind note from her yesterday, to ask me to come again & stay a night with them; I cannot do it, but I was pleased to find that she had the *power* of doing so right a thing. My going was to give them *both* Pleasure very properly.—I just saw Mr. Hayter at the Play, & think his face would please me on acquaintance. I was sorry he did not dine here. —It seemed rather odd to me to be in the Theatre, with nobody to *watch* for. I was quite composed myself, at leisure for all the agitation Isabella could raise.

Now my dearest Fanny, I will begin a subject which comes in very naturally.—You frighten me out of my wits by your reference. Your affection gives me the highest pleasure, but indeed you must not let anything depend on my opinion. Your own feelings & none but your own, should determine such an important point. —So far however as answering your question, I have no scruple.—I am perfectly convinced that your present feelings supposing you were to marry *now*, would be sufficient for his happiness;—but when I think how very, very far it is from a *Now*, & take everything that *may be*, into consideration, I dare not say, ' Determine to accept him.' The risk is too great for *you*, unless your own Sentiments prompt it.—You will think me perverse perhaps; in my last letter I was urging everything in his favour, & now I am inclining the other way; but I cannot help it; I am at present more impressed with the possible Evil that may arise to *you* from engaging yourself to him—in word or mind—than with anything else.—When I consider how few young Men you have yet seen much of—how capable you are (yes, I do still think you *very* capable) of being really in love—and how full of temptation the next 6 or 7 years of your Life will probably be—(it is the very period of Life for the *strongest* attachments to be formed)—I cannot wish you with your present very cool feelings to devote yourself in honour to him. It is very true that you never may attach another Man, his equal altogether, but if that other Man has the power of attaching you *more*, he will be in your eyes the most perfect.—I shall be glad if you *can* revive past feelings, & from your unbiassed self resolve to go on as you have done, but this I do not expect, and without it I cannot wish you to be fettered. I should not be afraid of your *marrying* him;—with all his worth, you would soon love him enough for the happiness of both; but I should dread the continuance of this sort of tacit engagement, with such an uncertainty as there is, of *when* it may be completed.—Years may pass, before he is Independant.—You like him well enough to marry, but not well enough to wait.—The unpleasantness of appearing fickle is certainly great—but if you think you want Punishment for past Illusions, there it is—and nothing can be compared to the misery of being bound *without* Love, bound to one, & preferring another. *That* is a Punishment which you do *not* deserve.—I know you did not meet—or rather will not meet today—as he called here yesterday—& I am glad of it.—It does not seem very likely at least that he sh[d] be in time for a Dinner visit 60 miles off. We did not see him, only found his card when we came home at 4.—Your Uncle H. merely observed that he was a day after the Fair.—He asked your Brother on Monday, (when Mr. Hayter was talked of) why he did not invite *him* too?—saying, 'I know he is in Town, for I met him the other day in Bond St.—'Edward answered that he did not know where he was to be found.—'Don't you know his chambers?—' 'No.'—I shall be most glad to hear from you again my dearest Fanny, but it must not be later than Saturday, as we shall be off on Monday long before the Letters are delivered—and

Mifs O'Neill

as Isabella.

write *something* that may do to be read or told. I am to take the Miss Moores back on Saturday, & when I return I shall hope to find your pleasant, little, flowing scrawl on the Table.—It will be a releif to me after playing at Ma'ams—for though I like Miss H. M. as much as one can at my time of Life after a day's acquaintance, it is uphill work to be talking to those whom one knows so little. Only *one* comes back with me tomorrow, probably Miss Eliza, & I rather dread it. We shall not have two Ideas in common. She is young, pretty, chattering, & thinking cheifly (I presume) of Dress, Company, & Admiration.—Mr. Sanford is to join us at dinner, which will be a comfort, and in the even[g] while your Uncle and Miss Eliza play chess, he shall tell me comical things & I will laugh at them, which will be a pleasure to both.—I called in Keppel Street & saw them all, including dear Uncle Charles, who is to come & dine with us quietly today.—Little Harriot sat in my lap—& seemed as gentle and affectionate as ever, & as pretty, except not being quite well.—Fanny is a fine stout girl, talking incessantly, with an interesting degree of Lisp and Indistinctness—and very likely may be the handsomest in time.—That puss Cassy, did not shew more pleasure in seeing me than her Sisters, but I expected no better;—she does not shine in the tender feelings. She will never be a Miss O'Neal;—more in the Mrs. Siddons line.—

Thank you—but it is not settled yet whether I *do* hazard a 2[d] Edition. We are to see Egerton today, when it will probably be determined.—People are more ready to borrow & praise, than to buy—which I cannot wonder at;—but tho' I like praise as well as anybody, I like what Edward calls *Pewter* too.—I hope he continues careful of his eyes & finds the good effect of it.

I cannot suppose we differ in our ideas of the Christian Religion. You have given an excellent description of it. We only affix a different meaning to the Word *Evangelical*.

Yours most affec^ly^

J. Austen

Miss Gibson is very glad to go with us.

107. *To Anna Lefroy. Wednesday* ⟨*Dec.* 1814⟩

No address or postmark.

Miss Isabel Lefroy. One leaf 8⁰, $7\frac{1}{4}\times4\frac{7}{16}$, the other leaf lost. Page 2 ends *some hint of St. Julian's early*. Lord Brabourne must have seen the missing leaf, unless he finished the sentence by conjecture.

Memoir[1] 121, *Memoir*[2] 92 (extract); *Brabourne* ii. 322; *Life* 361. The concluding paragraph printed by Lord Brabourne does not belong to this letter; see the next letter. The *Memoir* dates this letter November; but see *Life* 361.

Hans Place. Wednesday

My dear Anna

I have been very far from finding your Book an Evil I assure you; I read it immediately—& with great pleasure. I think you are going on very well. The description of Dr. Griffin & Lady Helena's unhappiness is very good, just what was likely to be.—I am curious to know what the end of *them* will be: The name of Newton-Priors is really invaluable!—I never met with anything superior to it.—It is delightful.—One could live upon the name of Newton-Priors for a twelvemonth.—Indeed, I *do* think you get on very fast. I wish other people of my acquaintance could compose as rapidly.—I am pleased with the Dog scene, & with the whole of George & Susan's Love;

but am more particularly struck with your *serious* conversations &c.—They are very good throughout.—St. Julian's History was quite a surprise to me ; You had not very long known it yourself I suspect—but I have no objection to make to the circumstance—it is very well told—& his having been in love with the Aunt, gives Cecilia an additional Interest with him. I like the Idea :—a very proper compliment to an Aunt !—I rather imagine indeed that Neices are seldom chosen but in compliment to some Aunt or other. I daresay Ben was in love with me once, & w[d] never have thought of *you* if he had not supposed me dead of a scarlet fever.—Yes, I was in a mistake as to the number of Books. I thought I had read 3 before the 3 at Chawton ; but fewer than 6 will not do.—I want to see dear Bell Griffin again.—Had not you better give some hint of St. Julian's early history in the beginning of the story ?

108. ⟨*To Anna Lefroy.*⟩

No address or postmark.

Miss Isabel Lefroy. A scrap of a 4⁰ leaf, $7\frac{1}{2}\times$(about) $2\frac{1}{4}$. One side begins *which is quite*, ends *not to be in print* ; the other begins *: natural.—M[lle] Cossart*, ends *wishes.* A lost fragment of the same letter is printed in the *Memoir*.

***Memoir*[1] 173, *Memoir*[2] 131 (begins *We have got 'Rosanne'*, ends *rather my passion*) ; *Memoir*[1] 116, *Memoir*[2] 89 (begins *So, Miss B. is actually married*, ends *not to be in print*) ; *Brabourne* ii. 323 (misplaced ; begins *We shall see nothing*, ends *not to be in print*) ; *Life* 362. The final scrap is distinct from that in the *Memoir* except for the sentence about M[lle] Cossart (which serves to unite them) and is unpublished. (See note on the foregoing letter.)**

. . . which is quite against my skin & conscience.—We shall see nothing of Streatham while we are in Town ;—M[rs] Hill is to lye-in of a Daughter early in

March.—Mrs Blackstone is to be with her. Mrs Heathcote & Miss Bigg are just leaving her; the latter writes me word that Miss Blachford *is* married, but I have never seen it in the Papers. And one may as well be single, if the Wedding is not to be in print.— . . .

We have got 'Rosanne' in our Society, and find it much as you describe it; very good and clever, but tedious. Mrs. Hawkins' great excellence is on serious subjects. There are some very delightful conversations and reflections on religion: but on lighter topics I think she falls into many absurdities; and, as to love, her heroine has very comical feelings. There are a thousand improbabilities in the story. Do you remember the two Miss Ormesdens, introduced just at last? Very flat and unnatural.—Mlle Cossart is rather my passion.—Miss Gibson returned to the G^t^ House last friday, & is pretty well, but not entirely so. Captn Clement has very kindly offered to drive her out, & she would like it very much, but no day has yet been quite good enough, or else she has not been otherwise equal to it.—She sends you her Love ⟨*nearly a line missing*⟩d wishes

109. *To Anna Lefroy.* ⟨*Nov. or Dec.* 1814?⟩

No address or postmark.
R. A. Austen-Leigh. A scrap.
Memoir[1] 173, *Memoir*[2] 131. (The writer of the *Memoir* gives the authors of the *opinions* as Mr. (*sic*) C. and Mr. D.) Part unpublished. The reference to Hendon fixes the date; J. A. was in Hans Place again in Oct.–Dec. 1815, but the Lefroys were then no longer at Hendon.

Mrs Creed's opinion is gone down on my list; but fortunately I may excuse myself from entering M^r^

⟨*word cut out*⟩ as my paper only relates to Mansfield Park. I will redeem my credit with him, by writing a close Imitation of ' Self-control ' as soon as I can ;—I will improve upon it ;—my Heroine shall not merely be wafted down an American river in a boat by herself, she shall cross the Atlantic in the same way, & never stop till she reaches Gravesent.— . . . that depends on us to secure it, but you mu⟨st be⟩ aware that in another person's house one cannot command one's own time or actions, & though your Uncle Henry is so kind as to give us the use of a Carriage while we are with him, it may not be possible for us to turn that Carriage towards Hendon without actually mounting the Box ourselves ;—Your Uncle arrived yesterday by the Gosport—(and only think of the Gosport not being here till 1/2 past 4 !—I ⟨*a line missing*⟩ and takes . . .

110. *To Anna Lefroy. Friday* 29 *September* ⟨1815⟩

No address or postmark.
Miss Isabel Lefroy. One leaf 4⁰, the other leaf lost. Facsimile in Constance Hill, *Jane Austen, Her Homes and her Friends*, 1902.
***Brabourne* ii. 324.**

Chawton, Friday Sept[r] 29.

My dear Anna

We told Mr. B. Lefroy that if the weather did not prevent us, we should certainly come & see you tomorrow, & bring Cassy, trusting to your being so good as to give her a dinner about one o'clock, that we might be able to be with you the earlier & stay the longer—but on giving Cassy her choice of the Fair or Wyards, it must be confessed that she has preferred the former, which we trust will not greatly affront you ;—if it does, you may hope that some little Anna hereafter may revenge the insult by a similar preference of an Alton Fair to her Cousin Cassy.—In the meanwhile, we have determined to put off our visit to you till Monday, which we hope will be not less convenient to you. I wish the weather may not resolve upon other put-offs. I *must* come to you before Wednesday if it be possible, for on that day I am going to London for a week or two with your Uncle Henry, who is expected here on Sunday. If Monday therefore should appear too dirty for walking, and Mr. B. L. would be so kind as to come & fetch me to spend some part of the morn[g] with you, I should be much obliged to him. Cassy might be of the Party, and your Aunt Cassandra will take another opportunity.

Your G. Mama sends her Love & Thanks for your note. She was very happy to hear the contents of your Packing Case.—She will send the Strawberry roots by Sally Benham, as early next week as the weather may allow her to take them up.—

Yours very affec:[ly]
My dear Anna
J. Austen

111. *To Cassandra Austen. Tuesday* 17 *Oct.* 1815

Address: To Miss Austen | Chawton | Alton
Postmark: 18 oc 1815
Mrs. Henry Burke; formerly in the collection described in *Times Literary Supplement* 14 Jan. 1926.
Life 309 (extracts). Mostly unpublished.

Hans Place Tuesday Oct. 17 [1815]

My dear Cassandra

Thank you for your two letters; I am very glad the new cook begins so well. Good apple pies are a considerable part of our domestic happiness. Mr. Murray's letter is come. He is a rogue of course, but a civil one. He offers £450 but wants to have the copyright of M. P. & S. & S. included. It will end in my publishing for myself I daresay. He sends more praise however than I expected. It is an amusing letter. You shall see it. Henry came home on Sunday & we dined the same day with the Herrieses—a large family party—clever & accomplished. I had a pleasant visit the day before. Mr. Jackson is fond of eating & does not much like M^r^ or Miss P. What weather we have! What shall we do about it. The 17th of October & summer still. Henry is not quite well—a bilious attack with fever. He came back early from H. S^t^ yesterday & went to bed—the comical consequence of which was that Mr Seymour & I dined together tête-à-tête. He is calomeling & therefore in a way to be better & I hope may be well to-morrow. The Creeds of Hendon dine here to-day, which is rather unlucky, for he will hardly be able to shew himself, & they are all strangers to me. He has asked Mr Tilson to come & take his place. I doubt our being a very agreeable pair. We are engaged to-morrow to Cleveland Row. I was there yesterday morning. There seems no idea now of Mr Gordan's going to Chawton—nor of any of the family coming here at present. Many of them are sick.

Wednesday. Henry's illness is more serious than I expected. He has been in bed since three o'clock on Monday. It is a fever—something bilious but chiefly inflammatory. I am not alarmed but I have determined to send this letter to-day by the post, that you may know how things are going on.

There is no chance of his being able to leave town on Saturday. I asked Mr Haydon that question to-day. Mr H. is the apothecary from the corner of Sloane S^t^, successor to Mr Smith, a young man, said to be clever, & he is certainly very attentive, & appears hitherto to have understood the complaint. There is a little pain in the chest, but it is not considered of any consequence. Mr H. calls it a general inflammation. He took twenty ounces of blood from Henry last night, & nearly as much more this morning, & expects to have to bleed him again to-morrow—but he assures me that he found him *quite* as much better to-day as he expected. Henry is an excellent patient, lies quietly in bed & is ready to swallow anything. He lives upon medicine, tea & barley-water. He has had a great deal of fever but not much pain of any sort, & sleeps pretty well. *His* going to Chawton will probably end in nothing, as his Oxfordshire business is so near : as for myself you may be sure I shall return as soon as I can—Tuesday is in my brain, but you will feel the uncertainty of it. I want to get rid of some of my things & therefore shall send down a parcel by Collier on Saturday. Let it be paid for on my own account. It will be mostly dirty cloathes, but I shall add Martha's lambswool, your muslin handks. (India at 3/6) your pens 3^d^ & some articles for Mary if I receive them in time from Mrs Hore. Cleveland Row of course is given up. Mr Tilson took a note there this morning. Till yesterday afternoon I was hoping that the medicine he had taken with a good night's rest would set him quite to rights. I fancied it only bile but they say the disorder must have originated in a cold. You must fancy Henry in the back-room upstairs, & I am generally there also, working or writing. I wrote to Edward yesterday to put off our nephews till Friday. I have a strong idea of their Uncle's being well enough to like seeing them [by] that time. I shall write to you next by my parcel—two days hence unless there is anything particular to be communicated before, always excepted. The post has this moment brought me a letter from Edward. He is likely to come here on Tuesday next for a day or two's necessary business in his cause.

Mrs. Hore wishes to observe to Frank & Mary that she doubts their finding it answer to have chests of drawers bought in London when the expense of carriage is considered. The two Miss Gibsons called here on Sunday & brought a letter for Mary, which shall also be put into the parcel. Miss G. looked particularly well. I have not been able to return their call. I want to get to Keppel S^t^ again if I can, but it must be doubtful. The Creeds are agreeable people themselves but I fear must have had a very dull visit. I long to know how Martha's plans go on. If you have not written before, write by Sunday's post to Hans Place. I shall be more than ready for news of you by that time. A change of weather at last—wind & rain. Mrs Tilson has just called. Poor woman—she is quite a wretch—always ill. God bless you.

Y^rs^ affec^tely^ J. A.

Uncle Henry was very much amused with Cassy's message, but if she were here now with the red shawl she would make him laugh more than would do him good.

112. *To Caroline Austen.* *Monday* 30 *Oct.* ⟨1815⟩

No address or postmark.
L. A. Austen-Leigh. One leaf 8⁰, the other leaf almost all lost.
***Life* 365. Part unpublished.**

Hans Place, Monday nig⟨ht⟩ Oct: 30.

My dear Caroline

I have not yet felt quite equal to taking up your Manuscript, but think I shall soon, & I hope my detaining it so long will be no inconvenience.—It gives us great pleasure that you should be at Chawton. I am sure Cassy must be delighted to have you.—You will practise your Music of course, & I trust to you for taking care of my Instrument & not letting it be ill used in any respect.—Do not allow anything to be put on it, but what is very light.—I hope you will try to make out some other tune besides the Hermit.—Tell your Grandmama that I have written to Mrs Cooke to congratulate her, & that I have heard from Scarlets today; they were much shocked by the preparatory Letter which I felt obliged to send last wednesday, but had been made comfortable in comparison, by the receipt of my friday's Letter. Your Papa wrote again by this Post, so that I hope they are now easy.—I am sorry you got wet in your ride; Now that you are become an Aunt, you are a person of some consequence & must excite great Interest whatever you do. I have always maintained the importance of Aunts as much as possible, & I am sure of your doing the same now.—Beleive me my dear Sister-Aunt,

Yours affec^ly^

J. Austen

113. *To James Stanier Clarke.* ⟨*Wednesday*⟩ 15 *Nov.* 1815

No address or postmark.
Pierpont Morgan Library (1925). Formerly in the collection described in *Times Literary Supplement* 14 Jan. 1926. One leaf. Endorsed 'Copy of my Letter to Mr Clarke, Nov: 15, 1815.'
Memoir^{1} 149, *Memoir*^{2} 112 ; *Life* 312.

Sir

I must take the liberty of asking you a question.—Among the many flattering attentions which I rec^{d} from you at Carlton House on Monday last, was the Information of my being at liberty to dedicate any future work to HRH. the P. R. without the necessity of any solicitation on my part. Such at least, I beleived to be your words ; but as I am very anxious to be quite certain of what was intended, I intreat you to have the goodness to inform me how such a Permission is to be understood, & whether it is incumbent on me to shew my sense of the Honour, by inscribing the Work now in the Press, to H.R.H.—I sh^{d} be equally concerned to appear either Presumptuous or Ungrateful.—

I am &c—

113*a*. *From James Stanier Clarke.* ⟨*Thursday*⟩ 16 *Nov.* 1815

Address : Miss Austen | N^{0} 23 | Hans Place | Sloane Street
Postmark : Jermyn St. and 16 NO 1815
Pierpont Morgan Library. From the same collection as N^{0} 113.

Carlton House Nov^{r}: 16th: 1815.

Dear Madam.

It is certainly not *incumbent* on you to dedicate your work now in the Press to His Royal Highness : but if you wish to do the Regent that honour either now or at any future period, I am happy to send you that permission which need not require any more trouble or solicitation on your Part.

Your late Works, Madam, and in particular Mansfield Park reflect the highest honour on your Genius & your Principles; in every new work your mind seems to increase its energy and powers of discrimination. The Regent has read & admired all your publications.

Accept my sincere thanks for the pleasure your Volumes have given me: in the perusal of them I felt a great inclination to write & say so. And I also dear Madam wished to be allowed to ask you, to delineate in some future Work the Habits of Life and Character and enthusiasm of a Clergyman—who should pass his time between the metropolis & the Country—who should be something like Beatties Minstrel

Silent when glad, affectionate tho' shy
And now his look was most demurely sad
& now he laughd aloud yet none knew why—

Neither Goldsmith—nor La Fontaine in his Tableau de Famille—have in my mind quite delineated an English Clergyman, at least of the present day—Fond of, & entirely engaged in Literature—no man's Enemy but his own. Pray dear Madam think of these things.

Believe me at all times
With sincerity & respect
Your faithful & obliged Servant
J. S. Clarke
Librarian.

P. S.

I am going for about three weeks to Mr. Henry Streatfeilds, Chiddingstone Sevenoaks—but hope on my return to have the honour of seeing you again.

114. ⟨*To John Murray.*⟩ *Friday* 3 *Nov.* ⟨1815⟩

No address or postmark.
Earl Stanhope, to whose ancestor the then Mr. Murray gave it in 1870.
Draft or copy, Bodleian.
Unpublished.

23 Hans Place, Friday Nov: 3d

Sir

My Brother's severe Illness has prevented his replying to Yours of Oct. 15, on the subject of the MS of *Emma*, now in your hands—and as he is though recovering, still in a state which we are fearful of harrassing by Business & I am at the same time desirous of coming to some decision on the affair in question, I must request the favour of you to call on me here, any day that may suit you best, at any hour in the Evening, or any in the Morning except from Eleven to One.—A short conversation may perhaps do more than much writing.

My Brother begs his Compts & best thanks for your polite attention in supplying him with a copy of Waterloo.

I am Sir
Your Ob. Hum: Servt
Jane Austen

115. *To John Murray.* *Thursday* 23 *Nov.* ⟨1815⟩

Address: lost.
Original not traced.
Memoir[2] 122 (from a copy communicated by Mr. Murray); *Life* 314.

23 Hans Place, Thursday, November 23 (1815).

Sir

My brother's note last Monday has been so fruitless, that I am afraid there can be but little chance of my writing to any good effect ; but yet I am so very much disappointed and vexed by the delays of the printers, that I cannot help begging to know whether there is no hope of their being quickened. Instead of the work being ready by the end of the present month, it will hardly, at the rate we now proceed, be finished by the end of the next ; and as I expect to leave London early in December, it is of consequence that no more time should be lost. Is it likely that the printers will be influenced to greater dispatch and punctuality by knowing that the work is to be dedicated, by permission, to the Prince Regent ? If you can make that circumstance operate, I shall be very glad. My brother returns ' Waterloo ' with many thanks for the loan of it. We have heard much of Scott's account of Paris. If it be not incompatible with other arrangements, would you favour us with it, supposing you have any set already opened ? You may depend upon its being in careful hands.

I remain, Sir, your ob[t] humble Se[t]

J. Austen

116. *To Cassandra Austen.* *Friday* 24 *Nov.* 1815

Address: Miss Austen, Chawton
Postmark: none.
Pierpont Morgan Library. 2 leaves 4⁰.
Brabourne ii. 249 ; *Life* 315 (extracts). One sentence unpublished.

Hans Place, Friday Nov: 24.

My dearest Cassandra

I have the pleasure of sending you a much better account of *my affairs*, which I know will be a great delight to you. I wrote to Mr. Murray yesterday myself, & Henry wrote at the same time to Roworth. Before the notes were out of the House, I received three sheets, & an apology from R. We sent the notes however, & I had a most civil one in reply from Mr. M. He is so very polite indeed, that it is quite overcoming. —The Printers have been waiting for Paper—the blame is thrown upon the Stationer—but he gives his word that I shall have no farther cause for dissatisfaction.—He has lent us *Miss Williams & Scott*, & says that any book of his will always be at *my* service.—In short, I am soothed & complimented into tolerable comfort.—

We had a visit yesterday from Edw[d] Knight, & Mr. Mascall joined him here ;—and this morning has brought Mr. Mascall's Compt[s] & two Pheasants.—We have some hope of Edward's coming to dinner today ; he will, if he can I beleive.—He is looking extremely well.—Tomorrow Mr. Haden is to dine with us.—There's Happiness !—We really grow so fond of Mr. Haden that I do not know what to expect.—He, & Mr. Tilson & Mr. Philips made up our circle of Wits last night ; Fanny played, & he sat & listened & suggested improvements, till Richard came in to tell him that 'the Doctor was waiting for him at Capt[n] Blake's'—and then he was off with a speed that you can imagine. He never does appear in the least above his Profession, or out of humour with it, or I should think poor Capt[n] Blake, whoever he is, in a very bad way.—

I must have misunderstood Henry, when I told you that *you* were to hear from him today. He read me what he wrote to Edward ;—part of it must have amused him I am sure ;—one part alas ! cannot be very amusing to anybody.—I wonder that with such

Q

Business to worry him, he can be getting better, but he certainly does gain strength, & if you & Edw[d] were to see him now I feel sure that you would think him improved since Monday. He was out yesterday, it was a fine sunshiney day *here*—(in the Country perhaps you might have Clouds & fogs—Dare I say so?—I shall not deceive *you*, if I do, as to my estimation of the Climate of London)—& he ventured, first on the Balcony, & then as far as the Greenhouse. He caught no cold, & therefore has done more today with great delight, & self-persuasion of Improvement; he has been to see Mrs. Tilson & the Malings.—By the bye, you may talk to Mr. T. of his wife's being better, I saw her yesterday & was sensible of her having gained ground in the last two days.—

Evening.—We have had no Edward.—Our circle is formed; only Mr. Tilson & Mr. Haden.—We are not so happy as we were. A message came this afternoon from Mrs. Latouche & Miss East, offering themselves to drink tea with us tomorrow—& as it was accepted, here is an end of our extreme felicity in our Dinner-Guest.—I am heartily sorry they are coming! It will be an Even[g] spoilt to Fanny & me. Another little Disappointment.—Mr. H. advises Henry's *not* venturing with us in the Carriage tomorrow;—if it were Spring, he says, it w[d] be a different thing. One would rather this had not been. He seems to think his going out today rather imprudent, though acknowledging at the same time that he is better than he was in the Morn[g].—Fanny has had a Letter full of commissions from Goodnestone; we shall be busy about them & her own matters I dare say from 12 to 4.—Nothing I trust will keep us from Keppel Street.—This day has brought a most friendly letter from Mr. Fowle, with a brace of Pheasants. I did not know before that Henry had written to him a few days ago, to ask for them. We shall live upon Pheasants ; no bad Life !—I send you five one pound notes, for fear you should be distressed for little Money.—Lizzy's work is charmingly done. Shall you put it to your Chintz ?—A *sheet* come in this moment. 1st & 3d vol. are now at 144.—2d at 48.—I am sure you will like Particulars.—We are not to have the trouble of returning the sheets to Mr. Murray any longer, the Printer's boys bring & carry.

I hope Mary continues to get well fast—& I send my Love to little Herbert.—You will tell me more of Martha's plans of course when you write again.—Remember me most kindly to everybody, & Miss Benn besides.—Yours very affecly J. Austen

I have been listening to dreadful Insanity.—It is Mr. Haden's firm beleif that a person *not* musical is fit for every sort of Wickedness. I ventured to assert a little on the other side, but wished the cause in abler hands.—

Supposing the weather shd be very bad on Sunday Eveng I shall not like to send Richard out you know—& in that case, my Dirty Linen must wait a day.

117. *To Cassandra Austen.* *Sunday* 26 *Nov.* ⟨1815⟩

Address : Miss Austen
Postmark : none.
New York Public Library, Berg Collection. 2 leaves 4o.
Brabourne ii. 253 ; *Life* 316 (extracts). A few lines unpublished.

Hans Place. Sunday Nov: 26.

My Dearest

The Parcel arrived safely, & I am much obliged to you for your trouble. It cost 2s 10—but as there is a certain saving of 2^{s} 4$\frac{1}{2}$ on the other side, I am sure it is well worth doing.—I send 4 p^{r} of silk stock^{gs}—but I do not want them washed at present. In the 3 neck-handfs. I include the one sent down before.—These things perhaps Edw. may be able to bring, but even if he is not, I am extremely pleased with his returning to you from Steventon. It is much better—far preferable.—I *did* mention the P. R—in my note to Mr. Murray, it brought me a fine compliment in return; whether it has done any other good I do not know, but Henry thought it worth trying.—The Printers continue to supply me very well, I am advanced in vol. 3. to my *arra*-root, upon which peculiar style of spelling there is a modest *qu:^{ry}?* in the Margin.—I will not forget Anna's arrow-root.—I hope you have told Martha of my first resolution of letting nobody know that I *might* dedicate, &c for fear of being obliged to do it—& that she is thoroughly convinced of my being influenced now by nothing but the most mercenary motives.—I have paid nine shillings on her account to Miss Palmer; there was no more oweing.—Well—we were very busy all yesterday; from $\frac{1}{2}$ past 11 to 4 in the Streets, working almost entirely for other people, driving from Place to Place after a parcel for Sandling which we could never find, & encountering the miseries of Grafton House to get a purple frock for Eleanor Bridges.—We got to Keppel St. however, which was all I cared for & though we could stay only a q^{r} of an hour, Fanny's calling gave great pleasure & her Sensibility still greater, for she was very much affected at the sight of the Children.—Poor little F. looked heavy.—We saw the whole party.—Aunt Har^{r} hopes Cassy will not forget to make a pincushion for Mrs. Kelly—

as *she* has spoken of its being promised her several times.—I hope we shall see Aunt H.—& the dear little Girls here on Thursday.—

So much for the morn^g; then came the dinner & Mr. Haden who brought good Manners & clever conversation ;—from 7 to 8 the Harp ; at 8 Mrs. L. & Miss E. arrived—& for the rest of the even^g the Draw^g-room was thus arranged, on the Sopha-side the two Ladies Henry & myself making the best of it, on the opposite side Fanny & Mr. Haden in two chairs (I *believe* at least they had *two* chairs) talking together uninterruptedly.—Fancy the scene ! And what is to be fancied next ?—Why that Mr. H. dines here again tomorrow.—To-day we are to have Mr. Barlow.—Mr. H. is reading Mansfield Park for the first time and prefers it to P. and P.—A Hare & 4 Rabbits from Gm. yesterday, so that we are stocked for nearly a week.—Poor Farmer Andrews ! I am very sorry for him, & sincerely wish his recovery.—A better account of the Sugar than I could have expected. I should like to help you break some more.—I am glad you cannot wake early, I am sure you must have been under great arrears of rest.—Fanny & I have been to B. Chapel, & walked back with Maria Cuthbert.—We have been very little plagued with visitors this last week, I remember only Miss Herries the Aunt, but I am in terror for to-day, a fine bright Sunday, plenty of Mortar & nothing to do.—Henry gets out in his Garden every day, but at present his inclination for doing more seems over, nor has he now any plan for leaving London before Dec: 18, when he thinks of going to Oxford for a few days ;—to-day indeed, his feelings are for continuing where he is, through the next two months. One knows the uncertainty of all this, but should it be so, we must think the best & hope the best & do the best—and my idea in that case is, that when *he* goes to Oxford *I* should go home & have nearly a week of you before *you* take my place.—This is only a silent project you know, to be gladly given up, if better things occur.—Henry calls himself stronger every day & Mr. H. keeps on approving his Pulse which seems generally better than ever—but still they will not let him be well.—The fever is not yet quite removed.—The Medicine he takes (the same as before you went) is chiefly to improve his Stomach, & only a little aperient. He is so well, that I cannot think why he is not perfectly well.—I should not have supposed his Stomach at all disordered but *there* the Fever speaks probably ;—but he has no headake, no sickness, no pains, no Indigestions !—Perhaps when Fanny is gone he will be allowed to recover faster.—I am not disappointed, I never thought the little girl at Wyards very pretty, but she will have a fine complexion & curling hair & pass for a beauty.—We are glad the Mama's cold has not been worse—& send her our Love—& good wishes by every convenient opportunity. Sweet amiable Frank ! why does *he* have a cold too ? Like Capt Mirvan to Me Duval, 'I wish it well over with him.'

Fanny has heard all that I have said to you about herself & Mr. H.—Thank you very much for the sight of dearest Charles's Letter to yourself. How pleasantly & how naturally he writes ! and how perfect a picture of his Disposition & feelings, his style conveys !—Poor dear Fellow !—not a Present !—I have a great mind to send him all the twelve Copies which were to have been dispersed among my near Connections—beginning with the P. R. & ending with Countess Morley.—Adieu.—Y^rs^ affec^ly^—

J. Austen

Give my Love to Cassy &
Mary Jane.—Caroline will
be gone when this reaches you.

118. *To Cassandra Austen.* *Saturday* 2 *Dec.* 1815

Address: Miss Austen | Chawton | Alton | Hants
Postmark: DE 2 1815
Pierpont Morgan Library. 2 leaves 4°.
Brabourne ii. 258; *Life* 317 (extracts). A few lines unpublished.

Hans Place, Saturday Dec: 2.

My dear Cassandra

Henry came back yesterday, & might have returned the day before if he had known as much in time. I had the pleasure of hearing from Mr. T. on wednesday night that Mr. Seymour thought there was not the least occasion for his absenting himself any longer.—I had also the comfort of a few lines on wednesday morning from Henry himself—(just after your Letter was gone) giving so good an account of his feelings as made me perfectly easy. He met with the utmost care & attention at Hanwell, spent his two days there very quietly & pleasantly, & being certainly in no respect the worse for going, we may beleive that he must be better, as he is quite sure of being himself.—To make his return a complete Gala, Mr. Haden was secured for dinner—I need not say that our Even^g^ was agreable.—But you seem to be under a mistake as to Mr. H.—You call him an Apothecary; he is no

Apothecary, he has never been an Apothecary, there is not an Apothecary in this Neighbourhood—the only inconvenience of the situation perhaps, but so it is—we have not a medical Man within reach—he is a Haden, nothing but a Haden, a sort of wonderful nondescript Creature on two legs, something between a Man & an Angel—but without the least spice of an Apothecary.—He is perhaps the only Person *not* an Apothecary hereabouts.—He has never sung to us. He will not sing without a P. Forté accompaniment. Mr. Meyers gives his three Lessons a week—altering his days & his hours however just as he chuses, never very punctual, & never giving good Measure.—I have not Fanny's fondness for Masters, & Mr. Meyers does not give me any Longing after them. The truth is I think, that they are all, at least Music Masters, made of too much consequence & allowed to take too many Liberties with their Scholar's time. We shall be delighted to see Edward on Monday—only sorry that you must be losing him. A Turkey will be equally welcome with himself.—He must prepare for his own proper bedchamber here, as Henry moved down to the one below last week; he found the other cold.—I am sorry my Mother has been suffering, & am afraid this exquisite weather is too good to agree with her.—*I* enjoy it all over me, from top to toe, from right to left, Longitudinally, Perpendicularly, Diagonally;—& I cannot but selfishly hope we are to have it last till Christmas;—nice, unwholesome, Unseasonable, relaxing, close, muggy weather!—Oh! thank you very much for your long Letter; it did me a great deal of good.—Henry accepts your offer of making his nine gallon of Mead, thankfully. The mistake of the Dogs rather vexed him for a moment, but he has not thought of it since.—Today, he makes a third attempt at his strengthening Plaister, & as I am sure he will now be getting out a great deal, it is to be wished that he may be able to keep it on.—He sets off this morning by the Chelsea Coach to sign Bonds and visit Henrietta S^t^, & I have no doubt will be going every day to Henrietta S^t^.—Fanny & I were very snug by ourselves, as soon as we were satisfied about our Invalid's being safe at Hanwell.—By Manœuvring & good luck we foiled all the Malings attempts upon us. Happily I caught a little cold on wednesday, the morn^g^ we were in Town, which we made very useful; & we saw nobody but our Precious, & Mr. Tilson.—This Evening the Malings are allowed to drink tea with us.—We are in hopes, that is, we *wish* Miss Palmer & the little girls may come this morning. You know of course, that she could *not* come on Thursday;—& she will not attempt to *name* any other day.—I do not think I shall send down any more Dirty Linen; it will not answer when the Car^ge^ is to be paid each way.—I have got Anna's arrow-root, & your gloves.

God bless you.—Excuse the shortness of this—but I must finish it now, that I may save you 2^d^—Best love.—

Y^rs^ affec^ly^

J. A.

It strikes me that I have no business to give the P.R. a Binding, but we will take Counsel upon the question.—

I am glad you have put the flounce on your Chintz, I am sure it must look particularly well, & it is what I had thought of.

119. *To Caroline Austen.* 6 *Dec.* ⟨1815⟩

No address or postmark.
L. A. Austen-Leigh. A scrap.
***Life* 363.**

My dear Caroline

I wish I could finish Stories as fast as you can.—I am much obliged to you for the sight of Olivia, & think you have done for her very well; but the good for nothing Father, who was the real author of all her Faults and Sufferings, should not escape unpunished. I hope *he* hung himself, or took the sur-name of *Bone* or underwent some direful penance or other.—

Yours affec[ly]

Dec: 6. J. Austen

120. *To James Stanier Clarke.* ⟨*Monday*⟩ 11 *Dec.* 1815

***Address*: lost.**
T. Edward Carpenter (1948); copy by J. A. Original not traced.
***Memoir*[1] 152, *Memoir*[2] 114; *Life* 319.**

Dec. 11.

Dear Sir

My 'Emma' is now so near publication that I feel it right to assure you of my not having forgotten your kind recommendation of an early copy for Carlton House, and that I have Mr. Murray's promise of its being sent to His Royal Highness, under cover to you, three days previous to the work being really out. I must make use of this opportunity to thank you, dear Sir, for the very high praise you bestow on my other novels. I am too vain to wish to convince you that you have praised them beyond their merits.

My greatest anxiety at present is that this fourth work should not disgrace what was good in the others. But on this point I will do myself the justice to declare that, whatever may be my wishes for its success, I am very strongly haunted with the idea that to those readers who have preferred 'Pride and Prejudice' it will appear inferior in wit, and to those who have preferred 'Mansfield Park' very inferior in good sense. Such as it is, however, I hope you will do me the favour of accepting a copy. Mr. Murray will have directions for sending one. I am quite honoured by your thinking me capable of drawing such a clergyman as you gave the sketch of in your note of Nov. 16th. But I assure you I am *not*. The comic part of the character I might be equal to, but not the good, the enthusiastic, the literary. Such a man's conversation must at times be on subjects of science and philosophy, of which I know nothing; or at least be occasionally abundant in quotations and allusions which a woman who, like me, knows only her own mother tongue, and has read very little in that, would be totally without the power of giving. A classical education, or at any rate a very extensive acquaintance with English literature, ancient and modern, appears to me quite indispensable for the person who would do any justice to your clergyman; and I think I may boast myself to be, with all possible vanity, the most unlearned and uninformed female who ever dared to be an authoress.

Believe me, dear Sir,

Your obliged and faithful hum^{bl} Ser^{t}.

Jane Austen

120a. *From James Stanier Clarke. Thursday* ⟨? 21⟩ *Dec.* 1815

Address: lost.
Pierpont Morgan Library. From the same collection as N⁰ 113.

Carlton House Thursday, 1815

My dear Madam

The Letter you were so obliging as to do me the Honour of sending, was forwarded to me in Kent, where in a Village, Chiddingstone near Sevenoaks, I had been hiding myself from all bustle and turmoil—and getting Spirits for a Winter Campaign—and Strength to stand the sharp knives which many a Shylock is wetting to cut more than a Pound of Flesh from my heart, on the appearance of James the Second.

On Monday I go to Lord Egremonts at Petworth—where your Praises have long been sounded as they ought to be. I shall then look in on the Party at the Pavilion for a couple of nights—and return to preach at Park Street Chapel Green St. on the Thanksgiving Day.

You were very good to send me Emma—which I have in no respect deserved. It is gone to the Prince Regent. I have read only a few Pages which I very much admired—there is so much nature—and excellent description of Character in every thing you describe.

Pray continue to write, & make all your friends send Sketches to help you—and Memoires pour servir—as the French term it. Do let us have an English Clergyman after *your* fancy—much novelty may be introduced—shew dear Madam what good would be done if Tythes were taken away entirely, and describe him burying his own mother—as I did—because the High Priest of the Parish in which she died—did not pay her remains the respect he ought to do. I have never recovered the Shock. Carry your Clergyman to Sea as the Friend of some distinguished Naval Character about a Court—you can then bring foreward like Le Sage many interesting Scenes of Character & Interest.

But forgive me, I cannot write to you without wishing to elicit your Genius ;—& I fear I cannot do that, without trespassing on your Patience and Good Nature.

I have desired Mr. Murray to procure, if he can, two little Works I ventured to publish from being at Sea—Sermons which I wrote & preached on the Ocean—& the Edition which I published of Falconers Shipwreck.

Pray, dear Madam, remember, that besides My Cell at Carlton House, I have another which Dr Barne procured for me at N^o^: 37. Golden Square—where I often hide myself. There is a small Library there much at your Service—and if you can make the Cell render you any service as a sort of Half-way House, when you come to Town—I shall be most happy. There is a Maid Servant of mine always there.

I hope to have the honour of sending you James the 2^d^ when it reaches a second Ed:—as some few Notes may possibly be then added.

Yours dear Madam, very sincerely

J. S. Clarke.

121. *To John Murray.* ⟨*Monday*⟩ 11 *Dec.* ⟨1815⟩

Address **: lost.**
Lt. Col. John Murray. One leaf 4°, the other lost.
***Memoir*[2] 122 (from a copy communicated by Mr. Murray) ; *Life* 318.**

Hans Place, Dec: 11th.

Dear Sir

As I find that *Emma* is advertized for publication as early as Saturday next, I think it best to lose no time in settling all that remains to be settled on the subject, & adopt this method of doing so, as involving the smallest tax on your time.—

In the first place, I beg you to understand that I leave the terms on which the Trade should be supplied with the work, entirely to your Judgement, entreating you to be guided in every such arrangement by your own experience of what is most likely to clear off the Edition rapidly. I shall be satisfied with whatever you feel to be best.—

The Title page must be Emma, Dedicated by Permission to H.R.H. The Prince Regent.—And it is my particular wish that one Set should be completed & sent to H.R.H. two or three days before the Work is generally public.—It should be sent under Cover to the Rev: J. S. Clarke, Librarian, Carlton House.—I shall subjoin a list of those persons, to whom I must trouble you to forward also a Set each, when the Work is out ;—all unbound, with From the Authoress, in the first page.

I return you, with very many Thanks, the Books you have so obligingly supplied me with.—I am very sensible I assure you of the attention you have paid to my Convenience & amusement. I return also

'Mansfield Park,' as ready for a 2^{d} edit: I beleive, as I can make it.—

I am in Hans Place till the 16th. From that day, inclusive, my direction will be, Chawton, Alton, Hants.

I remain dear Sir,
Y^{r} faithful Hum. Servt
J. Austen

I wish you would have the goodness to send a line by the Bearer, stating *the day* on which the set will be ready for the Prince Regent.—

122. *To John Murray.* ⟨*Monday*⟩ 11 *Dec.* ⟨1815⟩

Address : lost.
Original not traced.
Memoir[2] 124 (from a copy communicated by Mr. Murray) ; *Life* 319.

Hans Place, December 11 (1815).

Dear Sir

I am much obliged by yours, and very happy to feel everything arranged to our mutual satisfaction. As to my direction about the title-page, it was arising from my ignorance only, and from my having never noticed the proper place for a dedication. I thank you for putting me right. Any deviation from what is usually done in such cases is the last thing I should wish for. I feel happy in having a friend to save me from the ill effect of my own blunder.

Yours, dear Sir, &c.
J. Austen

122.1. *To Charles Thomas Haden. Thursday* ⟨14 *Dec.* 1815⟩. See p. 510

123a. *From the Countess of Morley.* ⟨*Wednesday*⟩ 27 *Dec.* 1815

Address : lost.
Postmark : lost.
Cambridge University Library. One leaf 8⁰.
See N⁰ 123.

Saltram 27th Decr

Madam

I have been most anxiously waiting for an introduction to Emma, & am infinitely obliged to you for your kind recollection of me, which will procure me the pleasure of her acquaintance some days sooner than I shd otherwise have had it.—I am already become intimate in the Woodhouse family, & feel that they will not amuse & interest me less than the Bennetts, Bertrams, Norriss & all their admirable predecessors. —I *can* give them no higher praise—

I am
Madam
Yr much obliged
F Morley

123. *To the Countess of Morley.* ⟨*Sunday*⟩ 31 *Dec.* 1815

No address or postmark.
Mrs. Henry Burke. One leaf 8⁰.—Cambridge University Library (1925): Copy by J. A.; Lady Morley's letter is preserved with it.
*Memoir*1 140, *Memoir*2 126; *Life* 326 (extract).

Chawton Dec: 31

Madam

Accept my Thanks for the honour of your note, & for your kind disposition in favour of Emma. In my present state of doubt as to her reception in the

World, it is particularly gratifying to me to receive so early an assurance of your Ladyship's approbation. —It encourages me to depend on the same share of general good opinion which Emma's Predecessors have experienced, & to believe that I have not yet—as almost every Writer of Fancy does sooner or later—overwritten myself.—I am Madam,

Your obliged & faith[l] Serv[t]

J. Austen

124. ⟨*To Anna Lefroy. ? Dec.* 1815⟩

No address.
R. A. Austen-Leigh. A scrap.
Memoir[1] 203, *Memoir*[2] 148. A few words unpublished. Copies of *Emma* were in circulation in December 1815. Anna Jemima Lefroy was born 20 Oct. 1815.

My dear Anna

As I wish very much to see *your* Jemima, I am sure you will like to see *my* Emma, & have therefore great pleasure in sending it for your perusal. Keep it as long as you chuse, it has been read by all here.—

125. *To Caroline Austen. Wednesday* 13 *March* ⟨1816⟩

Address: Miss C. Austen | Steventon
Postmark: none.
L. A. Austen-Leigh. 2 leaves 8[0].
Life 365 (misdated 1815). A few lines unpublished.

Chawton Wednesday March 13.

My dear Caroline

I am very glad to have an opportunity of answering your agreable little Letter. You seem to be quite my own Neice in your feelings towards M^{de} de Genlis. I do not think I could even now, at my sedate time of Life, read *Olimpe et Theophile* without being in a rage. It really is too bad !—Not allowing them to be happy together, when they *are* married.—Don't talk of it, pray. I have just lent your Aunt Frank the 1st vol. of Les Veilleès du Chateau, for Mary Jane to read. It will be some time before she comes to the horror of Olympe. We have had sad weather lately, I hope you have liked it.—Our Pond is brimfull & our roads are dirty & our walls are damp, & we sit wishing every bad day may be the last. It is not cold however. Another week perhaps may see us shrinking & shivering under a dry East Wind.

I had a very nice Letter from your Brother not long ago, & I am quite happy to see how much his Hand is improving.—I am convinced that it will end in a very gentlemanlike Hand, much above Par.—We have had a great deal of fun lately with Post-chaises stopping at the door ; three times within a few days, we had a couple of agreable Visitors turn in unexpectedly—your Uncle Henry & Mr. Tilson, Mrs Heathcote & Miss Bigg, your Uncle Henry and Mr Seymour. Take notice, that it was the same Uncle Henry each time.

I remain my dear Caroline,

Your affec: Aunt,

J. Austen

THE HALL CARLTON HOUSE.

London Pub. 1st April 1808 at R. Ackermann's Repository of Arts 101 Strand.

126a. *From James Stanier Clarke.* ⟨*Wednesday*⟩ 27 *March* 1816

Address: Miss Jane Austen | at Mr Murrays | Albemarle Street | London. *Redirected* Chawton Alton Hants. *Franked* Clarence.
Postmarks: 27 28 and 29 MR 1816
T. Edward Carpenter (1948); the wrapper, Pierpont Morgan Library (from the same collection as N° 113).
Life 322.

Pavilion: March 27, 1816.

Dear Miss Austen,

I have to return you the thanks of His Royal Highness, the Prince Regent, for the handsome copy you sent him of your last excellent novel. Pray, dear Madam, soon write again and again. Lord St. Helens and many of the nobility, who have been staying here, paid you the just tribute of their praise.

The Prince Regent has just left us for London; and having been pleased to appoint me Chaplain and Private English Secretary to the Prince of Cobourg, I remain here with His Serene Highness and a select party until the marriage. Perhaps when you again appear in print you may chuse to dedicate your volumes to Prince Leopold: any historical romance, illustrative of the history of the august House of Cobourg, would just now be very interesting.

Believe me at all times,
Dear Miss Austen,
Your obliged friend,
J. S. Clarke.

126. *To James Stanier Clarke.* ⟨*Monday*⟩ 1 *April* 1816

Address: lost.
T. Edward Carpenter (1948): copy by J. A.
Memoir[1] 156, *Memoir*[2] 116; *Life* 323.

My dear Sir

I am honoured by the Prince's thanks and very much obliged to yourself for the kind manner in which you mention the work. I have also to acknowledge a former letter forwarded to me from Hans Place. I assure you I felt very grateful for the friendly tenor of it, and hope my silence will have been considered, as it was truly meant, to proceed only from an unwillingness to tax your time with idle thanks. Under every interesting circumstance which your own talents and literary labours have placed you in, or the favour of the Regent bestowed, you have my best wishes. Your recent appointments I hope are a step to something still better. In my opinion, the service of a court can hardly be too well paid, for immense must be the sacrifice of time and feeling required by it.

You are very very kind in your hints as to the sort of composition which might recommend me at present, and I am fully sensible that an historical romance, founded on the House of Saxe Cobourg, might be much more to the purpose of profit or popularity than such pictures of domestic life in country villages as I deal in. But I could no more write a romance than an epic poem. I could not sit seriously down to write a serious romance under any other motive than to save my life; and if it were indispensable for me to keep it up and never relax into laughing at myself or other people, I am sure I should be hung before I had finished the first chapter. No, I must keep to my own style and go on in my own way; and though I may never succeed again in that, I am convinced that I should totally fail in any other.

I remain, my dear Sir,

Your very much obliged, and very sincere friend,

J. Austen

Chawton, near Alton, April 1, 1816.

127. *To John Murray.* ⟨*Monday*⟩ 1 *April* 1816

Address: lost.

Sotheby's, 24 June 1975, Lot 270 (illustrated in the sale catalogue); Mrs. D. H. Warren.

*Memoir*² 124 (from a copy communicated by Mr. Murray): *Life* 327.

Dear Sir,

I return you the Quarterly Review with many Thanks. The Authoress of *Emma* has no reason I think to complain of her treatment in it—except in the total omission of Mansfield Park.—I cannot but be sorry that so clever a Man as the Reveiwer of *Emma* should consider it as unworthy of being noticed.—You will be pleased to hear that I have received the Prince's Thanks for the *handsome* Copy I sent him of *Emma*. Whatever he may think of *my* share of the Work, *Yours* seems to have been quite right.

In consequence of the late sad Event in Henrietta S^t^ I must request that if you should at any time have anything to communicate by Letter, you will be so good as to write by the post, directing to me (Miss J. Austen) Chawton near Alton—and that for anything of a larger bulk, you will add to the same direction, by *Collier's Southampton Coach.*—

I remain, dear Sir,
Yours very faithfully
J. Austen

Chawton April 1.
1816.

128. *To Caroline Austen.* *Sunday* 21 *April* ⟨1816⟩

No address.

L. A. Austen-Leigh. Copy of the original. Another copy, by Mrs. Bellas, is in the possession of Miss Isabel Lefroy. Though apparently a complete letter, the copy seems to represent pages 1–2 only of a 4-page original. See the fragment following.

Unpublished.

Chawton Sunday April 21st

My dear Caroline

I am glad to have an opportunity of writing to you again, for my last Note was written so long before it was sent, that it seemed almost good for nothing. The note to your Papa is to announce the death of that excellent woman Miss Elizth Leigh; it came here this morning enclosed in a letter to Aunt Cassandra. We all feel that we have lost a most valued old friend; but the death of a person at her advanced age, so fit to die and by her own feelings so *ready* to die, is not to be regretted. She has been so kind as to leave a little remembrance of £20 to your Grandmama.

I have had a letter from Scarlets this morning, with a very tolerable account of health there. We have also heard from Godmersham, and the day of your Uncle and Fanny's coming is fixed; they leave home tomorrow se'night; spend two days in Town and are to be with us on Thursday May 2nd. We are to see your cousin Edward likewise, but probably not quite so soon. Your Uncle Henry talks of being in Town again on Wednesday. He will have spent a complete fortnight at Godmersham, and no doubt it will have done him good. Tell your Mama that he came back from Steventon much pleased with his visit to her. Your Grandmama is not *quite* well, she seldom gets through the 24 hours without some pain in her head, but we hope it is lessening, and that a continuance of such weather as may allow her to be out of doors and hard at work every day, will gradually remove it.

Cassy has had great pleasure in working *this*—whatever it may be—for you, I believe she rather fancied it might do for a quilt for your little wax doll, but you will find a use for it if you can I am sure. She often *talks* of you and we should all be very glad to see you again—and if your Papa comes on Wednesday, as we rather hope, and it suited everybody that you should come with him, it would give us great pleasure. Our Fair at Alton is next Saturday which is also Mary Jane's Birthday, and you would be thought an *addition* on such a great day.

Yours affec^{ly}

J. Austen

128·1. ⟨*To Caroline Austen.* *Sunday* 21 *April* 1816⟩

Address (fragmentary): Austen

L. A. Austen-Leigh. A fragment, $7\frac{3}{8} \times 4$, of a 4^{0} leaf. Endorsed 'The corresponding page dated Chawton Sunday April 21st sent to Miss Le Marchant Sep^{t} 20th 1852'. This seems to imply that the preceding letter occupied pages 1–2 of a 4-page letter, and that this fragment is a part of pp. 3–4, containing a postscript and the address.

Unpublished.

I shall say no more, because I know th⟨ere may be ?⟩ many circumstances to make it inconvenient at home.—We are almost ashamed to include your Mama in the invitation, or to ask *her* to be at the trouble of a long ride for so few days as we shall be having disengaged, for we *must* wash before the G^m Party come & therefore Monday would be last day that our House could be comfortable for her; but if she does feel disposed to pay us a little visit & you could *all* come, so much the better.—We do not like to *invite* her to come on wednesday, to be turned out of the house on Monday.

129. *To Anna Lefroy.* *Sunday* 23 *June* ⟨1816⟩

No address.
Miss Isabel Lefroy. Copy by Anna Lefroy's daughter.
***Brabourne* ii. 326.**

My dear Anna

Cassy desires her best thanks for the book. She was quite delighted to see it: I do not know when I have seen her so much struck by anybody's kindness as on this occasion. Her sensibility seems to be opening to the perception of great actions. These gloves having appeared on the Piano Forte ever since you were here on Friday, we imagine they must be yours. Mrs. Digweed returned yesterday through all the afternoon's rain and was of course wet through, but in speaking of it she never once said 'It was beyond everything,' which I am sure it must have been. Your Mama means to ride to Speen Hill tomorrow to see the Mrs. Hulberts who are both very indifferent. By all accounts they really are breaking now. Not so stout as the old Jackass.

Yours affec^ately J A

Chawton, Sunday, June 23rd. Uncle Charles's birthday.

130. *To James Edward Austen, son of James Austen.*
Tuesday 9 *July* 1816

Address: Mr Edward Austen | Steventon | By favour of | Mr W. Digweed.
No postmark.
L. A. Austen-Leigh. 2 leaves 4°.
Memoir[1] 208, *Memoir*[2] 151; *Life* 371. Part unpublished.

Chawton Tuesday July 9. 1816

My dear Edward

Many Thanks. A thank for every Line, & as many to Mr. W. Digweed for coming. We have been wanting very much to hear of your Mother, & are happy to find she continues to mend, but her illness must have been a very serious one indeed.—When she is really recovered, she ought to try change of air & come over to us.—Tell your Father I am very much obliged to him for his share of your Letter & most sincerely join in the hope of her being eventually much the better for her present Discipline. She has the comfort moreover of being confined in such weather as gives one little temptation to be out. It is really too bad, & has been too bad for a long time, much worse than anybody *can* bear, & I begin to think it will never be fine again. This is a finesse of mine, for I have often observed that if one writes about the weather, it is generally completely changed before the Letter is read. I wish it may prove so now, & that when Mr. W. Digweed reaches Steventon tomorrow, he may find you have had a long series of hot, dry weather. We are a small party at present, only G. Mama, Mary Jane & myself.—Yalden's coach cleared off the rest yesterday. I suppose it is known at Steventon that Uncle Frank & Aunt Cassandra were to go to Town on some business of Uncle Henry's—& that Aunt Martha had some business of her own which determined her to go at the same time ;—but that Aunt Frank determined to go likewise & spend a few days with her family, may not be known—nor that two other places in the Coach were taken by Capt. & Mrs Clement.—Little Cassy went also, & does not return at present. They are all going to Broadstairs again.—The Aunt Cass: & the Aunt Martha did not mean to stay beyond two whole days, but the Uncle Frank & his Wife proposed being pressed to remain till Saturday.

I am glad you recollected to mention your being come home. My heart began to sink within me when I had got so far through your Letter without its being mentioned. I was dreadfully afraid that you might be detained at Winchester by severe illness, confined to your Bed perhaps & quite unable to hold a pen, & only dating from Steventon in order, with a mistaken sort of Tenderness, to deceive me.—But now, I have no doubt of your being at home, I am sure you would not say it so seriously unless it actually were so.—We saw a countless number of Postchaises full of Boys pass by yesterday morn^g—full of future Heroes, Legislators, Fools, and Villains.—You have never thanked me for my last Letter, which went by the Cheese. I cannot bear not to be thanked. You will not pay us a visit yet of course, we must not think of it. Your Mother must get well first, & you must go to Oxford and *not* be elected ; after that, a little change of scene may be good for you, & your Physicians I hope will order you to the Sea, or to a house by the side of a very considerable pond. Oh ! it rains again ; it beats against the window.—Mary

ONE
No. 942 ALTON BANK No. 942
HANTS.
I Promise to pay the Bearer on demand
the Sum of ONE POUND here or at Messrs.
Austen, Maunde & Tilson, Bankers, London.
Value received. Alton the
10, HENRIETTA STREET
£ 1

Jane & I have been wet through once already today, we set off in the Donkey Carriage for Farringdon as I wanted to see the improvements Mr. Woolls is making, but we were obliged to turn back before we got there, but not soon enough to avoid a Pelter all the way home. We met Mr. Woolls—I talked of it's being bad weather for the Hay—& he returned me the comfort of it's being much worse for the Wheat.—We hear that Mrs. S— does not quit Tangier—why & wherefore ?—Do you know that our Browning is gone ?—You must prepare for a William when you come, a good looking Lad, civil & quiet, & seeming likely to do.—Good bye. I am sure Mr. W. D. will be astonished at my writing so much, for the Paper is so thin that he will be able to count the Lines, if not to read them.—Yours affec^{ly}

J. Austen

My dear James

We suppose the Trial is to take place this week, but we only feel sure that it cannot have taken place yet because we have heard nothing of it. A Letter from G^{m} today tells us that *Henry* as well as William K-- goes to France with his Uncle.—

Y^{rs} ever—J. A.

131. *To Caroline Austen.* *Monday* 15 *July* ⟨1816⟩

Address: Miss C. Austen | Steventon
Postmark: none.
L. A. Austen-Leigh. Two leaves 8^{0}, the signature cut away from the second leaf.
Life 364. A few words unpublished.

My dear Caroline

I have followed your directions & find your Handwriting admirable. If you continue to improve as much as you have done, perhaps I may not be obliged to shut my eyes at all half a year hence.—I have been very much entertained by your story of Carolina & her aged Father, it made me laugh heartily, & I am particularly glad to find you so much alive upon any topic of such absurdity, as the usual description of a Heroine's father.—You have done it full justice—or if anything *be* wanting, it is the information of the venerable old Man's having married when only Twenty one, & being a father at Twenty two.

I had an early opportunity of conveying your Letter to Mary Jane, having only to throw it out of window at her as she was romping with your Brother in the Back Court.—She thanks you for it—& answers your questions through me.—I am to tell you that she has passed her time at Chawton very pleasantly indeed, that she does not miss Cassy so much as she expected, & that as to Diana Temple, she is ashamed to say it has never been worked at since you went away.—She is very glad that you found Fanny again.—I suppose you had worn her in your stays without knowing it, & if she tickled you, thought it only a flea.

Edward's visit has been a great pleasure to us. He has not lost one good quality or good Look, & is only altered in being improved by being some months older than when we saw him last. He is getting very near our own age, for *we* do not grow older of course.

Chawton

Monday July 15.

132. *To Cassandra Austen.* ⟨*Wednesday*⟩ 4 *Sept.* 1816

Address : Miss Austen.
Postmark : none.
L. A. Austen-Leigh. One leaf 4°, fragmentary, containing parts of pages 3–4 of a letter. Endorsed ' Dated Chawton Sept. 4th 1816 ' and (pencil) ' For Caroline '.
Life 374. Part unpublished.

Letter today. His not writing on friday gave me some ⟨*room for* 12 *letters*⟩ coming makes me more than amends.—I know you heard from Edward yesterday, Henry wrote to me by the same post, & so did Fanny—I had therefore 3 Letters at once which I thought well worth paying for ! Yours was a treasure, so full of everything.—But how very much Cheltenham is to be preferred in May !—Henry does not write diffusely, but chearfully ;—at present he wishes to come to us as soon as we can receive him—is decided for Orders &c.—I have written to him to say that after this week, he cannot come too soon.—I do not really expect him however immediately ; they will hardly part with him at G^{m} yet.—Fanny does not seem any better, or very little ; she ventured to dine one day at Sandling & has suffered for it ever since.—I collect from her, that Mr Seymour is either married or on the point of being married to Mrs Scrane.—She is not explicit, because imagining us to be informed.—I am glad I did not know that you had no possibility of having a fire on saturday—& so glad that you have your Pelisse !—Your Bed room describes more comfortably than I could have supposed.—We go on very well here, Edward is a great pleasure to me ;—he drove me to Alton yesterday ; I went principally to carry news of you & Henry, &

made a regular handsome visit, staying there while Edwd went on to Wyards with an invitation to dinner; it was declined, & will be so again today probably, for I really beleive Anna is not equal to the fatigue.—The Alton 4 drank tea with us last night, & we were very pleasant:—Jeu de violon &c.—all new to Mr. Sweney—& he entered into it very well.—It was a renewal of former agreable evenings.—We all (except my Mother) dine at Alton tomorrow—& perhaps may have some of the same sports again—but I do not think M^r and Mrs D. will add much to our wit.—Edward is writing a Novel—we have all heard what he has written—it is extremely clever; written with great ease and spirit;—if he can carry it on in the same way, it will be a first-rate work, & in a style, I think, to be popular.—Pray tell Mary how much I admire it.—And tell Caroline that I think it is hardly fair upon her & myself, to have him take up the Novel Line, . . . but the coldness of the weather is enough to account for their want of power.—The Duchess of Orleans, the paper says, drinks at my Pump. Your Library will be a great resource.—Three Guineas a week for such Lodgings!—I am quite angry.—Martha desires her Love—& is sorry to tell you that she has got some Chilblains on her fingers—she never had them before.—This is to go for a Letter.—

Y^rs affcc^ly

J. Austen

I shall be perfectly satisfied if I hear from you again on Tuesday.

133. *To Cassandra Austen. Sunday* 8 *Sept.* ⟨1816⟩

Address: Miss Austen | Post Office | Cheltenham
Postmarks: ALTON and 10 SE (year illegible)
Pierpont Morgan Library. 2 leaves 4⁰.
Brabourne ii. 262; *Life* 375 (extracts).

Chawton, Sunday Sept: 8.

My dearest Cassandra

I have borne the arrival of your Letter today extremely well; anybody might have thought it was giving me pleasure.—I am very glad you find so much to be satisfied with at Cheltenham. While the Waters agree, everything else is trifling.—A Letter arrived for you from Charles last Thursday. They are all safe, & pretty well in Keppel S[t], the children decidedly better for Broadstairs, & he writes principally to ask when it will be convenient to us to receive Miss P.—the little girls & himself.—They w[d] be ready to set off in ten days from the time of his writing, to pay their visits in Hampshire & Berkshire—& he would prefer coming to Chawton *first.* I have answered him & said, that we hoped it might suit them to wait till the *last* week in Sept[r], as we could not ask them sooner, either on your account, or the want of room. I mentioned the 23[d], as the probable day of your return.—When you have once left Cheltenham, I shall grudge every half day wasted on the road. If there were but a coach from Hungerford to Chawton!—I have desired him to let me hear again soon.—He does not include a Maid in the list to be accomodated, but if they bring one, as I suppose they will, we shall have no bed in the house even then for Charles himself—let alone Henry—. But what can we do?—We shall have the G[t] House quite at our command;—it is to be cleared of the Papillons' Servants in a day or two;—they themselves have been hurried off into Essex to take possession—not of a large Estate left them by an Uncle—but to scrape together all they can I suppose of the effects of a Mrs. Rawstorn a rich old friend & cousin, suddenly deceased, to whom they are joint Executors. So, there is a happy end of the Kentish Papillons coming here.

No morning service today, wherefore I am writing between 12 & 1 o'clock.—Mr. Benn in the afternoon—& likewise more rain again, by the look & the sound of things. You left us in doubt of Mrs. Benn's situation, but she has bespoke her Nurse.—Mrs. F. A. seldom either looks or appears quite well.—Little Embryo is troublesome I suppose.—They dined with us yesterday, & had fine weather both for coming & going home, which has hardly ever happened to them before.—She is still unprovided with a Housemaid.—Our day at Alton was very pleasant—Venison quite right—Children well-behaved—& Mr. & Mrs. Digweed taking kindly to our Charades, & other Games.—I must also observe, for his Mother's satisfaction, that Edward at my suggestion, devoted himself very properly to the entertainment of Miss S. Gibson.—Nothing was wanting except Mr. Sweney; but he alas! had been ordered away to London the day before.—We had a beautiful walk home by Moonlight.—Thank you, my Back has given me scarcely any pain for many days.—I have an idea that agitation does it as much harm as fatigue, & that I was ill at the time of your going, from the very circumstance of your going.—I am nursing myself up now into as beautiful a state as I can, because I hear that Dr.

White means to call on me before he leaves the Country.—*Even^g^*.—Frank & Mary & the Child[n] visited us this morn[g].—Mr. & Mrs. Gibson are to come on the 23[d]—& there is too much reason to fear they will stay above a week.—Little George could tell me where you were gone to, as well as what you were to bring him, when I asked him the other day.—Sir Tho: Miller is dead. I treat you with a dead Baronet in almost every Letter.—So, you have C. Craven among you, as well as the Duke of Orleans & Mr. Pococke. But it mortifies me that *you* have not added one to the stock of common acquaintance. Do pray meet with somebody belonging to yourself.—I am quite weary of your knowing nobody.—

Mrs. Digweed parts with both Hannah and old Cook, the former will not give up her Lover, who is a man of bad Character, the Latter is guilty only of being unequal to anything.—Miss Terry was to have spent this week with her Sister, but as usual it is put off. My amiable friend knows the value of her company.—I have not seen Anna since the day you left us, her Father & Brother visited her most days.—Edward & Ben called here on Thursday. Edward was in his way to Selborne. We found him very agreable. He is come back from France, thinking of the French as one could wish, disappointed in everything. He did not go beyond Paris.—I have a letter from Mrs. Perigord, she & her Mother are in London again;—she speaks of France as a scene of general Poverty & Misery,—no Money, no Trade—nothing to be got but by the Innkeepers—& as to her own present prospects, she is not much less melancholy than before.—I have also a letter from Miss Sharp, quite one of her Letters;

R

—she has been again obliged to exert herself—more than ever—in a more distressing, more harrassed state—& has met with another excellent old Physician & his wife, with every virtue under Heaven, who takes to her & cures her from pure Love & Benevolence.—Dr. & Mrs. Storer are *their* Mrs. & Miss Palmer—for they are at Bridlington. I am happy to say however that the sum of the account is better than usual. Sir William is returned; from Bridlington they go to Chevet, & she *is* to have a Young Governess under her.—I enjoyed Edward's company very much, as I said before, & yet I was not sorry when friday came. It had been a busy week, & I wanted a few days quiet, & exemption from the Thought & contrivances which any sort of company gives.—I often wonder how *you* can find time for what you do, in addition to the care of the House;—and how good Mrs. West c^d^ have written such Books & collected so many hard words, with all her family cares, is still more a matter of astonishment! Composition seems to me Impossible, with a head full of Joints of Mutton & doses of rhubarb.—*Monday.* Here is a sad morn^g^.—I fear you may not have been able to get to the Pump. The two last days were very pleasant.—I enjoyed them the more for your sake.—But today, it is really bad enough to make you all cross.—I hope Mary will change her Lodgings at the fortnight's end; I am sure, if you looked about well, you would find others in some odd corner, to suit you better. Mrs. Potter charges for the *name* of the High S^t^.—Success to the Pianoforte! I trust it will drive you away.—We hear now that there is to be *no Honey* this year. Bad news for us.—We must husband our present stock of Mead;

—& I am sorry to perceive that our 20 Gal: is very nearly out.—I cannot comprehend how the 14 Gal: c[d] last so long.—

We do not much like Mr. Cooper's new Sermons;—they are fuller of Regeneration & Conversion than ever—with the addition of his zeal in the cause of the Bible Society.—Martha's love to Mary & Caroline, & she is extremely glad to find they like the Pelisse.—The Debarys are indeed odious!—We are to see my Brother tomorrow, but for only one night.—I had no idea that he would care for the Races, *without* Edward.—Remember me to all.

Yours very affec:[ly]
J. Austen

134. *To J. Edward Austen. Monday* 16 *Dec.* ⟨1816⟩

Address: James Edward Austen Esq[re] | Steventon
Postmark: none.
L. A. Austen-Leigh. 2 leaves 4°.
Biographical Notice in *Northanger Abbey* 1818 (extract); *Memoir*[1] 212, *Memoir*[2] 153; *Life* 377.

Chawton, Monday Dec: 16.

My dear Edward

One reason for my writing to you now, is that I may have the pleasure of directing to you *Esq[re]*.—I give you Joy of having left Winchester.—Now you may own, how miserable you were there; now, it will gradually all come out—your Crimes & your Miseries—how often you went up by the Mail to London & threw away Fifty Guineas at a Tavern, & how often you were on the point of hanging yourself—restrained only, as some illnatured aspersion upon poor old

Winton has it, by the want of a Tree within some miles of the City.—Charles Knight & his companions passed through Chawton about 9 this morning; later than it used to be. Uncle Henry and I had a glimpse of his handsome face, looking all health & good-humour.—

I wonder when you will come & see us. I know what I rather speculate upon, but I shall say nothing.—We think Uncle Henry in excellent Looks. Look at him this moment & think so too, if you have not done it before; & we have the great comfort of seeing decided improvement in Uncle Charles, both as to Health, Spirits & Appearance.—And they are each of them so agreable in their different way, & harmonize so well, that their visit is thorough enjoyment.—Uncle Henry writes very superior Sermons.—You and I must try to get hold of one or two, & put them into our Novels;—it would be a fine help to a volume; & we could make our Heroine read it aloud of a Sunday Evening, just as well as Isabella Wardour in the Antiquary, is made to read the History of the Hartz Demon in the ruins of St. Ruth—though I beleive, upon recollection, Lovell is the Reader.—By the bye, my dear Edward, I am quite concerned for the loss your Mother mentions in her Letter; two Chapters & a half to be missing is monstrous! It is well that *I* have not been at Steventon lately, & therefore cannot be suspected of purloining them;—two strong twigs & a half towards a Nest of my own, would have been something.—I do not think however that any theft of that sort would be really very useful to me. What should I do with your strong, manly, spirited Sketches, full of Variety and

Glow ?—How could I possibly join them on to the little bit (two Inches wide) of Ivory on which I work with so fine a Brush, as produces little effect after much labour ?

You will hear from uncle Henry how well Anna is. She seems perfectly recovered.—Ben was here on Saturday, to ask Uncle Charles & me to dine with them, as tomorrow, but I was forced to decline it, the walk is beyond my strength (though I am otherwise very well) & this is not a Season for Donkey Carriages ; & as we do not like to spare Uncle Charles, he has declined it too.—

Tuesday.—Ah, ha !—Mr Edward, I doubt your seeing Uncle Henry at Steventon today. The weather will prevent your expecting him I think.—Tell your Father, with Aunt Cass:'s Love & mine, that the Pickled Cucumbers are extremely good, & tell him also—' tell him what you will ' ; No, do'nt tell him what you will, but tell him that Grandmama begs him to make Joseph Hall pay his Rent if he can. You must not be tired of reading the word *Uncle*, for I have not done with it. Uncle Charles thanks your Mother for her Letter ; it was a great pleasure to him to know the parcel was received & gave so much satisfaction ; & he begs her to be so good as to give *Three Shillings* for him to Da⟨me⟩ Staples, which shall be allowed for in the payment of her debt here.—

I am happy to tell you that Mr. Papillon will soon make his offer, probably next Monday, as he returns on Saturday.—His *intention* can be no longer doubtful in the smallest degree, as he has secured the refusal of the House which Mrs Baverstock at present occupies in Chawton & is to vacate soon, which is of course intended for M[rs] Eliz[th] Papillon.—

Adeiu Amiable!—I hope Caroline behaves well to you.

Yours affec[ly]
J. Austen

135. *To Anna Lefroy. Thursday ⟨late in* 1816⟩

No address or postmark.
Miss Isabel Lefroy. Copy by Anna Lefroy (on paper with watermark dated 1854), who adds: 'This note was written the winter of 1816 & the original is in the possession of W. Chambers Lefroy the grandson of the Receiver.'
Unpublished.

My dear Anna

Your Grandmama is *very* much obliged to you for the Turkey, but cannot help grieving that you should not keep it for yourselves. Such Highmindedness is almost more than she can bear.—She will be very glad of better weather that she may see you again & so we shall all.

Yours affec[ately]

Thursday.   J. Austen

136. *To Cassandra, daughter of Charles Austen.* ⟨*Wednesday*⟩ 8 *Jan.* 1817

Address: Capt. C. J. Austen R.N. | 22 Keppel Street | Russel Square | London
Postmarks: ALTON and 9 JA 1817
Pierpont Morgan Library (1925). Formerly in the collection described in *Times Literary Supplement* 14 Jan. 1926. One leaf 4°.
Brabourne ii. 327.

Ym raed Yssac

I hsiw uoy a yppah wen raey. Ruoy xis snisuoc emac ereh yadretsey, dna dah hcae a eceip fo ekac.

Siht si elttil Yssac's yadhtrib, dna ehs si eerht sraey dlo. Knarf sah nugeb gninrael Nital. Ew deef eht Nibor yreve gninrom.—Yllas netfo seriuqne retfa uoy. Yllas Mahneb sah tog a wen neerg nwog. Teirrah Thgink semoc yreve yad ot daer ot Tnua Ardnassac.—Doog eyb ym raed Yssac.—Tnua Ardnassac sdnes reh tseb evol, dna os ew od lla.

Ruoy Etanoitceffa Tnua

Notwahc, Naj. 8. Enai Netsua

137. *To Caroline Austen.* *Thursday* 23 *Jan.* 1817

Address: Miss Caroline Austen
Postmark: none.
L. A. Austen-Leigh. Two leaves 4^0, a small piece cut away from the second leaf.
Memoir[2] 160 (short extract); *Life* 366. A large part unpublished.

Chawton Thursday Jan: 23. 1817—

My dear Caroline

I am always very much obliged to you for writing to me, & have now I beleive two or three Notes to thank you for; but whatever may be their Number, I mean to have this Letter accepted as a handsome return for all, for you see I have taken a complete, whole sheet of Paper, which is to entitle me to consider it as a very long Letter whether I write much or little.—We were quite happy to see Edward, it was an unexpected pleasure, & he makes himself as agreable as ever, sitting in such a quiet comfortable way making his delightful little Sketches.—He is generally thought grown since he was here last, & rather Thinner, but in very good Looks.—We have used Anna as ill as we could, by not letting him leave us before tomorrow morning, but it is a Vile World, we are all for Self & I expected no better from any of us.—But though *Better* is not to be expected, *Butter* may, at least from Mrs Clement's Cow, for she has sold her Calf.—Edward will tell you of the Grand Evening Party he has come in for. We were proud to have a young Man to accompany us, & he acquitted himself to admiration in every particular except selling his Deals at Vingt-un.—He read his two Chapters to us the first Evening;—both good—but especially the last in our opinion. We think it has more of the Spirit & Entertainment of the early part of his Work, the first 3 or 4 Chapters, than some of the subsequent.—Mr Reeves is charming—& Mr Mountain—& Mr Fairfax—& all their day's sport.—And the introduction of Emma Gordon is very amusing.—I certainly *do* altogether like this set of People better than those at Culver Court.

Your Anne is dreadful. But nothing offends me so much as the absurdity of not being able to pronounce the word *Shift*. I could forgive her any follies in English, rather than the Mock Modesty of that french word. She should not only place her Quilt in the Centre, but give it's Latitude & Longitude, & measure its Dimensions by a Lunar Observation if she chose.—Cook & Sally seem very properly pleased by your remembrance, & desire their Duty & Thanks. Sally has got a new red Cloak, which adds much to her happiness, in other respects she is unaltered, as civil & well meaning & talkative as ever.—Only think of your lost Dormouse being brought back to you!—I was quite astonished.—No time is fixed for Cassy's return, but *March* has always been her month hitherto for coming down. Aunt Cass:—had a letter from her very lately, extremely well written in a large hand, but as you may suppose containing little beyond her hope of every body's being well at Chawton, & Harriet & Fanny's love. Uncle Charles, I am sorry to say, has been suffering from Rheumatism, & now he has got a great eruption in his face & neck—which is to do him good however—but he has a sad turn for being unwell.—*I* feel myself getting stronger than I was half a year ago, & can so perfectly well walk to Alton, *or* back again, without the slightest fatigue that I hope to be able to do both when Summer comes. —I spent two or three days with your Uncle & Aunt lately, & though the Children are sometimes very noisy & not under such Order as they ought & easily might, I cannot help liking them & even loving them, which I hope may be not wholly inexcusable in their & ⟨your affectionate Aunt,

J. Austen⟩

The Piano Forté often talks of you ;—in various keys, tunes, & expressions I allow—but be it Lesson or Country Dance, Sonata or Waltz, *you* are really it's constant Theme. I wish you c[d] come and see us, as easily as Edward can.

138. *To Caroline Austen.* *Wednesday* ⟨1817⟩

Address : Miss Caroline Austen.
Postmark : none.
L. A. Austen-Leigh. 2 leaves 8⁰.
Life 367. Part unpublished.

You send me great News indeed my dear Caroline, about M[r] Digweed M[r] Trimmer, & a Grand Piano Forte. I wish it had been a small one, as then you might have pretended that Mr D.'s rooms were toc damp to be fit for it, & offered to take charge of it at the Parsonage.—I am sorry to hear of Caroline Wiggetts being so ill. Mrs Chute I suppose would almost feel like a Mother in losing her.—We have but a poor account of your Uncle Charles 2d Girl; there is an idea now of her having Water in her head. The others are well.—William was mistaken when he told your Mama we did not mean to mourn for Mrs Motley Austen. Living here we thought it necessary to array ourselves in our old Black Gowns, because there is a line of Connection with the family through the Prowtings & Harrisons of Southampton.—I look forward to the 4 new Chapters with pleasure.—But how can you like Frederick better than Edgar—You have some eccentric Tastes however I know, as to Heroes & Heroines.—Good bye.

Yrs affecly

Wed: Night. J. Austen

139. *To Alethea Bigg.* ⟨*Friday*⟩ 24 *Jan.* 1817

Address: Miss Bigg—The Revnd Herbert Hill's, Streatham, London.
Original not traced. Copy by R. A. Austen-Leigh of a copy made by Mary Augusta Austen-Leigh.
*Memoir*2 158 (extracts); *Life* 379 (extracts). Part unpublished.

Chawton Jany 24—1817

My dear Alethea

I think it time there should be a little writing between us, though I believe the epistolary debt is on *your* side, and I hope this will find all the Streatham party well, neither carried away by the flood, nor rheumatic through the damps. Such mild weather is, you know, delightful to *us*, and though we have a great many ponds, and a fine running stream through the meadows on the other side of the road, it is nothing but what beautifies us and does to talk of. We are all in good health & *I* have certainly gained strength through the winter and am not far from being well; and I think I understand my own case now so much better than I did, as to be able by care to keep off any serious return of illness. I am more & more convinced that *bile* is at the bottom of all I have suffered, which makes it easy to know how to treat myself. You will be glad to hear thus much of me, I am sure as I shall in return be very glad to hear that your health has been good lately. We have just had a few days' visit from Edward, who brought us a good account of his father, and the very circumstance of his coming at all, of his father's being able to spare him, is itself a good account. He is gone to spend this day at Wyards & goes home to-morrow. He grows still, and still improves in appearance, at least in the estimation of his aunts, who love him better and better, as they see the sweet temper and warm affections of the boy confirmed in the young man: I tried hard to persuade him that he must have some message for William, but in vain. Anna has not been so well or so strong or looking so much like herself since her marriage as she is now; she is quite equal to walking to Chawton, & comes over to us when she can, but the rain & dirt divide us a good deal. Her grandmama she can only see at Chawton as this is not a time of year for donkey-carriages, and our donkeys arc necessarily having so long a run of luxurious idleness that I suppose we shall find they have forgotten much of their education when we use them again. We do not use two at once however; don't imagine such excesses. Anna's eldest child just now runs alone, which is a great convenience with a second in arms, & they are both healthy nice children—I wish their Father were ordained & all the family settled in a comfortable Parsonage house. The Curacy only is wanting I fancy to complete the business. Our own new clergyman is expected here very soon, perhaps in time to assist Mr. Papillon on Sunday. I shall be very glad when the first hearing is over. It will be a nervous hour for our pew, though we hear that he acquits himself with as much ease and collectedness, as if he had been used to it all his life. We have no chance we know of seeing you between Streatham and Winchester: you go the other road and are engaged to two or three houses; if there should be any change, however, you know how welcome you would be. Edward mentioned one circumstance concerning you my dear Alethea, which I must confess has given me considerable astonishment & some alarm—your having left your best gown at Steventon. Surely if you do not want it at Streatham, you will be spending a few days with Mrs G. Frere, & must want it there. I would lay any wager that you have been sorry you left it. We have been reading the 'Poet's Pilgrimage to Waterloo,' and generally with much approbation. Nothing will please all the world, you know; but parts of it suit me better than much that he has written before. The opening—*the proem* I believe he calls it—is very beautiful. Poor man! one cannot but grieve for the loss of the son so fondly described. Has he at all recovered it? What do Mr. and Mrs.

Hill know about his present state ? I hear from more than one quarter that Miss Williams is really better, & I am very glad, especially as Charlotte's being better also must I think be the consequence of it. I hope your letters from abroad are satisfactory. They would not be satisfactory to *me*, I confess, unless they breathed a strong spirit of regret for not being in England. Kind love & good wishes for a happy New Year to you all, from all our four here. Give our love to the little Boys, if they can be persuaded to remember us. *We* have not at all forgot Herbert's & Errol's fine countenances. Georgiana is very pretty I daresay. How does Edward like school ? —I suppose his holidays are now over yet.[1]

Yours affec^{ly}

J. Austen

The real object of this letter is to ask you for a receipt, but I thought it genteel not to let it appear early. We remember some excellent orange wine at Manydown, made from Seville oranges, entirely or chiefly & should be very much obliged to you for the receipt, if you can command it within a few weeks.

[1] *Sic* in the copy.

140. *To Fanny Knight. Thursday* 20 *Feb.* ⟨1817⟩

Address: Miss Knight | Godmersham Park | Faversham | Kent
Postmarks: ALTON and 22 (month and year illegible)
Lord Brabourne. 2 leaves 4^{0}. Endorsed '3 Feb. 20 1816'; but see *Life* 347 note. The date 1816 is moreover inconsistent with the days of the week and month given for this letter and the two which follow. This letter is dated 20 Feb., and was begun on Thursday (for the later part dated Friday refers to the earlier part as written 'yesterday'). 20 Feb. was a Thursday in 1817.
Facsimile in *Five Letters from Jane Austen to Fanny Knight*, Oxford 1924.
Brabourne ii. 290; *Life* 348, 383 (extracts). Several sentences or parts of sentences unpublished; and Lord Brabourne disguised some names.

Chawton Feb: 20

My dearest Fanny,

You are inimitable, irresistable. You are the delight of my Life. Such Letters, such entertaining Letters as you have lately sent!—Such a description of your queer little heart!—Such a lovely display of what Imagination does.—You are worth your weight in Gold, or even in the new Silver Coinage.—I cannot express to you what I have felt in reading your history of yourself, how full of Pity & Concern & Admiration & Amusement I have been. You are the Paragon of all that is Silly & Sensible, common-place & eccentric, Sad & Lively, Provoking & Interesting.—Who can keep pace with the fluctuations of your Fancy, the Capprizios of your Taste, the Contradictions of your Feelings?—You are so odd!—& all the time, so perfectly natural—so peculiar in yourself, & yet so like everybody else!—It is very, very gratifying to me to know you so intimately. You can hardly think what a pleasure it is to me, to have such thorough pictures of your Heart.—Oh! what a loss it will be when you are married. You are too agreable in your single state, too agreable as a Neice. I shall hate you when your delicious play of Mind is all settled down into conjugal & maternal affections.

Mr. J. W. frightens me.—He will have you.—I see you at the Altar.—I have *some* faith in Mrs. C. Cage's observation, & still more in Lizzy's ; & besides, I know it *must* be so. He must be wishing to attach you. It would be too stupid & too shameful in him, to be otherwise ; & all the Family are seeking your acquaintance.—Do not imagine that I have any real objection, I have rather taken a fancy to him than not, & I like Chilham Castle for you ;—I only do not like you sh[d] marry anybody. And yet I do wish you to marry very much, because I know you will never be happy till you are ; but the loss of a Fanny Knight will be never made up to me ; My 'affec: Neice F. C. Wildman' will be but a poor Substitute. I do not like your being nervous & so apt to cry :—it is a sign you are not quite well, but I hope Mr. Scud—as you always write his name, (your Mr. *Scuds:* amuse me very much) will do you good.—What a comfort that Cassandra should be so recovered !—It is more than we had expected.—I can easily beleive she was very patient & very good. I always loved Cassandra, for her fine dark eyes & sweet temper.—I am almost entirely cured of my rheumatism ; just a little pain in my knee now and then, to make me remember what it was, & keep on flannel.—Aunt Cassandra nursed me so beautifully !—I enjoy your visit to Goodnestone, it must be a great pleasure to you, You have not seen Fanny Cage in any comfort so long. I hope she represents & remonstrates & reasons with you, properly. Why should you be living in dread of his marrying somebody else ?—(Yet, how natural !)—You did not chuse to have him yourself; why not allow him to take comfort where he can ?—In your conscience you *know* that he could not bear a comparison with a more animated Character.—You cannot forget how you felt under the idea of it's having been possible that he might have dined in Hans Place.—My dearest Fanny, I cannot bear you should be unhappy about him. Think of his Principles, think of his Father's objection, of want of Money, of a coarse Mother, of Brothers & Sisters like Horses, of sheets sewn across &c.—But I am doing no good—no, all that I urge against him will rather make you take his part more, sweet perverse Fanny.—And now I will tell you that we like your Henry to the utmost, to the very top of the Glass, quite brimful.—He is a very pleasing young Man. I do not see how he could be mended. He does really bid fair to be everything his Father and Sister could wish; and William I love very much indeed, & so we do all, he is quite our own William. In short we are very comfortable together—that is, we can answer for *ourselves*.—Mrs. Deedes is as welcome as May, to all our Benevolence to her Son; we only lamented that we c[d] not do more, & that the £50 note we slipt into his hand at parting was necessarily the Limit of our Offering.—Good Mrs. Deedes !—I hope she will get the better of this Marianne, & then I w[d] recommend to her & Mr. D. the simple regimen of separate rooms.—Scandal & Gossip;—yes I dare say you are well stocked; but I am very fond of Mrs. C. Cage, for reasons good. Thank you for mentioning her praise of Emma &c.—I have contributed the marking to

Uncle H.'s shirts, & now they are a complete memorial of the tender regard of many.—

Friday.—I had no idea when I began this yesterday, of sending it before your B^{r} went back, but I have written away my foolish thoughts at such a rate that I will not keep them many hours longer to stare me in the face.—Much obliged for the *Quadrilles*, which I am grown to think pretty enough, though of course they are very inferior to the Cotillions of my own day.—Ben & Anna walked here last Sunday to hear Uncle Henry, & she looked so pretty, it was quite a pleasure to see her, so young & so blooming & so innocent, as if she had never had a wicked Thought in her Life—which yet one has some reason to suppose she must have had, if we believe the Doctrine of original Sin, or if we remember the events of her girlish days.—

I hope Lizzy will have her Play. Very kindly arranged for her. Henry is generally thought very good-looking, but not so handsome as Edward.—I think *I* prefer his face.—Wm. is in excellent Looks, has a fine appetite & seems perfectly well. You will have a great Break-up at G^{m} in the Spring, You *must* feel their all going. It is very right however. One sees many good causes for it.—Poor Miss C.—I shall pity her, when she begins to understand herself.—Your objection to the Quadrilles delighted me exceedingly.—Pretty well, for a Lady irrecoverably attached to *one* Person !—Sweet Fanny, beleive no such thing of yourself.—Spread no such malicious slander upon your Understanding, within the Precincts of your Imagination.—Do not speak ill of your Sense, merely for the Gratification of your Fancy.—Yours is Sense, which deserves more honourable Treatment.—You are *not* in love with him. You never have been really in love with him.—Y[rs] very affec[ly]

J. Austen

Uncle H. & Miss Lloyd dine at Mr. Digweed's today, which leaves us the power of asking Uncle & Aunt F.—to come & meet their Nephews here.

141. *To Fanny Knight. Thursday* 13 *March* ⟨1817⟩

Address (fragment): ⟨Miss Knig⟩ht | ⟨Godmers⟩ham Park
Postmark: none.

Lord Brabourne. This letter consists of two distinct pieces, which are preserved together: (1) 2 leaves 4°, ending *an occupation & a comfort to him*; endorsed 'N° 4 March 13'; (2) a half leaf (the rest torn off) containing the remainder of the letter and the fragment of the address; endorsed '2'. The first paragraph of the letter shows that it did not go through the post, and that explains Miss Austen's allowing herself a second sheet. Facsimile in *Five Letters from Jane Austen to Fanny Knight*, Oxford 1924.

Brabourne ii. 295; *Life* 351, 383 (extracts). Lord Brabourne omitted large parts of the first sheet and (doubtless by inadvertence, or because it was mislaid) the whole of the second.

Chawton, Thursday March 13.

As to making any adequate return for such a Letter as yours my dearest Fanny, it is absolutely impossible; if I were to labour at it all the rest of my Life & live to the age of Methuselah, I could never accomplish anything so long & so perfect; but I cannot let William go without a few Lines of acknowledgement & reply. I have pretty well done with Mr. Wildman. By your description he *cannot* be in love with you, however he may try at it, & I could not wish the match unless there were a great deal of Love on his side. I do not know what to do about Jemima Branfill. What does her dancing away with so much spirit, mean ? that she does not care for him, or only wishes to *appear* not to care for him ?—Who can understand a young Lady ?—Poor Mrs. C. Milles, that she should die on a wrong day at last, after being about it so long !—It was unlucky that the Goodnestone Party could not meet you, & I hope her friendly, obliging, social Spirit, which delighted in drawing People together, was not conscious of the division and disappointment she was occasioning. I am sorry & surprised that you speak of her as having little to leave, & must feel for Miss Milles, though she *is* Molly, if a material loss of Income is to attend her other loss.—Single Women have a dreadful propensity for being poor—which is one very strong argument in favour of Matrimony, but I need not dwell on such arguments with *you*, pretty Dear, you do not want inclination.—Well, I shall say, as I have often said before, Do not be in a hurry ; depend upon it, the right Man will come at last ; you will in the course of the next two or three years, meet with somebody more generally unexceptionable than anyone you have yet known, who will love you as warmly as ever *He* did, and who will so completely attach you, that you will feel you never really loved before.—And then, by not beginning the business of Mothering quite so early in life, you will be young in Constitution, spirits, figure & countenance, while Mrs Wm Hammond is growing old by confinements & nursing. Do none of the Plumtres ever come to Balls now ?—You have never mentioned them as being at any ?—And what do you hear of the Gipps or of Fanny and her Husband ?—Mrs F. A. is to be confined the middle of April, & is by no means remarkably Large for *her*.—Aunt Cassandra walked to Wyards yesterday with Mrs. Digweed. Anna has had a bad cold, looks pale, & we fear something else. She has just weaned Julia.—How soon, the difference of temper in Children appears!—Jemima has a very irritable bad Temper (her Mother says so)—and Julia a very sweet one, always pleased & happy.—I hope as Anna is so early sensible of it's defects, that she will give Jemima's disposition the early & steady attention it must require.—*I* have also heard lately from your Aunt Harriot, & cannot understand their plans in parting with Miss S—whom she seems very much to value, now that Harriot & Eleanor are both of an age for a Governess to be so useful to;—especially as when Caroline was sent to School some years, *Miss Bell* was still retained, though the others were then mere Nursery Children.—They have some good reason I dare say, though I cannot penetrate it, & till I know what it is I shall invent a bad one, and amuse myself with accounting for the difference of measures by supposing Miss S. to be a superior sort of Woman, who has never stooped to recommend herself to the Master of the family by Flattery, as Miss Bell did.—I *will* answer your kind questions more than you expect. Miss Catherine is put upon the Shelve for the present, and I do not know that she will ever come out;—but I have a something ready for Publication, which may perhaps appear about a twelvemonth hence. It is short, about the length of Catherine.—This is for yourself alone. Neither Mr. Salusbury nor Mr. Wildman are to know of it.

I am got tolerably well again, quite equal to walking about & enjoying the Air; and by sitting down & resting a good while between my Walks, I get exercise enough. I have a scheme however for accomplishing more, as the weather grows springlike. I mean to take to riding the Donkey. It will be more independant & less troublesome than the use of the carriage, & I shall be able to go about with A[t] Cassandra in her walks to Alton and Wyards.—I hope you will think Wm. looking well. He was bilious the other day, and Aunt Cass: supplied him with a Dose at his own request, which seemed to have good effect.—I was sure *you* would have approved it. Wm. & I are the best of friends. I love him very much. Everything is so *natural* about him, his affections, his Manners & his Drollery. He entertains & interests us extremely. —Max: Hammond and A. M. Shaw are people whom I cannot care for, in themselves, but I enter into their situation & am glad they are so happy.—If I were the Duchess of Richmond, I should be very miserable about my son's choice. What can be expected from a Paget, born & brought up in the centre of conjugal Infidelity & Divorces ?—I will *not* be interested about Lady Caroline. I abhor all the race of Pagets.— Our fears increase for poor little Harriet ; the latest account is that Sir Ev: Home is confirmed in his opinion of there being water on the brain.—I hope Heaven in its mercy will take her soon. Her poor Father will be quite worn out by his feelings for her.— He cannot spare Cassy at present, she is an occupation & a comfort to him.

Adieu my dearest Fanny. Nothing could be more delicious than your Letter ; & the assurance of your feeling releived by writing it, made the pleasure perfect.—But how could it possibly be any new idea to you that you have a great deal of Imagination ?—

You are all over Imagination.—The most astonishing part of your Character is, that with so much Imagination, so much flight of Mind, such unbounded Fancies, you should have such excellent Judgement in what you do!—Religious Principle I fancy must explain it.-- Well, good bye & God bless you.

Yrs very affecly

J. Austen

141.1 *To Caroline Austen. ⟨Friday⟩* 14 *March* ⟨1817⟩. See p. 511

142. *To Fanny Knight. Sunday* 23 *March* ⟨1817⟩

Address: Miss Knight | Godmersham Park | Canterbury
Postmark: 25 M (the rest illegible)
Lord Brabourne. 2 leaves 4⁰. Endorsed '5 March 23 1816'; but in 1816 March 23 was not a Sunday. Facsimile in *Five Letters from Jane Austen to Fanny Knight*, Oxford 1924.
Brabourne ii. 299; *Life* 352, 383 (extracts). A few lines unpublished.

Chawton, Sunday March 23.

I am very much obliged to you my dearest Fanny for sending me Mr. Wildman's conversation, I had great amusement in reading it, & I *hope* I am not affronted & do not think the worse of him for having a Brain so very different from mine, but my strongest sensation of all is *astonishment* at your being able to press him on the subject so perseveringly—and I agree with your Papa, that it was not fair. When he knows the truth he will be uncomfortable.—You are the oddest Creature!—Nervous enough in some respects, but in others perfectly without nerves!—Quite unrepulsible, hardened & impudent. Do not oblige him to read any more.—Have mercy on him, tell him the truth & make him an apology. He & I should not in the least agree of course, in our ideas of Novels and Heroines;—pictures of perfection as you know make me sick & wicked—but there is some very good sense in what he says, & I particularly respect him for wishing to think well of all young Ladies; it shews an amiable & a delicate Mind.—And he deserves better treatment than to be obliged to read any more of my Works.—Do not be surprised at finding Uncle Henry acquainted with my having another ready for publication. I could not say No when he asked me, but he knows nothing more of it.—You will not like it, so you need not be impatient. You may *perhaps* like the Heroine, as she is almost too good for me.—Many thanks for your kind care for my health; I certainly have not been well for many weeks, and about a week ago I was very poorly, I have had a good deal of fever at times & indifferent nights, but am considerably better now, & recovering my Looks a little, which have been bad enough, black & white & every wrong colour. I must not depend upon being ever very blooming again. Sickness is a dangerous Indulgence at my time of Life. Thank you for everything you tell me;—I do not feel worthy of it by anything I can say in return, but I assure you my pleasure in your Letters is quite as great as ever, & I am interested & amused just as you could wish me. If there is a *Miss* Marsden, I perceive whom she will marry.

*Even^g^*.—I was languid & dull & very bad company when I wrote the above; I am better now—to my own feelings at least—& wish I may be more agreable. We are going to have Rain, & after that, very pleasant genial weather, which will exactly do for me, as my Saddle will then be completed—and air & exercise is what I want. Indeed I shall be very glad when the event at Scarlets is over, the expectation of it keeps us in a worry, your Grandmama especially; she sits brooding over Evils which cannot be remedied & Conduct impossible to be understood.—Now, the reports from Keppel St. are rather better; little Harriet's headaches are abated, & Sir Ev^d: is satisfied with the effect of the Mercury, & does not despair of a Cure. The Complaint I find is not considered Incurable nowadays, provided the Patient be young enough not to have the Head hardened. The Water in that case may be drawn off by Mercury. But though this is a new idea to us, perhaps it may have been long familiar to you, through your friend Mr. Scud:—I hope his high renown is maintained by driving away William's cough. Tell William that Triggs is as beautiful & condescending as ever, & was so good as to dine with us today, & tell him that I often play at *Nines* & think of him.—Anna has not a chance of escape; her husband called here the other day, & said she was *pretty* well but not *equal* to so long a walk; she *must come in* her *Donkey Carriage*.—Poor Animal, she will be worn out before she is thirty.—I am very sorry for her.—Mrs Clement too is in that way again. I am quite tired of so many Children.—Mrs Benn has a 13th.—The Papillons came back on friday night, but I have not seen them yet, as I do not venture to Church. I cannot hear however, but that they are the same Mr. P. & his sister they used to be. She has engaged a new Maidservant in Mrs. Calker's room, whom she means to make also Housekeeper under herself.—Old Philmore was buried yesterday, & I, by way of saying something to Triggs, observed that it had been a very handsome Funeral, but his manner of reply made me suppose that it was not generally esteemed so. I can only be sure of *one* part being very handsome, Triggs himself, walking behind in his Green Coat.—Mrs. Philmore attended as chief Mourner, in Bombasin, made very short, and flounced with Crape.

Tuesday.—I have had various plans as to this Letter, but at last I have determined that Un: Henry shall forward it from London. I want to see how Canterbury looks in the direction.—When once Unc. H. has left us I shall wish him with you. London is become a hateful place to him, & he is always depressed by the idea of it.—I hope he will be in time for your sick. I am sure he must do that part of his Duty as excellently as all the rest. He returned yesterday from Steventon, & was with us by breakfast, bringing Edward with him, only that Edwd staid to breakfast at Wyards. We had a pleasant family-day, for the Altons dined with us;—the last visit of the kind probably, which *she* will be able to pay us for many a month; —Very well, to be able to do it so long, for she *expects* much about this day three weeks, & is generally very exact.—I hope your own Henry is in France & that you have heard from him. The Passage once over, he will feel all Happiness.—I took my 1st ride yesterday & liked it very much. I went up Mounters Lane, & round by where the new Cottages are to be, & found the exercise & everything very pleasant, and I had the advantage of agreable companions, as A^t^ Cass: and Edward walked by my side.—A^t^ Cass. is such an excellent Nurse, so assiduous & unwearied!—But you know all that already.—

Very affec^ly^ Yours J. Austen

143. *To Caroline Austen. Wednesday* 26 *March* ⟨1817⟩

Address: Miss Caroline Austen
Postmark: none.
L. A. Austen-Leigh. 2 leaves 8°, a piece cut away from the second leaf.
Life 367. A few lines unpublished.

Chawton Wed^y March 26

My dear Caroline

Pray make no apologies for writing to me often, I am always very happy to hear from you, & am sorry to think that opportunities for such a nice little economical correspondence, are likely to fail now. But I hope we shall have Uncle Henry back again by the 1st Sunday in May.—I think you very much improved in your writing, & in the way to write a very pretty hand. I wish you could practise your fingering oftener.—Would not it be a good plan for you to go & live entirely at Mr. Wm. Digweed's?—He could not desire any other remuneration than the pleasure of hearing you practise. I like Frederick & Caroline better than I did, but must still prefer Edgar & Julia. Julia is a warm-hearted, ingenuous, natural Girl, which I like her for;—but I know the word *Natural* is no recommendation to you.—Our last Letter from Keppel St. was rather more chearful.—Harriet's head-aches were a little releived, & Sir Ed: Hume does not despair of a cure.—*He* persists in thinking it Water on the Brain, but none of the others are convinced.—I am happy to say that your Uncle Charles speaks of himself as quite well. How very well Edward is looking! You can have nobody in your Neighbourhood to vie with him at all, except Mr. Portal.—I have taken one ride on the Donkey & like it very much—& you must try to get me quiet, mild days, that I may be able to go out pretty constantly.—A great deal of Wind does not suit me, as I have still a tendency to Rheumatism. ⟨In⟩ short I am a poor Honey at present. I will be better when you can come & see us.—

144. *To Charles Austen. Sunday* 6 *April* 1817

***Address*: Captn C. J. Austen RN | 22 Keppel St. | Russell Sqre**
***Postmarks*: ALTON and 7 AP 1817**

British Museum (1925). Formerly in the collection described in *Times Literary Supplement* 14 Jan. 1926. 2 leaves 4°. Endorsed 'My last letter from dearest Jane C. J. A'.

***Memoir*[1] 207, *Memoir*[2] 150 (a short extract); *Life* 385 (extracts). Part unpublished.**

Chawton Sunday April 6.

My dearest Charles

Many thanks for your affectionate Letter. I was in your debt before, but I have really been too unwell the last fortnight to write anything that was not absolutely necessary. I have been suffering from a Bilious attack, attended with a good deal of fever. A few days ago my complaint appeared removed, but I am ashamed to say that the shock of my Uncle's Will brought on a relapse, & I was so ill on friday & thought myself so likely to be worse that I could not but press for Cassandra's returning with Frank after the Funeral last night, which she of course did, & either her return, or my having seen Mr Curtis, or my Disorder's chusing to go away, have made me better this morning. I live upstairs however for the present & am coddled. I am the only one of the

Legatees who has been so silly, but a weak Body must excuse weak Nerves. My Mother has born the forgetfulness of *her* extremely well ;—her expectations for herself were never beyond the extreme of moderation, & she thinks with you that my Uncle always looked forward to surviving her.—She desires her best Love & many thanks for your kind feelings ; and heartily wishes that her younger Child^{n} had more, & all her Child^{n} something immediately. My Aunt felt the value of Cassandras company so fully, & was so very kind to her, & is poor Woman ! so miserable at present (for her affliction has very much increased since the first) that we feel more regard for her than we ever did before. It is impossible to be surprised at Miss Palmer's being ill, but we are truly sorry, & hope it may not continue. We congratulate you on Mrs P.'s recovery.—As for your poor little Harriet, I dare not be sanguine for her. Nothing can be kinder than Mrs Cooke's enquiries after you & her, in all her Letters, & there was no standing her affectionate way of speaking of *your* Countenance, after her seeing you. —God bless you all. Conclude me to be going on well, if you hear nothing to the contrary.—Yours Ever truely

J. A.

Tell dear Harriet that whenever she wants me in her service again, she must send a Hackney Chariot all the way for me, for I am not strong enough to travel any other way, & I hope Cassy will take care that it is a green one.

I have forgotten to take a proper-edged sheet of Paper.

145. *To Anne Sharp.* ⟨*Thursday*⟩ 22 *May* ⟨1817⟩

Address: Miss Sharp | South Parade | Doncaster
Postmarks: ALTON and 23 MY 1817
Mrs. Henry Burke. 2 leaves 4°.
The Times 1 Feb. 1926.

Chawton May 22[d]

Your kind Letter my dearest Anne found me in bed, for in spite of my hopes & promises when I wrote to you I have since been very ill indeed. An attack of my sad complaint seized me within a few days afterwards—the most severe I ever had—& coming upon me after weeks of indisposition, it reduced me very low. I have kept my bed since the 13. of April, with only removals to a Sopha. *Now*, I am getting well again, & indeed have been gradually tho' slowly recovering my strength for the last three weeks. I can sit up in my bed & employ myself, as I am proving to you at this present moment, & *really* am equal to being out of bed, but that the posture is thought good for me.—How to do justice to the kindness of all my family during this illness, is quite beyond me!—Every dear Brother so affectionate & so anxious!—and as for my Sister!—Words must fail me in any attempt to describe what a Nurse she has been to me. Thank God! she does not seem the worse for it *yet*, & as there was never any sitting-up necessary, I am willing to hope she has no after-fatigues to suffer from. I have so many alleviations & comforts to bless the Almighty for!—My head was always clear, & I had scarcely any pain; my cheif sufferings were from feverish nights, weakness and Languor.—This Discharge was on me for above a week, & as our Alton Apoth[y] did not pretend to be able to cope with it, better advice was called in. Our nearest *very good*, is at Winchester, where there is a Hospital & capital Surgeons, & one of them attended me, & *his* applications gradually removed the Evil.—The consequence is, that instead of going to Town to put myself into the hands of some Physician as I sh[d] otherwise have done, I am going to Winchester instead, for some weeks to see what M[r] Lyford can do farther towards re-establishing me in tolerable health.—On Sat[y] next, I am actually going thither—my dearest Cassandra with me I need hardly say—and as this is only two days off you will be convinced that I am now really a very genteel, portable sort of an Invalid.—The Journey is only 16 miles, we have comfortable Lodgings engaged for us by our kind friend M[rs] Heathcote who resides in W. & are to have the accomodation of my elder Brother's Carriage which will be sent over from Steventon on purpose. Now, that's a sort of thing which M[rs] J. Austen does in the kindest manner!—But still she is in the main *not* a liberal-minded Woman, & as to this reversionary Property's amending that part of her Character, expect it not my dear Anne;—too late, too late in the day;—& besides, the Property may not be theirs these ten years. My Aunt is very stout.—M[rs] F. A. has had a much shorter confinement than I have—with a Baby to produce into the bargain. We were put to bed nearly at the same time, & she has been quite recovered this great while.—I hope *you* have not been visited with more illness my dear Anne, either in your own person or your Eliza's.—I must not attempt the pleasure of addressing her again, till my hand is stronger, but I prize the invitation to do so.—Beleive me, I was interested in all you wrote, though with all the Egotism of an Invalid I write only of myself.—Your Charity to the poor Woman I trust fails no more in effect, than I am sure it does in exertion. What an interest it must be to you all! & how gladly sh[d] I contribute more than my good wishes, were it possible!—But how you are worried! Wherever Distress falls, you are expected to supply Comfort. Ly P— writing to you even from Paris for advice!—It is the Influence of Strength over Weakness indeed. —Galigai de Concini for ever & ever.—Adeiu.—Continue to direct to Chawton, the communication between the two places will be frequent.—I have not mentioned my dear Mother; she suffered much for me when I was at the worst, but is tolerably well.—Miss Lloyd too has been all kindness. In short, if I live to be an old Woman, I must expect to wish I had died now; blessed in the tenderness of such a Family, & before I had survived either them or their affection.—You would have held the memory of your friend Jane too in tender regret I am sure.—But the Providence of God has restored me—& may I be more fit to appear before him when I *am* summoned, than I sh[d] have been now!—Sick or Well, beleive me ever y[r] attached friend

J. Austen

M[rs] Heathcote will be a great comfort, but we shall not have Miss Bigg, she being frisked off like half England, into Switzerland.

146. *To J. Edward Austen. Tuesday* 27 *May* 1817

Address : J. E. Austen Esq[re] | Exeter College | Oxford
Postmarks : WINCHESTER MY 27 181⟨7⟩ and 28 ⟨MY⟩ 1817
L. A. Austen-Leigh. 2 leaves 4°.
Memoir[2] 163 ; *Life* 389.

Mrs. Davids, College Street—Winton

Tuesday May 27.

I know no better way my dearest Edward, of thanking you for your most affectionate concern for me during my illness, than by telling you myself as soon as possible that I continue to get better.—I will not boast of my handwriting ; neither that, nor my face have yet recovered their proper beauty, but in other respects I am gaining strength very fast. I am *now* out of bed from 9 in the morn[g] to 10 at night—upon the sopha t'is true—but I eat my meals with aunt Cass: in a rational way, & can employ myself, and walk from one room to another.—Mr. Lyford says he will cure me, & if he fails I shall draw up a Memorial and lay it before the Dean & Chapter, & have no doubt of redress from that Pious, Learned, and Disinterested Body.—Our Lodgings are very comfortable. We have a neat little Drawing room with a Bow-window overlooking Dr. Gabell's garden. Thanks to the kindness of your Father & Mother in sending me their carriage, my Journey hither on Saturday was performed with very little fatigue, & had it been a fine day I think I should have felt none, but it distressed me to see uncle Henry & Wm. K— who kindly attended us on horseback, riding in rain almost all the way.—We expect a visit from them tomorrow, & hope they will stay the night, and on Thursday, which is Confirmation & a Holiday, we are to get Charles out to breakfast. We have had but one visit yet from *him* poor fellow, as he is in sick room, but he hopes to be out to-night.—

We see Mrs. Heathcote every day, & William is to call upon us soon.—God bless you my dear Edward. If ever you are ill, may you be as tenderly nursed as I have been, may the same Blessed alleviations of anxious, simpathising friends be yours, & may you possess—as I dare say you will—the greatest blessing of all, in the consciousness of not being unworthy of their Love. *I* could not feel this.

Your very affec: Aunt

J. A.

Had I not engaged to write to you, you w[d] have heard again from your Aunt Martha, as she charged me to tell you with her best Love.

147. *To* —— ⟨*end of May ?* 1817⟩

Original not traced.
***Biographical Notice* in *Northanger Abbey* 1818 ; *Memoir*[1] 207, 224, *Memoir*[2] 150, 164 ; *Life* 391.**

My attendant is encouraging, and talks of making me quite well. I live chiefly on the sofa, but am allowed to walk from one room to the other. I have been out once in a sedan-chair, and am to repeat it, and be promoted to a wheel-chair as the weather serves. On this subject I will only say further that my dearest sister, my tender, watchful, indefatigable nurse, has not been made ill by her exertions. As to what I owe to her, and to the anxious affection of all my beloved family on this occasion, I can only cry over it, and pray to God to bless them more and more.

[She next touches with just and gentle animadversion on a subject of domestic disappointment. Of this the particulars do not concern the public. Yet in justice to her characteristic sweetness and resignation, the concluding observation of our authoress thereon must not be suppressed.]

But I am getting too near complaint. It has been the appointment of God, however secondary causes may have operated. . . .

You will find Captain —— a very respectable, well-meaning man, without much manner, his wife and sister all good humour and obligingness, and I hope (since the fashion allows it) with rather longer petticoats than last year.

148. *To Catherine Ann Prowting*

***Address*: Miss Prowting**
***Postmark*: none.**
Miss Anne Tucker. Two leaves 8^{0}.
Unpublished.

My dear Miss Prowting

Had our poor friend lived these volumes would have been at her service, & as I know you were in the habit of reading together & have had the gratification of hearing that the *Works of the same hand* had given you pleasure, I shall make no other apology for offering you the perusal of them, only begging that, if not immediately disposed for such light reading, you would keep them as long as you like, as they are not wanted at home.

Yours very sincerely
J. Austen

Sunday Night—

ADDENDA

74.1. *To Martha Lloyd.* *Sunday* 29 *Nov.* ⟨1812⟩

Address: Miss Lloyd
Postmark: none
New York Public Library, Berg Collection. (Sotheby's 17 Apr. 1930). 2 leaves 4°.
Unpublished. See p. 291.

Chawton Sunday Novr 29th

My dear Martha

I shall take care not to count the lines of your *last* Letter; you have obliged me to eat humble-pie indeed; I am really obliged to you however, & though it is in general much pleasanter to reproach than to be grateful, I do not mind it now.—We shall be glad to hear, whenever you can write, & can well imagine that time for writing must be wanting in such an arduous, busy, useful office as you fill at present. You are made for doing good, & have quite as great a turn for it I think as for physicking little Children. The mental Physick which you have been lately applying bears a stamp beyond all common Charity, & I hope a Blessing will continue to attend it.—I am glad you are well & trust you are sure of being so, while you are employed in such a way;—I must hope however that your health may eer long stand the trial of a more common-place course of days, & that you will be able to leave Barton when Mrs D. D. arrives there.—There was no ready-made Cloak at Alton that would do, but Coleby has undertaken to supply one in a few days; it is to be Grey Woollen & cost ten shillings. I hope you like the *sim* of it.—Sally knows your kind intentions & has received your message, & in return for it all, she & I have between us made out that she sends her Duty & thanks you for your goodness & means to be a good girl if I please.—I have forgot to enquire as to her wanting anything particularly, but there is no *apparent* deficiency, she looks very neat & tidy. The Calico for her Mother shall be bought soon.—We have been quite alone, except Miss Benn, since 12 o'clock on wednesday, when Edward & his Harem drove from the door; & we have since heard of their safe arrival & happiness at Winchester.—Lizzy was much obliged to you for your message, but *she* has the little room. Her Father having his choice & being used to a very large Bed chamber at home, would of course prefer the ample space of yours.—The visit was a very pleasant one I really beleive on each side; they were certainly very sorry to go away, but a little of that sorrow must be attributed to a disinclination for what was before them. They have had favourable weather however, & I hope Steventon may have been better than they expected.—We have reason to suppose the change of name has taken place, as we have to forward a Letter to Edward Knight Esqre from the Lawyer who has the management of the business. I must learn to make a better K.—Our next visitor is likely to be William from Eltham in his way to Winchester, as Dr Gabell chuses he should come then before the Holidays, though it can be only for a week. If Mrs Barker has any farther curiosity about the Miss Webbs let her know that we are going to invite them for Tuesday even^{g}—also Capt. & Mrs Clement & Miss Benn, & that Mrs Digweed is already secured.—'But why not Mr Digweed ?'—Mrs Barker will immediately say—To that you may answer that Mr D. is going on tuesday to Steventon to shoot rabbits.—The 4 lines on Miss W. which I sent you were all my own, but James afterwards suggested what I thought a great improvement & as it stands in the Steventon Edition. P. & P. is sold.—Egerton gives £110 for it.—I would rather have had £150, but we could not both be pleased, & I am not at all surprised that he should not chuse to hazard so much.—It's being sold will I hope be a great saving of Trouble to Henry, & therefore must be welcome to me.—The Money is to be paid at the end of the twelvemonth.—You have sometimes expressed a wish of making Miss Benn some present;—Cassandra & I think that something of the Shawl kind to wear over her Shoulders within doors in very cold weather might be useful, but it must not be very handsome or she would not use it. Her long Fur tippet is almost worn out.—If you do not return in time to send the Turkey yourself, we must trouble you for Mr Morton's direction again, as we should be quite as much at a loss as ever. It becomes now a sort of vanity in us not to know Mr Morton's direction with any certainty.—We are just beginning to be engaged in another Christmas Duty, & next to eating Turkies, a very pleasant one, laying out Edward's money for the Poor; & the Sum that passes through our hands this year is considerable, as Mrs Knight left £20 to the Parish.—Your nephew William's state seems very alarming. Mary Jane, from whom I heard the other day, writes of him as very uneasy; I hope his Father & Mother are so too.—When you see Miss Murden, give her our Love & Good wishes, & say that we are very sorry to hear of her so often as an Invalid. Poor Mrs Stent I hope will not be much longer a distress to anybody.—All of you that are well enough to look, are now passing your Judgements I suppose on Mrs John Butler; & 'is she pretty? or is she not?' is the knotty question. Happy Woman! to stand the gaze of a neighbourhood as the Bride of such a pink-faced, simple young Man!—

Monday. A wettish day, bad for Steventon.—Mary Deedes I think must be liked there, she is so perfectly unaffected & sweet tempered, & tho' as ready to be pleased as Fanny Cage, deals less in superlatives & rapture.—Pray give our best comp[ts] to M[rs] Dundas & tell her that we hope soon to hear of her complete recovery.—Yours affect:[y]

J. Austen

78.1. *To Martha Lloyd.* *Tuesday* 16 *Feb.* ⟨1813⟩

Address: Miss Lloyd.
Postmark: none.
Sotheby's 1 Aug. 1933, 'the property of a Lady,' to whose courtesy I owe a copy. See p. 305.

Chawton Tuesday Feb: 16.

My dear Martha

Your long Letter was valued as it ought, & as I think it fully entitled to a second from me, I am going to answer it now in an handsome manner before Cassandra's return; after which event, as I shall have the benefit of all your Letters to her I claim nothing more. —I have great pleasure in what you communicate of Anna, & sincerely rejoice in Miss Murden's amendment; & only wish there were more stability in the Character of their two constitutions.—I will not say anything of the weather we have lately had, for if you were not aware of it 's being terrible, it would be cruel to put it in your head. My Mother slept through a good deal of Sunday, but still it was impossible not to be disordered by such a sky, & even yesterday she was but poorly. She is pretty well again today, & I am in hopes may not be much longer a Prisoner.—We are going to be all alive from this forenoon to tomorrow afternoon;—it will be over when you receive this, & you may think of me as one not sorry that it is so. George, Henry & William will soon be here & are to stay the night—and tomorrow the 2 Deedes' & Henry Bridges will be added to our party;—we shall then have an early dinner & dispatch them all to Winchester. We have no late account from Sloane S[t] & therefore conclude that everything is going on in one regular progress, without any striking change.—Henry was to be in Town again last Tuesday.—I have a Letter from Frank ; they are all at Deal again, established once more in fresh Lodgings. I think they must soon have lodged in every house in the Town.—We read of the Pyramus being returned into Port, with interest —& fear Mrs D.D. will be regretting that she came away so soon.—There is no being up to the tricks of the Sea.—Your friend has her little Boys about her I imagine. I hope their Sister enjoyed the Ball at Lady Keith—tho' I do not know that I do much hope it, for it might be quite as well to have her shy & uncomfortable in such a croud of Strangers.

I am obliged to you for your enquiries about Northamptonshire, but do not wish you to renew them, as I am sure of getting the intelligence I want from Henry, to whom I can apply at some convenient moment ' sans peur et sans reproche '.—I suppose all the World is sitting in Judgement upon the Princess of Wales's Letter. Poor woman, I shall support her as long as I can, because she *is* a Woman, & because I hate her Husband—but I can hardly forgive her for calling herself ' attached & affectionate ' to a Man whom she must detest—& the intimacy said to subsist between her & Lady Oxford is bad—I do not know what to do about it ; but if I must give up the Princess, I am resolved at least always to think that she would have been respectable, if the Prince had behaved only tolerably by her at first.—

Old Philmore is got pretty well, well enough to warn Miss Benn out of her House. His son is to come into it.—Poor Creature !—You may imagine how full of cares she must be, & how anxious all Chawton will feel to get her decently settled somewhere.—She will have

3 months before her.—& if anything else can be met with, she will be glad enough to be driven from her present wretched abode ;—it has been terrible for her during the late storms of wind & rain.—Cassandra has been rather out of luck at Manydown—but that is a House, in which one is tolerably independent of weather.—The Prowtings perhaps come down on Thursday or Saturday, but the accounts of *him* do not improve.—Now I think I may in *Quantity* have deserved your Letter. My ideas of Justice in Epistolary Matters are you know very strict.—with Love from my Mother, I remain. Y^rs^ very affec^ly^

J. Austen

Poor John Harwood !—One is really obliged to engage in Pity again on his account—& when there is a lack of money, one is on pretty sure grounds.—So after all, Charles, that thick-headed Charles is the best off of the Family. I rather grudge him his 2,500£.—My Mother is very decided in *selling* Deane—and if it is *not* sold, I think it will be clear that the Proprietor can have no plan of marrying.

99.1 *To Martha Lloyd. Friday* 2 *Sept.* 1814.

***Address*: Miss Lloyd Captn. Deans Dundas' R.N. Pulteney Street, Bath.**
***Postmark*: 3 SE 1814.**
Mrs. R. M. Mowll. Defective at end and where the seal has caused a tear.

23 Hans Place Friday Sepr. 2d.

My dear Martha

The prospect of a long quiet morning determines me to write to you. I have been often thinking of it before, but without being quite able to do it—and You are too busy, too happy and too *rich* I hope, to care much for Letters.—It gave me very great pleasure to hear that your money was paid, it must have been a circumstance to increase every enjoyment you can have had with your friends—and altogether I think you must be spending your time most comfortably. The weather can hardly have incommoded you by it's heat.—We have had many evenings here so cold, that I was sure there must be fires in the Country.—How many alterations you must perceive in Bath! and how many People and Things gone by, must be recurring to you!—I hope you will see Clifton. Henry takes me home tomorrow; I rather expect at least to be at Chawton before night, tho' it may not be till early on Sunday, as we shall lengthen the Journey by going round by Sunning Hill; his favourite Mrs Crutchley lives there, and he wants to introduce me to her.—We offered a visit in our way, to the Birches, but they cannot receive us, which is a disappointment.—He comes back again on Wednesday, and perhaps brings James with him; so it was settled, when James was here; he wants to see Scarman again, as his Gums last week were not in a proper state for Scarman's operations. I cannot tell how much of all this may be known to you already.—I shall have spent my 12 days here very pleasantly, but with not much to tell of them; two or three *very* little Dinner-parties at home, some delightful Drives in the Curricle, and quiet Tea-drinkings with the Tilsons, has been the sum of my doings. I have seen no old acquaintances I think, but Mr Hampson. Henry met with Sir Brook and Lady Bridges by chance, and they were to have dined with us yesterday, had they remained in Town. I am amused by the present style of female dress; the coloured petticoats with braces over the white Spencers and enormous Bonnets upon the full stretch, are quite entertaining. It seems to me a more marked *change* than one has lately seen.—Long sleeves appear universal, even as *Dress*, the Waists short, and as far as I have been able to judge, the Bosom covered.—I was at a little party last night at Mrs Latouche's, where dress is a good deal attended to, and these are my observations from it.—Petticoats short, and generally, tho' not always, flounced.—The broad-straps belonging to the Gown or Boddice, which cross the front of the Waist, over white, have a very pretty effect I think.—I have seen West's famous Painting, and prefer it to anything of the kind I ever saw before. I do not know that it *is* reckoned superior to his 'Healing in the Temple'. but it has gratified *me* much more, and indeed is the first representation of our Saviour which ever at all contented me. 'His Rejection by the Elders', is the subject.—I want to have You and Cassandra see it.—I am extremely pleased with this new House of Henry's, it is everything that could be wished for him, and I have only to hope he will continue to like it as well as he does now, and not be looking out for anything better.—He is in very comfortable health;—he has not been so well, he says, for a twelvemonth.—*His* view, and the veiw of those he mixes with, of Politics, is not chearful—with regard to an American war I mean;—they consider it as certain, and as what is to ruin us. The ⟨ ⟩ cannot be conquered, and we shall only be teaching them the skill in War which they may now want. We are to make them good Sailors and Soldiers, and g⟨ain?⟩ nothing ourselves. —If we *are* to be ruined, it cannot be helped—but I place my hope of better things on a claim to the protection of Heaven, as a Religious Nation, a Nation in spite of much Evil improving in Religion, which I cannot beleive the Americans to possess.—However this may be, Mr Barlowe is to dine with us today, and I am in some hope of getting Egerton's account before I go away—so we will enjoy ourselves as long as we can. My Aunt does not seem pleased with Capt. and Mrs D. D. for taking a House in Bath, I was afraid she would not like it, but I ⟨ ⟩ do. — When I get home, I shall hear ⟨more. I sh⟩all be very happy to find myself at ⟨ ⟩ Miss Benn ⟨ ⟩ to hear Mrs Digweed's goodhumoured communications. The language of London is flat; it wants her phrase.—Dear me! I wonder if you have seen Miss Irvine!—At this time of year, she is more likely to be out of Bath than in.

One of our afternoon drives was to Streatham, where I had the pleasure of seeing Mrs Hill as well and comfortable as usual;— but there is a melancholy disproportion between the Papa and the little Children.—She told me that the Audrys have taken that sweet St. Bo⟨niface⟩ hoped be ⟨ ⟩ Ventnor ⟨*two lines missing, with the conclusion*⟩.

Pray give my best ⟨com⟩pts. to your Friends.—I have not forgotten their parti⟨cular⟩ claim to my Gratitude as an Author.—We have j⟨ust learn⟩ed that Mrs C. Austen is safe in bed with a Girl.—It happened on board, a fortnig⟨ht⟩ before it was expected.

122.1. *To Charles Thomas Haden. Thursday* ⟨14 *Dec.* 1815⟩

Address: C. Haden Esq.
Mrs. Henry Burke. Not published.

Dear Sir

We return these volumes with many Thanks. They have afforded us great amusement.—As we were out ourselves yesterday Even[g] we were glad to find you had not called—but shall depend upon your giving us some part of this Even[g].—I leave Town early on Saturday, & must say 'Good bye' to you.—

y[r] obliged & faithful

J. Austen

Thursday.

141.1. *To Caroline Austen* *Friday* 14 *March* ⟨1817⟩

Address: Miss Caroline Austen. No postmark.
Lady Charnwood (1939).

My dear Caroline

You will receive a message from me Tomorrow, & today you will receive the parcel itself; therefore I should not like to be in that Message's shoes, it will look so much like a fool. I am glad to hear of your proceedings & improvements in the Gentleman Quack. There was a great deal of Spirit in the first part. Our objections to it You have heard, & I give your Authorship credit for bearing Criticism so well.—I hope Edwd is not idle. No matter what becomes of the Craven Exhibition provided he goes on with his Novel. In that, he will find his true fame & his true wealth. That will be the honourable Exhibition which no V. Chancellor can rob him of.—I have just rec^d^ nearly twenty pounds myself on the 2^d^ Edit: of S & S—which gives me this fine flow of Literary Ardour.—

Tell your Mama, I am very much obliged to her for the Ham she intends sending me, & that the Seacale will be extreemly acceptable—*is* I should say, as we have got it already; the future, relates only to our time of dressing it, which will not be till Uncles Henry & Frank can dine here together.—Do you know that Mary Jane went to Town with her Papa? They were there last week from Monday to Saturday, & she was as happy as possible. She spent a day in Keppel S^t^ with Cassy; & her Papa is sure that she must have walked 8 or 9 miles in a morn^g^ with him. Your Aunt F. spent the week with us, & one Child with her, changed every day. The Piano Forte's Duty, & will be happy to see you whenever you can come.

yrs affec[ly]

J. Austen

Chawton March 14.

149. ⟨*To Caroline Austen?*⟩. n.d.

From a copy at Frog Firle, where the late E. C. Austen-Leigh lived, headed 'Scrap in Jane Austen's handwriting pasted at foot of a framed engraving (portrait)'.

We four sweet Brothers & Sisters dine today at the G[t]. House. Is not that quite natural? Grandmama & Miss Lloyd will be by themselves, I do not exactly know what they will have for dinner, very likely some pork,

Addenda: *Letter* 10

Page 22. Add (from the MS., omitted by Lord Brabourne): (indisposed) 'from that particular kind of evacuation which has generally preceded her illnesses.'
(at Staines) '& felt a heat in her throat as we travelled yesterday morning, which seemed to foretell more Bile.—She bore her Journey however much' (better than).
(accordingly did.) 'It is by no means wonderful that her Journey should have produced some kind of visitation;—I hope a few days will entirely remove it.'

Page 23. (went to bed.) 'Lyford has promised to call in the course of a few days, & then they will settle about the Dandelion Tea; the receipts for which were shewn him at Basingstoke, & he approved of them highly, they will only require some slight alteration to be better adapted to my Mother's constitution.'
(visit.) 'Mary is quite all he says, & uncommonly large' [James Edward was born 17 November].
For 'Japan ink' read 'Japan silk'.

Page 26. (she is better.) 'I shall be able to be more positive on this subject I hope tomorrow.'
(good night, and) 'tho' she did not get up to breakfast,'.

APPENDIX

1. *Letters from Cassandra Austen to Fanny Knight on Jane Austen's death*

Brabourne ii. 333–41. The first letter has been collated, by the courtesy of Mr. Percy Dobell, with the original in the possession of his firm. The second I have not seen.

Winchester Sunday

My dearest Fanny—doubly dear to me now for her dear sake whom we have lost.

She did love you most sincerely, & never shall I forget the proofs of love you gave her during her illness in writing those kind, amusing letters at a time when I know your feelings would have dictated so different a style. Take the only reward I can give you in my assurance that your benevolent purpose *was* answer'd; you *did* contribute to her enjoyment. Even your last letter afforded pleasure, I merely cut the seal & gave it to her; she opened it & read it herself, afterwards she gave it me to read, & then talked to me a little & not unchearfully of its contents, but there was then a languor about her which prevented her taking the same interest in any thing, she had been used to do.

Since Tuesday evening, when her complaint re-turnd, there was a visible change, she slept more & much more comfortably, indeed during the last eight & forty hours she was more asleep than awake. Her looks altered & she fell away, but I perceived no material diminution of strength & tho' I was then hopeless of a recovery I had no suspicion how rapidly my loss was approaching.—I *have* lost a treasure, such a Sister, such a friend as never can have been

surpassed,—she was the sun of my life, the gilder of every pleasure, the soother of every sorrow, I had not a thought concealed from her, & it is as if I had lost a part of myself. I loved her only too well, not better than she deserved, but I am conscious that my affection for her made me sometimes unjust to & negligent of others, & I can acknowledge, more than as a general principle, the justice of the hand which has struck this blow. You know me too well to be at all afraid that I should suffer materially from my feelings, I am perfectly conscious of the extent of my irreparable loss, but I am not at all overpowerd & very little indisposed, nothing but what a short time, with rest & change of air will remove. I thank God that I was enabled to attend her to the last & amongst my many causes of self-reproach I have not to add any wilfull neglect of her comfort. She felt herself to be dying about half an hour before she became tranquil and aparently unconscious. During that half hour was her struggle, poor soul! she said she could not tell us what she sufferd, tho she complaind of little fixed pain. When I asked her if there was any thing she wanted, her answer was she wanted nothing but death & some of her words were 'God grant me patience, Pray for me oh Pray for me'. Her voice was affected but as long as she spoke she was intelligible. I hope I do not break your heart my dearest Fanny by these particulars, I mean to afford you gratification whilst I am relieving my own feelings. I could not write so to any body else, indeed you are the only person I have written to at all excepting your Grandmama, it was to her not your Uncle Charles I wrote on Friday.—
Immediately after dinner on Thursday I went into the

Town to do an errand which your dear Aunt was anxious about. I returnd about a quarter before six & found her recovering from faintness & oppression, she got so well as to be able to give me a minute account of her seisure & when the clock struck 6 she was talking quietly to me. I cannot say how soon afterwards she was seized again with the same faintness, which was followed by the sufferings she could not describe, but Mr. Lyford had been sent for, had applied something to give her ease & she was in a state of quiet insensibility by seven oclock at the latest. From that time till half past four, when she ceased to breathe, she scarcely moved a limb, so that we have every reason to think, with gratitude to the Almighty, that her sufferings were over. A slight motion of the head with every breath remaind till almost the last. I sat close to her with a pillow in my lap to assist in supporting her head, which was almost off the bed, for six hours,—fatigue made me then resign my place to Mrs J. A. for two hours & a half when I took it again & in about one hour more she breathed her last. I was able to close her eyes myself & it was a great gratification to me to render her these last services. There was nothing convulsed or which gave the idea of pain in her look, on the contrary, but for the continual motion of the head, she gave me the idea of a beautiful statue, & even now in her coffin, there is such a sweet serene air over her countenance as is quite pleasant to contemplate. This day my dearest Fanny you have had the melancholly intelligence & I know you suffer severely, but I likewise know that you will apply to the fountain-head for consolation & that our merciful God is never deaf to such prayers as you will offer.

The last sad ceremony is to take place on Thursday morning, her dear remains are to be deposited in the cathedral—it is a satisfaction to me to think that they are to lie in a Building she admird so much—her precious soul I presume to hope reposes in a far superior Mansion. May mine one day be reunited to it.—Your dear Papa, your Uncles Henry & Frank & Edw[d] Austen instead of his Father will attend, I hope they will none of them suffer lastingly from their pious exertions.—The ceremony must be over before ten o'clock as the cathedral service begins at that hour, so that we shall be at home early in the day, for there will be nothing to keep us here afterwards.—Your Uncle James came to us yesterday & is gone home to day—Uncle H. goes to Chawton to-morrow morning, he has given every necessary direction here & I think his company there will do good. He returns to us again on Tuesday evening. I did not think to have written a long letter when I began, but I have found the employment draw me on & I hope I shall have been giving you more pleasure than pain.

Remember me kindly to M[rs] J. Bridges (I am so glad she is with you now) & give my best love to Lizzy & all the others. I am my dearest Fanny

Most affect[ly] yrs

CASS. ELIZ[TH] AUSTEN

I have said nothing about those at Chawton because I am sure you hear from your Papa.

Chawton: Tuesday (July 29, 1817).

My dearest Fanny,

I have just read your letter for the third time, and thank you most sincerely for every kind expression to myself, and still more warmly for your praises of her who I believe was better known to you than to any human being besides myself. Nothing of the sort could have been more gratifying to me than the manner in which you write of her, and if the dear angel is conscious of what passes here, and is not above all earthly feelings, she may perhaps receive pleasure in being so mourned. Had *she* been the survivor I can fancy her speaking of *you* in almost the same terms. There are certainly many points of strong resemblance in your characters; in your intimate acquaintance with each other, and your mutual strong affection, you were counterparts.

Thursday was not so dreadful a day to me as you imagined. There was so much necessary to be done that there was no time for additional misery. Everything was conducted with the greatest tranquillity, and but that I was determined I would see the last, and therefore was upon the listen, I should not have known when they left the house. I watched the little mournful procession the length of the street; and when it turned from my sight, and I had lost her for ever, even then I was not overpowered, nor so much agitated as I am now in writing of it. Never was human being more sincerely mourned by those who attended her remains than was this dear creature. May the sorrow with which she is parted with on earth be a prognostic of the joy with which she is hailed in heaven!

I continue very tolerably well—much better than

any one could have supposed possible, because I certainly have had considerable fatigue of body as well as anguish of mind for months back; but I really am well, and I hope I am properly grateful to the Almighty for having been so supported. Your grand-mamma, too, is much better than when I came home.

I did not think your dear papa appeared unwell, and I understand that he seemed much more comfortable after his return from Winchester than he had done before. I need not tell you that he was a great comfort to me; indeed, I can never say enough of the kindness I have received from him and from every other friend.

I get out of doors a good deal and am able to employ myself. Of course those employments suit me best which leave me most at leisure to think of her I have lost, and I do think of her in every variety of circumstance. In our happy hours of confidential intercourse, in the cheerful family party which she so ornamented, in her sick room, on her death-bed, and as (I hope) an inhabitant of heaven. Oh, if I may one day be re-united to her there! I know the time must come when my mind will be less engrossed by her idea, but I do not like to think of it. If I think of her less as on earth, God grant that I may never cease to reflect on her as inhabiting heaven, and never cease my humble endeavours (when it shall please God) to join her there.

In looking at a few of the precious papers which are now my property I have found some memorandums, amongst which she desires that one of her gold chains may be given to her god-daughter Louisa, and a lock of her hair be set for you. You can need no assurance, my dearest Fanny, that every request of your beloved aunt will be sacred with me. Be so good as to say whether you prefer a brooch or ring. God bless you, my dearest Fanny.

Believe me, most affectionately yours,

CASS. ELIZTH. AUSTEN.

Miss Knight, Godmersham Park,
Canterbury.

2. *Jane Austen's Will.*

I JANE AUSTEN of the Parish of Chawton do by this my last Will and testament give and bequeath to my dearest sister Cassandra Eliz'th every thing of which I may die possessed or which may hereafter be due to me subject to the payment of my funeral expenses and to a legacy of £50 to my brother Henry and £50 to Mde Bijion which I request may be paid as soon as convenient and I appoint my said dear sister EXECUTRIX of this my last Will and testament JANE AUSTEN April 27; 1817.

STEVENTON MANOR
from a drawing by Anna Lefroy

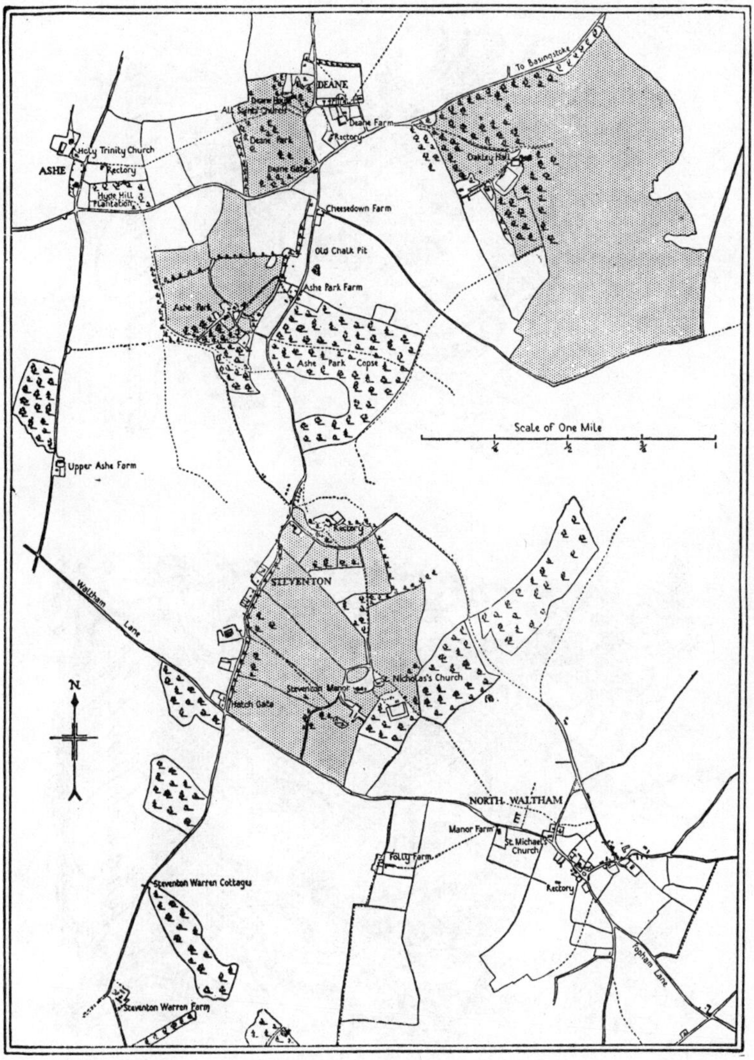

PLAN OF THE NEIGHBOURHOOD OF STEVENTON

QUI INVIDIT MINOR EST
John Austen Esqr.

Francis Motley Austen.

R
K
S
H
Wasing
Stratfield Mortimer
Part of Wilts
Silchester
Baughurst
Tadley
Kingsclere
Sydmonton
Ecchinswell
Woolverton
Pamber
Sherborne St. Johns
Sherfield
Rotherwick
Hartley Wespall
Mattingley
Stratfield Turgis
Bramley
Chinham
Old Basing
Newnham
Basingstoke
Worting
Oakley
Overton
Ash
Steventon
Cliddisden
Winslade
Tunworth
Upton Grey
Farleigh
Dummer
Ellisfield
North Waltham
Weston Patrick
Herriard
Popham
Nutley
Woodmancot
Preston Candover
Chilton Candover
Brown Candover
Bradley
Lasham
Shalden
Bentworth
Alton
Northington
Swarraton
Weld
Medstead
Chawton
Kings Worthy
Itchin Abbots
Itchin Stoke
Old Alresford
Bighton
New Alresford
Ropley
Newton Valence
Easton
Ovington
Bishops Sutton
Winchester
Tichborne
West Tisted
East Tisted
Colemore
Priors Dean
Chilcomb
Cheriton
Bramdean
Morested
Hinton Ampner
Kilmiston
Privet
Froxfield
Micheldever
Hunton
Whitchurch
Overton
Laverstock
Grewell
Nately
13
12
11
18
19
20
17
9

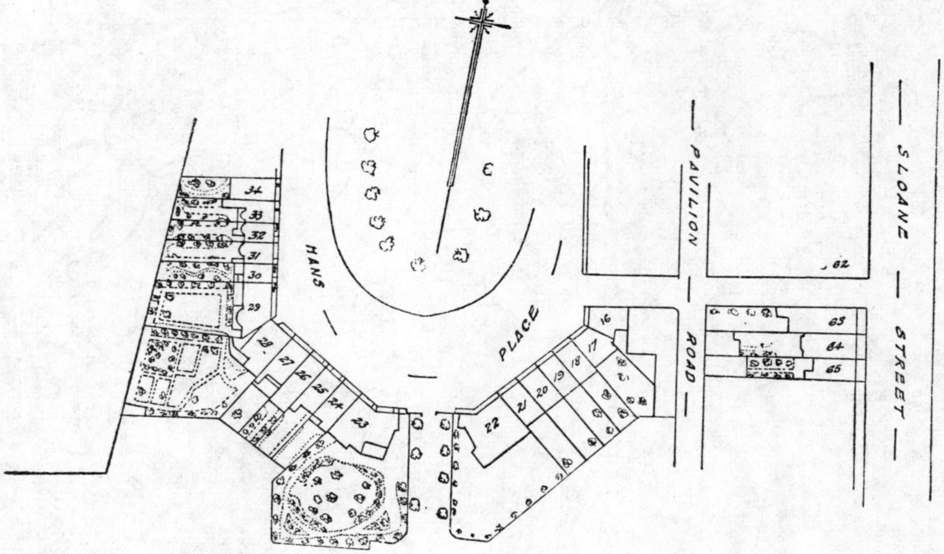

HANS PLACE (*c.* 1869)
before the modern reconstruction

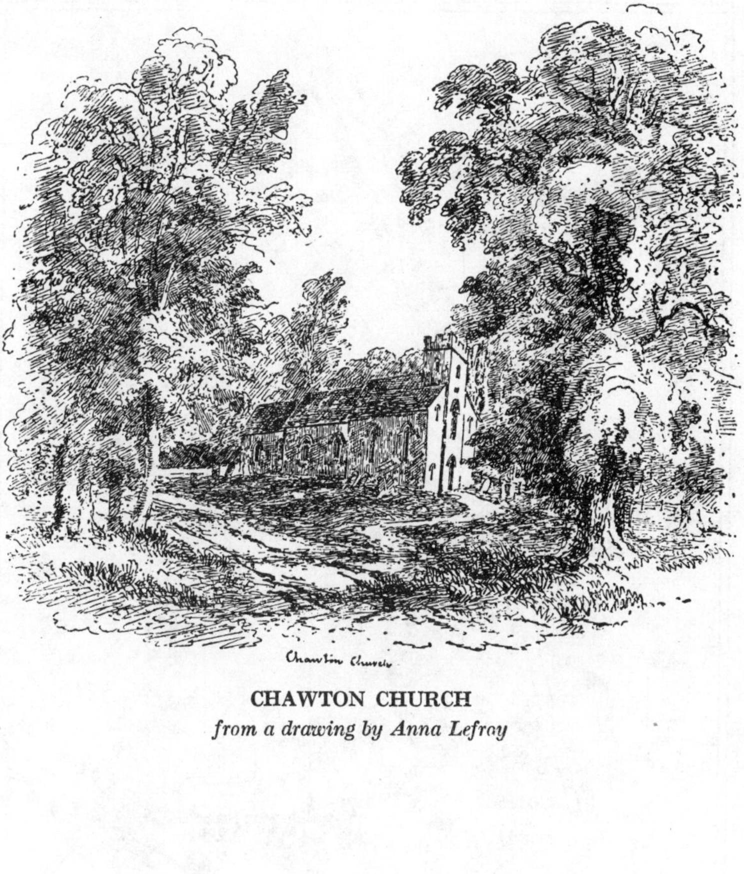

CHAWTON CHURCH

from a drawing by Anna Lefroy

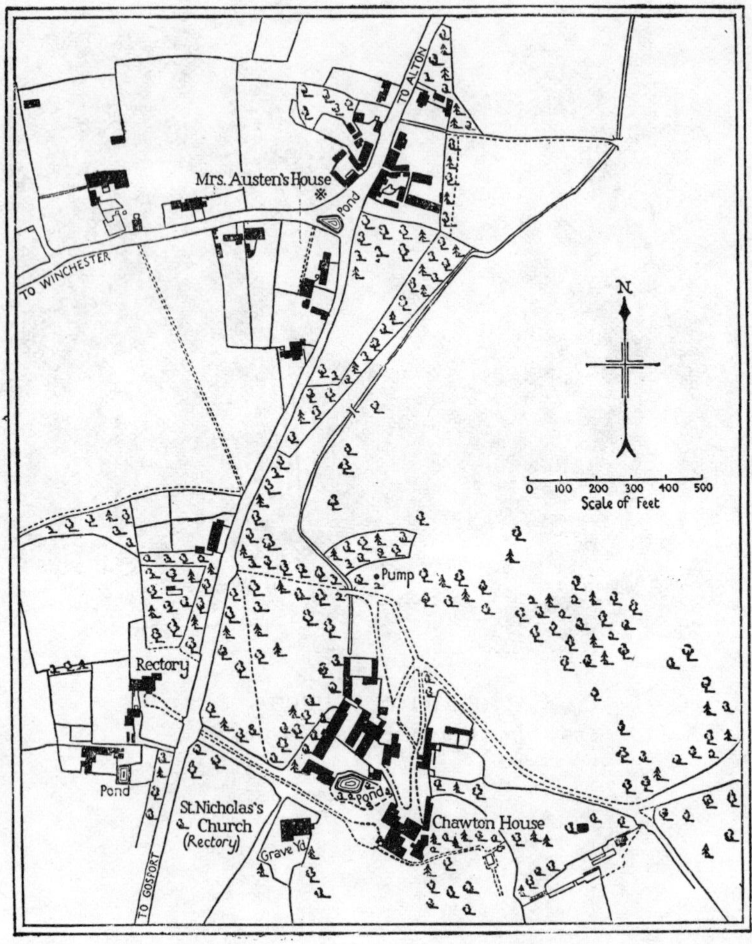

PLAN OF CHAWTON

NOTES

THE first object of these notes is to enable the reader to distinguish persons *ambiguously* named, and so to refer to the Indexes if more information is wanted. It may be borne in mind that 'my Uncle' and 'my Aunt' always mean Mr. and Mrs. Leigh Perrot; that 'Mary' may be either Mrs. James or Mrs. Frank Austen (often 'Mrs. J. A.' and 'Mrs. F. A.'); 'Elizabeth' either Mrs. Edward Austen (her daughter is always 'Lizzie') or Elizabeth Bigg, Mrs. Heathcote; 'Eliza' either Mrs. Henry Austen or Mrs. Fowle; 'Edward' either J. A.'s brother, or his son, or James's son James Edward.

The index of places indicates that 'Goodnestone' means the Bridges, 'Hamstall' the Coopers, &c.

1. *Sat.* 9 *Jan.* 1796

1. *very near of an age* is a playful exaggeration, for C. E. A. was born 9 Jan. 1773 and T. L. not until 1776 (unless the authorities err).

2. *my Irish friend*: Tom Lefroy.

Henry goes to Harden: to the Coopers. Caroline Cooper's mother recorded in her diary for May 1793, 'Edward and Caroline went to Harpsden to live, a very pretty place near Henley' (Diaries of Mrs. Lybbe Powys).

3. *Alithea*: Bigg.

Charles: Fowle, as p. 4 shows; but at the foot of this page, Charles Austen.

adjutancy: the project was successfully revived, see p. 31.

Tom Jones: Book 7, chapter 14. 'As soon as the sergeant was departed, Jones rose from his bed, and dressed himself entirely, putting on even his coat, which, as its colour was white, showed very visibly the streams of blood which had flowed down it.'

4. *Tom*: perhaps Williams; if so it could no doubt be determined what ship he is jocularly supposed to have named; perhaps the *Unicorn*. See, however, the note on p. 5.

Miss M.: perhaps Miss Murden, whose mother was a Fowle.

2. *Thur.* 14 *Jan.* 1796

Since this letter was printed I have received from Mr. Davidson Cook a collation with the original. There are no corrections of note. The postmark is 16 Jan. 1796.

5. *Anna*: James Austen's child.

Tom. It has been assumed, e.g. by the authors of *Sailor Brothers*, that this is Thomas Williams, R.N.; and the context here and on p. 4 makes this plausible. On the other hand, *Tom* in a letter from Jane to Cassandra at Kintbury, and just after a mention of Mr. and Mrs. Fowle, may well mean Cassandra's fiancé Tom Fowle; who at about this time went to the West Indies as chaplain to his kinsman Lord Craven's regiment. He died there in Feb. 1797. Cassandra no doubt destroyed any letters of that time; we have none for 1797. I have not been able to find any record of the embarkation, which would settle the point.

Friday, 8th: J. A. wrote *Friday the 8th.*

6. *don't*: J. A. wrote *do not.*

Tom: Chute.

Edward: Cooper.

3. *Tues.* — *Aug.* 1796

Since my text was printed I have learned that a facsimile is in the second edition of O. F. Adams, *The Story of Jane Austen's Life*, Boston, 1897. The facsimile supplies no verbal correction.

4. *Thur.* 1 *Sept.* 1796

8. *at school.* See *Memoir*, ch. 1, or *Life*, p. 26, for J. A.'s schooldays at Reading.

for Yarmouth: to join his regiment.

9. *Camilla.* See note on p. 13.

Fanny: Cage (and on p. 10).

10. *Louisa*: Bridges.

stout: probably *robust*, with no reference to girth, as (?) always; see Index VII.

5. *Mon.* 5 *Sept.* 1796

11. *Michael* looks more like a principal than a servant; possibly Michael Terry, one of a large family.

the Marys: Lloyd and Harrison.

Harriot and *Louisa* Bridges, *Frank* Austen, *Fanny* Cage; *George* is doubtful. (On p. 12 he looks like a Cage, but I cannot find a George C.)

Henry seems here, and on pp. 12, 18, to be Henry Austen, not Henry Bridges (the 'Mr. Bridges' of pp. 9, 12), though he too was of the party. Henry B. would not be writing to Steventon. The same ambiguity arises on pp. 163, 166, 219.

12. *Miss Bridges* is, perhaps, Marianne, then the oldest unmarried d. of Sir Brook III, and just 21. Lord Fitzwalter (to whom I owe this suggestion) knows of no other candidate; Sir Brook had no sister.

without fayl: perhaps Frank's spelling, or Charles's—hardly Henry's.

Crixhall ruff: not, as has naturally enough been assumed, a church, but a wood, which to-day has some fine oaks.

13. *Dr. Marchmont.* For his respectable meddling between Camilla and her young man see that work *passim*, and especially the last page of the last volume, where we are told that he at last 'acknowledged its injustice, its narrowness, and its arrogance'.

The name of 'Miss J. Austen, Steventon' is in the list of subscribers to *Camilla*. What is no doubt her copy was lately presented to the Bodleian by a descendant of Sir Francis Austen. It contains in each volume the inscription 'Cass. Eliz. Austen' and (also in Cassandra's hand) 'Given to Lady Austen May 1837'; Lady Austen is best known to us as Martha Lloyd; she became Lady Austen in Feb. 1837, when her husband became Sir Francis.

In the lower margin of the last page of the last volume is a pencil inscription which I have no doubt was written by the first owner. She, as a subscriber, received the volumes in boards, uncut, and probably she wrote her comment when she finished the book in 1796. Later it was half-bound (Cassandra's signature is on the end-paper) and the inscription was mutilated, slightly in the outer margin, but more severely in the lower margin, where I think it has lost a line or two lines. The inscription is also faint, but I read it thus:

> Since this work went to the Press a
> Circumstance of some Importance to the
> happiness of Camilla has taken place,
> namely that Dr. Marchmont has at last . . .

and I conjecture that in the missing conclusion J. A. pleased herself with the intelligence of Dr. Marchmont's death.

Of Mary Harrison's love affairs I know nothing, but there may be *some* connexion between this passage and p. 134.

6. *Thur.* 15 *Sept.* 1796

14. *Lucy*: Lefroy.

my Aunt Fielding. Members of Miss Austen's family and others have been puzzled by places in the letters where 'my aunt' or 'my cousin' is applied to persons not so related to the writer. Cf.

p. 279 our cousin Miss Payne
p. 280 our cousin Margt. Beckford
p. 282 my aunt Harding
p. 283 my cousin Flora Long
p. 310 my cousin Caro*line*

In most of these places it is clear that the personal pronoun is quoted as from a third person. Mrs. Fielding's husband was half-brother to Sir Brook Bridges III, and she would naturally be called aunt by Sir Brook's children. Mrs. Harding (282) and her niece Flora Long (283) are evidently connexions of the Terrys. 'My cousin Caro*line*' (310) is no doubt Mrs. Tilson's cousin; the italics indicate her pronunciation. See also note on p. 280.

15. *Jane*: Cooper.

Seward's coming over: from Chawton, no doubt.

Miss Holwell. Governor H. was one of the survivors of the Black Hole, of which in 1758 he published a *Genuine Narrative*.

Fly: Frank.

16. The last four paragraphs are marginal additions in various parts of the letter. *she accompanies* evidently refers to Miss Pearson, not to Miss Harrison.

7. *Sun.* 18 *Sept.* 1796

17. *commanded by the Triton*: a playful inversion.

Mary: Pearson. She was the elder daughter, elsewhere always *Miss Pearson.*

9. *Wed.* 24 *Oct.* 1798

20. *Daniel* was the Godmersham coachman. No doubt the first stage was accomplished in Edward Austen's own carriage.

Cax: not explained.

21. *Harry*: Digweed (p. 26).

Midnight Bell: by Francis Lathom.

and mother. I think J. A. wrote *& my mother.*

22. *Dordy*: her nephew George.

10. *Sat.* 27 *Oct.* 1798

24. *Mr. W.* Mrs. Austen wrote to Mary Lloyd a letter of congratulation on her engagement to James Austen, dated Steventon, 30 Nov. 1796, a copy of which is in the Lefroy MS. 'Tell Martha she too shall be my daughter, she does me honour in the request, and Mr. W. shall be my son if he pleases. Don't be alarmed my dear Martha, I have kept and will keep your secret.'

11. *Sat.* 17 *Nov.* 1798

27. *her nephew*: Tom Lefroy.

her friend. See Index II, s.v. *Blackall*, and *Life* 86.

28. *on the letter.* Lord Brabourne prints *in.*

29. *Miss Cuthbert*: Lord Brabourne (i. 228) explains that Miss C. and her sister Maria lived at Eggarton House near Godmersham, where they had charge of a weak-minded sister of Mr. Thomas Knight; see *Eggerton* in Index III.

30. *a fine little boy*: J. A. announces the birth of her biographer.

12. *Sun.* 25 *Nov.* 1798

31. *the qualification.* Henry 'joined the Oxford Militia as lieutenant in 1793, becoming adjutant and captain four years later'. *Life* 107. *Mr. Mowell* was probably Morrell, see Index II.

the Colonel: Gore-Langton.

32. *Oxford smack* has not been explained.

Egerton: Brydges.

13. *Sat.* 1 *Dec.* 1798

34. *East India Directors.* See p. 47.

You and my mother is, I think, an error for *You and my Brother*; *Br* in J. A.'s hand need not be very unlike *M.* It would be much more natural to 'address this advice' to two persons then in the same place than to one at a distance and one under the same roof as the writer; and the description 'tender-hearted' fits Edward and Cassandra particularly well.

35. *his mother and child* must be his mother-in-law Mrs. Lloyd (who lived at Ibthrop) and his daughter Anna; *the child* in l. 3 is clearly the baby at Deane, James Edward.

14. *Tues.* 18 *Dec.* 1798

37. *your Business*: connected perhaps with her legacy from her fiancé Tom Fowle. But his will was proved in May 1797.

38. *Sir Thos* : Williams.

a dish of Tea: in honour of her birthday 16 Dec.

15. *Mon.* 24 *Dec.* 1798

42. *happiness to Martha.* It has been confidently assumed (e.g. by the authors of *Sailor Brothers*) that Cassandra and Jane were making a match between Frank and Martha (who were actually married thirty years later). But we ought not to forget Mr. W. (see note on p. 24). Perhaps he, too, was a naval officer in need of promotion.

43. *Butcher . . . Temple.* See Index II. The Powlett correspondence has no letters of the winter 1798–9; but at other times Frank Temple was staying with his brother-in-law and sister, Mr. and Mrs. Charles Powlett; and letters from F. T. to Mrs. C. P. (at Hackwood Farm, Basingstoke; C. P. was

related to Lord Bolton) show that he and his friend Butcher had stayed with the Powletts in March or April 1797. They returned to Portsmouth; 'but Butcher poor fellow was very near being left behind, the Sans Paraeil had gone to St. Helens'. 'The horrid one of all' may be one of Frank's brothers, for whose careers and characters see Mr. Bettany's edition of W. J. Temple's *Diaries* (Oxford, 1929). There *was* a Butcher in the 11th Light Dragoons, but we need not pursue him.

Mr. Calland, Rector of Bentworth, excites curiosity because his behaviour is so like Darcy's—and this is the time at which *First Impressions* was composed. He was twelve years J. A.'s senior. His attachment to his hat is noticed in a versified account of a Basingstoke ball of 1794 'sent by Mrs. Austen to one of her Daughters staying from home' (Lefroy MS.):

> And Bentworth's Rector, with his hat,
> Unwillingly he parts from that.

He appears again in a letter from Nancy Powlett to her husband (Powlett correspondence, 5 April 1799):

> 'You know my dear Love the Beaux always find out your absence immediately—no sooner had you mounted your Horse than one made his appearance—he was let in, and exerted himself to entertain me for near an Hour; when I tell you this said Beau was *Mr. Calland* you will not be surprised that all his exertions were unsuccessful. . . . At last he took his leave. Perhaps for the sake of my vanity I ought to conceal that his motive for calling, I believe, was to ask your assistance next Sunday.'

44. *supped with the Prince*. See also p. 45. The Prince was clearly Prince William of Gloucester, whose military duties no doubt brought him into Kent. Mrs. Lybbe Powys's diary for the Canterbury race-week, 1798, is full of his affability and volubility. He dined with the Dean on 25 Aug. (the Dean was a bachelor, and on this occasion his sister-in-law Mrs. L. P. did the honours) and during the play which followed, 'for he there talked almost as much as during dinner, he told me he was to sup at Dr. Welsby's, and then . . . set off for Ashford'. It was at Ashford that C. E. A. supped with him.

Mrs. L. P. records the 'dinner for Prince William of Gloucester' as follows:

Salmon Trout
Soles
Fricando of Veal. Rais'd Giblet Pie
Vegetable Pudding
Chickens. Ham
Muffin Pudding
Curry of Rabbits. Preserve of Olives
Soup. Haunch of Venison
Open Tart Syllabub. Rais'd Jelly
Three Sweetbreads, larded
Maccaroni. Buttered Lobster
Peas
Potatoes
Baskets of Pastry. Custards
Goose

16. *Fri.* 28 *Dec.* 1798

47. *the India House.* See p. 34. Sir William Foster sends me these extracts from the Court Minutes of the Company:

5 Dec. 1798. The request of Lieut. Francis William Austen to be allowed passage money from India was referred to a committee.

10 Feb. 1801. A letter from Capt. F. W. A. 'stating the grounds of his former application' for an allowance 'to indemnify him for his expences in returning from India' in 1793 was referred to the same committee.

4 March 1801. On the committee's report the claim was disallowed.

His later relations with the Company were happier. In 1808 and 1809 substantial sums were voted to him 'for the Purchase of a Piece of Plate', or without such appropriation, with the Company's thanks for various services.

17. *Tues.* 8 *Jan.* 1799

49. *mamalone* is thought by Miss Constance Hill (p. 76) a misreading for *mamalouc*. 'The battle of the Nile had set the fashion in ladies' dress. In the fashion-plates we find Mamalouc cloaks and Mamalouc robes. . . . Ladies wear toupées, some-

what resembling a fez, which we recognize as the Mamalouc cap.'

F— has lost his election at B—. The blanks are Lord Brabourne's, no doubt. Failing to trace a parliamentary election (defeat in which might have deprived the candidate of immunity from arrest for debt—one reason for shunning company), I suggested (*Times Lit. Suppt.* 17 Sept. 1931) a scholarship or fellowship election. The name which most readily occurs is that of Fulwar (Craven Fowle). But he was too old, having taken his M.A. in 1788.

50. *on Harriet's account.* There was, I think, no Harriet at Eastwell; but H. Bridges may have joined the Finch-Hatton family for music lessons.

W—— W—— (the blanks may be Lord Brabourne's) is not identified.

giving her name to a set. J. A. means that she has called this house-party 'the Biggs', though only Catherine B. was strictly so named; for her father and brother were Bigg-Wither and her sister had become Mrs. Heathcote.

51. *act of generosity.* Mrs. Knight's abdication in favour of her adopted son was subject to an annuity for herself of £2,000.

52. *Mr. South.* The Bishop's name was North.

The Miss Charterises. I can make nothing of these ladies, nor of the Miss Edens whom they emulated.

53. *Jeffereys,* &c.: not identified.

18. *Mon.* 21 *Jan.* 1799

55. *Elizabeth Caroline*: Fowle.

Our first cousins. They had three—one on their father's side, Eliza Hancock (de Feuillide) who 31 Dec. 1797 became Mrs. Henry A., two on their mother's, Edward Cooper and his sister Jane, Lady Williams, who died Aug. 1798.

the other living: that of Ryton in Shropshire to which, no doubt, Lord Craven had meant to present his protégé Tom Fowle, Cassandra's fiancé. Mrs. Austen writes to Mary Lloyd, 30 Nov. 1796 (see note on p. 24), 'I look forward to you as a real comfort in my old age when Cassandra is gone into Shropshire and Jane—the Lord knows where'. Mary, fixed at Deane (and no doubt James's succession to Steventon was already foreseen) would always be near; for a move to Bath was not yet in contemplation.

Fulwar: Fowle.

56. *Harris* Bigg-Wither is mentioned three times, the last reference being Nov. 1800. The story of his proposing marriage to J. A. in 1802 is mentioned in *Memoir* (28), and is told in full in *Life* (92) but without the gentleman's name. This reticence is accounted for by a letter from Caroline Austen to her brother (?1869), in which she wishes 'that not any allusion should be made to the Manydown story, or at *least* that the reference should be so vague, as to give *no* clue to the place or person'—on the ground that Mr. Wither's children lived in the neighbourhood, and that other neighbours would be curious. But the name has been given, e.g. by Miss Constance Hill (240). The reasons given for J. A.'s change of mind are doubtless the true reasons; but it may be added that the gentleman was six years her junior and that his health seems at the time to have been uncertain.

57. *talobert* is unexplained; it may be nonsense.

19. *Fri.* 17 *May* 1799

59. *the children*: Fanny and Edward (p. 68), so the *three little boys* (p. 61) left at Godmersham were George, Henry, and William.

61. *dirty quilts.* *dimity* has been conjectured, but I hope J. A. wrote *dirty.*

carpenters. I suspect that Mrs. W. Fowle had relations named *Carpenter.* 1959: The MS. confirms me.

62. *prospective* is obscure to me, but the picturesque writers dealt much in *prospects.* The house has still a handsome interior, but I could see no poplars from the windows. 1959: The MS. reads *perspective*, as I had suspected.

20. *Sun.* 2 *June* 1799

64. *Eliza*: Fowle, no doubt.

65. *Martha's uncle*: probably Rev. John Craven, brother of Martha's mother; or possibly the husband of her mother's sister, Mrs. T. Fowle (see Index II).

21. *Tues.* 11 *June* 1799

67. *Fitzalbini*: by Egerton Brydges.

68. *Mr. Evelyn*: of St. Clere, near Wrotham, Kent. George Austen in 1775 wrote from Steventon: 'Mr. Evelyn is going to treat us with a plowing match in this neighbourhood... Kent against Hants . . . he sends for his own ploughman from St. Clair.'

22. *Wed.* 19 *June* 1799

72. *after all that had passed.* See the note on Miss Pearson, p. 180.

Earle: Harwood.

23. *Sat.* 25 *Oct.* 1800

75. *Heathcote & Chute for ever*: an election cry.

Catherine . . . Harris: Bigg-Wither.

76. *a fireplace.* Mr. A. H. Hallam Murray tells me that the window is still there, but the fireplace has been removed.

24. *Sat.* 1 *Nov.* 1800

80. *Mr. Peters* seems to have been a clergyman at Tichborne and later at Ovington. The Powlett correspondence contains letters from Anne Powlett to her friend Miss Peters in Truro, in which reference is frequently made to this clergyman, her brother. A letter of 1 Nov. 1800 speaks of talk about him and Miss Lyford; but a later letter, 5 Aug. 1801, reports that 'we have ceased to talk of your Brother and Miss Lyford'.

81. *Mrs. Cooper* may be the wife of J. A.'s first cousin, but they are regularly *Edward* and *Caroline*; I cannot find any other Mrs. Cooper living. J. A. may mean her mother's only sister Jane Cooper, who had died in 1783 and was perhaps too remote to be *Aunt Jane* (which besides would have been ambiguous, since Mrs. Leigh Perrot was also Jane).

25. *Sat.* 8 *Nov.* 1800

82. *Les Veillees*: by Madame de Genlis.

our constant Table. I could not be sure whether J. A. wrote *our* or *one*.

83. *a Cutter.* 'Grand Falconer cutter, Lieutenant Chilcott,

from Marcou' is the only suitable arrival from Marcou mentioned in the Portsmouth Report (27 Oct.–23 Nov.) in *Naval Chronicle* (1800, second part, p. 438).

85. *Anna.* I find from *The History of the Hawtrey Family* (1903), p. 107, that Mary, daughter of Charles Hawtrey, Sub-Dean of Exeter, married the Rev. John Marshall, and that their daughter Anna married 'Mr. Buller son to the Bishop of Exeter'.

Harris: Bigg-Wither.

87. *a Turkish ship.* For Frank's own account see *Sailor Brothers*, 100.

26. *Martha Lloyd. Wed.* 12 *Nov.* 1800

88. *Our invitations*: for the Hurstbourne ball. Lord Portsmouth, when Lord Lymington and aged five, had been a pupil at Steventon Rectory. His 'eccentricities afterwards became notorious'. *Life* 149.

hope at Manydown. The illness of both father and son has been mentioned in earlier letters; but they survived until 1813 and 1833 respectively.

89. *Henry's History*: published in six volumes quarto. The portion for Saturday is 'the history of the manners, virtues, vices, remarkable customs, language, dress, diet and diversions of the people'.

Mrs. Stent. 'With Mrs. Lloyd lived to the last Mrs. Stent, an earlier friend of rather inferior position in life, and reduced, from family misfortunes, to very narrow means.' Caroline Austen's *Reminiscences*.

27. *Thur.* 20 *Nov.* 1800

91. *Rosalie.* Mr. R. A. Austen-Leigh supplies a quotation from a letter of Eliza de Feuillide (later Mrs. Henry Austen) to her cousin Philadelphia Walter, Aug. 1788, asking her to come to Tunbridge Wells for a ball and 'accept half my bed. You will have my apartment to dress in and Miss Rosalie will be very happy to give you all the assistance she can.' We may guess that this Rosalie attracted Sir Thomas's notice.

Warren. In *Times Lit. Suppt.* 7 May 1931 I threw some light on Rev. Thomas Alston W., Rector of South Warnborough, Hants, and John Willing W., both of St. John's,

Oxford, and both contributors to *The Loiterer*, the Oxford periodical edited by James Austen; and I suggested that the Warren of this passage might be T. A. W. But I find that Mrs. Bellas, in a note, identifies this W. as 'Lt.-Col. W.' and his wife as a Maitland; and the dates (see Index II) and connexion with General Mathew make this certain. I still identify the Colonel's cousin, the familiar 'Warren' of the early letters, as J. W. W.; but cannot be sure of p. 46.

Anne: the first Mrs. James Austen.

92. *the General*: General Mathew, Mrs. Maitland's father.

93. *reconciled*. The MS. is mutilated; Lord Brabourne prints *resigned*, but it was a long word, and the third letter looks like *c*.

Lucy: Lefroy.

Mrs. Augusta: Bramstone; who, asked her opinion of *Mansfield Park*, 'owned that she thought S. & S. and P. & P. downright nonsense, but expected to like MP. better, & having finished the 1st vol. flattered herself she had got through the worst'. (*Opinions*.)

94. *George*: perhaps Edward's little boy; but there is an obscure George on p. 11.

Atkinsons of En . . .: probably Enham, cf. p. 91. In Nov. 1792 J. A. was just short of seventeen, and perhaps it was her 'first Hurstbourne ball'.

95. *Lady S & S*——: Saye and Sele. In a letter from Mrs. Austen to Mrs. J. A. written from Stoneleigh 13 Aug. 1806 (Lefroy MS.) I find: 'Poor Lady Saye & Sele to be sure is rather tormenting, tho' sometimes amusing, and affords Jane many a good laugh.'

28. *Sun.* 30 *Nov.* 1800

like Mrs Hastings: probably the wife of Warren Hastings; see Index II for other references, and, for the family connexion. *Life*, ch. 3. I have no clue to the faithful Maria; but Mrs. Hastings's name was Marian.

the Shrewsbury Clock: *I Henry IV*, Act V, Scene iv.

97. *the Eldest daughter*. J. A. is herself strict in observing this and similar rules; in writing to her niece Anna she always

calls her husband 'Mr. Ben Lefroy', because he had an elder brother. So in *Mansfield Park* Edmund is usually 'Mr. Edmund Bertram', even in his presence and in Tom's absence. There are some exceptions in the letters; 'Mrs. H. Digweed' is sometimes 'Mrs. Digweed'; but of that there may be an explanation.

98.

Delman is my misreading of Delmar. The Canterbury Librarian sends me a notice (*Kentish Gazette*, 4 Nov. 1800) of 'A Ball at Delmar's Rooms', the first of a series, to be held on 6 Nov. The subscription for six balls was a guinea.

29. *Sat.* 3 *Jan.* 1801

99. *Miss Lloyd* occurs also on pp. 142, 225, 235, 299, 357 (*Floyd*, see note), 412, 482, 495. In each place the context makes it natural that Martha Lloyd should be so styled. (At 225 J. A. is quoting the boys.)

101. *Mr. Nibbs*: not identified, and perhaps not the name of a real artist. But see Addenda after Index VIII.

102. *Miss Foote* is no doubt Harriet, younger sister of the reigning Lady Bridges; she became Mrs. Edward Bridges in 1809. Her cousin Frederick I have not identified.

103. *The threatened Act of Parliament.* The reference is probably (as Prof. Veitch suggests) to one of the measures proposed to meet the distress of the winter of 1800–1. One of these was the fixing of a maximum price of ten shillings a bushel for wheat. This was proposed by Lord Warwick, but met with vigorous opposition. (*Parl. Hist.* xxxv. 833–5.)

30. *Thur.* 8 *Jan.* 1801

105. *Peter.* Black Peter is the knave of spades, in a childish card game so called.

actually erected. Egerton Brydges was Mrs. Lefroy's brother. In his *Autobiography* (1834, i. 137) he states that 'when I first married, in 1786, I hired a small parsonage-house in the parish adjoining' Ashe. This was no doubt Deane Parsonage, later occupied by Mrs. Lloyd.

106. *the Farm*: probably Cheesedown.

Mrs. Laurel. This passage is perhaps hopelessly obscure. Sir William Foster has probably identified the rich

East Indian (see Index II). But since *this proof* may be either the wedding or the arrival of the letter which announced it, there is ample room for conjecture. I think *Mary* is Mrs. James Austen (who was given to self-torment), not Mary Cooke.

Mr. R. A. Austen-Leigh reminds me that one of Mrs. Lloyd's (Mrs. J. A.'s mother) sisters, *née* Craven, made a misalliance with one Hinxman (so spelled in the Lefroy MS.), and suggests that J. A. may be jocularly identifying the two H.'s. The Cravens lived in Berkshire, so *Wantage Downs* is suitable.

The wedding-day: James and Mary's.

Fulwar, Eliza: Fowle.

107. *Hugh Capet* and *Mr. Skipsey*: the former, I suppose, a horse; Mr. S. I do not recognize, but he may be a horse too.

31. *Wed.* 14 *Jan.* 1801

111. *singing Duetts with the Prince of Wales.* The *Morning Post* 12 Jan. reports 'H.R.H. . . . now on a visit to Sir Hy. Featherstonhaugh in Hampshire . . ., a large party . . . sports of the field'. Sir Henry lived at Up Park, which is in Sussex, but very near the Hampshire border. Sir Alfred Welby tells me that he has a recollection of hearing that his ancestress *was* musical. See also 72, note on p. 280.

Major Byng. Times, 13 Jan. 1801:

> 'We are extremely sorry to learn, by private letters received yesterday, the confirmation of the death of Mr. Byng, a cousin of Mr. Wickham, who was killed in the battle of the 14th near Salzburg. This gentleman was a Volunteer in the Austrian service', &c.

No previous notice has been found, and the Christian name is not given. *The Times* notice suggests that Mr. B. was *not* a member of the Torrington family; the only Edmund of that family who can be found died in 1854.

32. *Wed.* 21 *Jan.* 1801

115. *Caroline*: Cooper.

Mrs. G.: Girle.

the Square: Queen's Square.

J. D.: James Digweed.

the Boarding-school: a book, or a game? If a book, probably (as Miss M. Hope Dodds suggests) *The Governess; or Evening Amusements at a Boarding-School* (anon., 1800).

34. *Wed.* 11 *Feb.* 1801

119. *24 Upper Berkeley Street*: it is clear, from the references on pp. 118, 120, and 121, that Cassandra was staying with Henry at this address; p. 121 is the first mention of his keeping a carriage.

120. *their Royal Passenger*: the Duke of Sussex.

121. *Cath*: Bigg.

sunday-chaise: not explained.

35. *Tues.* 5 *May* 1801

123. *Gloucestershire*: *Life* 166, 373. The visit was perhaps to the Fowles at Elkstone, near Cheltenham. A visit to Adlestrop is an alternative.

36. *Tues.* 12 *May* 1801

126. *Mary*: Mrs. J. A.; Frank's Mary does not come on the scene for five years.

37. *Thur.* 21 *May* 1801

131. *Weston*: 'The Promenade to Weston; the Hyde-Park, or Kensington-Gardens, of Bath . . . attractive from the shortness of its distance, which does not exceed a mile and a half. . . . At the bottom of *Sion-Hill* . . . the Village of Weston . . . which is occupied by numerous laundresses, has altogether a superior appearance. . . . The Church is a small erection; but the numerous monuments in its Burying-Ground are highly attractive and interesting. . . . The visitor . . . can diversify the scene by turning off into *Barton's Fields*.' Egan, *Walks through Bath*, 1819.

132. *an absurd pretension*. But Mrs. Allen noted with approval that 'Miss Tilney always wears white'. *Northanger Abbey*, ch. 12.

38. *Tues.* 26 *May* 1801

134. *the Harrison family*. This obscure allusion may be connected with the reference to Mary Harrison on p. 13.

136. *Now this, says My Master* suggests a quotation from Mrs. Piozzi (cf. p. 66), but it does not seem to be in her Johnsonian writings.

137. *particularly scrupulous.* Perhaps because the Evelyns seem to be involved in the Twistleton scandal (p. 127) and because the Leighs of Stoneleigh were connected with the Twistletons.

Topaze crosses: now, alas, in America, but in good hands. There is a picture of them in *Sailor Brothers.* They are no doubt the archetype of the amber cross in *Mansfield Park.*

39. *Fri.* 14 *Sept.* 1804

138. *the Royal Family.* Mr. C. Wanklyn sends me this from the *Western Flying Post* for 10 Sept.:

> 'Weymouth Sept. 8th. Arrived here this town's original patron, his Royal Highness the Duke of Gloucester on a visit to the Royal Family, all of whom, we are happy to observe, enjoy good health and spirits. The King rises very early and visits the camps before breakfast, then embarks with the family for a cruise in the Royal Sovereign yacht, attended by the two others, the frigates, and a fleet of yachts of every description, returns to an evening parade and lastly visits the theatre. This is making the most of his time. The town was never known to be fuller of company than this season, since the Royal Family has been here.'

The *Morning Post* describes the embarkation of Tuesday:

> 'Weymouth Sept. 11. At half-past ten the Royal Family left the Lodge, and went to the shore in their carriages, when two boats were waiting to receive them, and convey them on board the Royal Yacht.'

139. *last evening.* Cf. p. 142, *yester morning.* Mr. Peter Debary seems to have been a purist.

Le Chevalier: not identified.

140. *uncle Toby's annuity*: *Tristram Shandy*, iii. 22.

141. *their infamous plate*: on No. 4 Sydney Place, which the Austens left (for Green Park Buildings) in Jan. 1805. See Index II, s.v. Cole.

142. *yester-morning.* J. A. uses *yester morn* in *Persuasion*,

ch. 13 (p. 126 of my edition). But I suspect that she there wrote *morn*[g] as was her custom, and that *morn* is a printer's error.

Fraser. The word is I think more like Leaver or Feaver.

Manhood: reading uncertain. *Hooper*: Holder.

40. *Francis Austen*. *Mon.* 21 *Jan.* 1805

145. *Brompton*. Henry lived from 1805 to 1809 at 16 Michael's-place, Brompton.

43. *Mon.* 8 *Apr.* 1805

148. *Miss Lefroy*: probably (in spite of the formality) Lucy L., now Mrs. Henry Rice.

149. *her end*. Mrs. Lloyd died 16 Apr.

152. *The Wallop race*. This is a flight of fancy, as Mr. Horrocks pointed out. Many of the ladies of the Portsmouth family were Camilla or Urania; and the ships so named reminded J. A. of this.

153. *Expedition*: a forty-four, built at Chatham 1784.

44. *Sun.* 21 *Apr.* 1805

156. *Bickerton* and *Amelia* (157), and their connexion with *Fulwar-William* (Fowle), are obscure. There was a Bickerton family at Chawton; Richard B., 1816–54, and his wife Sophia are buried in Chawton churchyard.

157. *the famous Saunders*. I have not traced this author, who may be fabulous.

158. *Lady Roden*. Why J. A. should with great justice be guessed to have visited this lady I do not know; but Robert Jocelyn, the second earl, married as his second wife a Northumberland Orde; and J. A. was acquainted with Lord Bolton (a Northumberland Orde by origin) and with other Hampshire Ordes, Powletts, and Orde-Powletts. The Powlett correspondence shows that a son of Lord R. was or might have been Charles Powlett's pupil.

45. *Sat.* 24 *Aug.* 1805

160. *Harriot*: Bridges.

161. *Palmerstone* was perhaps derived from *Letters from Mrs. Palmerstone to her Daughters, inculcating Morality by*

Entertaining Narratives, 1803, by Mrs. Rachel Hunter (whom J. A. is known to have laughed at, see p. 406 and note).

163. *Henry's picture of Rowling.* There is no other allusion to H. as an artist, and it is just possible that the picture was by Henry Bridges; but Henry Austen seems to have been staying at Godmersham (161, 162). I suppose that Daniel, the Godmersham coachman, drove him as far as Ospringe, where he caught a London coach. He may, however, have gone not to London but to Goodnestone, see **166**. See notes on pp. 11, 219.

46. *Tues.* 27 *Aug.* 1805

166. *Sophie*: probably Deedes.

John: Bridges.

Henry: the same ambiguity as on 163. Henry Bridges would be more likely than Henry Austen to pronounce on Marianne's symptoms.

47. *Fri.* 30 *Aug.* 1805

169. *the evil intentions of the Guards.* Sir John Fortescue tells me that on Friday, 30 Aug. (partridge-shooting began on the Monday following) the First and Second Grenadier Guards marched from Deal for Chatham, the First Coldstreams and First Scots Guards from Chatham for Deal. A movement on such a scale might well disturb the birds; and Mr. Edward Bridges may have apprehended that (in spite of the efforts of their officers) some of the men might do a bit of poaching. 'Yet (Sir John adds) the danger of invasion was only just past. Napoleon's orders for the march from Boulogne to the Danube were not issued until 22 August, and the camp at Boulogne was not finally evacuated until that same fateful 30 August.'

48. *Wed.* 7 *Jan.* 1807

171. *our guests*: apparently James (occasionally) and his wife and daughter (Caroline) and Frank and his wife. (But Frank and Mary were perhaps sharing Mrs. Austen's lodgings.)

172. *Mrs. Foote's baby's name.* J. A. had forgotten that Captain Foote had already a Caroline—a daughter by his first wife. He was first cousin of John Foote, banker of London, father of the three sisters, Eleanor, Harriet, and Lucy, two of

whom married Bridges brothers. This explains Fanny's interest.

the Williams: Sir Thomas and Lady W.

173. *Alphonsine*: by Madame de Genlis.

the 'Female Quixotte': by Charlotte Lennox.

the family treaty: a financial arrangement between Mr. Leigh Perrot and the Adlestrop Leighs; see 177, 'my Uncle's Business'; 182, 'the negociation between them & Adlestrop', 207 'Business', 232 'the Stoneleigh business', 316 'vile compromise', and *Life* 195.

Mrs. K.: Knight.

49. *Sun.* 8 *Feb.* 1807

176. *Queen Mary's Lamentation*. J. A. perhaps got her knowledge from Goldsmith's *History of England* (4 vols., 1771), her own copy of which has been preserved (*Life* 29; Keynes, *Bibliography* 274). See ii. 85: 'The unhappy princess continued her lamentations; but being informed of his (Rizzio's) fate, at once dried her tears, and said she would weep no more, for she would now think of revenge.' But there are other possibilities.

to see Peter Debary. Caroline Austen in her *Reminiscences* records a longer visit in May 1815: 'We visited the Debarys at Eversley. His sister lived with him. We were there Sunday 18 June' (i.e. for Waterloo).

178. *Our Garden*: in Castle Square.

Cowper's Line: *The Task*, vi. 150:

Laburnum, rich
In streaming gold; syringa, iv'ry pure.

the Castle: see the account of this eccentric building and its eccentric owner in *Memoir*. His portrait at Bowood shows a mild man, and has nautical accessories.

Catherine: Foote.

179. *Mrs. W. K.*: Wyndham Knatchbull.

Hastings: no doubt Warren Hastings; Henry Egerton was an acquaintance of his protégée Mrs. Henry Austen.

180. *the only Family . . . whom we cannot visit*. I have little doubt that the cause of this *unluckiness* was a youthful indis-

cretion not of Frank, but of Henry Austen. The references in 3, 6, and 7 (pp. 7, 9, 15, 16, 18) suggest that Henry was in 1796 either engaged, or thought likely to be engaged, to Miss Pearson. See p. 72, 'after all that had passed', and Index II, s.v. Pearson, for other references.

M[de] Duval: *Evelina*, vol. ii, Letter 3, 'Of all the unluckinesses that ever I met, this is the worst!'

Edward: Edward Austen's eldest boy.

Clarentine: by Sarah Burney.

Miss Harrison: presumably d. of John Butler H. II.

Mrs. Dusautoy (not Dusantoy or Durantoy as in Brabourne): a family of French origin. Members of the family were in trade in Hants, and it might be Louis D., teacher of French in Southampton, who took lodgers (p. 252). But a James D. of Winchester, Lt. of Marines, m. 1793 Mary Hinton of Chawton. The Hintons were connected with the Southampton Harrisons. This Mrs. D. may be ours, and the Misses D. of p. 391 her daughters. Mrs. James D. died at Taunton 1851, and I find a Rev. Frederic D. near Crewkerne. Taunton and Crewkerne are not far from Devonshire.

181. *Sir Tho.*: Williams.

Mary: Mrs. F. A.

like my dear Dr. Johnson: See Johnson's letter to Boswell 4 July 1774.

50. *Fri.* 20 *Feb.* 1807

182. *M[r] Austen . . . Mr. M[y] Austen*: John A. of Broadford and Francis Motley A. of Kippington.

Mary: Mrs. F. A.

183. Elizabeth (not Caroline) Coleman was baptized 1807.

184. *the 1st Lord*: Thomas Grenville.

185. *poor Mr. Sharpe.* For Samuel Sharp's controversy with Baretti see Index V. The sisters' sustained interest in this ancient quarrel invites explanation; and Mr. E. G. Bayford ingeniously suggests a connexion with their friend Ann Sharp, the governess at Godmersham. Samuel Sharp was a man of some note (see *D.N.B.*); but not much is known of his private

life. Baretti mentions that in 1765 he was accompanied in Italy by three young ladies, which looks like daughters. But if this Samuel Sharp, who died 24 March 1778, may be identified with Samuel Sharp of the Circus, Bath, whose will was proved on 4 Apr. 1778, his daughters were Eleanor and Frances, not Ann; and Sharp was too rich to have a governess daughter. There remains a possibility of a remoter relationship. (A Miss Sharpe of Bath is mentioned p. 157).

For further fact and speculation about Ann Sharp see *Doncaster Gazette* 9 Apr. (Mr. Bayford), *Times*, 12 Feb., and *Notes and Queries*, 27 Feb. 1926.

William: Fowle.

remedy: a holiday at Winchester, regularly 'asked' and granted on a Tuesday.

her Sister: Mrs. J. A. (not Mrs. Fowle).

Lady B.: Sir Brook's first wife, who died in 1806 leaving three children. Sir Brook did not accept the nomination suggested, though he did marry again.

51. *Wed.* 15 *June* 1808

187. *Our two brothers.* A coach left the Cross Keys, Gracechurch-street, daily at 5 a.m. and completed the journey to Dover (71 miles by this route) in 15 hours. So James would reach Canterbury (55 m.) in under 12 hours, and might well be at Godmersham before the carriage party.

since last year. Fanny Knight's diary shows that in Sept. 1807 'grandmamma and Aunts Cassandra and Jane Austen' paid a visit to Chawton House (*Brabourne*, ii. 116).

188. *John*: Bridges.

little Edward: James's boy James Edward, who was not yet ten years old; distinguished from his cousin of fourteen (*Edward* below). *Little Edward* is usually Edward's son, but on p. 68 must be James's.

at that time. A child was born in September.

189. *their carriage*: doubtless a chaise, which held three people without much to spare. On this occasion it conveyed the two ladies and two children (the *child of three* is James's

younger d. Caroline), unless, indeed, James Edward accompanied his father by coach.

the Temple Plantations. The Vicar of Godmersham tells me that in the 'wilderness' is a small building called the Temple—one of the places in which 'Jane Austen is supposed to have written'.

190. *Harriot*: Bridges, who became Mrs. Moore in 1806.

Mary: Mrs. F. A.

Huxham: from John H., physician, 1692–1768, whose tincture of cinchona bark is in the British Pharmacopoeia. An advertisement (*London Chronicle*, 31 Dec. 1807) of Newbery and Sons, proprietors of Dr. James's Powder, includes 'Huxham's Tinct. of Bark'.

191. *Louisa* in the first and third paragraphs is L. Bridges, in the last the little girl.

Mr. Jefferson's case. I cannot connect William Jefferson (see Index V) with the Austens; but Watt (*Bibliotheca Britannica*) mentions a Joseph J., dissenting minister at Basingstoke, who might perhaps be W. J.'s father.

Miss Austen: Harriet Lennard A.

Miss Maria: Cuthbert.

Mrs. Inman is said by Lord Brabourne (i. 338) to have been 'the aged widow of a former clergyman at Godmersham'; but the present vicar can trace no such clergyman, and the inscription on Rebecca Inman's tomb rather suggests a spinster.

in the Palace. I do not know how Sacree got there; Mrs. Edward Austen cannot have been present (Brook John was born in September) and I cannot find among the ladies at court any on whom Sacree would naturally be in attendance. Perhaps she was there by favour of Mrs. Charles Feilding, who was related to the Goodnestone family and was an inmate of the Palace.

192. *my brother James.* 'my brother' is regular, but this sounds formal. I imagine that J. A. wrote 'my brother' and then added 'James' to avoid ambiguity.

the nature of the road. I suppose there was no coach. Bookham is on the London–Farnham road by Leatherhead;

but James's natural route to Farnham (and so to Basingstoke and Steventon) would be direct by Maidstone. See p. 203.

52. *Mon.* 20 *June* 1808

193. *Mary Jane*: Frank's little girl, then at Southampton.

Caroline: possibly Hales (Mrs. Gore).

Edward Ju[n]: Edward's boy, not James Edward; see p. 199.

194. *Her very agreeable present*: Mrs. Knight's 'fee'.

195. *James-Edward*. James; Edward in Brabourne. But J. A. wrote *James:Edward*, using a colon where we use a hyphen.

the Dean: Powys.

on Tuesday: of the following week. Since Louisa Bridges 'goes home on Friday', she would be 'from Goodnestone' on the succeeding Tuesday.

197. It seems probable that the Mr. Lyford who attended the Austens in 1808 was the Basingstoke, not the Winchester surgeon; see pp. 210, 217.

bad pens. I have ascertained that J. A. wrote *pens*, not *puns*.

a sad story. The scandal cannot be found in the London *Courier*, but see *Morning Post*, 18 and 21 June 1808. 'Another elopement has taken place in high life. A Noble Viscount, Lord S., has gone off with a Mrs. P., the wife of a relative of a Noble Marquis' [of Winchester]. 'Mrs. P.'s *faux pas* with Lord S——e took place at an inn near Winchester.' Col. P. was awarded £3,000 damages. See *Mansfield Park*, ch. 46 (p. 440 of my edition).

198. *her duty*. Mrs. Knight was perhaps James Edward's godmother.

53. *Sun.* 26 *June* 1808

199. *young Edward* here means Edward's son, not James Edward, who was not yet at Winchester.

our Friends: probably the Biggs, see p. 194; why *secrecy* was needed does not appear.

201. *Mrs. M of Nackington*: Milles.

Mrs. Moore's. I conjecture that Mrs. M. of the Oaks was the Archbishop's widow and mother of the Rector of Wrotham. This would explain Harriot M.'s presence in Canterbury.

Ly. Knatchbull & her Mother: Mrs. Hawkins.

must keep it two. Perhaps letters were not sent to the post from Godmersham every day.

202. *into Somersetshire.* The Knatchbulls lived at Babington, which is about 5 miles north of Shepton Mallet on the Bath road. Thus it would be natural for them to leave the coast-road either at Fareham (for Winchester) or at Southampton (for Salisbury).

203. *her namesake*: Mrs. F. A.

to pass the door at Seale. The Walters lived at Seale.

54. *Thur.* 30 *June* 1808

204. *a silver knife* may remind us of Mary Price's silver knife in *Mansfield Park*, 'the gift of her good godmother, old Mrs. Admiral Maxwell'. Did Anna Austen furnish a hint for the character of Susan Price?

205. *glad to go home.* 'I remember the Godmersham visit well in many little points, and I don't think I was very happy there in a strange house. I recollect the model of a ship in a passage and my cousins' rabbits out of doors, in or near a long walk of high trees. I have been told it was the limestone path. I never visited the place again.'—Caroline Austen's *Reminiscences.* There is no mistaking the 'long walk of high trees'—a very narrow avenue of very tall limes, in the 'wilderness'. But the Vicar tells me that the term *limestone* is not used locally to describe the local limestones; if the path was named from its materials it would be the 'chalk path', or the 'rag path'. Probably, therefore, 'limestone path' is a mistake for 'lime path' or 'lime walk'.

206. *Fanny Austen's Match*: with Capt. Holcroft, R.A.; why this was *misconduct* is unknown.

207. *Business.* See note on 173.

Smalbone: 'My Father and Mother, taking my Brother and myself and Mary Smallbone who lived with us, went to Godmersham' (Caroline Austen's *Reminiscences*, 1808).

Mrs. Hastings' voyage down the Ganges. Mr. P. E. Roberts suggests that this is the voyage of 1781, when Mrs. H. got as far as Patna. See *Letters of W. H. to his Wife*, ed. S. C. Grier, 1905.

208. *Mrs. D.*: Deedes.

209. *the pleasures of Friendship*, &c., seems to point to a larger circle than the normal household in Castle Square; see note on *our Friends*, p. 199.

55. *Sun.* 1 *Oct.* 1808

210. *who the Godmother is to be* remains unsolved.

guessing the names. I do not know how Mrs. A. guessed Brook John's first name; but the second was perhaps obvious, since the child's elder maternal uncles—Sir Brook *William*, Brook *Henry*, and Brook *Edward*—already had namesakes in his brothers. Perhaps, again, since Edward Junior could not be regarded as named after his uncle of that name (since it was also his father's), *Brook John* was intended in compliment both to *Brook* Edward and to Brook *John*.

Eliza. There are two Elizas on this page. The first is a Maitland, the second, no doubt, Henry Austen's wife.

212. *if we ever have another garden here* does not imply that there was none in Castle Square (it was 'the best in the Town', p. 184), but that the Austens had decided to leave their house but had not decided whether to have another in Southampton or to go elsewhere.

something perfectly unexceptionable . . . through him. Henry's bank had an Alton branch, and his geese were apt to be swans.

Yarmouth Division: Frank and his wife.

Espriella: by Southey.

Miss B.: Bailey.

213. *my little Goddaughter*: Louisa Austen.

The Marquis: of Lansdowne. He put it off too long, for he died in 1809.

56. *Fri.* 7 *Oct.* 1808

214. *your Winchester Correspondent*: Edward junior, or possibly his brother George; *a very proper day*, being his father's birthday.

his 30th year is what J. A. wrote. Either she made a slip (for he was 40) or it is a joke.

215. *Eliza*: a maid.

Mrs. E. K.: I can think of nothing better than (Sir) Edward Knatchbull's first wife, who did not die until 1814. But see Index II (1949).

216. *those at Lyme.* I learn from C. Wanklyn's *Lyme Regis, a Retrospect* (second ed. 1927) that this is probably a reference to a big fire at L. on 5 Nov. 1803. If so, we can account for the family 'rambles' in each of the years 1801–4.

my two *companions*: her mother and Martha (see 215).

217. *the three boys*: Edward and George Austen and William Fowle.

Harriot: Moore.

her son Edward's 'invitation' may possibly, as Mr. Austen-Leigh suggests, have been an offer of marriage. The tone of p. 231 does not preclude the possibility.

218. *Catherine*: Bigg, now Mrs. Hill.

Miss Foote: Caroline.

to do with her is what J. A. wrote, but she perhaps intended *without*.

57. *Thur.* 13 *Oct.* 1808

219. *Henry*: the same uncertainty as is considered in notes on pp. 11, 163, 166. The reference to *anguish* (220) rather suggests a brother than a brother-in-law; and on p. 223 *Henry* is coupled with *John* Bridges. But 224 makes it clear that Henry Austen was at Godmersham, for Kintbury would not send apples to a Bridges (and cf. 244, his first *return* to Godmersham, i.e. since Elizabeth's death), and therefore his grief must be mentioned; and there is no reason to suppose that Henry Bridges was in Kent at the time. Henry Austen was of a mercurial temperament, and probably more demonstrative than his brothers and sisters.

58. *Sat.* 15 *Oct.* 1808; see Addenda

223. *Henry and John.* See note on p. 219.

to Edward, about their mourning: presumably Edward son of Edward, for J. A. would hardly write to James Edward, then under his own mother's roof, about his mourning. On the other hand the next sentence might suggest that *our nephew* may be James Edward. *The poor boys* are, of course, Edward's boys (Edward and George), who had been taken from Winchester to Steventon on the news of their mother's death.

224. *Mr. Fowle.* Since the Rev. Thomas Fowle the elder d. 1806, and his wife predeceased him 1798, the references 1808 and 1815 to *Mr.* or *Mrs. F.* must mean the *Fulwar* and *Eliza* of earlier letters. J. A.'s tone does not, however, suggest any diminution of friendliness. Fulwar on his father's death succeeded to the dignity of 'Mr. Fowle', as head of this family; and 'Eliza' may have been avoided as (until Henry Austen's wife's death 1813) ambiguous.

It appears from a letter of Charles Austen, 24 Dec. 1809, (printed in *Sailor Brothers*, 209), that Tom Fowle (not Fowler as there printed) was on board his ship. This explains Mr. F.'s consigning charts to the care of the Palmers (Mrs. Charles Austen's family).

59. *Mon.* 24 *Oct.* 1808

The italics in this letter (as printed in Brabourne) represent, I think, underlining by another hand—perhaps Fanny Knight's.

225. *Mr. Wise*: 'old Wyse, a civil, respectful mannered, elderly man, exceedingly fond of hunting, who drove Roger's coach every day, Sundays excepted, from Southampton to Popham Lane in the morning, and back to Southampton in the afternoon. He arrived at the Flower Pots, Popham Lane, soon after ten o'clock, and left it between three and four.' *Vine Hunt*, 66.

Miss Lloyd can only be Martha; J. A. is quoting the boys.

226. *poor Catherine*: Bigg, see 222, 228.

Fanny's letter must have betrayed knowledge of the intended move. *This proposal* is Edward's offer of the cottage at Chawton.

227. *Their aunt*: Mrs. J. A.

228. *Lake of Killarney*: by Anna Maria Porter.

noonshine: *moonshine* in Brabourne, but cf. 195.

229. ***summer evenings.*** See 226, *quite the evening.* I imagine Edward's *kind consideration* was an instruction that the boys should travel post.

60. *Sun.* 21 *Nov.* 1808

231. *John and Lucy.* Their marriage (it did not take place) would have been a third Bridges-Foote match.

for Edward's Manservant. I suppose so that Edward might pay occasional visits to the Cottage when he did not wish to open the Great House.

Alethea: Bigg.

232. *the Stoneleigh business.* See note on 173.

Chambers. A letter from Mrs. Leigh Perrot of 10 Nov. 1799, printed in *Notes and Queries for Somerset and Dorset*, Sept. 1924, p. 59, contains this passage: 'My Maid is a Welsh Woman. . . . Had my poor old quiet Chambers been living she would have been a real Comfort to me.' There may have been a second Chambers; but Mrs. L. P. was capable of repining for more than nine years.

233. Our *Brother*: presumably James.

234. *Mary Jane*: Frank's daughter, left behind when (233) 'Frank and Mary left us'.

61. *Fri.* 9 *Dec.* 1808

235. *Mrs. Piozzi*: *Letters to and from the late Samuel Johnson* (1788), i. 270; the quotation is substantially accurate.

a lately made Admiral: Thomas Bertie.

our Connections in West Kent: Austens of Broadford and elsewhere.

236. *I* will *marry Mr. Papillon*: the joke is repeated eight years later, p. 469.

237. *Sir Robert*: Sloper.

238. *Conscientious refusal.* The living of Hampstead Marshall fell vacant in 1806 by the death of Rev. Thomas Fowle, who, though he lived at Kintbury Vicarage after resigning that living to his son in 1798, retained the smaller living of Hampstead and did duty there up to his death. The patron, Lord Craven, asked James Austen to hold the living 'for some years,

until the young man for whom it was designed should be of age to take it'. James refused the living, 'not from any fear that he should be tempted to retain it dishonestly, but solely on account of the *words* which must be used in accepting it. He did not think the arrangement simoniacal in spirit; but there stood the ugly word' (Caroline Austen's *Reminiscences*).

the 4th of Septr. This precision, so far ahead, is perhaps jocular; but if Edward took his boys back to school he *might* visit Chawton on the day named. The 'election' (i.e. summer) holidays in 1809 ended before the 1st of September.

62. *Tues.* 27 *Dec.* 1808

239. *the party*: probably Mr. and Mrs. J. A.

240. *Eliza*: a maid.

Sir B.: Sir Brook Bridges.

241. *black butter.* Mr. F. C. Bell, writing in *The Times* of 8 Feb. 1930, thanks correspondents who had sent him 'recipes for apple butter'. He adds that 'this simple, uncostly, and delightful conserve' is in the Channel Islands 'called black butter, and has been known there for centuries'.

Miss Austen: probably C. E. A. (quoted from Eliza), not Miss A. of Southampton.

his godson: James Edward.

242. *Bermuda*: Charles and his family.

a day of sad remembrance. Edward was married on 27 Dec. 1791.

the boarding-house: kept, as Mr. Horrocks told me, by Mrs. B. Kelly at 17 High-street.

Corinna: by Madame de Stael.

244. *Eliza*: Mrs. Henry A.

boast no longer. See p. 184.

your godmother: Mrs. E. Leigh.

63. *Tues.* 10 *Jan.* 1809; see Addenda

245. *Mary*: Mrs. F. A.

246. *The 'Regency'.* Prof. Trevelyan tells me that this must refer to some rumour about the King's health; the expected regency became fact in 1810.

distinguished kindness seems an odd phrase. Did J. A. perhaps write *distinguishing*?

from one quarter: I suppose Paragon.

247. *Uncle John*: Bridges.

248. *The American lady.* J. A. doubtless wrote *Lady.* See Index V, s.v. Grant. Lord Brabourne's paragraphing is misleading; the report of the letter from Paragon ends at *mentioned*; what follows relates to family reading.

Margiana, or Widdrington Tower: by Mrs. S. Sykes (Minerva Press, five volumes, 1808).

very generous. The first edition of *Marmion*, in quarto, cost 31*s.* 6*d.*, but several octavo editions appeared in 1808, so we need not suppose that J. A. laid out more than 12*s.*

249. *many happy returns*: of C. E. A.'s birthday, 9 Jan. 1773.

64. *Tues.* 17 *Jan.* 1809

250. *her new Aunt*: Mrs. Brownlow Mathew.

251. *Mrs. Esten*: the wife of James Christie Esten, Chief Justice of Bermuda; his mother was a Palmer, and so connected with Charles Austen's wife (C. A.'s e.d. was Cassandra Esten).

William and *Mary Jane*: Fowle.

Ida of Athens and *Irish Girl*: by Sydney Owenson (Lady Morgan).

252. *Miss M. conveys*: I suppose Miss Murden, in the *basket* mentioned 250.

Alas! poor Brag. See 247.

253. *Mrs. Hy D.*: Digweed. I have not discovered the name of 'the next' (if any).

The Queen's Birthday fell on 19 May, but in 1809 (and always?) was celebrated on 18 Jan. (*London Gazette*).

Mr. Austen and Capt. Harwood: James A. and Earle H., see 250.

65. *Tues.* 24 *Jan.* 1809

254. *Miss Beverleys.* Miss B. is the heroine of *Cecilia.*

255. *a small prize.* 'In 1808 the *Indian*, Charles Austen's ship, captured *La Jeune Estelle*, a small privateer.' *Sailor Brothers*, 207.

a final e. I have seen letters of C. E. A. which show her fondness for final *e.*

Mary: Cooke.

yesterday: her birthday, 23 Jan. 1793.

256. *Caleb.* See p. 259.

Propria que Maribus: from the Eton Latin Grammar:

> Propria quae maribus tribuuntur, mascula dicas;
> ut sunt Divorum; Mars, Bacchus, Apollo—&c.

Miss C.: presumably Curling, cousin of Mrs. F. A. See 245.

257. *Mother.* J. A. invariably writes 'my Mother', and no doubt regarded 'Mother' as a vulgarism.

deputed by Capt. Smith. See 253.

the complacency of her Mama. There is no mention of a Mrs. Hammond in this matter of the ball; he was evidently a bachelor.

258. *Dr. M.*: Mant.

such a son: Sir John Moore.

The Portsmouth paper: Hampshire Telegraph, 23 Jan. 1809.

66. *Mon.* 30 *Jan.* 1809

259. *Cœlebs*: Hannah More's *Cœlebs in Search of a Wife.*

260. *Mrs. E. L.*: Leigh.

261. *Miss B.*: presumably Bailey.

Your plan for Miss Curling: perhaps that she should accompany Edward, who may have intended a visit to Chawton or Winchester.

Aunt Fanny. If 'the Fire' is Caroline Cooper's escape (260), Aunt Fanny should be a relation of that family. But if a Kentish fire, she would be Fanny Cage.

Sir J. Moore. See p. 258. I think 'no one nearer than Sir John himself' implies *some* family connexion; but some take the meaning to be that there was no connexion. None has been traced. A good deal is known of Deacon Morrell, but nothing of his relations with his mother.

Miss C. L. Thomson (*Jane Austen, a Survey*, 1929, p. 275)

thinks the reference to *Christian* and *Hero* 'not only conventional, but an offence against good taste'. But we do not know all that was in J. A.'s mind. Sir Charles Oman writes:

> 'What Jane was thinking of with regard to Sir John's deathbed—of which a rather full narrative survives—was that he is reported to have said nothing about God and the other world, but a good deal about public opinion in England, and his hope that it would acquit him; as well as some messages to Lady Hester Stanhope and other friends in London. I think she was hinting that it was not a very "Christian" end, and that her words have no further meaning.' Miss Lascelles suggests a reminiscence of *Rambler* 44 (Elizabeth Carter): 'The christian and the hero are inseparable'.

262. *Mrs. Seward* being Edward Austen's tenant, any application to her would naturally be made through Godmersham.

the Child: I suppose Frank's Mary Jane.

67. *Crosbie & Co. Wed.* 5 *Apr.* 1809

For a full account of the transaction see the *Life*, or my edition of *Northanger Abbey.*

particular circumstances. They did not reach Chawton until the end of July, and manuscripts would not accompany J. A. on visits.

68. *Francis Austen. Wed.* 26 *July* 1809

Since my text was printed off, extracts from this letter have appeared in *The Times* (16 Dec. 1930). Caroline Austen's *Reminiscences* record that the date of their arrival was 9 July.

265. *come to bide* is quoted again p. 113; see also p. 374.

Feel: the manuscript seems to show a final *s*, but I now think it merely an accidental stroke of the pen.

266. *over-right us*: i.e. in the Great House. But Charles did not reach England until April 1811.

TO

HIS ROYAL HIGHNESS

THE PRINCE REGENT,

THIS WORK IS,

BY HIS ROYAL HIGHNESS'S PERMISSION,

MOST RESPECTFULLY

DEDICATED,

BY HIS ROYAL HIGHNESS'S

DUTIFUL

AND OBEDIENT

HUMBLE SERVANT,

THE AUTHOR.

69. *Thur.* 18 *Apr.* 1811

268. *Manon*: possibly Eliza (though *Manon* has nothing to do with *Elizabeth*). But a letter from Eliza of 4 Aug. 1797, in Mr. Austen-Leigh's possession, rather suggests that Manon was her maid.

269. *Mr. Moore*: of Wrotham, no doubt.

Miss Beaty (here and 276) might be a Miss Beatrice (Smith, or Tilson).

the Col[n] might be Mr. James Tilson's brother, of whom we hear later; but 'the singing Smiths' (271) were plural, so probably it is Col. Smith; the article is accounted for by the following relative clause, 'you have been used to hear of'.

270. *Henry Egerton*. Eliza Austen was intimate with the Rev. Charles E., of Washington, Durham, and his wife; H. E. may have been a connexion. *W. Friars*: Mrs. Knight.

'*mais le moyen*' occurs in a letter of Chesterfield, 23 Oct. 1749.

271. *the 1*[st] *or 2*[d]. It appears (277) that the visit to the Hills at Streatham was fixed for 2 May.

out of humour. It will be remembered that the singing Smiths sang only 'if in good humour' (269).

James's verses. A good many of his verses are preserved; see my edition of the *Memoir*, note to p. 20. *Mrs. K.* is no doubt Mrs. Knight.

70. *Thur.* 25 *Apr.* 1811

272. *our new nephew*: Henry Edgar, son of Frank.

my Brother: Frank.

S & S: *Sense and Sensibility*.

273. *W.*: Willoughby. *Mrs. K.*: Mrs. Knight.

The Incomes were not 'altered' until the second edition, 1813; see my edition, p. 383.

274. *Mr. Cure*: perhaps a kinsman, for Henry and Eliza's common grandmother, Rebecca Hampson, had a sister who married a Cure.

Including everybody we were 66. The present 64 Sloane Street occupies the same site as that occupied by 64 in 1869 (see the plan of the district at that date, p. 267), and there seems no reason to suspect an earlier change of numbers. Unfortunately the house was (as I understand from its present owner) 'reconstructed' near the end of the century; and Mr. Ralph Edwards of the Victoria and Albert Museum, who kindly inspected the drawing-room, reported regretfully that 'nothing remains to recall the period of these festivities'. I gather, however, that the shell of the house was preserved; so we may still reconstruct the scene. The back drawing-room is a handsome octagon; the passage connecting it with a smaller, oblong, room facing the front of the house is short but spacious.

Poike pe Parp. For the nonsense language cf. 278. For what follows I am indebted to Mr. Archibald Jacob.

A chorus by Sir Henry Rowley Bishop (1786–1855) begins:

> Strike the harp in praise of my love
> The lovely sunbeam of Dunscaith,
> Strike the harp in praise of Bragela.

'In peace love tunes the shepherd's reed' is a glee by J. Attwood; *Lay of the Last Minstrel*, iii. 2.

'Rosabelle', a glee by John Wall Callcott (1766–1821); no doubt *Lay of the Last Minstrel*, vi. 23.

'The Red Cross Knight', a glee by Callcott, 1797, 'the words from Evans's Old English Ballads' ('Blow, Warder! blow thy sounding horn').

'Poor Insect': 'The May Fly', a glee by Callcott, 'Poor insect, poor insect'.

275. *the Hypocrite*: Bickerstaffe's adaptation of Cibber's version of *Tartuffe*.

Mrs. Siddons. Mr. C. B. Hogan tells me that *King John*, with Mrs. Siddons as Constance, had been announced at Covent Garden for Saturday 20 April; but, a day or two before, the play was changed for *Hamlet*, and Mrs. S. made her first appearance (since Dec. 1810) in *Macbeth* on the following Monday. J. A. was in London till the end of the month or later; but other engagements may have prevented her seeing Mrs. S. in *The Gamester* (27 April) or *Douglas* (1 May).

277. *Catherine*: Hill.

this morning's paper: 'On Tuesday, Mrs. H. AUSTIN had a musical party at her house in Sloane-street'.—*Morning Post*, 25 Apr.

71. *Tues.* 30 *Apr.* 1811

The shortness of this letter is explained by its costing nothing and by its following hard on another.

277. *much further expense* is, I suppose, jocular.

278. *Mr. W. K.*: Knatchbull.

Self-controul: by Mary Brunton.

her Estimate: not, as might be guessed, another novel, but Mrs. Knight's opinion of *Self-Control*.

Pery pell: 'Very well—or are they? or no.—or at the most, I hope they like it.' See 274.

279. *our cousin Miss Payne.* For *our cousin* see note on p. 14. But Miss P. probably *was* a distant cousin.

Mrs. Dundas's day: for coming to Town? See 261.

72. *Wed.* 29 *May* 1811; see Addenda

280. *Gloucester House*, where the first Duke of G. died in 1805, was the house in Grosvenor St. later called Grosvenor House. It there enjoyed (as Sir Alfred Welby points out to me) a view of Hyde Park, and more fresh air than at a later date. Since the Duke's widow died in 1807 at Brompton, and since it was not until his marriage in 1816 that the second Duke acquired (a different) Gloucester House, it seems safe to infer that in 1811 (the old) G. Ho. was not a ducal residence, and may have been rented by the Leigh Perrots. But see Addenda.

our cousin, Margt. Beckford. See Index II for the Beckfords, and for *our cousin* the note on p. 14. Margaret B. was daughter of the author of *Vathek*. His uncle Francis married Lady Albinia Bertie; the possibility occurs that 'our cousin' may be quoted from the second Mrs. James Austen, whose husband's first wife was a Bertie on her mother's side.

the papers say. The circumstances of the elopement are known, but I have not traced this newspaper scandal.

281. *plumb*: a link with Charles Lamb, who was attached to the *b*.

Cowes: Frank and Mary.

so large a party. We know (231) that there were six bedchambers. I do not know the interior of the cottage; but there are four large windows on the first floor (facing the road) and two small ones in the roof, i.e. two garrets (see 231). The distribution seems to be (1) Mrs. A., (2) C. E. A. and J. A., (3) Martha, (4) the Best, (5) two maids, (6) the manservant (231). On this occasion Mrs. A. offered to vacate (1) for (5). This confirms the statement of the *Memoir* (ch. 1; *Life*, p. 51) that C. and J. 'shared the same bedroom till separated by death'. And cf. 321 'our own room'.

distress of the family. Marianne Bridges died about the end of the month.

282. *Maria M.*: Middleton.

H. B.: Harriet Benn.

my aunt Harding, (283) *My cousin, Flora Long*. For *my* see note on p. 14. Mrs. H. and her niece F. L. were related to the Terrys.

283. *My name is Diana*. Perhaps J. A. wrote *her name*, i.e. Miss Harding's. Mrs. Harding's was actually Dyonisia.

very conveniently for my mother. We should say 'for us'; but J. A. would not claim property in her mother's gravel paths, or in Cassandra's mulberry trees (285), or in 'my father's mutton' (35). Mrs. Montagu Knight tells me that Mr. Prowting lived at 'Prowting's' until he sold that house to the Knights and built, on the opposite side of the road, a new house then called 'Denmead' and now known as Chawton Dower House. 'Prowting's' adjoins the Cottage, and the gravel pit still exists.

73. *Fri.* 31 *May* 1811

284. *conveyed hither*. Miss Sharpe was not at Godmersham; presumably she was in or near London. See 288.

285. *the Gaieties of Tuesday*. The 4th of June was the King's birthday (1738).

Harriot B.: Benn.

286. *the old Map*. Edward Austen no doubt, like Mr. Knightley, would often refer to a map of the Chawton estate.

Mary: Cooke.

74. *Thur.* 6 *June* 1811

288. *Cowes*: Frank and Mary.

289. *Lady B.*: Bridges; *the proposed party*: from Goodnestone, no doubt.

Harriot: Moore.

the Common: Selbourne.

290. *Abingdon St.*: Mrs. Dundas?

291. *Bombasin.* Mrs. Austen writes to Mrs. J. A. in July: 'Last week I bought a bombazeen thinking I should get it cheaper than when the poor King was actually dead.'

74.1. *Martha Lloyd. Sun.* 29 *Nov.* 1812

This, the only letter of 1812, was unknown to the authors of the *Life*, or to any writer on J. A., until its sale by a granddaughter of Sir Francis in 1930. It fetched the record price of £1,000. For the text see p. 499.

Martha Lloyd was then at Barton with her friend Mrs. Dundas, who died there on 1 Dec. *Mrs. D. D.* was her daughter Mrs. Deans Dundas. The letter had no full direction; doubtless it was enclosed in a cover to Mr. Dundas, who, being a member of parliament, would receive it free.

499. *sim*, i.e. *seem*; the short vowel occurs in many dialects.

500. *Edward & his Harem.* Fanny is not mentioned (she would be in charge at Godmersham) but Lizzie was of the party, and perhaps others of the children. They however do not justify the expression *Harem*, which is accounted for by Mary Deedes (who had a brother at Winchester) and perhaps Fanny Cage (502).

William: Edward's boy.

501. *Miss W.*: Camilla Wallop; see Index II. Mr. Austen-Leigh supplies the four lines, quoted in Stephen Terry's diary:

> Camilla, good humoured and merry and small,
> For a husband, it happened, was at her last stake,
> And having in vain danced at many a ball
> Is now very happy to jump at a Wake.

I have to thank Mrs. C. G. Stirling for leave to print this fragment of the 'Steventon edition', which has not hitherto been published with the true name; the *Memoir* (p. 93 of my edition) calls the lady *Maria*.

P. & P.: *Pride and Prejudice.* See Index VI.

William and *Mary Jane*: Fowle.

75. *Sun.* 24 *Jan.* 1813

292. *a Society octavo*: i.e. the property of the Chawton Reading Society.

Capt Pasley. It is *Military Policy* on the title-page, but Mr. Austen-Leigh's transcript (here and 294) is no doubt correct; the Oxford Dictionary has *police* in that sense at an even later date.

the Commissioner's: a reference to *Mansfield Park*, see Index VI.

293. *eleven altogether.* It appears from 295 that the 'party on Wednesday' (292) was Mr. Papillon's. So we have two Papillons (Mr. P. and his sister), Mr. and Mrs. H. Digweed, Mr. and Mrs. Clement, Miss Benn, J. A., and two 'strange gentlemen'—ten. Only Miss P. T. remains, and she is almost certainly the *Miss Terry* of 294. But there is no indication that any Miss Terry of Dummer was at this time staying with Mrs. H. Digweed or elsewhere in the neighbourhood. It occurred to me that Miss P. T. might be a daughter of a William Parker Terry of Alton, whose death (1810) I had noted in *Gent. Mag.* But I find that W. P. T. (1748–1810, a y. b. of Thomas T. of Dummer) had one d. only, who died in infancy.

294. *round table.* Eleven (293) less four for whist, and J. A., leaves six. The round table in *Mansfield Park* consisted of Lady Bertram and Edmund, two Prices, and two Crawfords.

295. *Bank Stock* may be a joke.

in a cover. The letter did not go through the post (if it had, a cover would have doubled the charge). No doubt it was sent by hand ('by J. Bond', 296).

296. *Brother Michael*: perhaps Terry.

76. *Fri.* 29 *Jan.* 1813

297. *my own darling child*: the first copy of *Pride and Prejudice.*

my two other sets suggests that the number of free copies was five. J. A. 'dispersed' (439) twelve of *Emma*; but she was then relatively famous, and *Emma* was published on a profit-sharing agreement.

Portsmouth: Frank.

my stupidest of all. J. A. looks forward to a crescendo of price and stupidity. In the event she feared that *Emma* would be thought 'inferior in good sense' to *M. P.* We do not know where she would have ranked *Persuasion* in point of stupidity. For the actual prices see Index VI.

two such people: I suppose Mrs. Austen and J. A. herself, for Martha was from home (299).

298. *I do not write*: *Marmion*, vi. 38.

I do not rhyme to that dull elf
Who cannot image to himself . . .

The second volume. The number of pages is: i. 307, ii. 239, iii. 323.

your enquiries. I guess that the subject of inquiry was the disposal of livings, on which the plot of *M. P.* largely turns. Cassandra was staying with her brother James, who would be an authority. The second inquiry, about hedgerows, suggests that J. A. thought of using in *M. P.* the device which she later used in *Persuasion.* The dialogue, I suppose, would have been between Edmund and Mary, overheard by Fanny. If J. A. abandoned the idea because there are no hedgerows in Northants, it is a striking example of her realistic scruples. See the note on *ships*, p. 317. See also note on 78.1.

your Charades. A collection of *Charades &c written a hundred years ago by Jane Austen and her family* was published by Spottiswoode & Co. in 1895.

beyond anything & everything quotes Mrs. H. Digweed.

77. *Thur.* 4 *Feb.* 1813

299. *fits of disgust*: a much less strong expression then than now. Dr. Johnson has lost reputation by describing *Lycidas* as disgusting.

300. *Mrs. D.*: Digweed.

blunder in the printing. See my edition, note on p. 343.

John M.: Middleton.

301. *the Harwoods*: of Deane (302).

'On the death of the old man sad disclosures were made, and ruin stared them in the face. . . . Old Mr. Harwood had contracted debts, quite unsuspected by his family. . . . There was nothing for his widow, and his sister's small portion had been left in his hands, and had gone with the rest of the money, so that both ladies were dependent on the Heir.' (Caroline Austen's *Reminiscences*.)

M. T.: perhaps Michael Terry, who became Rector of Dummer in 1811. I am not clear who Fanny is (perhaps Fanny Knight, though she was not staying at Steventon—see p. 303), nor how her faith was unsettled. If it was religious faith, it may be worth while to mention that Michael Terry is described in the Powlett correspondence as 'poor blundering Michael Terry'.

Edward: James Edward (302).

S. & P.: Steventon and Portsmouth (297).

78. *Tues.* 9 *Feb.* 1813

302. *Mrs. Heathcote.* Caroline Austen in her *Reminiscences* refers to this, without mentioning Mrs. Heathcote's name.

'It was generally supposed, I believe I might say, it was generally known among his (John Harwood's) intimate friends, that he had formed an attachment to a lady of good position in his own neighbourhood. It was also believed, though not of course with equal certainty, that this lady, a widow, and quite her own mistress, would be willing to accept him. Nor could it have been considered a bad match for *her*, if on his Father's death he could have offered her, as he had a right to expect, a home in the family mansion with an estate of at least £1000 a year around it. But . . . he then found himself a ruined man, and bound to provide as best he could for his Mother and Aunt.'

Maria may be a Heathcote; see Index II.

303. *the Boys*: Fanny's brothers, on the Winchester road.

I shall *tell Anna*: the secret of *Pride and Prejudice*?

304. *Lady W.*: Williams.

305. *work for one evening*: to finish *P. and P.*

78.1. *Tues.* 16 *Feb.* 1813

See at end of these notes.

79. *Thur.* 20 *May* 1813

307. *little Cass and her attendant* are no doubt Charles Austen's little girl (born Dec. 1808) and her attendant Betsy (351), who would have to be *distinguished* from her homonym (299) of Chawton Cottage. The end of the visit is mentioned 318. But the Cassy intending to sketch is presumably Edward's daughter (born Nov. 1806), now at the Great House.

308. *the watercoloured Exhibition*: that in Spring Gardens (309).

a 16th of the £20,000. Cf. 372, 'Fyfield estates'. I imagine the legacy may have been from Mrs. Dundas; but her will cannot be found at Somerset House.

the Guildford: *sic* in the copy; but J. A. may have written or intended *the Guildford road.*

80. *Mon.* 24 *May* 1813

309. *No. 10*: Henrietta-street.

the Exhibition in Spring Gardens: held by the Society of Painters in Oil and Water Colours. The catalogue (7855 dd in the British Museum) might lead to the identification of Mrs. Bingley's portrait, which would be indeed a triumph of research.

310. *the Great Exhibition*: doubtless that of the British Academy in Somerset-place, which was opened on 3 May.

Sir Joshua Reynolds. I find in the *Gentleman's Magazine* for May 1813, p. 480: 'The Managers of the British Institution, as a tribute to the memory of Sir Joshua Reynolds, have borrowed 130 of his performances, which are now on exhibition for the benefit of Students.'

shaped face is what J. A. wrote, but she may have intended *shape* (the modern *figure*).

*My cousin Car*oline. For *my* see the note on p. 14; the italics show that Car*oline* was Mrs. Tilson's pronunciation.

311. *a wild Beast.* The secret of authorship was leaking out.

come to bide: a quotation from Frank's childhood, as p. 265 shows.

312. *Miss D.*: Darcy.

81. *Francis Austen, Sat.* 3 *July* 1813

314. *a new Garden.* Chawton House faces west; in front of it, at a considerable distance and at a lower level, is the Alton-Southampton road. The Rectory is on the other side of the road. The present garden, which is large and enclosed by a beautiful brick wall, is 'at the top of the lawn' behind the house, and is no doubt of Edward's making. Mrs. Montagu Knight tells me that the old garden was in the church meadow.

315. *dishonourable accomodation.* I suppose because the boy's keep was saved.

Deputy Receiver. He had been promoted to Receiver-General for Oxfordshire.

his nephew: Edward's boy, not James Edward, as p. 338 shows.

316. *Mrs. L. P.*: Leigh Perrot.

that vile compromise. See note on 173.

Mr. Blackall. For J. A.'s interest in him see 11 (27 note).

317. *£250.* We now know (p. 501) that the copyright of *P. and P.* was sold for £110. Previously that figure depended on this passage.

not half so entertaining: *Mansfield Park.*

your old Ships. For his ships see Index VIII, and for the risk she took, p. 340. The ships borrowed for *Mansfield Park* were *Cleopatra*, *Elephant*, *Endymion*. See also my note on *hedgerows*, p. 298.

318. *not all off.* Sir Francis in extreme old age had still a quantity of hair.

82. *Wed.* 15 *Sept.* 1813

Since the text was printed I have received from Mr. Davidson Cook a collation with the original. The letter was on four leaves, and the conclusion—about six lines and the signature—has been cut away from the top of the fourth leaf. For a passage omitted by Lord Brabourne see note below on p. 322. Two corrections of the text are noticed below.

By favour of Mr. Gray. The letter went to Alton in 'the parcel' (322) and Mr. G. conveyed it thence.

319. *a little crowded.* J. A. wrote *a little crowd.*

his quarters: 'at an Hotel in the next street' (337).

Mr. Crabbe. See p. 323.

320. *Lady Robert*: Kerr.

the books may mean 'volumes', and need not imply that *S. and S.* was sent too; but see 323–4, which may refer to a presentation copy of the second edition of *S. and S.*

321. *Mrs. H. and Miss B.*: Mrs. Heathcote and her sister Alethea, who became *Miss* Bigg on her elder sister Catherine's becoming Mrs. Hill.

Clandestine Marriage: by Colman and Garrick.

Midas: by Kane O'Hara.

Five hours at Brighton: by Samuel Beazley.

322. *Harriot Byron's feather*: *Sir Charles Grandison*, Letter 22: 'A white Paris sort of cap, glittering with spangles, and encircled by a chaplet of artificial flowers, with a little white feather perking from the left ear, is to be my headdress.'

Thursday Morning. Just before this is, in the original, the following passage omitted by Lord Brabourne:

> 'This not seeing much of Henry, I have just seen him however for 3 minutes, & have read him the Extract from Mrs. F. A.'s Letter—& he says he will write to Mrs. Fra A. about it, & he has no doubt of being attended to as he knows they feel themselves obliged to him.—Perhaps you may see him on Saturday next. He has just started such an idea. But it will be only for a couple of days.

Mrs. Fra A. (the reading is not certain) is presumably the wife of Francis Motley Austen, or possibly the wife of their eldest son, who also was Francis.

323. *Madame B.*: Bigeon.

Mr. Crabbe: Huchon, *Crabbe and his Times* (Engl. trans. 1907, p. 375) states that the Crabbes were in London from July until just before Mrs. C.'s death in September.

crimson velvet. Mr. E. H. W. Meyerstein in *Times Lit. Suppt.* 31 March 1927 quoted the *Poems* of 1807 (p. 106, *The Lady*, in *Parish Register*, *Part iii*, *Burials*):

> Close on the case the crimson velvet 's press'd

(referring to a funeral pall). Perhaps a better parallel, and one more likely to be in J. A.'s mind, is *Tales*, 1812, p. 45, *The Gentleman Farmer*:

In full festoons the crimson curtains fell.

Gm (i.e. Godmersham) is Mr. Austen-Leigh's brilliant and certain correction of the *you* of Lord Brabourne's edition. Edward and his family spent the summer of 1813 at Chawton (see 80, 81, and p. 341 'five months'), but were at Godmersham in the autumn. (The correction is confirmed by the original.)

November collection. See p. 315 for Henry's Oxfordshire appointment; and p. 426.

Nothing has been done. I guess that there was a question of sending *Sense and Sensibility* to Warren Hastings, who had read and admired *Pride and Prejudice.* This would require the mediation of Henry (see 320). In the idiom of the time, which is not quite that of to-day, 'books' may mean either the set of three volumes (as on p. 320) or, as we say, 'copies', and especially presentation copies. 'Do not let us teize one another about books', wrote Dr. Johnson to his publisher.

324. *sent down to Alton.* Henry's bank had an Alton branch.

Mr. H.: Warren Hastings.

Poor F. Cage. The combination of the White Hart and susceptibility to noise reminds us of Louisa Musgrove's accident and subsequent nerves. I can find no report of the accident in the Bath newspapers.

83. *Thurs.* 16 *Sept.* 1813

327. *Mrs. T.*: Tilson.

from the Compting House. Mr. Tilson was a member of the firm, and Henry was now living 'over the shop'.

84. *Thur.* 23 *Sept.* 1813

329. *Mary P.*: Plumtre.

Ben: Lefroy.

every dinner-invitation. See p. 341.

330. *The Mr. Ks.* The Mr. Knatchbulls of pp. 330, 331, 339 are not, as Lord Brabourne (who had not seen 85) thought (ii. 123), sons of Sir Edward VIII, but his cousins, Mrs. Knight's brothers; 'their lovely Wadham' was their son and nephew.

331. *the two others*: Edward and George.

'Tis Night: from Beattie's *Hermit*.

Cambridge: probably R. B. Harraden's *Cantabrigia Depicta*: *A Series of Engravings*, quarto, 1809.

332. *the empty Pew.* The Knights spent five months at Chawton (341) and J. A. accompanied her brother and nieces to London on 14 Sept. Consequently on Sunday the 19th the pew in Chawton church was empty for the first time.

Bentigh (pronounce to rhyme with *high*), a wooded hill in Godmersham park. A map of 1769 shows, within a few miles, a *Clovertigh* and an *Ollantigh*.

333. *Mary O. nor Mary P.*: Oxenden, Plumtre.

Fanny C.: Cage.

Modern Europe: perhaps a work by John Bigland, q.v. in Index V.

334. *a* Thing *for measuring Timber with. An Olde Thrift Newly Revived* (London 1612) undertakes in its title-page to explain 'the use of a small portable Instrument for measuring of Board and the solid content and height of any Tree standing'.

Poor Dr. Isham. Mrs. Lybbe Powys records (p. 296) that Dr. I. was godfather, and Mrs. Austen godmother, to one of Edward Cooper's children (July 1797).

M^{de} Darblay's new Novel: *The Wanderer*.

335. *Mistress of all I survey.* Index V, s.v. Cowper.

85. *Francis Austen. Sat.* 25 *Sept.* 1813

337. *inside & out.* The barouche box was occupied by Lizzy (319).

338. *her Daughter*: probably Mme Perigord.

were sing-song. I could not be sure whether J. A. wrote *were* or *mere*.

339. *The Clerk*: John Hogben or Hogbin.

the Sherers are going. See 342, 366, 373. Clearly the proposed arrangement fell through; for Mr. S. continued to officiate till 1816, and the registers show no trace of Mr. P.

340. *my application.* See note on 317.

86. *Mon.* 11 *Oct.* 1813

342. *Mr. J. P.*: John Plumtre.

343. *triennial bliss* seems a malapropism.

344. *disgust me.* See note on 299.

Self Control: by Mary Brunton.

Such a long Letter! refers to Cassandra's; the 2nd page of J. A.'s own has only 36 lines.

like Harriot Byron: in *Sir Charles Grandison*, Letter 33: 'What shall I do with my gratitude! O my dear, I am *overwhelmed* with my gratitude; I can only express it in silence before them' (before Sir Charles who had rescued her from abduction, and his sister who had sheltered her).

345. *Mrs. H.*: Heathcote. *Alethea*: Bigg.

naming a Heroine. The heroine of 'Sanditon' *is* Charlotte.

346. *one Brother . . . & another Brother's Wife*: Charles at the Nore and Mrs. F. A. at Deal.

dined upon Goose. I am referred to *British Apollo*, 1708 (i. 74):

pray tell me whence
The Custom'd Proverb did commence,
That who eats Goose on Michael's Day,
Shan't Money lack, his Debts to pay.

Old Michaelmas Day was 11 Oct.

my 2[d] Edition: of *S. and S.*, not of *P. and P.* (they both appeared in 1813). See Index VI.

Uncle Edward: Bridges.

87. *Thur.* 14 *Oct.* 1813

347. *room for the seal.* A franked letter could be enclosed in an 'envelope', so that the seal need not be on the same piece of paper as the text.

348. *either House*: Chilham Castle (Wildman), and perhaps Dane Court—but it is a mile from the village—or the vicarage (Tylden).

the Footes. Edward Bridges's wife was a Foote.

349. *Lady B.*: Bridges.

350. *Hooper*: Holder.

354. *on board*: the *Namur*.

88. *Thur.* 21 *Oct.* 1813

357. *Miss Floyd.* 'It was my Grandfather who changed the pronunciation of Lloyd into Floyd as it was always spoken in my recollection. They said that was the true Welsh pronunciation of double L, but a Welshman and a scholar has assured me it was useless to try and imitate their accent—the English tongue could not give it, and that we had therefore better say Lloyd' (Caroline Austen's *Reminiscences*).

Key Street: not a London street as might be supposed, but a Kentish village.

Harriot: Moore.

358. *Mrs. Crabbe.* See Index II for the date of her death.

one of his prefaces: to *The Borough* (1810); in the third paragraph Crabbe likens an author's partiality for his manuscript to a parent's for his child, showing some familiarity with 'manuscripts in the study' and 'children in the nursery'.

89. *Tues.* 26 *Oct.* 1813

362. *Gloucestershire*: i.e. Adlestrop (383).

'*Whatever is, is best*' (right): Pope, *Essay on Man*.

directly: that is, I suppose, by the Bath road. The road-books name several houses called Harefield (Place, Park, &c.) in the neighbourhood of Uxbridge, but I have no means of telling which of these, if any, the party were to visit.

363. *Mde. B.*: Bigeon.

talk from books. J. A. perhaps remembered the *Tour to the Hebrides* (3 Nov.): 'He was pleased to say, "You and I do not talk from books."'

declined a curacy. 'My father although deeply attached to my mother was far too high-principled and conscientious to take Holy Orders for the sake of being immediately married. Possibly he had not yet quite decided on his profession, at all events he was not ordained until three years afterwards. As to my mother's reluctance to go to Chawton, sent away as she was to mark my G^d Mother's anger with him, it was not possible she should go with any other feelings.' *Bellas notes.*

Lady Elizabeth: Finch-Hatton.

90. *Wed.* 3 *Nov.* 1813

364. *this celebrated Birthday*: I do not know whose.

366. *Lady B.*: Bridges.

Dr. P.: Parry.

Bru of fcu the Archbishop puzzled Lord Brabourne; but *bru* is daughter-in-law, and Harriot Moore is meant.

367. *Lady B.*: the reigning Lady Bridges, not the dowager, who was in Bath.

her Mother's family. Anna's mother was, on *her* mother's side, a Bertie.

368. *five Tables, Eight & twenty Chairs & two fires.* For the various rooms at Godmersham Park see the references in Index III. The main entrance is on the north, and opens on the large hall. The room in which J. A. sat with these tables and chairs is probably what is now called the south drawing-room. It might escape identification to-day; for Lady Lewisham tells me that 'in putting up the old Adams bookcase at the end of this room, when we redecorated it, we closed up a second fireplace'. The *library* was probably a smaller room on the same side of the house. The *hall chamber* is above the hall, and the *yellow room* adjoins it.

The house is described in Zechariah Cozens, *Tour through the Isle of Thanet* (1793), as 'a modern building of a centre and two wings; one of which, the Eastern, contains a most excellent library; in the centre are some good apartments, particularly on the back front, which command exceeding delightful prospects of the hill and pleasure grounds'.

Charing Cross. Boswell's *Life of Johnson* (2 Apr. 1775).

Money for Printing: because the second edition of *S. and S.* was produced at the author's expense.

369. *Poor Lord Howard*: not identified, and I do not know whether it was a public or a private lament.

91. *Sat.* 6 *Nov.* 1813

370. *the famous Ball*: perhaps that of Jan. 1801 (pp. 104, 108).

371. *la Mere Beauté*: Mme de Sévigné.

to Cheltenham. Caroline Austen's *Reminiscences* record that her mother and she went from Kintbury (with the Fowles) to Cheltenham on 1 Nov. and returned 6 Dec.

372. *my 2ᵈ Edit.*: of *Sense and Sensibility*, not (*Life* 289) of *Pride and Prejudice*. The second edition of the latter was published at nearly the same time; but J. A. had sold the copyright to Egerton (see p. 501), and there is no evidence that she was consulted. The second edition (unlike those of *S. S.* and *M. P.*) contains no correction due to her. See my article, 'Jane Austen and her Publishers', in *London Mercury*, Aug. 1930.

what news! The Address was moved in both Houses on 4 Nov.; when the Marquis Wellesley 'concurred in the language of Mr. Pitt, that England had saved herself by her firmness and energies, and had saved other countries by her example'. On 8 Nov. Lord Bathurst 'in a neat speech' moved the thanks of the House of Lords to the Marquis of Wellington for the eminent skill and ability displayed in the operations succeeding the battle of Vittoria.

374. *Mrs. H.*: doubtless Mrs. Heathcote, staying with her sister Catherine (Mrs. Hill) at Streatham; though Mrs. H. *might* be Mr. Hill's mother.

I thought you would came: see note on p. 265.

92. *Wed.* 2 *March* 1814

376. *Henry's approbation.* It is generally assumed that Henry read *M. P.* in proof; and the assumption is natural in view of the dates—the book was read in the first week of March and published in May. The point is of the smallest importance; but I feel sure that H. read the MS. J. A. would hardly send it to the printer without first getting his approval. Again, the proofs would hardly be all in her hands before he had seen any of them; for they were no doubt sent to him by the printer as on former occasions (273). The fact that the book

as read was in three volumes proves nothing, for the division into volumes was not left to the printer.

the 'Heroine': by E. S. Barrett.

Miss P.: Papillon, or Prowting?

M^d B.: Bigeon.

377. *the willow.* See p. 398.

378. *Frederick.* See pp. 381, 386. General (Tilson) Chowne's name was Christopher. 'Frederick' seems to be an old nick-name, or perhaps some piece of make-believe; there is no trace of a Frederick Tilson in that family.

93. *Sat.* 5 *March* 1814

379. *Young Wyndham*: Knatchbull, second son of Sir Edward VIII. Fanny did better in marrying his elder brother, afterwards Sir Edward IX. But J. A. in March 1814 could not foresee the death of that gentleman's first wife, later in the year.

Mrs. L. and Miss E.: Latouche and East.

380. *second prosecution.* See 381.

6 weeks mourning. For the Queen's brother the Duke of Mecklenburg-Strelitz.

383. *Catherine*: Hill.

His opponent knocks under. This was too optimistic. In the end Edward had to pay a large sum to settle the claim on Chawton made by heirs of former Knights. (*Chawton Manor*, p. 171.) See Index II, s.v. Baverstock.

384. *'the Devil to pay'*: by Charles Coffey.

Artaxerxes: an Italian opera.

the Farmer's Wife: by Charles Dibdin.

94. *Wed.* 9 *March* 1814

385. *his new acquaintance*: Mr. J. P.; see the letters to Fanny of Nov. 1814.

386. *your little companion*: Charles's Cassy.

95. *Anna Austen. May or June* 1814

387. *sending your MS.* 'The story to which most of these letters of Aunt Jane's refer was never finished. It was laid aside for a season because my mother's hands were so full. . . . The

story was laid by for years, and then one day in a fit of despondency burnt. I remember sitting on the rug and watching its destruction, amused with the flame and the sparks which kept breaking out in the blackened paper. In later years when I expressed my sorrow that she had destroyed it, she said she could never have borne to finish it, but incomplete as it was Jane Austen's criticisms would have made it valuable.' *Bellas MS.*

388. *Lord Orville*: in *Evelina.*

96. *Tues.* 14 *June* 1814

389. *the Emperor*: of Russia.

97. *Thur.* 23 *June* 1814

390. *Miss B.*: perhaps Burdett.

391. *Berks*: i.e. Kintbury.

392. *Sir W. P.*: Pilkington.

98. *Anna Austen. Wed.* 10 *Aug.* 1814

393. *Enthusiasm* was perhaps relinquished on the discovery that Madame de Genlis had written 'Les Vœux Téméraires ou L'Enthousiasme' (1799 or earlier).

Desborough. The late baron's title dates from 1905.

W. D. and *H. D.*: Digweed.

99. *Tues.* ⟨23⟩ *Aug.* 1814

Lord Brabourne prints this letter without the day of the month, but states (ii. 221) that it was written on the 14th. He must have forgotten that the Canterbury Races were held late in Aug. The *Kentish Chronicle* for Friday 19 Aug. states that 'the grand Ball last night at Bellingham's Assembly Rooms was attended by all the principal families of the County'; naming among others our friends Sir Edward Knatchbull, Sir John Honywood, General Montresor, Sir H. Oxenden, Mr. Deedes, Mr. Lushington, Mr. Knight, Mr. Papillon—but no Finch-Hattons, see below. The year is not in doubt, for it is clear that Henry had just moved house. He was in Henrietta-street in June and in Hans-place in Nov. (see No. 106, where the date is *not* conjectural, though I have bracketed it, but is ascertained by the postmark). We may therefore date this letter, with some confidence, Tuesday, 23 Aug.

397. *Edinburgh & Sterling.* The intuition (*Life* 305) that this was an imaginary episode was confirmed by the publication of *Love and Freindship* (1790) in 1922. See p. 38: 'it would certainly have been much more agreeable to us, to visit the Highlands in a Postchaise than merely to travel from Edinburgh to Sterling and from Sterling to Edinburgh every other day in a crowded and uncomfortable Stage'.

397. *no Lady Charlottes.* Kirby was the Northamptonshire seat of Lord Winchilsea, so the reference is to the Finch-Hattons of Eastwell. Young George F.-H. married in 1814 Lady Charlotte Graham. I cannot be sure of the other Lady C.; there are several candidates. (The Lady Charlotte who was G. F.-H.'s great-aunt had died in 1813, as Lord Brabourne (ii. 124) correctly states, and as J. A. must have known.)

398. *the Willow*: doubtless 'willow sheets' or 'willow squares', sold ready plaited for hat-making (quotations in *O.E.D.*, 1819 and 1834).

399. *the parcel*: from Henrietta-street to the Alton bank. The letters sent 'by favour of Mr. Gray' were no doubt in the parcel; cf. 427. It did not go every day, as 425 shows.

Nunna Hat: J. A. herself, no doubt, but the etymology is unknown.

Mrs. C.: possibly Cooke or Craven, as this is Steventon news. 'farther & farther from Poverty' may be ironical.

Ben: Lefroy.

100. *Anna Austen. Fri.* 9 *Sept.* 1814

402. *Newton Priors.* Newton Valence and Priors Dean, both in the Chawton neighbourhood, may have suggested N. P.

this sad Event: Mrs. Charles Austen's death. Her fourth child was born and died this month.

Mr. D.: Digweed.

102. *Anna Austen.* n.d.

This obscure joke is only in form a letter to Anna. But since it is unpublished I have inserted it here.

'Aunt Jane and my Mother had been laughing over a most tiresome novel in eight volumes by a Mrs. Hunter, containing story within story, and of which the heroine was always in floods of tears.' *Bellas MS.* (I cannot find that Mrs. Hunter wrote anything above five volumes; but *Bibliotheca Britannica* certifies that 'all her works are of a strictly moral tendency'.)

406. The copy, on which I formerly relied, mis-read *Hunter* as *Hemter* and omitted the words *to Norwich* after *provided.*

407. *the Car of Falkenstein*: Falknor's coach, mentioned on p. 297.

103. *Fanny Knight. Fri.* 18 *Nov.* 1814

409. *Mr. J. P.*: Plumtre.

412. *Host & Hostess.* Edward had lent the Great House to Frank, and was now his brother's guest in his own house.

Aunt Louisa: Bridges.

Fanny C.: Cage.

104. *Anna Lefroy. Tues.* 22 *Nov.* 1814

413. *his Brother*: either Henry or William; *Cousins*: James Edward, and one or more of Edward's numerous cousins on his mother's side, Bridges or Deedes.

the Wen is Mr. R. A. Austen-Leigh's restoration of the mutilated MS. (Lord Brabourne printed *London*). The use is associated with Cobbett, who, however, does not seem to have it earlier than 1821. Dean Tucker, 1783, writing of London, has: 'no better than a wen or excrescence upon the body politic'.

105. *Anna Lefroy. Tues.* 29 Nov. 1814

414. *us both*: J. A. and Eliz. Gibson (422).

415. *Susan & Maria*: Middleton.

Your Uncle & Edw[d]: the Knights, no doubt in their way from Chawton (412) to Godmersham (416). For the *Cause* see 383, 427. In the final paragraph *your Uncle* is Henry.

Isabella: a tragedy adapted by Garrick from Southerne's *Fatal Marriage.*

106. *Fanny Knight.* *Wed.* 30 *Nov.* 1814

416. *to give them* both *Pleasure.* 'When first my father and mother married, they lived at Hendon with his next elder brother Edward who at that time had a house there. This will explain *why* Aunt Jane was glad she had the power of asking her friends to it and also that the "both" to whom it was "so proper that her visit should give pleasure" referred to the two gentlemen.' *Bellas notes.*

419. *a 2ᵈ Edition*: of *M. P.* The second edition was published in 1816 by Murray.

108. *Anna Lefroy.*

Since my text was printed Miss Lefroy has falsified the record by giving this characteristic scrap to its grateful editor.

421. *to lye-in of a Daughter*: a prediction falsified by the event, see Index II.

422. *Rosanne*: by Laetitia Matilda Hawkins.

serious subjects. The avowed purpose of *Rosanne* was 'to point out—though better illustrated by her Ladyship's example—the inestimable advantages attendant on the practice of pure Christianity'. (Her Ladyship, to whom the book was dedicated, was the Countess of Waldegrave.)

Mlle Cossart, like the Ormsdens, is a character in *Rosanne.*

109. *Anna Lefroy.* *Nov. or Dec.* 1814

422. *Mrs. Creed.* See p. 425. Probably Catherine Herries (see Herries in Index II) who 1813 m. Henry Knowles Creed; their d. Juliet m. Sir Frederick Pollock, 2nd Bart., and was the mother of the present Sir Frederick and of the late Walter Herries Pollock, author of an interesting book on J. A. This conjecture is Mr. Austen-Leigh's, and its probability is confirmed by Sir Frederick, though he knows of no residence at Hendon.

my list: of *Opinions* on *Mansfield Park.*

423. *Self-control*: by Mary Brunton.

110. *Anna Lefroy.* *Fri.* 29 *Sept.* 1815

423. Ben and Anna now lived in part of a farm-house, Wyards, close to Alton.

111. *Tues.* 17 *Oct.* 1815

425. *publishing for myself.* In the end Mr. Murray took the risk, such as it was.

Mr. or Miss P.: doubtless Papillon; Henry's second wife was a Jackson, and her mother was a Papillon.

comical consequence. It is believed that Mr. S. had at some time proposed marriage.

Henry's illness. Caroline Austen's *Reminiscences* tell us that J. A. sent for her brother James, who went to Chawton on 24 Oct. and took C. E. A. to London, leaving his wife to look after Mrs. A.—Martha Lloyd being then in Berkshire. The illness explains the 'preparatory Letter' (428) sent to Scarlets on 25 Oct.

427. *his cause.* See 383, 415.

112. *Caroline Austen. Mon.* 30 *Oct.* 1815

428. *at Chawton.* Caroline tells us (*Reminiscences*) that she joined her mother there soon after 24 Oct. and stayed about a month.

the Hermit: perhaps Goldsmith's ballad, of which there were settings; more probably (as Mr. Archibald Jacob tells me) Tommaso Giordani's very popular setting of Beattie's poem.

113. *J. S. Clarke. Wed.* 15 *Nov.* 1815

For the Clarke correspondence (and documents connected with it) I may refer to my *Plan of a Novel* (Oxford, 1926).

114. *John Murray. Nov.* 1815

431. *Waterloo*: Scott's *Field of Waterloo.*

115. *Thur.* 23 *Nov.* 1815

432. *delays of the printers*: Roworth, who printed vols. i–ii of *Emma.* The paper (see 433) has a watermark dated 1815.

116. *Fri.* 24 *Nov.* 1815

435. *Mary*: Mrs. F. A.

117. *Sun.* 26 *Nov.* 1815

436. arra-*root.* It is not so spelled in the first edition.

Aunt Har^{t}: Miss Palmer, Charles A.'s sister-in-law (later his second wife). Cassy was at Chawton.

437. *B. Chapel*: Belgrave.

plenty of Mortar. No plausible explanation of this has been suggested.

438. *the little girl at Wyards* cannot be Anna's daughter, who was born on 20 Oct. Probably Anna had taken charge of one of Frank's little girls (whose youngest brother was born this month); probably Cassandra, for the Cassy of the postscript is Charles's.

Me Duval. Brabourne prints Mr. I failed to correct this from the MS. when I had the chance; but probably J. A. wrote *M^{e}* for *Madame. Evelina,* vol. i, Letter 21.

118. *Sat.* 2 *Dec.* 1815

439. *Mr. T.*: Tilson.

absenting himself. The impending bankruptcy might make a temporary absence prudent.

441. *save you 2^{d}.* I cannot explain this. The charge for a 'single letter' to Alton was sixpence.

give the P.R. a binding. This was settled—no doubt on Mr. Murray's advice—in favour of a binding; see 451, 453. The other presentation copies were sent 'unbound', that is in publishers' boards.

121. *John Murray. Mon.* 11 *Dec.* 1815

446. *all unbound.* Collectors will note that presentation copies of *Emma* with 'From the Authoress' in a clerkly hand need not be suspected on that account.

127. *John Murray. Mon.* 1 *Apr.* 1816

453. *the 'Quarterly Review'.* The writer of this review was Sir Walter Scott. The history of the attribution is perplexed; but it was placed beyond all doubt by Mr. C. B. Hogan of Yale

in *Publications of the Modern Language Association of America*, 45 (1929), p. 1264.

the late event: the failure of Henry's bank.

130. *J. E. Austen. Tues.* 9 *July* 1816

458. *Little Cassy*: Frank's, not Charles's?

a very considerable pond. The pond has disappeared, but the ordnance map shows it.

459. *Mrs. S—*: Sclater.

the Trial: perhaps the 'Baigent business'.

132. *Wed.* 4 *Sept.* 1816

461. *to be preferred in May.* J. A. had spent three weeks at Cheltenham in May of this year, with Cassandra (Caroline's *Reminiscences*). She may have drunk the water from what she calls (462) 'my pump'.

decided for Orders. Caroline Austen's *Reminiscences* record that on 19 Dec. H. A. went to Winchester for his examination, and on the next day to Salisbury, 'where he was ordained to the Curacy of Alton' (of Bentley, near Alton, where for many years he was perpetual curate. *Life* 333).

462. *The Alton 4*: Frank, his wife, and (464) a Gibson, and the obscure Mr. Sweney?

133. *Sun.* 8 *Sept.* 1816

463. *Berkshire.* Presumably Kintbury.

a coach from Hungerford. Caroline Austen's *Reminiscences* show that Mrs. James Austen and C. E. A. took Caroline to Cheltenham via Kintbury, there picking up Mary Jane Fowle. In their return they left M. J. F. at Kintbury and then diverged, Mrs. J. A. returning to Steventon, C. E. A. taking Caroline to Chawton. J. A.'s sigh for a coach from Hungerford is no doubt connected with this division of the party.

465. *C. Craven.* The Cheltenham *Chronicle* of 1 Aug. mentions the Duke and Duchess of Orleans, and the issue of 8 Aug. mentions Charlotte Craven. But the Public Librarian, who kindly searched the files, could not find Miss Austen or Mr. Pococke.

Edward. Ben's brother Christopher Edward Lefroy.

134. *J. E. Austen. Mon.* 16 *Dec.* 1816

469. *'tell him what you will'*: from Hannah Cowley's *Which is the Man?* iv. 1.

Mr. Papillon. See p. 236, 'Mrs Eliz^th P.' is his (unmarried) sister.

136. *Cassandra* (*'Cassy'*). *Wed.* 8 *Jan.* 1817

470. The leaf containing the letter to Cassy and the direction was, no doubt, pp. 3–4 of the whole, pp. 1–2 being a letter to Charles.

137. *Caroline Austen. Thur.* 23 *Jan.* 1817

473. *your Uncle & Aunt*: Frank (at Alton).

139. *Alethea Bigg. Fri.* 24 *Jan.* 1817

475. *William*: Heathcote.

Her grandmama. The copy has:

'Her grandmama I can only see at Chawton', which is nonsense. I have put *she* for *I*; alternatives are:

'Her g. can only see her at C.'

or

'Her g. and I can only see her at C.'

476. *Our own new clergyman*: Henry.

between Streatham and Winchester. Miss Bigg was no doubt going to stay at W. with her other sister Mrs. Heathcote (495).

the 'Poet's Pilgrimage'. Southey, who was Mr. Hill's son-in-law, lost his eldest child Herbert in April 1816. The *proem* contains an affectionate description of the boy.

140. *Fanny Knight. Thur.* 20 *Feb.* 1817

478. *the new Silver Coinage* was announced by proclamation of 12 February; it replaced a debased currency.

(last line). *will be.* J. A. wrote *will be to me,* but erased the last two words.

480. *his marrying somebody else.* 'he' is now the 'Mr. J. P.' of the 1814 letters.

Henry (nearly 20) and *William* (18) had left Winchester, and were, I suppose, visiting their grandmother. There is no indication that the Great House was occupied at this time (though it might be used as an overflow? See pp. 463–4).

her praise of Emma. See *Opinions*.

'I like it better than any. . . . Miss Bates is incomparable, but I was nearly killed with those precious treasures! They are Unique, & really with more fun than I can express. I am at Highbury all day, & I can't help feeling I have just got into a new set of acquaintance. No one writes such good sense. & so very comfortable.'

481. *her girlish days*. A letter from one of her daughters (to Cholmeley, son of J. E. A. L.) reveals that Anna 'being dull when her brother went to school got engaged to Michael Terry, a good looking neighbour—to the displeasure of . . . her parents. Later she broke it off—also to their displeasure.'

Miss C.: perhaps Clewes.

141. *Fanny Knight. Thur.* 13 *March* 1817

483. *Fanny*: probably Plumtre.

484. *we fear something else*. Cf. p. 488: 'not a chance of escape'; but the next child was not born until May 1818.

your Aunt Harriot: Mrs. Moore.

485.

the race of Pagets. There is no evidence that J. A. had any acquaintance with Lord Anglesey's family; but one brother of the first marquis, Hon. Sir Arthur (1771–1840) married 1808 'Lady Augusta Fane, divorced wife of Lord Boringdon, at Hackfield, Hants' (*Gent. Mag.*); and another brother, Hon. Charles, was living at Fareham in 1807. (Lord Boringdon's second wife was J. A.'s correspondent Lady Morley.)

142. *Fanny Knight. Sun.* 23 *March* 1817

486. *Mr. Wildman's conversation* is not recorded in the *Opinions* on *M. P.* and *Emma*. Perhaps he was made to begin at the beginning with *S. and S.*

488. *the event at Scarlets*: Mr. Leigh Perrot's death.

489. *how Canterbury looks in the direction.* Mr. E. V. Hewkin of the G.P.O. kindly informs me that

'... there is no trace in the records here, of the route which would be taken by letters in transit between Chawton, Hants, and Godmersham, Kent, in the year 1817. In all probability such letters would circulate via London. Although "Feversham" was the correct address for letters for Godmersham, it appears to have been the practice of residents in the district to have their correspondence addressed "Canterbury" in spite of the fact that this entailed an extra penny postage. The advantage of the arrangement was that while letters addressed Canterbury were conveyed to addressees on the road to Ashford by a private van, those addressed "Feversham" had to be sent for.'

I note that Cassandra's letter to Fanny from Winchester (see Appendix), and one (but only one) of J. A.'s letters from London to Godmersham, are directed to Canterbury.

143. *Caroline Austen. Wed.* 26 *March* 1817

490. *opportunities.* Henry had been taking occasional duty at Chawton, and perhaps also at Steventon, for James's health was failing (he died 1819).

491. *I will be better.* J. A.'s use of *shall* and *will* is strict. This is a promise.

144. *Charles Austen. Sun.* 6 *Apr.* 1817

491. *my Uncle's Will.* Mr. L. P. left everything to his wife for her life, with the reversion of a large sum to James Austen and his heirs, and of £1,000 each to those of Mrs. Austen's younger children who should survive Mrs. L. P. (*Life* 385.)

145. *Anne Sharp. Thur.* 22 *May* 1817

My text depends on a photograph of the original. It should be noted, in justice to Miss Sharp's sense of humour, that, in spite of her admiration for the moral tendency of *M. P.*, she owned her preference for *P. & P.* (*Opinions*).

494. *your Eliza.* Had Miss S. adopted a daughter?

495. *Ly P*: Pilkington.

Galigai de Concini: Eléonore G., a maid of honour to

Marie de Médicis, married Concino Concini, and was burned as a sorceress in 1617. When one of her judges asked her what charm she had put on her mistress, she replied: 'Mon sortilège a été le pouvoir que les âmes fortes doivent avoir sur les esprits faibles' (Voltaire, *Essai sur les Mœurs*, ch. 175. I owe the reference to Mr. L. F. Powell). J. A. may have owed her knowledge to Lord Chesterfield: see his letter of 30 Apr. (O.S.) 1752; or to *The Absentee*, ch. 3 (M. Edgeworth).

in tender regret. The words are taken from the first publication of the letter in *The Times*. They are not legible in my photograph, but may well be in the original, which I have not seen. It is torn at this point, and perhaps creased. There is room for the words, and the photograph shows what may be *gret.*

147. *May* 1817

This is J. A.'s last known letter, and the first to be published. Its publication with *Northanger Abbey* suggests that the recipient may have been Henry Austen. But Captain —— looks like Capt. Clement of Chawton, whom H. A. must have known well enough.

148. *Miss Prowting.* n.d.

I have placed this letter here to avoid conjectural dating. The watermark is 1813, and the book sent was no doubt *M. P.* or *Emma*. I cannot identify *our poor friend*, but I do not know the date of Miss Benn's death; she is frequent in the Chawton letters up to 116 (Nov. 1815) but then disappears.

74.1. *Martha Lloyd. Sun.* 29 *Nov.* 1812

This letter was received too late to be correctly placed or included in the numerical series. The notes on it follow those on 74.

78.1. *Martha Lloyd. Tu.* 16 *Feb.* 1813; see next page.

NOTES: ADDENDA

28 (97). I had said 'always'; but a letter in *Times Lit. Suppt.* 26 Jan. 1933 (M. Joan Sargeaunt) reminded me of the passage in *M.P.* where Mary is glad that Tom Bertram is absent, so that his younger brother '*may* be Mr. Bertram again'.

31 (111). *Mr. Doricourt . . . best* is quoted from Hannah Cowley, *Belle's Stratagem* (1780), v. v.

39 (140). *James Selby.* Miss Tallmadge points out that he is Harriet Byron's 'cousin James Selby' in *Grandison* (1754, vi. 59, 75), who was 'on a sudden very earnest to go abroad; as if, silly youth, travelling would make him a Sir Charles Grandison'.

72 (280). *Gloucester House.* I owe to Miss Winifred Watson the discovery that I was on a wrong tack. The house is no doubt G. House at Weymouth. The king and queen, with them Fanny Burney, stayed there in 1789 (*Diary*, 1842, V. 32).

78.1 (503). *George &c.*: Knight.

(504). *Mrs. D. D.* (= *Your friend*): Deans Dundas.

(504). *Northamptonshire.* We now know that Mansfield Park may be identified with Cottesbrooke in that county, with whose owner Sir James Langham Henry was acquainted; see my *Jane Austen*, 1948, 82–4, and references there to *Times Lit. Suppt.* and *Country Life.*

141.1 (511).

The date is ascertained by J. A.'s record that on 7 March 1817 she received £19. 13*s.* 0*d.* for the second edition of *S.S.*

Craven Exhibition. In spite of nobler ambition J. E. A. became this year Craven Scholar.

Mary Jane, Cassy: daughters of Frank and Charles respectively. *Aunt F.* is Mrs. *Frank*, then staying (for the most part) at Alton, not Mrs. Charles (Frances).

149 (512). The provenance of this scrap makes it likely that it is part of a letter to Caroline Austen as a child. The two brothers are probably James and Henry, dining at Edward's house at Chawton; or possibly Edward himself and one of the two others. The rest of the letter may have been cut away and given to an autograph collector. This happened to other letters.

INDEXES

I. JANE AUSTEN'S FAMILY

References are to the numbers of the letters (or, within brackets, to the pages).

In this index the generations are thus distinguished:

AUSTEN, GEORGE
AUSTEN, JAMES
Austen, James Edward
Lefroy, Anna Jemima

For collateral Austens, Leighs, &c., see Index II.

AUSTEN, Rev. *GEORGE*, 1 May 1731–21 Jan. 1805, s. of William A., surgeon; scholar 1747 and fellow 1751 of St. John's Coll. Oxon.; rector of Steventon, Hants, from 1761, and of Deane, Hants, from (?)1773 to 1805; m. 26 Apr. 1764 at Walcot, Bath, Cassandra Leigh, q.v.; 6 s. 2 d.; buried at Walcot
1798: 10–12, 14 (24, 27, 32, 36 interest in pigs, 37, 38, 39 reads Cowper to us)
1799: 18 (57, 58)
1800: 25, 27 (82, 93)
1801: 29–31, 36–8 (99, 100, 101, 103 his income, 105 the curacy of Deane, 106, 109, 110, 111 'above 500 volumes' for sale, 126 at Godmersham, 129, 131 at Kintbury, 135)
1804: 39 (141 at Lyme)
1805: 40 and 41 *passim*, 42, 43 (147, 149 his peaceful end)
75 (293 his interest in scholarship)

AUSTEN, *CASSANDRA*, 26 Sept. 1739–1827, y. d. of Rev. Thomas Leigh of Harpsden (who d. 1763; for his other children see James Leigh Perrot and Jane Cooper); m. 26 Apr. 1764 Rev. George A., q.v.
1796: 1, 4, 7 (3, 10, 18)
1798: 9–15 (20 leaves Godmersham, 21, 22 her health, 23, 24, 26 health, 27, 28, 30, 31, 33, 34 'her *entrée* into the dressing-room', 36, 38, 39 imaginary ailments, 46 plans a hen-house)
1799: 18–21 (55, 57 health, 58 match-making, 60, 61, 63, 67)
1800: 25, 27, 28 (82, 83, 93, 96, 98)
1801: 29, 31, 33–8 (99 two maids, 'my father not in the secret', 100 avoidance of Trim Street, 101, 102 moves beds to Bath, 103, 109, 110, 111 quite stout, 116, 118, 119, 123, 125, 126, 129, 132, 138)

I. Jane Austen's Family

1804: 39 (139 pool of commerce, 140, 141)
1805: 40, 42–7 (145 the shock, 146, 147, 148, 149, 151, 152, 153 156, 159, 165 love of tidiness, 170 sure to be happy with Martha)
1807: 48–50 (171, 173 and 174 her finances, 177, 182, 184)
1808: 51–5, 58–62 (192, 193, 198, 199, 200, 201, 207, 210 guessing the names, 211 garden, 212 curing hams, 213 no ailments, though a wet Sunday, 223, 224, 226, 227 talking of a house at Wye, 229, 231 reconciled to a manservant, 232, 238, 239, 243, 244)
1809: 63–6 (246, 252, 256, 262)
1811: 70, 72–4 (275, 281, 283, 285, 287 not overpower'd by her Cleft Wood, 289, 290, 291)
1813: 75, 77–9, 83–5, 87, 88, 90 (292 reading, 294, 296, 299 'too rapid way of getting on' in reading *P. and P.* aloud, 300, 302, 303, 308, 325 no more in need of Leeches, 327, 329 every dinner-invitation he refuses will give her an indigestion, 334 Mrs. Cooke's diagnosis, 337, 352 in agonies (Mary's blue gown), 356, 357, 358, 367); 78.1.
1814: 92, 94, 95, 97, 100, 101 (377, 385, 387, 390, 392, 400 disturbed at Mrs. F.'s not returning the visit sooner, 402 making shoes for Anna, 403 her interest in Anna's MS.)
1815: 110, 112, 118 (424, 428, 440 weather too good to agree with her)
1816: 128, 130, 132, 134, 135 (454 Mrs. E. Leigh's legacy, 457, 462, 469, 470)
1817: 139, 144, 145 (475, 492 bears the shock of her brother's will 'extremely well', 495 ' suffered much for me . . . but is tolerably well')

I. AUSTEN, JAMES, 13 Feb. 1765–1819, e.s. of Rev. George A.; scholar 1779 of St. John's Coll. Oxon.; curate at Overton, and at Deane, Hants; Rector of Steventon, Hants, 1805–19; m. (1) 27 Mar. 1792 at Laverstoke, Anne, d. of General and Lady Jane Mathew, who d. 3 May 1795; 1 d.; (2) 17 Jan. 1797 at Hurstbourne Tarrant, Mary y.d. of Rev. Nowes Lloyd; 1 s. 1 d.
1796: 1 (1, 3) 2 (5) 5 (11) 6 (15)
1798: 10–15 (23, 25, 27, 30, 31, 35, 41, 46)
1799: 18, 21 (55, 68)
1800: 23–5, 27 (75, 81, 83, 84, 93)
1801: 29–31, 33, 34, 36 (99, 101, 107, 109, 110, 111, 118, 121, 126)
1805: 40, 41, 44 (145, 146, 154)

(or, within brackets, to the pages).

1807: 48, 49 (172, 173, 174, 176, 181)
1808: 51–5, 60–2 (186, 188, 189, 192, 195, 197, 202, 203, 205, 206, 207, 208, 210, 232, 237, 238, 241)
1809: 64 (250)
1811: 69 (271)
1812: 74.1 (501)
1813: 76, 82, 87, 89 (297, 325, 354, 363)
1814: 92, 98, 99, 104 (376, 394, 397, 398, 399, 412)
1815: 112 (428)
1816: 128, 130, 133, 134 (454, 455, 457, 459, 465, 467, 469)
1817: 139, 145, 146 (475, 494, 496)

AUSTEN, ANNE, 1st w. of James A., q.v.; 27 (91), 90 (367)

1. Austen, Jane Anna Elizabeth, 1793–1872, e.d. of James A. (and o.c. of his 1st wife), b. Laverstoke 15 Apr. 1793, m. 8 Nov. 1814 at Steventon, Ben Lefroy, q.v. in Index II; 1 s. 6 d.:
1796: 2 (5, 6), 4 (10)
1798: 13 (35 note)
1799: 18, 20, 21 (55, 56, 62, 68)
1800: 24 (81)
1801: 30 (107)
1808: 51–4, 61, 62 (189, 191, 192, 194, 198, 199, 200, 201, 202 204, 206, 207, 238, 241, 242)
1809: 63–5 (249, 250, 257, 258)
1811: 70–4 (275 an A. with variations, 279, 281, 282, 283, 285, 287, 289, 291)
1813: 75, 78, 83, 85, 86, 89, 90 (296, 302, 303, 328, 340 her engagement, 341, 343, 363, 367 an A. sent away and an A. fetched are different things), 78.1 (instability)
1814: 100–2 (letters to her), 103 (411), 104–5 (to her), 106 (416), 107–9 (to her)
1815: 110 (to her), 117 (436), 118 (441), 124 (to her)
1816: 129 (to her), 133 (465), 134 (469), 135 (to her)
1817: 137, 139–42 (471, 475, 476, 481 as if she had never had a wicked Thought in her Life, 488 Poor Animal)

i. *Lefroy, Anna Jemima,* 20 Oct. 1815, e.d. of Ben and Anna L.: 124, 139, 141.

ii. *Lefroy, Julia Cassandra,* 27 Sept. 1816, 2nd d. of Ben and Anna L.: 139, 141

AUSTEN, MARY, –1843, 2nd w. of James A., q.v.
1796: 1, 2, 5–7 (1, 4, 6, 11, 15, 18 the Lloyds)
1798: 10–14 (23, 25, 29, 30, 31, 33, 34, 35, 38, 40)
1799: 17–21 (49, 50, 55, 56, 60, 61, 62, 68, 69)

1800: 23–7 (75, 79, 81, 82, 84, 88, 92, 93)
1801: 29–33, 36 (99, 106, 108, 109, 110, 111, 114, 117, 119, 126, 128)
1805: 43 (149, 150)
1807: 48–50 (171, 173, 176, 181, 185)
1808: 51–5, 57–9, 61, 62 (187, 189, 190, 191, 192, 193, 194, 195, 198, 200, 202, 203, 204, 205, 210, 219, 223, 226, 227, 237, 241)
1809: 64–6 (250, 257, 261)
1813: 75, 76, 84, 87, 89, 91 (295, 296, 297, 329, 352 ?, 363, 371, 372)
1816: 128, 128.1, 129, 130, 132–4 (455, 456, 457, 458, 462, 464, 466, 467, 468)
1817: 138, 145, 146 (474, 494, 496)

2. Austen (-Leigh 1837), Rev. James Edward, 1798–1874, o.s. of James A.; b. Deane 17 Nov. 1798; commoner of Winchester 1814–16; Exeter Coll. Oxon.; Vicar of Bray 1851; author of the *Memoir* 1870; in his youth usually 'Edward':
1798: 11, 12, 15 (29, 30, 31, 46 the christening)
1799: 17, 18, 21 (50, 55, 68)
1800: 28 (98)
1801: 33 (117)
1808: 51, 52, 54, 62 (188 little E., 191, 195, 197, 205, 241 Edward A.'s godson, 242)
1813: 77, 78 (301, 302)
1814: 99 (397, 398, 399), 104 (413)
1816: 125 (450), 130 (letter to him), 131–3 (460, 461, 462 his novel, 464, 465, 466, 467), 134 (to him)
1817: 137 (471, 472 his novel, 473), 139 (475 his virtues, 476), 141.1 (his novel), 142 (489), 143 (490 his beauty?), 146 (to him at Oxford)

3. Austen, Caroline Mary Craven, 1805–80, y.d. of James A.; b. Steventon 18 June 1805; god-d. of Cassandra A.; author of *My Aunt Jane Austen*, published for the J. A. Society:
1807: 48 (173, 175)
1808: 51, 52, 54 (189, 190, 191, 194, 197, 205)
1813: 76 (299)
1815: 112 (letter to her), 117 (439), 119 (to her)
1816: 125, 128, 128.1, 131 (to her), 132 (462), 133 (467), 134
1817: 137, 138, 141.1 (to her; her Gentleman Quack), 143 (to her)

II. AUSTEN, GEORGE, 1766–1838, 2nd s. of George A., is not mentioned in the Letters.

III. AUSTEN (KNIGHT 1812), EDWARD, 7 Oct. 1768–1852, 3rd s.

of George A.; of Godmersham Park, Kent, and Chawton, Hants; m. 27 Dec. 1791, Elizabeth, 3rd d. of Sir Brook Bridges III; 6 s. 5 d.:
1796 in London 3; at Rowling 4–7 (8, 10, 12, 13, 15, 17)
1798 at Godmersham 11–16 (29, 31, 32, 36, 38, 39, 44, 46, 47)
1799 at Godmersham 17–18 (49, 51 his estate, 57); at Bath 19–22 (61 going out to taste a cheese, 63, 66, 68, 70, 71, 72)
1800 at Godmersham 23–7 (74, 75, 76, 79, 80, 82, 85, 88, 94)
1801 at Godmersham 29, 31, 33 (101, 109, 118)
1805 at Godmersham 43, 45–7 (149, 153, 161, 165, 167, 169)
1808 at Godmersham 51–62 *passim*
1809 at Godmersham 63, 64, 66 (246, 250, 261, 262)
1811 at Godmersham 70, 71, 73 (272, 276, 279, 281, 286)
1812 at Chawton Cottage 74.1 (500 change of name)
1813 at Godmersham 78 (303); at Chawton (April–Sept. 337, 341): 80, 81 (313, 314, 315, 317, 318); in London 82, 83 (319, 321, 326, 328); at Godmersham 84–91 *passim*
1814 in London 92–4 (376?, 379–85); at Chawton 96, 97 (388–90); 103, 104 (411–13); in London 105 (415); at Godmersham 106 (416)
1815 at Godmersham 111 (427); at Chawton 116–18 (433, 434, 436, 440)
1816: 132 (461)
1817: 142 (486)

AUSTEN, ELIZABETH, 23 May 1773–10 Oct. 1808, w. of Edward A., q.v.:
1796: 4–6 (8, 11, 14)
1798: 12–14 (31, 35, 38, 39)
1799: 17–21 *passim*
1800: 23, 26 (74, 88)
1801: 32, 33, 36 (114, 118, 126)
1805: 45–7 *passim*
1807: 48, 50 (170, 182)
1808: 51–7 *passim*; her wedding-day 62 (242)

1. Austen (Knight), Fanny Catherine ('Fag' p. 73), 23 Jan. 1793–1882, e.d. of Edward A.; m. 1820 Sir Edward Knatchbull Bt. of Mersham Hatch, Kent (their son the first Lord Brabourne edited 1884 the letters of J. A. in his mother's possession):
1796: 4 (9)
1798: 10 (26)
1799: 18, 19, 21–2 (55, 58, 59, 68, 70, 73 her letter to C. E. A.)
1800: 25 (87)

1801: 32 (115)
1805: 46 (161)
1807: 48, 50 (172, 183)
1808: 51–4, 56–9 *passim* (217 almost another Sister)
1809: 63–6 (246, 254, 255, 259)
1811: 69–74 (269, 274, 277, 278, 279, 283, 286, 289, 291)
1813: 78 (303), 80 (309, 312), 82–5 *passim*, 87–91 *passim*
1814: 93–4 *passim*, 96, 97, 99 (388, 390, 397), 103 and 106 to her
1815: 116–18 *passim*
1816: 128, 132 (454, 461)
1817: 140–2 letters to her

2. Austen (Knight), Edward, 10 May 1794–1879, e.s. of Edward A.; commoner of Winchester 1807–11; St. John's Coll. Oxon. 1811:
1796: 5 (13); 1798: 10, 12 (26, 33); 1799: 19, 21, 22 (59, 68, 70, 73 his letter to C. E. A.); 1800: 23 (74); 1805: 45–7 (161, 166, 167); 1807: 49 (180); 1808: 51–4 (188, 193, 199, 209), 56–8 *passim*, 62 (244); 1809: 63–5 (247, 252, 256); 1813: 78, 81, 83–6, 88, 91 (303, 315, 326, 331, 338, 344, 357, 358, 374); 1814: 103–6, 116 (412, 413, 415, 418, 420, 433, 434); 1816: 128 (454); 1817: 140 (481)

3. Austen (Knight), George, 22 Nov. 1795–1867, 2nd s. of Edward A.; commoner of Winchester 1808–12; St. John's Coll. Oxon. 1813:
1796: 4 (9); 1798: 9–11, 14 (22, 24, 26, 30, 38); 1799: 17, 19 (51, 61); 1800: 23, 24, 27 (74, 81, 94?); 1801: 30 (107); 1805: 45, 47 (161, 167); 1808: 54 (208), 56–9 *passim*, 62 (244); 1813: 78.1 (503), 81 (315), 84–8 *passim*, 91 (374)

4. Austen (Knight), Henry, 27 May 1797–1843, 3rd s. of Edward A.; commoner of Winchester 1810–14: 19 (61), 45 (161), 47 (167), 62 (244), 74, 78.1 (503), 81, 86, 97, 104?, 130, 140, 142

5. Austen (Knight), William, 10 Oct. 1798–, 4th s. of Edward A.; commoner of Winchester 1813–14: 11 (30 baby), 19 (61), 45, 51, 63, 64 (249), 74.1, 78.1 (503), 81, 87, 97, 104?, 130, 140, 141, 142, 146

6. Austen (Knight), Elizabeth (Lizzy), 27 Jan. 1800–   , 2nd d. of Edward A.: 45, 46, 48, 50, 51, 52, 54, 58, 65, 74.1, 82–6, 88, 90, 116, 140

7. Austen (Knight), Marianne, 15 Sept. 1801–96, 3rd d. of Edward A.: 46, 51, 54, 63, 65, 82–5, 90

8. Austen (Knight), Charles Bridges, 11 Mar. 1803–67, 5th s. of Edward A.; commoner of Winchester 1816–20: 51, 81, 134, 146

---

9. Austen (Knight), Louisa, 13 Nov. 1804–89, 4th d. of Edward A.; J. A.' s. god-d. (*Brabourne*, ii. 341): 51, 55, 84, 86, 88
10. Austen (Knight), Cassandra Jane, 16 Nov. 1806–42, 5th d. of Edward A.: 50 (182), 51, 63, 79 (307), 88, 140
11. Austen (Knight), Brook John, 28 Sept. 1808–78, 6th s. of Edward A.: 55, 58, 60

IV. AUSTEN, Rev. HENRY THOMAS, (bapt.) 8 June 1771–1850, 4th s. of George A.; scholar 1788 of St. John's Coll. Oxon.; Lieutenant Oxford Militia 1793, Captain and Adjutant 1797; Partner in Austen, Maunde and Tilson, bankers of 10 Henrietta-street, Covent Garden, 1807–16, and in Austen, Gray and Vincent, bankers of Alton, Hants; Receiver-General for Oxfordshire 1813; bankrupt March 1816; took orders and became curate of Bentley near Alton, Dec. 1816; m. (1) 31 Dec. 1797 his cousin Eliza, q.v.; (2) 1820, Eleanor Jackson
1796: 1, 3–7 (2 his Master's degree, 7 his attentions to Miss Pearson (cf. 16, and 180 note), 8 at Rowling, 9, 11, 12, 15, 18)
1798: 12 (31 his affairs, i.e. the militia)
1799: 18 (54)
1800: 27 (92, 95)
1801: 29, 30, 33, 34 (99 as agreeable as ever, 104, 107, 118 his office in Cleveland Court, 119 his house 24 Upper Berkeley Street, cf. 120 and 121)
1804: 39 (139 opinion of Weymouth)
1805: 40, 43, 45, 46 (145 note, Brompton, 152 cannot help being amusing, 153 rambles in 1804, 161, 162 his office in the Albany, 163 at Godmersham)
1808: 51–62 (186, 189, 191, 196, 199, 203, 206, 207, 208, 210, 212, 217, 219 at Godmersham, 220, 223, 224, 229, 232, 238, 244 at Godmersham)
1809: 63–5 (248 the progress of the bank, 250, 254 at Godmersham)
1811: 69–71, 74 (267 J. A. stays with him at 64 Sloane Street, 268 Life & Wit, 269, 271 his office in Henrietta Street, 273, 275, 276, 277 at Oxford, 278, 288 his Gig, 289 at Chawton)
1812: 74.1 (501)
1813: 75–7, 79–85, 88–91 (292, 297 sends early copies of *P. and P.*, 301 at Oxford, 305 drives J. A. from Chawton to Sloane St., 308, 309 No. 10 Henrietta St. all dirt & confusion (in preparation for his living there cf. 311), 313, 315 his promotion to be Receiver-General for Oxfordshire, his scheme for Scotland, his Mind not a Mind for affliction, 318 J. A. stays with him at

10 Henrietta St. cf. 337, 319, 320 stays with Warren Hastings at Daylesford, 320 plans for Chawton and Oxfordshire cf. 321, 361 and 364, 323 his November collection cf. 426, 324 a new clerk sent down to Alton, 325, 326, 332, 338 his enjoyment of Roxburghshire, 340 reveals the authorship of *P. and P.*, 353, 355 Cassandra stays with him in Henrietta St., 358, 359, 363, 364 his illness cf. 373, 368 his carriage, 369, 373, 374); 78.1

1814: 92–4, 97, 99, 103, 105, 106, 109 (375 J. A. with him in Henrietta St., 376, 377, 378, 380, 381, 382, 383, 384, 385, 386, 390 at White's, 391, 396 J. A. with him at 23 Hans Place, 397, 398 office in Henrietta St. cf. 327, 399 likely to marry again, 411, 414 to take J. A. to Chawton, 415, 418, 419, 423)

1815: 110, 111, 114–18 (424 J. A. with him in Hans Place, 425 his illness cf. 426, 427, 431, 432, 433, 434 Business to worry him, 435, 436, 437 convalescence, 439, 440, 441)

1816: 125, 127, 128, 130, 132–4 (450 at Chawton Cottage, 453 the late event in Henrietta Street, i.e. the bankruptcy, 454 at Godmersham, 458, 459 to visit France ?, 461 at Godmersham, decided for Orders (see note), 463, 468 writes very superior Sermons, 469)

1817: 139, 140, 142, 143, 146 (476 to assist Mr. Papillon on Sunday . . . ease and collectedness, 481 preaching at Chawton, 482, 487, 489 London hateful to him, 490, 496 attends her journey to Winchester)

AUSTEN, ELIZA, 22 Dec. 1761–25 Apr. 1813, o. d. of Tysoe Saul Hancock of Fort St. David (Madras) and of Philadelphia, o.s. of George Austen; m. (1) 1781 Jean Capotte Comte de Feuillide (guillotined 1794); 1 s., Hastings, 1786–1801; (2) 31 Dec. 1797, Henry Thomas Austen: 18 (55), 39 (139), 43 (153), 51 (191), 55 (210), 62 (244), 63 (248), 69–71 *passim* 81 (315), 82 (319, 324)

V. AUSTEN, CASSANDRA ELIZABETH, 9 Jan. 1773–1845, e.d. of George A.; engaged (?1795) to Rev. Thomas Fowle (q.v.), who d. Feb. 1797. (Such of the events of her life as are known from her sister's letters can be easily traced, and are not here set out)

Her engagement, 'making your wedding-clothes' (p. 10, Sept. 1796, and see p. 5, note, and p. 14), her comic powers (p. 8); her drawing (101); 'scraps of Italian and French' (135); charades (298); her starched notions (300); 'does not like desultory novels' (395); 'my tender, watchful, indefatigable nurse', 140–7 *passim*

VI. AUSTEN, Sir FRANCIS WILLIAM, 23 Apr. 1774–1865, 5th

s. of George A.; G.C.B. (K.C.B. 1837), Admiral of the Fleet; m. (1) at Ramsgate 24 July 1806, Mary, e.d. of John Gibson, who d. 1823; 6 s. 5 d.; (2) 1828, Martha Lloyd, q.v.
Childhood: 68 (see note)
1792: Lieutenant R.N.
1796: London and Rowling 3–7 (7, 8, 10, 11, 12, 15 'Fly', 16, 17 appointment to the frigate *Triton*, 18)
1798: off Cadiz in H.M.S. *London* 13–16 (33, 36, 38, 41, 42, 47 promoted to Commander and appointed to sloop *Petterel*)
1799: 17, 18, 20 (51, 56, 65)
1800: off Cyprus 24, 25, 27 (78, 87, 94; promoted to post rank in (?) April)
1801: 32–5 (112 'thrust out of the Petterel', 116, 120, 124); 36–8 in Kent (126, 130, 135)
1805: 40–1 letters to him in *Leopard* at Portsmouth; 43–5 in the Mediterranean, *Canopus* (153, 157, 161, 162 his engagement)
1807: at Southampton 48–50 (172, 174, 177, 178, 180, 184 still unemployed; appointed to *St. Albans*, then at Sheerness, in April)
1808: 52–5 (196 *St. Albans* expected—from St. Helena, 199, 203, 204 his return, 206 *St. Albans* in the Downes, 208, 212 at Yarmouth); 59–63 (226 *St. Albans* sailed, 230, 233 end of a visit to Southampton, 234, 240 at Portsmouth, 241, 246 disembarcation of Sir John Moore's army, superintended by F. W. A. in Jan, 1809)
1809: 63, 65, 68 (248 at Portsmouth, 256, 264; *St. Albans* ordered to China in April)
1811: at Cowes, May (Dec. 1810–May 1811, Flag-captain to Lord Gambier in *Caledonia*); 69–74 (270 superseded in *Caledonia*, 272, 281, 284, 288 invited to Chawton)
1813: 76 (297 at Portsmouth); 81, 85 letters to him with *Elephant* in the Baltic; 86 (344, 345); 91 (374); 78.1 (504) at Deal
1814: 93 (382); 97 (390 at Portsmouth, 392)
1815: at Chawton Manor 111, 117 (427, 438)
1816: at Alton 130, 133 (457, 464, 465)
1817: at Alton 137, 140, 142, 144 (473, 482, 489, 491)

AUSTEN, MARY (Gibson), 'Mrs. F. A.', 1st w. of Francis A.:
1805: 43 (153)
1807: at Southampton 48–50 (171–86)
1808: at Yarmouth, I. of Wight 51–6 (190, 199, 203, 204, 206, 207, 212, 215); 60–2 (233–5, 240 at Portsmouth, 241)
1809: 63, 65, 68 (245, 256, 264)

1811: at Cowes 72–4 (281, 284, 288)
1813: 81 (313), 85 (337 at Deal, 340), 86 (346), 90 (366), 91 (375)
1814: at Chawton 97 (392), 101 (405)
1815: at Chawton 111, 116 (426, 427, 435)
1816 at Alton: 125, 130, 133 (450, 458, 464–5)
1817 at Alton: 137, 140–2, 145 (473, 482, 483, 489, 494)
1. Austen, Mary Jane, b. Southampton 27 Apr. 1807, e.d. of Francis A.: 51 (190), 52, 53, 60, 68, 85, 99, 105, 117, 125, 128, 130, 131, 141.1
2. Austen, Francis William, b. Alton 12 July 1809, e.s. of Francis A.: 68, 85 (337), 99, 136
3. Austen, Henry Edgar, b. Portsmouth 21 Apr. 1811, 2nd s. of Francis A.: 70 (272), 85 (337), 136
4. Austen, George, b. Deal 20 Oct. 1812, 3rd s. of Francis A.: 99, 133, 136
5. Austen, Cassandra Eliza, b. Portsmouth 8 Jan. 1814, 2nd d. of Francis A.: 130, 131, 136
6. Austen, Herbert Grey, b. Chawton 8 Nov. 1815, 4th s. of Francis A.: 116, 136
7. Austen, Elizabeth, b. Alton 15 Apr. 1817, 3rd d. of Francis A.: 133 (464), 145 (494)

AUSTEN, MARTHA, –1843, e.d. of Rev. Nowes Lloyd, q.v. in Index II; 2nd w. (1828) of Francis A.
1796: 6, 7 (16, 18)
1798: 10, 14, 15 (23, 24, 40 removal from Ibthrop, 41, 42 happiness to Martha, 45 at Deane, 46 they continue at Ibthrop)
1799: 17, 18, 20–2 (50, 54, 58, 62, 65, 66 to spend the summer at Steventon, 67 reads 'First Impressions', 70)
1800: 24–8, 26 a letter to her (81 at Kintbury and Ibthrop, 85 at Steventon, 87 J. A. to visit Ibthrop cf. 92 and 96–7, 98 to return with J. A. to Steventon)
1801: 29–33, 35, 37, 38 (99 Miss Lloyd, see note, 102 to be at Steventon again cf. 103, 105, 106 return to Ibthrop, 108, 113 to be at Deane, 119, 123, 125, 133 her elegance, 134 to visit Chilton)
1804: 39 (139, 142 at Bath, 143)
1805: 43, 44, 47 (150 Mrs. Lloyd's death, 154, 157 our intended partnership with Martha, 170 at Bath with Mrs. Austen)
1807: 48–50 (175 at Kintbury, 176 Deane and Eversley, 177 will marry Peter Debary, 184 her room, 185, 186)
1808: 52–62 *passim*, at Southampton (199, 207, 213 and 217 her visit to the Island with Mrs Craven)
1809: 64–6 at Southampton (251 M. and Dr. Mant as bad as ever,

---

253, 254, 258 immoral attachment, 261 to be in Town with Mrs. Dundas)
1811: 70, 72–4 (275 at Chawton, 284 in London cf. 288 and 290)
1812: 74.1 to her at Barton
1813: 75 and 76 at Steventon, 77, 79, 83–8 at Chawton (295, 299, 300 at Barton ?, 308 a legacy cf. 391, 328, 335 Races, 337, 345, 353, 357 Miss Floyd); 78.1 to her
1814: 92, 94, 97, 103 (377, 385 at Chawton, 391 her legacy, to visit the Deans Dundases at Clifton, 412 her return to Chawton)
1815: 111, 116, 117 (426, 427, 435, 436)
1816: 130, 132, 133 (458 in London, 462 at Chawton, 467)
1817: 140, 145, 146 (482 at Chawton, 495, 497 with J. A. at Winchester)

VII. AUSTEN, JANE, b. Steventon 16 Dec. 1775, d. Winchester 18 July 1817, y.d. of George A.; see Indexes IV, VI, VII for her Novels, her Vocabulary, and her Opinions

References to events before 1796

Schooldays: (8; see *Life* 26)
Visit to Gloucestershire with C. E. A.: (123, see note)
1793, ?Dec: dancing at Southampton (236)
1794, summer: in Kent, perhaps Rowling, with C. E. A. (168 October; 186 'our hot journey into Kent')

1796–May 1801: Steventon

1796, Aug.: 3 in Cork Street; Sept.: 4–7 at Rowling with the Edward Austens
1797, Nov.: at Bath with the Leigh-Perrots (26, 59, 60, 148)
1798, Oct.: 9 end of a visit at Godmersham with the Edward Austens, cf. 13 (33)
1799, Jan.: 18 (58) plan to visit the Lloyds at Ibthrop in Feb.; May–June: 19–22 at 13 Queen Square, Bath, with the Edward Austens; Summer: ? at Godmersham 17 (50); Nov.: 28 at Ibthrop with the Lloyds
1801, Jan.: 29–33 plans for a house in Bath; Mr. A.'s income (103); sale of Steventon furniture and books (109, 111, cf. 126, 128, 133); 'a tall woman' (116); Feb.: 34 at Manydown

May 1801–July 1805: Bath (4 Sidney Terrace)

1801, May: 35–8 staying (with Mrs. A.) in Paragon with the Leigh-Perrots while house-hunting; Summer: at Sidmouth (101, 107 cf. 118, 132; see *Life*, 90, 172 and Thomson, *Survey* 202)

I. Jane Austen's Family

1802, Summer: at Dawlish (85 the D. scheme, 393; see *Life* 173); Nov.: at Steventon with C. E. A. (*Life* 92)

1803: at Ramsgate? (351 suggests that J. A. knew R.; and see *Life* 174); Nov.: ? at Lyme (216)

1804, Summer: rambles with the Henry Austens (153, cf. 138 C. E. A. at Weymouth); Sept.: 39 at Lyme with Mr. and Mrs. A.

1805, Jan.: 40–2 in Green Park Buildings (Mr. A.'s death); April: 43–4 at 25 Gay Street (157 intended Partnership with Martha, cf. 170); Aug.: 45 at Godmersham, 46–7 at Goodnestone

[1806, April: at Trim St., Bath; July–Aug., at Adlestrop and Stoneleigh; *Life*, 191, 194.]

July 1806–April 1809: *Southampton*

1806, July 2: the A.s left Bath for Clifton 'with what happy feelings of escape!' (208)

1807, Jan.–Feb.: 48–50 in lodgings at Southampton with Mrs. A.; preparations in Castle Square ('Our garden is putting in order' 178, 'our removal' 183); Sept.: at Chawton House (187; see *Life* 203)

1808, June: in Brompton with the Henry Austens (191 saw the ladies go to Court, 197 and 209 visit at Brompton; see also 145); June: 51–4 at Godmersham; Oct.–Dec.: 55–62 in Castle Square, Southampton (212 another house there, or a move to Alton cf. 217, 229 the Chawton plan cf. 226 the kitchen garden and 'this proposal', 227 'a house at Wye', 231 keeping a manservant, 235 'our approaching removal', 243 'we *will* have a pianoforte')

1809, Jan.: 63–6 in Castle Square; April: the A.s left Southampton (for Bookham and Godmersham; 246 gives 3 April as the date, but see 263; and cf. 336)

July 1809–May 1817: *Chawton*

1809, July: 68 at Chawton Cottage (266 'the many comforts'; see note on 281)

1811, April: 69–71 in Sloane Street with the Henry Austens; 2–9 May: at Streatham with the Hills (271, 277); May–June: 72–4 at Chawton

1812, Nov.: 74.1 at Chawton

1813, Jan.–Feb.: 75–8 at Chawton; May: 79–80 in Sloane Street; July: 81 at Chawton; 15 Sept.: 82–3 at 10 Henrietta Street

---

(*or, within brackets, to the pages*).

with Henry A. (for two days 337); 17 Sept.–13 Nov.: 84–91 at Godmersham; Nov.: ? at 10 Henrietta Street (342, 361, 365, 374)

1814, March: 92–4 at 10 Henrietta Street; April: ? at Streatham (383, 387); June, Aug.: 95–8 at Chawton; 24 June–? July: at Bookham with the Cookes (389, 390); Aug.: 99 at 23 Hans Place with Henry A.; Sept., Nov.: 100–4 at Chawton; Nov.–5 Dec.: 105–7, 109, at 23 Hans Place (418 'off on Monday' 5 Dec.); 26 Dec.–(?) 14 Jan. 1815: J. A. and C. E. A. at Winchester (Mrs. Heathcote) and Steventon (Letter from Mrs. A. in Bellas MS.)

1815, Sept.: 110 at Chawton; 4 Oct. –16 Dec.: 111–22 at 23 Hans Place (424 date of starting, 447 return to Chawton)

1816, March, April: 125–8 at Chawton; May: at Cheltenham with C. E. A. (*Life* 334, following Caroline's *Reminiscences*). They stopped at Steventon, where they left Cassy, and at Kintbury; and in their return at Steventon again, whence they took Cassy and Caroline to Chawton. *Bellas MS.*); June, July: 129–31 at Chawton; Sept.: 132–3 at Chawton; Dec.: 134 at Chawton

1817, Jan.–May: 136–45 at Chawton

May–July 1817: Winchester

1817, May: 146 in College Street (496, 24 May)

VIII. AUSTEN, CHARLES JOHN, 23 June 1779–1852, 6th s. of George A.; Admiral; m. (1) 1 May 1807 Frances Fitzwilliam Palmer, q.v.; 3 d.; (2) 1820, her sister Harriet, q.v. in Index II; 3 s. 1 d.

1796: 1 (3, the *last* Charles on this page) 4 (9 at Cork)

1798: 10 (26), 14–16 (38—he was then lieutenant in *Scorpion*, having been commissioned Dec. 1797—42, 46, 47 in *Tamar*)

1799: 17–20 (48, 52, 54 at Steventon, 56, 57, 58 with Capt. Sir Thomas Williams (q.v. in Index II), *Endymion*, 63)

1800: 24–7 (80, 81, 84 at Gosport, 87, 89, 90 at Steventon, 92, 94)

1801: 32, 34, 35, 38 (113 Capt. Durham, q.v. in Index II, 120, 124, 134 at Portsmouth, 137 prize-money)

1804: 39 (140; he took command of the *Indian* sloop in October; 141 E. Indies)

1805: 43, 44, 47 (152, 158, 159, 170; on the North American station)

1807: 48 (171)

1808: 52 (196), 62 (242 in Bermuda, 243)
1809: 63–5, 68 (248, 253, 254, 266 expected home)
1811: 69, 70 (270, 275; he arrived in April, in command of *Cleopatra*)
1813: 75–91 in command of *Namur* as Flag-captain to Sir T. Williams, C.-in-C. at the Nore (296, 297, 304, 308, 312 visit to Chawton Cottage, 316 at Southend, 330, 337, 345, 350–4 visit to Godmersham, 356–7, 360, 366, 373)
1814: 105–6 (414 in Hans Place, 419 Keppel Street)
1815: 117 (438)
1816: 129, 133, 134 (456, 463, 468–9 at Chawton)
1817: 137, 141, 143 (473, 485, 490), 144 J. A.'s last letter to him

AUSTEN, FRANCES FITZWILLIAM, 1790–6 Sept. 1814, 1st w. of Charles A.; see Index II s.v. Palmer. 'She died at the Nore, where her husband had the Guardship'—Caroline Austen's Reminiscences
1809: 64, 65, 68 (251, 255, 266)
1813: 78, 81, 87–90 (304, 316, 350–60, 366)
1814: 100 (402)
1. Austen, Cassandra Esten, b. Bermuda 22 Dec. 1808, e.d. of Charles A.:
1809: 64, 65 (251, 255)
1813: 78, 79, 81, 84, 87–90 (304 on board the *Namur*, 307 little Cass going to Chawton Cottage cf. 316, 330 not to go to Chawton, 351 at Godmersham, 352, 354 so very Palmery, 357 (Cassy, *not* Cass.), 360 return to the *Namur*, 366 not to stay at Chawton if she hates it)
1814: 92, 94, 103, 105, 106 (378 at Chawton, 386 to move to 22 Keppel Street, 411 Mr. Palmer gone off with Cassy, 415 Keppel Street, 419 that puss Cassy)
1815: 110–12, 117 (424 at Chawton, 427, 428, 439)
1816: 128, 129 (455 at Chawton, 456)
1817: 136, 137, 141, 144 (470 letter to her, 472 to return to Chawton in March as usual, 485 her father cannot spare her, 492 Keppel Street), 141.1
2. Austen, Harriet Jane, b. Bermuda 19 Feb. 1810, 2nd d. of Charles A.: 78 (304 'Middle'), 81, 106, 137, 138, 141, 142, 143, 144.
3. Austen, Frances Palmer, b. London 1 Dec. 1812, 3rd d. of Charles A.: 78, 81 (316 all at Southend), 87, 88 (356 little F.), 105, 106, 117, 137.

II. OTHER PERSONS

References are to the numbers of the letters (or, within brackets, to the pages).

In this index Jane Austen's relations of the preceding generation and her own are thus distinguished:

AUSTEN, JOHN (her father's cousin)

COOKE, GEORGE (her cousin).

Abercrombie, General Sir Ralph, 1734–1801: 34

Adams, the: 88

Ajax, a horse: 48

'Alford', Mrs. and Misses: 61

Allen, Miss, governess at Godmersham: 71

Amos, Will: 88

Anderton: Anderdon, Edmund, apothecary, 4 Queen-square, Bath: 22

Andrews, Farmer: 117

Andrews, Mrs. (and her daughter? Elizabeth): 96

Anne: 24

Anne, a maid: 43, 56, 59

Anne (a maid?) 'late of Manydown': 11

Anning, tradesman at Lyme: 39

Armstrong, Mr. Mrs. and Miss (at Lyme): 39; Miss A. (at Bath—? the same) 44

Arnold, Misses, of Chippenham: 37

Arnold, Miss; Arnold, Sam; evidently connected with Cookes and Leighs: 63, 69

Atkinson, Misses, of En——: presumably dd. of Rev. Arthur Atkinson, Rector of Knight's Enham 1782 (cf. p. 91): 27

AUSTEN, JOHN, –1807, o.s. of John A. of Broadford and c. of George A.; m. Joanna Weeks of Sevenoaks (d. 1811); 1 d., Mary (d. unm. 1803); he left his property to John, 3rd s. of his c. Francis Motley A., q.v.: 50

AUSTEN, FRANCIS MOTLEY, 1747–1815, of Kippington, Sevenoaks, o.s. of Francis A. and c. of George A; m. 1772 Elizabeth d. of Sir Thomas Wilson, who d. 1817; 7 s. (including Thomas and John, qq.v.) 4 d. (including Frances, q.v.): 36, 50, 82 (322 note), 138

AUSTEN, Col. THOMAS, 1775–1859, 2nd s. of Francis Motley A., m. 1803 Margaretta Morland: 81

AUSTEN, Rev. JOHN, 1777–1851, 3rd s. of Francis Motley A.; inherited Broadford 1807: 50

AUSTEN, FRANCES, 1783– , y.d. of Francis Motley A., m. 1808 Capt. Holcroft R. A.: 54

AUSTEN, HARRIET LENNARD, 1768–1839, y.d. of Rev. Henry A. (c. of George

II. Other Persons

A.) and s. of Mrs. John Butler Harrison (II), with whom she lived: 51, 52, 55, 58, 62 (? 241)

Austen, Miss, 'of a Wiltshire family' not identified: 87

B., Miss (possibly Burdett): 97

Badcock, Mr. and Mrs.: 36

Baigent: perhaps a son of John B., a farmer at Chawton: 93

Bailey, Eliza: 17

Bailey, Harriet: 25

Bailey, Miss: 51, 55, 66

Bailey, Mr.: 14

Baker, Misses, mantua-makers, High Street, Southampton: 58

Balgonie, Lord, 1785–1863, afterwards (1820) Earl of Leven and Melville: 44

Ballard, Misses, of Southampton, related to the Harrisons (the mother of J. B. H. (2) was a Ballard): 55

Barker, Mrs.: 74.1

Barlow(e), ——, presumably employed in H. Austen's bank: 80, 92, 94, 117

Barnwall, Hon. John Thomas, 1773–1839, afterwards Baron Trimleston, and Mrs. B.: 39

Baskerville, Mrs. shopkeeper at Canterbury: 52

Bather (Bathur), Rev. Edward, 1780–1847, vicar (sic) of Meol-Brace, near Shrewsbury, m. April 1805 Emma Hallifax: 44

Battys, the: 15

Baverstock (or -stoke), Jane, 1751–18 , d. of Rev. John Hinton, Rector of Chawton 1744–1802, and, as heiress of her mother Martha Hinton, 'sole representative of the Knights of Chawton'; she m. 1769 James Baverstock of Alton: 93 (383–see also Hinton), 134

Bayle, Mr.: 23, 31

Beach, — Hicks, d. 1796, sister of William Hicks Beach, 1783– , who (1832) inherited Oakley Hall at the death of Wither Bramston: 1

Beatrice, a maid: 101

Beaty, Miss: 69, 70 (269 note)

Beckford, Maria, y.d. of Francis Beckford of Basing Park, Hants (uncle of the author of *Vathek*) and s.-in-law of John Middleton (with whom she resided at Chawton 1808–12); of 17 Welbeck-street: 69, 70, 77, 105

Beckford, Margaret Maria Elizabeth, 1785–1818, e.d. of William B. of Fonthill, the author of *Vathek* (who m. in 1783); m. 15 May 1811 Col. James Orde: 72 (see note)

Beckford, Susanna Euphemia, 1786–1859, y.d. of William B. of Fonthill, m. 1810 the Marquess of Douglas: 72

Becky: 63

Bell, Miss, governess at Wrotham: 141

Bendish, Mr. and Miss (perhaps Mr. Bendyshe of 1 Upper Park-street,) Bath: 44

Benham, Sally: 110, 136

Benn, Rev. John, 1766–1857, Univ. Coll. Oxon., Rector

(*or, within brackets, to the pages*).

1797 of Faringdon near Chawton, m. Elizabeth ——, 1779–1867; 13 (or more) children, including Harriet, Elizabeth, Piercy: 73, 133, 142
Benn, Miss, of Chawton, no doubt s. of Mr. B. above: 72, 74, 74.1, 75, 76, 77, 78, 80, 86, 87, 96, 97, 116, 78.1
Benn, Harriet or Harriot, 1792–1830: 72, 73, 74, 77, 104
Benn, Margaret Elizabeth, (?)1801–30: 72, 73
Benn, Piercy (sic), second Lieut. R.A. 1821, Major-General 1862: 99
Bent, Mr.: 37
Bertie, Sir Albemarle, Bart. (cr. 1812), 1755–1824; Rear Admiral 23 April 1804, Vice Admiral 28 April 1808; m. 1782 Emma Heywood, who d. 1805; of Hill, near Southampton: 48
Bertie, Catherine Brownlow, 2nd d. of Albemarle B.; she d. at Hill 17 April 1808: 48
Bertie, Sir Thomas (né Hoare), 1758–1825, m. 1788 Catherine d. of Peregrine B. and took her name; Rear Admiral of the Blue 28 April 1808; Kt. 1813; the Polygon, Southampton (where Lady B. d. 1823): 61
Bertie, ——, sister of Thomas B., = Mrs. Dickens, q.v.
Best, Dora: 90
Betsy, maid at Chawton: 76, 78, 79
Betsy, nursemaid to Mrs. Charles Austen: 79, 87
Bickerton: 44 (see note)
Bigeon, Madame, Henry Austen's servant (J. A. left her £50): 82, 85, 89, 92, 93; her daughter (? Mrs. Perigord, q.v.) 85
Bigg Wither, Lovelace, 1741–1813, of Manydown, Hants; m. (1) 1764 Rachel Clitheroe (s. of Lady Blackstone) who d. s.p.; (2) 1766 Margaret Blachford who d. 1784; 2 s. 7 d. (the dd. did not take the name Wither): 17, 18, 26 (88)
Bigg Wither, Harris, 1781–1833, 2nd s. (but his e.b. Lovelace d. 1794) of Lovelace B. W.; m. 1804 Anne Frith: 17, 18 (note), 23, 25
Bigg, Elizabeth: see Heathcote, Elizabeth
Bigg, Catherine: see Hill, Catherine
Bigg, Alethea, 1777–1847, 6th d. of Lovelace Bigg Wither of Manydown: 1, 2, 5, 21, 47, 52, 58, 60, 78, 82, 85, 86, 91, 108, 125, 145; J. A.'s letter to her, 139; 78.1
Binns, John: 60, 63, 65
Birch, Mrs., of Barton Lodge. See at end of this Index: 12 (31, 33), 63, 86, 99
Birchall, R., music-seller and publisher, 133 New Bond-street: 83
Blachford, Winifred, e.d. of Robert Pope B. of Osborne, I. of W. (b. of the 2nd w. of Lovelace Bigg Wither, q.v.), m. 18 Feb. 1815 Rev. J. Mansfield: 15, 17, 18, 44, 108.

II. Other Persons

Blachford, Jane, 1795–1855, y.s. of the above, m. about 1814 Philip Williams, s. of Rev. Philip W. of Winchester and b. of Charlotte W., q.v.: 31

Blackall, Rev. Samuel, 1771–1842, Emmanuel Coll., Camb., Rector 1812 of North (not Great) Cadbury, Som.; m. 5 Jan. 1813 Susannah, 1780–1844, d. of James Lewis of Clifton, formerly of Jamaica (not Antigua): 11 (27, see note), 81

Blackstone, Margaret, 1769–1842, e.d. of Lovelace Bigg Wither, q.v., and s. of Mrs. Herbert Hill; m. 1792 Charles B., 1759–1800, Vicar 1789 of Andover, nephew of Sir William B.: 108

Blackstone, Mrs. H.: probably widow of Henry B., 1722–1776, who m. 1771 Jane Brereton of Winchester: 17

Blairs, the, of Canterbury: 84

Blake, Captain: 116

Blount, Mr. and Mrs.: perhaps Edward Walter B. of Kempshott Park, 1779–1860, and his w. Janet Shirley: 27

Bolton, Lord: Thomas Orde (1795 Powlett), 1740–1807, m. 1778 Jane Mary, natural d. and (ultimately) heiress of the 5th Duke of Bolton (his b. the 6th Duke dying s.m.p. 1794), cr. Baron B. 1797; of Hackwood, Basingstoke; his e.s., William: 13, 17, 18, 24

Bond, Miss, (perhaps of Upper Park-street; or a d. or s. of Sir James B., bart., 6 Henrietta-street?) Bath: 37

Bond, John, bailiff at Steventon Parsonage: 10, 13, 20, 29, 30, 31, 62, 76, 78; Lizzie (probably his d.; Elizabeth B. of Steventon m. 1809 Joseph Beal of Overton) 13

Bonham, Miss: 39

Bonham, Mr. F.: 44

Booth, Mr. and Misses: 55

Bourne, Robert, 1761–1829, professor of medicine at Oxford; his great-grandson informs me that he lived in the house that is now the Union Society's: 63

Bowen, William, M.D., 1761–1815, apothecary at Bath: 40, 41, 43, 50

Boyle, Courtenay, R.N., 1770–1844, 3rd s. of the seventh Earl of Cork, 'post captain 1797; m. 1799 Carolina Amelia, d. of William Poyntz, of Midgham, Berks.: 34

Bradshaws, the (perhaps of 13 Vineyards,) Bath: 38

Bramston, Wither, 1753–1832, of Oakley Hall, Hants; m. 1783 Mary Chute (1760–1821); no children (Mrs. B. is mentioned in *Opinions*): 17, 23, 24, 27, 31, 34, 37, 75, 82

Bramston, Augusta, 1751–1819, s. of Wither B. (mentioned in *Opinions*): 23, 27

Branfill, Jemima, (presumably) d. of Mrs. John Harrison of Denne Hill, q.v.: 91 (371), 141

Branfill, Jemima, o.d. of Charlotte (Branfill) Harrison, q.v.

Brecknell, Joseph, m. 9 Oct.

(*or, within brackets, to the pages*).

1810, Lady Catherine Colyear, d. of the Earl of Portmore: 51, 71

Brecknell: 94

Brett, of Spring Grove, Kent: 27, 45, 87; 'a Mr. Brett', 90

Bridges, Fanny, Lady, – 1825, d. of Edmund Fowler of Graces, Essex, m. 1765 Sir Brook Bridges III, who d. 1791; 7 s. 6 d. During her widowhood Lady B. lived at Goodnestone Farm with her unmarried daughters and her orphan grand-daughters the Cages: 5, 6, 29, 35, 46 (spelled *Brydges* according to Brabourne), 52, 54, 55, 56, 57, 59, 72, 74, 82, 87, 90, 91, 93

Bridges, Sir Brook William, 1767–1829, of Goodnestone, Kent, fourth baronet (1791); m. (1) 1800 Eleanor Foote who d. 1806; 3 s. 1 d.; (2) 1809 Dorothy Elizabeth, e.d. of Sir Henry Hawley of Leybourne, Kent, who d. 1816: 5, 50 (186), 62, 89, 90, 91; 'three little Bridgeses,' 54; '3 children', 50 (the three then surviving)

Bridges, Eleanor, Lady, – 1806, e.d. of John Foote, 1st w. of Sir Brook B. IV and s. of Mrs. Edward B.: 50 (185), 60 (231, Eleanor)

Bridges, Eleanor, b. 1805, o.d. of Sir Brook B. IV: 117

Bridges, Dorothy Elizabeth, Lady, 2nd w. of Sir Brook B. IV, q.v.: 90 (367), 91 (370, 371, 373)

Bridges, Rev. Brook Henry, 1770–1855, 3rd s. of Sir Brook III; m. 1795 Jane, d. of Sir Thomas Pym Hales of Beaksbourne, Kent; 2 s. 2 d.; Rector of Danbury, Essex: 4, 5, 82, 91, 78.1

Bridges, Jane, 1766– , w. of Rev. Brook Henry Bridges, q.v.: 4, 5

Bridges, Rev. Brook Edward, 1779–1825, 5th s. of Sir Brook III; m. 1809 Harriet Foote; Rector 1807 of Bonnington, Kent, and Vicar 1810 of Lenham, Kent: 5, 15, 45, 46, 47, 54, 56, 60, 85, 86, 87, 89, 91

Bridges, Harriet, y.d. of John Foote, s. of Lady Bridges (w. of Sir Brook IV) and of Lucy F.; w. of Edward B.: 29, 60 (231, 234), 87

Bridges, Rev. Brook John, – 1812, 6th s. of Sir Brook III; St. John's Coll., Cambridge (M.A. 1808); m. 1810 Charlotte d. of Sir Henry Hawley of Leybourne, Kent; Rector 1808 of Saltwood and Hythe, Kent; (mentioned in *Opinions*): 46, 51, 52, 53, 54, 58, 60, 63, 72

Bridges, Fanny, 1771– , see Cage

Bridges, Sophia, 1772–1844, see Deedes

BRIDGES, ELIZABETH, 1773-1808, see Austen in Index I

Bridges, Marianne, 1774–1811, 4th d. of Sir Brook Bridges III: 5, 6, 46, 47, 49

Bridges, Louisa, 1777–1856, 5th

d. of Sir Brook Bridges III: 4, 5, 51, 52, 53, 82, 87, 89, 91, 93, 103
Bridges, Harriot Mary, 1781–1840, see Moore
Bridges, Miss: 5 (see note)
Briggs, Mr.: 18
Britton, Dr. and Mrs.: 86, 91
Bromley, Mrs., lodging-house keeper, 12 (and 13) Queen-square, Bath: 19
Brown, Bob: 12
Browns or Brownes, the (perhaps the Hon. Mrs. B., of 3 Burlington-street,) Bath: 43
Brown, Captain A., R.N., and Mrs. B.: 49
Browning, servant at Chawton Cottage: 77, 78, 97, 130
Browning, Mrs.: 96
Brydges, Jemima, 1727–1809, of the Precincts, Canterbury, widow (1780) of Edward B. of Wootton Court, Kent, and mother of Sir Samuel Egerton B., of Anne Lefroy, and of Charlotte Harrison: 14 (39), 52, 53
Brydges, Sir Samuel Egerton, 1762–1837, first baronet (1814) of Denton Court, Kent. See also Index V: 12, 30 (note)
Brydges, Mrs. Jemima, unmarried daughter of Mrs. Brydges: 53
Brydges, Jemima, 2nd d. of Sir Samuel Egerton B. (He had two daughters called Jemima; but Mrs. Bellas's note states that the J. B. referred to is the younger, who in 1817 became Mrs. Quillinan): 86
Budd, Mrs.: 74
Budd, Harriot: 74
Buller, Rev. Richard, 1776 (?)–19 Dec. 1806, Vicar of Colyton, Devon, s. of William Buller, Bishop of Exeter, and of Anne, d. of John Thomas (1691–1766), Bishop of Winchester; b. at Winston, Hants; pupil of George Austen; m. Anna Marshall: 2, 25 (85 note), 39, 43, 44
Buller, Susanna Catherine, 1769–1840, s. of Richard B., m. 1808 Sir John Duckworth, Bt.; 43, 48
Bulmore, Captain: 51
Buonaparté: 77
Burdett, Miss: probably Frances, d. 1846, s. of Sir Francis B., Bt., and of Elizabeth B., who 1801 m. Sir James Langham, Bt., of Cottesbrooke, Northants (Sir J. L. is coupled, in *Opinions*, with H. Sanford, q.v.): 80, 97 (? 390), 99 (mentioned in *Opinions*)
Burdon: either John Burden, bookseller, College-street, or Thomas B., bookseller and wine-merchant, Kingsgate-street, both of Winchester: 12
Burton, Miss: 69
Busby, Mrs., (perhaps Mrs. Sarah B., 5 King-street,) Bath: 35, 36, 37
Bushell, Dame: 10
Butcher: probably Samuel B., 1770–   , Lt. R.N. 1794: 15 (43 note)
Butler, Mr. and Mrs. John: 74.1

II. Other Persons

Butler, Richard, hair-dresser of Basingstoke: 13
Byng, Major Edmund, 1774–1854: 31 (111 note)
C., Miss (perhaps Clewes, q.v.): 140
C., Miss (probably Curling, q.v.): 65
C., Mrs.: 99 (see note)
Cage, Lewis, of Milgate, Kent, m. 1791, Fanny e.d. of Sir Brook Bridges III; 2 d. (Fanny and Sophia, who after the early death of their parents lived with their grandmother Lady Bridges at Goodnestone Farm): 4, 5, 26
Cage, Fanny, 1771– , e.d. of Sir Brook Bridges III, m. 1791, Lewis Cage: 4, 5, 15 (but this may be L. C.'s mother), 26
Cage, Fanny, 1793 (?)–1874, e.d. of Lewis Cage, m. 1834 her cousin Sir Brook Bridges V (mentioned in *Opinions*): 74.1, 82, 84, 86, 91, 103, 140
Cage, Rev. Charles, y.b. of Lewis C.; m. —— Graham, s. of the second Lady Knatchbull, of Lady Oxenden, and of Charles G. (C. Cage is mentioned in *Opinions*): 30, 87, 90, 140
Calker, Mrs.: 142
Calland, Mr.: probably Rev. John C., 1763–1800, s. of John C. of Alverstoke, Hants; Rector of Bentworth: 15
Canterbury, Archbishop of: Charles Manners Sutton, 1755–1828, archbp. 1805–28: 84
Canterbury, Dean of, see Powys
Capet, Hugh (a horse): 30
Carnarvon, Henry George Herbert, 2nd Earl of, 1772–1833, of Highclere, Hants: 23
Carpenter, Mr., physician at Lyme: 39
Carrick, Mrs. (mentioned in *Opinions*): 90
Catherine, Lady, see Brecknell, Joseph
Cawthorn, publisher: C. and Hutt, 24 Cockspur-St: 10
Chalcraft, Lucy: 88
Chamberlayne, Mr. and Mrs.: 31, 35, 36, 37, 38, 43, 44; Richard C., 43; Miss C., 43 (perhaps the niece mentioned in the same letter)
Chambers, maid to Mrs. Leigh Perrot: 60
Chambers, William, silk-dyer, Canal-place, Southampton: 56
Champneys, Sir Thomas, 1745–1821, first baronet (1767) of Orchardley, Som.: 27
Champneys, Catherine Harriet, 1776–1812, d. of Sir Thomas C., m. J. Butcher: 27
Chaplin, Miss: 62
Chapman, Mrs. and Miss, from Margate: 87
Charde, George William, 1765–1849, assistant organist at Winchester Cathedral: 4
Charles XII: 81
Charlotte, Queen, 1744–1818: 64
Charlotte, perhaps maid at Deane: 24, 26
Charlottes, Lady: 99 (397 note)

References are to the numbers of the letters

II. Other Persons

Charterises, the Miss: 17
Chessyre, Mr.: 55
Children, John George, 1777–1852, of Ferox Hall, Tunbridge, m. 1798 Miss Holwell, grandd. of Governor H. of Bengal: 6 (15 note)
Chisholme, Rev. Charles, Rector 1812 of Eastwell, Kent: 86
Choles, the Austens' servant at Southampton: 55, 62, 66
Chowne(s), see Tilson
Christian's; probably C. and Son, Linen-drapers, 11 Wigmore St.: 80
Christina, Queen of Sweden: 81
Chute, William John, 1757–1824, of The Vyne, Hants, M.P. for Hants 1790–1806 and 1807–1820; M.F.H.; succeeded his f. 1791; m. 1793 Elizabeth Smith, who d. 1842; no issue: 2, 23, 24, 25, 71, 138
Chute, Rev. Thomas Vere, 1772–1827, y.b. of W. J. C.; unmarried: 2, 24, 29, 30, 44, 48
Clarinbould or Claringbould, farmer: 5, 6
Clarke (Clerk), John, 1759–1842, of Worting, Hants, m. Anne 2nd d. of Carew Mildmay and s. of Lady M., q.v.: 12, 15, 24, 27
Clarke, Rev. James Stanier, 1765 (?)–1834, author, naval chaplain (1795–9) and (1799) domestic chaplain to the Prince of Wales: 121; letters to and from, 113, 113 a, 120 a, 126 a, 126; see also Index V
Clayton, Mr.: 6
Clement, Benjamin, 1785–1835, Capt. R.N., of Chawton; m. 1811 Ann Mary (1788–1858) y.d. of William Prowting: 74.1, 75, 78, 84, 97, 104, 108, 130, 137, 142, 147(?)
Clement, Rev. Benjamin, 1813–73, Minor Canon of Winchester: 84 (329)
Clerk, see Clarke
Clewes, Miss (*Mrs. Clewes* in 84 p. 335 may be a title of honour), governess at Godmersham (1813); (mentioned in *Opinions*): 78, 80, 84, 88, 90, 91 (and perhaps 140 p. 481)
Cole, Benjamin, lodging-house keeper, Sydney-place, Bath: 39
Coleby, milliner at Alton: 74.1
Coleman, Mrs.: 50
Collier's coach: 97, 99, 111, 127
Conyngham, Lady: Elizabeth, d. of J. Denison, m. 1794 Baron C., 1766–1832, who became 1816 first Marquis C., 1821 Baron Minster of M. Abbey, Kent; Lady C. 'possessed great influence over George IV': 14.
COOKE, Rev. *SAMUEL*, 1741–1820, Rector of Cotsford, Oxon., and Vicar of Great Bookham, Surry, where he lived; m. Cassandra, 1744–1826, d. of Theophilus Leigh, Master of Balliol, and first cousin of Mrs. George Austen (see also Index V): 2 s. 1 d.: 10, 30, 43, 44, 51, 52, 54, 57, 63, 65, 66, 69, 73, 84, 90, 96, 112, 144
COOKE, Rev. THEOPHILUS LEIGH, 1776–1846, e.s. of

(or, within brackets, to the pages).

Rev. Samuel C.; Balliol, and Fellow of Magdalen Coll., Oxon.: 63, 69
COOKE, Rev. GEORGE LEIGH, 1780–1853, y.s. of Rev. Samuel C.; Balliol, and (1800) Fellow of Corpus Christi Coll., Oxon.: 44, 63, 66, 69, 70, 84
COOKE, MARY, o.d. of Rev. Samuel C.: 43, 44, 65, 66, 69, 70, 73, 84
COOPER, Rev. Dr. *EDWARD*, 1728–27 Aug. 1792; of Southcote near Reading; Rector of Whaddon near Bath, and 1784 of Sonning, Berks.; m. 1768 Jane Leigh, o.s. of Mrs. George Austen, who d. 1783; 1 s. 1 d.: 2
Cooper, Mrs.: perhaps w. of Rev. Edward Cooper the elder, q.v.: 24 (note)
COOPER, Rev. EDWARD, 1770–1835, o.s. of above; Rector 1799 of Hamstall-Ridware, Staffs.; m. 14 March 1793 Caroline Isabella Lybbe Powys, who d. 1838; curate at Harpsden (Harden) near Henley 1793–9; see also Index V; 1 (see note), 2, 18, 32, 33, 57, 58, 66, 72. Their children: Edward 2, 66; Caroline 2; nine children 72.
COOPER, CAROLINE, w. of Edward C. the younger, q.v.
COOPER, JANE, o.d. of Edward C. the elder, see Williams, Lady
Cope, Rev. Sir Richard, 1719–1806, ninth baronet, of Bramshill Park, rector of Eversley, Hants: 49
Corbett, a bailiff: 31
Corbett, Mary, maid at Ashe Park: 33
Cottrell, Mr.: probably Rev. Clement C., Rector 1800 of North Waltham, Hants: 75. The Miss C. of Waltham, 55, is no doubt his d.; see Lefroy, J. H. G.
Coulthard, Thomas, d. 1811, living at Basing Park 1797, and tenant 1800–7 of Chawton Manor, and later of Oakley Hall; 4 s., 2 or more d.: 24, 75
Coulthard, Mrs., d. 1800, presumably w. of the above: 11
Coulthard, Mrs.: 43
Courtenay, Captain, see Lefroy, Sarah
Cove, Mrs. and Miss Anna: 39
Cox(e), Misses: 27
Crabbe, Sarah, wife of the poet (q.v. in Index V), d. 21 Sept. 1813 (not Oct. as stated in *Gent. Mag.* and by Crabbe's son; see Huchon, *Crabbe and his Times*, Engl. trans. 1907, p. 375): 88
Craven, Lord: William Craven, 1770–1825, 7th Baron and 1st Earl of the 2nd creation, of Hamstead Marshall and Ashdown Park, Berks.; m. 1807 Louisa Brunton, an actress (mentioned in *Opinions*): 18, 30, 32
Craven, Rev. John (see Mrs. Craven): 20 (65, see note)
Craven, Mrs.: Catherine Hughes, d. 1839, second w. (1779) of

Rev. John C. (d. 1804) of Chilton, Wilts. (b. of Mrs. Fowle and Mrs. Lloyd); Mrs. C. as a widow lived at Speen Hill; 2 s. 1 d., Charlotte, who 1819 m. Sir J. Pollen, Bt. (both Mrs. and Miss C. mentioned in *Opinions*): 38, 43, 51, 53, 79, 87, 97, 133
Crawford, Mr.: 39
Creed, Mrs. (mentioned in *Opinions*): 109; Creeds of Hendon, 111 (422 note)
Criswick, Mr.: 60 (There is mention in Caroline Austen's Reminiscences of a Mrs. Creswick at Highclere, and of a Mr. Creswick 'formerly a servant in Governor Craven's family').
Crook and Besford's (John Crook, Son, and Besford, Haberdashers and Hosiers, 104 Pall-mall): 83
Crooke, young Mr. and the second Miss: 27
Crosby, Richard, of Crosby and Co., 4 Stationers' Court, Ludgate-street, publishers: 67, 67a
Croucher, Mary: 88
Crutchleys, the; possibly G. H. C. of Sunning Hill Park, which is 6 m. from Egham on the Reading road: 99
Cure, Mr.: 70 (274 note)
Curling, Miss and Miss Eliza, cousins of Mrs. Frank Austen: 61, 63, 65, 66, 70
Curtis, Mr., Apothecary at Alton: 96, 144, 145
Cuthbert, Miss, and brother: 11 (29 note)
Cuthbert, Maria: 117
Daniel, coachman at Godmersham: 9, 45, 51
D'Arblay, Alexander, 1794– , s. of General D'A. and Fanny Burney: 90
D'Auvergne, Corbet James, Commander R.N. 1807, appointed to the *Autumn* Sept. 1810; see J. W. Horrocks in *Times Lit. Suppt.* 23 Feb. 1928: 61, 65
Davis, Mrs., draper at Basingstoke: 18
Davis, Miss, a singer: 70
Dawes, Miss: 28
Dawkins, Betty: 15, 23
Day, Mrs.: 50
Daysh, George, clerk in the Ticket Office, Navy Office: 13, 15, 16, 18, 69
Deane, Mr., of Winchester: 13
Deanes, Miss (or Deane, Misses): 1
Deans Dundas, see Dundas
Debary, Rev. Peter, 1725–Jan. 1814, Vicar 1775 of Hurstbourne Tarrant, Hants, m. Ann Hayward, 1727–1809; 2 s. 4 d.: Rev. Peter, 1764–1841, Trin. Coll., Camb., Curate 1804 and Vicar Jan. 1807 of Eversley, Hants; Richard, 1767–1829; Ann, 1763–1834; Mary, 1766–1854; Susannah, 1768–1852; Sarah, 1770–1823: 11, 12, 14, 17, 24, 27, 28, 30, 37, 39, 49, 55, 133
Deedes, William, 1761–1834, of Sandling, Kent, m. 1791 Sophia 2nd d. of Sir Brook Bridges III; 'numerous issue':

(*or, within brackets, to the pages*).

23, 49, 54, 57, 61, 63, 84, 86, 89, 90, 91, 140; their children: 54, eleven children; 54, 74.1, Mary; 90, Isabella; 46, 91, Sophia; 140, Marianne; 78.1
Delman's Rooms, Canterbury: 28 (98 note)
'Dennis, Mrs. Ashton' ('M. A. D.'), assumed name of J. A.: 67, 67a
D'Entraigues (or D'Antraigues), Comte, 1756–July 1812; came to England with credentials from the Emperor of Russia 1806; m. 'the once celebrated Mad. St. Huberti, an actress at the Theatre François', who 'had amassed a very large fortune by her professional talents'; of Barnes-terrace, Barnes, Surry, and Queen Anne-street West; assassinated by their Italian servant; one son (1792–1861) 'studying the law at Manchester' (*Gent. Mag.* 1812, ii. 79): 69, 70 (Un Agent secret, par L. Pingaud, Paris, 1894; *Gent. Mag.*)
Dering, Sir Edward, 1732–8 Dec. 1798, sixth baronet, of Surrenden-Dering, Kent; succeeded by his s. the seventh baronet: 14
Dewar, Jane Charlotte, d. of Penelope Susannah Mathew (q.v.) who 1787 m. David Dewar of Enham House, Hants: 105
Dickens, Mrs. (née Bertie): 61
Dickson, Mrs. (mentioned in *Opinions*): 48, 49
Digweed, Hugh, 1738–98, of Steventon Manor, Hants; m. Ruth——, 1740–91; 5 s., of whom the eldest, John, succeeded to his father's property at Ecchinswell, and is not mentioned in the letters; only the 2nd, 3rd, and 4th sons concern us: 6
Digweed, Harry, 1771–1848, 2nd s. of Hugh D.; from 1798 tenant, in common with his b. William, of Steventon Manor; m. 3 March 1808 Jane Terry, and thereafter lived at Alton: 9, 10, 15, 27, 31, 59, 72, 74, 74.1, 75, 76, 100 (?), 132, 133, 140
Digweed, Jane, w. of Harry D., q.v. ('Mrs. Digweed' is mentioned in *Opinions*): 24 (80 ?), 62, 64, 72, 74, 74.1, 75, 76 (298 'beyond anything & everything' quotes Mrs. D.), 77, 78, 86, 98, 129, 132, 133, 141
Digweed, Rev. James, 1774–1862, of Dummer; 3rd s. of Hugh D.; m. June 1803 Mary Susannah, 1772–1840, o.d. of John Lyford of Basingstoke: 10, 14, 15, 18, 24, 25, 26, 27, 30, 31, 32, 72
Digweed, Mary Susannah, w. of James Digweed, q.v.: 14, 24, 30, 31, 34, 55
Digweed, William Francis, 4th s. of Hugh D.; from 1798 tenant, in common with his b. Harry, of Steventon Manor, and continued there when H. went to Alton 1808: 15, 27, 33, 62, 98, 104, 130, 138, 143
Dinah, maid at Kintbury: 23

II. Other Persons

Doe, Mary: 86, 88

Dolphins, the, probably of Eyford House, Glos.: 36

Dorchester, Lord: Guy Carleton, 1724–1808, C. in C. in America 1781–3, first Baron D. 1786; of Kempshott Park, Hants; m. 1772 Maria, d. of 2nd Earl of Effingham, who d. 1836: 16, 24

Doricourt, Mr.: 31

Dormer, Mrs.: 104

Douglas, Marchioness of, see Beckford

Dowdeswell, Mrs., 17 Marlborough-buildings, Bath: 19

Downes, the: 39

Dowton, William, 1764–1851, actor: 70

Drew, Mrs.: 62

Driver, Mrs., housekeeper (?) at Godmersham: 84, 97

Drummond Smith, Lady, 2nd w. of Sir D. S. Bt. of Tring Park: 80

Duer, Mrs., of Southampton, doubtless w. or widow of John D. of Antigua, and grandm. of Sir George Henry Rose, M.P. for the city: 55, 56

Duncan, Mr., Mr. John, their sisters (perhaps children of Lady Mary D., 44 Great Pulteney-street,) Bath: 43

Dundas, Charles, 1751–1832, M.P. for Berks. 1794–1832; cr. Baron Amesbury 1832; m. Ann Whitley, heiress of Barton Court, Berks., q.v.; 1 d.: 87

Dundas, Ann Whitley, 1752–1 Dec. 1812, of Barton Court, Berks., first w. of the above: 30 (106), 56, 61, 66, 71, 74.1

Dundas, Janet Whitley, o.d. of Charles D., m. April 1808 her first c. James Deans, R.N., who took the names of Whitley and Dundas; (mentioned in *Opinions*): 43, 74.1, 75 (295), 97, 78.1 (504)

Durham, Sir Philip, 1763–1845, Captain R.N., Admiral and G.C.B. 1830; appointed to the *Endymion* Feb. 1801: 32

Dusautoy, Mrs. and Misses: 49 (180 note), 64, 97

Dyson, Rev. Henry, Rector of Baugherst, Hants, 'a gentleman of the most wooden and inexpressive countenance imaginable' (*The Vine Hunt*, 1865, p. 63), and Mrs. D.; in 1807 he had 7 s.: 34

East, Sir William, 1738–1819, first baronet 1766, of Hall Place, Berks.; an unpublished poem by James Austen, written 1799, shows that Sir William's e.s. Gilbert was one of George Austen's pupils: 29

East, Miss, see Latouche, Mrs.: 70, 99, 116, 117

Eden(s), the Miss: 17

Edwards, Mr., and d., (Edwards, Rev. and Mrs., 7 Gay-street,) Bath: 37

Edwards, Mrs.: 77

Edwin, Mrs. John, jun., 1769–1854, actress: 70

Egerton, Henry: 49, 69 (270 note), 70

Egerton, Thomas, Military Library, Whitehall, J. A.'s first publisher (mentioned in *Opin-*

ions as admiring the morality of *M.P.*): 74.1, 85, 106
Ekins, Anne, see Holder, John Hooper
Eliza, protégée of Anne Sharpe: 145
Eliza, the Austens' maid at Southampton: 56, 62, 65
Elizabeth, Queen: 81
Elkington, Major: 15
Elliott, Mr.: 21
Elliott, Mrs. (perhaps Mrs. Grace E. of 4 Seymour-street, Bath; see Stanhope): 44
Ellis, Charles Rose, of Claremont, q.v.: 79
Elliston, Robert William, 1774–1831, actor; m. 1796 Elizabeth Rundall, a teacher of dancing in Bath, who 'in the height of his success continued her occupation' (D.N.B.): 50, 93
Elliston, Rev. Dr. William, 1732–1807, Master of Sidney College, Cambridge, 'uncle to Mr. E. the dramatic performer, to whom he has left considerable property, Report says 17,000l.': 50
Elton, James: 23
Emery, John, 1777–1822, actor: 94
Esten, Mrs.: 64 (see note)
Estwick, Mrs.: Cassandra Julia, e.d. of second Lord Hawke, and n. of Lady Saye and Sele, q.v., m. (1) 1793 Samuel E. of Barbados, (2) Sept. 1800 Rev. Stephen Sloane: 27
Evelyn, Alexander, and Mrs. E.: 22, 87
Evelyn, William, 1734–1 Nov. 1813, of St. Clere, Kent, and 10 Queen's Parade, Bath, and Mrs. E.: 21 (68 note), 22, 36, 38, 87, 91

F——: 17 (49 note)
Fagg, Rev. Sir John, *c.* 1760–1822, sixth baronet, of Mystole near Canterbury, m. 1789 Anne Newman; their family included 5 d., Elizabeth, Sarah Anne, Augusta, Lucy, Jemima: 84, 86, 87, 91; Miss Sally, 87
Falknor: 76, 102 (407 note)
Fanshawe, Miss, perhaps a fabulous person: 27
Fellowes, Dr. physician, 4 Paragon-buildings, Bath, and Mrs. F.: 20, 22
Fendall, banker in Gloucester: 30
Fielding or Feilding, Mrs. (née Finch), m. 1772 Hon. Charles F., son (by a second marriage) of the wife of Sir Brook Bridges, 2nd baronet of Goodnestone: 6
Filmer, Rev. Francis, 1773–1859, Rector of Crondale, Kent, and Mrs. F.: 52, 53
Finch-Hatton, George, 1747–1823, of Eastwell, Kent, m. 1785 Lady Elizabeth, d. of 2nd Earl of Mansfield: 45, 46, 53, 54, 84, 89, 91
Finch-Hatton, George, 1791–1858, e.s. of George F.-H. of Eastwell; m. 1814 Lady Charlotte Graham, d. of the Duke of Montrose; afterwards (1826) 10th Earl of Winchilsea: 45, 84, 87, 89, 93, 99 (397)
Finch-Hatton, Rev. Daniel, 1795–1866, y.s. of George F.-H. of Eastwell: 45

II. Other Persons

Finch-Hatton, Louisa, *c.* 1786–1875, e.d. of G. F.-H. of Eastwell; m. 1807 Major-Gen. Hon. Charles Hope: 45, 46, 50, 54
Finch-Hatton, Anna Maria, –1837, 2nd d. of G. F.-H. of Eastwell: 54, 91
Finch-Hatton, Elizabeth: perhaps a mistake for Emily Mary, 3rd d. of G. F.-H. of Eastwell: 54
Finch-Hatton, John Emilius Daniel Edward, 1755– , y.b. of G. F.-H. of Eastwell: 18, 45
Finch, the Misses (Anne and Mary), ss. of G. F.-Hatton of Eastwell: 5, 18, 45, 66, 89
Fitzhugh, Valentine, d. 1811, y.b. of William F., M.P.: 62
Fletcher, Miss: 6
Fletcher, Mrs., wife of William F. (matric. Trin. Coll. Dublin 1765), judge of Common Pleas, Ireland: 90
Floor, Mr., tradesman in Southampton?: 56
Floyd, Miss, i.e. Martha Lloyd, q.v. in Index I: 88 (note)
Foley, Mrs., 17 Marlborough-buildings, Bath: 19
Fonnereau, Miss: 24
Foote, Edward James 1767–1833, Captain R.N., Vice-Admiral 1821, K.C.B. 1831; of Highfield House, Southampton; m. (1) Nina Herries (children, Francis, Catherine and Caroline), (2) Mary Patton (children, Mary, Helena, Anne, Elizabeth); (Admiral F. is mentioned in *Opinions*): 48 (172 note)
Foote, Francis, Catherine and Caroline, children of Captain Foote by his first marriage: 49 (178); Catherine 1797–1813, 49 (179), 61
Foote, Mary (née Patton), 2nd w. of Captain F.: 48
Foote, Mary, Helena, Anne and Elizabeth (*not* Caroline), children (the last bapt. 27 Jan. 1807) of Captain Foote by his second marriage: 48
Foote, Caroline, s. of Captain F.: 48 (172), 56
Foote, Eleanor, see Bridges, Eleanor, Lady
Foote, Harriet, see Bridges, Harriet
Foote, Lucy, y.s. of Lady Bridges (1st w. of Sir Brook B. IV) and of Mrs. Edward B.: 60, 90, 91
Forbes, Lady: 46
Foresters, the: 87
Fowle, Rev. Thomas (1), 1727–1806, Vicar of Kintbury, Berks., Rector of Hampstead Marshall, Berks., and Allington, Wilts.; m. Jane Craven (d. 1798), d. of Hon. Charles C., Governor of S. Carolina, and s. of Mrs. Lloyd; 4 s.: 2.
Fowle, Rev. Fulwar Craven, 1764–1840, e.s. of Rev. Thomas F. (1); St. John's Coll., Oxon, 1781, Vicar of Kintbury and Rector of Elkstone, Glos., 1798–1840; m. his 1st c. Eliza Lloyd: 3 s. 3 d.; (mentioned in *Opinions*): 18, 30, 32, 33, 58 (see note) 74.1, 116
Fowle, Eliza, 1768–1839, 2nd d. of Rev. N. Lloyd, m. Fulwar

Craven F.: 1, 2, 13, 20, 30, 32, 33, 39, 58 (see note), 59, 60, 74.1, 91
Fowle, Fulwar William, 15 April 1791–1876, e.s. of Fulwar Craven F.; Winchester (scholar 1803–9) and Merton Coll., Oxon.; Rector of Allington 1816: 32, 44, 50, 56, 60, 64, 74.1, 87
Fowle, Thomas (3), –(?)1822, 2nd s. of Fulwar Craven F.; Lt. R.N. 1812: 32; see also *Sailor Brothers* p. 210 (where *Fowler* should be *Fowle*)
Fowle, Mary Jane, 1792–1883, e.d. of Fulwar Craven F.: 60, 74.1, 87
Fowle, Elizabeth Caroline, Dec. 1798–1860, 2nd d. of Fulwar Craven F.: 18, 32
Fowle, Rev. Thomas (2), 1766–Feb. 1797, 3rd s. of Rev. Thomas F. (1), Rector of Allington 1793; left £1,000 to his fiancée, Cassandra Austen: (?) 2 (5 note)
Fowle, Charles, –1806, 4th s. of Rev. Thomas F. (1); a barrister; m. 1799 Honoria Townsend of Newbury, who d. 1823: 1, 2, 17, 43, 66
Fowle, Mrs.: perhaps the w. of William F., M.D., 1766–1805, 2nd s. of Rev. Thomas F. (1) —did he m. a Miss *Carpenter* ?; or of William F. of Chute Lodge, Hants, and Durrington, Wilts., a cousin of Rev. Thomas F.: 19
Fowler, Miss: 49
Frances, a maid?: 19
Franfraddops, the: 87
Frank, Mr. Leigh Perrot's (negro ?) servant: 19, 35
Franklyn, Mrs., 3 Montpelier, Bath: 37
Fraser, Mrs.: 39
Frederick, see Tilson, Christopher
Freeman, Mrs.: 78
French, Peter William, of St. Lawrence, Reading, chemist, m. 1799 Mary Skeete, widow, of Basingstoke: 17
Frere, Mrs. G.: 139
Fust, Sir John, Bart., 1725–99, of Hill Court, Glos., m. Philippa d. of John Hamilton of Chilson, Kent., who d. 1803: 36, 37, 38

Gabell, Henry Dison, 1764–1831, Headmaster of Winchester 1810–23: 74.1, 146
Galigar de Concini (d. 1617): 145 (495 note)
Gambier, James, first Baron, Admiral, 1756–1833: 14, 15, 16, 69
Gardiner, Rev. Dr., 10 Paragon-buildings, Bath, m. June 1799 Mrs. J. Piersy: 21
Garnet, Dame, and children: 75
Garrett, Miss: 10
Gauntlett, Mr.: 25, 75
Gayleard's: 51
George III, 4 June (N.S.) 1738–1820, acceded 1760: 22 (71), 38 (137–8), 51 (191), 73 (285), 74
Gibbs (Gibbes), Dr., physician, 28 Gay-street, Bath: 40, 41
Gibson, Miss, see Austen, Mrs. Frank, in Index I: 43
Gibson, Elizabeth and S——, doubtless sisters of Mrs. F. Austen: 105, 108, 111, 133

II. Other Persons

Gibson, a young: 99

Gipps, Rev. H., m. (?1812) Emma Maria, 2nd d. (but her e. sister d. 1809) of John Plumtre: 71, 73, 74, 84, 86, 91, 103, 141

Girle, Mrs., 1712–8 Jan. 1801, grandm. of Caroline Cooper (Lybbe Powys diary): 32

Gloucester, H. R. H. William Henry, Duke of, 1743–1805, b. of George III; he died at 8.30 p.m., 25 Aug. 1805: 46, 47

Gloucester, Prince William Frederick of, 1776–1834, s. of above; second D. of G. 1805: 15

Glyn, Miss: probably d. of Sir James Glynne of Bugle Hall, Southampton: 65

Goddard, Dr. William Stanley, 1757–1844, Headmaster of Winchester 1796–1809: 53, 54, 58

Goodchild, Mary, 'under' to the Frank Austens: 97

Gordan, Mr., of Cleveland Row?: 111

Gordon, Sir Jenison William, 1748–1831, second baronet, of Haverholm Priory, Lincolnshire; m. 1781 Harriet, s. of George Finch-Hatton, q.v. (Lady G. is mentioned in *Opinions*): 45.

Gore, Captain John, R.N.: 7

Gore, Caroline, 1772–   , 5th d. of Sir Thomas Pym Hales of Beaksbourne, Kent, and y.s. of Mrs. Henry Bridges; m. 1798, Hon. William John Gore, 2nd s. of the Earl of Arran: 4, 52 (193?), 90

Gore-Langton, William, 1760–18   , s. of Edward Gore of Kiddington, Oxon.; Lt.-Col. Oxfordshire militia 4 Oct. 1798: 12

Gould, Rev. John, 1780–1866, Trin. Coll., Oxon. (matric. 6 Dec. 1798): 20

Graham, Rev. Charles, Rector of Barham and b.-in-law of Sir Edward Knatchbull VIII, q.v. (*Brabourne* i. 340): 53

Graham, Charlotte: 25

Granby, Marquis of (George John Frederick Manners), baptized 4 Jan. 1814 ('by the Archbishop of Canterbury, in the presence of the whole of the nobility and gentry at the [Belvoir] Castle: the sponsors were the Prince Regent, and the Duke of York; and the Duchess Dowager of Rutland, Proxy for the Queen'); died 15 June 1814 (*Gent. Mag.* 1814, pp. 88, 700): 97

Grants, the: 1

Granville, Mrs., and her son: 39

Gray, E. H., and E. W., of the banking firm of Austen, Gray, and Vincent, of Alton, Hants: 56, 78, 80, 82, 92, 93, 94, 96, 97

Greaves's, the (the Bath Directory 1800 gives four families of G.): 38

Gregory, Mrs. and Miss, of Canterbury?: 53

Gregorys, young, of Southampton?: 60

Grenville, Rt. Hon. Thomas, M.P., 1755–1846, First Lord of the Admiralty 1806–April 1807: 50

(or, within brackets, to the pages).

II. Other Persons

Guillemarde: (probably) John Lewis, 1765–1844, s. of John G. of Spitalfields, Middlesex, and of 27 Gower-st., Bedford-square; St. John's Coll.,Oxon.: 70

Gunthorpe, William, jnr., of Bugle Hall, Southampton; m. 28 Jan. 1807 Alicia (18) d. of Josias Jackson of Belle Vue, Southampton: 49

Gustavus Vasa: 81

Hacker, a gardener: 27

Hacket, Pierce, M.D., Above Bar, Southampton: 64

Haden (not Haydon), Charles Thomas, 1786–1824, surgeon, of 62 Sloane-street; (mentioned in *Opinions*): 111, 116, 117, 118; J. A. to him, 122.1

Halavant, M., Henry Austen's cook: 33

Hales, Caroline, see Gore, Caroline

Hales, Jane, see Bridges, Jane

Hales, Harriet, 1770– , 4th d. of Sir Thomas Pym Hales of Beaksbourne, Kent, and y.s. of Mrs. Henry Bridges: 4, 5, 50

Hales, Lady, –1803, widow (1773) of Sir Thomas Pym Hales of Beaksbourne, fourth baronet: 4

Halifax, Emma: see Bather

Hall, Joseph, apparently a tenant of Mrs. Austen: 134

Hall's (possibly Joseph?) meadow, Steventon: 25

Hall, Mr., hairdresser (London), 45, 82

Hall, Dr.: 19

Hall, Mr. and Mrs., of Sherborne: 10

Hall, Mrs., nursemaid (?) at Southampton: 49, 53

Hallett, James, of Higham, near Bridge, on the Canterbury–Folkestone road: 47

Hamilton, Mrs., of Canterbury: 87

Hammond, William, 1752–1821, of St. Alban's Court, near Wingham, Kent; 2 s. 5 d.: 47

Hammond, William Osmund, 1790–1863, e.s. of William H., m. 1815, Mary e.d. of Sir Henry Oxenden: 91, 99

Hammond, Mary, 1794– , e.d. of Sir Henry Oxenden, m. 15 July 1815, William Osmund H.: 84, 86, 99, 141

Hammond, Maximilian Dudley Diggs (Dalison), y.s. of William H.: 141

Hammond, Miss, and Julia, two of the d. of William H.: 91

Hammond, Rev. ——, presumably curate of Deane in 1808; perhaps James H., who became Rector of Hannington, Hants, 1814: 61

Hammond, Mr.: perhaps William H. of West Worldham, Hants: 64, 65

Hampson, Sir Thomas, seventh baronet, of Taplow, Bucks (but being a republican did not use the title), 1765–1820, g.s. of Sir George V (whose s. Rebecca m. (1) W. Walter, (2) William Austen, and was

George A.'s m.); 1 s.: 44, 70, 80, 91, 93, 99

Hampson, George, 1789–1833, o.s. of the above: 99

Hancock, Mrs.: 23

Hannah (? Hilliard), maid at Steventon: 21, 61 (d. of Nanny Hilliard?); the two Hannahs are perhaps distinct

Hannah, Mrs. Digweed's maid: 133

Hanson, Miss: see Portsmouth

Harding, Mrs.: Dyonisia, d. of Sir Bourchier Wrey, sister of Mrs. N. Toke, m. 1780 Robert H. of Upcott, Devon; her daughter; (see also Terry, Thomas): 72

Hare, Miss, milliner: 82, 92, 93, 103

Harpur, mistake for Hawker, q.v.

Harrison, Charlotte, 5th d. of Jemima Brydges and s. of Anne Lefroy; m. (1) Champion Branfill (d. 1792); 1 s. 1 d. (Jemima B., q.v.); (2) John Harrison of Denne Hill near Canterbury (d. 1818 s.p.): 90, 91, 93 (381?)

Harrison, John Butler (1), of Amery, Alton, Hants, friend of Gibbon and f. of J. B. H. (2), q.v.

Harrison, John Butler (2), 1767– , s. of J. B. H. (1), m. Elizabeth Matilda, d. of Rev. Henry Austen of Tunbridge (c. of J. A.'s father); of St. Mary's, Southampton; 6 s. (including J. B. H. (3) and Henry Austen H.), 4 d. See also Austen, Harriet Lennard: 49, 51, 52, 55, 56, 58, 65, 138

Harrison, John Butler (3), 1790– , e.s. of J. B. H. (2); Magd. Coll., Oxon.: 55, 56, 65

Harrisons of Andover: conjecturally I connect Mary H. of 5 (11, 13) and 6, the Mrs. Harrison (at Andover) of 28, 'the Harrison family' of 38, and the Rev. William, apparently curate of Overton near Andover, 72 (283; he was s. of Rev. John H. of Croydon, and became Vicar of Fareham, Hants, in 1811); see also Poore

Harvey, —— and Richard: 5, 6

Harwood, John, 1747–Jan. 1813, of Deane House, Hants; m. Anne ——, 1752–1842; 3 s.: 1, 6, 11, 17, 23, 24, 25, 30, 31, 49, 77

Harwood, Betty Anna Maria, 1751–1838, s. of John H. the elder ('Mrs. Anna H.' is mentioned in *Opinions*): 24, 27

Harwood, Rev. John, 1770–1846, e.s. of John H., Rector 1799 of Ewhurst; of Deane House from 1813; unmarried: 5, 14, 15, 17, 18, 25, 26, 27, 77, 78, 78.1

Harwood, Earle, R.M., 1773–1811, 2nd s. of John H.: 10, 14, 22, 25, 26, 62, 64

Harwood, Charles, 1783–1855, 3rd s. of John H.; m. 1810 Eliza 3rd d. of Thomas Terry of Dummer: 10, 78.1

Hastings, Warren, 1732–1818, of Daylesford, Worcestershire: 49 (? 179), 82 (320, 324, his ad-

miration of *Pride and Prejudice*; 324, 'never hinted at Eliza')
Hastings, Mrs.; Marian, second w. of Warren H.: 28 (95 note 'like Mrs. Hastings, I do not despair'), 54 (207 her voyage down the Ganges)
Hatton, see Finch Hatton
Hawker (not Harpur), Rev.: 86
Hawkins, Mrs., m. of the third Lady Knatchbull: 53
Hawley, Harriot, 2nd d. of Sir Henry H. and s. of Lady Bridges 2nd w. of Sir Brook B. IV: 90
Hayter, Sir William, 1792–1878, first bart. (*Brabourne* ii. 276): 106
Heartley, Mr.: 2
Heathcote, Sir William, 1746–1819, third baronet (1787), of Hursley near Winchester, M.P.; m. Frances Thorpe (d. 1816); 5 s. 3 d.: 23
Heathcote, Maria Frances, 1787– , y.d. of Sir William H., third baronet: 78 (302?)
Heathcote, Sir Thomas Freeman, 1769–1825, e.s. of Sir William H., third baronet; M.P. for Hants 1808–20; fourth baronet, 1819; d.s.p.: 25, 26, 60
Heathcote, Rev. William, 1772–1802, Prebendary of Winchester and Rector of Worting, Hants, 2nd s. of Sir William H., third baronet, and father of the fifth; m. 1797 Elizabeth Bigg; 1 s.: 1, 17, 18, 25
Heathcote, Elizabeth, 1773–1855, 4th d. of Lovelace Bigg Wither; m. 11 Jan. 1798 Rev. William H., Rector of Worting, who d. March 1802; 1 s.; from 1814 lived with her s. Alethea in the Close, Winchester: 1, 12, 17, 18, 21, 23, 27, 31, 38, 62, 78, 82 (321), 85, 86, 91, 108, 125, 145, 146
Heathcote, Sir William, 17 May 1801–81, fifth baronet (1825), o.s. of Rev. William H.: 38 (135), 62, 139, 146
Heathcote, Gilbert, Captain R.N., 1779–1831, 5th son of Sir William H., third baronet, m. 1809 Ann Lyell: 60
Heathcote, Harriet, 1775–1850, 2nd (but in 1796 eldest surviving) d. of Sir William H., third baronet: 1
Herington, Mr., innkeeper (?) at Guildford: 79, 80, 92
Herries, Miss and others (Miss Isabella H. is mentioned in *Opinions*); Miss I. H. (d. 1870) was sister of Rt. Hon. J. C. H., 1778–1855, of 21 Cadogan-place, Sloane-street: 111, 117
Hey, Dr. and Mrs., probably of Wingham House, Kent: 12
Heywood, Mrs., 1732–1824, of Above Bar, Southampton, widow of Lt.-Col. H., Mayor of Southampton 1800–1: 55
Hibbs, John, hosier in High-street, Southampton: 56
Hill, Rev. Herbert, 1749–1828, Rector 1810 of Streatham, Surry, and 1815 of Worting, Hants; m. Oct. 1808 Catherine Bigg (see Bigg and Bigg Wither); their children in-

cluded Herbert 1810 (who m. Southey's d. Bertha), Errol 1812, and Alfred Wither 14 March 1815: 58, 90, 108, 139

Hill, Catherine, 1773–18 , 5th d. of Lovelace Bigg Wither of Manydown, m. Oct. 1808 Rev. Herbert H., q.v.: 14, 15, 17, 18, 21, 23, 24, 26, 27, 28, 31, 32, 34, 35, 37, 47, 52, 55, 56, 57, 58, 59, 69, 70, 80, 89, 91, 93, 94, 108, 139

Hill, Rev. Hugh, D.D., Rector of Holy Rood, Southampton, and of Church Oakley (which is close to Deane), 1792–1824; Mrs. H.: 61

Hilliard, Nanny (probably of Steventon, where 1795 a John H. m. an Anne Knight): 61

Hinchman, Mr.: probably Thomas Henchman, 1748–1804 (Holzman, J. M., *The Nabobs in England*, New York 1926, p. 145): 30 (106 note)

Hinton, John Knight, 1774–1846, o.s. of Rev. John H., Rector of Chawton 1744–1802, whose wife (he m. his cousin, Martha Hinton) is described as sole representative of the Knights of Chawton (Burke's *Commoners*, 1831, i. 515; *Chawton Manor and its Owners*, 1911, 171 and 188): 75, 93 (383—see also Baverstock), 97

Hinton, Miss, a sister of the above: 84

Hoare, Mr. and Mrs.: 15

Hoblyn, Mrs. and others (perhaps Thomas H. of 125 Sloane-street): 79, 80, 99

Hogben or Hogbin, John, 1772–1841, parish clerk of Godmersham: 85 (339)

Holder, William Thorpe, *c.* 1745–87, e.s. of William T. (who died in Barbados 1752); Trin. Coll., Oxon.; m. Philippa Elliot ——, who after his death lived at Bathford and at 16 St. James Square, Walcot, Bath: 2 s. (John Hooper, q.v., and William Philip, 1772–97), 2 d. (Margaret Dehany, q.v., and Philippa Harbin, who d. before 1801); Mrs. Holder d. (Sept.?) 1813: 37, 38, 39, 43, 63, 87

Holder, John Hooper, s. of William Thorpe H.; of Cerney House, Glos.; m. (1) 1808 Elizabeth y.d. of Hon. William Hewitt (one d., Elizabeth Philippa), who d. Jan. 1810; (2) 1812 Anne, y.d. of Rev. Jeffery Ekins, Dean of Carlisle: 27, 39, 63, 87

Holder, Margaret Dehany, d. Oct. 1809, d. of William Thorpe H.: 37, 38, 39, 63

Holder, James (of Merton Coll., Oxon., b. 1747), y.b. of William Thorpe H. and u. of John Hooper H.; tenant of Ashe Park, Hants (see Portal, William) from 1790 or earlier to 1804 or later: 14, 17, 25, 30, 31, 32, 33, 87

Holder, Mr. (a second): perhaps Joseph H. of Deane, who 1805 m. Mary Tolfree of Ashe: 32

Holwell, see Children

Home [Hume], Sir Everard,

(or, within brackets, to the pages).

Bart., 1750–1832, of 30 Sackville-street: 141, 142, 143
Honeywood, Sir John, 1787–1832, fifth baronet, of Evington, Kent, m. 1808, Mary Anne, d. of Sir William Henry Cooper, Bart.: 91
Hook, Miss M., –1816, d. of Brig.-Gen. H.: 62
Hookey, Mrs., widow, chemist and lodging-house keeper, Southampton: 62, 64
Hope, Mrs., see Finch-Hatton, Louisa
Hore, Mrs.: 111
Howard, Lord: 90
Hughes, Mrs., and children: 53
Hulbert, the two Mrs., of Speen Hill, Berks.: 17, 60, 61, 62, 84, 129
Humphries, Mrs.: 8
Husket, Mr.: 49
Hussey, Ed——: 87
Hutchins, Mary: 15

Inglis, Capt. R.N.: 32, 34
Inman, Rebecca, 1738–1815, of Ashford; buried at Godmersham: 51 (191 note), 52, 53
Iremonger, Miss, presumably of Wherwell Priory, near Andover: 27
Irvine, Mrs. and Miss, Lansdown (probably 19 New Crescent), Bath: 39, 43, 44, 47, 48, 50, 63
Isaac: 44
Isham, Rev. Dr. Edmund, d. 1819, Warden of All Souls 1793–1817: 84

Jackson, Alicia: see Gunthorpe
Jackson, Mr.: 111
James, the Austens' servant at Lyme: 39
Jeffereys, Toomer, and Legge: 17
Jenkins, Mr.: 18
Jenny, Mrs. James Austen's maid: 11
Jenny, the Austens' maid at Lyme, Bath, and Southampton: 39, 43, 48, 49, (?) 66
Jervoise, Colonel George Purefoy, of Herriard, Hants, m. 1798 Elizabeth Hall of Preston Candover: 18
John, the Austens' coachman at Steventon: 19, 34
John, Henry Austen's coachman: 92, 99
Johncock, butler at Godmersham: 86, 90
Johnson, Rev. Augustus, d. 1799, Rector 1791–9 of Hamstall-Ridware, Staffs.: 18
Jordan, Mrs.: 30
Julien, Comte: see D'Entraigues

K., Mrs. E.: 56 (215 note)
Kean, Edmund, 1787–1833, actor: 92, 93
Keith, Lord: George Keith Elphinstone, 1746–1823, admiral; Baron K., 1797: 27
Kelly, Mrs.: 117
Kemble, Mr.: 31
Kendall, R.N.: 87
Kennet, Mrs.: 51
Kerr, Lady Robert: Lord R. K., 1780–1843, y.s. of 5th Marquis of Lothian, m. 1806 Mary Gilbert, of Cornwall, who d. 1861 (mentioned *Opinions*): 82, 85
Keith, Lady: see after Index II
Kew, Dame: 15

II. Other Persons

Knatchbull, Sir Edward, eighth baronet of Mersham Hatch, Kent, 1759–1819; succeeded his f. 1789; m. (1) Mary Hugesson, co-heiress of Provender, Kent, who d. 1784 (1 s., Sir Edward IX); (2) Frances Graham, who d. 1799 (several children, including Rev. Dr. Wyndham K., q.v.); (3) Mary Hawkins, co-heiress of Nash Court, Kent, who d. 1850 (2 s. 6 d.); the Knatchbulls of 91 are no doubt members of this family

Knatchbull, Edward, 1781–1849, of Provender, Kent, e.s. of Sir Edward VIII, whom he succeeded 1819 as ninth baronet; m. (1) 1806 Annabella Christiana d. of Sir John Honeywood, who d. 1814 (several children); (2) 1820 Fanny Knight, q.v. in Index I (several children, including Edward first Lord Brabourne, editor of the *Letters*): 53

Knatchbull, Charles, 1747–1818, Capt. R.N., e.b. of Wyndham K. of Russell-place and c. of Sir Edward VIII; m. his cousin Frances, heiress of Babington, Som., who d. 1818: 45, 46, 52, 53, 84, 85

Knatchbull, Wyndham, 1750–1833, of Russell-place, merchant, cousin of Sir Edward VIII; m. his cousin Catherine Maria (s. of Sir Edward) who d. 1807; his children included Wyndham and Wadham, q.v.: 49, 70, 71, 84, 85, 89

Knatchbull, Wyndham, d. 1813, s. of Wyndham K. of Russell-place, Ensign in the first regiment of foot-guards: 89

Knatchbull, Wadham, 1794–1876, s. of Wyndham K. of Russell-place: 84

Knatchbull, Rev. Dr. Wyndham, 1786–1868, s. of Sir Edward VIII (by his second wife): 92, 93

Knatchbull, Lady, the third w. of Sir Edward VIII, q.v.: 53

Knatchbull, Joan Elizabeth, d. 1801, of Canterbury, cousin of Sir Edward VIII: 6

Knight, Mrs. Catherine, 1753–14 Oct. 1812, s. of Charles Knatchbull R.N. and of Wyndham K. (c. of Sir Edward K. VIII) and widow of Thomas Knight of Godmersham, who d. 1794; of White Friars, Canterbury: 4, 17, 32, 45, 47, 48, 49, 51, 52, 53, 54, 58, 60, 61, 69, 70, 71, 73, 74.1, 85

Knight, Hannah (a maid): 84

Knight, Harriet (perhaps a village child, cf. Hannah K.): 136

L., Dame: perhaps Libscombe, q.v.

Lambould, Mr. (a tradesman): 31

Lance, of Netherton: 21(?), 48

Lance, David, of Chessel (Chiswell), Lance's Hill, Bitterne, near Southampton; m. Mary, o.d. of Valentine Fitzhugh; their daughters, Mary (1798) and Emma (1799): 48, 60, 61, 62, 65

or within brackets, to the pages).

Lane, Mr.: 18
Langley, Miss: 36
Lansdowne, John Henry, 1765–1809, second (and 'wicked') Marquis of, m. Mary Arabella, d. of Rev. Hinton Maddox and widow of Sir Duke Gifford; d.s.p.: 49, 55
Latouche, Mrs., probably of 14 Portman-street, Portman-square (but a Miss La T. is recorded as living at Barnes next door to Comte D'Entraigues, q.v.): 70, 99, 116, 117
Laurel, Mrs.: 30
Layton and Shears, mercers, Bedford House, 11 Henrietta-street, Covent-garden: 80, 82, 90
Ledger, Misses: 1
Lee, Miss; probably a sister of Richard L., who 1801 m. Elizabeth e.d. of William Prowting, q.v.: 73
Lee, Miss: 91
Lefevre, Mrs., w. of C. Shaw L., of Heckfield, Hants: 1
Lefroy, Rev. Isaac Peter George, 1745–1806, s. of Anthony L. (1703); of Ewshot; Rector of Ashe, Hants; m. 1778, Anne, s. of Sir Samuel Egerton Brydges; 3 s. 1 d.: 24, 29
Lefroy, Anne, 1749–16 Dec. 1804, s. of Sir Samuel Egerton Brydges and w. of Isaac Peter George L.: 1, 11, 14, 15, 16, 18, 20, 24, 31, 91
Lefroy, Rev. John Henry George, 1782–1823, of Ewshot; e.s. of I. P. G. L.; Rector 1806 of Ashe, Hants; m. 1806 Sophia, y.d. of Rev. Charles Cottrell, Rector of Hadley, Middlesex ('Mrs. Lefroy' is in *Opinions*); numerous issue: 1, 15, 17
Lefroy, Christopher Edward, 1785– , y.s. of I. P. G. L.: 133
Lefroy, Rev. Benjamin, 1791–1829, y.s. of Isaac Peter George L.; Merton Coll., Oxon.; Rector 1823 of Ashe, Hants; m. Nov. 1814, Anna, e.d. of James Austen, q.v. in Index I; 1 s. 6 d.: 84, 85, 89, 90, 99, 101, 105, 106 (p. 416), 110, 133, 134, 139, 140, 142
Lefroy, Lucy, see Rice, Lucy
Lefroy, Thomas Langlois, 1776–1869, s. of Anthony Peter L. (1742) and n. of I. P. G. L.; Ch. Justice of Ireland: 1, 2, 11
Lefroy, Sarah, 1773–1836, 3rd d. of Anthony Peter L. of Carrigglas, co. Longford, and s. of Thomas Langlois L.; 'the third Miss Irish Lefroy'; m. 1799 Capt. Thomas Courtenay: 14
Leigh, Theophilus, of Adlestrop, Glos., d. 1724, grandfather of (1) Rev. Thomas L. of Adlestrop, q.v.; (2) Cassandra L. (Cooke), q.v.; (3) James (Leigh Perrot), Jane Leigh (Cooper), and Cassandra Leigh (Austen), qq.v.: *not mentioned*
Leigh, Hon. Mary, d. 1806, s. of Edward, fifth and last Baron Leigh, who d. s.p. 1786; life-heir to the Stoneleigh estates: 18, 60
LEIGH, Rev. *THOMAS*, –1813, Rector of Adlestrop;

succeeded to the Stoneleigh estates on the death 1806 of Hon. Mary L.; m. his c. Mary L. (d. 1797), but d. s.p.: 50 (182), 54, 60, 81

LEIGH, ELIZABETH, – Apr. 1816, s. of Rev. Thomas Leigh; always referred to as 'Mrs. E. Leigh' (except 128, where it is 'Miss'); godmother to Cassandra Austen: 12, 27, 49, 56, 62 (244), 63, 65, 66, 81 (316), 84, 128

LEIGH, JAMES HENRY, 1765–1823, of Adlestrop and (1813) of Stoneleigh (succeeding his uncle Rev. Thomas L.); m. 1786 Hon. Judith Julia Twisleton, e.d. of the 13th Lord Saye and Sele (d. 1843): 75, 81 (316), 84

Leigh, Rev. Thomas, d. 1763, Rector of Harpsden (Harden), Oxon.; s. of Theophilus L. of Adlestrop, q.v.; m. Jane Walker, 1704–68; f. of James Leigh (Perrot), of Jane Cooper, and of Cassandra Austen, qq.v.: *not mentioned*

LEIGH PERROT, JAMES, 17 –1817, o.s. (?) of Thomas L. of Harpsden; of Scarlets, Berks., and Paragon, Bath; later, 49 Pulteney-st., Bath; m. Jane Cholmeley; d. s.p.; commonly referred to as 'my Uncle': 20, 22, 35, 36, 37, 38, 39, 40, 43, 44, 49, 50, 54, 61, 72, 78, 112, 128, 142, 144

LEIGH PERROT, JANE, 1744–1836, w. of the above; commonly referred to as 'my Aunt': 10, 22, 27, 29, 30, 31, 35, 36, 37, 38, 39, 40, 44, 50, 60, 61, 63, 72, 78, 81, 112, 128, 144, 145

LEIGH, JANE, e.d. of Thomas L. of Harpsden: see Cooper

LEIGH, CASSANDRA, y.d. of Thomas L. of Harpsden: see Austen in Index I

Letty (a maid ?): 13

Leven and Melville, Alexander, earl of, 1749–1820; his countess, and d. Lady Marianne Leslie-Melville; see also Balgonie: 44

Lewis: see Blackall

Libscombe, Dame: 84 (? 332), 88

Lillingstone, Mrs., *née* Dottin, of 10 Rivers-street, Bath: 35, 36, 37, 38

Limprey, Mr.: 4

Linneus: 81

Liston, John, 1776 (?)–1846, actor: 94

Littlehales, Dr.: 25

Littlewart, Nanny: 12 (see also Nanny)

Littleworth, J.: 84

Lloyd, Martha, –16 Apr. 1805, d. of Hon. Charles Craven, Governor of S. Carolina (who m. Elizabeth Staples), and s. of Mrs. Thomas Fowle (1), q.v.; m. 1763 Rev. Nowis (or Noyes) L., 1720–89, R. (? 1771) of Enborne near Newbury; as a widow rented the parsonage at Deane and later moved to Ibthrop; 3 d. (1) Eliza Fowle, q.v.; (2) Martha, 2nd w. of Francis Austen, see Index I; (3) Mary, 2nd w. of James Austen, see Index I:

13 (35), 24, 25, 26, 30, 35, 36, 39, 43
Lloyd, Mrs., apparently a friend of Miss Sharpe, not connected with Martha L.: 73
Lockyer (Locker): see Pearson
Lodge, Jane: see Lyford, Jane
Long, Flora: presumably d. of Florentina Wrey, sister of Mrs. Harding and Mrs. N. Toke, who m. Richard Long of Rood Aston: 72
Louch, Mr.: 97
Louis XIV: 70
Lovett, John: 4, 5
Lucan, Richard, second Earl of, 1764–1839: 49
Ludlow, Mr.: Arnold, widower, of Andover, m. Jan. 1799 Sal Pugh, of Andover: 17
Lushington, Stephen Rumbold, 1776–1868, of Norton Court, Kent, 4th s. of Sir Stephen L., first baronet; M.P. for Canterbury 1812: 86, 87
Lyddy: 56
Lyell, Mrs., widow of Charles L. of Kinnordy, Forfarshire, settled in Southampton 1808 with her s. and 2 d., Mary and Anne (Mrs. Gilbert Heathcote, q.v.): 55, 60
Lyford, John, 1740–1829, surgeon of Basingstoke; probably s. of Giles L. (1700–83, mayor of Basingstoke) and b. of Charles L. (surgeon of Winchester); m. 1766 Mary Windover; 2 s. 1 d.: 10, 13, 52 (see note), 55, 56; his wife, 31
Lyford, John, 1769–12 June 1799, e.s. of the above; Eton, Queen's Coll., Oxon., Lincoln's Inn; m. 19 April 1799 Jane d. of John Lodge of Great Blakenham, Suffolk: 1, 2, 14, 18, 22
Lyford, Jane, w. of the above; 14, 22, 30
Lyford, Charles, 1778–1859, y.s. of John L. of Basingstoke, whose partner and successor he became: 55, 98
Lyford, Mary Susannah, see Digweed
Lyford, Giles King, *c.* 1764–1837, surgeon of Winchester; s. of Charles L., surgeon of W., and probably n. of John L. of Basingstoke; surgeon in ordinary at the County Hospital: 145, 146, 147
Lynch, John, 1735–1803: 6
Lysons, Mrs., (probably w. of Dr. L., 3 Paragon-buildings,) Bath: 38

M., Miss: 1
Mackays: 44
Maitland, Jane, 1757–1830, d. of General Mathew, sister of James Austen's first w., and widow (1797) of Thomas M. of Lyndhurst; 5 s. 3 d.; of Albion-place, Southampton: 27, 51, 54, 55, 56, 66
Maitland, Sir Peregrine, 1777–1854, e.s. of Thomas and Jane M.; Lt.-Col. 1803: 66
Maitland, Caroline, 1782–1830, 2nd d. of Thomas M., m. 1812 Capt. William Roberts, R.A.: 27, 51, 55, 56, 65, 66
Maitland, Eliza, 3rd d. of Thomas

II. *Other Persons*

M. (unmarried at the date of her sister Caroline's wedding 1812): 27, 51, 55, 56, 66

Maitland, Mr. Mrs. and 3 (not 10) children: 37

Malings, the: probably Mrs. M. of 21 Hans-place, or C.T.M. of 146 Sloane-street: 116, 118

Manon: 69 (268 note)

Manhood (?), Mr. and Mrs.: 39

Mant, Rev. Richard, D.D., –1817, Rector (1793) of All Saints, Southampton, and Mrs. M.; the unmarried dd. kept school in his house: 59, 64, 65, 91

Mant, Mr.: doubtless Henry M., attorney, 23 Gay-street, Bath: 44

Mapleton, ——, M.D., physician, 14 Belmont, Bath; his dd., Jane, Marianne (d. 18 May 1801), Christian(a): 11, 20, 22, 36, 37, 38

March, Charles Earl of, e.s. of the Duke of Richmond, m. 10 April 1817, Lady Caroline Paget, e.d. of the Marquis of Anglesey: 141

Marlow, Rev. Dr. Michael, 1769–1828, President 1795–1828 of St. John's Coll., Oxon., Prebendary of Canterbury. (The copy of the *Loiterer* referred to in the note on p. 91 identifies 'Marlow' as the ideal college tutor described in No. 58 of that periodical): 54

Marriot, Mrs.: 23

Marsden, Miss (hypothetical): 142

Marshall, Mr. and Mrs., of The George, Sittingbourne, Kent: 18, 51

Martha, the Leigh-Perrots' maid: 63

Martin, Mrs., circulating library: 14, 23

Mary, Queen (of Scots?): 49

Mary, at Rowling: 7

Mary: a maid at Chawton?: 87

Mascall, Robert: 86, 87, 116

Mathew, Brownlow (Bertie 1819), –1826, o.s. of Edward M.; Univ. Coll., Oxon.; m. 1807 Henrietta Anne d. of North Taylor; 16, 27, 64

Mathew, Edward, 1728–1805 (born in Antigua), of Clanville Lodge near Andover, and Argyll-street; General 1797; C.-in-C. of the Windward and Leeward Is.; m. (not in 1743 as is usually stated, but *c.*1760) Lady Jane Bertie, 3rd d. of the 2nd Duke of Ancaster (who d. 1793); 1 s., Brownlow; 3 d., Jane (Maitland), Anne (Austen), and Penelope Susannah (Dewar): 16, 27

Mathews, Charles, 1776–1835, actor: 70, 94

Maxwell, Mr.: 60

May, Mr.: 13

Meyer, ——, junior, of Upper Marylebone-street, teacher of the harp: 118

Middleton, John Charles, of Hinton Ampner, Hants; m. 1793 Charlotte, e.d. of Francis Beckford of Basing (and s. of Maria B., q.v.), who d. 1803; tenant 1808–12 of Chawton Manor: 77, 81

Middleton, John, s. of John Charles M.: 77

(or, within brackets, to the pages).

Middleton, Susan, e.d. of John Charles M.: 70, 105
Middleton, Charlotte Maria, y.d. of John Charles M.: 72, 73, 74, 105
Middleton, Mrs., a farmer's wife; 63
Mildmay, Jane, e.d. and co-heiress of Carew M. of Shawford, Hants; m. 1786 Sir Henry Paulet St. John of Moulsham, Essex, 3rd baronet, who 1790 took the name of M.; her e.s. was Henry, afterwards (1808) 4th baronet: 15, 17
Miller, Robert, pastry-cook, 143 High-street, Southampton: 56
Miller, Sir Thomas, Bart., d. 4 Sept. 1816: 133
Milles, Richard, –1818, of Nackington, Kent, M.P. for Canterbury; m. Mary, d. of Rev. Thomas Tanner, Prebendary of Canterbury; 1 d., Mary Lady Sondes, q.v.: 6, 31, 53, 54, 66 (262), 84
Milles, Mrs. Charles, 1723–6 March 1817, widow (1749) of Charles M., uncle of Richard M. of Nackington; her d. 'Molly' or 'Moy': 45, 47, 52 (193, 195), 74, 84, 86, 89, 141
Millman, — M.D.: 22
Mitchell, Sarah: 92
Moira, Lord, 1754–1826, first Marquis of Hastings: 50
Molly, the Austens' maid: 10, 24, 39, 48
Montresor, General Sir Henry Tucker, 1767–1837, K.C.B.; of Nash Court, Kent.; m. Jan. 1809 Lady Sondes, q.v.: 62
Montresor, Mary Lucy, s. of Henry M.; m. Sept. 1801 Lt.-Gen. Sir F. W. Mulcaster: 13, 17
Moore, Dr. 1729–1802, and Mrs. M., f. and m. of Sir John M.: 65, 66
Moore, General Sir John, 1761–1809: 65, 66
Moore, Rt. Rev. John, 1730–1805, son of a butcher in Gloucester, Archbishop of Canterbury 1783–1805; m. Catherine, d. of Sir Robert Eden: 90
Moore, Rev. George, e.s. of John Archbishop of Canterbury; Rector of Wrotham, Kent; m. 1806 Harriot Mary, 6th d. of Sir Brook Bridges III: 49, 51, 52, 53, 54, 69, 86, 87, 88, 89
Moore, Harriot Mary, 1781–1840, 6th d. of Sir Brook Bridges III, m. 1806, Rev. George Moore: 5, 15, 17, 45, 46, 47, 49, 51, 52, 53, 56, 57, 74, 87, 88, 89, 90, 93, 141
Moore, Caroline, Eleanor, George, Harriot, children of Rev. George M.: 52, 87, 89, 141
Moore, Mrs., of the Oaks, Canterbury: 53 (201 note), 54
Moore, Miss H. and Miss Eliza, of Hanwell (Miss Harriet M. is mentioned in *Opinions*): 93, 105, 106
Morgan, schoolmaster in Bath: 43
Morgan, Miss: 13
Morley, Countess of: second wife, 1809, of Lord Boringdon, who became 1815 Earl of Morley;

(mentioned in *Opinions*): 117, 123a, 123
Morley, the Misses: 27
Morrell, James (conjecture for *Mowell* in *Brabourne*), of 1 St. Giles, Oxford; and Mrs. M.; parents of Deacon M., q.v.: 12, 66
Morrell, Rev. Deacon, 1775–1854, e.s. of the above; of Christ Church, Oxon. (M.A. 1799, and student) and of Lincoln's Inn; of Moulsford, Berks., and Sackville-st.: 66
Morrises: perhaps Morrices of Betshanger: 52
Morton, Mr.: 74.1
Mowell, Mr.: perhaps a mistake for Morrell, q.v.: 12
Mulcaster, Miss, see Montresor, Mary: 13
Murden, Jane, d. of —— M. and Christian (sister of Rev. Thomas Fowle (1), q.v.); of Southampton: 61, 62, 64, 66, 74.1 (for her opinion of *Emma* see *Opinions*), 78.1
Murray, John, 1778–1843, publisher: 111, 115, 116, 117, 120
Musgrove, Miss: 5
Mussell, Mrs., dressmaker in Bath (perhaps w. of William M., hairdresser, 9 Queen-street): 35, 38
Nanny, at Steventon: 10, 12, 33 (perhaps Littlewart, q.v.)
Newton, Isaac, linen-draper, 14 Leicester-square: 83, 93
Nibbs, Mr.: 29 (see Addenda after Index VIII)
North, Rt. Rev. Brownlow, 1741–1820, Bishop of Winchester 1781–1820: 13, 72
North, Miss: 20
Nottley, Mr. (? landlord of the Bull and George, Dartford): 9
Nunes, Mrs.: 60, 64
Nutt, Mr.: 22

Ogle, Mr.: 90
O'Neal: Eliza O'Neill, 1791–1872, actress: 105, 106
O'Neil, Mr., drawing-master: 86
Orde, William: 15
Orde, Rev. John 1770– , Lincoln Coll., Oxon., V. (1802?) of Kingsclere, Hants: 15
Orde, James, Lt.-Col. 90th Foot, m. 15 May 1811 Margaret, e.d. of W. Beckford of Fonthill: 72
Orleans, Duke and Duchess of: 132, 133
Osborne, Mr. and Mrs.: 91
Owen, Mrs.: 36
Oxenden, Sir Henry, 1756–1838, seventh baronet (1803) of Deane Park, Wingham, and Broome House, Kent.; m. 1795, Mary Graham; 9 children: 12
Oxenden, Mary, see Hammond, Mary
Oxenden, Miss: 91
Oxford: see at end of Index II
P., Mr. and Miss: 111
Paget, Rev. —— and Mrs. P.: 85, 86, 91
Paget, Lady Caroline: see March
Paine, Farmer: 29
Painter and Pridding, Andover: 28
Palmer, John Grove, –1832, Attorney-General of Bermuda; of 22 Keppel-street, Russell-square; m. Dorothy Ball; their dd. Frances and Harriet

were the wives of Charles Austen, q.v. in Index I: 58, 62, 103, 117, 118, 133 (463), 144

Palmer, Mrs. and Miss (perhaps not the same as above): 133 (466)

Papillon, Thomas, 1757–1838, of Acrise, Kent.; a distant connexion of the Knights of Chawton; he, or one of his brothers (other than John R. P., q.v.) is presumably the 'Kentish Papillon' occupying Chawton House in 1816: 91, 133

Papillon, Rev. John Rawston (or Rawstorne), y.b. of Thomas P., Rector of Chawton 1801–37; his s. Elizabeth (p. 469); their niece Eleanor: 61, 74, 75, 76, 81, 92 (? 376), 97, 100, 111 (? 425), 134, 139, 142

Parry, Caleb Hillier, M.D., 1756–1822, physician, 27 Circus, Bath: 82, 87, 90, 91, 93

Paul, St.: 85

Payne, Mr.; Payne, Miss, 'our cousin': probably descendants of Capel P., who m. Jane, s. of Sir George Hampson V and of Rebecca (Walter) Austen; see Hampson: 30, 71

Payne, of Ashford: 65

Peach, Rev. ——, Curate of Wootton: 72

Pearson, Sir Richard, 1731–1805, Capt. R.N., Kt.; officer of Greenwich Hospital, and Lt.-Governor 3 Jan. 1801 (suceeding Capt. Locker); 2 d., Mary and Hannah Frances: 3, 4, 6, 7, 22, 29, 49 (see note)

Pellew, Admiral Sir Edward, first Baron Exmouth, 1757–1833: 69

Penlington, Tallow Chandler, Crown & Beehive, Charles-street, Covent-Garden: 6, 24, 32

Percival, Edward, M.B., 1783–1819, physician at Southampton, s. of Dr. P. (see Index V): 56

Percy [Piersy], Mrs., see Gardiner

Perigord, Mrs., Henry Austen's servant; 79, 82, 89, 92, 133; her mother (? Mme. Bigeon, q.v.), 79, 133

Peters, Mr.: 24 (80, note)

Phebe, the Austens' maid at Southampton: 48

Philip V of Spain: 70

Philips, Mr., proprietor of 12 Green Park Buildings, Bath: 38

Philips or Phillips, Mr.: 80, 89, 116

Phillott, Ven. James, D.D., 1749–1815, Rector and Archdeacon of Bath; Parsonage-house, Borough-Walls; m. Oct. 1808 Lady Frances St. Lawrence, 3rd d. of the first Earl of Howth; she died 1842; Lord Howth in 1800 resided at 1 Russell-street: 59

Philmore, John, 1747–17 March 1817, yeoman, of Chawton, m. Rachel Stubbington, 1737–1809, of Chawton; 'Mrs. P', their daughter?: 78, 142, 78.1

Pickford, Mr. and Mrs.: 37, 38

Pilkington, Sir Thomas, 1773–1811, seventh baronet, of Chevot near Wakefield, m.

1797, Elizabeth Anne Tufnell (who d. 1842); four d.: 97, 145

Pilkington, Lady, w. of Sir Thomas P., q.v.

Pilkington, Sir William, – 1850, eighth baronet, y.b. of Sir Thomas P.: 97, 133

Pinckards, the: 39

Plumtre (Plumptre, Plumtree, Plumbtree), John, *c.* 1760–1827, of Fredville, Kent, m. 1788 Charlotte Pemberton; numerous issue: 89

Plumtre, John Pemberton, 1791–1864, e.s. of John P.; St. John's Coll., Camb.; m. 1818; (mentioned in *Opinions*): 84, 86, 93, 94, 99, 103, 106, 140 (480), 141 (483)

Plumtre, Emma, see Gipps

Plumtre, Mary Louisa, 3rd d. of John P.: 73, 74, 84, 86, 89, 91, 103 (410?)

Plumtre, Frances Matilda, y.d. of John P., m. 29 July 1816 Robert Ramsden: 141 (483?)

Pococke, Mr.: 133

Pollens, two Mrs., of Above Bar, Southampton: 55

Poore, Philip Henry, surgeon, of Andover, m. Sept, 1797 Mary Harrison; her m., Mrs. H.: 28. See also Harrison, Mary

Portal, William, 1755–1846, of Laverstoke, Hants, and owner of Ashe Park; 1 d.; (Mrs. P. is mentioned in *Opinions*): 24, 25, 30, 143

Portal, John, 1764–1848, y.b. of William P.; of Freefolk, Hants; twice married, and several children: 1, 24

Portal, Rev. Benjamin William, 1768–1812, e.s. of William Portal of Camberwell, and connected with the Hants Portals; of St. John's Coll., Oxon.; contributed to *The Loiterer* edited by James Austen; Fellow 1788; Rector of Wasing: 1, 21

Portman, Mrs., presumably w. of Edward Berkley P., of Brianstone, Dorset, who m. Aug. 1798: 11

Portmore, William Charles Colyear, 3rd Earl, 1745–1823, of Ham Haw Park near Chertsey, Surry; see also Brecknell: 51

Portsmouth, Lord: John Charles, 1767–1853, third earl 1797; of Hurstbourn, Hants; George Austen's pupil, as Lord Lymington, 1773 (*Life* 21); m. (1) 19 Nov. 1799, Grace, d. of first Lord Grantley; (2) 7 March 1814, Anne, d. of John Hanson of Bloomsbury-place; see also Wallop: 24, 25, 26 (88), 94

Potter, Mrs., lodging-house keeper, High-street, Cheltenham: 133

Pottinger, Mrs.: 66

Powlett, Thomas Norton, Lt.-Col. 1802, Major-General 1814, d. 1824; of Southampton (at 'Argyle's inner house', Albion-place, 1808); m. Miss Percival: 52, 55

Powlett, ——, b. of Lt.-Col. P.: 55

Powlett, Mrs. née Percival, w. of Lt.-Col. P.; eloped 1808: 52 (note)

Powlett, Rev. Charles, 1765–

1834, apparently curate at Winslade, Hants, in 1798, and later at Dummer, Itchinstoke, Twyford; m. 1796 Anne, 1772–1827, e.d. of Rev. William Johnstone Temple, Vicar of St. Gluvias, Cornwall (Boswell's correspondent): 2, 13, 14, 30

Powys, Thomas, 1736–1809, Dean of Canterbury 1797–1809: 52

Price, see Rice

Prince Regent, the, afterwards George IV: 31, 96 (389), 97 (see Granby), 113, 113a, 115, 117, 118, 120, 121, 126a, 126, 127; the Princess, 78.1

Prowting, William, d. 1821, J.P., D.L., of Chawton; his e.d. Elizabeth m. 1801 Richard Lee; his 2nd d. Catherine Ann, q.v.; his y.d. Ann Mary m. B. Clement, q.v.: 72, 73, 74, 78, 78.1, 97, 138

Prowting, Catherine Ann, 1783–1848, 2nd d. of the above: 148

Pugh, Miss, see Ludlow

Pyne, Mr.: 39

Rawstorn (or Rawston), see Papillon

Rebecca, Mrs. Edward Austen's maid: 19

Remmington, Wilson and Co., Silk-manufacturers, 30 Milk-street: 83

Remnant, T., Glover, &c., 126 Strand: 80

Reynolds, Sir Joshua, P.R.A., 1723–92: 80

Rice: sometimes printed *Price* in *Brabourne*; J. A. writes *R* with an exaggerated tail, easily misread as *Pr*

Rice, Mrs., of Dover, Kent, widow of Henry R. of Bramling, near Canterbury, m. of Rev. Henry R.: 31, 33

Rice, Rev. Henry, –1860, e. s. of the above; of Tollard Royal, Wilts.; m. 20 July 1801 Lucy Lefroy: 15, 27, 30, 31, 33, 38

Rice, Jemima Lucy, 1779–1862, o.d. of Isaac P. G. Lefroy, m. 20 July 1801 Rev. Henry Rice: 6, 14, 27, 33, 38, 44

Richard, Henry Austen's servant: 93, 99, 116

Richis, servant at Rowling: 5

Richmond, Duchess of, see March, Earl of

Rider or Ryder, Mr. and Mrs., tradespeople at Basingstoke: 10, 23, 32

Ripley, Rev. Thomas, d. 20 Oct. 1813, Rector of Wootton Bassett, Wilts.; and his widow: 89

Ripley, a young: 43

Rivers, Lady: presumably Martha Coxe, m. 1768 d. *c.* 1835, widow 1790 of Rev. Sir Peter R., sixth baronet of Chafford, Kent, and Prebendary of Winchester; 3 s. 4 d. alive in 1796, including Sir Thomas VII (d. 1805), Sir James VIII (d. 1805), and Rev. Sir Peter IX, Rector of Martyr Worthy, Hants, who m. 1812: 1, 2, 87 (? 348)

Robert, the Leigh-Perrots' servant: 43, 63

Robert (at Steventon): 13 (perhaps Littlewart, q.v.)
Robinson, Mary: 4
Robinson, Rev. Matthew, *c.* 1775–1827, Rector 1800 of Burghfield near Reading; cousin of Lord Rokeby and b.-in-law of Sir Egerton Bridges: 27
Robinson, Dr., physician at Lyme: 39
Roden, Lady: 44 (see note)
Rogers, Mrs.: 32
Roland, Mr.: 23
Rolle(s), Misses: 69
Roope, Mr., music-master: 17
Rosalie: 27 (91 note)
Rowe, Miss: see Woodward
Roworth, C., printer, 38 Bell-yard, Temple-bar: 116, 117
Russell, Mrs.: probably a d.-in-law of Rev. Dr. Russell, who was Rector of Ashe 1720–83; his widow d. 1785: 11, 14, 18
Russell (at Godmersham): 52
Russia, Emperor of: 96, 97

S., Miss, governess at Wrotham: 141
Sace or Sayce, Mrs., lady's-maid at Godmersham: 45, 82, 84
Sacree, Susanna, 1761–1851, nursemaid at Godmersham (a tablet on the north buttress of the chancel records her virtues): 22, 45, 51, 66, 78, 84, 86, 97
Sackville, Viscount (last Duke of Dorset 1815), 1768–1843; see Powlett: 52
St. John, Rev. Henry Ellis, Rector 1800 of Winchfield, Hants, and his (?) brother: 1, 11, 27
St. Lawrence, Lady Frances, see Phillot
St. Vincent, John Jervis, Earl of, 1735–1823: 13
Salkeld, Mrs., housekeeper at Godmersham: 45, 87
Sally, name of various maids: 33 (Deane), 65 (Southampton), 74.1, 136, 137 (Chawton)
Salusbury, Mr.: 141
Sanford, Mr. (Mr. Henry S. is mentioned in *Opinions*): 106 (see Tilson, James)
Sankey, Mr. (? apothecary): 46
Saunders, Mr.: 44
Sawbridge, Miss: see Maxwell
Saye and Sele, Lady: Elizabeth Turner, d. 1816, grandd. of William Leigh of Adlestrop, m. 1767 Thomas Twisleton, 13th baron (who d. 1788); see Twisleton, and Leigh, James Henry: 27
Schuylers, the: 39
Sclater: Mrs. Penelope Lutley Sclater, 1750–1840, tenant of Tangier Park, Hants (the property of Mr. Bigg Wither of Manydown); mentioned in *Opinions*: 78, 130
Scott, Mr.: 6
Scrane, Mrs.: 132
Scudamore, Mr., physician: 52, 58, 81, 83, 89 (and Mrs. S.), 140, 142
Seagraves, the: 87 [Richardson
Selby, James: See Index V,
Serle, of Bishop's Stoke: 23
Seward, ——, steward to Edward Austen (*Life* 236) and

(or, within brackets, to the pages).

tenant of Chawton Cottage; Mrs. S.: 6, 12, 59, 66
Seymour, Mr., Henry Austen's man of business; 67, 67a, 70, 111 (see note), 118, 125, 132 (perhaps a different person)
Seymour, Miss, see Terry, Stephen
Sharpe, Miss, of Bath: 44
Sharp(e), Ann, governess at Godmersham and elsewhere: at Godmersham 45, 47, 49, 51, 52; with Miss Bailey 51, 55, 58, 66; projected visit to Chawton 72, 73, 74; her letters 82, 90; in Yorkshire 97, 133; J. A.'s letter to her at Doncaster 145; see also 44 (157) and 50 (185 note)
Shaw, A. M., see Hammond, Maximilian
Sherer, Rev. Joseph Godfrey, 1770–1823, Vicar of Godmersham (Jan. 1811) and Westwell, Kent; mentioned in *Plan of a Novel* and in *Opinions* (see *Plan* p. 10 and p. 20, where *Shean* is an error); Mrs. S., and their s. Joseph (Admiral, d. 1879): 84, 85, 86, 88, 90, 91
Shipley, Mr.: 24, 27
Sibley, Misses, probably dd. of Joseph S. of Hall Place, West Meon, Hants: 75
Siddons, Mrs., 1755–1831: 70, 106
Simpson, Capt. R.N.: 70
Simpson, Capt. R.N., b. of the above: 70
Skeete, Mrs., of Basingstoke, see French
Skipsey, Mr. (? a horse): 30
Sloane, Mr., see Estwick
Sloper, Mr.: probably Robert Orby S., only legitimate s. of General Sir Robert S., K.B., 1728–1802, of West Woodhay, Berks., who left 3 natural s., 2 natural d.: 61
Small, Miss, dressmaker: 13
Smalbone, Jenny, and her d. Mary (maid to the James Austens): 54
Smith, Robert, apothecary, 62 Sloane-street: 111
Smith, Mr., Mrs.; Colonel and Mrs. *Cantelo* S. (perhaps jocular, in allusion to singing; a Cantelo was singing in public in Bath about this time): 69, 70
Smith, Captain: probably Matthew S., Captain R.N. April 1808: 64, 65
Smith, actress: 93
Smithson, Mr.: 30, 34
Somerville, Mrs. Maria, (perhaps a sister of Rev. Mr. S., 21 Belvidere,) Bath: 37
Sondes, Lady: Mary, o.d. of Richard Milles of Nackington, m. (1) 1785 the e.s. of the first Baron (who became the second Baron and d. 1806); 4 s. 2 d. (of whom the elder, b. 1786, m. 1808, and the younger, b. 1802, was still a child in 1808); (2) Jan. 1809 Sir Henry Montresor, q.v.: 6, 62, 66
South, Mr., of Winchester: 17 (see North)
Southey, Herbert, 1806–16, son of the poet (q.v. in Index V): 139
Spence, G., dentist to his

Majesty, 17 Old Bond-st.; or S. and Son, dentists, 1 Arlington-st.: 82, 83
Spencer, George John, second Earl, 1758–1834, First Lord of the Admiralty 1794–1801: 13, 15
Spencer, Mr. and Miss: 82, 92, 93, 94
Spicer, J., see Esher in Index III
Stacey, Mary: 84
Stanhope, Admiral and Mrs., at Bath (a Capt. S. lived at 10 Seymour-street in 1800): 36, 44
Staples, Dame, and Hannah: 10, 15, 134
Stent, Mrs.: 26 (see note), 28, 44, 74.1
Stephens, Catherine, 1794–1882, actress; m. 1838 the 5th Earl of Essex: 93, 94
Stephens, John: 10
Stephens, Mary: 15
Stockwell, Mrs.: 86
Storer, Dr., physician at Bridlington, and Mrs. S.: 133
Street, Mr.: 18
Street, Mr., purser, Key-street: 88
Sukey: 10
Summers, Miss, dressmaker: 27
Sussex, H. R. H. Augustus Frederick, Duke of, 1773–1843, m. 1793 Lady Augusta Murray d. of the 4th Earl of Dunmore: 34
Sweden, King of (Charles XIII, 1809–18): 85
Sweney, Mr.: 132, 133

Taylor, Edward; his cousin Charlotte: 6, 14, 25
Temple: probably Frank T., 1771–1863, Lt. R.N. 1793 (Admiral 1854), y.s. of William Johnston T. (Boswell's correspondent) and b. of Mrs. Charles Powlett: 15 (43, note)
Terry, Thomas, 1741–1829, of Dummer, Hants; m. Elizabeth (1751–1811), o.d. of Robert Harding of Upcott, Devon, and was survived by 5 s. 6 d.: 24, 72
Terry, Stephen, 1774–1867, e.s. of Thomas T.; Fellow of King's Coll., Camb.; Captain in the 62nd Regiment; m. Maria Bridget Seymer, 1785–1841: 24, 43, 74
Terry, Rev. Michael, 1776–1848, 2nd s. of Thomas T.; Rector of Dummer 1811: 5 (? 11), 75 (? 296), and see note on p. 481, 77 (? 301)
Terry, Col. Robert, 1782–1869, 3rd s. of Thomas T.: 72
Terry, Jane, d. of Thomas T.; m. 1808 Harry Digweed, q.v.
Terry, Eliza, 1788–1841, 3rd d. of Thomas T., m. 1810 Charles Harwood, q.v.
Terry, Mary, d. of Thomas T. ('Miss Terry' 282, so presumably e., or e. surviving, d.): 72, 133 ('Miss Terry' 465). This is probably the 'Miss Terry' mentioned in *Opinions*
Terry, Anne, d. of Thomas T. (Anne T. is mentioned in the Powlett correpondence): 24
Terry, Daniel, 1780 (?)–1829, actor: 82
Thistlethwaite, Thomas, M.P. for Hants 1806–7: 60

II. Other Persons

Thomas, Edward Austen's servant: 19

Thomas, the Austens' servant at Southampton and (if the same) at Chawton: 66, 75, 77, 78

Tickars, Mrs., dressmaker: 82

Tilbury, Dame: 10

Tilson, John Henry, 1776–1836, e.s. of John T. of Watlington Park, Oxon.; Lt.-Col. of Oxfordshire Militia 1803; m. 1809 (?) Mrs. Sophia Langford: 64

Tilson, Christopher, d. 1834, third s. of John T.; took the name of Chowne 1812; Brigadier-General 1804, Major-General 1810: 43, 92 (see note 378 on 'Frederick'), 93, 94

Tilson, James, y.s. of John T.; partner in the banking firm of Austen, Maunde and Tilson; of Upper Berkeley-st. and later of 4, and then of 26 Hans-place; m. Feb. 1797 —— Sanford; 5 s. 7 d.: 55, 69, 70, 71, 74, 79, 80, 82, 83, 86, 88, 89, 92, 94, 99, 111, 116, 118, 125 (Mrs. James Tilson is mentioned in *Opinions*)

Tincton, Mr.: 5

Toke, John, 1738–1819, of Godinton, Kent, m. Margaretta Roundell, who d. 1780: 6, 53, 54, 87, 89

Toke, Nicholas Roundell, 1763–1837, e.s. of above; m. 1791 Anne Maria y.d. of Sir Bourchier Wrey (and s. of Mrs. Harding): 27, 72

Toke, Rev. John, 1766–1820, 2nd s. of J. T. above, Vicar of Beaksbourne: 6

Torrington, Lord, see Byng

Triggs, gamekeeper at Chawton: 83, 96, 97, 142

Trimmer, Mr., of Alton, Hants: 51, 82, 85

Trimmer, Mr., s. of the above: 85, 138

Turner, G.: 96

Turner: perhaps William Turner of 85 High-street, Portsmouth, and identical with the Turner of *Mansfield Park*, ch. 38: 43, 63

Twining: 93, 94

Twisleton, Hon. and Rev. Dr. Thomas James, 1772–1824, y.s. of the 13th Lord Saye and Sele, Rector 1821 of Broadwell, Glos., with Adlestrop (q.v.); first Archdeacon of Colombo: 84

Twisleton, Hon. Mary Cassandra, y.d. of the 13th Lord Saye and Sele; see also Leigh, James Henry: 27. 36

Twitchen, Farmer: 30

Twyford, Rev., Curate of Great Worldham, Hants: 75

Tylden, Richard, *c.* 1755–1832, of Milsted, Kent; his sons, Richard Osborne T. (Caius Coll., Camb. M.A. 1809), Vicar of Chilham, Kent, 1809–62, and Sir John Maxwell T. (Kt. 1812); his brother, Rev. Richard Cooke T., d. 1819, Rector of Milsted, in 1799 took the additional name of Pattenson: 84

II. Other Persons

Utterson, Alfred, s. of John U. of Fareham, Hants; St. John's Coll., Oxon., matric. 1810: 91

Valentine, ——, R.N.: 32
Vincent, Mr.: 80 (309)

W., W.: 17
W., Mr.: 10 (24 note)
W., Miss, 74.1 (501 note)
Wabshaw (Wapshare), see Williams, Sir Thomas
Wakeford, Jos.: 24
Wales, Prince and Princess of, see Prince Regent
Waller, Richard, of Bevis-hill, Southampton, d. 11 June 1808: 52
Wallop, family name of Earl of Portsmouth, q.v.
Wallop, Coulson, 1774 – 1807, M.P. for Andover 1796–1802, y.b. of the 3rd Earl of Portsmouth, q.v.: 29
Wallop, Hon. Mrs. Camilla Powlett, d. 1820, widow (1781) of Hon. and Rev. Barton W.; of High-street, Southampton: 43 (152 note), 56, 64
Wallop, Camilla, o.d. of the above, m. at Southampton 26 March 1813 Rev. Henry Wake: 43, 56, 64, 74.1 (501 note)
Walsby, Dr. and Mrs.: 54
WALTER, WILLIAM HAMPSON, d. 1798, half-brother of George Austen; of Seale, near Sevenoaks; m. Susanna Weaver; 8, 53 (203)
WALTER, PHILADELPHIA, d. of W. H. W.: 8, 29
Walter, Rev. Henry, grandson of W. H. W.; Fellow of St. John's Coll., Camb.: 69, 70, 75
Waltham, Lady, 1743 – 1819, widow (1787) of the second Baron W.; died at Goodnestone, Kent: 5
Wapshire (Wapshare), see Williams, Sir Thomas
Wapshire (Wapshare), William: 87 (354)
Warneford, of Dorking: 73
Warren, John Willing, of St. John's Coll., Oxon. (matric. 1786); a charity commissioner: 1, 2, 15 (?), 27, 62, 92
Warren, Lt.-Col., of the third foot-guards, m. 25 Feb. 1800 ——, d. of Thomas Maitland [presumably e.d., see Maitland, Jane] and g.d. of General Mathew (q.v.); their daughter b. 15 March 1801 at Houghton, Hants: 15 (?), 27 (note)
Watkins, Charles and (?) his e.b.: 1
Webb, Thomas, pastry-cook, 153 High-street, Southampton: 56
Webb, Mrs., Miss Harriot and sisters: 73, 74.1, 101
Wedgwood, Josiah, potter, York-street, St. James's: 69, 74, 83
Welby, Mrs.: Wilhelmina, 1773–1847, o.d. of William Spry, Governor of Barbadoes (who m. Katherine Cholmeley, s. of Mrs. Leigh Perrot, q.v.), m. 1792 William Earle W., 1768–1852, who became 1815 second baronet, of Denton Hall, Lincolnshire: 31, 48, 72

Welby, William Earle, 1794–1806, e.s. of the above: 48
Wemyss, Miss: 87
Wethered: Anne Eliza Weatherhead, d. or s. of Robert W., Collector of Excise, Southampton: 56
Whitby, Julia and Mary: 44
White, John, 1765–1855, of Selborne, Hants; n. of Gilbert W.: 73, 75 (but this might be his e.b. Edmund, Vicar of Newton Valence)
White, Dr.: probably Dr. John W., 'Gibraltar Jack', n. of Gilbert White (and c. of the above), surgeon at Alton (*c.* 1785) and afterwards at Salisbury and elsewhere; he would be likely to be staying with his Selborne relations: 133
White, Mrs. (of Canterbury?): 53
Whitfield: Rev. Francis Whitfeld, –1811, Vicar of Godmersham, Kent, 1778–1811; and Mrs. W.: 49, 51, 53, 58
Whitworth, Charles, Earl W., 1752–1825, Lord Lieutenant of Ireland 1813–17: 81
Wickham, Mr.: 93
Wiepart: Weippart, M., professor of the harp, 8 Foley-street, Portland-chapel: 70
Wiggett, Caroline, related to the Chutes: 138
Wigram, Sir Robert, 1744–1830, first baronet (cr. 1805), of Belmont, Worcestershire (he *had* 23 children): 87
Wigram, Henry Loftus, 1791–1866, y.s. of Sir Robert W.: 87
Wildman of Chilham Castle, near Godmersham: 30, 31, 83, 84, 86, 90; Mrs. and Miss W. 87; Miss and Mr. James 91; Mr. J. 93, 140–2
Wilkes: presumably John Golding W., of St. John's Coll., Cambridge (LL.B. 1816): 75
William: Henry Austen's servant: 82, 90
William, the Austens' servant at Chawton: 130
WILLIAMS, Admiral Sir THOMAS, 1762–1841; knighted 1796; captain H.M.S. *Endymion*; commanded the sea-fencibles of the Gosport division 1806–7; m. (1) at Steventon, 11 Dec. 1792, Jane, d. of Rev. Dr. Edward Cooper, q.v., who d. 9 Aug. 1798; (2) 1800 Miss Wapshare of Salisbury, who d. 1825; of Brooklands near Southampton: possibly the 'Tom' of 1 (4) and 2 (5), but see note; 6, 14, 26, 27, 28, 48, 49, 66, 78
WILLIAMS, JANE Lady, 1st w. of Sir Thomas W., q.v.: 2 (5, Jane Cooper), 6 (15, Jane), 18 (55 her death, see note)
Williams, Lady, 2nd w. of Sir Thomas W., q.v.: 27 (92 Emma Wabshaw), 28 (97 Wapshire), 48 (172), 87
Williams, Thomas, 1 Grosvenor-square, Knightsbridge; his son (?) Edmund: 82
Williams, Misses, of Southampton: 64 (250 Miss W., Miss Grace; 252 Miss Mary), 77
Williams, Miss and Miss Char-

lotte (associated with the Biggs of Manydown): 78, 86, 139
Williams, Mrs. (at Steventon?): 22, 53 (perhaps two persons)
Williams, ——: 138 (perhaps the same as the preceding)
Willoughby, Lady, second wife of Sir Christopher W. first baronet: 20
Wilmot, see Wylmot
Wilson, ——: 23
Winchester, Bishop of, see North
Winstone, Miss; the Winstones: perhaps Capt. Hayward W., 10 Great Bedford-street, Bath: 36, 37
Wise, Mr.: 59 (note)
Wither, see Bigg Wither
Wood, John: 15, 17
Wood, Miss: 38
Wood, Miss, of Basingstoke: 10
Woodd, Miss: 63
Woodford, Captain: 46
Woodward, Rev. James, of Brasenose Coll., Oxon., m. at Bath May 1801 Miss Wroe d. of the late Major W. of Calcutta: 36
Woolls, Mr. and Miss: 77, 130
Wren, Mr., dyer, Southampton: 56
Wright, Mr. and Mrs.: 5
Wylmot, ——, M.D., of Ashford, Kent, and Mrs. W.: 32, 45, 49
Wynne, Mr.: 62

Yalden's coach: 99, 130
Yates, Lady, probably widow of Sir Joseph Y., 1722–70; 1 s. 1 d.: 45
Yates, Miss, perhaps d. of the above: 86
York, H.R.H. Duchess of: Princess Frederica Charlotte of Prussia, 1767–1820, m. 1791 Frederick Augustus Duke of York: 35
Young, Charles Mayne, 1777–1856, actor: 94, 105

(*or, within brackets, to the pages*).

INDEX II

ADDENDA

Baigent: perhaps a son of William Baigen, a Chawton farmer, who m. *c.* 1802 (*Hampshire Allegations for Marriage Licences*): 93

Birch. Identification was impeded by an error in the Brabourne text of 63 (246), Baiton for Barton. This obstacle is now removed. Miss Tallmadge noted an entry in Mrs. Lybbe-Powys's diary for 1788 (p. 234): 'Went to pay a visit to the Birch's, St. Leonards Hill near Windsor.' Following this clue Sir Owen Morshead has referred me to various authorities. Near St. Leonards Hill is a modern house called Barton Lodge, and there was a house of the same name on the same site as early as 1823 (H. Walter's map of Windsor Forest and Vicinity). The 'great house' was at one time called Sophia Farm (it had belonged to the Duke of Gloucester); and 'I. Birch Esq' is named as its former proprietor in James Hakewill's *Views of the Neighbourhood of Windsor* 1820, 19. J. A.'s Mrs. Birch was presumably a dowager or a spinster, living in a dower-house.

Coleman: the Vicar of Godmersham told me that Elizabeth (*not* Caroline) C. was baptized there in 1807.

Fonnereau: in 1810 there was a Henry F. at Kiln Green, which is very near Scarlets, the Leigh-Perrot place: 24.

Gayleard: James Gaylard and Son, Hatters and Habit-makers, 82 New Bond Street (*P.O. Directory* 1808): 51

Grants: perhaps Sir Alexander G. of Dalvey, 7th Bart., *c.* 1750–1825, of Malshanger near Worting, and Lady G. (their 3 children, 1782+, too young?): 1

Hammond, Arthur Atherley, 1772–1852, s. of Arthur H. of Southampton; M.A. Oxon.; curate of Deane 1806–15: 61

Jefferson: I owe the solution of this to Miss Elvira Slack, who found *Two Sermons* by the Rev. T. Jefferson of Tunbridge, 1808, the list of subscribers to which includes Mr. and Mrs. Edward Austen of Godmersham and Miss Jane Austen. For another, I fear inferior, solution see R. W. C. in *Times Lit. Suppt.* 20 April 1943: 51, 53

Keith: Hester Maria Thrale, 1764–1857, m. Admiral George Keith Elphinstone, Viscount Keith: 78.1 (504)

K., Mrs. E.: probably Elizabeth, s. of Thomas Knight, who was buried at Godmersham in March 1809; see 11 (29, note): 56

References are to the numbers of the letters

Knatchbull, Wyndham, 1750–1833: presumably of Knatchbull, Rule, Cunningham, and Paterson, merchants, of 52 Gracechurch St. (*P.O. Directory* 1808). The Gardiners in *P.P.* were of Gracechurch St.

Louch: Austen, Blunt, and Louch, bankers, of Petersfield, Hants (*P.O. Directory* 1815), evidently a branch of the Austen, &c., banks in London and Alton; like them it disappears from the Directory in 1817. See Tilson: 97

May: brewer of Basingstoke (then and now): 13

Oxford: Edward Harley, 5th Earl of O., 1773–1848, m. 1794 Jane Elizabeth, 1773–1824, d. of James Scott, Vicar of Itchen Stoke, Hants. Her reputation may be judged by the name given to the children brought up in the house—the Harleian Miscellany.

Serle: possibly a relation. The *Memoir* (ed. 1926, 51) prints a letter of 1686 to J. A.'s great-grandmother from her mother, which mentions 'Cousin Robbert Serle': 23

Steele: Steel and Meyer, Lavender-Water-wareh., Catherine St., Strand (*P.O. Directory* 1815): 31

Walsby (Wolsby in Lybbe-Powys diary s.a. 1798): Dr. Edward Walsby, 1750–1815, Prebendary of Canterbury Cathedral 1793: 54

Mr. Austen Leigh has since printed (in *Austen Papers* 1942, 135) a letter from Eliza's mother, which mentions 'our Maid Rosalie'. As the letter was written in Paris, contemplating a visit to London, we may infer that Rosalie was French; the Hancocks, mother and daughter, lived in France for many years.

For Further Addenda see after Index VIII.

(*or, within brackets, to the pages*).

III. PLACES

References are to the pages

Cross-references to names of persons are to Indexes I and II

Adlestrop, Glos., see Leigh: 66, 182, 207, 245, 248, 301, 316, 321, 334, 383

Albany, see London

Alexandria: 78, 94, 95

Alton, Hants, 47½ m. from Hyde Park Corner on the London–Winchester road, 1¼ m. from Chawton: 188, 203, 212, 217, 246, 283, 291, 293–5, 300, 304–5, 324, 388–9, 407, 424, 455, 461, 462, 464, 473, 485

Andover, Hants, 63½ m. from Hyde Park Corner and 18¼ m. from Basingstoke on the London–Exeter road: 52, 59, 60, 96, 98, 106, 139

Antigua: 317

Appleshaw, 5 m. N.W. of Andover on the Devizes road: 106

Ash(e), Hants, 6¾ m. W. of Basingstoke on the London–Exeter road, 2 m. from Steventon, see Lefroy: 2, 5, 25, 29, 81, 93

Ash(e) Park, see Holder: 49, 84, 99, 114, 117

Ashdown Park, near Lambourn, Berks., see Craven, Earl of: 106

Ashford, Kent, 53¼ m. from London Bridge on the London–Hythe road, 7 m., from Godmersham: 44–5, 94, 163, 258, 344, 368

Astley's, see London: 7

B——: 49

Bagshot, Surry, 26 m. from Hyde Park Corner on the London – Basingstoke road: 308, 320

Barton Lodge, see Birch: 246

Baltic, the: 339, 375

Barbadoes: 5

Barton Court, Berks., between Speen and Hungerford on the Bath Road, see Dundas: 106, 261, 295

Basingstoke, Hants, 45¼ m. from Hyde Park Corner on the London–Exeter road, 8¾ m. from Steventon: 22, 29, 52, 56, 79, 81, 84, 92, 98, 99, 103, 121, 127, 185, 226, 343

BATH, Som., 107¼ m. from Hyde Park Corner by Maidenhead, Reading, Hungerford and Devizes. See also Bristol.

General References: 26, 49, 94, 95, 118, 119, 123 (the view), 172, 208, 232, 239, 334, 365, 366, 375, 381, 391 (J. & Cassandra's dislike of), 395

The Baths: Hetling Pump 63; Cross Bath 324, 349; Hot Bath 324; Hot Pump 349

Concerts: 65, 154

The Rooms: 127

Alfred St. 153; Axford Buildings 101; Bath St. 63, 150; Brock St. 62; Canal, the, 126; Chapel, the, 100, 148, 153; Chapel row 100; Charitable Repository 111; Charles St. 100; Crescent, the, 65, 127, 148; Gay St. 100, 148 (No. 25), 154, 157; Green Park Buildings 124, 130, 136 (No. 12), 145, 147, 157; Green Park St. 100; Henrietta St. 324; Kingsmead fields 100; Laura Place 100, 109, 115, 324; New King St. 124, 132; Paragon, see Leigh-Perrot; Prince's St. 100; Pulteney St. 100, 304; Pump Room 64; Queen's Parade 62, 68; Queen('s) Square 59 (No. 13), 62, 66, 68, 70, 115; Queen Square Chapel 100; Row, the, i.e. Westgate Buildings (still a single row, with no houses opposite) 109; Riding-house, the 148; St. James' Square (see Holder, William); 151; Seymour St. 124, 127, 136; South Parade 103; Square, the: doubtless Queen Square; Sydney Gardens 61, 65, 71, 115, 136, 155; Trim St. 100; Walcot Church 64, 147; Westgate Buildings 100, 109; White Hart, the 324; Upper Crescent 151

The Neighbourhood: Beacon Hill 64; Cassoon, the 129; Charlcombe 64; Kingsdown 60, 123, 137; Lansdown 148; Lyncombe 134; Sion Hill 131; Twerton 150; Weston 68, 129, 131 (see note), 155; Widcombe: 134

Battersea: 22

Baugherst, Hants, near Silchester, see Dyson: 121

Beaulieu, Hants: 205

Beckenham: 269

Bedfont, Middlesex, near Staines on the London–Basingstoke road: 308

Bentigh: 189, 332 note

Bentley Green, Hants, 5½ m. N.E. of Alton on the London–Southampton road: 376, 396

Bermuda: 242, 254

Bifrons, Kent, near Bridge on the Canterbury–Dover road, see Taylor: 14

Birmingham: 290

Bishopstoke, Hants, on the Winchester – Southampton road: 76

Bishop's Waltham, Hants, 10 m. from Southampton on the Alton road: 214

Blackheath, Kent, 5 m. from London Bridge on the London–Dover road: 186

Blandford, Dorset, 39¾ m. from Lyme Regis on the Bridport–Dorchester – Salisbury road: 138

Bookham, Surry, near Leatherhead, off the London–Guildford road, see Cooke: 66, 192, 203, 208, 220, 244–6, 248–50, 255, 286, 365, 374, 391

Brentford: 211

Bridlington, Yorks.: 466

Brighton, Sussex: 'I dread the idea of going to B.' 49; 334, 348

Bristol: 'one of the first houses in B.' 94; 'all over Bath—B. included': 102

Broadstairs, Isle of Thanet, 20 m. from Canterbury: 190, 458, 463
Brompton, see London
Brooklands, near Southampton, see Williams, Sir Thomas: 172 (and see 92)
Broome Park, Kent, near Dorringstone on the Canterbury – Folkestone road, see Oxenden: 168
Buckwell Pond, near Godmersham: 195
Builting or Bilting, a hamlet in Godmersham parish: 356

Cadbury, North (*not* Great), Som., see Blackall: 317
Cadiz: 33, 34
Calcutta: 15
Cambridge: 27, 205, 293, 331
Canterbury: 14, 54, 57, 115, 161, 163, 169, 170, 171, 189, 192, 195, 200, 203, 204, 205, 207, 208, 237, 270, 332, 333, 342, 348, 350, 357, 360, 364, 365, 397, 489
Cape of Good Hope: 3
Carlscroon: 314
Charlcombe: see Bath
Charmouth, Dorset, 1¾ m. from Lyme Regis: 143
Chawton, Hants, 48¾ m. from Hyde Park Corner on the London – Winchester – Southampton road, and at the junction of this road with the other road to Southampton (by Bishop's Waltham); 1¼ m. from Alton: *passim* from 24 Oct. 1808; the kitchen garden at C. Cottage 226; Cassandra's description 229; six bedchambers 231; J. A.'s verses on 266; the chimneys at the Great House 283; the Park 289; a new garden (at the Great House) 314 (see note); the new Coin 345, 346; the Round Tower &c. 349
Cheesedown, part of the Steventon estate: 57, 106 (?), 110
Chelsea: 441
Cheltenham: 142, 189, 196, 274, 355, 371, 372; letters to C. E. A. at, 461, 463; the High St.: 466
Chevet (or -ot), see Pilkington
Chilham Castle, see Wildman
Chilton House, near Hungerford, see Craven: 134, 308
Chippenham, Wilts., 12½ m. from Bath on the London–Calne–Bath road: 131
Chiswell, near Southampton, see Lance: 237, 238
Clanville Lodge, near Andover, see Mathew: 250
Clapham: 22
Claremont Park, Esher, Surry, on the London–Guildford road; built (and 'the grounds improved') by Brown for Lord Clive *c.* 1770; bought by the Commissioners of Woods and Forests 1816; 'Kent's last designs were in a higher style . . . the north terras at Claremont was much superior to the rest of the garden'. Walpole, *Anecdotes* vol. iv (1771), p. 142: 307
Clifton, near Bristol: 'we left

Bath for Clifton' (1806) 208, 317, 391
Cobham, Surry, 19½ m. from London Bridge on the London–Guildford road: 375–7
Colyton, see Buller: 85, 150
Cork: 9, 15
Cowes, Isle of Wight: 281, 288
Cranford Bridge, Middlesex, 12¼ m. from Hyde Park Corner on the London–Bath road: 379
Crixhall ruff, a wood near Rowling: 12
Crondale, near Godmersham, see Filmer: 198
Croydon, Surry, on the Dartford-Bromley–Croydon–Kingston–Staines road: 22, 250 ('the other road' is the Dorking–Maidstone road, cf. 203), 333
Cyprus: 78, 87, 94

Danbury, Essex, see Bridges, Brook Henry: 12
Dartford, Kent, 15 m. from London Bridge on the London–Dover road, 39 m. from Staines on the Dartford–Bromley–Croydon–Kingston–Staines road: 20, 186, 250, 381
Dawlish, Devon, 13 m. from Exeter on the Exeter–Teignmouth road: 85, 393–6, 402
Daylesford, see Hastings: 320
Deal, Kent, 19 m. from Canterbury by Bramling and Sandwich: 54, 58, 164, 337
Dean(e), near Steventon; see Austen, George and James, and Harwood: 24, 25, 29, 34, 39, 46, 66, 74, 79, 83, 84, 87, 90, 99, 104, 107, 111, 113, 117, 302
Dean(e) Gate, Hants, near Ashe on the Basingstoke–Andover road; 1½ m. from Steventon: 2, 54
Deptford, Kent, 4½ m. from London Bridge on the London–Dover road: 18, 186
Devizes, Wilts., 27¼ m. from Andover on the Andover–Bath road: 59, 122, 123
Doncaster, Yorks., see Sharpe: 493
Dorking, Surry, 11¾ m. from Guildford on the Maidstone–Guildford road: 203, 286
Dorsetshire: 12
Dover, Kent, 15¾ m. from Canterbury: 12, 162, 164
Downs, the: 54, 58, 206, 207
Dummer House, Hants, near Popham Lane, off the Basingstoke–Winchester road, see Terry: 26, 282, 300

East Indies: 141
Eastling, near Faversham, Kent; Edward Cage was the rector: 357
Eastwell Park, near Ashford, Kent, see Finch-Hatton: 50, 160, 164, 195, 331, 342, 350, 370
Edinburgh: 397 (see note), 405
Eggerton (Eggarton), Kent, near Godmersham, see Cuthbert: 94, 191
Egham, Surry, 19½ m. from Hyde Park Corner on the Lon-

don-Exeter road (from which the road to Farnham and Alton branches off at Golden Farmer): 397
Eltham School, Kent, on the Lewisham–Dartford road: 180, 191 (cf. 161, 167)
Egypt: 78, 137
Enham Place, Knight's Enham, 2 m. N. of Andover on the Newbury road: 91
En . . . , see Atkinson
Esher, Surry, 16 m. from London Bridge on the London–Guildford road. Esher Place ('T. Spicer, Esq.', *Paterson's Roads* 1824 p. 21); 'At Esher, "Where Kent and nature vied for Pelham's love", the prospects more than aided the painter's genius.—They marked out the points where his art was necessary or not'. Walpole, *Anecdotes* vol. iv (1771) p. 142): 306–8
Eton College, Bucks: 171
Everley, Wilts., 11¾ m. from Andover on the Andover–Bath road: 122
Eversley, Hants (in the N.E. corner of the county), see Cope, Sir Richard, and Debary, Peter: 176, 181, 185
Evington, Kent, 8 m. S. of Canterbury, W. of the Hythe road, see Honeywood: 333
Exeter: 104, 394

Falmouth: 5
Fareham, Hants, 18½ m. W. of Chichester on the Margate-Weymouth road: 202 (see note), 283
Faringdon, Hants, 1 m. S. of Chawton and 2½ from Selbourne, see Benn: 281–5, 289, 459
Farnham, Surry, 9¼ m. N.E. of Alton; two roads to London branch at F.: 36, 376, 396
Faversham, near Ospringe, Kent, off the London–Dover road; post-town for Godmersham: 93
Folly Farm: 75
France: 459, 'a scene of general Poverty and Misery' 465, 489
Fredville, near Knowlton, Kent, off the Canterbury–Deal road, see Plumtre: 358, 362
Friars, see White Friars
Fyfield: 372

Ganges: 208
Gibraltar: 34, 43, 47
Glencoe: 105
Gloucester: 105, 139
Gloucestershire, J. A.'s visit in: 123
Godington, near Great Chart, Kent, on the Ashford–Tenterden road, see Toke: 283, 351
Godmersham Park, Kent., 8¼ m. S.E. of Canterbury on the Ashford road; see Austen, Edward, in Index I: letters to and from Kent *passim*, and especially 8, 187 the yellow room, 189 (note) the Temple plantation, 194 the library, 197 the hall chamber, 200 the dressing-room, 206 the library, 205 (note) the limestone path, 330 the 'little chintz', the

white room, 333 improvements, the chintz room, 335 alone in the library, 352 hall and library, 353 the breakfast room, the billiard room, 368 the drawing-room (?). For the various rooms see 368 note; and see also Bentigh, Buckwell, Eggerton, Seaton Wood, Winnigates
Goodnestone, Kent, 6¾ m. from Canterbury on the Deal road, see Bridges: 11, 12, 116, 160, 161, 162, 203, 223, 230, 279, 333 the Fair, 339 the famous Fair, 352, 367, 434, 479, 483
Gosport, Hants, 31 m. from Alton by Fareham, about 41 m. from Steventon by Winchester: 83, 88, 90, 388, 423
Gravesend (-t), Kent, 7 m. E. of Dartford on the London–Dover road: 21, 423
Greenwich, Kent: 17
Guil(d)ford, Surry, 29½ m. from London Bridge on the London–Portsmouth road, 19½ m. from Alton; 42 m. from Maidstone on the Maidstone–Reigate–Guildford road: 203, 267, 286, 306, 308, 357, 360, 375, 389

Hackwood Park, near Basingstoke, Hants, see Bolton, Lord: 49
Hadley, Middlesex, see Lefroy, John Henry George: 413
Halifax, Nova Scotia: 152, 275
Hampstead, Middlesex: 311
Hampstead Marshall, Berks., see Fowle: 238
Hamstall Ridware, Staffs, see Cooper: 55, 118, 220, 252, 260, 280
Hanwell, Middlesex, 8½ m. from Tyburn Turnpike on the London–Wycombe road, see Moore: 398, 414, 439, 441
Harden, see Harpsden
Harefield (probably) near Uxbridge: 362
Harpsden (Harden, as formerly pronounced) near Henley-on-Thames; see Leigh, Rev. Thomas, and Cooper, Rev. Edward: 2 (see note), 66
Hartley Row, Hants, 9 m. from Basingstoke on the London–Basingstoke road: 23
Hatch, see Mersham Hatch
Hendon, Middlesex, 7 m. from Holborn Bars on the Mill Hill road: 413, 416, 423, 425
Henley, Oxon., 35 m. from Hyde Park Corner on the Bath road: 312
Hertford (Hartford) Bridge, Hants, 9¾ m. from Basingstoke on the Basingstoke–London road: 7
Hinckley (near Nuneaton ?): 212
Hog's-back, the, between Farnham and Guildford: 306, 307
Holybourn, Hants, 1½ m. from Alton on the Farnham road: 397
Horsham, Sussex: 306
Hungerford, Berks.: 463
Hurstbourne (Prior), Hants, 5 m. E. of Andover on the Basingstoke road; H. Park, see

Portsmouth, Earl of: 29, 87, 90, 94 (?)
Hurstbourne Tarrant, N. of Andover on the Newbury road; 126 (the same as Up H., 87, 122, 138, 148, 154; see Ibthrop)
Hythe, Kent, 12 m. from Ashford on the Folkestone road: 10, 12

Ibthrop (Ibthorp; *pron.* Ibtrop), a hamlet in the parish of Hurstbourne Tarrant, Hants, see Lloyd: 4, 23, 35, 40, 46, 58, 81, 87, 96, 101, 106, 109, 113, 126, 138, 148–50
Ilford, Essex: 268
Ireland: 368, 395
Itchen, the: 175; Itchen Ferry, Southampton: 228
Itchingswell, near Kingsclere, Hants: 174; see Digweed, Hugh

Jaffa: 78

Katherine, Lake: 105
Kempshott Park, near Basingstoke, see Dorchester, Lord: 48, 49
Kent, East and West, 359; the West Kent scheme 129; our Connexions in West K., 235
Key Street, Kent, 2 m. W. of Sittingbourne: 357
Kingsclere, Hants, 7 m. from Whitchurch on the Reading road: 43
Kingston, Surry, 10 m. from London Bridge on the London–Guildford road; also on the Dartford–Bromley–Croydon–Kingston–Staines road: 22, 307, 318, 376, 377, 382
Kintbury, Berks., see Fowle: 4, 23, 35, 54, 75, 81, 106, 131, 134, 175, 177, 224, 229, 233, 242, 251
Kippington, near Sevenoaks, Kent, see Austen, Motley: 126
Kirby, Northants: 397 (note)

Larnica, Cyprus: 94
Lenham, Kent, 9½ m. from Ashford on the Maidstone road (Wrotham lies near a continuation of this road), see Bridges, Brook Edward: 339, 343, 348, 374
Lisbon: 34, 43, 120
Litchfield, Hants, 2 m. N. of Whitchurch on the Newbury road, or South L., West of Steventon: 6
LONDON: Abingdon-street (? Dundas) 290; Albany 162; Astley's 7; Bath Hotel 186; Bedford House (Layton and Shears) 319, 366; Belgrave Chapel 310, 437; Bentinck-street 267; Berkeley-street (Upper 119), 121, 395, see Austen, Henry; Bond-street 418; British Gallery 267; Brompton 145, 197, 209, see Austen, Henry; Carlton House 429, 442; Charing Cross 366, 368; Charles-street, Covent Garden 16; Cleveland Court 118; Cleveland Row 425, 426; Cork-street 7; Coventry-street 383; Cranbourn Alley 384; Crown and Beehive 16; Glou-

cester Ho. 280 (but see note); Grafton House 268, 323, 325, 326, 328, 436; Grosvenor Place 324; Hans Place, No. 23, see Austen, Henry; Hans Place, No. 26: 278, 327, see Tilson; Henrietta-street, see Austen, Henry; Hertford-street 386; Hyde Park Corner, H.P. Gate: 276, 308; Kensington Gardens 275; Keppel-street, see Palmer, and Austen, Charles; Leicester Square 327; Liverpool Museum 267; Opera House 107, 118; Palace, the, 191; Pall Mall 310; Russel Square 395; St. James's 17; St. James's Church 207, 311; St. Paul's, Covent Garden 363; Sloane-street, see Austen, Henry; Somerset House 310; Spring Gardens 309; Tavistock-street 398; Temple 17; White's: 390

Luggershall (Ludgershall), Wilts., 7¼ m. from Andover on the Andover–Bath road: 122

Lyme Regis, Dorset, 29½ m. from Exeter by Honiton (and therefore 42½ m. from Dawlish): 138–43, 216, 394

Lyncombe, near Bath: 134

Madeiras, the: 142

Maidstone, Kent: 368

Malta: 34

Manydown, Hants, 1 m. from Worting on the Basingstoke–Andover road; 6 m. from Steventon, see Bigg Wither: 3, 5, 40, 43, 56, 69, 88, 115, 116, 217, 222, 241, 242, 249, 294, 298, 300–2, 304, 477

Marcou (St. Marcouf), two small islands off the coast of Normandy, occupied by the British: 83

Margate, Kent, 16¼ m. from Canterbury: 14, 348

Matlock, Derbyshire: 320, 326

Mecklenberg: 336

Mersham Hatch, Kent, 2¾ m. from Ashford on the Ashford–Folkestone road, see Knatchbull, Sir Edward: 361

Midgham House, Berks., between Reading and Newbury (a traveller to Midgham from Portsmouth would go by Winchester, Popham Lane, and Basingstoke); see Boyle: 120

Milgate, Kent, 3 m. from Maidstone on the Ashford road, see Cage: 77, 131, 368

Minorca: 34

Mounter's Lane, near Chawton: 489

Mystole, Kent, 4 m. from Godmersham on the Canterbury road, see Fagg: 346, 347

Nackington, Kent, 2 m. S. of Canterbury, off the Dover road, see Milles: 13, 166, 202, 205, 331, 332

Neatham, Hants, part of the Chawton estate: 210, 214, 301

Netherton, see Lance: 175

Netley: perhaps N. Lodge on Southampton Water ('J. Smith Esq.' *Paterson's Roads* 1824

p. 368), see Southampton: 197
Netley Abbey, see Southampton
Newbury, Berks., 13 m. N. of Whitchurch, 20 m. from Steventon: 119, 154, 204–5
North Cadbury, see Cadbury
Northam Bridge, Hants, 1 m. from Southampton on the Bishop's Waltham road: 228
Northamptonshire: 298, 504
Norton Court, Kent, near Ospringe on the London–Dover road, see Lushington: 342
Norwich: 406
Nova Scotia: 152

Oakley, Hants, S. of the Basingstoke–Andover road, between Worting and Ashe, near Manydown, see Bramston: 74, 75, 294
Ospringe, Kent, 9¼ m. from Canterbury on the London–Canterbury road; 9 m. from Godmersham by Chilham: 20, 54, 162, 163, 357
Overton, Hants, 7¾ m. from Basingstoke on the Basingstoke–Andover road, 3½ m. from Steventon (for which it was the post-town): 32, 72, 283
Oxford: 64, 245, 277, 301, 362, 374, 437–8, 458

Pains Hill Park, near Cobham, Surry, on the London–Guildford road. ('Mr. Charles Hamilton, at Pain's-hill, in my opinion has given a perfect example [of the alpine scene] in the utmost boundary of his garden. All is great and foreign and rude'. Walpole, *Anecdotes*, vol. iv (1771) p. 145): 307
Paris: 465
Penzance: 158
Petersfield, Hants, 11¾ m. from Chawton on the Alton–Petersfield road: 391
Pett Place, near Charing, Kent, on the Canterbury–Brighton road ('George Sayer, Esq.' *Paterson's Roads* 1813): 351
Popham Lane, Hants, 5 m. from Basingstoke off the Basingstoke–Winchester road, 2 m. from Steventon, see Midgham: 120
Portsmouth, Hants, 4½ m. S. of Cosham, which is 17 m. from Southampton by Fareham: 26, 39, 89, 120, 134, 152, 175, 233, 235, 240, 253, 258, 262, 290, 297, 301, 361, 389
Provendar, Kent, see Knatchbull, Edward: 200

Ramsgate, Kent: 166, 339, 343, 348, 351
Reading, Berks., 39 m. from Hyde Park Corner on the Bath road, 14¼ m. from Basingstoke: 52, 313
Rhodes: 120
Ripley, Surry, 23¾ m. from London Bridge on the London–Guildford road: 306, 360
Rochester, Kent, 29 m. from London Bridge on the London–Dover road: 20
Rostock: 336

Rowling, Kent, 1 m. E. of Goodnestone, see Austen, Edward: 7, 54, 163, 164, 168
Roxburghshire: 338
Rugby, Warwickshire: 260
Rugen: 313
Rumsey (Romsey), Hants, 10½ m. S.W. of Winchester: 388

St. Alban's Court, near Wingham, on the Canterbury–Sandwich road, see Hammond: 168
St. Bo⟨niface⟩, a house in the Isle of Wight, the seat, 1810, of 'Thos. Bowdler Esq.' (*Carey's New Itinerary*) 33
St. Helen's (Bay), Isle of Wight:
St. Maries, see Southampton
Salisbury, Wilts.: 97, 227
Sandling, Kent, 10 m. from Ashford on the Folkestone road, see Deedes: 76, 167, 188, 203, 206, 331, 332, 360, 436, 461
Scarlets (-tts), Berks., near Hare Hatch, 6 m. from Maidenhead on the Reading road, see Leigh-Perrot: 107, 141, 296, 304, 428, 454, 488
Scotland: 315
Seale, near Sevenoaks, on the Maidstone–Guildford road: see Walter: 203
Seaton Wood, on the Godmersham estate: 353
Selbo(u)rne, Hants, 3½ m. S. of Chawton: 285, 286, 289, 465
Shalden, Hants, part of the Chawton estate: 210, 345
Sheerness, Isle of Sheppey, Kent: 58, 354
Sherborne St. John, Hants, near Basingstoke: 24
Shrewsbury: 95
Sidmouth, Devon: 107
Sittingbourne, Kent, 15¼ m. from Canterbury on the London–Canterbury road; 16 m. from Godmersham: 20, 21, 187, 353–4, 359
Southend: 316
Southampton: *passim* in letters of 1807–9; 92; preferred to Canterbury 171; the Castle 178 (see note); St. Mary's (the district surrounding the parish church) 212 (see Harrison); fire in the High Street 216; Netley Abbey (a favourite excursion 'most frequently made by water . . . but those who prefer crossing the ferry and walking thither, will find the round extremely pleasant, and the distance about three miles') 228; the Theatre 233; Bellevue 233; the Polygon 235; date of departure 246
Spain: 258
Speen Hill, Berks., near Newbury on the Bath road, see Craven, Mrs., and Hulbert: 107, 149, 231
Spithead, 153
Staines, Middlesex, 16½ m. from Hyde Park Corner on the London–Basingstoke road: 7, 22, 24
Star Cross, Devon, 3¾ m. from Dawlish on the Exeter–Teignmouth road: 394
Start, the, Devon, 120
Steventon, Hants, 1½ m. off the Basingstoke–Andover road, S. of Ash, and 2 m. N.W. of Popham Lane on the Basing-

stoke–Winchester road, see Austen, George and James: *passim*; the Elm walk 76, 86; the little parlour 132; the Book Society 294
Stirling (Sterling) Scotland (the reference is to an imaginary visit, see *Love and Freindship*, 1922, p. 38): 397
Stoneleigh Abbey, Warwickshire, near Kenilworth, see Leigh, J. H.: 174, 189, 232
Streatham, Surry, 5¼ m. from Westminster Bridge on the London–Croydon road; see Hill: 271, 367, 374, 383, 392, 474–7
Sweden: 314, 336
Switzerland: 495

Tangier, Hants, see Sclater: 459
Tenby, Pembrokeshire: 190
Tewkesbury, Glos.: 96
Tollard Royal, Wilts., see Rice, Henry: 343, 402
Tunbridge: 182
Twerton, near Bath: 150

Uxbridge, Middlesex, 15 m. from Tyburn Turnpike on the London–Wycombe–Oxford road: 278

Vienna: 95

Wales: 103, 151
Waltham, see Bishop's Waltham
Wantage Down, Berks.: 106
Weston, near Bath: 68, 129, 131 (see note), 155
Westwell, Kent, W. of Eastwell, q.v.: 339
Weyhill, Hants, 3¼ m. W. of Andover on the Devizes road: 106, 343
Weymouth, 8¼ m. S. of Dorchester, which is on the Bridport–Salisbury road: 138, 280
Wheatfield, Oxon., near Stokenchurch on the Uxbridge–Oxford road: 278
Whit(e)church, Hants, 6¾ m. E. of Andover on the Basingstoke road: 98
White Friars, Canterbury, see Knight, Mrs.: 193, 194, 200, 270, 339
Widcombe, near Bath: 134
Wight, Isle of ('the Island'): 92, 199, 200, 202, 207
Winchester (Winton), Hants, 6¼ m. from Chawton, 14 m. from Steventon: 25, 55, 75, 92, 173, 180, 188, 200, 214, 219, 226, 238, 251, 458, 467, 476, 494, 496
Windsor, Berks., near Slough, off the London–Maidenhead–Henley road: 41, 312
Winnigates, or Wintergates, a wood on the Godmersham estate: 353
Wintney: Hartley Wintney, about 9 m. E. of Basingstoke, off the Basingstoke–Staines road: 56
Wood Barn, near Chawton: 285
Wootton St. Lawrence, Hants: 283
Woolwich, Kent: 72, 397
Worldham, Great (or East), E. of Chawton, Hants: 293
Worthing, Sussex, 12 m. W. of

III. Places

Brighton and so 82 m. from Canterbury by Charing and Highgate: 161, 167, 169
Worting, Hants, 2¼ m. from Basingstoke on the Andover road, see Clarke: 43, 81
Wrotham, Kent, 10½ m. W. of Maidstone; on the Maidstone–London road (by Eltham), and just off the Maidstone–Guildford road; see Moore: 203, 206, 231, 350, 358, 361, 364, 374
Wrotham Gate: 203
Wyards, a farmhouse near Alton, see Lefroy, Benjamin: 423, 438, 462, 475, 484, 485
Wye, Kent, 9½ m. S. of Canterbury, 1 m. from Godmersham: 227

Yarmouth, Isle of Wight: 8, 212, 215, 226
York: 104, 405

References are to the pages.

IV. GENERAL TOPICS

References are to pages

SUMMARY

- Balls
- Carriages
- Charities
- Dress
- Duelling
- Food and Drink (see also Meals)
- French
- Games and Pastimes
- Hair and Hairdressing
- Handshaking
- Handwriting (see also Letters)
- Houses
- Jewelry and Plate
- Letters (see also Handwriting)
- Literature (see also Indexes V and VI)
- Meals (see also Food)
- Music
- Names
- Nature, Gardens, Weather
- Newspapers
- OPINIONS
  - Beauty
  - Children
  - Clergy
  - Death
  - Education
  - Explanations
  - Family ties
  - Likenesses
  - Liking
  - Liveliness
  - Luxury
  - Marriage
  - Match-making
  - Money
  - Mothering
  - Old Age
  - Public Affairs (see also Newspapers)
  - Religion
  - Virtues and Vices
  - Youth
- Painting
- Prices
- Races
- Remedies
- Schools
- Shooting
- Spelling
- Teeth and Dentists
- Tips
- Transport
- Travel (see also Carriages)
- Visits
- Work

IV. General Topics

Balls: the early letters *passim*; 2 'sitting down', 6 'draw for partners', 11 'the Boulangeries' (cf. *P. P.* ch. 3), 29 Basingstoke assemblies, 44, 163 Ashford balls, 48 'a partner' for Charles A., 49 Hackwood, 51 'not very much in request', 55, 90, 91 'I called the last', 92, 98 Canterbury, 93 Faversham, 104 and 108 Chilham Castle (cf. 370?), 119 Newbury Assembly, 123 and 127 Upper Rooms, Bath, 141 Lyme, 164 Deal, 225, 253, 257 Southampton, 249 Manydown, 344 Ashford, 481 quadrilles and cotillions.

Carriages (see also Travel): 11 coach, 111 'Coach box, Basket & Dickey', 121 riding on the Bar, a Sunday chaise, 133 the Debary's coach, 136 and 137 Mr. Evelyn's Phaeton & four, 161, 189 the Godmersham chair, 173 James Austen's chair, 190 the Godmersham carriage, 195 John Bridges' gig, 280 Mrs. Welby's barouche. 288 Henry A.'s gig, 293 Mr. Clement's tax-cart, 306 Henry A.'s curricle, 313 and 398 his barouche, 318 and 397 hackney coach, 319 barouche box, 'four within' too many for comfort, 331 painting, 337 Edward Knight's barouche

Charities: 25 baby clothes, 45 'my charities to the poor' enumerated, 203 'If she wants sugar, I sh[d] like to supply her with it', 295 'an old shift & . . . a set of our Linen'

DRESS, &c. (The student is warned that the compiler of this mechanical list has no pretension to knowledge): band (head-dress) 81; beaver bonnet 111; *beds* (? bed-gowns) 172; boa 189; bombazeen (-sin, -zin) 222, 291, 301, 362; bonnet 37, 125, 133, 181, 215, 222, 250, 269; bugle 269, 277; button-holes 382; calico 115; cambric 98, 116, 125; cap 35, 37, 40, 44, 49, 65, 113, 154, 322, 323, 326, 330, 335, 380, 384; cawl 37; China, see crape; christening robe, &c. 172; cloak 63, 77, 125, 133; cloud 116; coarse spot 44; comb 77, 81; coquelicot 37; crape 154, 222, (China) 298, 301, 371, 381; cravat 249; cruels 268; dimity 310; fan 51; flounce 185, 358, 352, 362, 441; flowers and fruit 67; frock 98; gauze 125; gloves 3, 10, 24, 306; gore 279; gown 9, 35, 40, 49, 77, 99, 121, 124, 128, 132, 172; handkerchief: 125, (shirt h.) 204, (neckhandkerf) 257, (pocket) 415, (muslin) 426, (neckhandfs.) 436; hat 23, 31, 64, 131, 269; Irish 56, 327; kerseymere 204; lace 25, 63, 67, 328; lambswool 426; linon 185; list 257; mamalone 49 (note); mantle 250; mantua 49; mittens 162; mourning 115, 169, 215, 222, 315, 380, 381; muslin 251, 268, 276, 279; nightcap 162, 333, 358; parasol 131; pelisse 173, 215, 219, 222, 269, 277, 366, 399, 416, 461; perl edge 384; persian 3, 339; poplin 321, 324, 328; robe 40;

References are to the pages.

sarsenet 308, 310, 381; shawl 155, 295; shift 198; shoes 51, 63, 77, 242, 257, 402; slate 327; sleeves 386; spencer 133, 204; sprig 67; statues 92; stays 322, 357; stockings 3, 77, 269, 327, 436; strip (white) 125; tippet 383; veils 69, 328, 377, 380; velvet 219; Vine leaves and paste 386; white in the morning 99, cf. 132 and note
Duelling 83

Food and Drink (see also Meals): cold souse 6, 58; Edward A. goes out 'to taste a cheese himself' 61; black butter 241 note; syllabub 285; honey 330; 'very bad Baker's bread' 367; 'arra-root' 436; loaf sugar 345; breaking sugar 437. Wine: orange 209, 477; currant 290; white 330; liqueurs 10; mead 305, 363, 382, 441, 466; small beer 18; spruce beer 215; tea 14, 286
French words and phrases: 34, 72, 78, 89, 99, 110, 121, 130, 149, 180, 189, 270, 311, 345, 346, 362, 366, 462, 78.1

GAMES and other pastimes: backgammon 331; battledore and shuttlecock 161; bilbocatch 225; billiards 351, 362; brag 247, J. A.'s verses on b. and speculation 252; casino 93; charades 298; commerce 93, 139, 211, 215; conundrums 225; cribbage 126, 161, 302; nines 488; quadrille 215; riddles 225; speculation 229, 244, 247, J. A.'s verses 252; spillikins, -ens, 179, 211, 225; transparencies 75; turning 8, 10; vingt-un 117, 472; whist 93

Hair and Hairdressing: 54 powder, 57 'a crop', 113 cut too short, 162 Mr. Hall, '5*s.* for every time', 192 Anna A.'s cut off, 308 Charlotte Craven's does 'credit to any education', 323 Mr. Hall 'curled me out at a great rate', 327 'my hair was dressing'
Handshaking: 131, 158
Handwriting (see also Letters): 25 'sprawly', 115, 134 (?), 196, 197 bad pens (cf. 319, 366), 228, 336, 367 beauty of Cassandra's, 500 'I must learn to make a better K'
Houses: Dressing room 34, 35, 55, 200, 208, 260

Jewelry and Plate: 'gold chains & Topaze crosses' 137; the family silver 243; Cassandra's locket 310; broches 153, 204, 219

LETTERS (These references are for the most part noteworthy only as they illustrate the normal epistolary practice of the day).
Consequences of the expense of postage and of limitation of an unfranked letter to a single sheet: a long sheet 22; writing as closely as possible 44; materials to fill a sheet 95; 'very clever to write

such long Letters' (i.e. so closely-written) 196, cf. 118, 347; 'ashamed of my wide lines' 228; 'not filling my sheet' 53, cf. 95; 'my paper will be my own' 82, 'will hardly hold it all' 235, 'will put my lines very close together' 364, 'I have not time or paper for half that I want to say' 374; foolscap 104; crossing 295, 'obliged to write down the whole of this page'; gratitude to Cassandra for 'Such a long Letter! Two & forty lines in the 2[d] Page' 344; counting the lines 499

Envelope (the word is not in the Letters, but see *P. and P.* ch. 35): 295 'something in a cover' no doubt implies that the letter went by hand and cost the recipient nothing

Franking: 78, 82, 104, 277, 292, 347

Seal and Wafer: 51, 70, 347

Direction: 120, 141, 489

Cost: 47 'letter expences', 111 overcharge, 336, 441, 376 two-penny post (London)

Local arrangements: 154 Newbury, 489 Canterbury, 223 'by the coach'

Foreign letters: 95 'open'd at Vienna'; 162 numbered outside (to check losses—a practice repeated in the War of 1914–18)

Literary aspects: 102 'the true art of letter-writing', 181 'want of Materials', cf. 244–5, 186 'important nothings'

Various: 69, 70, 73 letters for children; 186 forced to be abusive for want of subject; 325 Sunday post; 492 mourning

Family letters for general consumption: 226 'we all saw what she wrote'; 306 'I hope somebody cares for these minutiæ'; 332 'I read him the cheif of your Letter'; 343 'we had all the reading of it of course'; 419 'write *something* that may do to be read or told'; 463 a letter from Charles to Cassandra opened by J. A. and not forwarded. See on the other hand 140

LITERATURE (see also Index V, Literary Allusions, Index VI, Jane Austen's Novels, and the letters to Anna, Nos. 95, 98, 100, 101, 107, *passim*)

Anonymity: precautions and risks 300; 'if I *am* a wild Beast, I cannot help it. It is not my own fault' 311; regrets at disclosure 320, 'I am trying to harden myself. After all, what a trifle it is . . .' 340; 'perhaps I may marry young Mr. D'arblay' 368

Classical Allusions: 'Homer and Virgil, Ovid and Propria que Maribus' 256; 'her sister in Lucina' 329

Composition: 'an artist cannot do any thing slovenly' (1798, of another art-form) 30; at work (Jan. 1809) 'could my Ideas flow as fast as the rain in the Store closet it would be charming' 256; 'wish other people of my acquaintance could compose as rapidly' 420; 'Impossible, with a head full of Joints of Mutton & doses of rhubarb' 466; 'the little bit (two Inches wide) of Ivory . . .' 468–9

Fancy and Imagination: 345

Libraries: Mrs. Martin's subscription l. (at Basingstoke?) opened 1799, 38; the 'particularly pitiful' l. at Dawlish 393

Names and Titles: 'I will compliment her by naming a Heroine after her' 345; '*Enthusiasm* was something so very superior that every common title must appear to disadvantage' 393

Novels: the A. family 'great Novel-readers & not ashamed of being so' 38; Cassandra's dislike of desultory n. 395; 'novel slang' 404

Octavos and Quartos: 304 'I detest a quarto'

Parody: of Mrs. Piozzi 235, and perhaps 136 line 3

Puns: 133, 335

Reading in general: 'I come to be talked to, not to read or hear reading, I can do *that* at home' 89; 'very little variety of Books or Gowns' 96

Reading Aloud: 'My father reads Cowper to us in the evening' 39; 'to read or hear reading' 89; 'the "Female Quixotte" . . . now makes our evening amusement' 173; 'James reads [*Marmion*] aloud in the Even[g]' 197; 'I read [*Espriella's Letters*] aloud by candlelight' 212; 'Our second evening's reading to Miss Benn' 299

Reading Clubs: the Chawton Book Society, its rival in the Steventon district, and its imitator elsewhere 294, 304

Subject: 'my preference for Men & Women, always inclines me to attend more to the company than the sight' 267; excuses herself to Mr. Clarke, 'the comic part of the character I might be equal to, but not the good, the enthusiastic, the literary'; ignorance of science, of philosophy, of languages and literature, &c. 443, and see 452–3; Pictures of Perfection make me sick and wicked 486; 'the dirty Shaving Rag was exquisite!—Such a circumstance ought to be in print' 412; fears of having 'overwritten' herself 449, 453; digressions might have improved *Pride and Prejudice*; Cassandra's 'starched notions' on this 300

Style: solicitude about 256, use of third person in dialogue 387, Charles A.'s (naively revealing) 438

Verses: on Brag and Spec. 252; 'I am in a Dilemma' 278; on the Weald of Kent Canal Bill 279; lines on Miss W. 501

IV. General Topics

MEALS (see also Food):

Breakfast: visiting before b. 23; shopping before b. 321; at 10 A.M. 188, 206, cf. 326; coffee at 68

Luncheon: 362; *Noonshine*: 195, 228; *The Tray*: 367

Dinner: 39 (1798, at 3.30); 164–5 (1805, at 5, but delayed till 6); 166 (at 4, 'that we may walk afterwards); 235 (1808, 'we never dine now till five'); 293 (1813, no fixed places); 303 (at 3, to suit children); 319 (London, soon after 5); 359 (Godmersham, at 6.30); 398 (London, at 4.30, 'that our Visitors may go to the Play')

Tea: at 6.30 (after dinner at 3.30) 39

Supper: 165 (1805, after dinner at 6); 197 (1808, ? 10.30); 241 (1808, 'the tray' at 10 or 10.30); 285 (1811, hot supper); 300 'at Longbourn'

Music: 10 'I practise every day', 48 'writing music', 65 Concert in Sydney Gardens, 111 singing Duetts, 126 'my Pianoforte' sold (1801) for 8 guineas, 132 'no taste for Music' a recommendation, 154 Concert, 243 'we *will* have a pianoforte' (1808, to cost 30 guineas), 274 Mrs. Henry A.'s party ,'Lessons on the Harp', 282 pleasure in another's playing, 370 Concert, 385 no pleasure in singing, 'being what Nature made me on that article', 412 F. Knight learning the Harp cf. 437, 416 Anna Lefroy's Instrument (24 guineas), 428 'my Instrument', 435 resists Mr. Haden's doctrine 'that a person *not* musical is fit for every sort of Wickedness', 440 music masters

Names: Caroline 172, 183; Charlcombe 'in a little green Valley, as a Village with such a name ought to be' 64; Diana 'my name is D.' 283 (see note); Emma 97, 'it went to my heart that the Miss Lances (one of them too named Emma!) should have partners only for two' dances 236; Henry 348 'a proof how unequally the gifts of Fortune are bestowed. I have seen many a John & Thomas much more agreeable'; Lesley '*is* a noble name' 400; Newton Priors 'is really a Nonpareil. Milton w^{d} have given his eyes to have thought of it' 402, cf. 420; Rachael 'as much as I can bear' 401; Richard 15 'till he has got a Better Christian name', cf. the first page of *Northanger Abbey*; Robert 231 'his name shall be R., if you please; 'no taste in names' 4; surnames of young men used without prefix 2 (Warren), 5 (Buller), 93 (Rice)

NATURE, GARDENS, WEATHER: 'a little green Valley' 64; a beautiful walk 135; beauty of Kent 189, of Surrey 306–8, of

---

Roxburghshire 338; envies the wives of sailors and soldiers (the power of spending their summers where they choose) 103; the Sea 103, 118, 153; Wales 103

The Picturesque: 'prospective view' 62; view of Bath criticized 123 (cf. *Northanger Abbey*); question if certain ladies had 'any right by Taste or Feeling to go their late Tour' 211;

Gardens: 'improvements' at Steventon 76; at Chawton ('I could not do without a Syringa') 178, 182, 281, 287; trees in London 275

Weather: 'what the 5th & 6th of October should always be' 218; 'a Prince of days' (in November), 'did not know how to turn back' 233; 'like an old Feby come back again' 300; 'nice unwholesome, Unseasonable, relaxing, close, muggy weather' 440

Walking: 39, 64, 96 'desperate walkers', 135, 153, 168, 233, 289, 295, 300, 464

Newspapers: 15 'the Papers say', 61 the Bath paper, 87 'Mr. Holder's paper', the *Sun*, 113, 143 'the Pinckards newspaper' (Lyme), 152 'in the papers' (Bath), 197 'yesterday's Courier', 227 'the Salisbury paper' (Southampton), 248 'your newspaper' (to Cassandra at Godmersham), 258 'the Portsmouth paper' (Southampton), 277 'this morning's paper' (London), 279 'as I have just had the pleasure of reading', 280 'the papers say' (Chawton), 297 'our paper' (Chawton)

OPINIONS on various topics

Beauty: 'whose eyes are as handsome as ever' 2; 'those beautiful dark eyes' 87; 'he must write a great deal better than those eyes indicate . . .' 117; 'pleased with his black eyes' 236; 'a pleasing looking young woman' (i.e. J. A.) 278; 'those large dark eyes' 345; 'Lady B. found me handsomer than she expected' 371; 'her fine dark eyes' 479

Children: the change from beauty and 'interesting manners' to 'an ungovernable, ungracious fellow' 24–5; 'what is become of all the Shyness in the World?' 179; praise of 'the best Children in the present day' (1807) 'so unlike anything that I was myself at her age' 179

Clergy: wisdom of residence 55; residence the only means of ejecting a bad curate 339; eagerness in delivery preferred to want of animation, in preaching 339

Death: 'not even Death itself can fix the friendship of the World' 114

IV. General Topics

Education: humorously defined (music, drawing and astronomy) 50

Explanations: 'Heaven forbid that I should ever offer . . . encouragement to Explanations' 64

Family Ties: 'could not have supposed that a neice would ever have been so much to me' 217; 'I like first Cousins to be first Cousins' 415; 'neices seldom chosen but in compliment to some Aunt or other' 421; 'now that you are become an Aunt, you are a person of some consequence . . . I have always maintained the importance of Aunts' 428; 'blessed in the tenderness of such a Family, & before I had survived either them or their affection' 495

Likenesses: 168; 'I wish she were not so very Palmery' 354

Liking: 'trouble of liking' people 43; merit in not liking 51; 'cannot anyhow continue to find people agreable' 129; 'seems to like people rather too easily' 142

Liveliness defined: 'the proper selection of adverbs, & due scraps of Italian & French' 135

Luxury: 'to sit in idleness over a good fire in a well-proportioned room' 84; 'pleasures of friendship . . . make good amends for Orange Wine' 209; 'these two Boys who are out with the Fox-hounds will come home & disgust me again by some habit of Luxury or some proof of sporting Mania' 344

Marriage: 'a great Improver' 231; every body has 'a right to marry *once* in their lives for love' 240; 'anything to be preferred or endured rather than marrying without affection' 410; '*parade* of happiness' in young married women 411; 'nothing can be compared to the misery of being bound *without* love' 418; poverty of single women an argument for marriage 483

Match-making: 58; 'so natural that I have no ingenuity in planning it' 210; 'a Southampton Match . . . I . . . like it, because I had made it before' 231

Money: 'so horridly poor & economical' 41; 'they live in a handsome style and are rich, and she seemed to like to be rich' 175; legacies are very wholesome diet' 188; 'the rich are always respectable' 195; 'As to Money, that will come you may be sure, because they cannot do without it' 231; 'I *had* thought with delight of saving you the postage, but money is dirt' 361; 'you are much above caring about money' 411; '*Pewter*' 420

Mothering: 'poor Woman! how can she be honestly breeding again?' 210; 'the simple regimen of separate rooms' 480; 'poor Animal, she will be worn out before she is thirty' 488; 'by not beginning the business of Mothering quite so early in life, you will be young . . . when . . . is growing old by confinements & nursing' 483; 488

Old Age: 'perhaps in time we may come to be Mrs Stents ourselves, unequal to anything & unwelcome to everybody' (1805) 154; 'at her age, perhaps, one may be as friendless oneself, and in similar circumstances quite as captious' (1808) 243; 'if I live to be an old Woman, I must expect to wish I had died now' (1817) 495

Public Affairs: (see also Newspapers); 'critical state' of 'our poor army' (Jan. 1809) 246; 'my most political correspondents' say nothing of the (rumoured, Jan. 1809) Regency 246; death of Sir John Moore; 'thank Heaven! we have had no one to care for particularly among the Troops' 261–2; 'This is greivous news from Spain' (Jan. 1809) 258; 'How horrible it is to have so many people killed!—And what a blessing that one cares for none of them!' (May 1811) 286; 'What weather! & what news!—We have enough to do to admire them both' (Nov. 1813) 372; letters from abroad (1817) 'would not be satisfactory to *me*, I confess, unless they breathed a strong spirit of regret for not being in England' 477, cf. 212, *Espriella's Letters* 'horribly anti-english'; state of France (1816) 465

Religion: 'her solid principles, her true devotion' 220; 'letters of cruel comfort' 222; I do not like the Evangelicals' (1809) 256; 'I am by no means convinced that we ought not all to be Evangelicals (1814) 410, cf. 420; 'I wish Sir John [Moore] had united something of the Christian with the Hero in his death' 261; 'We do not much like Mr. Cooper's new Sermons; they are fuller of Regeneration & Conversion than ever—with the addition of his zeal in the cause of the Bible Society' (1816) 467; 'Religious Principle' 486; humility 495; 'If ever you are ill, may you . . . possess . . . the greatest blessing of all, in the consciousness of not being unworthy of their [i.e. friends'] Love. *I* could not feel this' (1817) 497; the Sacrament 197, 344

Virtues and Vices: selfishness and unselfishness: 'as *you* are happy, all this is selfishness, of which here is enough for one page' 183; 'for one's own dear self, one ascertains & remembers every thing' 262; 'While she gives happiness to those about her, she is pretty sure of her own share' 256

ill-nature: 'This is an ill-natured sentiment to send all over the Baltic!' 339

narrow-mindedness: difficulty of persuading 'a perverse and narrow-minded woman to oblige those whom she does not love' 118, cf. 494

IV. General Topics

vanity: 'The pleasures of Vanity are more within your comprehension' 411

wisdom: better than Wit 410

Youth: 'she goes on now as young ladies of seventeen ought to do, admired and admiring' (1798) 45; 'like other young ladies she is considerably genteeler than her parents' 142; 'one of the sweet taxes of Youth to chuse in a hurry & make bad bargains' 330

Painting: rouge 128; 'employed about my Lady's face' 178

Prices (see also Dress, Letters): Apples 25s. a sack 334, Books 111 (a joke), 126, Bread 336, 2s. 6d. 352, Butter 12d. 124, Cheese 9½d. 124, Cows 126, Furniture 126, Hops 82, Meat 8d. 124, 336, 352, Salmon 2s. 9d. 124, Sugar 306, an Instrument 24 guineas 416

Races: 7, 204, 205, 335, 343, 397, 408, 467

Remedies: Bleeding 375 (Dr. Parry of Bath), 426; Calomel 335; Cupping 144, 335; Electricity 63; Hartshorn 170; Huxham (Dr. H.'s tincture of bark) 190; Laudanum 26; Leeches 325, 390; Magnesia 133; Mercury 488; Oil of sweet almonds 210; Physic 159; Plaister, strengthening, 441; Rhubarb 466; Steele's Lavender Water 108; Waters 66, 133, 349, 463

Schools: 'I could die of laughter . ., as they used to say at school' (1796) 8; 'the ignorant class of school mistresses' 151; a fashionable London school 309

Shooting: 15, 357

Spelling: final *e* 255, 'adding a vowel' 259; (note J. A.'s own spelling of e.g. *Plumtre*)

Teeth and Dentists: 322, 327, 328

Tips: 'half a guinea or only five shillings' 12, 'ten shillings for Sackree' 163

Transport (of goods): 23 'our trunk nearly slipped off'; 60 a trunk too heavy for the coach, to be sent by waggon; 102 cost of moving heavy furniture prohibitive; 115 'an opportunity of sending'; 311 trunk to be sent by coach

Travel (see also Carriages): 16 '*I* want to go in a Stage Coach, but Frank will not let me' (1796); 54 'both the coaches were full'; the night coach to Deal, 'the unpleasantness of returning by myself deters me' (1799); 57 the London coach; 99 'the Mail for London'; 121 'Henry would send you in his carriage a stage or

---

References are to the pages.

two, where you might be met'; 192 a visit impracticable from 'the nature of the road' (because no coach, cf. 463); 203 prohibitive cost of travelling; 225 'travelled on the outside'; 246 'these plans depend of course upon the weather, but I hope there will be no settled cold to delay us'; 318 'delayed for horses' in travelling post; 337 journey from Chawton to Godmersham: five in and on the barouche, eight in two post chaises, two in the chair, two on horseback and the rest by coach; 374 an early start 'as Edward takes his own Horses all the way'; 382 Henry A. desires Cassandra 'to come post at his expense, & added something of the Carriage meeting you at Kingston'; 396–7 J. A. travels from Chawton to Sloane St. by coach, 'Yalden', 4 in the kitchen part, 15 on top, (changing coaches at Farnham) and so to Hans Place by hackney coach; 397 'my own [imaginary] Coach between Edinburgh & Sterling; 398 Henry A. rides daily from Hans Place to Covent Garden; Edward Knight and his son arrive from Canterbury, 'cd not get Places the day before'; 441 the Chelsea Coach

Visits (duration of): 118, 188, cf. 199, 284, 337

Work (i.e. needle &c. w.): 10, 50, 210; cross-stitch 247; dressing dolls 81; glove-knitting 292; netting 344; notting 23, 57; patchwork 286; rugs 177; sattin-stitch 249; spinning-wheel 285; 'unpicking' 217

References are to the pages.

V. AUTHORS, BOOKS, PLAYS

References are to the pages

Books and plays are in general indexed here under their author's names only; but if the authorship of a book is unknown to the reader, it may be found in the *notes*.

For Songs, see the notes, 274, 428

Artaxerxes (an opera translated from Metastasio): 384

Baretti, Joseph (1719–89): *Account of the Manners and Customs of Italy* (1768; the second edition 1769 has an *Appendix added, in Answer to Samuel Sharp, Esq.*); *Journey from London to Genoa* (1770): 185

Barrett, Eaton Stannard (1786–1820): *The Heroine, or Adventures of a Fair Romance Reader* (1813): 376, 377

Barrow, Sir John (1764–1848): editor of (Lord Macartney's) *Journal of the Embassy to China* (1807): 294

Beattie, James (1735–1803): *The Hermit*: 331, (?)428

Beazley, Samuel (1786–1851): *The Boarding House ; or, Five Hours at Brighton* (1811): 321, 338

Beehive (a musical farce attributed to Millingen): 321, 338

Bickerstaffe, Isaac (fl. c. 1735–c. 1782): *The Hypocrite* (1768, adapted from Cibber's version of *Tartuffe*): 275

Bigland, John (1750–1832): perhaps *History of Spain* (1810) or *System of Geography and History* (1812): 294; perhaps *Letters on the Modern History and Political Aspect of Europe* (1804): 333

Boarding-School, The (?): 115 (note)

Boswell, James (1740–95): *Journal of a Tour to the Hebrides* (1785); *Life of Johnson* (1791; probably the second edition, 1793, published at 24s.): 32, 33, 49, 181; see also Johnson.

Brunton, Mary (1778–1818): *Self-Control: a Novel* (1810): 278, 344, 423

Brydges, Sir Samuel Egerton (1762–1837): *Arthur Fitz-Albini: a Novel* (1798): 32, 67; see also Index II.

Buchanan, Claudius (1766–1815); perhaps *Christian Researches in Asia* (1811), a very popular book, or *Apology for Promoting Christianity in India* (1813): 292

Burney, Frances (1752–1840): *Evelina, or a Young Lady's Entrance into the World* (1778): 'written by Dr. Johnson' 64; quoted 180, 438; Lord Orville

388; *Cecilia, or Memoirs of an Heiress* (5 vols. 1782): 254; *Camilla, or a Picture of Youth* (5 vols. 1796): 9, 13, 14; *The Wanderer, or Female Difficulties* (5 vols. 1814): 334
Burney, Sarah Harriet (1770?–1844): *Clarentine; a Novel* (1798): 180
Byron, Lord (1788–1824): *The Corsair* (1814): 379

Carr, Sir John (1772–1832): *Descriptive Travels in the Southern and Eastern Parts of Spain and the Balearic Isles, in the year 1809* (1811): 292
Clarke, James Stanier (1765?–1834): *Life of James II* (1816; there seems to have been no second edition): 444, 445; see also Index II.
Clarkson, Thomas (1760–1846): perhaps *Abolition of the African Slave Trade* (1808), or more probably *Life of William Penn* (1813, reviewed by Jeffrey in the July *Edinburgh*): 292
Coffey, Charles (d. 1745): *The Devil to Pay* (1731; Covent Garden, March 1814): 384
Colman, George, the elder (1732–94): *The Clandestine Marriage* (with Garrick, 1766; Covent Garden, Sept. 1813): 321, 323, 338
Combe, William (1741–1823): *The Tour of Dr. Syntax in Search of the Picturesque* (1812): 378
Cooke, Mrs. (see Index II): *Battleridge, an historical tale founded on facts. By a lady of quality.* (Cawthorn, 1799): 24
Cooper, Edward (see also Index II): *Examination of the Necessity of Sunday-drilling* (1803); *Sermons, chiefly designed to elucidate . . . Doctrines* (1804); *Practical and Familiar Sermons; designed for parochial and domestic Instruction* (1809); *Two Sermons preached at Wolverhampton* (1816): 252, 255, 467
Cowley, Hannah (1743–1809): *Which is the Man? a Comedy* (1783): 469
Cowper, William (1731–1800): read aloud, 39; 'Syringa, iv'ry pure', 178; *Verses on Alexander Selkirk*, 335; 'tame hares and blank verse', 368
Crabbe, George (1754–1832): *The Borough* (1810); *Tales* (1812): 319, 323 note, 358 note, 370 (for Mrs. C. see Index II)

d'Arblay, Madame: see Burney
Defoe, Daniel (1661?–1731): *Robinson Crusoe* (1719): 143
de Genlis, Madame (1746–1830): *Les Veillées du Château* (1784), translated as *Tales of the Castle* (? 1785), contains as one of its parts *Olympe et Théophile*, translated as *Theophilus and Olympia; or the Errours of Youth and Age; Alphonsine, ou la Tendresse maternelle* (1806), translated as *Alphonsine: or Maternal Affection*

(second edition 1807): 82, 173, 450
de Sévigné, Mme (1626–96): *Lettres* (1726; in English 1758): 371
de Stael, Mme (1766–1817): *Corinne, ou l'Italie* (1807); two translations into English published in 1807: 242
Dibdin, Charles (1745–1814): *The Farmer's Wife* (Covent Garden, Feb. 1814): 384, 385
Dodsley, Robert (1703–64): *A Collection of Poems in Six Volumes by Several Hands* (1758): 133
Don Juan, or the Libertine Destroyed (1792, a pantomime founded on Shadwell's *Libertine*): 321, 338

Edgeworth, Maria (1767–1849): probably *Tales from Fashionable Life* (second series, 1812): 305; *Patronage* (1814): 398; J. A.'s fondness for her novels, 405

Fielding, Henry (1707–54): *Tom Jones* (1749): 3

Garrick, David (1717–79); *Isabella, or the Fatal Marriage* (1776; a tragedy adapted from Southerne's *Fatal Marriage*): 414, 415, 417
Gisborne, Thomas (1758–1846): probably *An Enquiry into the Duties of the Female Sex* (1797): 169
Godwin, William (1756–1836): J. A. was probably acquainted with *Caleb Williams* (1794) and *St. Leon* (1799): 133
Grant, Mrs. Anne (1755–1838), of Laggan: *Letters from the Mountains, being the real correspondence of a Lady, between the years* 1773 *and* 1807 (1807); *Memoirs of an American Lady* (Catalina Schuyler) (1808): 184, 248, 292, 294, 305

Hamilton, Elizabeth (1758–1816): J. A. had probably read *The Cottagers of Glenburnie* (1808) and 'respectable' suggests knowledge of *Popular Essays on the Elementary Principles of the Human Mind* (1812), at least of the reputation of that and similar works: 372
Hawkins, Laetitia Matilda (1760–1835): *Rosanne; or a Father's Labour Lost* (1814): 422
Henry, Robert (1718–90): *History of Great Britain* (1771–93): 89 (note)
Homer: 256
Hook: perhaps James H. (1746–1827), *Guida di Musica, being a complete book of instruction for the Harpsichord or Pianoforte* (1790; new edition 1810): 328
Hunter, Mrs. Rachel, of Norwich (1754–1813): ?161 (note), 406 (note)

Illusion, or the Trances of Nourjahad ('a melodramatic spec-

References are to the pages.

tacle', *Genest*: Drury Lane Nov. 1813): 380

Jefferson: probably William J.: *Entertaining Literary Curiosities* (1808): 191 (note), 199

Jenner, Edward (1749–1823): pamphlets on cow-pox, 1798–1800; a second edition of the original *Inquiry* was dedicated to the King in 1800: 93

Johnson, Samuel (1709–84): *Evelina* written by him, 64; 'my dear Dr. Johnson', 181 (note); 'full tide of human existence at Charing Cross', 368 (note); 'talk from books', 362 (note); see Boswell, Piozzi

Lathom, Francis (1777–1832): *The Midnight Bell, a German Story, Founded on Incidents in Real Life* (1798): 21

Lennox, Charlotte (1720–1804): *The Female Quixote; or, the Adventures of Arabella* (1752): 173

Macartney, Lord (1737–1806): see Barrow

Mackenzie: probably Sir George Steuart M. (1780–1848): *Travels in Iceland* (1811): 294

Metastasio: see *Artaxerxes*

Milton (1608–74): 353; 'would have given his eyes to have thought of it' 402

Molière: *Tartuffe, ou l'Imposteur* (1664): 275

More, Hannah (1745–1833): *Cœlebs in Search of a Wife* (1809): 256, 259; 'Mrs. H. More's recent publication', no doubt *Practical Piety* (1811): 287

Nourjahad, see *Illusion*

O'Hara, Kane (1714?–82): *Midas: an English Burletta* (1764, and often revived): 321, 338

Ovid: 256

Owenson, Sydney, Lady Morgan (1783?–1859): *The Wild Irish Girl* (1806), *Woman, or Ida of Athens* (1809): 251

Pasley, Sir Charles William, R.E. (1780–1861): *Essay on the Military Policy and Institutions of the British Empire* (1810): 292 (note), 294, 304

Percival, Thomas (1740–1804), M.D., of Manchester: *A Father's Instructions; consisting of Moral Tales, Fables, and Reflections, designed to promote the Love of Virtue* (1768): 219

Piozzi, Hester Lynch (1741–1831, Dr. Johnson's Mrs. Thrale): *Letters to and from the late Samuel Johnson* (1788): imitated 66, quoted (i. 270) 235

Pope, Alexander (1688–1744): *Essay on Man* (1733): 362 (note)

Porter, Anna Maria (1780–1832): *Lake of Killarney* (1804): 228

Quarterly Review (first published Feb. 1809): 453

Radcliffe, Ann (1764–1823): 377

V. Authors, Books, Plays

Richardson, Samuel (1689–1761) *Sir Charles Grandison* (1753): 322, 344

Saunders: 157 (note)

Scott, Sir Walter (1771–1832): *The Lay of the Last Minstrel* (1805) 274 (note); *Marmion* (1808) 197, 248, parodied 298; *The Lady of the Lake* (1810) 290; 'a critique on Walter Scott' 300; 'has no business to write novels', i.e. *Waverley* (1814) 404; *The Field of Waterloo* (1815) 431, 432; 'Scott's account of Paris', i.e. *Paul's Letters to his Kinsfolk* (Murray, 1815) 432, 433; *The Antiquary* (1816) 468; review of *Emma* 453

Shakespeare: 1 *Henry IV*, 95; *Hamlet, King John, Macbeth*, 271; *King John*, 275; *Merchant of Venice*, 290, 377, 381; *Richard III* (Covent Garden, March 1814), 386

Sharp, Samuel (1700 ?–1778): *Letters from Italy* (1766); see Baretti

Sherlock, Thomas (1678–1761): *Several Discourses preached at the Temple Church* (1754–97; new edition, Oxford 1812): 406

Smith, James (1775–1839) and Horatio (1779–1849): *Rejected Addresses: or the new Theatrum Poetarum* (1812): 292–4

Southey, Robert (1774–1843): *Letters from England; by Dom Manuel Alvarez Espriella* (1807) 212; *Life of Nelson* (1813) 345; *The Poet's Pilgrimage to Waterloo* (1816) 476 (note)

Sterne, Laurence (1713–68): *Tristram Shandy* (1760–5): 140

Swift, Jonathan (1667–1745): *Gulliver's Travels* (1726): 70

Sykes, Mrs. S.: *Margiana, or Widdrington Fair* (1808): 248

Virgil: 256

West, Mrs. Jane (1758–1852), author of 'novels of good moral tone' (*D.N.B.*): 466; *Alicia de Lacy, an Historical Romance* (1814): 405

Williams, Helen Maria (1762–1827): *A Narrative of the Events which have lately taken place in France* (1815): 433

References are to the pages.

VI. JANE AUSTEN'S NOVELS

References are to the pages

SENSE AND SENSIBILITY (published on commission by Egerton Nov. 1811. 3 vols., 15s. Second edition Nov. 1813): J. A.'s 'sucking child' 272; correction of proofs, sent by the printer to Henry A. 273; 'the *Incomes*' 273, see note; 'my Elinor' 273; imagines *S. S.* to be longer than *P. P.* 298; first edition sold out and brings £140 317; J. A. retains the copyright 317, 425; a copy sent, or not sent, to Warren Hastings (?) 323, see note; second edition contemplated 341; prospects of sale 346; advertised 366; payment for printing 368; published 372, see note

PRIDE AND PREJUDICE (sold to Egerton Nov. 1812 for £110, 501, and published Jan. 1813. 3 vols., 18s. Second (1813) and third (1817) editions not mentioned by J. A., see 372 and note). *First Impressions* (the original draft) read by Cassandra (before 1799) 52, by Martha Lloyd 67; the first copy, 'my own darling child' 297; copies for the family 297; advertisement and price 297; read at Chawton 297; Elizabeth 'as delightful a creature as ever appeared in print' 297; typical errors 297; 'lop't and crop't', imagined shorter than *S.S.* 298; 'fits of disgust', self-criticism 299; 'playfulness and epigrammatism of the general style' 300; anonymity 300; 'the greatest blunder in the printing' 300; 'suppers at Longbourn' 300; Fanny Knight's admiration of Darcy and Elizabeth, 'she might hate all the others if she would' 303; 'portrait of Mrs. Bingley' at the Exhibition 309, 310; but none of Mrs. Darcy 309, 310; the secret gets out, 'if I *am* a wild Beast, I cannot help it' 311; conjectures—'the sort of letter that Miss D. would write' and Darcy's reason for not allowing his wife's portrait to 'be exposed to the public eye' 312; reputation of *P.P.* to sell *M.P.* 317; Henry A. betrays the secret of authorship 320; J. A. 'trying to harden' herself 340; praised by Warren Hastings 320; his admiration of Elizabeth 324; Dr. Isham's admiration 334; imitation by Anna A. 394; Mr. Haden prefers *M.P.* 437; J. A. fears *Emma* will be thought 'inferior in wit' 443

(Possible origin of the episode of Darcy at the ball 43, note)

MANSFIELD PARK (published on commission by Egerton, May 1814. 3 vols., 18s. Second edition published by John Murray 1816). No Government House at Gibraltar 292; 'agreeable set' for the 'round table at Mrs. Grants' 294; 'a complete change of subject [i.e. from that of *P.P.*]—ordination' 298; Cassandra's enquiries 298 note; uses the names of Frank A.'s ships 317, 340; read by Henry A. 376 note, 378, 381, 386 ('the most entertaining part' 376; H. A. 'foresees how it will all be' 376; 'admires H. Crawford: I mean properly' 378; 'has changed his mind as to foreseeing the end' 381; admires the conclusion 386); treatment of the clergy approved by Mr. Cooke 389; Fanny Price 391; the private theatricals imitated by Anna A. 395; first edition sold out, a second contemplated 411; mentioned 413; second edition doubtful 419; opinions of *M.P.* 423; copyright of 425; Mr. Clarke's admiration 430, Mr. Haden's 437; J. A. fears *Emma* will be thought 'inferior in good sense' 443; sends a corrected copy to John Murray for a second edition 446; regrets its 'total omission' by the Quarterly reviewer 453

(Original of Fanny Price's amber cross 137; possible hint for the circumstances of Maria Rushworth's elopement 197 note)

EMMA (published by John Murray Dec. 1815, dated 1816. 3 vols., 21s.). Negotiations with Murray, 'a rogue of course' 425, 431; correspondence with Mr. Clarke about the dedication to the Prince Regent 429; delays in printing 433; the three volumes printing concurrently, 436; 'the Printer's boys bring and carry' 435, 436; twelve presentation copies 439; early copy for the P.R. 442; fears it may be thought 'inferior in wit' to *P.P.* and 'inferior in good sense' to *M.P.* 443; directions about the dedication and presentation copies 446, 447; Lady Morley's copy 448; hopes she has not yet 'overwritten' herself 449; lent to Anna Lefroy 449; Mr. Clarke sends the P.R.'s thanks and 'the just tribute of their praise' from 'many of the nobility' 451; the 'Quarterly' review 453; the binding of the P.R.'s copy 441, 451, 453; Mrs. C. Cage's praise 480

(J. A. said 'I am going to take a heroine whom no one but myself will much like'. *Memoir* (1926), p. 157)

(The late A. B. Walkley saw in Mrs. and Miss 'Molly' Milles of Canterbury the original of Mrs. and Miss Bates.)

(*Emma* was 'read' for Murray by William Gifford, who offered to 'undertake the revision' of 'many little omissions' and other blemishes in the MS. *Life* 310. There is no indication that he read the proofs; but that J. A. had some communication from him appears from the *Plan of a Novel* (*Life* 337).)

NORTHANGER ABBEY AND PERSUASION (published posthumously by John Murray 1818. 4 vols., 24s.). Correspondence 1809 with Crosbie & Co. about the sale of *Susan* 263, 264; 'Miss Catherine is put upon the shelve for the present' 484; 'a something ready for Publication' 484; Fanny Knight 'may *perhaps* like the Heroine, as she is almost too good for me' 487

VII. JANE AUSTEN'S ENGLISH

This list may be read with the list in my edition of the novels (*Sense and Sensibility*, p. 388), and is subject to the same provisos.

References are to the pages.

about: 344 they are each a. a rabbit net

account: 315 when all the circumstances . . . are taken into the a.

accustomary: 124 his a. eager interest

affected: 332 Edward does not seem well a.—he would rather not be asked to go anywhere

altogether: 203 I really hope Harriot is a. very happy

anti-english: 212

bavins: 390

beauty: 58 He is a b. of my mother's

being: 152 your b. looking well

being that: 345 I am tired of Lives of Nelson, b. that I never read any

big: 121 Mrs. Dyson as usual looked b.

booking: 177 I insist upon treating you with the B.

bore: 50 this complaint in my eye has been a sad b. to me

boulangeries: 11

bring and carry: 435 the Printer's boys b. and c.

bring in: 233 requesting that he will b. in Mr. Heathcote (cause to be elected to Parliament)

call in: 279 Miss Payne called in on Saturday

capital: 131 in climbing a hill Mrs. C. is very c.; 270 one of the Hirelings is a C. on the Harp; 380, 494

carry: 74 left behind . . . the drawing . . . which he had intended to c. to George; 399 I must finish this (letter) and c. it with me

chief: 332 I read him the c. of your Letter; 364

cleft: 287 c. wood

closet: 416 her bed-room and her Drawers and her C.

collect: 461 I c. from her, that. . .

comparison: 104 as if Deane were not near London in c. of Exeter

country: 2 before he leaves the c. (i.e. Hampshire), 403

course: 330 I consider it (changing one's mind) as a thing of c. at her time of Life

crop: 57 Charles being a c.

curious: 36 Lord Bolton is particularly c. in his pigs

daresay: 87 you will see the account in the Sun I d.; 173, 281 bis, 384, 425; 497 may you possess—as I d. you will—the greatest blessing. (Always, I think, a confident expression of opinion)

deedily: 344

direct: 114 you may d. to me there; 399 you need not d. it (a parcel) to be left any where
direction: 137 remembering my Uncle's d.; 141; 489 I want to see how Canterbury looks in the d. (also = instruction, 447)
discontentedness: 232
discourse: 173 a great deal of unreserved d. with Mrs. K.
disgust: 299 some fits of d. (when reading *Pride and Prejudice*); 408 There was a little disgust I suspect, at the Races; cf. 344
division: 212 our Yarmouth D.; 289 a d. of the proposed party; 337 this d. of the Family
do: 380 she was doing about last night . . . a little after one
drank: 377 we have d. tea; 391
dress: 319 dressing us a most comfortable dinner
drink: 123 we drank tea as soon as we arrived; 391

engage: 285 from Monday to Wednesday Anna is to be engaged at Faringdon; 425 we are engaged tomorrow to Cleveland Row; 476 engaged to two or three houses
epigrammatism: 300
event: 241 such being the e. of the first pot; 258 I wish her happy at all events (= in any event, cf. 47)
evil: 232 looks about . . . for Inconvenience and E.; 297 the only e. is the delay
except: 185 e. William should send her word

fall: 57 conceal it from him . . . lest it might f. on his spirits; 332 he does not in general f. *within* a doubtful Intention
fee: 194 a letter . . . containing the usual F.; 301 I did not forget Henry's f. to Thomas
feel: 298 your miserable feeling feet
felicity: 247 the letter . . . was . . . like those which had preceded it, as to the f. of its writer; 285 Volunteers and Felicities of all kinds
fencibles: 181
finish: 177 help them in their finishing purchases
fly: 238 my Expectations for my Mother do not rise with this Event. We will allow a little more time, however, before we f. out (in indignation)

genius: 142 I do not perceive wit or g., but she has sense and some degree of taste
give: 372 (*Sense and Sensibility*) was very much admired at Cheltenham, and . . . was given to Miss Hamilton (i.e. as author)
govern: 278 hard at it, governing away (acting as governess; perhaps a jocular formation)
great: 228 one of our g. chairs

half: 122 h. after seven; 205; 217 an hour and half
high: 218 the interior of her High Drawers (= tallboy)
hither: 496 my Journey h. on Saturday, cf. 8 Godmersham,

whither Edward and Elizabeth are to remove . . . in October; 365 thither

honey: 339 she is a poor H.— the sort of woman who gives me the idea of being determined never to be well; 491 I am a poor H. at present

hotel-master: 192

ill: 292 a very ill-looking man

improvements: 76 our I. have advanced very well; — the Bank along the *Elm Walk* is sloped down for the reception of Thorns and Lilacs . . . (technical of landscape gardening)

incessantly: 170 of your visit there I must now speak 'incessantly' (a quotation?); cf. Fr. *incessamment*

instrument: 416 she *is* to have an I.

keep: 301 Thomas was married on Saturday, the wedding was kept at Neatham; 304 by keeping house ever since, it (my cold) is almost gone

kitchen: 397 there were 4 in the K. part of Yalden (the coach)

lay: 35 to l. in; 305 it can make no difference to *her*, which of the 26 fortnights in the year the 3 vols. lay in her house

lay down: 29 ever since we laid down the carriage

lay out: 501 laying out Edward's money for the Poor

lesson: 274 Lessons on the Harp (not instructional)

like: 73 pray will you send me another printed letter . . . if you l. it; 305 kill . . . Mrs. Sclater if you l. it; 335

liquor: 275 in l.

little: 435 for fear you should be distressed for l. Money

long: 113 hopes . . . to see you before it is l.

look: 82 (a table) holds a great deal . . . without looking awkwardly

looks: 127 wearing my new bonnet and being in good looks

make: 203 Harriot is very earnest with Edward to m. Wrotham in his Journey (this is like a common American use); 42 I really think he will soon be made, 47 Frank is made; 284 I shall m. the invitation directly; 204 m. our kind Love and Congratulations to her; 299 m. her best thanks etc. to Miss Lloyd; 212 she does not doubt your making out the Star pattern very well—I think this means *accomplish*, not *understand*, cf. 360 we were obliged to saunter about . . . to m. out the time (*fill in*, *put in*)

manager: 344 M. of the Lodge Hounds

mercantile: 348 a great rich m. Sir Robert Wigram (Lord Brabourne's edition has a comma after *mercantile*, which misled O.E.D.; there is no comma in the MS.)

References are to the pages.

mortar: 437 (obscure, see the context)

neck: 185 not more than you like of Miss Hatton's n.

nice: 191, 200, 217 she is a n. Woman (the modern sense, pilloried by Henry Tilney)

nidgetty: 37 my Cap . . . was too *nidgetty* to please me

noonshine: 195, 228

open: 432 supposing you have any set already opened (of a book opened with a paper-knife)

over-right: 266 to fancy them just o. us (verse)

overturn: 49

Oxford: 32 O. smack (not explained)

parlour: 301 Breakfast p., 337 an excellent Dining and common sitting p. (J. A. I think always writes *drawing-room*, *dining-parlour*)

'participle': 178 our Dressing-Table is constructing on the spot; 226 their (clothes) are making here; 276 the Tea is this moment setting out

particular: 359 your . . . Letter . . . was quite as long and as p. as I could expect

particularity: 180 the p. of this made us talk (see the context; the visitor's behaviour was regarded as pointed, or perhaps merely as odd)

perfect: 91 being p. indifferent

pewter: 420 tho' I like praise . . . I like what Edward (a young man) calls *P.* too

physic: 159 taking p.

place: 171 placing my silence to the want of subject

private: 316 any other p. Man in the United Kingdom

prospective: 62 a p. view of the left side of Brock Street

put forward: 159 I could not help putting f. to invite them

regale: 346 Fanny and I regale on them (Tomatas) every day

regard: 207 I do not at all r. Martha's disappointment

remedy: 185 (see note)

Richard Snow: 382

scheme: 360 our Canterbury s. took place as proposed; 205 our s. to Beaulieu

sensible: 306 this wet morning makes one more s. of it (the weather of the day before)

set down: 191 desires to have his name set down for a guinea

sim: 499 the *sim* of it (= *seem*, i.e. appearance)

sit down: 2 dancing and sitting down together (the modern *sit out*)

situation: 242 a s. . . . which bids very fair for comfort. . . . she comes to board and lodge with Mrs. Hookey

solicit: 342 they are not solicited till after Edward's return (invited)

solicitude: 220 grief and s.; 262 there is no entering much into the solicitudes of that family;

345 a narrow door to the Pantry is the only subject of s.
stationer: 433 the Printers have been waiting for Paper—the blame is thrown upon the S.
stout: 10 Louisa's figure is very much improved; she is as s. again as she was; 20 seems quite s.; 36 seems to cook very well, is uncommonly s., . . .; 111 my mother has been quite s.; 156 not feeling quite s.; 363; 419; 494 (perhaps never = *fat*; but see 158)
supersede: 52 Charles never came . . . I suppose he could not get superseded in time

talking: 363 friendly and t. and pleasant as usual
talobert: 57 the t. skin (family nonsense?)
thinking: 382 such t., clear, considerate Letters as Frank might have written
throw at: 349 Dr. Parry's opinion . . . throws their coming away at a greater Uncertainty than we had supposed
too: 380 too much tired
tough: 129 the three old *Toughs*
try for: 162 Harriot cannot be insincere, let her try for it ever so much
turn off: 365 a delightful morning . . . but the Day turned off . . . and we came home in . . . rain
typical: 297 a few t. errors (typographical)

willow: 377, 398, see note
wish: 244 I w. this (letter) may not have the same deficiency; 300 I w. it may be the means of saving you
within: 158 Lady Leven was not w.; 162 your mittens . . . were folded up w. my clean night-cap; 304 by staying w.
worthy: 338 no Actor w. naming

yester: 142 yesterday morning (ought it not in strict propriety to be termed yester-morning?) —cf. 139 last evening (avoiding yesterday evening?)

References are to the pages

ADDENDUM

strength: 172 the s. of our dinner

VIII. SHIPS

F = Francis, C = Charles. For further information see Hubback, *Jane Austen's Sailor Brothers.*

Ambuscade 149; Caledonia (F) 270; Camilla 152; Cleopatra (C) 275; Elephant (F) 313, 336; Endymion (C) 58, 80, 87, 113, 120, 134, 137; Excellent 33; Expedition 153; Haarlem 112; Leopard (F) 143, 145; London (F) 33, 42; Mercury 95; Namur (C) 304, 354, 360; Neptune 260; Petterel (F) 47, 78, 87, 112, 120; St. Albans (F) 196, 206, 207, 208, 226, 246; Scorpion (C), 42; Tamer (ar) (C) 47, 54, 58; Triton (F) 17, 18; Urania 152
Pyramus 504

References are to the pages.

ADDENDA INDEX II

The identifications, &c., following are drawn from an article by Mr. C. S. Emden in *Oriel Record* 1950:

Nibbs. Probably George N., whose father and J. A.'s were at St. John's together. G. N. was perhaps a pupil. See East.

East. Sir William's son was a pupil at Steventon. Mr. Emden conjectures that J. A. names the pictures (see Nibbs above) from their (conjectured) donors.

Mascall. Robert Curteis M., of Oriel.